THE

WORLD

OF

TIERS

VOLUME TWO

Tor Books by Philip José Farmer

The Cache
Dayworld Breakup
Father to the Stars
More Than Fire
The Other Log of Phileas Fogg
Riders of the Purple Wage
Red Orc's Rage
Time's Last Gift
Traitor to the Living
The World of Tiers, Volume One
(comprising *The Maker of Universes, The Gates of Creation,*
and *A Private Cosmos*)
The World of Tiers, Volume Two
(comprising *Behind the Walls of Terra, The Lavalite World,*
and *More Than Fire*)

THE
WORLD
OF
TIERS

VOLUME TWO

BEHIND THE WALLS OF TERRA
THE LAVALITE WORLD
MORE THAN FIRE

PHILIP JOSÉ FARMER

A TOM DOHERTY ASSOCIATES BOOK / NEW YORK

THE WORLD OF TIERS: VOLUME TWO

This is an omnibus edition, consisting of the novels: *Behind the Walls of Terra*, copyright © 1970, 1982 by Philip José Farmer; *The Lavalite World*, copyright © 1977, 1983 by Philip José Farmer; and *More Than Fire*, copyright © 1993 by Philip José Farmer.

This book is printed on acid-free paper.

Edited by David G. Hartwell

A Tor Book
Published by Tom Doherty Associates, Inc.
175 Fifth Avenue
New York, NY 10010

Tor Books on the World Wide Web:
http://www.tor.com

Tor® is a registered trademark of Tom Doherty Associates, Inc.

ISBN 0-312-86377-2 (pbk)
ISBN 0-312-86376-4 (hc)

First Edition: December 1997

Printed in the United States of America

0 9 8 7 6 5 4 3 2 1

CONTENTS

BEHIND
THE
WALLS OF TERRA

*This adventure of Kickaha is dedicated to
Jack Cordes, who lives in the pocket
universes of Peoria and Pekin.*

THE SKY HAD BEEN GREEN FOR TWENTY-FOUR YEARS. SUDDENLY, it was blue.

Kickaha blinked. He was home again. Rather, he was once more on the planet of his birth. He had lived on Earth for twenty-eight years. Then he had lived for twenty-four years in that pocket universe called The World of Tiers. Now, though he did not care to be here, he was back "home."

He was standing in the shadow of an enormous overhang of rock. The stone floor was swept clean by the wind that traveled along the face of the cliff. Outside the semi-cavern were mountains covered with pine and fir trees. The air was cool but would get warmer, since this was morning of a July day in southern California. Or it should be, if his calculations were correct.

Since he was high on the face of a mountain, he could see very far into the southwest. There was a great valley far beyond the nearer smaller valleys, a valley that he supposed was one near the Los Angeles area. It surprised and unnerved him, because it was not at all what he had expected. It was covered with a thick gray poisonous-looking cloud, that gave the impression of being composed of many many thousands of fumes, as if the floor of the valley below the cloud were jammed with geysers boiling and bubbling and pouring out the noxious gases of internal Earth.

He had no idea of what had occurred on Earth since that night in 1946 when he had been transmitted accidentally from this universe to that of Jadawin. Perhaps the great basins of the Los Angeles area were filled with poison gas that some enemy nation had dropped. He could not guess what enemy could do this, since both Germany and Japan had been wrecked and utterly defeated when he left this world, and Russia was sorely wounded.

He shrugged. He would find out in time. The memory banks below the great fortress-palace at the top of the only planet in the universe of the green sky had said that this "gate" opened into a place in the mountains near a lake called Arrowhead.

The gate was a circle of indestructible metal buried a few inches below the rock of the floor. Only a dimly stained ring of purple on the stone marked its presence.

Kickaha (born Paul Janus Finnegan) was six feet one inch in height, weighed one hundred and ninety pounds, and was broad-shouldered, lean-waisted, and massively thighed. His hair was red-bronze, his eyebrows were thick, dark, and arching, his eyes were leaf-green, his nose was straight but short, his upper lip was long, and his chin was deeply cleft. He wore hiking clothes and a bag on his back. In one hand he held the handle of a dark leather case that looked as if it contained a musical instrument, perhaps a horn or trumpet.

His hair was shoulder-length. He had considered cutting it before he returned to Earth, so he would not look strange. But the time had been short, and he had decided to wait until he got to a barber shop. His cover story would be that he and Anana had been in the mountains so long he had not had a chance to clip his hair.

The woman beside him was as beautiful as it was possible for a woman to be. She had long dark wavy hair, a flawless white skin, dark-blue eyes, and a superb figure. She wore hiking garb: boots, Levi's, a lumberman's checked shirt, and a cap with a long bill. She also carried a pack on her back in which were shoes, a dress, undergarments, a small handbag, and several devices that would have startled or shocked an Earth scientist. Her hair was done in the style of 1946, as Kickaha remembered it. She wore no make-up nor needed it. Thousands of years ago, she had permanently reddened her lips, as every female Lord had done.

He kissed the woman on the lips and said, "You've been in a number of worlds, Anana, but I'll bet in none more weird than Earth's."

"I've seen blue skies before," she said. "Wolff and Chryseis have a five-hour start on us. The Beller has a two-hour start. And all have a big world in which to get lost."

He nodded and said, "There was no reason for Wolff and Chryseis to hang around here, since the gate is one-way. They'll take off for the nearest two-way gate, which is in the Los Angeles area, if the gate still exists. If it doesn't, then the closest ones will be in Kentucky or Hawaii. So we know where they should be going."

He paused and wet his lips and then said, "As for the Beller, who knows? He could have gone anywhere or he may still be around here. He's in an absolutely strange world, he doesn't know anything about Earth, and he can't speak any of the languages."

"We don't know what he looks like, but we'll find him. I know the Bellers," she said. "This one won't cache his bell and then run away to hide with the idea he'll come back later for it. A Beller cannot endure the idea of being very far away from his bell. He'll carry it around as long as he can. And that will be our only means of identifying him."

"I know," Kickaha said. He was having trouble breathing, and his eyes were beginning to swim. Suddenly, he was weeping.

Anana was alarmed for a minute, and then she said, "Cry! I did it when I went back to my home world once. I thought I was dry forever, that tears were for mortals. But coming back home after so long exposed my weakness."

Kickaha dried his tears and took the canteen from his belt, uncapped it and drank deeply.

"I love my world, the green-skied world," he said. "I don't like Earth; I don't remember it with much affection. But I guess I had more love for it than I thought. I'll admit that, every once in a while, I had some nostalgia, some faint longing to see it again, see the people I knew. But . . ."

Below them, perhaps a thousand feet down, a two-lane macadam road curved around the side of the mountain and continued upward until it was lost around the other side. A car appeared on the upgrade, sped below them, and then was lost with the road. Kickaha's eyes widened, and he said, "I never saw a car like that before. It looked like a little bug. A beetle!"

A hawk swung into view and, riding the currents, passed before them not more than a hundred yards.

Kickaha was delighted. "The first red-tail I've seen since I left Indiana!"

He stepped out onto the edge, forgetting for a second, but a second only, his caution. Then he jumped back in under the protection of the overhang. He motioned to Anana, and she went to one end of the ledge and looked out while he did so at the other.

There was nobody below, as far as he could see, though the many trees could conceal anybody who did not want to be seen. He went out a little farther and looked upward then but could not see past the overhang. The way down was not apparent at first, but investigation revealed projections just below the right side of the ledge. These would have to do for a start, and once they began climbing down, other hand and footholds had to appear.

Kickaha eased himself backward over the ledge, feeling with his foot for a projection. Then he pulled himself back up and lay down on the edge, and again scrutinized the road and the forest a thousand feet below. A number of blue jays had started screaming somewhere below him; the air acted as a funnel to siphon the faint cries to him.

He took a pair of small binoculars from his shirt pocket and adjusted three dials on their surface. Then he removed an ear phone and a thin wire with a male jack on one end and plugged the jack into the receptacle on the side of the binoculars. He began to sweep the forest below and eventually centered it on that spot where the jays were raising such a ruckus.

Through the device, the distant forest suddenly became close, and the faint noises were loud. Something dark moved, and after he readjusted the binoculars, he saw the face of a man. More sweepings of the device and more adjusting enabled him to see parts of three other men. Each was armed with a rifle with a scope, and two had binoculars.

Kickaha gave the device to Anana so she could see for herself. He said, "As far as you know, Red Orc is the only Lord on Earth?"

She put the glasses down and said, "Yes."

"He must know about these gates, then, and he's set up some sort of alarm device, so he knows when they're activated. Maybe his men are stationed close, maybe far off. Maybe Wolff and Chryseis and the Beller got away before his men could get here. Maybe not. In any case, they're waiting for us."

They did not comment about the lack of a permanent trap at the gates or a permanent guard. Red Orc, or whatever Lord was responsible for these men, would make a game out of the invasion of his home territory by other Lords. It was deadly but nevertheless a game.

Kickaha went back to viewing the four beneath the trees. Presently, he said, "They've got a walkie-talkie."

He heard a whirring sound above him. He rolled over to look up and saw a strange machine that had just flown down over the mountain to his right.

He said, "An autogyro!" and then the machine was hidden by a spur of the mountain. He jumped up and ran into the cavern with Anana behind him.

The chopping sound of a plane's rotors became a roar and then the machine was hovering before the ledge. Kickaha became aware that the machine was not a true autogyro. As far as he knew, a gyro could not stand still in the air, or, as this was doing, swing from side to side or turn around one spot.

The body of the craft was transparent; he could see the pilot and three men inside, armed with rifles. He and Anana were trapped; they had no place to run or hide.

Undoubtedly, Orc's men had been sent to find out what weapons the intruders carried. Under these conditions, the intruders would have to use their weapons, unless they preferred to be captured. They did not so prefer. They spoke the activating code word, aimed the rings at the machine, and spoke the final word.

The needle-thin golden rays spat once, delivering the full charges in the rings' tiny powerpacks.

The fuselage split in two places, and the plane fell. Kickaha ran out and looked down over the ledge in time to see the pieces strike the side of the mountain below. One section went up in a white and red ball which fissioned into a dozen smaller fire globes. All the pieces eventually fell not too far apart near the bottom and burned fiercely.

The four men under the trees were white-faced, and the man with the walkie-talkie spat words into the transmitter. Kickaha tried to tighten the beam so he could pick them up, but the noise from the burning machine interfered.

Kickaha was glad that he had struck the first blow, but his elation was darkened. He knew that the Lord had deliberately sacrificed the men in the gyro in order to find out how dangerous his opponents were. Kickaha would have preferred to have gotten away undetected. Moreover, getting down the mountainside would be impossible until night fell. In the meantime, the Lord would attack again.

He and Anana recharged their rings with the tiny powerpacks. He kept a watch on the men below while she scanned the sides of the mountain. Presently, a red convertible appeared on the left, going down the mountain road. A man and a woman sat in it. The car stopped near the flaming wreckage and the two got out to investigate. They stood around talking and then they got back into the car and sped off.

Kickaha grinned. No doubt they were going to notify the authorities. That meant that the four men would be powerless to attack. On the other hand, the authorities might climb up here and find him and Anana. He could claim that they were just hikers, and the authorities could not hold them for long. But just to be in custody for a while would enable the Lord to seize them the moment they were released. Also, he and Anana would have a hard time identifying themselves, and it was possible that the authorities might hold them until they could be identified.

They would have no record of Anana, of course, but if they tracked down his fingerprints, they would find something difficult to explain. They would discover that he was Paul Janus Finnegan, born in 1918 near Terre Haute, Indiana, that he had served in a tank corps of the Eighth Army during World War II, and that he had mysteriously disappeared in 1946 from his apartment in a building in Bloomington while he was attending the University of Indiana, and that he had not been seen since.

He could always claim amnesia, of course, but how would he explain that he was fifty-two years old chronologically yet only twenty-five years old physiologically? And how would he explain the origin of the peculiar devices in his backpack?

He cursed softly in Tishquetmoac, in Half-Horse Lakotah, in the Middle High German of Dracheland, in the language of the Lords, and in English, because he had half-forgotten that language and had to get accustomed to its use. If those four men stuck there until the authorities showed up . . .

But the four were not staying. After a long conversation, and obvious receipt of orders from the walkie-talkie, they left. They climbed up onto the road, and within a minute a car appeared from the right. It stopped, and the four got in and drove off.

Kickaha considered that this might be a feint to get him and Anana to climb down the mountain. Then another gyro would catch them on the mountainside, or the men would come back. Or both.

But if he waited until the police showed up, he could not come down until nightfall. Orc's men would be waiting down there, and they might have some of the Lords' advanced weapons to use, because they would not fear to use them at night and in this remote area.

"Come on," he said to Anana in English. "We're going down now. If the police see us, we'll tell them we're just hitchhikers. You leave the talking to me; I'll tell them you're Finnish and don't speak English yet. Let's hope there'll be no Finns among them."

"What?" Anana said. She had spent three and a half years on Earth in the 1880s and had learned some English and more French but had forgotten the little she had known.

Kickaha repeated slowly.

"It's your world," she said in English. "You're the boss."

He grinned at that, because very few female Lords ever admitted that there was any situation in which the male was their master. He let himself down again over the ledge. He was beginning to sweat. The sun was coming over the mountain now and shining fully on them, but this did not account for his perspiration. He was sweating out the possible reappearance of the Lord's men.

He and Anana had gotten about one-third of the way down when the first police car appeared. It was black and white and had a big star on the side. Two men got out. Their uniforms looked like those of state police, as he remembered those of the Midwest.

A few minutes later, another patrol car and an ambulance appeared. Then two more cars stopped. After a while, there were ten cars.

Kickaha found a path that was sometimes precarious but led at an angle to the right along the slope. He and Anana could keep hidden from the people below part of the time. If they should be seen, they would not have to stop. The police could come after them, but they would be so far behind that their pursuit would be hopeless.

Or so it seemed until another gyro appeared. This one swept back and forth, apparently looking for bodies or survivors. Kickaha and Anana hid behind a large boulder until the craft landed near the road. Then they continued their sidewise descent of the mountain.

When they reached the road, they drank some water and ate some of the concentrated food they had brought from the other world. Kickaha told her that they would walk along the road, going downward. He also reminded her that Red Orc's men would be cruising up and down the road looking for them.

"Then why don't we hide out until nightfall?" she said.

"Because in the daylight I can spot a car that definitely won't be Orc's. I won't mind being picked up by one of them. But if Orc's men show up and try anything, we have our rays and we can be on guard. At night, you won't know who's stopping to pick you up. We could avoid the road altogether and hike alongside it in the woods, but that's slow going. I don't want Wolff or the Beller to get too far ahead."

"How do we know they didn't both go the other way?" she said. "Or that Red Orc didn't pick them up?"

"We don't," he said. "But I'm betting that this is the way to Los Angeles. It's westward, and it's downhill. Wolff would know this, and the instinct of the Beller would be to go down, I would think. I could be wrong. But I can't stand here forever trying to make up my mind what happened. Let's go."

They started off. The air was sweet and clean; birds sang; a squirrel ran out onto the branch of a tall and half-dead pine and watched them with its bright eyes. There were a number of dead or dying pines. Evidently, some plant disease had struck them. The only signs of human beings were the skeletal power transmission towers and aluminium cables going up the side of a mountain. Kickaha explained to Anana what they were; he was going to be doing much explaining from now on. He did not mind. It gave her the opportunity to learn English and him the opportunity to relearn it.

A car passed them from behind. On hearing it, Kickaha and Anana withdrew from the side of the road, ready to shoot their ray rings or to leap down the slope of the mountain if they had to. He gestured with his thumb at the car, which held a man, woman, and two children. The car did not even slow down. Then a big truck pulling a trailer passed them. The driver looked as if he might be going to stop but he kept on going.

Anana said, "These vehicles! So primitive! So noisy! And they stink!"

"Yes, but we *do* have atomic power," Kickaha said. "At least, we had atomic bombs. America did anyway. I thought that by now they'd have atomic-powered cars. They've had a whole generation to develop them."

A cream-colored station wagon with a man and woman and two teenagers passed them. Kickaha stared after the boy. He had hair as long as Kickaha's and considerably less disciplined. The girl had long yellow hair that fell smoothly over her shoulders, and her face was thickly made up. Like a whore's, he thought. Were those really green eyelids?

The parents, who looked about fifty, seemed normal. Except that she had a hairdo that was definitely not around in 1946. And her make-up had been heavy, too, although not nearly as thick as the girl's.

None of the cars that he had seen were identifiable. Some of them had a GM emblem, but that was the only familiar thing. This was to be expected, of course. But he was startled when the next car to pass was the beetle he had seen when he first looked down from the ledge. Or at least it looked enough like it to be the same. VW? What did that stand for?

He had expected many changes, some of which would not be easy to understand. He could think of no reason why such an ugly cramped car as the VW would be accepted, although he did remember the little Willys of his adolescence. He shrugged. It would take too much energy and time to figure out the reasons for everything he saw. If he were to survive, he would have to concentrate on the immediate problem: getting away from Red Orc's men. If they were Red Orc's.

He and Anana walked swiftly in a loose-jointed gait. She was beginning to relax and to take an interest in the beauty of their surroundings. She smiled and squeezed his hand once and said, "I love you."

He kissed her on the cheek and said, "I love you, too."

She was beginning to sound and act like an Earth-woman, instead of the superaristocratic Lord.

He heard a car coming around the bend a quarter of a mile away and glanced back at it. It was a black-and-white state police car with two golden-helmeted men. He looked straight ahead but out of the side of his mouth said, "If this car stops, act easy. It's the police. Let me handle things. If I hold up two fingers, run and jump down the side of the mountain. No! On second thought . . . listen, we'll go with them. They can take us into town, or near it, and then we'll stun them with the rings. Got it?"

The car, however, shot by without even scowling.

Kickaha breathed relief and said, "We don't look as suspicious as I feel."

They walked on down the road. As they came onto a half-mile stretch, they heard a faint roar behind them. The sound became louder, and then Kickaha grinned with pleasure. "Motorcycles," he said. "Lots of them."

The roaring became very loud. They turned, and saw about twenty big black cycles race like a black cloud around the corner of the mountain. Kickaha was amazed. He had never seen men or women dressed like these. Several of them aroused a reflex he had thought dead since peace was declared in 1945. His hand flew to the handle of the knife in his belt sheath, and he looked for a ditch into which to dive.

Three of the cyclists wore German coalscuttle helmets with big black swastikas painted on the gray metal. They also wore Iron Crosses or metal swastikas on chains around their necks.

All wore dark glasses, and these, coupled with the men's beards or handlebar mustaches and sideburns, and the women's heavy make-up, made their faces seem insectile. Their clothing was dark, although a few men wore dirty once-white T-shirts. Most wore calf-length boots. A woman sported a kepi and a dragoon's bright-red, yellow-piped jacket. Their black-leather jackets and T-shirts bore skulls and crossbones that looked like phalluses, and the legend: LUCIFER'S LOUTS.

The cavalcade went roaring by, some gunning their motors or waving at the two, and several wove back and forth across the road, leaning far over to both sides with their arms folded. Kickaha grinned appreciatively at that; he had owned and loved a motorcycle when he was going to high school in Terre Haute.

Anana, however, wrinkled up her nose. "The stink of fuel is bad enough," she said. "But did you smell *them?* They haven't bathed for weeks. Or months."

"The Lord of this world has been very lax," Kickaha said.

He referred to the sanitary habits of the human inhabitants of the pocket universes that the other Lords ruled. Although the Lords were often very cruel with their human property, they insisted on cleanliness and beauty. They had established laws and religious precepts that saw to it that cleanliness was part of the base of every culture.

But there were exceptions. Some Lords had allowed their human societies to degenerate into dirt-indifference.

Anana had explained that the Lord of Earth was unique. Red Orc ruled in strictest secrecy and anonymity, although he had not always done so. In the early days, in man's dawn, he had often acted as a god. But he had abandoned that role and gone into hiding—as it were. He had let things go as they would. This accounted for the past, present, and doubtless future mess in which Earthlings were mired.

Kickaha had had little time to learn much about Red Orc, because he had not even known of his existence until a few minutes before he and Anana stepped through the gates into this universe.

"They all looked so ugly," Anana said.

"I told you man had gone to seed here," he said. "There has been no selective breeding, either by a Lord or by humans themselves."

Then they heard the muted roar of the cycles again, and in a minute they saw eight coming back up the road. These held only men.

The cycles passed them, slowed, turned, and came up behind them. Kickaha and Anana continued walking. Three cycles zoomed by them, cutting in so close that he could have knocked them over as they went by. He was beginning to wonder if he should not have done so and therefore cut down the odds immediately. It seemed obvious that they were going to be harassed, if not worse.

Some of the men whistled at Anana and called out invitations, or wishes, in various obscene terms. Anana did not understand the words but she understood the tones and gestures and grins that went with them. She scowled and made a gesture peculiar to the Lords. Despite their unfamiliarity with it, the cyclists understood. One almost fell off his cycle laughing. Others, however, bared their teeth in half-grins, half-snarls.

Kickaha stopped and faced them. They pulled up around the pair in an enfolding crescent and turned off their motors.

"OK," Kickaha said. "What do you want?"

A big-paunched, thick-necked youth with thick coarse black hair spilling out of the V of his shirt and wearing a goatee and an Afrika Korps hat, spoke up. "Well, now, Red, if we was Satan's Slaves, we'd want you. But we ain't fags, so we'll take your *la belle dame con, voila.*"

"Man, that chick is the most!" said a tall skinny boy with acne scars, big Adam's apple, and a gold ring in a pierced ear. His long lank black hair hung down past his shoulders and fell over his eyes.

"The grooviest!" a bushy-bearded gap-toothed scar-faced man said.

Kickaha knew when to keep silent and when to talk, but he sometimes had a hard time doing what he knew was best. He had no time or inclination for brawls now, his business was serious and important. In fact, it was vital. If the Beller got loose and adapted to Earth well enough to make other bells, he and his kind would literally take over Earth. The Beller was no science-fiction monster; he existed, and if he were not killed, good-bye Earth! Or good-bye mankind! The bodies would survive but the brains would be emptied and alien minds would fill them.

It was unfortunate that salvation could not discriminate. If others were saved, then these would be too.

At the moment, it looked as if there could be some doubt about Kickaha being able to save even himself, let alone the world. The eight had left their cycles and were approaching with various weapons. Three had long chains; two, iron pipes; one, a switchblade knife; one, brass knuckles; another, an ice pick.

"I suppose you think you're going to attack her in broad daylight and with the cops so close?" he said.

The youth with the Afrika Korps cap said, "Man, we wouldn't bother you, ordinarily. But when I saw that chick! It was too much! What a doll! I ain't never seen a chick could wipe her. Too much! We gotta have her. You dig?"

Kickaha did not understand what this last meant but it did not matter. They were brutal men who meant to have what they wanted.

"You better be prepared to die," Kickaha said.

They looked surprised. The Afrika Korps youth said, "You got a lotta class, Red, I'll give you that. Listen, we could stomp the guts outta you and enjoy it, really dig it, but I admire your style, friend. Let us have the chick, and we return her in an hour or so."

Then Afrika Korps grinned and said, " 'Course, she may not be in the same condition she is now, but what the hell. Nobody's perfect!"

Kickaha spoke to Anana in the language of the Lords.

"If we get a chance, we'll make off on one of those cycles. It'll get us to Los Angeles."

"Hey, what kinda gook talk is that?" Afrika Korps said. He gestured at the men with the chains, who, grinning, stepped in front of the others. They drew their arms back to lash out with the chains and Kickaha and Anana sprayed the beams from their rings, which were set at "stun" power. The three dropped their chains, grabbed their middles, and bent over. The rays caught them on the tops of the heads then, and they fell forward. Their faces were red with suddenly broken blood vessels. When they recovered, they would be dizzy and sick for days and their stomachs would be sore and red with ruptured veins and arteries.

The others became motionless and went white with shock.

Kickaha snatched the knife out of his sheath and threw it at the shoulder of Afrika Korps. Afrika Korps screamed and dropped the ice pick. Anana knocked him out with her ray; Kickaha sprayed the remaining men.

Fortunately, no cars came by in the next few minutes. The two dragged the groaning half-conscious men to the edge of the road and pushed them over. They rolled about twenty feet and came to rest on a shelf of rock.

The cycles, except for one, were then pushed over the edge at a place where there was nothing to stop them. They leaped and rolled down the steep incline, turned over and over, came apart, and some burst into flames.

Kickaha regretted this, since he did not want the smoke to attract anybody.

Anana had been told what the group had planned for her. She climbed down the slope to the piled-up bodies. She set the ring at the lowest burn power and burned off the pants, and much outer skin, of every male. They would not forget Anana for a long time. And if they cursed her in aftertimes, they should have blessed Kickaha. He kept her from killing them.

Kickaha took the wallet of Afrika Korps. The driver's license gave his name as Alfred Roger Goodrich. His photograph did not look at all like Kickaha, which could not be helped. Among other things, it contained forty dollars.

He instructed Anana on how to ride behind him and what to expect when they were on the road. Within a minute, they were out on the highway, heading toward Los Angeles. The roar of the engine did not resurrect the happy memories of his cycling days in Indiana. The road disturbed him and the reek of gasoline and oil displeased him. He had been in a quiet and sweet-aired world too long.

Anana, clinging to his waist, was silent for a long while. He glanced back once to see her black hair flying. Her lids were half shut behind the sunglasses she had taken from one of the Louts. The shadows made them impenetrable. Later, she shouted something at him, but the wind and the engine noise flicked her words away.

Kickaha tested the cycle out and determined that a number of items had been cut out by the owner, mostly to reduce weight. For one thing, the front brakes had been taken off.

Once he knew what the strengths and weaknesses of the vehicle were, he drove along with his eyes inspecting the road ahead but his thoughts inclined to be elsewhere.

He had come on a long and fantastic road from that campus of the University of Indiana to this road in the mountains of southern California. When he was with the Eighth Army in Germany, he had found that crescent of hard silvery metal in the ruins of a local museum. He took it back with him to Bloomington, and there, one night, a man by the name of Vannax had appeared and offered him a fantastic sum for the crescent. He had refused the money. Later that night he had awakened to find Vannax had broken into his apartment. Vannax was in the act of placing another crescent of metal by his to form a circle. Kickaha had attacked Vannax and accidentally stepped within the circle. The next he knew, he was transported to a very strange place.

The two crescents had formed the gate, a device of the Lords that permitted a sort of teleportation from one universe to another. Kickaha had been transmitted into an artificial universe, a pocket universe, created by a Lord named Jadawin. But Jadawin was no longer in his universe; he had been forced out of it by another Lord, dispossessed and cast into Earth. Jadawin had lost his memory. He became Robert Wolff.

The stories of Wolff (Jadawin) and Kickaha (Finnegan) were long and involved. Wolff was helped back into his universe by Kickaha, and, after a series of adventures, Wolff regained his memory. He also regained his Lordship of the peculiar universe he had constructed, and he settled down with his lover, Chryseis, to rule in the palace on top of the Tower-of-Babel-like planet that hung in the middle of a universe whose "walls" contained a volume of less than that within the solar system of Earth.

Recently, Wolff and Chryseis had mysteriously disappeared, probably because of the machinations of some Lord of another universe. Kickaha had run into Anana, who, with two other Lords, was fleeing from the Black Bellers. The Bellers had originally been devices created in the biolabs of the Lords and intended for housing of the minds of the Lords during mind transference from one body to another. But the bell-shaped and indestructible machines had developed into entities with their own intelligence. These had succeeded in transferring their minds into the bodies of Lords and then began to wage a secret war on the Lords. They were found out, and a long and savage struggle began, with all the Bellers supposedly captured and imprisoned in a specially made universe. However, fifty-one had been overlooked, and these, after ten thousand years of dormancy, had gotten into human bodies again and were once more loose.

Kickaha had directly or indirectly killed all but one. This one, its mind in the body of a man called Thabuuz, had gated through to Earth. Wolff and Chryseis had returned to their palace just in time to be attacked by the Bellers and had escaped through the gate that Thabuuz later took.

Now Kickaha and Anana were searching for Wolff and Chryseis. And they were also determined to hound down and kill the last of the Black Bellers. If Thabuuz succeeded in eluding them, he would, in time, build more of the bells and with these begin a secret war against the humans of Earth, and, later, invade the private universes of the Lords and discharge their minds and occupy their bodies also. The Lords had never forgotten the Black Bellers, and every one still wore a ring that could detect the metal bells of their ancient enemies and transmit a warning to a tiny circuit-board and alarm in the brain of every Lord.

The peoples of Earth knew nothing of the Bellers. They knew nothing of the Lords. Kickaha was the only Earthling who had ever become aware of the existence of the Lords and their pocket universes.

The peoples of Earth would be wide open to being taken over, one by one, their minds discharged by the antennas of the bells and the minds of the Bellers possessing the brains. The warfare would be so insidious that only through accident would the humans even know that they were being attacked.

The Black Beller Thabuuz had to be found and killed.

In the meantime, the Lord of Earth, the Lord called Red Orc, had learned that five people had gated through into his domain. He would not know that one of them was the Black Beller. He would be trying to capture all five. And Red Orc could not be notified that a Black Beller was loose on Earth because Red Orc could not be found. Neither Anana nor Kickaha knew where he lived. Indeed, until a few hours ago, Kickaha had not known that Earth had a Lord.

In fifteen minutes, they had come down off the slope onto a plateau. The little village at the crossroads was a pleasant place, though highly commercialized. It was clean and bright, with many white houses and buildings. However, as they passed through the main street, they passed a big hamburger stand. And there were the rest of Lucifer's Louts lounging by the picnic tables, eating hamburgers and drinking cokes or beer. They looked up on hearing the familiar Harley-Davidson and then, seeing the two, did a double take. One jumped onto his cycle and kicked over the motor. He was a tall frowzy-haired long-mustachioed youth wearing a Confederate officer's cavalry hat, white silk shirt with frills at the neck and wrists, tight black shiny pants with red seams, and fur-topped boots.

The others quickly followed him. Kickaha did not think they would be going to the police; there was something about them which indicated that their relations with the police were not friendly. They would take vengeance in their own dirty hands. However, it was not likely that they would do anything while still in town.

Kickaha accelerated to top speed.

When they had gone around a curve that took them out of sight of the village, Anana half-turned. She waited until the leader was only ten feet behind her. He was bent over the bars and grinning savagely. Evidently he expected to pass them and either force them to stop or to knock them over. Behind him, side by side so that two rode in the other lane, were five cycles with individual riders. The engines burdened down with couples were some twenty yards behind.

Kickaha glanced back and yelled at Anana. She released the ray just long enough to cut the front wheel of the lead cycle in half. Its front dropped, and the rider shot over the bars, his mouth open in a yell no one could hear. He hit the macadam and slid for a long way on his face and body. The five cycles behind him tried to avoid the first, which lay in their path. They split like a school of fish, but Anana cut the wheels of the two in the lead and all three piled up while two skidded on their sides off the road. The other cycles slowed down in time to avoid hitting the fallen engines and drivers.

Kickaha grinned and shouted, "Good show, Anana!"

And then his grin fell off and he cursed. Around the corner of the road, now a half-mile away, a black-and-white car with red lights on top had appeared. Any hopes that he had that it would stop to investigate the accident quickly faded. The car swung to the shoulder to avoid the fallen vehicles and riders and then twisted back onto the road and took off after Kickaha, its siren whooping, its red lights flashing.

The car was about fifty yards away when Anana swept the ray down the road and across the front tires. She snapped the ray off so quickly that the wheels were probably only disintegrated a little on the rims, but the tires were cut in two. The car dropped a little but kept going on, though it decreased speed so suddenly that the two policemen were thrown violently forward. The siren died; the lights quit flashing; the car shook to a halt. And Kickaha and Anana sped around a curve and saw the policemen no more.

"If this keeps up, we're going to be out of charges!" Kickaha said. "Hell, I wanted to save them for extreme emergencies! I didn't think we'd be having so much trouble so soon! And we're just started!"

They continued for five miles and then he saw another police car coming toward them. It went down a dip and was lost for a minute. He shouted "Hang on" and swung off the road, bouncing across a slight depression toward a wide field that grew more rocks than grass. His goal was a clump of trees about a hundred yards away, and he almost made it before the police came into view. Anana, hanging on, yelled that the police car was coming across the field after them. Kickaha slowed the cycle. Anana ran the ray down the field in front of the advancing car. Burning dirt flew up in dust along a furrow and then the tires exploded and the front of the radiator of the car gushed water and steam.

Kickaha took the cycle back toward the road at an angle away from the car. Two policemen jumped out and, steadying their pistols, fired. The chances of hitting the riders of the machine at that distance were poor, but a bullet did penetrate the rear tire. There was a bang; the cycle began fishtailing. Kickaha cut the motor, and they coasted to a stop. The policemen began running toward them.

"Hell, I don't want to kill them!" Kickaha said. "But . . ."

The policemen were big and blubbery-looking and looked as if they might be between forty and fifty years old. Kickaha and Anana were wearing packs of about thirty pounds, but both were physically about twenty-five years old.

"We'll outrun them," he said, and they fled together toward the road. The two men fired their guns and shouted but they were slowing down swiftly and soon they were trotting. A half-mile later, they were standing together watching the two dwindle.

Kickaha, grinning, circled back toward the car. He looked back once and saw that the two policemen realized that he had led them astray. They were running again but not too swiftly. Their legs and arms were pumping at first but soon the motions became less energetic, and then both were walking toward him.

Kickaha opened the door to the car, tore off the microphone of the transceiver, reached under the dashboard and tore loose all the wires connected to the radio. By that time, Anana had caught up with him.

The keys were still in the ignition lock, and the wheels themselves had not been cut into deeply. He told Anana to jump in, and he got behind the steering wheel and started the motor. The cops speeded up then and began firing again, but the car pulled away from them and bumped and shook across the field, accelerating all the time. One bullet pierced and starred a rear window, and then the car was bump-bumping down the road.

After two miles of the grinding noise and piston-like movement, Kickaha decided to call it quits. He drove the car to the side of the road, got out, threw the ignition keys into the weeds, and started to hike again. They had walked perhaps fifty yards when they turned at the noise of a vehicle. A bus shot by them. It was painted all over with swirls, dots, squares, circles, and explosions of many bright colors. In bright yellow-and-orange-trimmed letters was a title along the front and the sides of the bus: THE GNOME

KING AND HIS BAD EGG. Above the title were painted glowing red and yellow quarter notes, bars, small guitars and drums.

For a moment, looking at the faces against the windows, he thought that the bus had picked up Lucifer's Louts. There were long hairs, fuzzy hairs, mustaches, beards, and the heavy make-up and long straight lank hair of the girls.

The bus slowed down with a squealing of brakes. It stopped, a door swung open, and a youth with a beard and enormous spectacles leaned out and waved at them. They ran to the bus and boarded with the accompaniment of much laughter and the strumming of guitars.

The bus, driven by a youth who looked like Buffalo Bill, started up. Kickaha looked around into the grinning faces of six boys and three girls. Three older men sat at the rear of the bus and played cards on a small collapsible table. They looked up and nodded and then went back to their game. Part of the bus was enclosed; there were, he later found out, a toilet and washroom and two small dressing rooms. Guitars, drums, xylophone, saxophones, flute, and harp were stored on seats or on the racks above the seats.

Two girls wore skirts that barely covered their buttocks, and dark gray stockings, bright frilly blouses, many varicolored beads, and heavy make-up: green or silver eyelids, artificial eyelashes, panda-like rings around the eyes, and green (!) and pale mauve (!) lips. The third girl had no make-up at all. Long straight black hair fell to her waist and she wore a tight sleeveless green-and-red-striped sweater with a deep cleavage, tight Levi's, and sandals. Several of the boys wore bell-bottom trousers, very frilly shirts, and all had long hair.

The gnome king was a very tall, tubercular-looking youth with very curly hair, handlebar mustache, and enormous spectacles perched on the end of his big nose. He also wore an earring. He introduced himself as Lou Baum (born Goldbaum).

Kickaha gave his name as Paul Finnegan and Anana's as Ann Finnegan. She was his wife, he told Baum, and had only recently come from Finnish Lapland. He gave this pedigree because he did not think that it was likely they would run into anyone who could speak Laplander.

"From the Land of the Reindeer?" Baum said. "She's a dear, all right." He whistled and kissed his fingertips and flicked them at Anana. "Groovy, me boy! Too much! Say, either of you play an instrument?" He looked at the case Kickaha was carrying.

Kickaha said that they did not. He did not care to explain that he once played the flute but not since 1945 or that he had played an instrument like a pan-pipe when he lived with the Bear Folk on the Amerindian level of the World of Tiers. Nor did he think it wise to explain that Anana played a host of instruments, some of which were similar to Earth instruments and some of which were definitely not.

"I'm using this instrument case as a suitcase," Kickaha said. "We've been on the road for some time since leaving Europe. We just spent a month in the mountains, and now we've decided to visit L.A. We've never been there."

"Then you've got no place to stay," Baum said. He talked to Kickaha but stared at Anana. His eyes glistened, and his hands kept moving with gestures that seemed to be reshaping Anana out of the air.

"Can she sing?" he said suddenly.

"Not in English," Kickaha replied.

The girl in Levi's stood up and said, "Come on, Lou. You aren't going to get anywhere with that chick. Her boyfriend'll kill you if you lay a hand on her. Or else she will. That chick can do it, you know."

Lou seemed to be shaken. He came very close and peered into Kickaha's eyes as if he were looking through a microscope. Kickaha smelled a strange acrid odor on his breath. A moment later, he thought he knew what it was. The citizens of the city of Talanac on the Amerind level, carved out of a mountain of jade, smoked a narcotic tobacco that left the same odor on their breath. Kickaha did not know, of course, since he had had no experience on Earth, but he had always suspected that the tobacco was marijuana, and that the Talanacs, descendants of the ancient Olmecs of Mexico, had brought it with them when they had crossed through the gates provided by Wolff.

"You wouldn't put me on?" Lou said to the girl, Moo-Moo Nanssen, after he had backed away from Kickaha's leaf-green eyes.

"There's something very strange about them," Moo-Moo said. "Very attractive, very virile, and very frightening. Real alien."

Kickaha felt the back of his scalp chill. Anana, moving closer to him, whispered in the language of the Lords, "I don't know what she's saying, but I don't like it. That girl has a gift of seeing things; she is *zundra*."

Zundra had no exact or near-exact translation into English. It meant a combination of psychologist, clairvoyant, and witch, with a strain of madness.

Lou Baum shook his head, wiped the sweat off his forehead, and then removed and polished his glasses. His weak, pale-blue eyes blinked.

"The chick is psychic," he said. "Weird. But in the groove. She knows what she's talking about."

"I get vibrations," Moo-Moo said. "They never fail me. I can read character like that!" She snapped her fingers loudly. "But there's something about you two, especially her, I don't get. Maybe like you two ain't from this world, you know. Like you're Martians . . . or something."

A short stocky youth with blond hair and an acne-scarred face, introduced only as Wipe-Out, looked up from his seat, where he was tuning a guitar.

"Finnegan's no Martian," he said, grinning. "He's got a flat Midwestern accent like he came from Indiana, Illinois, or Iowa. A hoosier, I'd guess. Right?"

"I'm a hoosier," Kickaha said.

"Close your eyes, you good people," Wipe-Out said loudly. "Listen to him! Speak again, Finnegan! If his voice isn't a dead ringer for Gary Cooper's, I'll eat the inedible!"

Kickaha said something for their benefit, and the others laughed and said, "Gary Cooper! Did you ever?"

That seemed to shatter the crystal tension that Moo-Moo's words had built. Moo-Moo smiled and sat down again, but her dark eyes flicked glances again and again at the two strangers, and Kickaha knew that she was not satisfied. Lou Baum sat down by Moo-Moo. His Adam's apple worked as if it were the plunger on a pump. His face was set in a heavy, almost stupefied expression, but Kickaha could tell that he was still very curious. He was also afraid.

Apparently, Baum believed in his girlfriend's reputation as a psychic. He was also probably a little afraid of her.

Kickaha did not care. Her analysis of the stranger may have been nothing but a maneuver to scare Baum from Anana.

The important thing was to get to Los Angeles as swiftly as possible, with as little chance of being detected by Orc's men as possible. This bus was a lucky thing for him, and as soon as they reached a suitable jumping-off place in the metropolitan area, they would jump. And hail and farewell to the Gnome King and His Bad Eggs.

He inspected the rest of the bus. The three older men playing cards looked up at him but said nothing. He felt a little repulsed by their bald heads and gray hair, their thickening and sagging features, red-veined eyes, wrinkles, dewlaps, and big bellies. He had not seen more than four old people in the twenty-four years he had lived in the universe of Jadawin. Humans lived to be a thousand there, if they could avoid accident or homicide, and did not age until the last hundred years. Very few survived that long, however. Thus, Kickaha had forgotten about old men and women. He felt repelled, though not as much as Anana. She had grown up in a world that contained no physically aged people, and though she was now ten thousand years old, she had lived in no universes that contained unhandsome humans. The Lords were an esthetic people and so they had weeded out the unbeautiful among their chattel and given the survivors the chance for a long, long youth.

Baum walked down the aisle and said, "Looking for something?"

"I'm just curious," Kickaha said. "Is there any way out other than the door in front?"

"There's an emergency inside the women's dressing room. Why?"

"I just like to know these things," Kickaha said. He did not see why he should explain that he always made sure he knew exactly the number of exits and their accessibility.

He opened the doors to the two dressing rooms and the toilet and then studied the emergency door so that he would be able to open it immediately.

Baum, behind him, said, "You sure got guts, friend. Didn't you know curiosity killed the cat?"

"It's kept this cat alive," Kickaha said.

Baum lowered his voice and came close to Kickaha. He said, "You really hung up on that chick?"

The phrase was new to Kickaha but he had no trouble understanding it. He said, "Yes. Why?"

"Too bad. I've really flipped for her. No offense, you understand," he said when Kickaha narrowed his eyes. "Moo-Moo's a real doll, but a little weird, you know what I mean. She says you two are weirdos, and there is something a little strange about you, but I like that. But I was going to say, if you need some money, say one or two thousand, and you'd just, say, give me a deed to your chick, in a manner of speaking, let me take over, and walk out, much richer, you know what I mean."

Kickaha grinned and said, "Two thousand? You must want her pretty bad!"

"Two thousand doesn't grow on the money tree, my friend, but for that doll . . . !"

"Your business must be very good, if you can throw that much away," Kickaha said.

"Man, you kidding!" Baum said, seemingly genuinely surprised. "Ain't you really heard of me and my group before? We're famous! We've been everywhere, we've made the top ten thirty-eight times, we got a Golden Record, we've given concerts at the Bowl! And we're on our way to the Bowl again. You don't seem to be with it!"

"I've been away for a long time," Kickaha said. "So what if I take your money and Ann doesn't fall for you? I can't force her to become your woman, you know."

Baum seemed offended. He said, "The chicks offer themselves to me by the dozens every night. I'm not jesting. I got the pick! You saying this Ann, Daughter-of-Reindeer, or whatever her name, is going to turn *me* down? Baum, the Gnome King?"

Baum's features were not only unharmonious, he had several pimples, and his teeth were crooked.

"Do you have the money on you?"

Baum's voice had been questioning, even wheedling before. Now it became triumphant and, at the same time, slightly scornful.

"I can give you a thousand; maybe Solly, my agent, can give you five hundred. And I'll give you a check for the rest."

"White slavery!" Kickaha said. And then, "You can't be over twenty-five, right? And you can throw money around like that?"

He remembered his own youth during the Depression and how hard he had worked to just survive and how tough so many others had had it.

"You are a weirdo," Baum said. "Don't you know anything? Or are you putting me on?"

His voice was loaded with contempt. Kickaha felt like laughing in his face and also felt like hitting him in his mouth. He did neither. He said, "I'll take the fifteen hundred. But right now. And if Ann spits on you, you don't get the money back."

Baum glanced nervously at Moo-Moo, who had moved over to sit with Anana.

He said, "Wait till we get to L.A. We'll stop off to eat, and then you can take off. I'll give you your money then."

"And you can get up your nerve to tell Moo-Moo that Ann is joining you but I'm taking off?" Kickaha said. "Very well. Except for the money. I want it now! Otherwise, I tell Moo-Moo what you just said."

Baum turned a little pale and his undershot jaw sagged. He said, "You slimy . . . ! You got a nerve! You think I'd double-cross you, turn you in to the fuzz?"

"And I want a signed statement explaining why I'm getting the money. Any legitimate excuse will do," Kickaha said, wondering if the "fuzz" was the police.

"You may have been out of it for a long time, but you haven't forgotten any of the tricks, have you?" Baum said, not so scornfully now.

"There are people like you everyplace," Kickaha said.

He knew that he and Anana would need money, and they had no time to go to work to earn it, and he did not want to rob to get it if he could avoid doing so. If this nauseating specimen of arrogance thought he could buy Anana, let him pay for the privilege of finding out whether or not he could.

Baum dug into his jacket and came up with eight one-hundred-dollar bills. He handed these to Kickaha and then interrupted his manager, a fat bald-headed man with a huge cigar. The manager gestured violently and shot some hard looks at Kickaha but he gave in. Baum came back with five one-hundred-dollar bills. He wrote a note on a piece of paper, saying that the money was in payment for a debt he owed Paul J. Finnegan. After giving it to Kickaha, he insisted that Kickaha write him a receipt for the money. Kickaha also took the check for the rest of the money, although he did not think that he would be able to cash it. Baum would stop payment on it, he was sure of that.

Kickaha left Baum and sat down on a seat on which were a number of magazines, paperback books, and a *Los Angeles Times*. He spent some time reading, and when he had finished, he sat for a long time looking out the window.

Earth had certainly changed since 1946.

Pulling himself out of his reverie, he picked up a road map of Los Angeles, which he'd noticed among the magazines. As he studied it, he realized Wolff and Chryseis could be anywhere in the great sprawl of Los Angeles. He was certain they were headed in that direction though, rather than Nevada or Arizona, since the nearest gate was in the L.A. area. They might even be in a bus only a few miles ahead.

Since Wolff and Chryseis had taken the gate to Earth from the palace in Wolff's universe as an emergency exit to avoid being killed by the invaders, they were dressed in the clothes of the Lords. Chryseis may have been wearing no clothes at all. So the two would have been forced to obtain clothes from others. And they would have had to find some big dark glasses immediately, because anyone seeing Chryseis' enormous violet eyes would have known that she was not Earth-born. Or would have thought her a freak, despite her great beauty.

Both of them were resourceful enough to get along, especially since Wolff had spent more time on Earth as an adult than Kickaha had.

As for the Beller, he would be in an absolutely strange and frightening world. He could speak no word of the language, and he would want to cling to his bell, which would be embarrassing and inconvenient for him. But he could have gone in any direction.

The only thing Kickaha could do was to head toward the nearest known gate in the hope that Wolff and Chryseis would also be doing that. If they met there, they could team up, consider what to do next, and plan the best way of locating the Beller. If Wolff and Chryseis did not show, then everything would be up to Kickaha.

Moo-Moo sat down by him. She put her hand on his arm and said, "My, you're muscular!"

"I have a few," he said, grinning. "Now that you've softened me up with your comments on my hardness, what's on your mind?"

She leaned against him, rubbing the side of her large breast against his arm, and said, "That Lou! He sees a new chick that's reasonably good-looking, and he flips every time. He's been talking to you, trying to get you to give your girlfriend to him, hasn't he? I'll bet he offered you money for her?"

"Some," Kickaha said. "What about it?"

She felt the muscles of his thigh and said, "Two can play at that game."

"You offering me money, too?" he said.

She drew away from him, her eyes widening, and then she said, "You're putting me on! *I* should pay *you?*"

At another time, Kickaha might have played the game out to the end. But, corny as it sounded, the fate of the human race on Earth really depended on him. If the Beller adjusted to this world, and succeeded in making other bells, and then the minds in these possessed the bodies of human beings, the time would come when . . . Moo-Moo herself would become a mindless thing and then a body and brain inhabited by another entity.

It might not matter, however. If he were to believe half of what he read in the magazines and newspaper, the human race might well have doomed itself. And all life on the planet. Earth might be better off with humans occupied by the minds of Bellers. Bellers were logical beings and, given a chance, they would clean up the mess that humans seemed to have made of the entire planet.

Kickaha shuddered a little. Such thinking was dangerous. There could be no rest until the last of the Bellers died.

"What's the matter with you?" Moo-Moo said, her voice losing its softness. "You don't dig me."

He patted her thigh and said, "You're a beautiful woman, Moo-Moo, but I love Ann. However, tell you what! If the Gnome King succeeds in turning Ann into one of his Bad Eggs, you and I will make music together. And it won't be the cacophony that radio is vomiting."

She jerked with surprise and then said, "What do you mean? That's the Rolling Stones!"

"No moss gathered here," he said.

"You're not with it," she said. "Man, you're square, square, square! You sure you're not over thirty?"

He shrugged. He had not cared for the popular music of his youth, either. But it was sometimes pleasant, when compared to this screeching rhythm that turned his teeth in on himself.

The bus had moved out of the desert country into greener land. It sped along the freeway despite the increasing traffic. The sun was shining down so fiercely now, and the air was hot. The air was also noisy with the roar of cars, and stinking with fumes. His eyes stung, and the insides of his nostrils felt needled. A grayish haze was lying ahead; then they were in it, and the air seemed to clear somewhat, and the haze was ahead again.

Moo-Moo said something about the smog really being fierce this time of the year and especially along here. Kickaha had read about smog in one of the magazines, although he did not know the origin of the word as yet. If this was what the people of southern California lived in, he wanted no more to do with it. Anana's eyes were red and teary, and she was sniffing and complaining of a headache and clogging sinuses.

Moo-Moo left him, and Anana sat down by him.

"You never said anything about this when you were describing your world to me," she said.

"I didn't know anything about it," he said. "It developed after I left Earth."

The bus had been traveling swiftly and too wildly. It had switched lanes back and forth as it squeezed between cars, tailgating and cutting in ahead madly. The driver crouched over his wheel, his eyes seeming to blaze, his mouth hanging open and his tongue flicking out. He paid no attention to the sound of screeching brakes and blaring horns, but leaned on his own horn when he wanted to scare somebody just ahead of him. The horn was very loud and deep and must have sounded like a locomotive horn to many a startled driver. These usually pulled over to another lane, sometimes doing it so swiftly, they almost sideswiped other cars.

After a while, the press of cars was so heavy that the bus was forced to crawl along or even stop now and then. For miles ahead, traffic was creeping along. The heat and the gray haze thickened.

Moo-Moo said to Baum, "Why can't we get air conditioning on this bus? We certainly make enough money!"

"How often do we get on the freeway?" the manager said.

Kickaha told Anana about Baum's proposal.

Anana said, "I don't know whether to laugh or to throw up."

"A little of both might help you," he said. "Well, I promised I wouldn't try to argue you out of it if you decided to take him in preference to me. Which, by the way, he seemed one-hundred-percent sure would happen."

"You sell me; you worry a while until I make up my mind," she said.

"Sure. I'll do that," he replied. He rose and sauntered down the aisle and looked out the back of the bus. After a while he came back and sat down again with Anana.

In a low voice, he said, "There's a big black Lincoln Continental, I believe, behind us. I recognize one of the men in it. I saw him through the binoculars when I looked down from the cave."

"How could they have found us?" she said. Her voice was steady but her body was rigid.

"Maybe they didn't," he said. "It might be just a coincidence. They may have no idea they're so close to us. And then, again . . ."

It did not seem at all likely. But how had they caught up with them? Had they been posted along the road and seen them go by in the bus? Or did Orc have such a widespread organization that someone on the bus had reported to him?

He dismissed this last thought as sheer paranoia. Only time would show whether or not it was coincidence.

So far, the men in the car had not seemed interested in the bus. They were having a vigorous dispute. Three of them were dark and between forty and fifty-five years old. The fourth was a young man with blond hair cut in a Julius Caesar style. Kickaha studied them until he had branded their features on his mind. Then he returned to the seat near the front.

After a while, the traffic speeded up. The bus sped by grim industrial sections and the back ends of run-down buildings. The grayish green-tinged smog did not thicken, but its corrosive action became worse. Anana said, "Do your people live in this all the time? They must be very tough!"

"You know as much as I do about it," he said.

Baum suddenly rose from his seat beside Moo-Moo and said to the driver, "Jim, when you get near Civic Center, pull off and look for a hamburger stand. I'm hungry."

The others protested. They could eat at the hotel when they got there. It would only take about a half hour more. What was his hurry?

"I'm hungry!" he shouted. He looked wild-eyed at them and stomped his foot hard. "I'm hungry! I don't want to wait any longer! Besides, if we got to fight our way through the usual mob of teenyboppers, we may be held up for some time! Let's eat now!"

The others shrugged. Evidently they had seen him act this way before. He looked as if he were going to scream and stamp through the floor, like in a tantrum, if he did not get his way.

It was not a whim this time, however. Moo-Moo rolled her eyes and then came up to Kickaha and said, "He's letting you know it's time to bow out, Red. You better take your worldly goods and kiss your girlfriend goodbye."

"You've been through this before?" Kickaha said, grinning. "What makes you so sure Ann'll be staying?"

"I'm not so sure about her," Moo-Moo said. "I sensed something weird about you two, and the feeling hasn't gone away. In fact, it's even stronger."

She surprised Kickaha then by saying, "You two are running away, aren't you? From the fuzz. And from others. More than the fuzz. Somebody close behind you now. I smell danger."

She squeezed his arm, bent lower, and whispered, "If I can help you, I'll be at the Beverly Hilton for a week, then we go to San Francisco. You call me. I'll tell the hotel to let you through. Any time."

Kickaha felt warmed by her interest and offer of help. At the same time, he could not keep from considering that she might know more than any would-be friend of his should. Was it possible that she was tied in with Red Orc?

He rejected that. His life had been so full of danger, one perilous situation after another, and he had gotten into the pro-survival habit of always considering the worst and planning possible actions to avoid it. In this case, Moo-Moo could be nothing more than a psychic, or at least, a very sensitive person.

The bus pulled off the freeway and drove to the Music Center. Kickaha would have liked to study the tall buildings here, which reminded him of those of Manhattan, but he was watching the big black Lincoln and its four occupants. It had turned when the bus turned and was now two cars behind. Kickaha was willing to concede that its getting off the freeway here might be another coincidence. But he doubted it very much.

The bus pulled into a corner of a parking lot in the center of which was a large hamburger stand. The bus doors opened, and the driver got out first. Baum took Anana's hand and led her out. Kickaha noted this out of the corner of his eye; he was watching the Lincoln. It had pulled into a parking place five cars down from the stand.

Baum was immediately surrounded by five or six young girls who shrieked his name and a number of unintelligible exclamations. They also tried to touch him. Baum smiled at them and waved his hands for them to back away. After a minute's struggle, he and the older men succeeded in backing them off.

Kickaha, carrying the instrument case, followed Moo-Moo off the bus and across the lot to the picnic table under a shady awning, where Baum and Anana were seated. The waitress brought hamburgers, hot dogs, milk shakes, and Cokes. He salivated when he saw his hamburger. It had been, God, over twenty-four years since he had tasted a hamburger! He bit down and then chewed slowly. There was something in the meat, some unidentified element, that he did not like. This distasteful substance also seemed to be in the lettuce and the tomato.

Anana grimaced and said, in the language of the Lords, "What do you put in this food?"

Kickaha shrugged and said, "Insecticide, maybe, although it doesn't seem possible that we could detect one part in a million or whatever it was. Still, there's something."

They fared better with the chocolate milk shake. This was as thick and creamy and delicious as he remembered it. Anana nodded her approval, too.

The men were still in the Lincoln and were looking at him and Anana. At the group, anyway.

Baum looked across to Kickaha and said, "OK, Finnegan. This is it. Take off!"

Kickaha glanced up at him and said, "The bargain was, I take off if she agrees to go with you."

Baum laughed and said, "Just trying to spare your feelings, my Midwestern rustic. But have it your own way. Watch me, maybe you'll learn something."

He leaned over Anana, who was talking with Moo-Moo. Moo-Moo glanced once at Baum's face, then got up, and walked off. Kickaha watched Baum and Anana. The conversation was short; the action, abrupt and explosive.

Anana slapped Baum so hard across the face that its noise could be heard above the gabble of his fans and the roar of the traffic. There was a short silence from everybody around Baum and then a number of shrieks of anger from the girl fans. Baum shouted angrily and swung with his right fist at Anana. She dodged and slid off the bench, but then the people around her blocked Kickaha's view.

He scooped off some change on the table, left by customers. Putting this in his pocket, he jumped into the fray. He was, however, almost knocked down by the press of bodies trying to get away. The girls rammed into him, clawed at him, shrieked, gouged, and kicked.

Suddenly, there was an opening. He saw Baum lying on the cement, his legs drawn up and his hands clenching his groin. A girl, bent over, was sitting by him and holding her stomach. Another girl was leaning over a wooden table, her back to him and retching.

Kickaha grabbed Anana's hand and shouted, "Come on! This is the chance we've been looking for!"

The instrument case in his other hand, he led her running toward the back of the parking lot. Just before they went down a narrow alley between two tall buildings, he looked back. The car containing his shadowers had pulled into the lot, and three of the men were getting out. They saw their quarry, and ran toward them. But they were not stupid enough to pull out weapons before they caught up with them. Kickaha did not intend that they should catch up with them.

And then, as he ran out of the alley and into the next street, he thought, *Why not? I could spend years trying to find Red Orc, but if I can get hold of those who work for him . . . ?*

The next street was as busy as the one they had just left. The two stopped running but did walk swiftly. A police car, proceeding in the same direction, suddenly accelerated, its lights coming into red life. It took the corner with squealing tires, pursued by the curses of an old man who looked like a wino.

He looked behind him. The three men were still following but making no effort to overtake them. One man was talking into something concealed in his hand. He was either speaking to the man in the car or to his boss. Kickaha understood by now that radio sets were much smaller than in 1946 and that the man might be using a quite common miniature transceiver. On the other hand, he might be using a device unknown on Earth except to those who worked for Red Orc.

They continued walking. He looked back once more when they had covered two blocks. The big black Lincoln had stopped, and the three men were getting into it. Kickaha halted before a pawn shop and looked through the dirty plate-glass window at the backwash of people's hopes. He said, "We'll give them a chance to try to pick us up. I don't know that they'll have guts enough to do it in broad daylight but if they do, here's what we do . . ."

The Lincoln drew up even with them and stopped.

Kickaha turned around and grinned at the men in the Lincoln. The front and back doors on the right side opened, and three men got out. They walked toward the couple, their hands in their coat pockets. At that moment a siren wailed down the street. The three jerked their heads to look at the police car that had suddenly appeared. It shot between cars, swerved sharply to cut around the Lincoln, and went on through the traffic light just as it was turning red. It kept on going; evidently it was not headed for the trouble around the corner.

The three men had turned casually and walked back toward the Lincoln. Kickaha took advantage of their concern over the police car. Before they could turn around again, he was behind them. He shoved his knuckles into the back of the oldest man and said, "I'll burn a hole through you if you make any trouble."

Anana had her ring finger against the back of the young man with the tangled blond hair. He stiffened, and his jaw dropped, as if he could not believe that not only had their hunted turned against them, they were doing so before at least fifty witnesses.

Horns started blaring at the Lincoln. The driver gestured at the three to hurry back, then he saw that Kickaha and Anana were pressed up closely against the backs of two of the men. The third man, who had overheard Kickaha, waved at the driver to go on. The Lincoln took off with a screeching and burning of tires and swung around the corner without coming to a stop first.

"That was a smart move!" Kickaha said to the man just in front of him. "One-up for you!"

The third man began to walk away. Kickaha said, "I'll kill this guy if you don't come back!"

"Kill him!" the man said and continued walking.

Kickaha spoke in Lord language to Anana. "Let your man go! We'll keep this one and herd him to a private place where we can talk."

"What's to keep the others from following us?"

"Nothing. I don't care at this moment if they do."

He did, but he did not want the others to think so.

The blond sneered at them and swaggered off. There was something in his walk, however, that betrayed him. He was very relieved to have gotten away unhurt.

Kickaha then told the remaining man just what would happen if he tried to run away. The man said nothing. He seemed very calm. A genuine professional, Kickaha thought. It would have been better to have kept the blond youth, who might not be so tough to crack. It was too late to do anything about that, however.

The problem was: where to take the man for questioning? They were in the center of a vast metropolis unfamiliar to either Kickaha or Anana. There should be some third-rate hotels around here, judging by the appearance of the buildings and many of the pedestrians. It might be possible to rent a room and interrogate their captive there. But he could ruin everything if he opened his mouth and screamed. And even if he could be gotten into a hotel room, his buddies would have trailed them there and would call in reinforcements. The hotel room would be a trap.

Kickaha gave the order and the three started walking. He was on one side of the man and Anana was on the other. He studied his captive's profile, which looked brutish but strong. The man was about fifty, had a dark sallow skin, brown eyes, a big curved nose, a thick mouth, and a massive chin. Kickaha asked his name, and the man growled, "Mazarin."

"Who do you work for?" Kickaha said.

"Somebody you'd better not mess around with," Mazarin said.

"You tell me who your boss is and how I can get to him, and I'll let you go scot-free," Kickaha said. "Otherwise, I burn you until you tell. You know everybody has their limits, and you might be able to take a lot of burning, but you'll give in eventually."

The man shrugged big shoulders and said, "Sure. What about it?"

"Are you really that loyal?" Kickaha said.

The man looked at him contemptuously. "No, but I don't figure you'll get the chance to do anything. And I don't intend to say anything more."

He clamped his lips shut and turned his eyes away.

They had walked two blocks. Kickaha looked behind him. The Lincoln had come around and picked up the two men and now was proceeding slowly on the lane nearest the sidewalk.

Kickaha did not doubt that the three had gotten into contact with their boss and were waiting for reinforcements. It was an impasse.

Then he grinned again.

He spoke rapidly to Anana, and they directed Mazarin to the edge of the road. They waited until the Lincoln drew even and then stepped out. The three were staring from the car as if they could not believe what they were seeing. They also looked apprehensive. The car stopped when Kickaha waved at them. The two on the right side of the car had their guns out and pointed through the window, although their other hands concealed the barrels as best they could.

Kickaha pushed Mazarin ahead of him, and they walked around in front of the car and to the driver's side. Anana stopped on the right side of the car about five feet away.

Kickaha said, "Get into the car!"

Mazarin looked at him with an unreadable expression. He opened the rear door and began to climb in. Kickaha shoved him on in and came in with him. At the same time, Anana stepped up to the car. The driver had turned around and the other two had turned to watch Kickaha. She pressed the ring, which was set to stun power again, against the head of the man in the front right seat. He slumped over, and at the same time, Kickaha stunned Mazarin.

The blond youth in the right rear seat pointed his gun at Kickaha and said, "You must be outta your mind! Don't move or I'll plug you!"

The energy from the ring hit the back of his head and spread out over the bone of the skull, probably giving the skin a first-degree burn through all the layers of cells. His head jerked forward as if a fist had hit it; his finger jerked in reflex. The .38 automatic went off once, sounding loudly inside the car. Mazarin jerked, fell back, his arms flying out and his hand hitting Kickaha in the chest. Then he fell over, slowly, against Kickaha.

The driver yelled and gunned the car. Anana leaped back to keep from being run over. Kickaha shouted at the driver, but the man kept the accelerator pressed to the floor. He screamed back an obscenity. He intended to keep going, even through the red light ahead at the intersection, on the theory that Kickaha would be too frightened of the results if he knocked him out.

Kickaha stunned him anyway, and the car immediately slowed down. It did not stop, however, and so rolled into the rear end of a car waiting for the red light to change. Kickaha had squatted down on the floor behind the driver's seat to cushion the impact. He was thrown forward, with the back of the seat and the driver's body taking up most of the energy.

Immediately thereafter, he opened the door and crawled out. The man in the car in front of him was still sitting in his seat, looking stunned. Kickaha reached back into the car and took out Mazarin's wallet from his jacket pocket. He then removed the driver's wallet. The registration card for the car was not on the steering-wheel column, nor was it in the glove compartment. He could not afford to spend any more time at the scene. Kickaha walked away and then began running when he heard a scream behind him.

He met Anana at the intersection, and they took a left turn around the corner. Only one man had pursued Kickaha, but he had halted when Kickaha had glared at him, and he did not continue his dogging.

He hailed a cab, and they climbed in. Remembering the map of Los Angeles he had studied on the bus, he ordered the driver to drop them off on Lorraine, south of Wilshire.

Anana did not ask him what he was doing, because he had told her to keep quiet. He did not want the cab driver to remember a woman who spoke a foreign language, although her beauty and their hiking clothes would make them stand out in his memory.

He picked out an apartment building to stop in front of, paid the driver, and tipped him with a dollar bill. Then he and Anana climbed the steps and went into the lobby, which was empty. Waiting until they were sure the cab would be out of sight, they walked back to Wilshire. Here they took a bus.

After several minutes, Kickaha led Anana off the bus and she said, "What now?" although she did not seem to be too interested at the moment in their next move. She was looking at the gas station across the street. Its architecture was new to Kickaha also. He could compare it only to something out of the Flash Gordon serials. Anana, of course, had seen many different styles. A woman didn't live ten thousand years and in several different universes without seeing a great variety of styles in buildings. But this Earth was such a hodgepodge.

Kickaha told her what he planned next. They would go toward Hollywood and look for a motel or hotel in the cheaper districts. He had learned from a magazine and from newspapers that the area contained many transients—hippies, they called them now—and the wilder younger element. Their clothing and lack of baggage would not cause curiosity.

They caught a cab in two minutes, and it carried them to Sunset Boulevard. Then they walked for quite a while. The sun went down; the lights came on over the city. Sunset Boulevard began to fill up with cars bumper to bumper. The sidewalks were beginning to be crowded, mainly with the "hippies" he'd read about. There were also a number of "characters," which was to be expected in Hollywood.

They stopped and asked some of the aimlessly wandering youths about lodging. A young fellow with shoulder-length hair and a thick 1890 mustache and sideburns, but dressed in expensive-looking clothes, gave them some sound information. He wanted to talk some more and even invited them to have dinner with him. It was evident that he was fascinated by Anana, not Kickaha.

Kickaha said to him, "We'll see you around," and they left. A half hour later, they were inside their room in a motel on a side street. The room was not plush, but it was more than adequate for Kickaha, who had spent most of the past twenty-four years in primitive conditions. It was not as quiet as he wished, since a party was going on in the next room. A radio or record player was blasting out one of the more screechy examples of Rock, many feet stomped, and many voices shrieked.

While Anana took a shower, he studied the contents of the wallets he'd taken from the two men. Frederic James Mazarin and Jeffrey Velazquez

Ramos, according to their drivers' licenses, lived on Wilshire Boulevard. His map showed him that the address was close to the termination of Wilshire downtown. He suspected that the two lived in a hotel. Mazarin was forty-eight and Ramos was forty-six. The rest of the contents of the wallets were credit cards (almost unknown in 1946, if he remembered correctly), a few pictures of the two with women, a photo of a woman who might have been Ramos' mother (three hundred and twenty dollars), and a slip of paper in Mazarin's wallet with ten initials in one column and telephone numbers in others.

Kickaha went into the bathroom and opened the shower door. He told Anana that he was going across the street to the public telephone booth.

"Why don't you use the telephone here?"

"It goes through the motel switchboard," he said. "I just don't want to take any chances of being traced or trapped."

He walked several blocks to a drugstore where he got change. He stood for a moment, considering using the drugstore phones and then decided to go back to the booth near the motel. That way, he could watch the motel front while making his calls.

He stopped for a moment by the paperback rack. It had been so long since he'd read a book. Well, he had read the Tishquetmoac books, but they didn't publish anything but science and history and theology. The people of the tier called Atlantis had published fiction, but he had spent very little time among them, although he had planned to someday. There had been some books in the Semitic civilization of Khamshem and the Germanic civilization of Dracheland, but the number of novels was very small and the variety was limited. Wolff's palace had contained a library of twenty million books—or recordings of books—but Kickaha had not spent enough time there to read very many.

He looked over the selection, aware that he shouldn't be taking the time to do so, and finally picked three. One was a Tom Wolfe book (but not the Thomas Woolfe he had known), which looked as if it would give him information about the zeitgeist of modern times. One was a factual book by Asimov (who was, it seemed, the same man as the science-fiction writer he remembered), and a book on the black revolution. He went to the magazine counter and purchased *Look, Life, The Saturday Review, The New Yorker,* the *Los Angeles* magazine, and a number of science-fiction magazines.

With his books, magazines, and an evening *Times,* he walked back to the telephone booth. He called Anana first to make sure that she was all right. Then he took pencil and paper and dialed each of the numbers on the slip of paper he had found in Mazarin's wallet.

Three of them were women who disclaimed any knowledge of Mazarin. Three of the numbers did not reply. Kickaha marked these for late calls. One might have been a bookie joint, judging from the talking in the background. The man who answered was as noncommittal as the women. The eighth call got a bartender. Kickaha said he was looking for Mazarin.

The bartender said, "Ain't you heard, friend? Mazarin was killed today!"

"Somebody *killed* him?" Kickaha said, as if he were shocked. "Who done it?"

"Nobody knows. The guy was riding with Fred and some of the boys, and all of a sudden the guy pulls Charley's gun out of his pocket, shoots Fred in the chest with it, and takes off, but only after he knocks out Charley, Ramos, and Ziggy."

"Yeah?" Kickaha said. "Them guys was pros, too. They must've got careless or something. Say, ain't that gonna make their boss mad? He must be jumping up and down!"

"You kiddin', friend? Nothin' makes Cambring jump up and down. Look, I gotta go, a customer. Drop around, buy me a drink, I'll fill you in on the gory details."

Kickaha wrote the name Cambring down and then looked through the phone book. There was no Cambring in the Los Angeles directory or any of the surrounding cities.

The ninth phone number was that of a Culver City garage. The man who answered said he'd never heard of Mazarin. Kickaha doubted that that was true, but there was nothing he could do about it.

The last number was opposite the letters *R.C.* Kickaha hoped that these stood for R.R. Cambring. But the woman who answered was Roma Chalmers. She was as guarded as the others in her replies to his questions.

He called Anana again to make doubly sure that she was all right. Then he returned to the room, where he ordered a meal from Chicken Delight. He ate everything in the box, but the food had that taste of something disagreeable and of something missing. Anana also ate all of hers but complained.

"Tomorrow's Saturday," he said. "If we haven't found any promising leads, we'll go out and get some clothes."

He took a shower and got dried just before a bottle of Wild Turkey and six bottles of Tuborg were delivered. Anana tried both and settled for the Danish beer. Kickaha sipped a little of the bourbon and made a wry face. The liquor-store owner had said that the bourbon was the best in the world. It had been too long since he had tasted whisky; he would have to learn to like it all over again. If he had time, that is, which he doubted. He decided to drink a bottle or two of the Tuborg, which he found tasty, probably because beer-making was well known on the World of Tiers and he had not gotten out of the habit of drinking it.

He sat in a chair and sipped while he slowly read out loud in English from the newspaper to Anana. Primarily, he was looking for any news about Wolff, Jadawin, or the Beller. He sat up straight when he came across an item about Lucifer's Louts. These had been discovered, half naked, beaten up, and burned, on the road out of Lake Arrowhead. The story they gave police was that a rival gang had jumped them.

A page later, he found a story about the crash of a helicopter near Lake Arrowhead. The helicopter, out of the Santa Monica airport, was owned by a Mister Cambring, who had once been put on trial, but not convicted, for bribery of city officials in connection with a land deal. Kickaha whooped with delight and then explained to Anana what a break this was.

The news story did not give Cambring's address. Kickaha called the office of Top Hat Enterprises, which Cambring owned. The phone rang for a long time, and he finally gave up. He then called the *Los Angeles Times* and, after a series of transfers from one person and department to another, some of them involving waits of three or four minutes, he got his information. Mr. Roy Arndell Cambring lived on Rimpau Boulevard. A check of the city map showed that the house was several blocks north of Wilshire.

"This helps," he said. "I would have located Cambring if I had to hire a private eye to find him. But that would have taken time. Let's get to bed. We have a lot to do tomorrow."

However, it was an hour before they fell asleep. Anana wanted to lie quietly in his arms while she talked of this and that, about her life before she had met Kickaha, but mostly of incidents after she had met him. Actually, they had not known each other more than two months and their life together had been hectic. But she claimed to be in love with Kickaha and acted as if she were. He loved her but had had enough experience with the Lords to wonder how deep a capacity for love anybody ten thousand years old could possess. It was true, though, that some of the Lords could live for the moment far more intensely than anybody he had ever met simply because a man who lived in eternity had to eat up every moment as if it were his last. He could not bear to think about the unending years ahead.

In the meantime, he was happy with her, although he would have been happier if he could have some leisure and peace so he could get to know her better. Which was exactly what she was complaining about. She did not complain too much. She knew that every situation ended sooner or later.

He fell asleep thinking about this. Sometime in the night, he awoke with a jerk. For a second, he thought somebody must be in the room, and he slid out the knife that lay sheathless by his side under the sheet covering him. His eyes adjusted to the darkness, which was not too deep because of the light through the blinds from the bright neon lights outside and the street lamps. He could see no one.

Slowly, so the bed would not creak, he got out and moved cautiously around the room, the bathroom, and then the closet. The windows were still locked on the inside, the door was locked, and the bureau he had shoved against it had not moved. Nor was there anyone under the bed.

He decided that he had been sleeping on a tightwire too long. He expected, even if unconsciously, to fall off.

There must be more to it than that, however. Something working deep inside him had awakened him. He had been dreaming just before he awoke. Of what?

He could not get his hook into it and bring it up out of the unconscious, though he cast many times. He paced back and forth, the knife still in his hand, and tried to recreate the moment just before awakening. After a while he gave up. But he could not sleep when he lay back down again. He rose again, dressed, and then woke Anana up gently. At his tender touch on her face, she came up off the bed, knife in hand.

He had wisely stepped back. He said, "It's all right, lover, I just wanted to tell you that I'm leaving to check out Cambring's house. I can't sleep anymore; I feel as if I have something important to do. I've had this feeling before and it's always paid off."

He did not add that it had sometimes paid off with grave, almost fatal, trouble.

"I'll go with you."

"No, that won't be necessary. I appreciate your offer, but you stay here and sleep. I promise I won't do anything except scout around it, at a safe distance. You won't have anything to worry about."

"All right," she said, half drowsily. She had full confidence in his abilities. "Kiss me good night again and get on with you. I'm glad I'm not a restless soul."

The lobby was empty. There were no pedestrians outside the motel, although a few cars whizzed by. The droning roar of a jet lowering for International Airport seemed to be directly overhead, but its lights placed it quite a few miles southeastward. He trotted on down the street toward the south and hoped that no cops would cruise by. He understood from what he'd read that a man running was suspected anywhere in the city and a man walking at night in the more prosperous districts was also suspect.

He could have taken a taxi to a place near his destination, but he preferred to run. He needed the exercise; if he continued life in this city long, he would be getting soft rapidly.

The smog seemed to have disappeared with the sun. At least, his eyes did not burn and run, although he did get short-winded after having trotted only eight blocks. There must be poisonous oxides hanging invisibly in the air. Or he was deteriorating faster than he had thought possible.

By the map, the Cambring house lay about three and one-half

miles from the motel, not as the crow flies but as a ground-bound human must go.

Once on Rimpau he was in a neighborhood of fairly old mansions. The neighborhood looked as if only rich people had lived here, but it was changing. Some of the grounds and houses had deteriorated, and some had been made into apartment dwellings. But a number were still very well kept up.

The Cambring house was a huge three-story wooden house that looked as if it had been built circa 1920 by someone nostalgic for the architecture popular among the wealthy of the Midwest. It was set up on a high terrace with a walk in the middle of the lawn and a horseshoe-shaped curving driveway. Three cars were parked in the driveway. There were a dozen great oaks and several sycamores on the front lawn and many high bushes, beautifully trimmed, set in among the trees. A high brick wall enclosed all but the front part of the property.

There were lights behind closed curtains in the first and second stories. There was also a light in the second story of the garage, which he could partially see. He walked on past the front of the house to the corner. The brick wall ran along the sidewalk here. Partway down the block was another driveway that led to the garage. He stopped before the closed iron gates, which were locked on the inside.

It was possible that there were electronic detecting devices set on the grounds among the trees, but he would have to chance them. Also, it would be well to find out now.

He doubted that this house was lived in by Red Orc. Cambring must be one of Orc's underlings, probably far down in the hierarchy. The Lord of Earth would be ensconced in a truly luxurious dwelling and behind walls that would guard him well.

He set his ring for flesh-piercing powers at up to two hundred feet and placed his knife between his teeth. Instead of returning to the front, he went over the wall on the side of the house. It was more difficult to enter here, but there was better cover.

He backed up into the street and then ran forward, bounded across the sidewalk, and leaped upward. His fingers caught the edge of the wall and he easily pulled himself up and over onto the top of the wall. He lay stretched out on it, watching the house and garage for signs of activity. About four minutes passed. A car, traveling fast, swung around the corner two blocks away and sped down the street. It was possible that the occupants of the house might see him in the beams. He swung on over and dropped onto soft grassy ground behind an oak tree. If he had wished, he could have jumped to the nearest branch, which had been sawed off close to the wall, and descended by the tree. He noted it as a means of escape.

It was now about three in the morning, if his sense of time was good.

He had no watch but meant to get one, since he was now in a world where the precise measurement of time was important. The next ten minutes he spent in quietly exploring the area immediately outside the house and the garage. Three times he went up into a tree to try to look through windows, but he could see nothing. He poked around the cars but did not try to open their doors because he thought that they might have alarms. It seemed likely that a gangster like Cambring would be more worried about a bomb being placed in his car than he would about an invasion of his house. The big black Lincoln was not there. He assumed it had been impounded by the police as evidence in the murder. He read the license numbers several times to memorize them, even though he had a pencil and a piece of paper. During his years in the universe next door, he had been forced to rely on his memory. He had developed it to a power that he would have thought incredible twenty-five years ago. Illiteracy had its uses. How many educated men on Earth could recall the exact topography of a hundred places or draw a map of a five-thousand-mile route or recite a three-thousand-line epic?

In fifteen minutes he had checked out everything he could on the outside and knew exactly where things were in relation to each other. Now was the time to leave. He wished he had not promised Anana that he would only observe the exterior. The temptation to get inside was almost overwhelming. If he could get hold of Cambring and force some information from him . . . but he had promised. And she had gone back to sleep because she trusted him to keep his word. That in itself indicated how much she loved him, because if there was one thing a Lord lacked, it was trust in others.

He crouched for a while behind a bush in the side yard, knowing that he should leave but also knowing that he was hoping something would happen that would force him to take action. Minutes passed.

Then he heard a phone ringing inside the house. A light went on in a second-story window behind a curtain. He rose and approached the house and applied a small bell-like device to the side of the house. A cord ran from it to a plug, which he stuck in one ear. Suddenly, a man said, "Yes, sir. I got you. But how did you find them, if I may ask?"

There was a short silence, then the man said, "I'm sorry, sir. I didn't mean to be nosy, of course. Yes, sir, it won't happen again. Yes, sir, I got you the first time. I know exactly what to do. I'll call you when we start the operation, sir. Good night, sir."

Kickaha's heart beat faster. Cambring could be talking directly to Red Orc. In any event, something important was happening. Something ominous.

He heard footsteps and buzzers ringing. The voice said—presumably over an intercom—"Get dressed and up here! On the double! We got work to do! Jump!"

He decided what to do. If he heard anything that indicated that they were not going after him, he would wait until they left and then enter the house. Conditions would have changed so much that it would be stupid for him not to take advantage of their absence. Anana would have to understand that.

If he heard anything that indicated that he and Anana were concerned, he would take off for the nearest public phone booth.

He felt in his pocket for change and cursed. He had one nickel left over from the calls made that previous evening.

Seven minutes later, eight men left by the front door. Kickaha watched them from behind a tree. Four men got into a Mercedes-Benz and four into a Mercury. He could not be sure which was Cambring, because nobody spoke when they left the house. One man did hold the door open for a tall man with a high curly head of hair and a bold sweeping nose. He suspected that that was Cambring. Also he recognized two: the blond youth and Ramos, the driver of the Lincoln. Ramos had a white bandage over his forehead.

The cars drove off, leaving one car in the driveway. There were also people in the house. He had heard one woman sleepily asking Cambring what was wrong, and a man's voice surlily asking why he had to stay behind. He wanted some action. Cambring had curtly told him to shut up. They were under orders never to leave the house unguarded.

The cars had no sooner disappeared than Kickaha was at the front door. It was locked, but a quick shot of energy from the ring cut through the metal. He swung the door inward slowly, and stepped inside into a room lit only by a light from a stairwell at the far end. When his eyes adjusted, he could see a phone on a table at the far wall. He went to it, lit a match, and by its light, dialed Anana. The phone rang no more than three times before she answered.

He said softly, "Anana, I'm in Cambring's house! He and his gang are on the way to pick us up. You grab your clothes and get out of there, fast, hear! Don't even bother to dress! Put everything in a bag and take off! Dress behind the motel. I'll meet you where we arranged. Got it?"

"Wait!" she said. "Can't you tell me what's happened?"

"No!" he said and softly replaced the receiver on the phone. He had heard footsteps in the hall upstairs and then the creaking caused by a big man descending the steps slowly.

Kickaha reset the ring for stunning power. He needed someone to question, and he doubted that the woman would know as much about operations as this man.

The faint creakings stopped. Kickaha crouched by the foot of the steps and waited. Suddenly, the lights in the great room went on, and a man catapulted outward from behind the wall that had hidden him. He came down off the steps in a leap, whirling as he did so. He held a big automatic, probably a .45, in his right hand. He landed facing Kickaha and then fell backward, unconscious, his head driven back by the impact of the beam. The gun fell from his hand onto the thick rug.

Kickaha heard the woman upstairs saying, "Walt! What's the matter? Walt! Is anything wrong?"

Kickaha picked up the gun, flicked on the safety, and stuck it in his belt. Then he walked up the steps and got to the head of the stairwell just as the woman did. She opened her mouth to scream, but he clamped his hand over it and held the knife before her eyes. She went limp as if she thought she could placate him by not struggling. She was correct, for the moment, anyway.

She was a tall, very well built blonde, about thirty-five, in a filmy negligee. Her breath stank of whiskey. But good whiskey.

"You and Cambring and everybody else in this house mean only one thing to me," he said. "As a means of getting to the big boss. That's all. I can let you go without a scratch and care nothing about what you do from then on if you don't bother me. Or I can kill you. Here and now. Unless I get the information I want. You understand me?"

She nodded.

He said, "I'll let you go. But one scream, and I'll rip out your belly. Understand?"

She nodded again. He took his hand away from her mouth. She was pale and trembling.

"Show me a picture of Cambring," he said.

She turned and led him to her bedroom, where she indicated a photograph on her bureau dresser. It was of the man he had suspected was Cambring. "Are you his wife?" he said.

She cleared her throat and said, "Yes."

"Anybody else in this house besides Walt?"

She said huskily, "No."

"Do you know where Cambring went tonight?"

"No," she said. She cleared throat again. "I don't want to know those things."

"He's gone off to pick up me and my woman for your big boss," Kickaha said. "The boss would undoubtedly kill us, after he'd tortured us to get everything he wanted to know. So I won't have mercy on anybody connected with him—if they refuse to cooperate."

"I don't know anything!" she gasped. "Roy never tells me anything! I don't even know who the big boss is!"

"Who's Cambring's immediate superior?"

"I don't know. Please believe me, I don't know! He gets orders from somebody, I'll admit that! But I don't know!"

She was probably telling the truth. So the next thing to do was to rouse Walt and find out what he knew. He did not have much time.

He went downstairs with Cara ahead of him. The man was still unconscious. Kickaha told Cara to get a glass of water from the nearest bathroom. He threw it over Walt's face. Walt recovered a moment later, but he looked too sick to be a threat. He seemed to be on the verge of throwing up. A big black mark was spreading over the skin on his forehead and nose, and his eyes looked a solid red.

The questioning did not last long. The man, whose full name was Walter Erich Vogel, claimed he also did not know who Cambring's boss was. Nor did he even know where Cambring was going. Kickaha believed this, since Cambring had not said anything about the destination. Apparently, he meant to tell his men after they got started. Cambring called his boss now and then but he carried the phone number in his head.

"It's the old Commie cell idea," Vogel said. "So you could torture me from now until doomsday and you wouldn't get anything out of me because I don't know anything."

Kickaha went to the phone again and, while he kept an eye on the two, dialed Anana's number again. He wasn't surprised when Cambring answered.

"Cambring," he said, "this is the man you were sent after. Now hear me out because this message is intended for your big boss. You tell him, or whoever relays messages to him, that a Black Beller is loose on Earth."

There was a silence, one of shock, Kickaha hoped, and then Cambring said, "What? What the hell you talking about? What's a Black Beller?"

"Just tell your boss that a Black Beller got loose from Jadawin's world. The Beller's in this area, or was yesterday, anyway. Remember, a Black Beller. Came here yesterday from Jadawin's world."

There was another silence and then Cambring said, "Listen. The boss knows you got away. But he said that if I got a chance to talk to you, you should come on in. The boss won't hurt you. He just wants to talk to you."

"You might be right," Kickaha said. "But I can't afford to take the chance. No, you tell your boss something. You tell him that I'm not out to get him; I'm not a Lord. I just want to find another Lord and his woman, who came to this world to escape from the Black Bellers. In fact, I'll tell you who that Lord is. It's Jadawin. Maybe your boss will remember him. It's Jadawin, who's changed very much. Jadawin isn't interested in challenging your boss; he couldn't care less. All he wants to do is get back to his own world. You tell him that, though I doubt it'll do any good. I'll call your home tomorrow about noon, so you can relay more of what I have to say to your boss. I'll call your home. Your boss might want to be there so he can talk to me directly."

"What the hell you gibbering about?" Cambring said. He sounded very angry.

"Just tell your boss what I said. He'll understand," Kickaha said, and he hung up. He was grinning. If there was one thing that scared a Lord, it was a Black Beller.

The sports car was, as he had suspected, hers. She said she would have to go upstairs to get the keys. He said that that was all right, but he and Vogel would go with her. They went into the bedroom, where Kickaha gave Vogel a slight kick in the back of the head with a beam from the ring. He took Vogel's wallet and dragged him into the closet, where he left him snoring. He then demanded money from the woman, and she gave him six hundred dollars in twenties and fifties. It pleased him that he had been able to live off the enemy so far.

To keep her occupied, he tore down some curtains, and set them on fire with a sweep from the ring. She screamed and dashed into the bathroom to get water. A moment later, he was driving the Jaguar off the driveway. Behind him, screams came through the open doorways as she fought the flames.

At a corner a few blocks east from the motel, he flashed his lights twice to alert Anana. A dark figure emerged from between two houses. She approached warily until she recognized him. She threw their packs and the instrument case into the back seat, got in and said, "Where did you get this vehicle?"

"Took it from Cambring." He chuckled and said, "I left a message with Cambring for Red Orc. Told him that a Black Beller was loose. That ought to divert him. It might even scare him into offering an armistice."

"Not Red Orc," she said. "Not unless he's changed. Which is possible. I did. My brother Luvah did. And you say Jadawin did."

He told her about his idea for contacting Wolff. "I should have thought of it sooner, but we have been occupied. And, besides, I've forgotten a lot about Earth."

For the moment, they would look for new lodgings. However, he was not so sure that they could feel safe even there. It was remarkable that they had been located. Red Orc must have set into action a very large organization to have found them.

"How could he do that?" she said.

"For all I know, his men called every hotel and motel in the Los Angeles area. That would be such a tremendous job, though, I doubt they could have gone through more than a small percentage of them. Maybe they were making random spot calls. Or maybe they were going through them all, one by one, and were lucky."

"If that is so, then we won't be safe when we check in at the next place."

"I just don't believe that even the Lord of the Earth would have an organization big enough to check out all the motels and hotels in so short a time," he said. "But we'll leave the area, go to the Valley, as they so quaintly call it here."

When they found a motel in Laurel Canyon, he ran into difficulties. The clerk wanted his driver's license and the license number of his car. Kickaha did not want to give him the license number, but since the clerk showed no signs of checking up on him, Kickaha gave him a number made up in his head. He then showed him Ramos' driver's license. The clerk copied down the number and looked once at the photograph. Ramos had a square face with a big beaky nose, black eyes, and a shock of black hair. Despite this, the clerk did not seem to notice.

Kickaha, however, was suspicious. The fellow was too smooth. Perhaps he did not really care whether or not Kickaha was the person he claimed to be, but then again, he might.

Kickaha said nothing, took the keys, and led Anana out of the lobby. Instead of going to their room on the second floor, he stood outside the door, where he could not be seen. A minute later, he heard the clerk talking to somebody. He looked in. The clerk was sitting at the switchboard with his back to the door. Kickaha tiptoed in closer.

". . . not his," the clerk was saying. "Yeah, I checked out the license, soon as they left. The car's parked near here. Listen, you . . ."

He stopped because he had turned his head and had seen Kickaha. He turned it away, slowly, and said, "OK. See you."

He took off the earphones and stood up and said, smiling, "May I help you?"

"We decided to eat before we went to bed; we haven't eaten all day," Kickaha said, also smiling. "Where's the nearest good restaurant?"

The clerk spoke slowly, as if he were trying to think of one that would suit them. Kickaha said, "We're not particular. Any place'll do."

A moment later, he and Anana drove off. The clerk stood in the front door and watched them. He had seen them put their packs and the case in the car, so he probably did not believe that they were coming back.

Kickaha was thinking that they could sleep in the car tonight, provided the police weren't looking for it. Tomorrow they would have to buy clothes and a suitcase or two. He would have to get rid of this car, but the problem of renting or buying a car without the proper papers was a big one.

He pulled into a service station and told the attendant to fill her up. The youth was talkative and curious; he wanted to know where they'd been, up in the mountains? He liked hiking, too.

Kickaha made up a story. He and his wife had been bumming around but decided to come down and dig L.A. They didn't have much money;

they were thinking about selling the car and getting a secondhand VW. They wanted to stay the night someplace where they didn't ask questions if the color of your money was right.

The attendant told them of a motel near Tarzana in Van Nuys that fit all Kickaha's specifications. He grinned and winked at them, sure they were engaged in something illegal (or rebellious), and wished them luck. Maybe he could get them a good bargain on the Jag.

A half hour later, he and Anana fell into a motel bed and were asleep at once.

He got up at ten. Anana was sleeping soundly. After shaving and showering, he woke her long enough to tell her what he planned. He went across the street to a restaurant, ate a big breakfast, bought a paper, and then returned to the room. Anana was still sleeping. He called the *Los Angeles Times* ad department and dictated an item for the personal column. He gave as his address the motel and also gave a fictitious name. He had thought about using Ramos' name in case the *Times* man checked out the address. But he did not want any tie between the ad and Cambring, if he could help it. He promised to send his check immediately, and then, hanging up, forgot about it.

He checked the personals of the morning's *Times*. There were no messages that could be interpreted as being from Wolff.

When Anana woke, he said, "While you're eating breakfast, I'll use a public phone booth to call Cambring. I'm sure he's gotten word to Red Orc."

Cambring answered at once as if he had been waiting by the phone. Kickaha said, "This is your friend of last night, Cambring. Did you pass on my information about the Black Beller?"

Cambring's voice sounded as if he were controlling anger.

"Yes, I did."

"What did he say?"

"*He* said that he'd like to meet you. Have a conference of war."

"Where?"

"Wherever you like."

Good, thought Kickaha. *He doesn't think I'm so dumb that I'd walk into his parlor. But he's confident that he can set up a trap no matter where I meet him. If, that is, he himself shows up. I doubt that. He'd be far too cagey for that. But he'll have to send someone to represent him, and that someone might be higher up than Cambring and a step closer to the Lord.*

"I'll tell you where we'll meet in half an hour," Kickaha said. "But, before I hang up, did your boss have anything else to say I should hear?"

"No."

Kickaha clicked the phone down. He found Anana in a booth in the restaurant. He sat down and said, "I don't know whether Orc's got hold of

Wolff or not. I don't even know for sure whether Cambring repeated my message about Wolff and Chryseis, but Orc knows the gate was activated twice before we came through and that one of the people coming through was a Black Beller. I don't think he's got Wolff and Chryseis, because if he did, he'd use them as a way to trap me. He'd know I'd be galloping in to save them."

"Perhaps," she said. "But he may feel that he doesn't have to let you know he has Wolff and Chryseis. He may feel confident that he can catch us without saying anything about them. Or perhaps he's withholding his knowledge until a more suitable time."

"You Lords sure figure out the angles," he said. "As suspicious a lot as the stars have ever looked down on."

"Look who's talking," she said in English.

They returned to their room, picked up their bags and the case, and went to the car. They drove off without checking out, since Kickaha did not think it wise to let anybody know what they were doing if it could be helped. In Tarzana, he went into a department store and checked out clothes for himself and Anana. This took an hour, but he did not mind keeping Cambring waiting. Let him and his boss sweat for a while.

While he was waiting for his trousers to be altered, he made the call. Again, Cambring answered immediately.

"Here's what we'll do," Kickaha said. "I'll be at a place fairly close to your house. I'll call you when I get there, and I'll give you twelve minutes to get to our meeting place. If you aren't there by then, I move on. Or if it looks like a trap, I'll take off, and that'll be the last you'll see of me—at a meeting place, that is. Your boss can take care of the Beller himself."

"What the hell is this Beller you're talking about?" Cambring said angrily.

"Ask your boss," Kickaha said, knowing that Cambring would not dare do this. "Look, I'm going to be in a place where I can see on all sides. I want just two men to meet me. You, because I know you, and your boss. You'll advance no closer than sixty yards, and your boss will then come ahead. Got it? So long!"

At noon, after eating half a hamburger and drinking a glass of milk, he called Cambring. He was at a restaurant only a few blocks from the meeting place. Cambring answered again before the phone had finished its third ring. Kickaha told him where he was to meet him and under what conditions.

"Remember," he said. "If I smell anything fishy, I take off like an Easter bunny with birth pangs."

He hung up. He and Anana drove as quickly as traffic would permit. His destination was the Los Angeles County Art Museum. Kickaha parked the car around the corner and put the keys under the floor mat, in case only one of them could get back to it. They proceeded on foot behind the museum and walked through the parking lot.

Anana had dropped behind him so that anyone watching would not know she was with Kickaha. Her long glossy black hair was coiled up into a Psyche knot, and she wore a white low-cut frilly blouse and very tight green-and-red-striped culottes. Dark glasses covered her eyes, and she carried an artist's sketch pad and pencils. She also carried a big leather purse that contained a number of items that would have startled any scientifically knowledgeable Earthling.

While Kickaha hailed down a cab, she walked slowly across the grass. Kickaha gave the cab driver a twenty-dollar bill as evidence of his good intentions and of the tip to come. He told him to wait in the parking lot, motor running, ready to take off when Kickaha gave the word. The cab driver raised his eyebrows and said, "You aren't planning on robbing the museum?"

"I'm planning on nothing illegal," Kickaha said. "Call me eccentric. I just like to leave in a hurry sometimes."

"If there's any shooting, I'm taking off," the driver said. "With or without you. And I'm reporting to the cops. Just so you know, see?"

Kickaha liked to have more than one avenue of escape. If Cambring's men should be cruising around the neighborhood, they might spot their stolen car and set a trap for Kickaha. In fact, he was betting that they would. But if the way to the cab was blocked, and he had to take the route to the car, and that wasn't blocked, he would use the car.

However, he felt that the driver was untrustworthy, not that he blamed him for feeling suspicious.

He added a ten to the twenty and said, "Call the cops now, if you want. I don't care, I'm clean."

Hoping that the cabbie wouldn't take him up, he turned and strode across the cement of the parking lot and then across the grass to the tar pit. Anana was sitting down on a concrete bench and sketching the mammoth, which seemed to be sinking into the black liquid. She was an excellent artist, so that anybody who looked over her shoulder would see that she knew her business.

Kickaha wore dark glasses, a purple sleeveless and neckless shirt, a big leather belt with fancy silver buckle, and Levi's. Under his long red hair, against the bone behind his ear, was a receiver. The device he wore on his wrist contained an audio transmitter and a beamer six times as powerful as that in his ring.

Kickaha took his station at the other end of the tar pit. He stood near the fence beyond which was the statue of a huge prehistoric bear. There were about fifty people scattered here and there, none of whom looked as if they would be Cambring's men. This, of course, meant nothing.

A minute later, he saw a large gray Rolls-Royce swing into the parking lot. Two men got out and crossed the grass in a straight line toward him. One was Ramos. The other was tall and gangly and wore a business suit, dark glasses, and a hat. When he came closer, Kickaha saw a horse-faced man of about fifty. Kickaha doubted then that he would be Red Orc, because no Lord, not even if he were twenty thousand years old, looked as if he were over thirty.

Anana's voice sounded in his ear. "It's not Red Orc."

He looked around again. There were two men on his left, standing near the fountain by the museum and two men on his right, about twenty yards beyond Anana. They could be Cambring's men.

His heart beat faster. The back of his neck felt chilled. He looked through the fence across the pit at Wilshire Boulevard. Parking was forbidden there at any time. But a car was there, its hood up and a man looking under it. A man sat in the front seat and another in the rear.

"He's going to try to grab me," Kickaha said. "I've spotted seven of his men, I think."

"Do you want to abandon your plan?" she said.

"If I do, you know the word," he said. "Watch it! Here they come!"

Ramos and the gangly man stopped before him. The gangly man said, "Paul?" using the name Kickaha had given Cambring.

Kickaha nodded. He saw another big car enter the parking lot. It was too far for him to distinguish features, but the driver, wearing a hat and dark glasses, could be Cambring. There were three others in his car.

"Are you Red Orc?" Kickaha said, knowing that the tall man was probably carrying a device that would transmit the conversation to the Lord, wherever he was.

"Who? Who's Reddark?" the tall man said. "My name is Kleist. Now, Mr. Paul, would you mind telling me what you want."

Kickaha spoke in the language of the Lords, "Red Orc! I am not a Lord but an Earthling who found a gate to the universe of Jadawin, whom you may remember. I came back to Earth, though I did not want to, to hunt down the Beller. I have no desire to stay here; I wish only to kill the Beller and get back to my adopted world. I have no interest in challenging you."

Kleist said, "What the hell you gibbering about? Speak English, man!"

Ramos looked uneasy. He said, "He's flipped."

Kleist suddenly looked dumbfounded. Kickaha guessed that he was getting orders.

"Mr. Paul," Kleist said, "I am empowered to offer you complete amnesty. Just come with us and we will introduce you to the man you want to see."

"Nothing doing," Kickaha said. "I'll work with your boss, but I won't put myself in his power. He may be all right, but I have no reason to trust him.

I would like to cooperate with him, however, in tracking down the Beller."

Kleist's expression showed that he did not understand the reference to the Beller.

Kickaha looked around again. The men on his left and right were drifting closer. The two men in the car on Wilshire had gotten out. One was looking under the hood with the other man, but the third was gazing through the fence at Kickaha. When he saw Kickaha looking at him, he slowly turned away.

Kickaha said angrily, "You were told that only two of you should come! You're trying to spring a trap on me! You surely don't think you can kidnap me here in the middle of all these people?"

"Now, now, Mr. Paul!" Kleist said. "You're mistaken! Don't be nervous! There's only two of us, and we're here to talk to you, only that."

Anana said, "A police car has just pulled up behind that car on the street."

Kleist and Ramos looked at each other; it was evident that they had also seen the police car. But they looked as if they had no intention of leaving.

Kickaha said, "If your boss would like me to help, he'll have to think of some way of guaranteeing me passage back."

He decided he might as well spring his surprise now. The Lord knew that there was a woman with Kickaha, and while he had no way of knowing that she was a Lord, he must suspect it. Kickaha had only been on Earth a short time when the Lord's men had seen her with him. And since he knew that the gate had been activated twice before Kickaha came along, he must suspect that the other party—or parties—was also a Lord.

Now was the time to tell Red Orc about them. This would strengthen Kickaha's bargaining position and it might stop the effort to take him prisoner now.

"You tell your boss," he said, "that there are four other Lords now on Earth."

Kickaha was not backward about exaggerating if it might confuse or upset the enemy. There might come a time when he could use the two nonexistent Lords as leverage.

"Also," he added, "there are two Earthlings who have come from Jadawin's world. Myself and a woman who is with Jadawin."

That ought to rock him, he thought. Arouse his curiosity even more. He must be wondering how two Earthlings got into Jadawin's world in the first place and how they got back here.

"You tell your boss," Kickaha said, "that none of us, except for the Beller, mean him any harm. We just want to kill the Beller and get the hell out of this stinking universe."

Kickaha thought that Red Orc should be able to understand that. What Lord in his right mind would want to take control of Earth from another

Lord? What Lord would want to stay here when he could go to a much nicer, if much smaller, universe?

Kleist was silent for a moment. His head was slightly cocked as if he were listening to an invisible demon on his shoulder. Then he said, "What difference does it make if there are four Lords?"

It was obvious that Kleist was relaying the message and that he did not understand the references.

Kickaha spoke in the language of the Lords. "Red Orc! You have forgotten the device that every Lord carries in his brain. The alarm that rings in every Lord's head when he gets close to the metal bell of a Beller! With four Lords searching for the Beller, the chances of finding him are greater!"

Kleist had dropped any pretence that he was not in direct communication with his chief. He said, "How does he know that *you* are not a Beller?"

"If I were a Beller, why would I get into contact with you, let you know you had a dangerous enemy loose in your world?"

"He says," Kleist reported, his face becoming blanker as he talked, as if he were turning into a mechanical transceiver, "that a Beller would try to locate all Lords as quickly as possible. After all, a Lord is the only one besides a Beller who knows that Bellers exist. Or who can do anything about them. So you would try to find him, just as you are now doing. Even if it meant your life. Bellers are notorious for sacrificing one of their numbers if they can gain an advantage thereby.

"He also says, how does he know that these so-called Lords are not your fellow Bellers?"

Kickaha spoke in the Lords' tongue. "Red Orc! You are trying my patience. I have appealed to you because I know of your vast resources! You haven't got much choice, Red Orc! If you force me to cut off contact with you, then you won't know that I'm not a Beller and your sleep will be hideous nightmares about the Bellers at large! In fact, the only way you can be sure that I'm not a Beller is to work with me, but under my terms! I insist on that!"

The only way to impress a Lord was to be even more arrogant than he.

Anana's voice said, "The car's gone. The police must have scared them out. The police car's going now."

Kickaha raised his arm and muttered into the transceiver, "Where are the others?"

"Closing in. They're standing by the fence and pretending to look at the statues. But they're working toward you."

He looked at Kleist and Ramos across the grass. The two cars he had suspected were now empty, except for one man, whom he thought would be Cambring. The others were among the picnickers on the grass. He saw two men who looked grim and determined and tough; they could be Cambring's.

"We'll take off to my left," he said. "Around the fence and across Wilshire. If they follow us, it'll have to be on foot. At first, at least."

He flicked a look toward Anana. She had gotten up from the bench and was strolling towards him.

Kleist said, "Very well. I am authorized to accept your terms."

He smiled disarmingly and stepped closer. Ramos tensed.

"Couldn't we go elsewhere? It's difficult to carry on a conversation here. But it'll be wherever you say."

Kickaha was disgusted. He had just been about to agree that it would be best to tie in with Red Orc. Through him, the Beller and Wolff and Chryseis might be found, and after that, the dam could break and the devil take the hindmost. But the Lord was following the bent of his kind; he was trusting his power, his ability to get anything or anybody he wanted.

Kickaha made one last try. "Hold it! Not a step closer! You ask your boss if he remembers Anana, his niece, or Jadawin, his nephew? Remembers how they looked? If he can identify them, then he'll know I'm telling the truth."

Kleist was silent and then nodded his head. He said, "Of course. My boss agrees. Just let him have a chance to see them."

It was no use. Kickaha knew then what Red Orc was thinking. It should have occurred to Kickaha. The brains of Anana and Wolff could be housing the minds of the Bellers.

Kleist, still smiling, reached into his jacket slowly, so that Kickaha would not be thinking he was reaching for a gun. He brought out a pen and pad of paper and said, "I'll write down this number for you to call, and . . ."

Not for a second did Kickaha believe that the pen was only a pen. Evidently Orc had entrusted Kleist with a beamer. Kleist did not know it, but he was doomed. He had heard too much during the conversation, and he knew about a device that should not be existing on Earth as yet.

There was no time to tell Kleist that in the hope that he could be persuaded to desert the Lord.

Kickaha leaped to one side just as Kleist pointed the pen at him. Kickaha was quick, but he was touched by the beam on the shoulder and hurled sideways to the ground. He rolled on, seeing Kleist throw his hands up into the air, the pen flying away, and then Kleist staggered back one step and fell onto his back. Kickaha leaped up and dived toward the pen, even though his left shoulder and arm felt as if a two-by-four had slammed into it. Ramos, however, made no effort to grab the pen. Probably, he did not know what it really was.

Women were shrieking and men were yelling, and there was much running around.

When he got to his feet, he saw why. Kleist and three of his men were unconscious on the ground. Six men were running toward them— these must have been the late-comers—and were shoving people out of their way.

The fourth man who had been sneaking up on him was pulling a gun from an underarm holster.

Ramos, seeing this, shouted, "No! No guns! You know that!"

Kickaha aimed the beamer-pen, which, fortunately, was activated by pressing a slide, not by code words, and the man seemed to fold up and be lifted off the ground. He sailed back, hit on his buttocks, straightened out, and lay still, arms outspread, his face gray. The gun lay on the ground several feet before him.

Kickaha turned and saw Anana running toward him. She had shot a beam at the same time that Kickaha shot his, and the gunman had gotten a double impact.

Kickaha leaped forward, scooped up the gun, and hurled it over the fence into the tar pit. He and Anana ran around the fence and up the slope onto the sidewalk. There was no crosswalk here, and the traffic was heavy. But it was also slow because the traffic light a half block away was red.

The two ran between the cars, forcing them to slam on their brakes. Horns blasted, and several people yelled at them out the windows.

Once they reached the other side, they looked behind them. The traffic had started up again, and the seven men after them were, for the moment, helpless.

"Things didn't work out right," Kickaha said. "I was hoping that I could grab Kleist and get away with him. He might've been the lead to Red Orc."

Anana laughed, though a little nervously. "Nobody can accuse you of being underconfident," she said. "What now?"

"The cops'll be here pretty quick," he said. "Yeah, look, Cambring's men are all going back. I bet they got orders to get Kleist and the others out before the cops get here."

He grabbed Anana's hand and began running east toward the corner. She said, "What're you doing?"

"We'll cross back at the traffic light while they're busy and then run like hell down Curson Street. Cambring's there!"

She did not ask any more. But to get away from the enemy and then to run right back into his mouth seemed suicidal.

The two were now opposite the men about a hundred yards away. Kickaha looked between the trees lining the street and saw the unwounded men supporting Kleist and three others. In the distance, a siren wailed. From the way Cambring's men hurried, they had no doubt that it was coming after them.

Cambring, looking anxious, was standing by the car. He stiffened when he felt the pen touch his back and heard Kickaha's voice.

Cambring did not look around but got into the front seat as directed. Anana and Kickaha got into the rear seat, and ducked down. Kickaha kept the pen jammed against Cambring's back.

Cambring protested once. "You can't get away with this! You're crazy!"

"Just shut up!" Kickaha said.

Thirty seconds later, Kleist, supported by two men, reached the car. Kickaha swung out the back door and pointed the pen at them, saying, "Put Kleist into the front seat."

The two holding Kleist halted. The others, forming a rear guard, reached for their guns, but Kickaha shouted, "I'll kill Kleist and Cambring both. And you, too, with this!"

He waved the pen. The others knew by now that the pen was a weapon of some sort even if they did not know its exact nature. They seemed to fear it more than a gun, probably because its nature was in doubt.

They stopped. Kickaha said, "I'm taking these two! The cops'll be here in a minute! You better take off, look out for yourselves!"

The two holding Kleist carried him forward and shoved him into the front seat. Cambring had to push against Kleist to keep him from falling on him like a sack full of garbage. Kickaha quickly got out of the car and went around to get into the driver's seat, while Anana held the pen on the others.

He started the motor, backed up with a screech of tires, jerked it to a stop, turned, and roared out of the parking lot. The car went up and down violently as they jumped the dip between the lot entrance and the street. Kickaha shouted to Anana, and she reached over the seat, felt behind Kleist's ear, and came up with the transceiver. It was a metal disc thin as a postage stamp and the size of a dime.

She stuck it behind her ear and also removed Kleist's wristwatch and put it on her own wrist.

He now had Cambring and Kleist. What could he do with them?

Anana suddenly gasped and pushed at Cambring, who had slumped over against Kickaha. In a swift reaction, he had shoved out with his elbow, thinking for a second that Cambring was attacking him. Then he understood that Cambring had fallen against him. He was unconscious.

Another look convinced him that Cambring was dead or close to death. His skin was the gray-blue of a corpse.

Anana said, "They're both dead."

Kickaha pulled the car over to the curb and stopped. He pointed frantically at her. She stared a moment, and then saw what he was trying to communicate. She quickly shed the receiver and Kleist's wristwatch as if she had discovered that she was wearing a leper's clothing.

Kickaha reached over and pulled her close to him and whispered in her ear, "I'll pick up the watch and receiver with a handkerchief and stick them in the trunk until we can get rid of them. I think you'd be able to hear Red Orc's voice now, if you still had that receiver behind your ear. He'd be telling you he'd just killed Cambring and he was going to kill you unless we surrendered to him."

He picked up Cambring's wrist and with a pencil pried up the watch compartment. There was a slight discoloration under it on the skin. With the pencil, he pried loose the disc from behind Cambring's ear and exposed a brown-blue disc-shaped spot.

Kleist groaned. His eyelids fluttered, and he looked up. Kickaha started the car again and pulled away from the curb, and then turned north. As they drove slowly in the heavy traffic, Kleist managed to straighten himself. To do this, he had to push Cambring over against Kickaha. Anana gave a savage order, and Kleist got Cambring off the seat and onto the floor. Since the body took up so much space, Kleist had to sit with his knees almost up to his chin.

He groaned again and said, "You killed him."

Kickaha explained what had happened. Kleist did not believe him. He said, "What kind of a fool do you think I am?"

Kickaha grinned and said, "Very well, so you don't believe in the efficacy of the devices, the workings of which I've just explained to you. I could put them back on you and so prove the truth of what I've told you. You wouldn't know it, because you'd be dead and your boss would've scored one on us."

He drove on until he saw a sign that indicated a parking lot behind a business building. He drove down the alley and turned into it. The lot was a small one, enclosed on three sides by the building. There were no windows from which he could be seen, and, for the moment, there was no one in the lot or the alley. He parked, then got out and motioned to Kleist to get out. Anana held the pen against his side.

Kickaha dragged Cambring's body out and rolled it under a panel truck. Then they got back into the car and drove off, toward the motel.

Kickaha was worried. He may have pushed Red Orc to the point where he would report the Rolls as stolen. Up to now he had kept the police out of it, but Kickaha did not doubt that the Lord would bring them in if he felt it necessary. The Lord must have great influence, both politically and financially, even if he remained an anonymous figure. With Kickaha and Anana picked up by the police, the Lord could then arrange for his men to seize them. All he had to do was to pay the bail and catch them after they'd gone a few blocks from the police station.

And if Kleist knew anything that might give Kickaha a lead to Red Orc, the Lord might act to make sure that Kleist could not do so.

Kleist, at this moment, was not cooperating. He would not even reply to Kickaha's questions. Finally, he said, "Save your breath. You'll get nothing from me."

When they reached the motel, Kleist got out of the car slowly. He looked around as if he would like to run or shout, but Kickaha had warned him that if he tried anything, he would get enough power from the pen to knock his head off. He stepped into the motel room ahead of Kickaha, who did not even wait for Anana to shut the door before stunning his prisoner with a minimum jolt from the pen.

Before he could recover, Kleist had been injected with a serum that Kickaha had brought from Wolff's palace in that other world.

During the next hour, they learned much about the working and the people of what Kleist referred to as The Group. His immediate boss was a man named Alfredo Roulini. He lived in Beverly Hills, but Kleist had never been in his home. Always, Roulini gave orders over the phone or met Kleist and other underlings at Kleist's or Cambring's home.

Roulini, as described by Kleist, could not be Red Orc.

Kickaha paced back and forth, frowning, running his fingers through his long red hair.

"Red Orc will know, or at least surmise, that we've gotten Roulini's name and address from Kleist. So he'll warn Roulini, and they'll have a trap set for us. He may have been arrogant and overconfident before, but he knows now we're no pushovers. We've given him too hard a time. We won't be able to get near Roulini, and even if we did, I'll bet we'd find out that he has no more idea of the true identity or location of Red Orc than Kleist."

"That's probably true," Anana said. "So the only thing to do is to force Red Orc to come into the open."

"I'm thinking the same thing," he said. "But how do you flush him out?"

Anana exclaimed, "The Beller!"

Kickaha said, "So far, we don't know where the Beller is, and much as I hate to think about it, may never."

"Don't say that!" she said. "We have to find him!"

Her determination, he knew, did not originate from concern for the inhabitants of Earth. She was terrified only that the Bellers might one day become powerful enough to gate from Earth into other universes, the pocket worlds owned by the Lords. She was concerned only for herself and, of course, for him. Perhaps for Luvah, the wounded brother left behind to guard Wolff's palace. But she would never be able to sleep easily until she was one-hundred-percent certain that no Bellers were alive in the one thousand and eight known universes.

Nor would Red Orc sleep any more easily.

Kickaha tied Kleist's hands behind him, tied his feet together, and taped his mouth. Anana could not understand why he didn't just kill the man. Kickaha explained, as he had done a number of times, that he would not do so unless he thought it was necessary. Besides, they were in enough trouble without leaving a corpse behind them.

After removing Kleist's wallet, he put him in the closet.

"He can stay there until tomorrow when the cleaning woman comes in. But I think we'll move on. Let's go across the street and eat. We have to put something in our bellies."

They walked across the street at the corner, and went down half a block to the restaurant. They got a booth by the window, from which he could see the motel.

While they were eating, he told her what his plans were. "A Lord will come as swiftly for a pseudo-Beller as for the real thing, because he won't know for sure which is which. We make our own Beller and get some publicity, too, and so make sure that Red Orc finds out about it."

"There's still a good chance that he won't come personally," she said.

"How's he going to know whether or not the Beller is for real unless he does show?" he said. "Or has the Beller brought to him."

"But you couldn't get out then!" she said.

"Maybe I couldn't get out, but I'm not there yet. We've got to play this by ear. I don't see anything else to do, do you?"

They rose, and he stopped at the register to pay their bill. Anana whispered to him to look through the big plate-glass window at the motel. A police car was turning into the motel grounds.

Kickaha watched the two policemen get out and look at the license plate on the rear of the Rolls. Then one went into the manager's office while the other checked out the Rolls. In a moment, the officer and the manager came out, and all three went into the motel room that Anana and Kickaha had just left.

"They'll find Kleist in the closet," Kickaha murmured. "We'll take a taxi back to L.A. and find lodgings somewhere else."

They had the clothes they were wearing, the case with the Horn of Shambarimen, their beamer rings with a number of power charges, the beamer-pen, their ear receivers and wrist chronometer transmitters, and the money they'd taken from Baum, Cambring, and Kleist. The latter had provided another hundred and thirty-five dollars.

They went outside into the heat and the eye-burning, sinus-searing smog. He picked up the morning *Los Angeles Times* from a corner box, and then waited for a taxi. Presently, one came along, and they rode out of the Valley. On the way, he read the personals column, which contained his ad. None of the personals read as if they had been planted by Wolff. The two got out of the taxi, walked two blocks and took another taxi to a place chosen at random by Kickaha.

They walked around for a while. He got a haircut and purchased a hat and also talked the clerk out of a woman's hatbox. At a drugstore, he bought some hair dye and other items, including shaving equipment, toothbrushes and paste, and a nail file. In a pawnshop he bought two suitcases, a knife that had an excellent balance, and a knife sheath.

Two blocks away, they checked in at a third-rate hotel. The desk clerk seemed interested only in whether they could pay in advance or not. Kickaha, wearing his hat and dark glasses, hoped that the clerk wasn't paying them much attention. Judging from the stink of cheap whiskey on his breath, he was not very perceptive at the moment.

Anana, looking around their room, said, "The place we just left was a hovel. But it's a palace compared to this!"

"I've been in worse," he said. "Just so the cockroaches aren't big enough to carry us off."

They spent some time dyeing their hair. His red-bronze became a dark brown, and her hair, as black and glossy as a Polynesian maiden's, became corn-yellow.

"It's no improvement, but it's a change," he said. "So now to a metal-worker's."

The telephone books had given the addresses of several in this area. They walked to the nearest place advertising metalworking, where Kickaha gave his specifications and produced the money in advance. During his conversation, he had studied the proprietor's character. He concluded that he was open to any deal where the money was high and the risk low.

He decided to cache the Horn. Much as he hated to have it out of his sight, he no longer cared to risk the chance of Red Orc's getting his hands on it. If he had not carried it with him when he left the motel, it would be in the hands of the police by now. And if Orc heard about it, which he was bound to do, Orc would quickly enough have it.

The two went to the Greyhound Bus station, where he put the case and Horn in a locker.

"I gave that guy an extra twenty bucks to do a rush job," he said. "He promised to have it ready by five. In the meantime, I propose we rest in the tavern across the street from our palatial lodgings. We'll watch our hotel for any interesting activities."

The Blue Blottle Fly was a sleazy beer joint, which did, however, have an unoccupied booth by the front window. This was covered by a dark blind, but there was enough space between the slats for Kickaha to see the front of the hotel. He ordered a Coke for Anana and a beer for himself. He drank almost none of the beer but every fifteen minutes ordered another one just to keep the management happy. While he watched, he questioned Anana about Red Orc. There was so little that he knew about their enemy.

"He's my *krathlrandroon*," Anana said. "My mother's brother. He left the home universe over fifteen thousand Earth years ago to make his own. That was five thousand years before I was born. But we had statues and photos of him, and he came back once when I was about fifteen years old, so I knew how he looked. But I don't remember him now. Despite which, if I were to see him again, I might know him immediately. There is the family resemblance, you know. Very strong. If you should ever see a man who is the male counterpart of me, you will be looking at Red Orc. Except for the hair. His is not black, it is a dark bronze. Like yours. Exactly like yours.

"And now that I come to think of it . . . I wonder why it didn't strike me before . . . you look much like him."

"Come on now!" Kickaha said. "That would mean I'd look like you! I deny that!"

"We could be cousins, I think," she said.

Kickaha laughed, though his face was warm and he felt anxious for some reason.

"Next, you'll be telling me I'm the long-lost son of Red Orc."

"I don't know that he has any son," she said thoughtfully. "But you could be his child, yes."

"I know who my parents are," he said. "Hoosier farm folk. And they knew who their ancestors were, too. My father was of Irish descent—what else, Finnegan, for God's sake?—and my mother was Norwegian and a quarter Catawba Indian."

"I wasn't trying to prove anything," she said. "I was just commenting on certain undeniable resemblances. Now that I think about it, your eyes are that peculiar leaf-green . . . yes, exactly like it . . . I'd forgotten . . . Red Orc's eyes are yours."

Kickaha put his hand on hers and said, "Hold it!"

He was looking through the slats. She turned and said,

"A police car!"

"Yeah, double-parked outside the hotel. They're both going in. They could be checking on someone else. So let's not get panicky."

"Since when did I ever panic?" she said coldly.

"My apologies. That's just my manner of speaking."

Fifteen minutes passed. Then a car pulled up behind the police car. It contained three men in civilian clothes, two of whom got out and went into the hotel. The car drove away.

Kickaha said, "Those two looked like plainsclothesmen to me."

The two uniformed policemen came out and drove away. The two suspected detectives did not come out of the hotel for thirty minutes. They walked down to the corner and stood for a minute talking, and then one returned. He did not, however, reenter the hotel. Instead, he crossed the street.

Kickaha said, "He's got the same idea we had! Watch the hotel from here!" He stood up and said, "Come on! Out the back way. Saunter along, but fast!"

The back way was actually a side entrance, which led to a blind alley the open end of which was on the street. The two walked northward toward the metalworking shop.

Kickaha said, "Either the police got their information from Red Orc or they're checking us out because of Kleist. It doesn't matter. We're on the run, and Orc's got the advantage. As long as he can keep pushing us, we aren't going to get any closer to him. Maybe."

They had several hours yet before the metalworker would be finished. Kickaha led Anana into another tavern, much higher class, and they sat down again. He said, "You just barely got started telling me the story of your uncle."

"There isn't really much to tell," she said. "Red Orc was a figure of terror among the Lords for a long time. He successfully invaded the universes of at least ten Lords and killed them. Then he was badly hurt when he got into the world of Vala, my sister. Red Orc is very wily and a man of many resources and great power. But my sister Vala combines all the qualities of a cobra and a tiger. She hurt him badly, as I said, but in doing so got hurt herself. In fact, she almost died. Red Orc escaped, however, and came back to this universe, which was the first one he made after leaving the home world."

Kickaha sat up and said, "*What!*"

His hand, flailing out, knocked over his glass of beer. He paid no attention but stared at her.

"What did you say?"

"You want me to repeat the whole thing?"

"No, no! That final . . . the part where you said he came back to *this* universe, the first one he *made!*"

"Yes? What's so upsetting about that?"

Kickaha did not stutter often. But now he could not quite get the words out.

Finally, he said, "L-listen! I accept the idea of the pocket universes of the Lords, because I've lived in one half my life and I know others exist because I've been told about them by a man who doesn't lie and I've seen the Lords of other universes, including you! And I know there are at least one thousand and eight of these relatively small manufactured universes.

"But I had always thought . . . I still think . . . it's impossible . . . my universe is a natural one, just as you say your home universe, Gardzrintrah, was."

"I didn't say *that*," she said softly. She took his hand and squeezed it. "Dear Kickaha, does it really upset you so much?"

"You must be mistaken, Anana," he said. "Do you have any idea of the *vastness* of *this* universe? In fact, it's infinite! No man could *make* this incredibly complex and gigantic world! My God, the nearest star is four and some light-years away and the most distant is billions of light-years away, and there must be others billions of billions of light-years beyond these!

"And then there is the age of this universe! Why, this planet alone is two and one-half billion years old the last I heard! That's a hell of a lot older than fifteen thousand years, when the Lords moved out of their home world to make their pocket universes! A hell of a lot older!"

Anana smiled and patted his hand as if she were his grandmother and he a very small child.

"There, there. No reason to get upset, lover. I wonder why Wolff didn't tell you. Probably he forgot it when he lost his memory. And when he got his memory back, he did not get all of it back. Or perhaps he took it so for granted that he never considered that you didn't know, just as I took it for granted."

"How can you explain away the infinite size of this world, and the age of Earth? And the evolution of life?" he said triumphantly. "There, how do you explain evolution? The undeniable record of the fossils. Of carbon-14 dating and potassium-argon dating? I read about these new discoveries in a magazine on that bus, and their evidence is scientifically irrefutable!"

He fell silent as the waitress picked up their empty glasses. As soon as she left, he opened his mouth, and then he closed it again. The TV above the bar was showing the news and there on the screen was a drawing of two faces.

He said to Anana, "Look there!"

She turned just in time to see the screen before the drawing faded away.

"They looked like us!" she said.

"Yeah. Police composites," he said. "The hounds have really got the scent now! Take it easy! If we get up now, people might look at us. But if we sit here and mind our own business, as I hope the other customers are doing . . ."

If it had been a color set, the resemblance would have been much less close, since they had dyed their hair. But in black and white, their pictures were almost photographic.

However, no one even looked at them and it was possible that no one except the drunks at the bar had seen the TV set. And they were not about to turn around and face them.

"What did that thing say?" Anana whispered, referring to the TV.

"I don't know. There was too much noise for me to hear it. And I can't ask anybody at the bar."

He was having afterthoughts about his plans. Perhaps he should give up his idea of tricking Red Orc out of hiding. Some things were worth chancing, but with the police actively looking for him, and his and Anana's features in every home in California, he did not want to attract any attention at all. Besides, the idea had been one of those wild hares that leaped through the brier patches of his mind. It was fantastic, too imaginative, but for that very reason might have succeeded. Not now, though. The moment he put his plan into action, he would bring down Orc's men and the police, and Red Orc would not come out himself because he would know where Kickaha was.

"Put on the dark glasses now," he said. "Enough time has gone by that nobody'd get suspicious and connect us with the pictures."

"You don't have to explain everything," she said sharply. "I'm not as unintelligent as your Earthwomen."

He was silent for a moment. Within a few minutes, so many events had dropped on his head like so many anvils. He wanted desperately to pursue the question of the origin and nature of this universe, but there was no time. Survival, finding Wolff and Chryseis, and killing the Beller, these were the important issues. Just now, survival was the most demanding.

"We'll pick up some more luggage," he said. "And the bell, too. I may be able to use it later, who knows?"

He paid the bill, and they walked out. Ten minutes later, they had the bell. The metalworker had done a good enough job. The bell wouldn't stand a close-up inspection by any Lord, of course. But at a reasonable distance, or viewed by someone unfamiliar with it, it would pass for the prized possession of a Beller. It was bell-shaped but the bottom was covered, was one and a half times the size of Kickaha's head, was made of aluminium, and had been sprayed with a quick-dry paint. Kickaha paid the maker of it and put the bell in the hatbox he had gotten from the shop.

A half hour later, they walked across MacArthur Park.

Besides the soap-box speakers, there were a number of winos, hippie types, and some motorcycle toughs. And many people who seemed to be there just to enjoy the grass or to watch the unconventionals.

As they rounded a big bush, they stopped.

To their right was a concrete bench. On it sat two bristly-faced, sunken-cheeked, blue-veined winos and a young man. The young man was a well-built fellow with long dirty-blond hair and a beard of about three days' growth. He wore clothes that were even dirtier and more ragged than the winos.

A cardboard carton about a foot and a half square was on the bench by his side.

Anana started to say something and then she stopped.

Her skin turned pale, her eyes widened, she clutched her throat, and she screamed.

The alarm embedded in her brain, the alarm she had carried since she had become an adult ten thousand years ago, was the only thing that could be responsible for this terror.

Nearness to the bell of a Beller touched off that device in her brain. Her nerves wailed as if a siren had been tied into them. The ages-long dread of the Beller had seized her.

The blond man leaped up, grabbed the cardboard box, and ran away.

Kickaha ran after him. Anana screamed. The winos shouted, and many people came running.

At another time, he would have laughed. He had originally planned to take his box and the pseudo-bell into some such place as this, a park where winos and derelicts hung out, and create some kind of commotion, which would make the newspapers. That would have brought Red Orc out of his hole, Kickaha had hoped.

Ironically, he had stumbled across the real Beller.

If the Beller had been intelligent enough to cache his bell someplace, he would have been safe. Kickaha and Anana would have passed him and never known.

Suddenly, he stopped running. Why chase the Beller, even if he could catch up with him? A chase would draw too much attention.

He took out the beamer disguised as a pen and set the little slide on its barrel for a very narrow flesh-piercing beam. He aimed it at the back of the Beller and, at that moment, as if the Beller realized what must happen, he dropped to the ground. His box went tumbling, he rolled away and then disappeared behind a slight ridge. Kickaha's beam passed over him, struck a tree, drilled a hole in it. Smoke poured out of the bark. Kickaha shut the beamer off. If it was kept on for more than a few seconds, it needed another powerpack.

The Beller's head popped up, and his hand came out with a slender dark object in it. He pointed it at Kickaha, who leaped into the air sideways and at the same time threw the hatbox away. There was a flash of something white along the box, and the box and its contents, both split in half, fell to the ground. The hatbox burst into flames just before it struck.

Kickaha threw himself onto the ground and shot once. The grass on the ridge became brown. The next instant, the Beller was shooting again. Kickaha rolled away and then was up and away, zigzagging.

Anana was running toward him, her hand held up with the huge ring pointed forward. Kickaha whirled to aid her and saw that the Beller, who had retrieved the cardboard box, was running away again. Across the grass toward them, from all sides, people were running. Among them were two policemen.

Kickaha thought that his antics and those of the Beller must have seemed very peculiar to the witnesses. Here were these two youths, each with a box, pointing ballpoint pens at each other, dodging, ducking, playing cowboy and Indian. And the woman who had been screaming as if she had suddenly seen Frankenstein's monster was now in the game.

One of the policemen shouted at them.

Kickaha said, "Don't let them catch us! We'll be done for! Get the Beller!"

They began running at top speed. The cops shouted some more. He looked behind him. Neither had their guns out but it would not be long before they did.

They were overtaking the Beller, and the policemen were dropping behind. He was breathing too hard, though.

Whatever his condition, the Beller's was worse. He was slowing down fast. This meant that very shortly he would turn again, and Kickaha had better be nimble. In a few seconds, he would have the Beller within range of the beamer, and he would take both legs off. And that would be the end of possibly the greatest peril to man, other than man himself, of course.

The Beller ran up concrete steps in a spurt of frantic energy and onto the street above. Kickaha slowed down and stopped before ascending the last few steps. He expected the Beller to be waiting for his head to appear. Anana came up behind him then. Between deep gasps, she said, "Where is he?"

"If I knew, I wouldn't be standing here," he said.

He turned and left the steps to run crouching across the steep slope of the hill. When he was about forty feet away from the steps, he got down on his belly and crawled up to the top of the slope. The Beller would be wondering what he was doing. If he were intelligent, he would know that Kickaha wasn't going to charge up and over the steps. He'd be looking on both sides of the steps for his enemy to pop up.

Kickaha looked to his right. Anana had caught on and was also snaking along. She turned her head and grinned at him and waved. He signaled that they should both look over the ledge at the same time. If the Beller was paralysed for just a second by the double appearance, and couldn't make up his mind which one to shoot at first, he was as good as dead.

That is, if the cops behind them didn't interfere. Their shouts were getting louder, and then a gun barked and the dirt near Kickaha flew up.

He signaled, and they both stuck their heads up. At that moment, a gun cracked in the street before them.

The Beller was down on his back in the middle of the street. There was a car beside him, a big black Lincoln, and several men were about to pick the Beller up and load him into the car. One of the men was Kleist.

Kickaha swore. He had run the Beller right into the arms of Orc's men, who were probably cruising this area and looking for a man with a big box.

Or maybe somebody had—oh, irony of ironies—seen Kickaha with his box and thought he was the Beller!

He gestured at Anana and they both jumped up and ran off toward the car. More shouts but no shots from the policemen. The men by the limousine looked up just as they hurled the limp form of the Beller into the car. They climbed in, and the car shot away with a screaming of burning rubber into the temporarily opened lane before it.

Kickaha aimed at the back of the car, hoping to pierce a tire or to set the gasoline tank on fire. Nothing happened, and the car was gone yowling around a corner. His beamer was empty.

There was nothing to do except to run once more, and now the policemen would be calling in for help. The only advantage for the runners was the very heavy rush-hour traffic. The cops wouldn't be able to get here too fast in automobiles.

A half hour later, they were in a taxi, and in another twenty minutes, they were outside a motel. The manager looked at them curiously and raised his eyebrows when he saw no luggage. Kickaha said that they were advance agents for a small rock group and their baggage was coming along later. They'd flown in on fifteen minutes' notice from San Francisco.

They took the keys to their room and went down the court and into their room. Here they lay down on the twin beds and, after locking the door and pushing the bureau against it, slept for fifteen minutes. On awakening, they took a shower and put their sweaty clothes back on. Following the manager's directions, they walked down to a shopping area and purchased some more clothes and necessary items.

"If we keep buying clothes and losing them the same day," Kickaha said, "we're going to go broke. And I'll have to turn to robbery again."

When they returned to the motel room, he eagerly opened the latest copy of the *Los Angeles Times* to the personals column. He read down and then, suddenly, said, "Yay!" and leaped into the air. Anana sat up from the bed and said, "What's the matter?"

"Nothing's the matter! This is the first good thing that's happened since we got here! I didn't really believe that it'd work! But he's a crafty old fox, that Wolff! He thinks like me! Look, Anana!"

He shoved the paper at her. Blinking, she moved away so she could focus and then slowly read the words:

Hrowakas Kid. You came through. Stats. Wilshire and San Vicente. 9 p.m. C sends love.

Kickaha pulled her up off the bed and danced her around the room. "We did it! We did it! Once we're all together, nothing'll stop us!"

Anana hugged and kissed him and said, "I'm very happy. Maybe you're right, this is the turning point. My brother Jadawin! Once I would have tried to kill him. But no more. I can hardly wait."

"Well, we won't have long to wait," he said. He forced himself to become sober. "I better find out what's going on."

He turned the TV on. The newscaster of one station apparently was not going to mention them, so Kickaha switched channels. A minute later, he was rewarded.

He and Anana were wanted for questioning about the kidnapping of Kleist. The manager of the motel in which Kleist had been tied up had described the two alleged kidnappers. Kleist himself had made no charges at first, but then Cambring's body had been found. The police had made a connection between Cambring and Kickaha and Anana because of the ruckus at the La Brea Tar Pits. There was also an additional charge: the stealing of Cambring's car.

Kickaha did not like the news but he could not help chuckling a little because of the frustration that Red Orc must feel. The Lord would have wanted some less serious charge, such as the car stealing only, so that he would pay the bail of the two and thus nab them when they walked out of the police station. But on charges such as kidnapping, he might not be able to get them released.

These charges were serious enough, though not enough to warrant their pictures and descriptions on TV newscasts. What made this case so interesting was that the fingerprints of the male in the case had checked out as those of Paul Janus Finnegan, an ex-serviceman who had disappeared in 1946 from his apartment in Bloomington, Indiana, where he had been attending the university.

Twenty-four years later, he had shown up in Van Nuys, California, in very mysterious, or questionable, circumstances. And this was the kicker according to the newscaster—Finnegan was described by witnesses as being about twenty-five, yet he was fifty-two years old!

Moreover, since the first showing of his picture over TV, he had been identified as one of the men in a very mysterious chase in MacArthur Park.

The newscaster ended with a comment supposed to be droll. Perhaps this Finnegan had returned from the Fountain of Youth. Or perhaps the witnesses may have been drinking from a slightly different fountain.

"With all this publicity," Kickaha said, "we're in a bad spot. I hope the motel manager didn't watch this show."

It was eight-thirty. They were to meet Wolff at nine at Stats Restaurant on Wilshire and San Vicente. If they took a taxi, they could get there with plenty of time to spare. He decided they should walk, he did not trust the taxis. And while he would use them if he had to, he saw no reason to take one just to avoid a walk. Especially since they needed the exercise.

Anana complained that she was hungry and would like to get to the restaurant as soon as possible. He told her that suffering was good for the soul and grinned as he said it. His own belly was contracting with pangs, and his ribs felt more obtrusive than several days ago. But he was not going to be rushed into anything if he could help it.

While they walked, Kickaha questioned her about Red Orc and the "alleged" creation of Earth.

"There was the universe of the Lords in the beginning, and that was the only one we knew about. Then, after ten thousand years of civilization, my ancestors formulated the theory of artificial universes. Once the mathematics of the concept was realized, it was only a matter of time and will until the first pocket universe was made. Then the same 'space' would hold two worlds of space-matter, but one would be impervious to the inhabitants of the other, because each universe was 'at right angles to the other.' You realize that the term 'right angles' does not mean anything. It is just an attempt to explain something that can really only be explained to one who understands the mathematics of the concept. I myself, though I designed a universe of my own and then built it, never understood the mathematics of even how the world-making machines operated.

"The first artificial universe was constructed about two hundred years before I was born. It was made by a group of Lords—they did not call themselves Lords then, by the way—among whom were my father Urizen and his brother Orc. Orc had already lived the equivalent of two thousand Terrestrial years. He had been a physicist and then a biologist and finally a social scientist.

"The initial step was like blowing a balloon in non-space. Can you conceive that? I can't either, but that's the way it was explained to me. You blow a balloon in non-space. That is, you create a small space or a small universe, one to which you can 'gate' your machines. These expand the space next to, or in, the time-space of the original universe. The new world is expanded so that you can gate even larger machines into it. And these expand the universe more, and you gate more machines into the new larger space.

"From the beginning of this making of a new world, you have set up a world which may have quite different physical 'laws' than the original universe. It's a matter of shaping the space-time-matter so that, say, gravity works differently than in the original world.

"However, the first new universe was crude, you might say. It embodied no new principles. It was, in fact, an exact imitation of the original. Well, not exact in the sense that it was not a copy of the world as it was but as it had been in our past."

"The copy was this—my—world?" Kickaha said. "Earth's?"

She nodded and said, "It—this universe—was the first. And it was made approximately fifteen thousand Earth years ago. This solar system deviated only in small particulars from the solar system of the Lords. This Earth deviated only slightly from the native planet of the Lords."

"You mean . . . ?"

He was silent while they walked a half block, then he said, "So that explains what they meant when you said this world was fairly recent. I knew that that could not be so, because potassium-argon and xenon-argon dating prove irrefutably that this world is more than two and a half billion years old, and hominid fossils have been found that are at least one million seven hundred and fifty thousand years old. And then we have carbon-14 dating, which is supposed to be accurate up to fifty thousand years ago, if I remember that article correctly.

"But you're saying that the rocks of your world, which were four and a half billion years old, were reproduced in this universe. And so, though they were really made only fifteen thousand years ago, they would seem to be four and a half billion years old.

"And we find fossils that prove indubitably that dinosaurs lived sixty million years ago, and we find stone tools and the skeletons of men who lived a million years ago. But these were duplicated from your world."

"That is exactly right," she said.

"But the stars!" he said. "The galaxies, the super-novas, the quasars, the millions, billions of them, billions of light-years away! The millions of stars in this galaxy alone, which is one hundred thousand light-years across! The red shift of light from galaxies receding from us at a quarter of the speed of light and billions of light-years away! The radio stars, the—my God, everything!"

He threw his hands up to indicate the infinity and eternity of the universe. And also to indicate the utter nonsense of her words.

"This universe is the first, and the largest, of the artificial ones," she said. "Well, not the largest, the second one was just as large. Its diameter is three times that of the distance from the sun to the planet Pluto. If men ever build a ship to voyage to the nearest star, they will get past the orbit of Pluto and then to a distance twice that of Pluto from the sun. And then . . ."

"Then?"

"And then the ship will enter an area where it will be destroyed. It will run into a—what shall I call it?—a force field is the only term I can think of. And it would disappear in a blaze of energy. And so will any other ship, or ships, coming after it. The stars are not for men. Mainly because there are no stars."

Kickaha wanted to protest violently. He felt outraged. But he forced himself to say calmly, "How do you explain that?"

"The space-matter outside the orbit of Pluto is a simulacrum. A tiny simulacrum. Relatively tiny, that is."

"The effects of the light from the stars, the nebulas, and so forth? The red shift? The speed of light? All that."

"There's a warping factor that gives all the necessary illusions."

All extra-Plutonian astronomy, all cosmogony, all cosmology, was false. "But why did the Lords feel it necessary to set up this simulacrum of an infinite ever-expanding universe with its trillions of heavenly bodies? Why didn't they just leave the sky blank except for the moon and the planets? Why this utterly cruel deception? Or need I ask? I had forgotten for the moment that the Lords are *cruel*."

She patted his hand, looking up into his eyes, and said, "The Lords are not the only cruel ones. You forget that I told you that this universe was an exact copy of ours. I meant exact. From the center, that is, the sun, to the outer walls of this universe, your world is a duplicate of ours. That includes the simulacrum of extra-solar-system space."

He stopped and said, "You mean . . . ? The native world of the Lords was an artificial universe, too?"

"Yes. After three ships had been sent out past our outermost planet, to the nearest star, only four-point-three light-years away—we thought—a fourth ship was sent. But this had disappeared in a burst of light. It was not destroyed, but it could progress no farther than the first three. It was repelled by a force field. Or was turned away by the structure of the space-matter continuum at that point.

"After some study, we reluctantly came to the realization that there were no stars or outer space. Not as we had thought of them.

"This revelation was not accepted by many people. In fact, the impact of this discovery was so great that our civilization was in a near-psychotic state for a long while.

"Some historians have maintained that it was the discovery that we were in an artificial, comparatively finite, universe that spurred us—stung us—into searching for means of making our own synthetic universes. Because, if we were ourselves the product of a people who made our universe and therefore made us, then we, too, could make our worlds. And so . . ."

"Then Earth's world is not even secondhand!" Kickaha said. "It's thirdhand! But who could have made your world? Who are the Lords of the Lords?"

"So far, we do not know," she said. "We have found no trace of them or their native worlds or any other artificial worlds they might have made. They exist on a plane of polarity that was beyond us then, and as far as I know, will always be beyond us."

Kickaha thought that this discovery should have humbled the Lords. Perhaps, in the beginning, it did. But they had recovered and gone on to their own making of cosmoses and their solipsist way of life.

And in their search for immortality, they had made the Bellers, those Frankenstein's monsters, and then, after a long war, had conquered the Bellers and disposed of the menace forever—they had thought. But now there was a Beller loose and . . . No, he was not loose. He was in the hands of Red Orc, who surely would see to it that the Beller died and his bell was buried deep somewhere, perhaps at the bottom of the Pacific.

"I'll swallow what you told me," he said, "though I'm choking. But what about the people of Earth? Where did they come from?"

"Your ancestors of fifteen thousand years ago were made in the biolabs of the Lords. One set was made for this Earth and another set, exact duplicates, for the second Earth. Red Orc made two universes that were alike, and he put down on the face of each Earth the same peoples. Exactly the same in every detail.

"Orc set down in various places the infants, the Caucasoids, the Negroids and Negritos, the Mongolians, Amerinds, and Australoids. These were infants who were raised by Lords to be Stone Age peoples. Each group was taught a language, which, by the way, were artificial languages. They were also taught how to make stone and wooden tools, how to hunt, what rules of behavior to adopt, and so forth. And then the Lords disappeared. Most of them returned to the home universe, where they would make plans for building their own universes. Some stayed on the two Earths to see but not be seen. Eventually, all of these were killed or run out of the two universes by Red Orc, but that was a thousand years later."

"Wait a minute," Kickaha said. "I never thought about it, just took it for granted, I guess. But I thought all Lords were Caucasians."

"That is just because it so happened that you met only Caucasoid Lords," she said. "How many have you met, by the way?"

He grinned and said, "Six."

"I would guess that there are about a thousand left, and of these, about a third are Negroid and a third Mongolian, to use Terrestrial terms. On our world, our equivalent of Australoids became extinct and our equivalent of Polynesians and Amerinds became absorbed by the Mongolians and Caucasoids."

"That other Earth universe?" he said. "Have the peoples there developed on lines similar to ours? Or have they deviated considerably?"

"I couldn't tell you," she said. "Only Red Orc knows."

He had many questions, including why there happened to be a number of gates on Earth over which Red Orc had no control. It had occurred to him that these might be gates left over from the old days, when many Lords were on Earth.

There was no time to ask more questions. They were crossing San Vicente at Wilshire now, and Stats was only a few dozen yards away. It was a low brick-and-stone building with a big plate-glass window in front. His heart was beating fast. The prospect of seeing Wolff and Chryseis again made him happier than he had been for a long time. Nevertheless, he did not lose his wariness.

"We'll walk right on by the first time," he said. "Let's case it."

They were opposite the restaurant. There were about a dozen people eating in it, two waitresses, and a woman at the cash register. Two uniformed policemen were in a booth; their black-and-white car was in the plaza parking lot west of the building. Neither Wolff nor Chryseis was there.

It was still not quite nine o'clock, however, and Wolff might be approaching cautiously.

They halted before the display window of a dress shop. From their vantage point, they could observe anybody entering or leaving the restaurant. Two customers got up and walked out. The policemen showed no signs of leaving. A car drove into the plaza, pulled into a slot, and turned its lights out. A man and a woman, both white-haired, got out and went into the restaurant. The man was too short and skinny to be Wolff, and the woman was too tall and bulky to be Chryseis.

A half hour passed. More customers arrived and more left. None of them could be his friends. At a quarter to ten, the two policemen left.

Anana said, "Could we go inside now? I'm so hungry, my stomach is eating itself."

"I don't like the smell of this," he said. "Nothing looks wrong, except Wolff not being here yet. We'll wait a while, give him a chance to show. But we're not going inside that place. It's too much like a trap."

"I see a restaurant way down the street," she said. "Why don't I go down there and get some food and bring it back?"

They went over her pronunciation of two cheeseburgers, everything except onions, and two chocolate milk shakes, very thick. To go. He told her what to expect in change and then told her to hurry.

For a minute, he wondered if he should not tell her to forget it. If something unexpected happened, and he had to take off without her, she'd be in trouble. She still did not know the way of this world.

On the other hand, his own belly was growling.

Reluctantly he said, "Okay. But don't be long, and if anything happens so we get separated, we'll meet back at the motel."

He alternated watching the restaurant to his left and looking down the street for her.

About five minutes later she appeared with a large white paper bag. She crossed the street twice to get back on the same block and started walking toward him. She had taken a few steps from the corner when a car that had passed her stopped. Two men jumped out and ran toward her. Kickaha began running toward them. Anana dropped the bag and then she crumpled. There was no sound of a gun or spurt of flame or anything to indicate that a gun had been used. The two men ran to her. One picked her up; the other turned to face Kickaha.

At the same time, another man got out of the car and ran toward Kickaha. Several cars came up behind the stopped car, honked, and then pulled around it. Their lights revealed one man inside the parked car in the driver's seat.

Kickaha leaped sideways and out into the street. A car blew its horn and swerved away to keep from hitting him. The angry voice of its driver floated back, "You crazy son . . . !"

Kickaha had his beamer-pen out by then. A few hasty words set it for piercing effect. His first concern was to keep from being hit by the beamers of the men and his second was to cripple the car.

He dropped on the street and rolled, catching out of the corner of his eye a flash of needle-thin, sun-hot ray. A beam leaped from his own pen and ran along the wheels of the car on the street side. The tires blew with a bang, and the car listed to one side as the bottom parts of the wheels fell off.

The driver jumped out and ran behind the car.

Kickaha was up and running across the street toward a car parked by the curb. He threw himself forward, hit the macadam hard, and rolled. When he had crawled behind the car and peered from behind it, he saw that a second car was stopped some distance behind the first. Anana was being passed into it by the men from the first car.

He jumped up and shouted, but several cars whizzed by, preventing him from using the beam. By the time they had passed, the second car was making a U-turn. More cars, coming down the other lane, passed between him and the automobile containing her. He had no chance now to beam the back wheels of the departing car. And just then, as if the Fates were against him, a police car approached on the lane on his side and stopped. Kickaha knew that he could not be questioned. Raging, he fled.

Behind him, a siren started whooping. A man shouted at him, and fired into the air.

He increased his pace, and ran out onto San Vicente, almost stopping traffic as he dodged between the streaming cars. He crossed the divider, and as he reached the other side of the street, he spared a glance behind and saw one of the policemen on the divider, blocked by the stream of cars.

The police car had made a U-turn and was coming across. Kickaha ran on, turned the corner, ran between two houses, and came out behind them on San Vicente again. The cop on foot was getting into the car. Kickaha crouched in the shadows until the car, siren still whooping, took off again. It went around the same corner he had turned.

He doubled to Stats and looked inside. There was no sign of Wolff or Chryseis. Another police car was approaching, its lights flashing but its siren quiet.

He went across the parking lot and around a building. It took him an hour, but by then, dodging between houses, running across streets, hiding now and then, he had eluded the patrol cars. After a stop at a drive-in to pick up some food, he returned to his motel.

There was a police car parked outside it. Once more he abandoned his luggage and was gone into the night.

There was one thing he had to do immediately. He knew that Red Orc would give Anana a drug that would make her answer any question Orc asked. It just might happen that Orc would become aware that the Horn of Shambarimen had been brought through into this world and that it now was in a locker in the downtown bus station. He would, of course, send men down to the station, and would not hesitate to have the whole station blown up. Orc would not care what he had to do to get that Horn.

Kickaha caught a taxi and went down to the bus station. After emptying the locker, he walked seven blocks from the bus station before he took another taxi, which carried him to the downtown railroad station. Here he placed the Horn in a locker. He did not want to carry the key with him. He purchased a package of gum and chewed all the sticks until he had a big ball of gum. While he was chewing, he strolled around outside the station, inspected a tree on the edge of the parking lot, and decided he had found an excellent hiding place. He stuck the key, embedded in the ball of gum, into a small hollow in the tree just above the line of his vision.

He took another taxi to the Sunset and Fairfax area.

He awoke about eight o'clock on an old mattress on the bare floor of a big moldy room. Beside him slept Rod (short for Rodriga). Rodriga Elseed, as she called herself, was a tall thin girl with remarkably large breasts, a pretty but overfreckled face, big dark-blue eyes, and lank yellow-brown hair that fell to her waist. She was wearing a red-and-blue-checked lumberman's shirt, dirty bell-bottoms, and torn moccasins. Her teeth were white and even, but her breath reeked of too little food and too much marijuana.

While walking along Sunset Boulevard in the Saturday-night crowds, Kickaha had seen her sitting on the sidewalk talking to another girl and a boy.

The girl, seeing Kickaha, had smiled at him. She said, "Hello, friend. You look as if you've been running for a long time."

"I hope not," he said, smiling back. "The fuzz might see it, too."

It had been easy to make the acquaintanceship of all three, and when Kickaha said he would buy them something to eat, he felt a definite strengthening of their interest.

After eating they had wandered around Sunset, "grooving" on everything. He learned much about their sub-world that night. When he mentioned that he had no roof over his head, they invited him to stay at their pad. It was a big run-down spooky old house, they said, with about fifty people, give or take ten, living in it and chipping in on the rent and utilities, if they had it. If they didn't, they were welcome until they got some bread.

Rodriga Elseed (he was sure that wasn't her real name) had recently come here from Dayton, Ohio. She had left two uptight parents there. She was seventeen and didn't know what she wanted to be. Just herself for the time being, she said.

Kickaha donated some more money for marijuana, and the other girl, Jackie, disappeared for a while. When she returned, they went to the big house, which they called the Shire, and retired to this room. Kickaha smoked with them, since he had the feeling that he would be a far more accepted comrade if he did. The smoke did not seem to do much except to set him coughing.

After a while, Jackie and the boy, Dar, began to make love. Rodriga and Kickaha went for a walk. She said she liked Kickaha, but did not feel like going to bed with him on such short acquaintance.

Kickaha said that he understood. He was not at all disgruntled. He just wanted to get some sleep. An hour later, they returned to the room, which was then empty, and fell asleep on the dirty mattress.

But the night's sleep had not lessened his anxiety. He was depressed because Anana was in Red Orc's hands, and he suspected that Wolff and Chryseis were also his prisoners. Somehow, Red Orc had guessed that the ad was from Kickaha and had answered. But he would not have been able to answer so specifically unless he had Wolff and had gotten out of him what he knew about Kickaha.

Knowing the Lords, Kickaha felt it was likely that Red Orc would torture Wolff and Chryseis first, even though he had only to administer a drug that would make them tell whatever Orc asked for. After that, he would torture them again and finally kill them.

He would do the same with Anana. Even now . . .

He shuddered and said, "No!"

Rodriga opened her eyes and said, "What?"

"Go back to sleep," he said, but she sat up and hugged her knees to her breasts. She rocked back and forth and said, "Something is bugging you, *amigo*. Deeply. Look, I don't want to bug you, too, but if there's anything I can do . . ."

"I've got my own thing to do," he said.

He could not involve her in this even if she could help him in any way. She would be killed the first time they contacted Red Orc's men. She wasn't the fast, extremely tough, many-resourced woman that Anana was. Yes, that's right, he said to himself. *Was*. She might not be alive at this very moment.

Tears came to his eyes.

"Thanks, Rod. I've got to be going now. Dig you later, maybe."

She was up off the floor then and said, "There's something a little strange about you, Paul. You're young but you don't use our lingo quite right, you know what I mean? You seem to me to be just a little weird. I don't mean a creep. I mean, as if you don't quite belong to this world. I know how that is; I get the same feeling quite a lot. That is, I don't belong here, either. But it isn't quite the same thing with you, I mean, you are *really* out of this world. You aren't some being off a flying saucer, are you now?"

"Look, Rod, I appreciate your offer. I really do. But you can't go with me or do anything for me. Not just now. But later, if anything comes up that you can help me with, I sure as hell will let you do something for me and be glad to do so."

He bent over and kissed her forehead and said, "*Hasta la vista*, Rodriga. Maybe *adiós*. Let's hope we see each other again, though."

Kickaha walked until he found a small restaurant. As he ate breakfast, he considered the situation.

One thing was certain. The problem of the Beller was solved. It did not matter whether Kickaha or Orc killed him. Just so he was killed and the Bellers forever out of the way.

And Red Orc now had all but one of his enemies in his hands, and he would soon have that last one. Unless that enemy got to him first. Red Orc had not been using all his powers to catch Kickaha because his first concern was the Beller. But now, he could concentrate on the last holdout.

Somehow, Kickaha had to find the Lord before the Lord got to him. Very soon.

When he had finished eating, he bought a *Times*. As he walked along the street, he scanned the columns of the paper. There was nothing about a girl being kidnapped or a car on Wilshire with the bottom halves of the left wheels sliced off. There was a small item about the police sighting Paul J. Finnegan, the mystery man, his getting away, and a résumé of what was known about him in his pre-1946 life.

He forced himself to settle down and to think calmly. Never before had he been so agitated. He was powerless to stop the very probable torture of his lover and his friends, which might be happening right now.

There *was* no way to get into the Lord's house and face him. If he gave himself up, he could then rely upon his inventiveness and his boldness after he was brought before the Lord.

His sense of reality rescued him. He would be taken in only after a thorough examination to make sure he had no hidden weapons or devices. And he would be brought in bound and helpless.

Unless the Lord followed the custom of always leaving some way open for an exceptionally intelligent and skilled man. Always, no matter how effective and powerful the traps the Lords set about their palaces, they left at least one route open, if the invader was perceptive and audacious enough. That was the rule of the deadly game they had played for thousands of years. It was, in fact, this very rule that had made Red Orc leave the gate in the cave unguarded and untrapped.

Because he had nothing else to do, he went into a public phone booth on a gas station lot and dialed Cambring's number. The phone was picked up so swiftly that Kickaha felt, for a second, that Cambring was still alive and was waiting for his call. It was Cambring's wife who answered, however.

Kickaha said, "Paul Finnegan speaking."

There was a pause and then, "You murderer!" she screamed.

He waited until she was through yelling and cursing him and was sobbing and gasping.

"I didn't kill your husband," he said, "although I would have been justified if I had, as you well know. It was the big boss who killed him."

"You're a liar!" she screamed.

"Tell your big boss I want to speak to him. I'll wait on this line. I know you have several phones you can use."

"Why should I do that?" she said. "I'll do nothing for you!"

"I'll put it this way. If he gets his hands on me, he'll see to it that you get your revenge. But if I don't get into contact with him right now, I'm taking off for the great unknown. And he'll never find me."

She said, "All right," sniffed, and was gone. About sixty seconds later, she was back. "I got a loudspeaker here, a box, what you call it?" she said. "Anyway, you can speak to him through it."

Kickaha doubted that the man he was going to talk to was actually the "big boss" himself. Although Mrs. Cambring had revealed that she now had information that she had not possessed when he had drugged her. Could this be because the Lord had calculated that Kickaha would call her?

He felt a chill sweep over the back of his scalp. If Red Orc could anticipate him so well, then he would also know Kickaha's next step.

He shrugged. There was only one way to find out if Red Orc was that clever.

The voice was deep and resonant. Its pronunciation of English was that of a native, and its use of vocabulary seemed to be "right." The speaker did not introduce himself. His tone indicated that he did not need to do so, that just hearing him should convince anyone immediately of his identity. And of his power.

Kickaha felt that this was truly Red Orc, and the longer he heard him, the more he identified certain characteristics that reminded him of Anana's voice. There was a resemblance there, which was not surprising, since the family of Urizen was very inbred.

"Finnegan! I have your friends Wolff and Chryseis and your lover, my niece, Anana. They are well. Nothing has happened to them, nothing harmful, that is. As yet! I drugged the truth from them; they have told me everything they know about this."

Then it is good, Kickaha thought, *that Anana does not know where the Horn of Shambarimen really is.*

There was a pause. Kickaha said, "I'm listening."

"I should kill them, after some suitable attentions, of course. But they don't really represent any threat to me; they were as easily caught as just-born rabbits."

A Lord always had to do some bragging. Kickaha said nothing, knowing that the Lord would get to the point when he became short-winded. But Red Orc surprised him.

"I could wait until I caught you, and I would not have to wait very long. But just now, time is of the essence, and so I am willing to make a trade."

He paused again. Kickaha said, "I'm all ears."

"I will let the prisoners go and will allow them to return to Jadawin's world. And you may go with them. But on several conditions. First, you will hand over the Horn of Shambarimen to me!"

Kickaha had expected this. The Horn was not only unique in all the universes, it was the most prized item of the Lords. It had been made by the fabled ancestor of all the Lords now living, though it had been in the possession of his equally fabled son so long that it was sometimes referred to as the Horn of Ilmarwolkin. It had a unique utility among gates. It could be used alone. All other gates had to exist in pairs. There had to be one in the universe to be left and a sister, a resonant gate, in the universe to be entered. The majority of these were fixed, though the crescent type was mobile. But the Horn had only to be blown upon, with the keys of the Horn played in the proper coded sequence, and a momentary way between the universes would open. That is, it would do so if the Horn were played near a "resonant" point in the "walls" between the two worlds.

A resonant point was the path between two universes, but these universes never varied. Thus, if a Lord used the Horn without knowing where the resonant point would lead him, he would find himself in whichever universe was on the other side, like it or not.

Kickaha knew of four places where he could blow the Horn and be guaranteed to open the way to the World of Tiers. One was at the gate in the cave near Lake Arrowhead. One was in Kentucky, but he would need Wolff to guide him to it. Another would be in his former apartment in Bloomington, Indiana. And the fourth would be in the closet in the basement of a house in Tempe, Arizona. Wolff knew that, too, but he had described to Kickaha how to get to it from Earth's side, and Kickaha had not forgotten.

Red Orc's voice was impatient. "Come, come! Don't play games with *me*, Earthling! Say yes or say no, but be quick about it!"

"Yes! provisionally, that is. It depends upon your other conditions."

"I have only one." Red Orc coughed several times and then said, "And that is, that you and the others first help me catch the Beller!"

Kickaha was shocked, but a thousand experiences in being surprised enabled him to conceal it. Smoothly, he said, "Agreed! In fact, that's something I had wished you would agree to do, but at that time, I didn't see working with you. Of course, you had no whip hand then."

So the Beller had either been caught by Orc's men and had then escaped or somebody else had captured him. That somebody else could only be another Lord.

Or perhaps it was another Beller.

At that thought, he became cold.

"What do we do now?" he said, unwilling to state the truth, which was, "What do *you* wish now?"

Orc's voice became crisp and restrainedly triumphant. "You will present yourself at Mrs. Cambring's house as soon as possible, and my men will conduct you here. How long will it take you to get to Cambring's?"

"About half an hour," Kickaha said. If he could get a taxi at once, he could be there in ten minutes, but he wanted a little more time to plan.

"Very well!" the Lord said. "You must surrender all arms, and you will be thoroughly examined by my men. Understood?"

"Oh, sure."

While he was talking, he had been as vigilant as a bird. He looked out the glass of the booth for anything suspicious, but had seen nothing except cars passing. Now a car stopped by the curb. It was a big dark Cadillac with a single occupant. The man sat for a minute, looked at his wristwatch, and then opened the door and got out. He sauntered toward the booth, looking again at his watch. He was a very well built youth about six-foot-three and dressed modishly and expensively. The long yellow hair glinted in the sun as if it were flecked with gold. His face was handsome but rugged.

He stopped near the booth and pulled a cigarette case from his jacket. Kickaha continued to listen to the instructions from the phone but he kept his eye on the newcomer. The fellow looked at the world through half-lidded arrogant eyes. He was evidently impatient because the booth was occupied. He glanced at his watch again and then lit his cigarette with a pass of the flame over the tip and a flicking away of the match in one smooth movement.

Kickaha spoke the code that prepared the ring on his finger to be activated for a short piercing beam. He would have to cut through the glass if the fellow were after him.

The voice on the phone kept on and on. It seemed as if he were dictating the terms of surrender to a great nation instead of to a single man. Kickaha must approach the front of the Cambring house and advance only halfway up the front walk and then stand until three men came out of the house and three men in a car parked across the street approached him from behind at the same time. And then . . .

The man outside the booth made a disgusted face as he looked at his watch again and swung away. Evidently he had given up on Kickaha.

But he took only two steps and spun, holding a snub-nosed handgun.

Kickaha dropped the phone and ducked, at the same time speaking the word that activated the ring.

The gun barked, the glass of the booth shattered, and Kickaha was enveloped in a white mist. It was so unexpected that he gasped once, knew immediately that he should hold his breath, and did so. He also lunged out of the booth, cutting down the door with the ring. The door fell outward from his weight, but he never heard it strike the ground.

When he recovered consciousness, he was in the dark and hard confines of a moving object. The odor of gas and the cramped space made him believe that he was in the trunk of a car. His hands were tied behind him, his legs were tied at the ankles, and his mouth was taped.

He was sweating from the heat, but there was enough air in the trunk. The car went up an incline and stopped. The motor stopped, doors squeaked, the car lifted as bodies left it, and then the lid of the trunk swung open. Four men were looking down at him, one of whom was the big youth who had fired the gas gun.

They pulled him out and carried him from the garage, the door of which was shut. The exit led directly into the hall of a house, which led to a large room, luxuriously furnished and carpeted. Another hall led them to a room with a ceiling a story and a half high, an immense crystal chandelier, black-and-white parquet floor, heavy mahogany furniture, and paintings that looked like original old masters.

Here he was set down in a big high-backed chair and his legs were untied. Then he was told by one of the men to walk. A man behind urged him on with something hard and sharp against his back. He followed the others from the room through a doorway set under the great staircase. This led down a flight of twelve steps into a sparsely furnished room. At one end was a big massive iron door that he knew led to his prison cell. And so it was, though a rather comfortable prison. His hands were untied and the tape was taken from his mouth.

The beamer-ring had been removed, and the beamer-pen taken from his shirt pocket. While the big man watched, the others stripped him naked, cutting the shirt and his undershirt off. Then they explored his body cavities for weapons but found nothing.

He offered no resistance since it would have been futile.

The big man and another held guns on him. After the inspection, a man closed a shackle around one ankle. The shackle was attached to a chain that was fastened at the other end to a ring in the wall. The chain was very thin and lightweight, and long enough to permit him to move anywhere in the room.

The big man smiled when he saw Kickaha eyeing it speculatively and said, "It's as gossamer as a cobweb, my friend, but strong as the chain that bound Fenris."

"I am Loki, not Fenris," Kickaha said, grinning savagely. He knew that the man expected him to be ignorant of the reference to the great wolf of the old Norse religion, and he should have feigned ignorance. The less respect your imprisoner has for you, the more chance you have to escape. But he could not resist the answer.

The big man raised his eyebrows and said, "Ah, yes. And you remember what happened to Loki?"

"I am also Logi," Kickaha said, but he decided that that sort of talk had gone far enough. He fell silent, waiting for the other to tell him who he was and what he meant to do.

The man did not look quite so young now. He seemed to be somewhat over thirty. His voice was heavy, smooth, and very authoritative. His eyes were beautiful; they were large and leaf-green and heavily lashed. His face seemed familiar, though Kickaha was sure that he had never seen it before.

The man gestured, and the others left the room. He closed the door behind him and then sat on the edge of the table. This was bolted down to the floor, as were the other pieces of furniture. He dangled one leg while he held the gun on his lap. It looked like a conventional weapon, not a gas gun or a disguised beamer, but Kickaha had no way of determining its exact type at that moment. He sat down on a chair and waited. It was true that this left the man looking down on him, but Kickaha was not one to allow a matter of relative altitude to give another a psychological advantage.

The man looked steadily at him for several minutes. Kickaha looked back and whistled softly.

"I've been following you for some time," the man suddenly said. "I still don't know who you are. Let me introduce myself. I am Red Orc."

Kickaha stiffened, and he blinked.

The man smiled and said, "Who did you think I was?"

"A Lord who'd gotten stuck in this universe and was looking for a way out," Kickaha said. "Are there two Red Orcs, then?"

The man lost some of his smile. "No, there is only one! I am Red Orc! That other is an imposter! A usurper! I was careless for just one moment. But I got away with my life, and because of his bad luck, I will kill him and get back everything!"

"Who is that other?" Kickaha said. "I had thought . . . but then he never named himself . . . he let me think . . ."

"That he was Red Orc, I thought so! But his name is Urthona, and he was once Lord of the Shifting World. Then that demon-bitch Vala, my niece, drove him from his world, and he fled and came here, to this world, my world. I did not know who it was, although I knew that some Lord had come through a gate in Europe. I hunted for him and did not find him and then I forgot about him. That was a thousand years ago; I presumed he had gotten out through some gate I did not know about or else had been killed.

"But he was lying low and all the time searching for me. And finally, only ten years ago, he found me, surveyed my fortress, my defenses, watched my comings and goings, and then he struck!

"I had grown careless, but I got away, although all my bodyguards died. And he took over. It was so simple for him because he was in the seat of power, and there was no one to deny him. How could there be anyone to say no to him? I had hidden my face too well. Anyone in the seat of power could issue orders, pull the strings, and he would be obeyed, since the Earthlings who are closest to him do not know his real name or his real face.

"And I could not go to the men who had carried out my orders and say, 'Here I am, your own true Lord! Obey me and kill that fool who is now giving you orders!' I would have been shot down at once, because Urthona had described me to his servants, and they thought I was the enemy of their leader.

"So I went into hiding, just as Urthona had done. But when I strike, I will not miss! And I shall again be in the seat of power!"

There was a pause. Orc seemed to be expecting him to comment. Perhaps he expected praise or awe or terror.

Kickaha said, "Now that he has this seat of power, as you call it, is he Lord of both Earths? Or of this one only?"

Orc seemed set aback by this question. He stared, then his face got red. "What is that to you?" he finally said.

"I just thought that you might be satisfied with being Lord of the other Earth. Why not let this Urthona rule this world? It looks to me, from the short time I've been here, that this world is doomed. The humans are polluting the air and the water and, at any time, they may kill off all life on Earth with an atomic war. Apparently, you are not doing anything to prevent this. So why not let Urthona have this dying world while you keep the other?"

He paused and then said, "Or is Earth Number Two in as bad a condition as this one?"

Red Orc's face had lost its redness. He smiled and said, "No, the other is not as bad off. It's much more desirable, even though it got exactly the same start as this one. But your suggestion that I surrender this world shows you don't know much about us, *leblabbiy*."

"I know enough," Kickaha said. "But even Lords change for the better, and I had hoped . . ."

"I will do nothing to interfere here except to protect myself," Orc said. "If this planet chokes to death on its man-made foulness, or if it goes out in a thousand bursts of radiation, it will do so without any aid or hindrance from me. I am a scientist, and I do not influence the direction of natural development one way or another on the two planets. Anything I do is on a microscale level and will not disturb macroscale matters.

"That, by the way, is one more reason why I must kill anyone who invades my universes. They might decide to interfere with my grand experiments."

"Not me!" Kickaha said. "Not Wolff or Chryseis or Anana! All we want is to go back to our own worlds! After the Beller is killed, of course. He's the only reason we came here. You must believe that!"

"You don't really expect me to believe that?" Orc said.

Kickaha shrugged and said, "It's true, but I don't expect you to believe it. You Lords are too paranoid to see things clearly."

Red Orc stood up from the table. "You will be kept prisoner here until I have captured the others and defeated Urthona. Then I'll decide what to do with you."

By this, Kickaha knew, he meant just what delicate tortures he could inflict upon him. For a moment, he thought about informing Orc of the Horn of Shambarimen's presence on Earth in this area. Perhaps he could use it for a bargaining point. Then he decided against it. Once Orc knew that it was here, he would just get the information from his captive by torture or drugs.

"Have you killed the Beller yet?" he said.

Orc smiled and said, "No."

He seemed very pleased with himself. "If it becomes necessary, I will threaten Urthona with him. I will tell Urthona that if he does not leave, I will let the Beller loose. That, you understand, is the most horrible thing a Lord could do."

"You would do this? After what you said about getting rid of anybody that might interfere with the natural development?"

"If I knew that my own death was imminent, unavoidable, yes, I would! Why not? What do I care what happens to this world, to all the worlds, if I am dead? Serve them right!"

There were more questions to which Kickaha wanted answers, but he was not controlling the interview. Orc abruptly walked out, leaving by the other door. Kickaha strained at the end of the chain to see through it, but the door swung out toward him and so shut off his view.

He was left with only his thoughts, which were pessimistic. He had always boasted that he could get loose from any prison, but it was, after all, a boast. He had, so far, managed to escape from every place in which he had been imprisoned, but he knew that he would someday find himself in a room with no exit. This was probably it. He was being observed by monitors, electronic or human or both, the chain was unbreakable with bare hands, and it also could be the conductor for some disabling and punishing agent if he did not behave.

This did not prevent him from trying to break it and twist it apart, because he could not afford to take anything for granted. The chain was unharmed, and he supposed that any human monitors would be amused by his efforts.

He stopped struggling, and he used the toilet facilities. Then he lay down on the sofa and thought for a while about his predicament. Though he was naked, he was not uncomfortable. The air was just a few degrees below his body temperature and it moved slowly enough so that it did not chill him. He fell asleep after a while, having found no way out, having thought of no plan that could reasonably work.

When he awoke, the room was as before. The sourceless light still made it high noon, and the air had not changed temperature. However, on sitting up, he saw a tray with dishes and cups and table utensils on top of the small thin-legged wooden table at the end of the sofa. He did not think that anyone could have entered with it unless he had been drugged. It seemed more likely that a gate was embedded in the wooden top and that a tray had been gated through while he slept.

He ate hungrily. The utensils were made of wood, and the dishes and the cups were of pewter and bore stylized octopuses, dolphins, and lobsters. After he ate, he walked back and forth within the range of the chain for about an hour. He tried to think of what he could do with the gate, if there was a gate inside the wooden table top. At the end of the hour, as he turned back toward the table, he saw that the tray was gone. His suspicion was correct; the top did contain a gate.

There had been no sound. The Lords of the old days had solved the problem of noise caused by sudden disappearance of an object. The air did not rush into the vacuum created by the disappearance because the gate arrangement included a simultaneous exchange of air between the gate on one end and that at the other.

About an hour later, Orc entered through the door by which he had left. He was accompanied by two men, one carrying a crossbow and the other a hypodermic needle. They wore kilts. One kilt was striped red and black and the other was white with a stylized black octopus with large blue eyes. Other than the kilts, leather sandals, and beads and metal medallions at the end of the necklace of beads, they wore nothing. Their skins were dark, their faces looked somewhat Mediterranean but also reminded him of Amerindians, and their straight black hair was twisted into two pigtails. One pigtail fell down the back and the other was coiled on the right side of the head.

Orc spoke to them in a language unknown to Kickaha. It did seem vaguely Hebrew or Arabic to him but that was only because of its sounds. He knew too little of either language to be able to identify them.

While the one with the crossbow stood to one side and aimed it at Kickaha, the other approached from the other side. Orc commanded him to submit to the injection, saying that if he resisted, the crossbow would shoot its hypodermic into him. And the pain that followed would be long-lasting and intense. Kickaha obeyed, since there was nothing else he could do.

He felt nothing following the injection. But he answered all of Orc's questions without hesitation. His brain did not feel clouded or bludgeoned. He was thinking as clearly as usual. It was just that he could not resist giving Orc all the information he asked for. But that was what kept him from mentioning the Horn of Shambarimen. Orc did not *ask* him about it nor was there any reason for him to do so. He had no knowledge that it had been in the possession of Wolff, or Jadawin, as Orc knew him.

Orc's questions did, however, reveal almost everything else of value to him. He knew something of Kickaha's life on Earth before that night in Bloomington when Paul Janus Finnegan had been accidentally catapulted out of this universe into the World of Tiers. He learned more about Finnegan's life since then, when Finnegan had become Kickaha (and also Horst von Horstmann and a dozen other identities). He learned about Wolff-Jadawin and Chryseis and Anana, the invasion of the Black Bellers, and other matters pertinent. He learned much about Kickaha's and Anana's activities since they had gated into the cavern near Lake Arrowhead.

Orc said, "If I did allow you and Anana and Wolff and Chryseis to go back to your world, would you stay there and not try to get back here?"

"Yes," Kickaha said. "Provided that I knew for sure that the Beller was dead."

"Hmm. But your World of Tiers sounds fascinating. Jadawin always was very creative. I think that I would like to add it to my possessions."

This was what Kickaha expected.

Orc smiled again and said, "I wonder what you would have done if you had found out where I used to live and where Urthona now sits in the seat of power."

"I would have gone into it and killed you or Urthona," Kickaha said.

"And I would have rescued Anana and Wolff and Chryseis and then searched for the Beller until I found him and killed him. And then we would have returned to my world, that is to Wolff's, to be exact."

Orc looked thoughtful and paced back and forth for a while. Suddenly, he stopped and looked at Kickaha. He was smiling as if a brilliant idea were shining through him.

"You make yourself sound very tricky and resourceful," he said. "So tricky that I could almost think you were a Lord, not just a *leblabbiy* Earthling."

"Anana has the crazy idea that I could be the son of a Lord," Kickaha said. "In fact, she thinks I could be your son."

Orc said, "What?" and he looked closely at Kickaha and then began laughing. When he had recovered, he wiped his eyes and said, "That felt good! I haven't laughed like that for . . . how long? Never mind. So you really think *you* could be my child?"

"Not me," Kickaha said. "Anana. And she likes to speculate about it because she still needs some justification for falling in love with a *leblabbiy*. If I could be half-Lord, then I'd be more acceptable. But this idea is one-hundred-percent wishful thinking, of course."

"I have no children because I want to interfere as little as possible with the natural development here, although a child or two could really make little difference," Orc said. "But you could be the child of another Lord, I suppose. However, you've gotten me off the subject. I was saying that you were very tricky, if I am to believe your account of yourself. Perhaps I could use you."

He fell silent again and paced back and forth once more with his head bent and his hands clasped behind him. Then he stopped, looked at Kickaha, and smiled. "Why not? Let's see how good you are. I can't lose by it no matter what happens, and I may gain."

Kickaha had guessed, correctly, what he was going to propose. He would tell him the address of Urthona, would take him there; in fact, provide him with some weapons, and allow him to attack Urthona as he wished. And if Kickaha failed, he still might so distract Urthona that Orc could take advantage of the distraction.

In any event, it would be amusing to watch a *leblabbiy* trying to invade the seat of power of a Lord.

"And if I do succeed?" Kickaha said.

"It's not very likely, since *I* have not had any success yet. Though, of course, I haven't really tried yet. But if you should succeed, and I'm not worried that you will, I will permit you and your lover and your friends to return to your world. Provided that the others also swear, while under the influence of the proper drugs, that they have no intention of returning to either Earth."

Kickaha did not believe this, but he saw no profit in telling Orc so. Once he was out of this cell and had some freedom of action—though closely watched by Orc—he would have some chance against the Lords. Orc spoke the unknown language into a wristband device, and a moment later another entered. His kilt was red with a black stylized bird with a silver fish in its claws. He carried some papers that he gave to Orc, then bowed, and withdrew.

Orc sat down by Kickaha.

The papers turned out to be maps of the central Los Angeles area and of Beverly Hills. Orc circled an area in Beverly Hills.

"That is the house where I lived and where Urthona now lives," he said. "The house you were searching for and where Anana and the others are now undoubtedly held. Or, at least, where they were taken after being captured."

Orc's description of the defenses in the house made Kickaha feel very vulnerable. It was true that Urthona would have changed the defense setup in the house. But, though the configuration on the traps might be different, the traps would remain fundamentally the same.

"Why haven't you tried to attack before this?"

"I have," Red Orc replied. "Several times. My men got into the house, but I never saw them again. The last attempt was made about three years ago.

"If you don't succeed," Orc continued, "I will threaten Urthona with the Beller. I doubt, however, that that will do much good, since he will find it inconceivable that a Lord could do such a thing."

His tone also made it evident that he did not think Kickaha would succeed.

He wanted to know Kickaha's plans, but Kickaha could only tell him that he had none except to improvise. He wanted Orc to use his devices to ensure a minute's distortion of Urthona's detection devices.

Orc objected to loaning Kickaha an antigravity belt. What if it fell into the hands of the Earthlings?

"There's not much chance of that," Kickaha said. "Once I'm in Urthona's territory, I'll either succeed or fail. In either case, the belt isn't going to get into any outsider's hands. And if it did, whoever is Lord will have the influence to see that it is taken out of the hands of whoever has it. I'm sure that even if the FBI had it in their possession, the Lord of the Two Earths could find a way to get it from them. Right?"

"Right," Orc said. "But do you plan on running away with it instead of attacking Urthona?"

"No. I won't stop until I'm dead, or too incapacitated to fight, or have won," Kickaha said.

Orc was satisfied, and by this Kickaha knew that the truth drug was still effective. Orc stood up and said, "I'll prepare things for you. It will take some time, so you might as well rest or do whatever you think best. We'll go into action at midnight tonight."

Kickaha asked if the cord could be taken off him. Orc said, "Why not? You can't get out of here, anyway. The cord was just an extra precaution." One of the kilted men touched the shackle around his leg with a thin cylinder. The shackle opened and fell off. While the two men backed away from Kickaha, Orc strode out of the room. Then the door was shut, and Kickaha was alone.

He spent the rest of the time thinking, exercising, and eating lunch and supper. Then he bathed and shaved, exercised some more, and lay down to sleep. He would need all his alertness, strength, and quickness and there was no use draining these with worry and sleeplessness.

He did not know how long he had slept. The room was still lighted, and everything seemed as when he had lain down. The tray with its empty plates and cups was still on the table, and this, he realized, was a wrong note. It should have been gated out.

The sounds that had awakened him had seemed to be slight tappings. When coming out of his sleep, he had dreamed, or thought he dreamed, that a woodpecker was rapping a tree trunk.

Now there was only silence.

He rose and walked toward the door used by Orc and his servants. It was of metal, as he had ascertained after being loosed from the cord. He placed his ear against it and listened. He could hear nothing. Then he jumped back with an oath. The metal had suddenly become hot!

The floor trembled as if an earthquake had started. The metal of the door gave forth a series of sounds, and he knew where the dream of a woodpecker had originated. Something was striking the door on the other side.

He stepped away from it just as the center of the door became cherry-red and began to melt. The redness spread, became white, and then the center disappeared, leaving a hole the size of a dinner plate. By then, Kickaha was crouching behind the sofa and looking out around its corner. He saw an arm reach in through the hole and the hand grope around the side. Evidently it was trying to locate a lock. There was none, so the arm withdrew and a moment later, the edge of the door became cherry-red. He suspected that a beam was being used on it, and he wondered what the metal was. If it had been the hardest steel, it should have gone up in a puff of smoke at the first touch of a beam.

The door fell inward with a clang. A man jumped in, a big cylinder with a bell-like muzzle and rifle-type stock in his hands. The man was one of the kilted servants. But he carried on his back a black bell-like object in a net attached to the shoulders with straps.

Kickaha saw all this at a glance and withdrew his head. He crouched on the other side, hoping that the intruder had not seen him and would not, as a matter of precaution, sweep the sofa with the beamer to determine if anyone would be behind it. He knew who the man *now* was. Whatever he *may* have been, he was now the Black Beller, Thabuuz. The mind of the Beller was housed in the brain of the servant of the Lord, and the mind of the servant was discharged.

Somehow, the Beller had gotten the bell and managed to transfer his mind from the wounded body of the Drachelander to the servant of the Lord. He had gotten hold of a powerful beamer, and he was on his way out of the stronghold of Red Orc.

The odor of burnt flesh filled the room; there must be bodies in the next room.

Kickaha wanted desperately to find out what the Beller was doing, but he did not dare to try to peek around the corner of the sofa again. He could hear the man's breathing, and then, suddenly, it was gone. After waiting sixty seconds and hearing nothing, Kickaha peeked around the corner. The room seemed to be empty. A moment later, he was sure of it. The other door, the door by which Kickaha and Orc and his men had originally entered, was standing wide open, its lock drilled through.

Kickaha looked cautiously around the side of the opposite door. There were parts of human bodies here, arms, trunks, a head, all burned deeply. There seemed to have been four or five men originally. There was no way of telling which was Red Orc or if he was among the group, since all clothes and hair had been burned off.

Somewhere, softly, an alarm was ringing.

He was torn between the desire to keep on the trail of the Beller so that he would not lose him and by the desire to find out if Red Orc was still alive. He also wanted very much to confirm his suspicions that he was not on the Earth he knew. He suspected that the door through which he had entered was a gate between the two worlds and that this house was on Earth Number Two.

He went into the hallway. There were some knives on the floor, but they were too hot to pick up. He went down the hall and through a doorway into a large room. It was dome-shaped, its walls white with frescoes of sea life, its furniture wooden and lightly built with carved motifs he did not recognize, and its floor a mosaic of stone with more representations of sea creatures.

He crossed the room and looked out the window. There was enough light from the moon to see a wide porch with tall round wooden pillars, painted white, and beyond that, a rocky beach that sloped for a hundred yards from the house to the sea. There was no one in view.

He prowled the rest of the house, trying to combine caution with speed. He found a hand-beamer built to look like a conventional revolver. Its butt bore markings that were not the writing of the Lords or of any language that he knew. He tested it out against a chair, which fell apart down the middle. He could find no batteries to recharge it and had no way of knowing how much charge remained in the battery.

He also found closets with clothes, most of them kilts, sandals, beads, and jackets with puffed sleeves. But in one closet he found Earth Number One-type clothing, and he put on a shirt and trousers too large for him. Since he could not wear the big shoes, he put on a pair of sandals.

Finally, in a large bedroom luxuriously provided with alien furniture, he discovered how Red Orc had escaped. A crescent lay in the center of the floor. The Lord had stepped into a circle formed of two crescents of a gate and been transported elsewhere. That he had done so to save himself was evident. The door and the walls were crisscrossed with thin perforations and charred. It was not likely that Orc would be caught without a weapon on him, but he must have thought that the big beamer was too much to face.

He had gated, but where? He could have gone back to Earth Number One, but not necessarily to the same house. Or he could have gated to another place on Earth Number Two. Or, even, to another room in this house.

Kickaha had to get out of this house and after the Beller. He ran downstairs, through the big room, down the hall, and into the room where he had been kept prisoner. The door through which the Beller had gone was still open. Kickaha hesitated before it, because the Beller might be waiting for someone to follow. Then it occurred to him that the Beller would think that everybody in the house had fled or gone and that nobody would be following him. He had not known about the other prisoner, of course, or he would have looked around to dispose of him first.

He returned to the hallway. One knife lying on the floor had cooled off by then and seemed to be undamaged. He hefted it, determined that it had a good balance, and stuck it in his belt. He leaped through the doorway, his gun ready if somebody should be waiting for him. There was no one. The short and narrow hallway was quiet. The door beyond had been closed, and he pushed it open gently with the tip of his dagger. After the door had swung open, he waited a minute, listening. Before going through, he inspected the room. It had changed. It was larger, and the gray-paper walls were gray smooth stone. He had expected that this might happen. Red Orc would change the resonance of the gates so that if a prisoner did escape, he would find himself in a surprising, and probably unpleasant, place.

Under other circumstances, Kickaha would have turned back and looked for the switch that would set the gate to the frequency he desired. But now his first duty was to those in the hands of Urthona. To hell with the Beller! It would really be best to get back to Earth Number One and to get started on the attack against Urthona.

He turned and started to reenter the room where he had been held, and again he stopped. That room had changed, though he would not have known it if the door to the opposite side had not been removed by the Beller's weapon. This door looked exactly the same, but it was upright and in its place. Only this kept Kickaha from stepping into it and so finding himself gated to another place where he would be cut off from both the Beller and Urthona's captives.

He set his teeth together and hissed rage and frustration. Now he could do nothing but take second-best and put himself in with the Beller and hope that he could figure a way out.

He turned and went back through the door after the Beller, though no less cautiously.

This room seemed to be safe, but the room beyond that would probably tell him where he was. However, it was just like the one he had left except that there were some black metal boxes, each about six feet square, piled along the walls almost to the ceiling. There were no locks or devices on them to indicate how they were opened.

He opened the next door slowly, looked through, and then leaped in. He was in a large room furnished with chairs, divans, tables, and statuary. A big fountain was in the middle. The furniture looked as if it had been made by a Lord; though he did not know the name of the particular style, he recognized it. Part of the ceiling and one side of the right wall were curved and transparent. The ground outside was not visible for some distance and then it abruptly sprang into view. It sloped down for a thousand feet to end in a valley that ran straight and level for several miles and then became the side of a small mountain.

It was daylight outside, but the light was pale, though it was noon. The sun was smaller than Earth's, and the sky was black. The earth itself was rocky with some stretches of reddish sand, and there were a few widely separated cactus-looking plants on the slope and in the valley. They seemed small, but he realized after a while that they must be enormous.

He examined the room carefully and made sure that the door to the next room was closed. Then he looked through the window again. The scene was desolate and eerie. Nothing moved, and probably nothing had moved here for thousands of years. Or so it seemed to him. He could see past the end of the mountain. The horizon was closer than it should have been.

He had no idea where he was. If he had been gated into another universe, he would probably never know. If he had been gated to another planet in his native universe, or its double, then he was probably on Mars. The size of the sun, the reddish sand, the distance of the horizon, the fact that there was enough air to support plant life—if that was plant life—and, even as he watched, the appearance of a swift whitish body coming from the western sky indicated that this was Mars.

For all he knew, this building had been on Mars for fifteen thousand years, since the creation of this universe.

At that moment, something came flapping over the mountain on the opposite side and then glided toward the bottom of the valley. It had an estimated wing span of fifty yards and looked like a cross between a kite, a pterodactyl, and a balloon. Its wing bones gave the impression of being thin as tin foil, though it was really impossible to be sure at that distance. The skin of the wings looked thinner than tissue paper. Its body was a great sac that gave the impression, again unverifiable, of containing gas. Its tail spread out in a curious configuration like six box kites on a rod. Its lower limbs were exceedingly thin but numerous and spread out below it like a complicated landing gear, which it probably was. Its feet were wide and many-toed.

It glided down very gracefully and swiftly. Even with the lift of its great wings and tail and the lighter-than-air aspect of the swollen gas-containing body, it had to glide at a steep angle. The air must be so thin.

The thing threw an enormous shadow over one of the gigantic cactusoids, and then it was settling down, like a skyscraper falling, on the plant. Red dust flew into the air and came down more swiftly than it would have on Earth.

The plant was completely hidden under the monster's bulk. It thrust its rapier-like beak down between two of its legs and, presumably, into the plant. And there it squatted, as motionless as the cactusoids.

Kickaha watched it until it occurred to him that the Beller might also be watching it. If this were so, it would make it easier for Kickaha to surprise him. He went through the next door in the same manner as the last and found himself in a room ten times as large as the one he had just left. It was filled with great metal boxes and consoles with many screens and instruments. It, too, had a window with a view of the valley.

There was no Beller, however.

Kickaha went into the next room. This was small and furnished with everything a man would need except human companionship. In the middle of the floor lay a skeleton.

There was no evidence of the manner of death. The skeleton was that of a large male. The teeth were in perfect condition. It lay on its back with both bony arms outstretched.

Kickaha thought that it must have been some Lord who had either entered this fortress on Mars from a gate in some other universe or had been trapped elsewhere and transported here by Red Orc. This could have happened ten thousand years ago or fifty years ago.

Kickaha picked the skull up and carried it in his left hand. He might need something to throw as a weapon or as a distraction to his enemy. It amused him to think of using a long-dead Lord, a failed predecessor, against a Beller.

The next room was designed like a grotto. There was a pool of water about sixty yards wide and three hundred long in the center and a small waterfall on the left that came down from the top of a granite cone. There were several of the stone cones and small hills, strange-looking plants growing here and there, a tiny stream flowing from a spring on top of another cone, and huge lilypad-like plants in the pool.

As he walked slowly along the wet and slimy edge of the pool, he was startled by a reddish body leaping from a lily pad. It soared out, its legs trailing behind frog-fashion and then splashed into the water. It arose a moment later and turned to face the man. Its face was froglike but its eyes were periscopes of bone or cartilage. Its pebbly skin was as red as the dust on the surface outside.

There were several shadowy fishlike bodies in the depths. There had to be something for the frog to eat, and for the prey of the frog to eat. The ecology in this tiny room must be delicately but successfully balanced. He doubted that Red Orc came here very often to check up on it.

He was standing by the edge of the pool when he saw the door at the far end begin to open. He had no time to run forward or backward because of the distance he would have to traverse. There was no hiding place to his right and only the pool close by on his left. Without more than a second's pause, he chose the pool and slid over the slimy edge into the water. It was warm enough not to shock him but felt oily. He stuck the beamer in his belt and, still holding the skull in one hand, submerged with a shove of his sandaled feet against the side of the pool. He went down deep, past the thick stems of the lily pads, and swam as far as he could under the water. When he came up, he did so slowly and alongside the stem of a lily. Emerging, he kept his head under the pad of the plant and hoped that the Beller would not notice the bulge. The other rooms had been bright with the equal-intensity, hidden-source lighting of the Lords. But this room was lit only by the light from the window and so had a twilight atmosphere on this side.

Kickaha clung with one hand to the stem of the plant and peered out from under the lifted edge of the pad. What he saw almost made him gasp. He was fortunate to have restrained himself, because his mouth was underwater.

The black bell was floating along the edge of the pool at a height of about seven feet above the floor.

It went by slowly and then stopped at the door. A moment later, the Beller entered and walked confidently toward it.

Kickaha began to get some idea of what had happened in Red Orc's house.

The Beller, while in the laboratories of Wolff, must have equipped his bell with an antigravity device. And he must have added some device for controlling it at a distance with his thoughts. He had not been able to use it while on Earth, nor had any reason to do so until he was taken prisoner by Orc. Then, when he had recovered enough from the wound, he saw his chance and summoned the bell to him with his thoughts. Or, to be more exact, by controlled patterns of brainwaves that could be detected by the bell. The control must be rough and limited, but it had been effective enough.

Somehow, the bell, operating at the command of the Beller's brainwave patterns, had released him. And the Beller had seized one of Orc's men, discharged the neural pattern of the man's mind, and transferred his mind from the wounded body of Thabuuz to the brain of the servant.

The bell could detect the mental call of the Beller when it extended the two tiny drill-antennas from two holes in its base. The stuff of which the bell was made was indestructible, impervious even to radiation. So the antennas must have come out automatically at certain intervals to "listen" for the brainwaves of the Beller. And it had "heard" and had responded. And the Beller had gotten out and obtained a weapon and started to kill. He had succeeded; he may even have killed Red Orc, though Kickaha did not think so.

And then he had been shunted through the escape gate into a building on Mars.

Kickaha watched the Beller approach. Unable to hang onto the skull any longer and handle his gun at the same time, he let the skull drop. It sank silently into the depths while he held on to the stem with his left hand and pulled the beamer from his belt with the other. The Beller went on by him and then stopped at the door. After opening this, he waited until the bell had floated on through ahead of him.

Apparently, the bell could detect other living beings, too. Its range must be limited, otherwise it would have detected Kickaha in the water as it went by. It was possible, of course, that the water and the lily pad shielded him from the bell's probe.

Kickaha pulled himself higher out of the water with his left hand and lifted the beamer above the surface. From under the darkness of the pad, he aimed at the Beller. It would be necessary to get him with the first beam. If it missed, the Beller would get through the door and then Kickaha would be up against a weapon much more powerful than his.

If he missed the Beller, the beam would slice through the wall of the building, and the air would boil out into the thin atmosphere of Mars. And both of them would have had it.

The Beller was presenting his profile. Kickaha held his beamer steadily as he pointed it so that the thread-thin ray would burn a hole through the hip of the man. And then, as he fell, he would be cut in two.

His finger started to squeeze the trigger. Suddenly, something touched his calf and he opened his mouth to scream. So intense was the pain, it almost shocked him into unconsciousness. He doubled over, and water entered his mouth and nostrils, and he choked. His hand came loose from the plant stem and the beamer fell from the other hand.

In the light-filled water, he saw a froglike creature swim away swiftly, and he knew that it was this that had bitten him. He swam upward because he had to get air, knowing even as he did that the Beller would easily kill him, if the Beller had heard him.

He came up and, with a massive effort of will, kept himself from blowing out water and air and gasping and thrashing around. His head came up under the pad again, and he eased the water out. He saw that the Beller had disappeared.

But in the next second he doubled over again with agony. The frog had returned and bitten him on the leg again. His blood poured out from the wounds and darkened the water. He swam quickly to the edge of the pool and pulled himself out with a single smooth motion. His legs tingled.

On the walk, he pulled off his shirt and tore it into strips to bind around his wounds. The animal must have had teeth as sharp as a shark's; they had sheared through the cloth of his pants and taken out skin and flesh. But the wounds were not deep.

The Lord must have been greatly amused when he planted the savage little carnivore in this pool.

Kickaha was not amused. He did not know why the Beller was in the next room, but he suspected that he would soon be back. He had to get away, but he also needed his beamer. Not that he would be able to get it. Not while that frog-thing was in the pool.

At least he had the knife. He took it from his belt and put it between his teeth while he splashed water on the walk where his blood had dripped. Then he straightened up and limped past the pool and into the next room.

He passed through a short bare-walled hall. The room beyond was as large as the one with the pool. It was warm and humid and filled with plant life that looked neither Terrestrial nor Martian. It was true that he had not seen any Martian vegetation other than the cactusoids in the valley. But these plants were so tall, green, stinking, fleshy, and so active, they just did not look as if they could survive on the rare-aired Marsscape.

One side of the wall was transparent, and this showed a gray fog. That was all. Strain his eyes as much as he could, he could see nothing but the grayness. And it did not seem to be a watery fog, but one composed of thousands upon thousands of exceedingly tiny particles. More like dust of some kind, he thought.

He was surely no longer on Mars. When he had passed from the hall into this room, he had stepped through a gate that had shot him instantaneously into a building on some other planet or satellite. The gravity seemed no different than Earth's, so he must be on a planet of similar size. That, plus the cloud, made him think that it must be Venus.

With a start, he realized that the gravity in the Martian building should have been much less than Earth's. How much? A sixth? He did not remember, but he knew that when he had leaped, he should have soared far more than he did.

But that building was on Mars. He was sure of that. This meant that the building had been equipped with a device to ensure an Earth-gravity locally. Which meant that this building could be on, say, Jupiter, and yet the titanic drag of the planet would be nullified by the Lord's machines.

He shrugged. It really did not matter much where he was if he could not survive outside the building. The problem he had to solve was staying alive and finding a way back to Earth. He went on to another short and bare hall and then into a twilit room the size of Grand Central Station. It was dome-shaped and filled with a silvery-gray metal liquid except for a narrow walk around the wall and for a small round island in the middle. The metal looked like mercury, and the walk went all the way around the room. Nowhere along the wall was there any sign of any opening.

The island was about fifty yards from the wall. Its surface was only a foot above the still lake of quicksilver. The island seemed to be of stone, and in its exact center was a huge hoop of metal set vertically in the stone. He knew at once that it was a gate and that if he could get to it, he would be transported to a place where he would at least have a fighting chance. That was the rule of the game. If the prisoner was intelligent enough and strong enough and swift enough—and, above all, lucky enough—he just might get free.

He waited by the door because there was no other place to hide. While he waited, he tried to think of anything in the other rooms that could be converted into a boat. Nothing came to his mind except one of the sofas, and he doubted that it would float. Still, he might try it. But how did you propel a heavy object that was slowly sinking, or perhaps swiftly sinking, through mercury?

He would not know until he tried it. The thought did not cheer him up. And then he thought, could a man swim in mercury? In addition, there were poisonous vapors rising from mercury, if he remembered his chemistry correctly.

Now he remembered some phrases from his high-school chemistry class. That was back in 1936 in a long-ago and truly different world: *Does not wet glass but forms a convex surface when in a glass container . . . is slightly volatile at ordinary temperatures and a health hazard due to its poisonous effect . . . slowly tarnishes in moist air. . . .*

The air in this dome was certainly moist, but the metal was not tarnished. And he could smell no fumes and did not feel any poisonous effects. Not as yet.

Suddenly, he stiffened. He heard, faintly, the slapping of leather on stone. The door had been left open by the Beller, so Kickaha had not moved it. He was on the other side, waiting, hoping that the bell would not enter first.

It did. The black object floated through about four feet off the floor. As soon as it had passed by, it stopped. Kickaha leaped against the door and slammed it shut. The bell continued to hover in the same spot.

The door remained shut. It had no lock, and all the Beller had to do was to kick it. But he was cautious, and he must have been very shaken by finding the door closed. He had no idea who was on the other side or what weapons his enemy had. Furthermore, he was separated from his bell, his most precious possession. If it was true that the bell could not be destroyed, it was also true that it could be taken away and hidden from him.

Kickaha ran in front of the door, hoping that the Beller would not fire his heavy beamer at it at that moment. He seized the bell and plunged on. The bell resisted but went backward all the same. It did not, however, give an inch on the vertical.

At that moment, the metal of the edge of the door and the wall began to turn red, and Kickaha knew that the Beller was turning the full power of his beamer on the door and that the metal must be very resistant indeed.

But why didn't the Beller just kick the door open and then fire through it?

Perhaps he was afraid that his enemy might be hiding behind the door when it swung open, so he was making sure that there would be nothing to swing. Whatever his motives, he was giving Kickaha a little more time, not enough though to swim across to the island. The Beller would be through the door about the time he was halfway to the island.

Kickaha took hold of the bell with both hands and pushed it up against the wall. It did not go easily on the horizontal, but he did not have to strain to move it. He pulled it toward him and then away, estimating its resistance. Then he gave it a great shove with both hands in the direction along the wall. It moved at about two feet per second but then slowed as it scraped along the curved wall. Another shove, this time at an angle to take it away from the curve but to keep it from going out over the pool, resulted in its moving for a longer distance.

He looked at the door. The red spot was a hole now with a line of redness below it. Evidently the Beller intended to carve out a large hole or perhaps to cut out the door entirely. He could stop at any moment to peek through the hole, and if he did, he would see his enemy and the bell. On the other hand, he might be afraid to use the hole just yet because his enemy might be waiting to blast him. Kickaha had one advantage. The Beller did not know what weapons he had.

Kickaha hurried after the bell, seized it again, backed up, stopped at the wall, and then drew his feet up. He hung with his knees and toes almost touching the walk. But the bell did not lose a fraction of altitude.

"Here goes everything!" he said and shoved with all the power of his legs against the wall.

He and the bell shot out over the pool, straight toward the vertical hoop on the island. They went perhaps forty feet and then stopped. He looked down at the gray liquid below and slowly extended his feet until they were in the metal. He pushed against it, and it gave way to his feet, but he and the bell moved forward a few feet. And so he pushed steadily and made progress, though it was slow and the sweat poured out over his body and ran into his eyes and stung them, and his legs began to ache as if he had run two miles as fast as he could.

Nevertheless, he got to the island, and he stood upon its stone surface with the hoop towering only a few feet from him. He looked at the door. A thin line ran down one side and across the bottom and up the other side. It curved suddenly and was running across the top of the door. Within a minute or two, the door would fall in and then the Beller would come through.

Kickaha looked back through the hoop. The room was visible on the other side, but he knew that if he stepped through it, he would be gated to some other place, perhaps to another universe. Unless the Lord had set it here for a joke.

He pushed the bell ahead of him and then threw himself to one side so he would not be in front of the hoop. He had had enough experience with the Lords to suspect that the place on the other side was trapped. It was always best to throw something into the trap to spring it.

There was a blast that deafened him. His face and the side of his body were seared with heat. He had shut his eyes, but light flooded them. And then he sat up and opened them in time to see the bell shooting across the pool, though still at its original height. It sped above the mercury pool and the walk and stopped only when it slammed into the wall. There it remained, a few inches from the wall because of its rebound.

Immediately thereafter, the door fell outward and down against the wall. He could not hear it; he could hear only the ringing in his ears from the blast. But he saw the Beller dive through, the beamer held close to him, hit the floor, roll, and come up with the beamer held ready. By then, Kickaha had jumped up. As he saw the Beller look around and suddenly observe him, he leaped through the hoop. He had no choice. He did not think it would be triggered again, since that was not the way the Lords arranged their traps. But if the trap on the other side was reset, it would blow him apart, and his worries would be over.

He was through, and he was falling. There were several thousands of feet of air beneath him, a blue sky above, and a thin horizontal bar just before him. He grabbed it, both hands clamping around smooth cold iron, and he was swinging at arm's length below a bar, the ends of which were set in two metal poles that extended about twenty feet out from the cliff.

It was a triumph of imagination and sadism for Red Orc. If the prisoner was careless enough to go through the hoop without sending in a decoy, he would be blown apart before he could fall to death. And if he did not jump, but stepped through the gate, he would miss the bar.

And, having caught the bar, then what?

A man with lesser nerve or muscle might have fallen. Kickaha did not waste any time. He reached out with one hand and gripped the support bar. And as quickly let loose while he cursed and swung briefly with one hand.

The support pole was almost too hot to touch.

He inched along the bar to the other support pole and touched it. That was just as hot.

The metal was not quite too hot to handle. It pained him so much that Kickaha thought about letting go. But he stuck to it, and finally, hurting so much that tears came to his eyes and he groaned, he pulled himself up over the lip of the cliff. For a minute he lay on the rock ledge and moaned. The palms of his hands and the inner sides of his fingers felt as if they had third-degree burns. They looked, however, as if they had only been briefly near a fire, not in it, and the pain quickly went away.

His investigation of his situation was short because there was not much to see. He was on the bare top of a pillar of hard black rock. The top was wider than the bottom, and the sides were smooth as the barrel of a cannon. All around the pillar, as far as he could see, was a desolate rock plain and a river. The river split the circle described by the horizon and then itself split when it came to the column. On the other side, it merged into itself and continued on toward the horizon.

The sky was blue, and the yellow sun was at its zenith.

Set around the pillar near its base, at each of the cardinal points of the compass, was a gigantic hoop. One of these meant his escape to a place where he might survive if he chose the right one. The others probably meant certain death if he went through them.

They were not an immediate concern. He had to get down off the pillar first, and at that moment he did not know how he was going to do that.

He returned to the bar projecting from the cliff. The Beller could be about ready to come through the gate. Even if he was reluctant, he would have to come through. This was the only way out.

Minutes passed and became an hour, if he could trust his sense of time. The sun curved down from the zenith. He walked back and forth to loosen his muscles and speed the blood in his legs and buttocks. Suddenly a foot and a leg came out of the blue air. The Beller, on the other side of the gate, was testing out the unknown.

The foot reached here and there for substance and found only air. It withdrew, and a few seconds later, the face of the Beller, like a Cheshire Cat in reverse, appeared out of the air.

Kickaha's knife was a streak of silver shooting toward the face. The face jerked back into the nothingness, and the knife was swallowed by the sky at a point about a foot below where the face had been.

The gate was not one-way. The entrance of the knife showed that. The fact that the Beller could stick part of his body through it and then withdraw it did not have anything to do with the one-way nature of some gates. Even a one-way gate permitted a body to go halfway through and then return. Unless, of course, the Lord who had designed it wished to sever the body of the user.

Several seconds passed. Kickaha cursed. He might never find out if he had thrown true or not.

Abruptly, a head shot out of the blue and was followed by a neck and shoulders and a chest and a solar plexus from which the handle of the knife stuck out.

The rest of the body came in view as the Beller toppled through. He fell through and out and his body became smaller and smaller and then was lost in distance. But Kickaha was able to see the white splash it made as it struck the river.

He took a deep breath and sat down, trembling. The Beller was at last dead, and all the universes were safe forever from his kind.

And here I am, Kickaha thought. *Probably the only living thing in this universe. As alone as a man can be. And if I don't think of something impossible to do before my nonexistent breakfast, I will soon be one of the only two dead things in this universe.*

He breathed deeply again and then did what he had to do.

It hurt just as much going back out on the pole as it had coming in. When he reached the bar, he rested on it with one arm and one leg over it. After the pain had gone away in his hands and legs, he swung up onto the bar and balanced himself standing on it. His thousands of hours of practicing on tightwires and climbing to great heights paid off. He was able to maintain his equilibrium on the bar while he estimated again the point through which the Beller had fallen. It was only an undefined piece of blue, and he had one chance to hit his target.

He leaped outward and up, and his head came through the hoop, and then the upper part of his body, and he went "Whoof!" as his belly struck on the edge of the hoop. He reached out and gripped the stone with his fingertips and pulled himself on through. For a while, he lay on the stone until his heart resumed its normal beat. He saw that the bell was above him and the beamer was on the floor of the island only a foot from him.

He rose and examined the bell. It was indestructible, and the tips of the antennas were encased in the same indestructible stuff. When the antennas were withdrawn, the tips plugged up the two tiny holes at the base of the bell. But the antennas themselves were made of less durable metal, and they had suffered damage from the blast. Or so he supposed. He could see no damage. In fact, he could not even see the antennas, they were so thin, though he could feel them. But the fact that the Beller had not sent the bell ahead through the gate proved to Kickaha that something had damaged the bell. Perhaps the blast had only momentarily impaired the relatively delicate brainwave and flight-governing apparatus inside the bell. This was, after all, something new, something that the Beller had not had time to field-test.

Whatever had happened, it was fixed at its altitude above the island. And it still put up a weak resistance against a horizontal push.

Kickaha presumed that its antennas must still be operative to some degree. Otherwise, the bell would not know how to maintain a constant height from the ground.

It gave him his only chance to get to the ground several thousand feet below. He did not know how much of a chance. It might just stay at this level even if the ground beneath it were to suddenly drop away. If that happened, he still might be able to get to the top of the stone pillar.

He put the strap of the beamer over one shoulder, hugged the bell to his chest, and stepped out through the hoop.

His descent was as swift as if he were dangling at the end of a parachute, a speed better than he had hoped for. From time to time, he had to kick against the sides of the pillar because the bell kept drifting back toward it, as if the mass of the pillar had some attraction for it.

Then he was ten feet above the river and released his hold on the bell. He fell a little faster, hit the water, which was warm, and came up in a strong current. He had to fight to get to shore but managed it. After he had regained some of his strength, he walked along the shore until he saw the bell. It was stopped against the side of the pillar, like a baby beast nuzzling its gigantic mother. There was no way for him to get to it, nor did he see any reason why he should.

A few yards on, he found the body of the Beller. It had come to rest against a reef of rock that barely protruded above the surface of the small bay. Its back was split open, and the back of the head was soft, as if it had struck concrete instead of water. The knife was still in its solar plexus. Kickaha pulled it out, and cleaned it on the wet hair of the Beller. The fall had not damaged the knife.

He pulled the body from the river. Then he considered the giant gates set hooplike in the rock like the smaller one in the island in that other world. Two were on this side of the river and two on the other. Each was at the corner of a square two miles long. He walked to the nearest one and threw a stone into it. The stone went through and landed on the rock on the other side. It was one of Red Orc's jokes. Perhaps all four were just hoops and he would be stuck on this barren world until he starved to death.

The next hoop, in the northeast corner also proved to be just that, a hoop.

Kickaha was beginning to get tired and hungry. He now had to swim over the river, through a very strong current, to get to the other two hoops. The walk from one to the other was two miles, and if he had to test all four, he would walk eight miles. Ordinarily, he would not have minded that at all, but he had been through much in the past few hours.

He sat down for a minute and then he jumped up, exclaiming and cursing himself for a fool. He had forgotten that gates might work when entered in one direction but not work in the other. Picking up a stone, he went around to the other side of the big hoop and cast the stone through it. The hoop was still just a hoop.

There was nothing to do then but to walk back to the first hoop and to test that from the other side. It, too, gave evidence that it was no gate.

He swam the river and got to the other side after having been carried downstream for a half-mile, thus adding to his journey. The beamer made the swimming and the walking more difficult, since it weighed about thirty pounds. But he did not want to leave it behind.

The southwest hoop was only a huge round of metal. He went toward the last one while the sun continued westward and downward. It shone in a silent sky over a silent earth. Even the wind had died down, and the only sound was the rushing of the river, which died as he walked away from it, and his own feet on the rocks and his breathing.

When he got to the northwest hoop, he felt like putting off his rock-throwing for a while. If this proved to be another jest of Red Orc, it might also prove to be the last jest that Kickaha would ever know. So he might as well get this over with.

The first stone went through and struck the rock beyond.

The second went through the other side and fell on the ground beyond.

He jumped up and down and yelled his frustration and hit the palm of one hand with the fist of the other. He kicked at a small boulder and then went howling and hopping away with pain. He pulled his hair and slapped the side of his head and then turned his face toward the blind blue sky and the deaf bright-yellow sun and howled like a wolf whose tail was caught in a bear trap.

After a while he became silent and still. He might as well have been made of the light-red rock that was so abundant on this earth, except that his eyelids jumped and his chest rose and fell.

When he broke loose from the mold of contemplation, he walked briskly but unemotionally to the river. Here he drank his fill and then he looked for a sheltered place to spend the night. After fifteen minutes, he found a hollow in the side of a small hill of hard rock that would protect him from the wind. He fell asleep after many unavoidable thoughts of the future.

In the morning, he looked at the Beller's body and wondered if he was going to have to eat it.

To give himself something to do, and also because he never entirely gave up hope or quit trying, he waded around in the shallows of the river and ran his hands through the waters. No fish were touched or scared into revealing their presence. It did not seem likely that there would be any, especially when there was an absolute absence of plant life.

He walked to the top of the hill in the base of which he had slept. He sat on the hard round peak for a while, moving only to ease the discomfort of the stone on his buttocks. His situation was desperate and simple. Either Red Orc had prepared a way for his prisoner to escape if he was clever and agile enough or he had not. If he had not, then the prisoner would die here. If he had, then the prisoner—in this case, Kickaha—was just not bright enough. In which case, the prisoner was going to die soon.

He sat for a long while and then he groaned. What was the matter with his brain? Sure, the stone had gone through the gates, but no flesh had passed through them. He should have tried them himself instead of trickily testing them only with the stones. The gates could be set up to trigger only if matter above a certain mass passed through them, or sometimes only if protein passed through them. Or even only if human brainwaves came close enough to set them off. But he had been so concerned with traps on the other side that he had forgotten about this possibility.

However, any activated gate might be adjusted to destroy the first large mass that entered, just as the gate from the room with the mercury pool had been booby-trapped.

He groaned at the thought of the strain and sweat involved, but he had not survived thus far by being lazy. He lifted the body of the Beller onto his shoulders, thanking his fortunes that the man was small, and set off toward the nearest gate.

It was a long, hot, and muscle-trembling day. The lack of food weakened him, and every failure at each gate took more out of him. The swim across the river with the deadweight of the corpse and the beamer drained him of even more. But he cast the body six times through the three gates, once through each side.

And now he was resting beside the fourth. The Beller lay near him, its arms spread out, its face upturned to the hot sun, its eyes open, its mouth open, and a faint odor of corruption rising like invisible flies from it. At least, there were no real flies in this world.

Time passed. He did not feel much stronger. He had to get up and throw the body through both sides. Just rolling it through was out of the question because he did not want to stand in the path of any explosion. It was necessary to stand by the edge of the hoop, lift the body up and throw it through and then leap to one side.

For the seventh time, he did so. The body went through the hoop and sprawled on the ground. He had one last chance, and this time, instead of resting, he picked up the corpse and lifted it up before him until it was chest-high and heaved.

When he raised his head from his position on the rock, he saw that the body was still visible.

So much for that theory. And so much for him. He was done for.

He sat up instead of just lying there with his eyes closed. This move, made for no motive of which he was aware, saved his life.

Even so, he almost lost it. The tigerish beast that was charging silently over the hard rock roared when it saw him sit up and increased the length of its bounds and its speed. Kickaha was so surprised that he froze for a second and thus gave the animal an edge. But he did not give enough. The beamer fired just as the animal rose for its final arc, and the ray bored through its head, sliced it, cut through the neck and chest, took off part of a leg, and drilled into the rock beyond. The body struck the ground and slid into him and knocked him off his feet and rolled him over and over. He hurt in his legs and his back and chest and hands and nose when he arose. Much skin had been burned off by his scraping against the rock, and where the body of the beast had slammed into his legs was a dull pain that was to get sharper.

Nevertheless, the animal looked edible. And he thought he knew where it had come from. After he had cut off several steaks and cooked and eaten them, he would return to the northwest gate and investigate again.

The beast was about a quarter larger than a Siberian tiger, had a catlike build, thick long fur with a tawny undercoat, and pale red zigzag stripes on head and body, and black stocking-like fur on the lower part of the legs and the paws. Its eyes were lemonade-yellow, and its teeth were more those of a shark than a cat.

The steaks tasted rank, but they filled him with strength. He took the Beller by the arm and dragged him the two miles to the gate. The corpse, by this time, was in a badly damaged condition. It stank even stronger when he lifted it up and threw it through the gate.

This time, it disappeared, and it was followed by a spurt of oil from the gate that would have covered him if he had been standing directly before it within a range of ten yards. Immediately after, the oily substance caught fire and burned for fifteen minutes.

Kickaha waited until long after the fire was out and then he jumped through with his beamer ready. He did not know what to expect. There might be another of the tigers waiting for him. It was evident that the first time he had thrown the Beller through it, he had set off a delaying activation that had released the beast through it sometime after he had given up on it. It was a very clever and sadistic device and just the sort of thing he could expect from Red Orc. It seemed to him, however, that Red Orc might have given up setting any more machines. He would believe that it was very unlikely that anybody could have gotten this far.

For a second, he was in a small bare room with a large cage, its door open, and a black dome on three short legs. Then he was in another room. This one was larger and was made of some hard gray metal or plastic and lacked any decoration and had no furniture except a seatless commode, a washbowl and a single faucet, and a small metal table fastened to the floor with chains.

The transition from one room to the other shocked him, although he could explain how it happened. On jumping through the hoop into this room, he had triggered a delayed gate. This, activated, had sent him into this seemingly blind-alley chamber.

The light had no visible source; it filled the room with equal intensity. It was bright enough so that he could see that there were no cracks or flaws in the walls. There was nothing to indicate a window or door. And the walls were made of sturdy stuff. The ray from the beamer, turned to full power, only warmed the wall and the air in the chamber. He turned the weapon off and looked for the source of air, if there was one.

After an extensive inspection, he determined that fresh air moved in slowly from a point just above the table top. This meant that it was being gated in through a device embedded inside the solid table top. And the air moved out through another gate that had to be embedded in the wall in an upper corner of wall and ceiling. The gates would be operating intermittently and were set for admission only of gases.

He turned the full power of the beamer on the table top, but that was as resistant as the walls. However, unless his captor intended him to starve, he would have provided a gate through which to transmit food to his captive. It probably would be the same gate as that in the table top, but when the time came for the meal, the gate would be automatically set for passage of solid material.

Kickaha considered this for a while and wondered why no one had thought of this idea for escape. Perhaps the Lord had thought of it and was hoping that his prisoner also would. It would be just the kind of joke a Lord would enjoy. Still, it was such a wild idea, it might not have occurred to the Lord.

He imagined that alarms must be flashing and sounding somewhere in the building that housed this chamber. That is, if the chamber was in a building and not in some deserted pocket universe. If, however, the Lord should be away, then he might return too late to keep his prisoner imprisoned.

He had no exact idea of how much time passed, but he estimated that it was about four hours later when the tray appeared on the table. It held Earth food, a steak medium well-done, three pieces of brown European bread with genuine butter, and a dish of chocolate ice cream.

He felt much better when he finished, indeed almost grateful to his captor. He did not waste any time after swallowing the last spoonful of ice cream, however. He climbed onto the top of the table, the beamer held on his shoulder with the strap, and the tray in his hands. He then bent over and, balancing on one leg, set the tray down and then stepped onto it. He reasoned that the gate might be activated by the tray and dishes and not by a certain mass. He was betting his life that the influence of the gate would extend upward enough to include him in it. If it did not, somebody on the other end was going to be surprised by half a corpse. If it did, somebody was still going to be surprised and even more unpleasantly.

Suddenly, he was on a table inside a closet lit by one overhead light. If he had not been crouching, he would have been deprived of his head by the ceiling as he materialized.

He got down off the table and swung the door open and stepped out into a very large kitchen. A man was standing with his back to him, but he must have heard the door moving because he wheeled around. His mouth was open, his eyes were wide, and he said, "What the . . . ?"

Kickaha's foot caught him on the point of the chin, and he fell backward, unconscious, onto the floor. After listening to make sure that the noise of the man's fall had not disturbed anyone, Kickaha searched the man's clothes.

He came up with a sawed-off Smith & Wesson .38 in a shoulder holster and a wallet with a hundred and ten dollars in bills, two driver's licenses, the omnipresent credit cards, and a business card. The man's name was Robert di Angelo.

Kickaha put the gun in his belt after checking it and then inspected the kitchen. It was so large that it had to be in a mansion of a wealthy man. He quickly found a small control board behind a sliding panel in the wall that was half open. Several lights were blinking on it.

The fact that di Angelo had sent down a meal to him showed that the dwellers of this house knew they had a prisoner. Or at least, that the Lord knew it. His men might not be cognizant of gates, but they would have been told to report to Red Orc if the lights on this panel and others flashed out and, undoubtedly, sound alarms were activated. The latter would have been turned off by now, of course.

There must be a visual monitor of the prison, so the Lord, Urthona, in this case, must know whom he held. Why hadn't Urthona at once taken steps to question his captive? He must surely be burning to know how Kickaha had gotten in there.

He ran water into a glass and dashed it in the face of the man on the floor. Di Angelo started and rolled his head, and his eyes opened. He jerked again when he saw Kickaha over him and felt the point of the knife at his throat.

"Where is your boss?" Kickaha said.

Di Angelo said, "I don't know."

"Ignorance isn't bliss in your case," Kickaha said. He pushed the knife in so that blood trickled out from the side of the neck.

The man's eyes widened, and he said, "Take it easy," and then, "What difference does it make? You haven't got a chance. Here's what happened . . ."

Di Angelo was the cook, but he was also aware of what was going on in the lower echelons. He had been told long ago to inform the boss, whom he called Mr. Callister, if the alarms were activated in the kitchen. Until tonight, they had been dormant. When they did go off, startling him, he had called Mr. Callister, who was with his gang on business di Angelo knew nothing about. It must have something to do with the recent troubles, those that had come with the appearance of Kickaha and the others. Callister had told him what to do, which was only to prepare a meal, set it on the table in the closet, close the closet door, and press a button on the control panel.

Kickaha asked about Wolff, Chryseis, and Anana. Di Angelo said, "Some of the guys took them into the boss's office and left them there and that's the last anybody's seen of them. Honest to God, I'm telling the truth! If anybody knows where they went, it's Callister. Him and him only!"

Kickaha made di Angelo get up and lead him through the house. They went through some halls and large rooms, all luxuriously furnished, and then up a broad winding marble staircase to the second floor. On the way, di Angelo told him that this house was in a walled estate in Beverly Hills. The address was that which Red Orc had said was Urthona's.

"Where are the servants?" he said.

"They've either gone home or to their quarters over the garage," di Angelo said. "I'm not lying, mister, when I say I'm the only one in the house."

The door to Callister's office was of heavy steel and locked. Kickaha turned the beamer on it and sliced out the lock with a brief quick rotation of the barrel. Di Angelo's eyes bulged, and he turned paler. Evidently he knew nothing of the weapons of the Lord.

Kickaha found some tape in a huge mahogany desk and taped di Angelo's hands behind him and his ankles together. While di Angelo sat in a chair, Kickaha made a quick but efficient search of the office. The control panel for what he hoped were the gates popped out of a section of the big desk when a button in a corner of the desk was pressed. The pushbuttons, dials, and lights were identified by markings that would have mystified any Earthling but Kickaha. These were in the writing of the Lords.

However, he did not know the nature of Gates Number One through Ten, nor what would happen if he pressed a button marked with the symbol for *M*. That could mean many thousands of things, but he suspected that it stood for *miyrtso,* meaning death.

The first difficulty in using the panel was that he did not know where the gates were even if he activated them. The second was that he probably could not activate them. The Lord was not foolish enough to leave an operable system that was also relatively accessible. He would carry on his person some device that had to be turned on before the control panel would be energized. But at least Kickaha knew where the panel was so that if he ever got hold of the activator, he could use the panel. That is, if he also located the gates.

It was very frustrating because he was so sure that Anana and his two friends, if they were still alive, were behind one of the ten gates.

The telephone rang. Kickaha was startled but quickly recovered. He picked up the phone and carried it over to di Angelo and put the receiver at a distance between both their ears. Di Angelo did not need to be told what was expected of him. He said, "Hello!"

The voice that answered was Ramos'.

"Di Angelo? Just a minute."

The next voice was that of the man Kickaha had talked to when he thought he was speaking to Red Orc. This must be Urthona, and whatever it was that had brought him out in the open had to be something very important. The only thing that would do that would be a chance to get Red Orc.

"Angelo? I'm getting an alarm transmission here. It's coming from my office. Did you know that?"

Kickaha shook his head and di Angelo said, "No, sir."

"Well, someone is in my office. Where are you?"

"In the kitchen, sir," di Angelo said.

"Get up there and find out what's going on," Urthona said. "I'll leave this line open. And I'm sending over men from the warehouse to help you. Don't take any chances. Shoot to kill unless you're dead certain you can get the drop on him. You understand?"

"Yes sir," di Angelo said.

The phone clicked. Kickaha did not feel triumphant. Urthona must realize that anyone in the office could have picked up the phone to listen in. He knew this cut down any chance of di Angelo's surprising the intruder and meant that the reinforcements would have to be rushed over as swiftly as possible.

Kickaha taped di Angelo's mouth and locked him in the closet. He then destroyed the control panel for the gates with a flash from the beamer. If Urthona meant to transfer his other prisoners—if he had any—or to do anything to them, he would be stopped for a while. He would have to build another panel—unless he had some duplicates in storage.

His next step was to get out of the house quickly and down to the railroad station, where the Horn was in a locker. He wished that he could have gotten the Horn first, because then he might have been able to use it unhindered. Now, Urthona would be certain to guard his house well.

Kickaha had to leave the house and go downtown. He decided to cache the beamer on the estate grounds. He found a depression in the ground behind a large oleander bush near the wall. The estate was excellently gardened; there were no loose leaves or twigs with which to cover the weapon. He placed it in the depression and left it there. He also decided to leave the gun that he had taken from di Angelo. It was too bulky to conceal under his shirt.

He left without incident except having to return to the beamer's hiding place so he could use it to burn through the lock on the iron gate that was the exit to the street. This was set in a high brick wall with spikes on top. The guardhouse by the big iron gate to the driveway was unoccupied, apparently because Urthona had pulled everybody except di Angelo from the house. There were controls in the guardhouse, and he easily identified those that worked both gates. But the power or the mechanisms had been shut off, and he did not want to take the time to return to the house to question di Angelo. He burned through the lock mechanism and pushed the gate open. Behind him, a siren began whooping and he could see lights flashing on the control board in the guardhouse. If the noise continued, the police would be called in. Kickaha smiled at that thought. Then he lost his smile. He did not want the police interfering any more than Urthona did.

After hiding the beamer behind the bush again, he walked southward. After five blocks, he came to Sunset. He was apprehensive that a police car might notice him, because he understood that any pedestrians in this exclusive and extremely wealthy neighborhood were likely to be stopped by the police. Especially at night.

But his luck held out, and he was able to hail a taxi. The driver did not want to go that far out of Beverly Hills, but Kickaha opened the back door and got in the car. "This is an emergency," he said. "I got a business appointment that involves a lot of money."

He leaned forward and handed the driver a twenty-dollar bill from di Angelo's wallet. "This is yours, over and above the fare and the regular tip. Think you can detour a little?"

"Can do," the cabbie said.

He let Kickaha off three blocks from the railroad station, since Kickaha did not want him to know where he was going if the police should question him. He walked to the station, removed the ball of gum and the key from the hollow in the tree, and then went inside the station.

He removed the instrument case from the locker without interference or attention, other than from a four-year-old girl who stared at him with large deep-blue eyes and then said, "Hello!" He patted her on the head as he went by, causing her mother to pull her away and lecture her in a loud voice about being friendly to strangers.

Kickaha grinned, though he did not really think the incident amusing. During his long years on the World of Tiers, he had become used to children being treated as greatly valued and much-loved beings. Since Wolff had put into the waters of that great world a chemical that gave the humans a thousand-year youth but also cut down considerably on the birth rate, he had ensured that children were valued. There were very few cases of child killings, abuses, or deprivation of love. And while this sort of rearing did not keep the children from growing into adults who were quite savage in warfare—but never killed or maltreated children—it did result in people with many fewer neuroses and psychoses than the civilized Earthlings. Of course, most societies in Wolff's world were rather homogeneous, small, and technologically primitive, not subject to the many-leveled crisscross current modes of life in Earth's highly industrial societies.

Kickaha left the station and walked several blocks before coming to a public phone booth in the corner of a large service-station area. He dialed Urthona's number. The phone had rung only once when it was picked up and an unfamiliar voice answered. Kickaha said, "Mr. Callister, please."

"Who is this?" the rough voice said.

"Di Angelo can describe me," Kickaha said. "That is, if you've found him in the closet."

There was an exclamation and then, "Just a minute."

A few seconds later, a voice said, "Callister speaking."

"Otherwise known as Urthona, present Lord of Earth," Kickaha said. "I am the man who was your prisoner."

"How did you . . . ?" Urthona said and then stopped, realizing that he was not going to get a description of the escape.

"I'm Kickaha," Kickaha said. There was no harm in identifying himself, since he was sure that Urthona had gotten both his name and description from Anana. "The Earthling who did what you supposed Lords of Creation could not do. I killed directly, or caused to be killed, all fifty-one of the Bellers. They are no longer a menace. I got out of Red Orc's house in that other Earth, got through all his traps and got into your house. If you had been there, I would have captured or killed you. Make no mistake about that.

"But I didn't call you just to tell you what I have done. I want only to return in peace to Wolff's world with Wolff, Chryseis, and Anana. You and Red Orc can battle it out here and may the best Lord win. Now that the Beller is dead, there is no reason for us to stay here. Nor for you to keep my friends."

There was a long silence and then Urthona said, "How do I know that the Beller is dead?"

Kickaha described what had happened, although he left out several details that he did not think Urthona should know.

"So you now know how you can check out my story," he said. "You can't follow my original route as I did, since you don't know where Red Orc's house is, and I don't either. But I think that all the gates are two-way, and you can backtrack, starting from that room in which I ended."

He could imagine the alternating delight and alarm Urthona was feeling. He now had a route to get into Red Orc's dwelling, but Red Orc could get into his house through that same route, too.

Urthona said, "You're wrong, I know where Red Orc lives. Did live, that is. One of my men saw him on the street only two hours ago. He thought at first it was me and that I was on some business he'd better keep his nose out of. Then he returned here and saw me and knew I couldn't have gotten here so quickly.

"I realized what good fortune had done for me. I got my men and surrounded the house and we broke in. We had to kill four of his men, but he got away. Gated out, I suppose. And when he did, he eliminated all the gates in the house. There was no way of following him."

"I had thought that one of the burned corpses might be Red Orc's," Kickaha said. "But he is still alive. Well . . ."

"I'm tired of playing this game," Urthona said. "I would like to see my brother become one of those charred corpses. I will make a bargain with you again. If you will get Red Orc for me, deliver him to me in a recognizable condition, I will release your friends and guarantee safe passage to your World of Tiers. That is, if I can satisfy myself that your story about the Beller is true."

"You know how to do that," Kickaha said. "Let me speak to Anana and Wolff, so that I can be sure they're still alive."

"I can't do that just at this moment," Urthona said. "Give me, say, ten minutes. Call back then."

"Okay," Kickaha said. He hung up and left the phone booth in a hurry. Urthona might and might not have some means of quickly locating the source of the call, but he did not intend to give him a chance. He hailed a taxi and had it drop him off near the La Brea Tar Pit. From there, he walked up Wilshire until he came to another booth. Fifteen, not ten, minutes had passed. Di Angelo answered the phone this time. Although he must have recognized Kickaha's voice, he said nothing except for him to wait while he switched the call. Urthona's voice was the next.

"You can speak to my niece, the *leblabbiy*-lover, first," Urthona said.

Anana's lovely voice said, "Kickaha! Are you all right?"

"Doing fine so far!" Kickaha said. "The Beller is dead! I killed him myself. And Red Orc is on the run. Hang on. We'll get back to the good world yet. I love you!"

"I love you, too," she said.

Urthona's voice, savage and sarcastic cut in. "Yes, I love you too, *leblabbiy!* Now, do you want to hear from Wolff?"

"I'm not about to take your word that he's OK," Kickaha said.

Wolff's voice, deep and melodious, came over the phone. "Kickaha, old friend! I knew you'd be along, sooner or later!"

"Hello, Robert, it's great to hear your voice again! You and Chryseis all right?"

"We're unharmed, yes. What kind of deal are you making with Urthona?"

The Lord said, "That's enough. You satisfied, Earthling?"

"I'm satisfied that they're alive as of this moment," Kickaha said. "And they had better be when the moment of payment comes."

"You don't threaten me!" Urthona said. And then, in a calmer tone, "Very well. I shall assist you in any way I can. What do you need?"

"The address of Red Orc's house," Kickaha said.

"Why would you need that?" Urthona said, surprised.

"I have my reasons. What is the address?"

Urthona gave it to him but he spoke slowly as if he were trying to think of Kickaha's reasons for wanting it. Kickaha said, "That's all I need now. So long."

He hung up. A minute later, he was in a taxi on his way to Urthona's house. Two blocks away, he paid the driver and walked the rest of the way. The small iron gate was chained now, and the lights in the little guardhouse near the big gate showed three men inside. The mansion was also ablaze with lights, although he could see nobody through the windows.

There did not seem to be any way of getting in just then. He was capable of leaping up and grabbing the top of the wall and pulling himself over, but he did not doubt that there would be alarms on top of the wall. On second thought, so what? At this time, he did not intend to invade the house. All he wanted was to get the beamer and then get out. By the time Urthona's men arrived, he could be back over the wall.

It was first necessary to cache the Horn somewhere, because it would be too awkward, in fact, impossible, to take it with him in scaling the wall. He could throw it over the wall first but did not want to do that. A minute's inspection showed him that he could stick the case in the branches of a bush growing on the strip of grass between the sidewalk and the street. He returned to the spot by the wall opposite where he had hidden the beamer. He went across the street, stood there a minute waiting until a car went by, and then dashed full speed across the street. He bounded upward and his fingers closed on the rough edge of the wall. It was easy for him to pull himself upward then. The top of the wall was about a foot and a half across and set with a double row of spikes made of iron and about six inches high. Along these was strung a double row of thin wires that glinted in the light from the mansion.

He stepped gingerly over the wires and turned and let himself down over the edge and then dropped to the soft earth. For a few seconds, he looked at the guardhouse and the mansion and listened. He heard nothing and saw no signs of life.

He ran into the bush and picked up the beamer. Getting back over the wall was a little more difficult with the beamer strapped over his shoulder, but he made it without, as far as he knew, attracting any attention from inside the walls.

With the beamer and the Horn, he walked down toward Sunset again. He waited on the corner for about ten minutes before an empty cab came by. When he entered the taxi, he held the case with the beamer against it so that the driver would not see it. Its barrel was too thick to be mistaken for even a shotgun, but the stock made it look too much like a firearm of some sort.

Red Orc's address was in a wealthy district of Pacific Palisades. The house was, like Urthona's, surrounded by a high brick wall. However, the iron gate to the driveway was open. Kickaha slipped through it and toward the house, which was dark. Urthona had not mentioned whether or not he had left guards there, but it seemed reasonable that he would. He would not want to miss a chance to catch Red Orc if he should return for some reason.

The front and rear main entrances were locked. No light shone anywhere. He crouched by each door, his ear against the wood. He could hear nothing. Finally, he bored a hole through the lock of the rear door and pushed it open. His entry was cautious and slow at first and then he heard some noises from the front. These turned out to have been made by three men sitting in the dark in the huge room at the front of the house. One had fallen asleep and was snoring softly, and the other two were talking in low voices.

He sneaked up the winding staircase, which had marble steps and so did not squeak or groan under his feet. Finding a bedroom, he closed the door and then turned on a lamp. He dialed one of the numbers of the house.

When the phone was answered, Kickaha, an excellent mimic, spoke in an approximation of Ramos' voice.

"The boss is calling you guys in," he said. "Get out of here on the double! Something's up, but I can't tell you over the phone!"

He waited until the man had hung up before he himself hung up. Then he went to the window. He saw the three walk down the driveway and go through the gate. A moment later, the headlights of a car came on a half block down. The car pulled away, and he was, as far as he knew, alone in the house. He would not be for more than thirty-five minutes, at least, which was the time it would take to get to Urthona's, find out they had been tricked, and return with reinforcements.

All he needed was a few minutes. He went downstairs and turned on the lights in the kitchen. Finding a flashlight, he turned the kitchen lights off and went into the big front room. The door under the stairs was open. He stepped through it into the little hall. At its end, he opened the door and cast the flashlight beam inside. The room looked just like the one he had entered when he was Red Orc's prisoner, but it was not. This room really was set inside this house. The gate embedded in the wood and plaster of the doorway had been inactivated.

He opened the instrument case and took the Horn out. In the beams of the flashlight, it glistened silvery. It was shaped like the horn of an African buffalo except at the mouth, where it flared broadly. The tip was fitted with a mouthpiece of soft golden material, and on top along the axis were seven small buttons in a row. Inside the flared mouth was a silvery web of some material. Halfway along the length of the Horn was an inscribed hieroglyph, the mark of Shambarimen, maker of the Horn.

He raised the Horn to his lips and blew softly through it while he pressed the little buttons. The flare on the other end was pointed at the walls, and, as he finished one sequence of notes, he moved it to his left until it pointed at a place on the wall about twelve feet from the first. He hoped that the inactive gates were in this room. If they were, they had set up a resonant point that had weakened the walls between the universes. And so the frequencies from the Horn would act as a skeleton key and open the gates. This was the unique ability of the Horn, the unreproduced device of Shambarimen, greatest of the scientist-inventors of the Lords.

Softly the Horn spoke, and the notes that issued from the mouth seemed golden and magical enough to open doors to fairyland. But none appeared on the north or east walls. Kickaha stopped blowing and listened for sounds of people approaching the house. He heard nothing. He put the mouthpiece to his lips again and once more played the sequence of notes that was guaranteed to spread wide any break in the walls between the worlds.

Suddenly, a spot on the wall became luminous. The white spot enlarged, inched outward, and then sprang to the limits of the circle that defined the entrance. The light faded and was replaced by a softer darker light. He looked into it and saw a hemispherical room with no windows or doors. The walls were scarlet, and the only furniture was a bed that floated a few feet above the floor in the center of the room and a transparent booth, also floating, that contained a washbowl, faucet, and toilet.

Then the walls regrew swiftly, the edges of the hole sliding out toward each other, and in thirty seconds, the wall was as solid as before.

The Horn swung away, and the white spot appeared again and grew, and then the light died to be replaced by the greenish light of a green sun over a green moss-tinted plain and sharp green mountains on a horizon twice as distant as Earth's. To the right were some animals that looked like gazelles with harp-shaped horns. They were nibbling on the moss.

The third opening revealed a hallway with a closed door at its end. There was nothing else for Kickaha to do but to investigate, since the door might lead to Anana or the others. He jumped through the now swiftly decreasing hole and walked down the hall and then cautiously opened the door. Nothing happened. He looked around the edge of the door into a large chamber. Its floor was stone mosaic, a small pool flush with the floor was in the center, and furniture of airy construction was around it. The light was sourceless.

Anana, unaware that anybody had entered, was sitting on a chair and reading from a big book with thick covers that looked like veined marble. She looked sleek and well fed.

Kickaha watched her for a minute, though he had to restrain himself from running in and grabbing her. He had lived too long in worlds where traps were baited.

His inspection did not reveal anything suspicious, but this meant only that dangers could be well hidden. Finally, he called softly, "Anana!"

She jumped, the book fell out of her hands, and then she was out of the chair and rushing toward him. Tears glimmered in her eyes and on her cheeks though she was smiling. Her arms were held out to him, and she was sobbing with relief and joy.

His desire to run toward her was almost overwhelming. He felt tears in his own eyes and a sob welling up. But he could not get rid of his suspiciousness that Red Orc might have set this room to kill a person who entered without first activating some concealed device. He had been lucky to get this far without tripping off some machine.

"Kickaha!" Anana cried and came through the door and fell into his embrace.

He looked over her shoulder to make sure that the door was swinging shut and then bent his head to kiss her.

The pain on his lips and nose was like that from burning gasoline. The pain on the palm of his hand, where he had pressed it against her back, was like that from sulphuric acid.

He screamed and threw himself away and rolled on the floor in his agony. Yet, half-conscious though he was from the searing, he knew that his tortured hand had grabbed the beamer from the floor, where he had dropped it.

Anana came after him but not swiftly. Her face had melted as if it were wax in the sun; her eyes ran; her mouth drooped and furrowed and made runnels and ridges. Her hands were spread out to seize him, but they were dripping with acid and losing form. The fingers had elongated, so much so that one had stretched down, like taffy, to her knee. And her beautiful legs were bulging everywhere, giving way to something like gas pressing the skin outward. The feet were splaying out and leaving impresses of something that burned the stone of the floor and gave off faint green wisps of smoke.

The horror of this helped him overcome the pain. Without hesitation, he lifted the beamer and pressed the button that turned its power full on her. Rather, on *it*.

She fell into two and then into four parts as the beam crisscrossed. The parts writhed on the floor, silently. Blood squirted out from the trunks and from the legs and turned into a brownish substance that scorched the stone. An odor as of rotten eggs and burning dog excrement filled the room.

Kickaha stepped down the power from piercing to burning. He played the beam like a hose, squirting flaming kerosene over the parts, and they went up in smoke. The hair of Anana burned with all the characteristic odor of burning human hair, but that was the only part of her—of it—that gave off a stench of human flesh in the fire. The rest was brimstone and dog droppings.

In the end, after the fire burned out, there were only some gristly threads left. Of bones there was no sign.

Kickaha did not wish to enter the room from which it had come, but the pain in his lips and nose and hand was too intense. Besides, he thought that the Lord should have been satisfied with the fatality of the thing he had created to look like Anana. There was cool-looking water in that room, and he had to have it. It was possible to blow the Horn and go back into Orc's office, but he didn't think he could endure the agony long enough to blow the sequence of notes. Moreover, if he encountered anyone in that office, he wanted to be able to defend himself adequately. In his present condition, he could not.

At the pool, he stuck his face and one hand under the water. The coolness seemed to help at once, although when he at last removed his face and breathed, the pain was still intense. With the good hand, he splashed water on his face. After a long while, he rose from the pool. He was unsteady and felt as if he were going to vomit. He also felt a little disengaged from everything. The shock had nudged him one over from reality.

When he raised the Horn gently to his lips, he found that they were swelling. His hand was also swelling. They were getting so big and stiff they were making him clumsy. It was only at the cost of more agony that he could blow upon the Horn and press the little valves, and the wall opened before him. He quickly put the Horn in its case, and shoved it through the opening with his foot, then leaped through with the beamer ready. The office was empty.

He found the bathroom. The medicine cabinet above the washbowl was a broad and deep one with many bottles. A number were of plastic, marked with hieroglyphs. He opened one, smelled the contents, tried to grin with his blistered swollen lips and squeezed out a greenish salve onto his hand. This he rubbed over his nose and lips and on the palm of his burned hand. Immediately, the pain began to dissolve in a soft coolness and the swelling subsided as he watched himself in the mirror.

He squeezed a few drops from another bottle onto his tongue, and a minute later the shakiness and the sense of unreality left him. He recapped the two bottles and put them in the rear pockets of his pants.

The business of the gates and the Anana-thing had taken more time than he could spare. He ran out of the bathroom and directed the Horn at the next spot on the wall. This failed to respond, so he tried the next one. This one opened, but neither this nor the one after it contained those for whom he was looking.

The bedroom yielded a gate at the first place he directed the Horn. The wall parted like an opening mouth, a shark's mouth, because the hillside beyond was set with rows of tall white sharp triangles. The vegetation between the shark's teeth was a purplish vine-complex and the sky beyond was mauve.

The second gate opened to another hallway with a door at its end. Again, he had no choice but to investigate. He pushed the door open silently and peered around it. The room looked exactly like the one in which he had found the thing he had thought was Anana. This time, she was not reading a book, although she was in the chair. She was leaning far forward, her elbows on her thighs and her chin cupped by her hands. Her stare was unmoving and gloomy.

He called to her softly, and she jumped, just like the first Anana. Then she leaped up and ran toward him, tears in her eyes and on her cheeks and her mouth open in a beautiful smile and her arms held toward him. He backed away as she came through the door and harshly told her to stop. He held the beamer on her. She obeyed but looked puzzled and hurt. Then she saw the still slightly swelled and burned lips and nose, and her eyes widened.

"Anana," he said, "what was that ten-thousand-year-old nursery rhyme your mother sang to you so often?"

If this was some facsimile or artificial creature of Red Orc's, it might have a recording of what Orc had learned from Anana. It might have a memory of a sort, something that would be sketchy but still adequate enough to fool her lover. But there would be things she had not told Red Orc while under the influence of the drug, because he would not think to ask her. And the nursery song was one thing. She had told Kickaha of it when they had been hiding from the Bellers on the Great Plain of the World of Tiers.

Anana was more puzzled for a few seconds, and then she seemed to understand that he felt compelled to test her. She smiled and sang the beautiful little song that her mother had taught her in the days before she grew up and found out how ugly and vicious the adult family life of the Lords was.

Even after this, he felt restrained when he kissed her. Then, as it became apparent that she had to be genuine flesh and blood, and she murmured a few more things that Red Orc was highly unlikely to know, he smiled and melted. They both cried some more, but he stopped first.

"We'll weep a little later," he said. "Do you have any idea where Wolff and Chryseis could be?"

She said no, which was what he had expected.

"Then we'll use the Horn until we've opened every gate in the house. But it's a big house, so . . ."

He explained to her that Urthona and his men would be coming after them. "You look around for weapons, while I blow the Horn."

She joined him ten minutes later and showed him what looked like a pen but was a small beamer. He told her that he had found two more gates but both were disappointments. They passed swiftly through all the rooms in the second story while he played steadily upon the Horn. The walls remained blank.

The first floor of the house was as unrewarding. By then, forty minutes had passed since the men had left the house. Within a few more minutes, Urthona should be here.

"Let's try the room under the stairs again," he said. "It's possible that reactivating the gate might cause it to open on to still another world."

A gate could be set up so that it alternated its resonances slightly and acted as a flip-flop entrance. At one activation, it would open to one universe and at the next activation, to another. Some gates could operate as avenues to a dozen or more worlds.

The gates activated upstairs could also be such gates, and they should return to test out the multiple activity of every one. It was too discouraging to think about at that moment, though they would have to run through them again. That is, they would if this gate under the stairs did not give them a pleasant surprise.

Outside the door, he lifted the Horn once more and played the music that trembled the fabric between universes. The room beyond the door suddenly was large and blue-walled, with bright light streaming from chandeliers carved out of single Brobdingnagian jewels: hippopotamus-head-sized diamonds, rubies, emeralds, and garnets. The furniture was also carved out of enormous jewels set together with some kind of golden cement.

Kickaha had seen even more luxurious rooms. What held his attention was the opening of the round door at the far end of the room and the entrance through it of a cylindrical object.

This was dark red, and it floated a foot above the floor. At its distant end, the top of a blond head appeared. A man was pushing the object toward them.

That head looked like Red Orc's. He seemed to be the only one who would be in another world and bringing toward this gate an object that undoubtedly meant death and destruction to the occupants of this house.

Kickaha had his beamer ready, but he did not fire it. If that cylinder was packed with some powerful explosive, it might go up at the touch of the energy in a ray from a beamer.

Quickly, but silently, he began to close the door. Anana looked puzzled, since she had not seen what he had. He whispered, "Take off out the front door and run as far as you can as fast as you can!"

She shook her head and said, "Why should I?"

"Here!"

He thrust the Horn and the case at her. "Beat it! Don't argue! If he . . ."

The door began to swing open. A thin curved instrument came around the side of the door. Kickaha fired at it, cutting it in half. There was a yell from the other side, cut off by the door slamming. Kickaha had shoved it hard with his foot.

"Run!" he yelled, and he took her hand and pulled her after him. Just as he went through the door, he looked back. There was a crash as the door under the stairs and part of the wall around it fell broken outward, and the cylinder thrust halfway through before stopping.

That was enough for Kickaha. He jumped out onto the porch and down the steps, pulling Anana behind him with one hand, the other holding the beamer. When they reached the brick wall by the sidewalk, he turned to run along it for its protection.

The expected explosion did not come immediately.

At that moment, a car screeched around the corner a block away. It straightened up, swaying under the streetlights, and shot toward the driveway of the house they had just left. Kickaha saw the silhouettes of six heads inside it; one might have been Urthona's. Then he was running again. They rounded the corner from which the speeding automobile had come, and still nothing happened. Anana cried out, but he continued to drag her on. They ran a complete block and were crossing the street to go around another corner, when a black-and-white patrol car came by. It was cruising slowly and so the occupants had plenty of time to see the two runners. Anybody walking on the streets after dark in this area was suspect. A running person was certain to be taken to the station for questioning. Two running persons carrying a large musical instrument case and something that looked like a peculiar shotgun were guaranteed capture by the police. If they could be caught, of course.

Kickaha cursed and darted toward the house nearest them. Its lights were on, and the front door was open, though the screen door was probably locked. Behind them, brakes squealed as the patrol car slid to a stop. A loud voice told them to halt.

They continued to run. They ran onto the porch and Kickaha pulled on the screen door. He intended to go right through the house and out the back door, figuring that the police were not likely to shoot at them if innocents were in the way.

Kickaha cursed, gave the handle of the screen door a yank that tore the lock out. He plunged through with Anana right behind him. They shot through a vestibule and into a large room with a chandelier and a broad winding staircase to the second story. There were about ten men and women standing or sitting, all dressed semiformally. The women screamed; the men yelled. The two intruders ran through them, unhindered, while the shouts of the policemen rose above the noise of the occupants.

The next moment, all human noise was shattered. The blast smashed in the glass of the windows and shook the house as if a tidal wave had struck it. All were hurled to the floor by the impact.

Kickaha had been expecting this, and Anana had expected something enormously powerful by his behavior. They jumped up before anybody else could regain their wits and were going out the back door in a few seconds. Kickaha doubled back, running along the side of the house toward the front. There was much broken glass on the walk, flicked there by the explosion from some nearby house. A few bushes and some lawn furniture also lay twisted on the sidewalk.

The patrol car, its motor running, and lights on, was still by the curb. Anana threw the instrument case into the rear seat and got in and Kickaha laid the beamer on the floor and climbed in. They strapped themselves in, and he turned the car around and took off. In the course of the next four blocks, he found the button switches to set the siren off and the light whirling and flashing.

"We'll get to Urthona's house, near it, anyway," he yelled, "and then we'll abandon this. I think Red Orc'll be there now to find out if Urthona was among those who entered the house when that mine went off!"

Anana shook her head and pointed at her ears. She was still deaf.

It was no wonder. He could just faintly hear the siren, which must be screaming.

A few minutes later, as they shot through a red light, they passed a patrol car, lights flashing, going the other way. Anana ducked down so that she would not be seen, but evidently the car had received notice by radio that this car was stolen. It screamed as it slowed down and turned on the broad intersection and started after Kickaha and Anana. A sports car that had sped through the intersections, as if its driver intended to ignore the flashing red lights and sirens, turned away to avoid a collision, did not quite make it, scraped against the rear of the police car, and caromed off over the curb and up onto the sidewalk.

Kickaha saw this in the mirror as he accelerated. A few minutes later, he went through a stop sign south of a very broad intersection with stop signs on all corners. A big Cadillac stopped in the middle of the intersection so suddenly that its driver went up over the wheel. Before he could sit back and continue, the patrol car came through the stop sign.

Kickaha said, "Can you hear me now?"

She said, "Yes. You don't have to shout quite so loudly!"

"We're in Beverly Hills now. We'll take this car as far as we can and then we'll abandon it, on the run," he said. "We'll have to lose them on foot. That is, if we make it."

A second patrol car had joined them. It had come out of a side street, ignoring a stop sign, causing another car to wheel away and ram into the curb. Its driver had hoped to cut across in front of them and bar their way, but he had not been quite fast enough. Kickaha had the car up to eighty now, which was far too fast on this street with its many intersecting side streets.

Then the business section of Beverly Hills was ahead. The light changed to yellow just as Kickaha zoomed through. He blasted the horn and went around a sports car and skidded a little, and then the car hit a dip and bounced into the air. He had, however, put on the brakes to slow to sixty. Even so, the car swayed so that he feared they were going over.

Ahead of them, a patrol car was approaching. It swung broadside when over a half block away and barred most of the street. There was very little clearance at either end of the patrol car, but Kickaha took the rear.

Both uniformed policemen were out of the car, one behind the hood with a shotgun and the other standing between the front of the car and the parked cars. Kickaha told Anana to duck and took the car between the narrow space on the other side. There was a crash. One side of the car struck the bumper of the patrol car and the other side struck the side of a parked car. But they were through with a grinding and clashing of metal. The shotgun boomed; the rear window starred.

At the same time, another patrol car swung around the corner on their left. The car angled across the street. Kickaha slammed on the brakes. They screamed, and he was pushed forward against his belt and the wheel. The car fishtailed, rocked, and then it slammed at an obtuse angle into the front of the patrol car.

Both cars were out of commission. Kickaha and Anana were stunned, but they reacted on pure reflex. They were out of the car on either side, Kickaha holding the beamer, and Anana the instrument case. They ran across the street, between two parked cars, and across the sidewalk before they heard the shouts of the policemen behind them. Then they were between two tall buildings on a narrow sidewalk bordered by trees and bushes. They dashed down this until they came to the next street. Here Kickaha led her northward, saw another opening between buildings, and took that. There was an overhang of prestressed concrete about eight feet up over a doorway. He threw his beamer upon it, threw the instrument case up, turned, held his locked hands out, and she put her foot in it and went up as he heaved. She caught the edge of the overhang: he pushed, and she was up on it. He leaped and swung on up, lying down just in time.

Feet pounded; several men, breathing hard, passed under them. He risked a peep over the edge and saw three policemen at the far end of the passageway, outlined by the streetlights. They were talking, obviously puzzled by the disappearance of their quarry. Then one started back, and Kickaha flattened out. The other two went around the corner of the building.

But as the man passed below him, Kickaha, taken by a sudden idea, rose and leaped upon the man. He knocked him sprawling, hitting the man so hard he knocked the wind out of him. He followed this with a kick on the jaw.

Kickaha put the officer's cap on and emptied the .38 that he took from his holster. Anana swung down after him, having dropped the beamer and the Horn to him. She said, "Why did you do this?"

"He would have blocked our retreat. Besides, there's a car that isn't damaged, and we're going to take that."

The fourth policeman was sitting in the car and talking over a microphone. He did not see Kickaha until he was about forty paces away. He dropped the microphone, grabbed for the shotgun on the seat, and jumped out. The beamer, set for stunning power, hit him in the shoulder and knocked him against the car. He slumped down, the shotgun falling on the street.

Kickaha pulled the officer away from the car, noting that blood was seeping through his shirtsleeve. The beamer, even when set on "stun" power, could smash bone, tear skin, and rupture blood vessels.

As soon as Anana was in the car, Kickaha turned it northward. Down the street, coming swiftly toward him, on the wrong side because the other lane was blocked, were two police cars.

At the intersection ahead, as Kickaha shot past the red light, he checked his rearview mirror and saw the police cars had turned and were speeding after him.

Ahead, the traffic was so heavy, he had no chance of getting through it. There was nothing to do but to take the alley to the right or the left, and he took the left. This was by the two-story brick wall of a grocery-store building.

Then he was down the alley. Kickaha applied his brakes so hard, the car swerved, scraping against the brick wall. Anana scrambled out after Kickaha on his side of the car.

The police cars, moving more slowly than Kickaha's had when it took the corner into the alley, turned in. Just as the first straightened out to enter, Kickaha shot at the tires. The front of the lead car dropped as if it had driven off a curb, and there was a squeal of brakes.

The car rocked up and down, and then its front doors opened like the wings of a bird just before taking off.

Kickaha ran away with Anana close behind him. He led her at an angle across the the parking lot of the grocery store, and through the driveway out onto the street.

The light was red now, and the cars were stopped. Kickaha ran up behind a sports car in which sat a small youth with long black hair, huge round spectacles, a hawkish nose, and a bristly black mustache. He was tapping on the instrument panel with his right hand to the raucous cacophonous radio music, which was like Scylla and Charybdis rubbing against each other. He stiffened when Kickaha's arm shot down, as unexpectedly as a lightning stroke from a clear sky, over his shoulder and onto his lap. Before he could do more than squeak and turn his head, the safety belt was unbuckled. Like a sack of flour, he came out of the seat at the end of Kickaha's arm and was hurled onto the sidewalk. The dispossessed driver lay stunned for a moment and then leaped screaming with fury to his feet. By then, Kickaha and Anana were in his car, on their way.

Anana, looking behind, said, "We got away just in time."

"Any police cars after us?" he said.

"No. Not yet."

"Good. We only have a couple of miles to go."

There was no sign of the police from there on until Kickaha parked the car a block and a half from Urthona's.

He said, "I've described the layout of the house, so you won't get confused when we're in it. Once we get in, things may go fast and furious. I think Red Orc will be there. I believe he's gated there just to make sure that Urthona is dead. He may be alive, though, because he's a fox. He should have scented a trap. I know I would've been skittish about going into that house unless I'd sniffed around a lot."

The house was well lit, but there was no sign of occupants. They walked boldly up the front walk and onto the porch. Kickaha tried the door and found it locked. A quick circling of the beamer muzzle, with piercing power turned on, removed the lock mechanism. They entered a silent house and when they were through exploring it, they had found only a parrot in a cage and it broke the silence only once to give a muffled squawk.

Kickaha removed the Horn from the case and began to test for resonant points as he had at Red Orc's. He went from room to room, working out from Urthona's bedroom and office because the gates were most likely to be there. The Horn sent out its melodious notes in vain, however, until he stuck it into a large closet downstairs just off the bottom of the staircase. The wall issued a tiny white spot, like a tear of light, and then it expanded and suddenly became a hole into another world.

Kickaha got a glimpse of a room that was a duplicate of the closet in the house in which he stood. Anana cried out softly then and pulled at his arm. He turned, hearing the noise that had caused her alarm. There were footsteps on the porch, followed by the chiming of the doorbell. He strode across the room, stopped halfway, turned and tossed the Horn to her, and said, "Keep that gate open!" While the notes of the Horn traveled lightly across the room, he lifted the curtain a little. Three uniformed policemen were on the porch and a plainclothesman was just going around the side. On the street were two patrol cars and an unmarked automobile.

Kickaha returned to her and said, "Urthona must have had a man outside watching for us. He called the cops. They must have the place surrounded!"

They could try to fight their way out, surrender, or go through the gate. To do the first was to kill men whose only fault was to mistake Kickaha for a criminal.

If Kickaha surrendered, he would sentence himself and Anana to death. Once either of the Lords knew they were in prison, they would get to their helpless victims one way or the other and murder them.

He did not want to go through the gate without taking some precautions, but he had no choice. He said, "Let's go," and leaped through the contracting hole with his beamer ready. Anana, holding on to the Horn, followed him.

He kicked the door open and jumped back. After a minute of waiting, he stepped through it. The closet was set near the bottom of a staircase, just like its counterpart on Earth. The room was huge, with marble walls on which were bright murals and a many-colored marble mosaic floor. It was night outside; the light inside came from many oil-burning lamps and cressets on the walls and the fluted marble pillars around the edges of the room. Beyond, in the shadows cast by the pillars, were entrances to other rooms and to the outside.

There was no sound except for a hissing and sputtering from the flames at the ends of the cressets.

Kickaha walked across the room between the pillars and through an antechamber, the walls of which were decorated with dolphins and octopuses. It was these that made him expect the scene that met him when he stepped out upon the great pillared porch. He was back on Earth Number Two.

At least, it seemed that he was. Certainly, the full moon near the zenith was Earth's moon. And, looking down from the porch, which was near the edge of a small mountain, he would swear that he was looking down on the duplicate of that part of southern California on which Los Angeles of Earth Number One was built. As nearly as he could tell in the darkness, it had the same topography. The unfamiliarity was caused by the differences in the two cities. This one was smaller than Los Angeles; the lights were not so many nor so bright, and were more widely spaced. He would guess that the population of this valley was about one thirty-second of Earth Number One.

The air looked clear; the stars and the moon were large and bright. There was no hint of the odor of gasoline. He could smell a little horse manure, but that was pleasant, very pleasant.

Of course, he was basing his beliefs on very small evidence, but it seemed that the technology of this Earth had not advanced nearly as swiftly as that of his native planet.

Evidently, Urthona had found gates leading to this world.

He heard voices then from the big room into which he had emerged from the closet. He took Anana's arm and pulled her with him into the shadow of a pillar. Immediately thereafter, three people stepped out onto the porch. Two were men, wearing kilts and sandals and cloth jackets with flared-out collars, puffed sleeves, and swallowtails. One was short, dark and

Mediterranean, like the servants of Red Orc. The other was tall, ruddy-faced and reddish-haired. The woman was a short blonde with a chunky figure. She wore a kilt, buskins and a jacket also, but the jacket, unbuttoned, revealed bare breasts held up by a stiff shelf projecting from a flaming-red corselet. Her hair was piled high in an ornate coiffure, and her face was heavily made up. She shivered, said something in a Semitic-sounding language, and buttoned up the jacket.

If these were servants, they were able to ride in style. A carriage like a cabriolet, drawn by two handsome horses, came around the corner and stopped before the porch. The coachman jumped down and assisted them into the carriage. He wore a tall tricorn hat with a bright red feather, a jacket with huge gold buttons and scarlet piping, a heavy blue kilt, and calf-length boots.

The three got into the carriage and drove off. Kickaha watched the oil-burning lamps on the cabriolet until they were out of sight of the road that wound down the mountain.

This world, Kickaha thought, would be fascinating to investigate. Physically, it had been exactly like the other Earth when it had started. And its peoples, created fifteen thousand years ago, had been exactly like those of the other Earth. Twins, they had been placed in the same locations, given the same languages and the same rearing, and then were left to themselves. He supposed that the deviations of the humans here from those on his world had started almost immediately. Fifteen millennia had resulted in very different histories and cultures.

He would like to stay here and wander over the face of this Earth. But now, he had to find Wolff and Chryseis and to do this, he would have to find and capture Urthona. The only action available was to use the Horn, and to hope it would reveal the right gate to the Lord.

This was not going to be easy, as he found out a few minutes later. The Horn, though not loud, attracted several servants. Kickaha fired the beamer once at a pillar near them. They saw the hole appear in the stone and, shouting and screaming, fled. Kickaha urged Anana to continue blowing the Horn, but the uproar from the interior convinced him that they could not remain here. This building was too huge for them to leisurely investigate the first story. The most likely places for gates were in the bedroom or office of the master, and these were probably on the second story.

When they were halfway up the steps, a number of men with steel conical helmets, small round shields, and swords and spears, appeared. There were, however, three men who carried big heavy clumsy-looking firearms with flared muzzles, wooden stocks, and flintlocks.

Kickaha cut the end of one blunderbuss off with the beamer. The men scattered, but they regrouped before Kickaha and Anana had reached the top of the steps. Kickaha cut through the bottom of a marble pillar and then through the top. The pillar fell over with a crash that shook the house, and the armed men fled.

It was a costly rout, because a little knob on the side of the beamer suddenly flashed a red light. There was not much charge left, and he did not have another powerpack.

They found a bedroom that seemed to be that of the Lords. It was certainly magnificent enough, but everything in this mansion was magnificent. It contained a number of weapons: swords, axes, daggers, throwing knives, maces, rapiers, and—delight!—bows and a quiver of arrows. While Anana probed the walls and floors with the Horn, Kickaha chose a knife with a good balance for her and then strung a bow. He shouldered a quiver and felt much better. The beamer had enough left in it for several seconds of full piercing power or a dozen or so rays of burn power or several score rays of stun power. After that, he would have to depend on his primitive weapons.

He also chose a light ax that seemed suitable for throwing for Anana. She was proficient in the use of all weapons, and while she was not as strong as he, she was as skillful.

She stopped blowing the Horn. There was a bed that hung by golden chains from the ceiling, and beyond it on the wall was a spreading circle of light. The light dissolved to show delicate pillars supporting a frescoed ceiling and, beyond, many trees.

Anana cried out with surprise in which was an anguished delight. She started forward but was held back by Kickaha. He said, "What's the hurry?"

"It's home!" she said. "Home!"

Her whole being seemed to radiate light.

"Your world?" he said.

"Oh, no! Home! Where I was born! The world where the Lords originated!"

There did not seem to be any traps, but that meant nothing. However, the hubbub outside the room indicated that they had better move on or expect to fight. Since the beamer was so depleted, he could not fight them off for long, not if they were persistent.

He said, "Here we go," and leaped through. Anana had to bend low and scoot through swiftly, because the circle was closing. When she got up on her feet, she said, "Do you remember that tall building on Wilshire, near the tar pits? The big one with the big sign, *California Federal*? It was always ablaze with lights at night?"

He nodded and she said, "This summerhouse is exactly on that spot. I mean, on the place that corresponds to that spot."

There was no sign here of anything corresponding to Wilshire Boulevard, nothing resembling a road or even a footpath. The number of trees here certainly did take away from the southern California lowlands look, but she explained that the Lords had created rivers and brooks here so that this forest could grow. The summerhouse was one of many built so that the family could stop for the night or retire for meditation or the doing of whatever virtue or vice they felt like. The main dwellings were all on the beach.

There had never been many people in this valley, and when Anana was born, only three families lived here. Later, at least as far as she knew, all the Lords had left this valley. In fact, they had left this world to occupy their own artificial universes and from thence to wage their wars upon each other.

Kickaha allowed her to wander around while she exclaimed softly to herself or called to him to look at something that she suddenly remembered. He wondered that she remembered anything at all, since her last visit here had been three thousand and two hundred years ago. When he thought of this, he asked her where the gate was through which she had entered at that time.

"It's on top of a boulder about a half mile from here," she said. "There are a number of gates, all disguised, of course. And nobody knows how many others here. I didn't know about the one under the stone floor of the summerhouse, of course. Urthona must have put it there long ago, maybe ten thousand years ago."

"This summerhouse is that old?"

"That old. It contains self-renewing and self-cleaning equipment, of course. And equipment to keep the forest and the land in its primeval state is under the surface. Erosion and buildup of land are compensated for."

"Are there any weapons hidden here for your use?" he said.

"There are a number just within the gate," she said. "But the charges will have trickled off to nothing by now, and besides, I don't have an activator. . . ."

She stopped and said, "I forgot about the Horn. It can activate the gate, of course, but there's really nothing in it to help us."

"Where does the gate lead to?"

"It leads to a room that contains another gate, and this one opens directly to the interior of the palace of my own world. But it is trapped. I had to leave my deactivator behind when the Bellers invaded my world and I escaped through another gate into Jadawin's world."

"Show me where the boulder is, anyway. If we have to, we could take refuge inside its gate and come back out later."

First, they must eat and, if possible, take a nap. Anana took him into the house, although she first studied it for a long time for traps. The kitchen contained an exquisitely sculptured marble cabinet. This, in turn, housed a fabricator, the larger part of which was buried under the house. Anana opened it cautiously and set the controls, closed it, and a few minutes later, opened it again. There were two trays with dishes and cups of delicious food and drink. The energy-matter converters below the earth had been waiting for thousands of years to serve this meal and would wait another hundred thousand years to serve the next one if events so proceeded.

After eating, they stretched out on the bed that hung on chains from the ceiling. Kickaha questioned her about the layout of the land. She was about to go to sleep when he said, "I've had the feeling that we got here not entirely by accident. I think either Urthona or Red Orc set it up so that we'd get here if we were fast and clever enough. And he also set it up so that the other Lord is alive. I feel that this is the showdown, and that Urthona or Orc arranged to have it here for poetic or aesthetic reasons. It would be like a Lord to bring his enemies back to the home planet to kill them—if he could. This is just a feeling, but I'm going to act as if it were definite knowledge."

"You'd act that way, anyway," she said. "But I think you may be right."

She fell asleep. He left the bed and went to the front room to watch. The sun started down from the zenith. Beautiful birds, most of whose ancestors must have been made in the biolabs of the Lords, gathered around the fountain and pool before the house. Once a large brown bear ambled through the trees and near the house. Another time, he heard a sound that tingled his nerves and filled him with joy. It was the shrill trumpet of a mammoth. Its cry reminded him of the Amerind tier of Wolff's world, where mammoths and mastodons by the millions roamed the plains and the forests of an area larger than all of North and South America. He felt homesick and wondered when—if—he would ever see that world again. The Hrowakas, the Bear People, the beautiful and the great Amerinds who had adopted him, were dead now, murdered by the Bellers. But there were other tribes that would be eager to adopt him, even those who called him their greatest enemy and had been trying for years to lift his scalp or his head.

He returned to the bedroom and awoke Anana, telling her to rouse him in about an hour. She did so, and though he would have liked to sleep for the rest of the day and half the night, he forced himself to get up.

They ate some more food and packed more in a small basket. They set off through the woods, which were thick with trees but only moderately grown with underbrush. They came onto a trail that had been trampled by mammoths, as the tracks and droppings showed. They followed this, sensitive to the trumpetings or squealings of the big beasts. There were no flies or mosquitoes, but there was a variety of large beetles and other insects on which the birds fed.

Once they heard a savage yowl. They stopped, then continued after it was not repeated. Both recognized the cry of the saber-tooth.

"If this was the estate of your family, why did they keep the big dangerous beasts around?" he said.

"You should know that. The Lords like danger; it is the only spice of eternity. Immortality is nothing unless it can be taken away from you at any moment."

That was true. Only those who had immortality could appreciate that. But he wished, sometimes, that there were not so much spice. Lately, he did not seem to be getting enough rest, and his nerves were raw from the chafing of continuous peril.

"Do you think that anybody else would know about the gate in the boulder?"

"Nothing is sure," she replied. "But I do not think so. Why? Do you think that Urthona will know that we'll be going to the boulder?"

"It seems highly probable. Otherwise, he would have set up a trap for us at the summerhouse. I think that he may expect and want us to go to the boulder because he is also leading another toward the same place. It's to be a trysting place for us and our two enemies."

"You don't know that. It's just your highly suspicious mind believing that things are as you would arrange them if you were a Lord."

"Look who's calling who paranoid," he said, smiling. "Maybe you're right. But I've been through so much that I can hear the tumblers of other people's minds clicking."

He decided that Anana should handle the beamer and he would have his bow and arrows ready.

Near the edge of the clearing, Kickaha noted a slight swelling in the earth. It was almost a quarter inch high and two inches wide, and it ran for several feet, then disappeared. He moved in a zigzagging path for several yards and finally found another swelling that described a small part of a very large circle before it disappeared, too.

He went back to Anana, who had been watching him with a puzzled expression.

"Do you know of any underground work done around here?" he said.

"No," she said. "Why?"

"Maybe an earthquake did it," he said and did not comment any more on the swelling.

The boulder was about the size of a one-bedroom bungalow and was set near the edge of a clearing. It was of red-and-black granite and had been transported here from the north along with thousands of other boulders to add variety to the landscape. It was about a hundred yards northeast of a tar pit. This pit, Kickaha realized, was the same size and in the same location as the tar pit in Hancock Park on Earth Number One.

They got down on their bellies and snaked slowly toward the boulder. When they were within thirty yards of it, Kickaha crawled around until he was able to see all sides of the huge rock. Coming back, he said, "I didn't think he'd be dumb enough to hide *behind* it. But *in* it would be a good move. Or maybe he's out in the woods and waiting for us to open the gate because he's trapped it."

"If you're right and he's waiting for a third party to show . . ."

She stopped and clutched his arm and said, "I saw someone! There!"

She pointed across the clearing at the thick woods where the Los Angeles County Art Museum would have been if this had been Earth Number One. He looked but could see nothing.

"It was a man, I'm sure of that," she said. "A tall man. I think he was Red Orc!"

"See any weapon? A beamer?"

"No. I just got a glimpse, and then he was gone behind a tree."

Kickaha began to get even more uneasy.

He watched the birds and noticed that a raven was cawing madly near where Anana though she had seen Red Orc. Suddenly, the bird fell off its branch and was seen and heard no more. Kickaha grinned. The Lord had realized it might be giving him away and had shot it.

A hundred yards to their left near the edge of the tar pit, several blue jays screamed and swooped down again and again at something in the tall grass. Kickaha watched them, but in a minute a red fox trotted out of the grass and headed into the woods southward. The jays followed him.

With their departure, a relative quiet arrived. It was hot in the tall saw-bladed grass. Occasionally, a large insect buzzed nearby. Once a shadow flashed by them, and Kickaha, looking upward, saw a dragon fly, shimmering golden-green, transparent copper-veined wings at least two feet from tip to tip, zooming by.

Now and then, a trumpeting floated to them and a wolf-like howl came from far beyond. And, once, a big bird high above screamed harshly.

Neither saw a sign of the man Anana had thought was Red Orc. Yet, he must be out there somewhere. He might even have spotted them and be crawling toward their hiding place. This caused Kickaha to move away from their position near the boulder. They did this very slowly so they would shake the tall grasses as unviolently as possible. When they had gotten under the trees at the edge of the clearing, he said, "We shouldn't stay together. I'm going to go back into the woods about fifty feet or so. I can get a better view."

He kissed her cheek and crawled off. After looking around, he decided to take a post behind a bush on a slight rise in the ground. There was a tree behind it that would hide him from anybody approaching in that direction. It also had the disadvantage that it could hide the approaching person from him, but he took the chance. And the small height gave him a better view while the bush hid him from those below.

He could not see Anana even though he knew her exact position. Several times, the grasses moved just a little bit contrary to the direction of the breeze. If Orc or Urthona were watching, they would note this and perhaps . . .

He froze. The grass was bending, very slightly and slowly and at irregular intervals, about twenty yards to the right of Anana. There was no movement for what seemed like ten minutes, and then the grass bent again. It pointed toward Anana and moved back up gently, as if somebody were slowly releasing it. A few minutes later, it moved again.

Kickaha was absorbed in watching the progress of the person in the grass, but he did not allow it to distract him from observation elsewhere. During one of his many glances behind him, he saw a flash of white skin through the branches of a bush about sixty feet to his left. At first, he considered moving away from his position to another. But if he did so, he would very probably be seen by the newcomer. It was possible that he had been seen already. The best action just now was no action.

The sun slid on down the sky, and the shadows lengthened. The person creeping toward Anana moved rarely and very slowly but within an hour, he was about twelve feet from her. Whether or not she knew it, Kickaha could not tell.

He removed the Horn from its case. And he placed the nock of an arrow in the string of the bow and waited. Again, the grass bent down toward Anana, and the person moved a foot closer.

Behind him, nothing showed except the flash of a bright blue-and-red bird swooping between the trees.

Presently, on the other side of the clearing, keeping close to the trees on its edge, a huge black wolf trotted. It stood at least four and a half feet high at the shoulder, and it could remove the leg of a man at the ankle bone with one bite. It was a dire wolf, extinct on Earth some ten thousand years, but plentiful on Jadawin's world and recreated in the Lords' biolabs for restocking of this area. The giant he-wolf trotted along as stealthily and vibrantly as a tiger, its red tongue hanging out like a flag after a heavy rain. It trotted warily but confidently along for twenty yards and then froze. For a few seconds, it turned its head to scan a quarter of the compass, and then it moved ahead, but crouchingly. Kickaha watched it, while keeping tabs on the persons unknown before and behind him—or tried to do so. Thus, he almost missed the quick action of the wolf.

It suddenly charged toward a spot inside the woods and just as suddenly abandoned its charge and fled yowling across the clearing toward Anana. The fur on its back and hind legs was aflame.

Kickaha grasped immediately that a fifth person was in the game and that he had tried to scare the wolf away with a brief power-reduced shot from a beamer. But in his haste he had set the power too high and had burned the wolf instead of just stunning it.

Or perhaps the burning was done deliberately. The newcomer might have set the beast on fire and be guiding it this way with stabs of beamer power to see what he could flush up.

Whatever his intent, he had upset the plans of the person sneaking up on Anana. He had also upset Anana, who, hearing the frantic yowls approaching her with great speed, could not resist raising her head just high enough to see what was happening.

Kickaha wanted to take another quick look behind him, but he did not have time. He rose, bent the bow and released the shaft just as something dark reared up a little way above the grass about forty feet from Anana. It was dressed in black and had a black helmet with a dark faceplate, just like the helmets with visors that the Los Angeles motorcyclists wore. The man held the stock of a short-barreled beamer to his shoulder.

At the same time, the wolf ran howling by, the flames leaping off onto the dry grass and the grass catching fire. The arrow streaked across the space between the trees and the edge of the clearing, the sun sparkling off the metal head. It struck the man just under the left arm, which was raised to hold the barrel of the beamer. The arrow bounced off, but the man, although protected by some sort of flexible armor, was knocked over by the impact of the arrow.

The beamer fell out of his hands. Since it had just been turned on, it cut a fiery tunnel through the grass. It also cut off the front legs of the wolf, which fell down howling but became silent as the beam sliced through its body. The fire, originating from the two sources, quickly spread. Smoke poured out, but Kickaha could see that Anana had not been hit and that she was crawling swiftly through the grass toward the fallen man and the beamer.

Kickaha whirled then, drawing another arrow from the quiver and starting to set it to the bowstring. He saw the tall figure of the man lean from around behind the trunk of a tree. A hand beamer was sticking out, pointing toward Kickaha. Kickaha jumped behind his tree and crouched, knowing that he could not get off an arrow swiftly or accurately enough.

There was a burning odor, a thump. He looked up. The beam had cut through the trunk, and the upper part of the tree had dropped straight down for two inches, its smoothly chopped butt against the top of the stump.

Kickaha stepped to the left side of the tree and shot with all the accuracy of thousands of hours of practice under deliberately difficult conditions and scores of hours in combat. The arrow was so close to the tree, it was deflected by the slightest contact. It zoomed off, just missing the arm of the man holding the beamer. The beamer withdrew as the man jumped back. And then the tree above Kickaha fell over, pulled to one side by the unevenness of the branches' weight. It came down on Kickaha, who jumped back and so escaped the main weight of the trunk. But a branch struck him, and everything became as black and unknowing as the inside of a tree.

When he saw light again, he also saw that not much time had passed. The sun had not moved far. His head hurt as if a root had grown into it and was entangled with the most sensitive nerves. A branch pressed down his chest, and his legs felt as if another branch was weighting them down. He could move his arms a little to one side and turn his head, but otherwise he was unable to move as if he were buried under a landslide.

Smoke drifted by and made him cough. Flames crackled, and he could feel some heat on the bottom of his feet. The realization that he might burn to death sent him into a frenzy of motion. The result was that his head hurt even more and he had not been able to get out from under the branches at all.

He thought of the others. What had happened to Anana? Why wasn't she here trying to get him free? And the man who had severed the tree? Was he sneaking up now, not sure that he had hit the archer? And then there was the man in black he'd knocked down with the arrow and the person across the clearing who had set fire to the wolf and precipitated the action. Where were they?

If Anana did not do something quickly, she might as well forget about him. The smoke was getting thicker, and his feet and the lower part of his legs were getting very uncomfortable. It would be a question of whether he choked to death from smoke or burned first. Could this be the end? The end came to everybody, even those Lords who had survived fifteen thousand years. But if he had to die, let him do it in his beloved adopted world, the World of Tiers.

Then he stopped thinking such thoughts. He was not dead and he was not going to quit struggling. Somehow, he would get this tree off his chest and legs and would crawl away to where the fire could not reach him and where he would be hidden from his enemies. But where was Anana?

A voice made him start. It came a foot away from his left ear. He turned his head and saw the grinning face of Red Orc.

"So the fox was caught in my deadfall," Red Orc said in English.

"Of course, you planned it that way," Kickaha said.

The Lords were cruel, and this one would want him to die slowly. Moreover, Orc would want him to fully savor the taste of defeat. A Lord never killed a foe swiftly if he could avoid it.

He must keep Red Orc talking as long as he could. If Anana were trying to get close, she would be helped if Red Orc were distracted.

The Lord wanted to talk, to taunt his victim, but he had not relaxed his vigilance. While he lay near Kickaha, he held his beamer ready, and he looked this way and that as nervously as if he were a bird.

"So you've won?" Kickaha said, although he did not believe that Red Orc had won and would not think so until he was dead.

"Over you, yes," Red Orc said. "Over the others, not yet. But I will."

"Then Urthona is still out there," Kickaha said. "Tell me, who set up this trap? You or Urthona?"

Red Orc lost his smile. He said, "I'm not sure. The trap may be so subtle that I was led into thinking that I set it. And then again, perhaps I did. What does it matter? We were all led here, for one reason or another, to this final battleground. It has been a good battle, because we are not fighting through our underlings, the *leblabbiy*. We are fighting directly, as we should. You are the only Earthling in this battle, and I'm convinced that you may be half-Lord. You certainly do have some family resemblances to us. I could be your father. Or Urthona. Or Uriel. Or even that dark one, Jadawin. After all, he had the genes for red hair."

Red Orc paused and smiled, then said, "And it's possible that Anana could be your mother, too. In which case, you might be all-Lord. That would explain your amazing abilities and your successes."

A thick arm of smoke came down over Kickaha's face and set him coughing again. Red Orc looked alarmed and he backed away a little, turning his back to Kickaha, who was recovering from another coughing fit. Something had happened to his legs. Suddenly, they no longer felt the heat. It was as if dirt had been piled on them.

Kickaha said, "I don't know what you're getting at, Orc, but Anana could not possibly be my mother. Anyway, I know who my parents are. They were Indiana farmers who come from old American stock, including the oldest, and also from Scotch, Norwegian, German, and Irish immigrants. I was born in the very small rural village of North Terre Haute, and there is no mystery. . . ."

He stopped, because there had been a mystery. His parents had moved from Kentucky to Indiana before he was born and, suddenly, he remembered the mysterious Uncle Robert who had visited their farm from time to time when he was very young. And then there was the trouble with his birth certificate when he had volunteered for the Army cavalry. And when he had returned to Indiana after the war, he had been left ten thousand dollars from an unknown benefactor. It was to put him through college and there had been a vague promise of more to come.

"There is no mystery?" Red Orc said. "I know far more about you than you would dream possible. When I found out that your natal name was Paul Janus Finnegan, I remembered something, and I checked it out. And so . . ."

Kickaha began coughing again. Orc quit talking. A second later, a shape appeared through the smoke above him, coming from the other side of the tree where he had thought nothing could be living. It dived through the cloud and sprawled on top of Red Orc, knocking him on his back and tearing the beamer from his hands.

Orc yelled with the surprise and shock and tried to roll after the beamer but the attacker, in a muffled voice, said, "Hold it! Or I cut you in half!"

Kickaha bent his head as far to one side and as far back as he could. The voice he knew, of course, but he still could not believe it. Then he realized that Anana had piled dirt on them or covered them up with something.

But what had kept her from coughing and giving herself away?

She turned toward him then, though still keeping the beamer turned on Red Orc. A cloth was tied around her nose and mouth. It was wet with some liquid that he suspected was urine. Anana had always been adaptable, making do with whatever was handy.

She gestured to Orc to move away from his beamer. He scooted away backward on his hands and buttocks, eyeing her malevolently.

Anana stepped forward, tossed her beamer away with one hand as she picked up Orc's with the other. Then, aiming the weapon at him with one hand, she slipped the cloth from her face to around her neck. She smiled slightly and said, "Thanks for your beamer, Uncle. Mine was discharged."

Orc looked shocked.

Anana crouched down and said, "All right, Uncle. Get that tree off him. And quick!"

Orc said, "I can't lift that! Even if I broke my back doing it, I couldn't lift it!"

"Try," she said.

His face set stubbornly. "Why should I bother? You'll kill me, anyway. Do it now."

"I'll burn your legs and scorch your eyes out," she said, "and leave you here legless and blind if you don't get him from under that tree."

"Come on, Anana," Kickaha said. "I know you want to make him suffer, but not at my expense. Cut the branches off me with the beamer so he won't have so much weight to lift. Don't play around. There are two others out there, you know."

Anana moved away from the smoke and said, "Stand to one side, Uncle!" She made three passes with the ray from the beamer. The huge branch on his chest was cut in two places; he could not see what she had done to the branch on his legs. Orc had no difficulty removing the trunk and dragging him out of the smoke. He lifted him in his arms and carried him into the woods, where the grass was sparser and shorter.

He let Kickaha down very gently and then put his hands behind his neck at her orders.

"The stranger is out on the boulder," she said. "He got up and staggered away just after I got his beamer. He ran there to get away from me and the fire. I didn't kill him; maybe I should have. But I was curious about him and thought I could question him later."

That curiosity had made more than one Lord lose the upper hand, Kickaha thought. But he did not comment, since the deed was done and, besides, he understood the curiosity. He had enough of it to sympathize.

"Do you know where Urthona is?" he said, wheezing and feeling a pain in his chest as if a cancer had grown there within the last few seconds. His legs were numb but life was returning in them. And with the life, pain.

"I'm not going to be much good, Anana," he said. "I'm hurting pretty badly inside. I'll do what I can to help, but the rest is up to you."

Anana said, "I don't know where Urthona is. Except he's out there. I'm sure he was the one who set the wolf on fire. And set this up for us. Even the great Red Orc, Lord of the two Earths, was lured into this."

"I knew it was a trap," Orc said. "I came into it, anyway. I thought that surely I . . . I . . ."

"Yes, Uncle, if I were you, I wouldn't brag," she said. "The only question, the big question anyway, is how we get away from him."

"The Horn," Kickaha said. He sat up with great effort, despite the clenching of a dragon's claw inside his chest. Smoke drifted under the trees and made him cough again. The pain intensified.

Anana said, "Oh!" She looked distressed. "I forgot about it."

"We'll have to get it. It must be under the tree back there," he said. "And we'll open the gate in the boulder. If worse comes to worst, we'll go through it."

"But the second room past it is trapped!" she said. "I told you I'd need a deactivator to get through it."

"We can come out later," he said. "Urthona can't follow us and he won't hang around because he'll think we definitely escaped into another universe."

He stopped talking because the effort pained him so much.

Red Orc, at Anana's orders, helped him up. He did it so roughly that a low cry was forced from Kickaha. Anana, glaring, said, "Uncle, you be gentle, or I'll kill you right now!"

"If you do," Orc said, "you'll have to carry him yourself. And what kind of position will that put you in?"

Anana looked as if she were going to shoot him anyway. Before Kickaha could say anything, he saw the muzzle end of the beamer fall onto the ground. Anana was left with half a weapon in her hand.

A voice called out from the trees behind them. "You will do as I tell you now! Walk to that boulder and wait there for further orders!"

Why should he want us to do that? Kickaha thought. *Does he know about the trap inside the gate, know that we'll be stuck there if he doesn't go away as I'd planned? Is he hoping we'll decide to run the trap and so get ourselves killed? He will wait outside the boulder while we agonize inside, and he'll get his sadistic amusement thinking about our dilemma.*

Clearly, Urthona thought he had them in his power, and clearly, he did. But he was not going to expose himself or get closer.

That's the way to manage it, Kickaha thought. Be cagey, be foxy, never take anything for granted. That was how he had survived through so much. Survive? It looked as if his days were about ended.

"Walk to the boulder!" Urthona shouted. "At once! Or I burn you a little!"

Anana went to Kickaha's other side and helped Orc move him. Every step flicked pain through Kickaha, but he shut his mouth and turned his groans into silence. The smoke still spread over the air and made him cough again and caused even deeper pain.

Then they passed the tree where the Horn was sticking out from a partially burned branch.

"Has Urthona come out from the trees yet?" he asked.

Anana looked around slowly, then said, "No more than a step or two."

"I'm going to stumble. Let me fall."

"It'll hurt you," she said.

"So what? Let me go! Now!"

"Gladly!" Orc said and released him. Anana was not so fast, and she tried to support his full weight for a second. They went down together, she taking most of the impact. Nevertheless, the fall seemed to end on sharpened stakes in his chest, and he almost fainted.

There was a shout from Urthona. Red Orc froze and slowly raised his hands above his head. Kickaha tried to get up and crawl to the Horn, but Anana was there before him.

"Blow on it now!" he said.

"Why?" Red Orc and Anana said in unison.

"Just do what I say! I'll tell you later! If there is a later!"

She lifted the mouthpiece to her lips and loudly blew the sequence of seven notes that made the skeleton key to turn the lock of any gate of the Lords within range of its vibrations.

There was a shout from Urthona, who had begun running toward them when they had fallen. But as the first note blared out, and he saw what Anana held in her mouth, he screamed.

Kickaha expected him to shoot. Instead, Urthona ran away toward the woods.

Red Orc said, "What is happening?"

The last of the golden notes faded away.

Urthona stopped running and threw his beamer down on the ground and jumped up and down.

The immediate area around them remained the same. There was the clearing with its burned grasses, the boulder on top of which the darkly clothed stranger sat, the fallen tree, and the trees on the edge of the clearing.

But the sky had become an angry red without a sun.

The land beyond the edge of the clearing had become high hills covered with a rusty grass and queer-looking bushes with green-and-red-striped swastika-shaped leaves. There were trees on the hills beyond the nearest ones; these were tall and round and had zebra stripes of black, white, and red. They swayed as if they were at the bottom of the sea responding to a current.

Urthona's jumping up and down had resulted in his attaining heights of at least six feet. Now he picked up his beamer and ran in great bounds toward them. He seemed in perfect control of himself.

Not so with Red Orc, who started to whirl toward them, his mouth open to ask what had happened. The motion carried him on around and toppled him over. But he did not fall heavily.

"Stay down," Kickaha said to Anana. "I don't know where we are, but the gravity's less than Earth's."

Urthona stopped before them. His face was almost as red as the sky. His green eyes were wild.

"The Horn of Shambarimen," he screamed. "I wondered what you had in that case! If I had known! If I had known!"

"Then you would have stayed outside the rim of the giant gate you set around the clearing," Kickaha said. "Tell me, Urthona, why did you step inside it? Why did you drive us toward the boulder, when we were already inside the gate?"

"How did you know?" Urthona screamed. "How could you know?"

"I didn't really *know*," Kickaha said. "I saw the slight ridge of earth at several places on the edge of the clearing before we came on in. It didn't mean much, although I was suspicious. I'm suspicious of everything that I can't explain at once.

"Then you hung back, and that in itself wasn't too suspicious, because you wouldn't want to get too close until you were certain we had no hidden weapons. But you wanted to do more than just get us inside this giant gate and then spring it on us. You wanted to drive us into our own gate, in the boulder, where we'd be trapped. You wanted us to hide inside there and think we'd fooled you and then come out after a while, only to find ourselves in this world.

"But you didn't know that Anana had no activator and you didn't know that we had the Horn. There was no reason why you would think of it even if you saw the instrument case, because it must be thousands of years since you last saw it. And you didn't know Jadawin had it, or you would have connected that with the instrument case, since I am Jadawin's friend.

"So I got Anana to blow the Horn even if she didn't know why she was doing it. I didn't want to go into your world, but if I could take you with me, I'd do it."

Anana got up slowly and carefully and said, "The Shifting World! Urthona's World!"

In the east, or what was the east in the world they'd just left, a massive red body appeared over the hills. It rose swiftly and revealed itself as a body about four times the size of the Earth's moon. It was not round but oblong, with several blobby tentacles extending out from it. Kickaha thought that it was changing shape slightly.

He felt the earth under him tilting. His head was getting lower than his feet. And the edge of the high hills in the distance was sagging.

Kickaha sat up. The pains seemed to be slightly attenuated. Perhaps it was because the pull of gravity was so much reduced. He said, "This is a one-way gate, of course, Urthona?"

"Of course," Urthona said. "Otherwise I would have taken the Horn and reopened the gate."

"And where is the nearest gate out of this world?"

"There's no harm in telling you," Urthona said. "Especially since you won't know any more than you do now when I tell you. The only gate out is in my palace, which is somewhere on the surface of this mass. Or perhaps on that," he added, pointing at the reddish metamorphosing body in the sky. "This planet splits up and changes shape and recombines and splits off again. The only analogy I can think of is a lavalite. This is a lavalite world."

Red Orc went into action then. His leap was prodigious and he almost went over Urthona's head. But he rammed into him and both went cartwheeling. The beamer, knocked out of Urthona's hand by the impact, flew off to one side. Anana dived after it, got it, and landed so awkwardly and heavily that Kickaha feared for her. She rose somewhat shakily but grinning. Urthona walked back to them; Red Orc crawled.

"Now, Uncles," she said. "I could shoot you and perhaps I should. But I need someone to carry Kickaha, so you two will do it. You should be thankful that the lesser gravity will make the task easier. And I need you, Urthona, because you know something of this world. You should, since you designed it and made it. You two will make a stretcher for Kickaha, and then we'll start out."

"Start out where?" growled Urthona. "There's no place to go to. Nothing is fixed here. Can't you understand that?"

"If we have to search every inch of this world, we'll do it," she said. "Now get to work!"

"Just one moment," Kickaha said. "What did you do with Wolff and Chryseis?"

"I gated them through to this world. They are somewhere on its surface. Or on that mass. Or perhaps another mass we haven't seen yet. I thought that it would be the worst thing I could do to them. And, of course, they do have some chance of finding my palace. Although . . ."

"Although even if they do, they'll run into some traps?" Kickaha said.

"There are other things on this world . . ."

"Big predators? Hostile human beings?"

Urthona nodded and said, "Yes. We'll need the beamer. I hope its charge lasts. And . . ."

Kickaha said, "Don't leave us in suspense."

"I hope that we don't take too long finding my palace. If you're not a native, you're driven crazy by this world!"

THE LAVALITE

WORLD

1

KICKAHA WAS A QUICKSILVER PROTEUS.
Few could match his speed in adapting to change. But on Earth and on other planets of the pocket universes, the hills, mountains, valleys, plains, the rivers, lakes, and seas, seldom altered. Their permanence of form and location were taken for granted.

There were small local changes. Floods, earthquakes, avalanches, tidal waves reshaped the earth. But the effects were, in the time scale of an individual, in the lifetime of a nation, minute.

A mountain might walk, but the hundreds of thousands of generations living at its foot would not know it. Only God or a geologist would see its movements as the dash of a mouse for a hole.

Not here.

Even cocksure, unfazed Kickaha, who could react to change as quickly as a mirror reflects an image, was nervous. But he wasn't going to let anyone else know it. To the others, he seemed insanely cool. That was because they were going mad.

2

THEY HAD GONE TO SLEEP DURING THE "NIGHT." KICKAHA HAD taken the first watch. Urthona, Orc, Anana, and McKay had made themselves as comfortable as they could on the rusty-red tough grass and soon had fallen asleep. Their camp was at the bottom of a shallow valley ringed by low hills. Grass was the only vegetation in the valley. The tops of the hills, however, were lined with the silhouettes of trees. These were about ten feet tall. Though there was little breeze, they swayed back and forth.

When he had started the watch, he had seen only a few on the hilltops. As time passed, more and more had appeared. They had ranged themselves beside the early comers until they were a solid line. There was no telling how many were on the other side of the hills. What he was sure of was that the trees were waiting until "dawn." Then, if the humans did not come to them, they would come down the hills after them.

The sky was a uniform dark red except for a few black slowly floating shapes. Clouds. The enormous reddish mass, visually six times the size of Earth's moon, had disappeared from the sky. It would be back, though he didn't know when.

He sat down and rubbed his legs. They still hurt from the accident that had taken place twelve "days" ago. The pain in his chest had almost ceased, however. He was recovering, but he was not as agile and strong as he needed to be.

That the gravity was less than Earth's helped him, though.

He lay down for a minute. No enemy, human or beast, was going to attack. They would have to get through those killer trees first. Only the elephants and the giant variety of moosoids were big enough to do that. He wished that some of these would show up. They fed upon trees. However, at this distance, Kickaha couldn't determine just what type of killer plants they were. Some were so fearsomely armed that even the big beasts avoided them.

How in hell had the trees detected the little party? They had a keen olfactory sense, but he doubted that the wind was strong enough to carry the odor of the party up over the hills. The visual ability of the plants was limited. They could see shapes through the multifaceted insectine eyes ringing the upper parts of their trunks. But at this distance and in this light, they might as well be blind.

One or more of their scouts must have come up a hill and caught a molecule or two of human odor. That was, after all, nothing to be surprised about. He and the others stank. The little water they had been able to find was used for drinking only. If they didn't locate more water tomorrow, they'd have to start drinking their own urine. It could be recycled twice before it became poisonous.

Also, if they didn't kill something soon, they would be too weak from hunger to walk.

He rubbed the barrel of the hand-beamer with the fingers of his left hand. Its battery had only a few full-power discharges available. Then it would be exhausted. So far, he and Anana had refrained from using any of the power. It was the only thing that allowed them to keep the upper hand over the other three. It was also their only strong defense against the big predators. But when "dawn" came, he was going to go hunting. They had to eat, and they could drink blood to quench their thirst.

First, though, they had to get through the trees. Doing that might use up the battery. It also might not be enough. There could be a thousand trees on the other side of the hills.

The clouds were thickening. Perhaps, at long last, rain would come. If it rained as hard as Urthona said it did, it might fill this cup-shaped valley. They'd have to drown or charge into the trees. Some choice.

He lay on his back for a few minutes. Now he could hear faint creaks and groans and an occasional mutter. The earth was moving under him. Heat flowed along his back and his legs. It felt almost as warm as a human body. Under the densely packed blades and the thick tangle of roots, energy was being dissipated. The earth was shifting slowly. In what direction, toward what shapes, he did not know.

He could wait. One of his virtues was an almost-animal patience. Be a leopard, a wolf. Lie still and evaluate the situation. When action was called for, he would explode. Unfortunately, his injured leg and his weakness handicapped him. Where he had once been dynamite, he was now only black gunpowder.

He sat up and looked around. The dark reddish light smoldered around him. The trees formed a waving wall on the hilltops. The others of the party lay on their sides or their backs. McKay was snoring. Anana was muttering something in her native language, a speech older than Earth itself. Urthona's eyes were open, and he was looking directly at Kickaha. Was he hoping to catch him unawares and get hold of the beamer?

No. He was sleeping, his mouth and eyes open. Kickaha, having risen and come close to him, could hear the gentle burbling from his dry lips. The eyes looked glazed.

Kickaha licked his own sandpaper lips and swallowed. He brought the wristwatch, which he'd borrowed from Anana, close to his eyes. He pressed the minute stud on its side, and four glowing figures appeared briefly on the face. They were the numerical signs of the Lords. In Earth numerals, 15:12. They did not mean anything here. There was no sun; the sky provided light and some heat. In any event, this planet had no steady rotation on any one plane, and there were no stars. The great reddish mass that had moved slowly across the sky, becoming larger ever day, was no genuine moon. It was a temporary satellite, and it was falling.

There were no shadows except under one peculiar condition. There was no north, south, east and west. Anana's watch had compass capabilities, but they were useless. This great body on which he stood had no nickel-steel core, no electromagnetic field, no north or south pole. Properly speaking, it wasn't a planet.

And the ground was rising now. He could not detect that by its motion, since that was so slow. But the hills had definitely become lower.

The watch had one useful function. It did mark the forward movement of time. It would tell him when his hour and a half of sentinel duty was over.

When it was time to rouse Anana, he walked to her. But she sat up before he was within twelve feet. She knew that it was her turn. She had told herself to wake at the proper time, and a well-developed sense, a sort of biological clock within her, had set off its alarm.

Anana was beautiful, but she was beginning to look gaunt. Her cheekbones protruded, her cheeks were beginning to sink in, her large dark-blue eyes were ringed with the shadows of fatigue. Her lips were cracked, and that once soft white skin was dirty and rough-looking. Though she had sweated much in the twelve days they'd been here, there were still traces of smoke on her neck.

"You don't look so good yourself," she said, smiling.

Normally, her voice was a rich contralto, but now it was gravelly.

She stood up. She was slim but broad-shouldered and full-breasted. She was only two inches shorter than his six feet one inch, was as strong as any man her weight, and inside fifty yards, she could outrun him. Why not? She had had ten thousand years to develop her physical potentialities.

She took a comb from the back pocket of her torn bell-bottom trousers and straightened out her long hair, as black as a Crow Indian's.

"There. Is that better?" she said, smiling. Her teeth were very white and perfect. Only thirty years ago, she'd had tooth buds implanted, the hundredth set in a series.

"Not bad for a starving dehydrated old woman," he said. "In fact, if I was up to it . . ."

He quit grinning, and waved his hand to indicate the hilltops. "We've got visitors."

It was difficult in this light to see if she'd turned pale. Her voice was steady. "If they're bearing fruit, we'll eat."

He thought it better not to say that they might be eaten instead.

He handed her the beamer. It looked like a six-shooter revolver. But the cartridges were batteries, of which only one now had a charge. The barrel contained a mechanism that could be adjusted to shoot a ray that could cut through a tree or inflict a slight burn or a stunning blow.

Kickaha went back to where his bow and a quiver of arrows lay. He was an excellent archer, but so far, only two of his arrows had struck game. The animals were wary, and it had been impossible, except twice, to get close enough to any to shoot. Both kills had been small gazelles, not enough to fill the bellies of five adults in twelve days. Anana had gotten a hare with a throw of her light ax, but a long-legged baboon had dashed out from behind a hill, scooped it up, and run off with it.

Kickaha picked up the bow and quiver, and they walked three hundred feet away from the sleepers. Here he lay down and went to sleep. His knife was thrust upright into the ground, ready to be snatched in case of attack. Anana had her beamer, a light throwing ax, and a knife for defense.

They were not worried at this time about the trees. They just wanted to keep distance between them and the others. When Anana's watch was over, she would wake up McKay. Then she'd return to lie down by Kickaha. She and her mate were not overly concerned about one of the others trying to sneak up on them while they slept. Anana had told them that her wristwatch had a device that would sound an alarm if anybody with a mass large enough to be dangerous came close. She was lying, though the device was something that a Lord could have. They probably wondered if she was deceiving them. However, they did not care to test her. She had said that if anyone tried to attack them, she would kill him immediately. They knew that she would do so.

3

HE AWOKE, SWEATING FROM THE HEAT, THE BRIGHT LIGHT OF "day" plucking at his eyes. The sky had become a fiery light red. The clouds were gone, taking their precious moisture elsewhere. But he was no longer in a valley. The hills had come down, flattened out into a plain. And the party was now on a small hill.

He was surprised. The rate of change had been greater than he'd expected. Urthona, however, had said that the reshaping occasionally accelerated. Nothing was constant or predictable here. So he shouldn't have been surprised.

The trees still ringed them. There were several thousand, and now some scouts were advancing toward the just-born hill. They were about ten feet tall. The trunks were barrel-shaped and covered with a smooth greenish bark. Large round dark eyes circled the trunk near its top. On one side was an opening, the mouth. Inside it was soft flexible tissue and two hard ridges holding sharklike teeth. According to Urthona, the plants were half protein, and the digestive system was much like an animal's. The anus was the terminus of the digestive system, but it was also located in the mouth.

Urthona should know. He had designed them.

"They don't have any diseases, so there's no reason why the feces shouldn't pass through the mouth," Urthona had said.

"They must have bad breath," Kickaha had said. "But then, nobody's going to kiss them, are they?"

He, Anana, and McKay had laughed. Urthona and Red Orc had looked disgusted. Their sense of humor had atrophied. Or perhaps they'd never had much.

Above the head of the tree was a growth of many slender stems rising two feet straight up. Broad green leaves, heart-shaped, covered the stems. From the trunk radiated six short branches, each three feet long, a pair on each side, in three ranks. These had short twigs supporting large round leaves. Between each ring of branches was a tentacle, about twelve feet long and as supple as an octopus's. A pair of tentacles also grew from the base.

The latter helped balance the trunk as it moved on two short kneeless legs ending in huge round barky toeless feet. When the tree temporarily changed from an ambulatory to a sedentary state, the lower tentacles bored into the soil, grew roots, and sucked sustenance from the ground. The roots could be easily broken off and the tentacles withdrawn when the tree decided to move on.

Kickaha had asked Urthona why he had had such a clumsy unnatural monster made in his biolabs.

"It pleased me to do so."

Urthona probably was wishing he hadn't done so. He had wakened the others, and all were staring at the weird—and frightening—creatures.

Kickaha walked up to him. "How do they communicate?"

"Through pheromones. Various substances they emit. There are about thirty of these, and a tree smelling them receives various signals. They don't think; their brains are about the size of a dinosaur's. They react on the instinctive—or robotic—level. They have a well-developed herd instinct, though."

"Any of these pheromones stimulate fear?"

"Yes. But you have to make one of them afraid, and there's nothing in this situation to scare them."

"I was thinking," Kickaha said, "that it's too bad you don't carry around a vial of fear-pheromones."

"I used to," Urthona said.

The nearest scout had halted thirty feet away. Kickaha looked at Anana, who was sixty feet from the group. Her beamer was ready for trouble from the three men or the tree.

Kickaha walked to the scout and stopped ten feet from it. It waved its greenish tentacles. Others were coming to join it, though not on a run. He estimated that with those legs, they could go perhaps a mile an hour. But then, he didn't know their full potentiality. Urthona didn't remember how fast they could go.

Even as he walked down toward the tree, he could feel the earth swelling beneath him, could see the rate of its shaping increase. The air became warmer, and spaces had appeared between the blades of grass. The earth was black and greasy-looking. If the shaping stopped and there was no change for three days, the grass would grow enough to fill in the bare spots.

The thousand or so plants were still moving but more slowly. They leaned forward on their rigid legs, their tentacles extended to support them.

Kickaha looked closely at the nearest one and saw about a dozen apple-red spheres dangling from the branches. He called to Urthona. "Is their fruit good to eat?"

"For birds, yes," Urthona said. "I don't remember. But I can't think why I should have made them poisonous for humans."

"Knowing you, I'd say you could have done it for laughs," Kickaha said.

He motioned to Angus McKay to come to him. The black came to him warily, though his caution was engendered by the tree, not Kickaha.

McKay was an inch shorter than Kickaha but about thirty pounds heavier. Not much of the additional weight was fat, though. He was dressed in black Levi's, socks, and boots. He'd long ago shed his shirt and the leather jacket of the motorcyclist, but he still carried his helmet. Kickaha had insisted that it be retained to catch rainwater in, if for nothing else.

McKay was a professional criminal, a product of Detroit, who'd come out to Los Angeles to be one of Urthona's hired killers. Of course, he had not known then that Urthona was a Lord. He had never been sure what Urthona, whom he knew as Mr. Callister, did. But he'd been paid well, and if Mr. Callister wasn't in a business that competed with other mobs, that was all to the good. And Mr. Callister certainly seemed to know how to handle the police.

That day which seemed so long ago, he'd had a free afternoon. He'd started drinking in a tavern in Watts. After picking up a good-looking if loud-mouthed woman, he'd driven her to his apartment in Hollywood. They'd gone to bed almost at once, after which he fell asleep. The telephone woke him up. It was Callister, excited, obviously in some kind of trouble. Emergency, though he didn't say what it was. McKay was to come to him at once. He was to bring his .45 automatic with him.

That helped to sober him up. Mr. Callister must really be in trouble if he would say openly, over a phone that could be tapped, that he was to be armed. Then the first of the troubles started. The woman was gone, and with her, his wallet—five hundred dollars and his credit cards—and his car keys.

When he looked out the window into the parking space behind the building, he saw that the car was gone, too. If it hadn't been that he was needed so quickly, he would have laughed. Ripped off by a hooker! A dumb one at that, since he would be tracking her down. He'd get his wallet back and its contents, if they were still around. And his car, too. He wouldn't kill the woman, but he would rough her up a bit to teach her a lesson. He was a professional, and professionals didn't kill except for money or in self-defense.

So he'd put on his bike clothes and wheeled out on it, speeding along in the night, ready to outrun the pigs if they saw him. Callister was waiting for him. The other bodyguards weren't around. He didn't ask Callister where they were, since the boss didn't like questions. But Callister volunteered, anyway. The others were in a car that had been wrecked while chasing a man and a woman. They were not dead, but they were too injured to be of any use.

Callister then had described the couple he was after, but he didn't say why he wanted them.

Callister had stood for a moment, biting his lip. He was a big handsome honky, his curly hair yellow, his eyes a strange bright green, his face something like the movie actor, Paul Newman's. Abruptly, he went to a cabinet, pulled a little box about the size of a sugar cube from his pocket, held it over the lock, and the door swung open.

Callister removed a strange-looking device from the cabinet. McKay had never seen anything like it before, but he knew it was a weapon. It had a gunstock to which was affixed a short thick barrel, like a sawed-off shotgun.

"I've changed my mind," Callister said. "Use this, leave your .45 here. We may be where we won't want anybody to hear gunfire. Here, I'll show you how to use it."

McKay, watching him demonstrate, began to feel a little numb. It was the first step into a series of events that made him feel as if he'd been magically transformed into an actor in a science-fiction movie. If he'd had any sense, he would have taken off then. But there wasn't one man on Earth who could have foreseen that five minutes later, he wouldn't even *be* on Earth.

He was still goggle-eyed when, demonstrating the "beamer," Callister had cut a chair in half. He was handed a metal vest. At least, it looked and felt like steel. But it was flexible.

Callister put one on, too, and then he said something in a foreign language. A large circular area on the wall began glowing; then the glow disappeared, and he was staring into another world.

"Step through the gate," Callister said. He was holding a hand weapon disguised as a revolver. It wasn't pointed at McKay, but McKay felt that it would be if he refused.

Callister followed him in. McKay guessed that Callister was using him as a shield, but he didn't protest. If he did, he might be sliced in half.

They went through another "gate" and were in still another world or dimension or whatever. And then things really began to happen. While Callister was sneaking up on their quarry, McKay circled around through the trees. All of a sudden, hell broke loose. There was this big red-haired guy with, believe it or not, a bow and arrows.

He was behind a tree, and McKay sliced the branches of the tree off on one side. That was to scare the archer, since Callister had said that he wanted the guy—his name was Kickaha, crazy!—alive. But Kickaha had shot an arrow and McKay certainly knew where it had been aimed. Only a part of his body was not hidden by the tree behind which he was concealed. But the arrow had struck McKay on the only part showing, his shoulder.

If he hadn't been wearing that vest, he'd have been skewered. Even as it was, the shock of the arrow knocked him down. His beamer flew away from his opening hands and, its power still on, it rolled away.

Then, the biggest wolf—a wolf!—McKay had ever seen had gotten caught in the ray, and it had died, cut into four different parts. McKay was lucky. If the beamer had fallen pointing the other way, it would have severed him. Though he was stunned, his shoulder and arm completely numb, he managed to get up and to run, crouching over, to another tree. He was cursing because Callister had made him leave his automatic behind. He sure as hell wasn't going into the clearing after the beamer. Not when Kickaha could shoot an arrow like that.

Besides, he felt that he was in over his head about fifty fathoms.

There was a hell of a lot of action after that, but McKay didn't see much of it. He climbed up on a house-sized boulder, using the projections and holes in it, hauling himself up with one hand. Later, he wondered why he'd gone up where he could be trapped. But he had been in a complete panic, and it had seemed a logical thing to do. Maybe no one would think of looking for him up there. He could lie down flat and hide until things settled down. If the boss won, he'd come down. He could claim then that he'd gone up there to get a bird's-eye view of the terrain so he could call out to Callister the location of his enemies.

Meanwhile, his beamer burned itself out, half-melting a large boulder fifty feet from it while doing so.

He saw Callister running toward the couple and another man, and he thought Callister had control of the situation. Then the red-haired Kickaha, who was lying on the ground, had said something to the woman. And she'd lifted a funny-looking trumpet to her lips and started blowing some notes. Callister had suddenly stopped, yelled something, and then he'd run like a striped-ass ape away from them.

And suddenly they were in *another* world. If things had been bad before, they were now about as bad as they could be. Well, maybe not quite as bad. At least, he was alive. But there had been times when he'd wished he wasn't.

So here he was, twelve "days" later. Much had been explained to him, mostly by Kickaha. But he still couldn't believe that Callister, whose real name was Urthona, and Red Orc and Anana were thousands of years old. Nor that they had come from another world, what Kickaha called a pocket universe. That is, an artificial continuum, what the science-fiction movies called the fourth dimension, something like that.

The Lords, as they called themselves, claimed to have made Earth.

Not only that, the sun, the other planets, the stars—which weren't really stars, they just looked like they were—the whole damn universe.

In fact, they claimed to have created the ancestors of all Earth people in laboratories.

Not only that—it made his brain bob up and down, like a cork on an ocean wave—there were many artificial pocket universes. They'd been constructed to have different physical laws than those on Earth's universe.

Apparently, some ten thousand or so years ago, the Lords had split. Each had gone off to his or her own little world to rule it. And they'd become enemies, out to get each other's ass.

Which explained why Urthona and Orc, Anana's own uncles, had tried to kill her and each other.

Then there was Kickaha. He'd been born Paul Janus Finnegan in 1918 in some small town in Indiana. After World War II, he'd gone to the University of Indiana as a freshman, but before a year was up, he was involved with the Lords. He'd first lived on a peculiar world he called the World of Tiers. There he'd gotten the name of Kickaha from a tribe of Indians that lived on one level of the planet, which seemed to be constructed like the Tower of Babel or the leaning tower of Pisa. Or whatever.

Indians? Yes, because the Lord of that world, Jadawin, had populated various levels with people he'd abducted from Earth.

It was very confusing. Jadawin hadn't always lived on the home planet of the Lords or in his own private cosmos. For a while he'd been a citizen of Earth, and he hadn't even known it because of amnesia. Then . . . to hell with it. It made McKay's head ache to think about it. But someday, when there was time enough, if he lived long enough, he'd get it all straightened out. If he wasn't completely nuts before then.

4

KICKAHA SAID, "I'M A HOOSIER APPLE KNOCKER, ANGUS. SO I'm going to get us some fresh fruit. But I need your help. We can't get close because of those tentacles. However, the tree has one weak point in its defense. Like a lot of people, it can't keep its mouth shut.

"So, I'm going to shoot an arrow into its mouth. It may not kill it, but it's going to hurt it. Hopefully, the impact will knock it over. This bow packs a hell of a wallop. As soon as the thing's hit, you run up and throw this ax at a branch. Try to hit a cluster of apples if you can. Then I'll decoy it away from the apples on the ground."

He handed Anana's light throwing ax to McKay.

"What about those?" McKay said, pointing at three trees that were only twenty feet below their intended victim. They were coming slowly but steadily.

"Maybe we can get their apples, too. We need that fruit, Angus. We need the nourishment, and we need the water in them."

"You don't have to explain that," McKay said.

"I'm like the tree. I can't keep my mouth shut," Kickaha said, smiling.

He fitted an arrow to the string, aimed, and released it. It shot true, plunging deep into the O-shaped orifice. The plant had just raised the two tentacles to take another step upward and then to fall slightly forward to catch itself on the rubbery extensions. Kickaha had loosed the shaft just as it was off balance. It fell backward, and it lay on its hinder part. The tentacles threshed, but it could not get up by itself. The branches extending from its side prevented its rolling over even if it had been capable, otherwise, of doing so.

Kickaha gave a whoop and put a hand on McKay's shoulder.

"Never mind throwing the ax. The apples are knocked off. Hot damn!"

The three trees below it had stopped for a moment. They moved on up. There had not been a sound from their mouths, but to the two men, the many rolling eyes seemed to indicate some sort of communication. According to Urthona, however, the creatures were incapable of thought. But they did cooperate on an instinctual level, as ants did. Now they were evidently coming to assist their fallen mate.

Kickaha ran ahead of McKay, who had hesitated. He looked behind him. The two male Lords were standing about sixty feet above them. Anana, beamer in hand, was watching, her head moving back and forth to keep all within eye-range.

Urthona had, of course, told McKay to kill Anana and Kickaha if he ever got the chance. But if he hit the redhead from behind with the ax, he'd be shot down by Anana. Besides, he was beginning to think that he had a better chance of survival if he joined up with Anana and Kickaha. Anyway, Kickaha was the only one who didn't treat him as if he was a nigger. Not that the Lords had any feeling for blacks as such. They regarded *everybody* but Lords as some sort of nigger. And they weren't friendly with their own kind.

McKay ran forward and stopped just out of reach of a thrashing tentacle. He picked up eight apples, stuffing four in the pockets of his Levi's and holding two in each hand.

When he straightened up, he gasped. That crazy Kickaha had leaped onto the fallen tree and was now pulling the arrow from the hole. As he raised the shaft, its head dripping with a pale sticky fluid, he was enwrapped by a tentacle around his waist. Instead of fighting it, he rammed his right foot deep into the hole. And he twisted sideways.

The next moment he was flying backward toward McKay, flung by a convulsive motion of the tentacle, no doubt caused by intense pain.

McKay, instead of ducking, grabbed Kickaha and they both went down. The catcher suffered more punishment than the caught, but for a minute or more, they both lay on the ground, Kickaha on top of McKay. Then the redhead rolled off and got to his feet.

He looked down at McKay. "You okay?"

McKay sat up and said, "I don't think I broke anything."

"Thanks. If you hadn't softened my fall, I might have broken my back. Maybe. I'm pretty agile. Man, there's real power in those tentacles."

Anana was with them by then. She cried, "Are you hurt, Kickaha?"

"No. Black Angus here, he seems okay, too."

McKay said, "Black Angus? Why, you son of a bitch!"

Kickaha laughed. "It's an inevitable pun. Especially if you've been raised on a farm. No offense, McKay."

Kickaha turned. The three advance scouts were no closer. The swelling hill had steepened its slopes, making it even more difficult for them to maintain their balance. The horde behind them was also stalled.

"We don't have to retreat up the hill," Kickaha said. "It's withdrawing for us."

However, the slope was becoming so steep that if its rate of change continued, it would precipitate everybody to the bottom. The forty-five-degree angle to the horizontal could become ninety degrees within fifteen minutes.

"We're in a storm of matter-change," Kickaha said. "If it blows over quickly, we're all right. If not . . ."

The tree's tentacles were moving feebly. Apparently, Kickaha's foot had injured it considerably. Pale fluid oozed out of its mouth.

Kickaha picked up the ax that McKay had dropped. He went to the tree and began chopping at its branches. Two strokes per limb sufficed to sever them. He cut at the tentacles, which were tougher. Four chops each amputated these.

He dropped the ax and lifted one end of the trunk and swung it around so that it could be rolled down the slope.

Anana said, "You're wasting your energy."

Kickaha said, "Waiting to see what's going to happen burns up more energy. At this moment, anyway. There's a time for patience and a time for energy."

He placed himself at the middle of the trunk and pushed it. It began rolling slowly, picked up speed, and presently, flying off a slight hump, flew into a group of trees. These fell backward, some rolling, breaking their branches, others flying up and out as if shot out of a cannon.

The effect was incremental and geometrical. When it was done, at least five hundred of the things lay in a tangled heap in the ravine at the foot of the slope. Not one could get up by itself. It looked like the result of a combination of avalanche and flood.

"It's a log jam!" Kickaha said.

No log jam, however, on Earth featured the wavings of innumerable octopus-tentacles. Nor had any forest ever hastened to the aid of its stricken members.

"Birnham Wood on the march," Kickaha said.

Neither Anana nor McKay understood the reference, but they were too tired and anxious to ask him to explain it.

By now, the humans were having a hard time keeping from falling down the slope. They clung to the grass while the three advance guards slid down on their "backs" toward the mess in the hollow at the base.

"I'm getting down," Kickaha said. He turned and began sliding down on the seat of his pants. The others followed him. When the friction became too great on their buttocks, they dug in their heels to brake. Halfway down, they had to halt and turn over so their bottoms could cool off. Their trouser seats were worn away in several spots.

"Did you see that water?" Kickaha said. He pointed to his right.

Anana said, "I though I did. But I assumed it was a mirage of some sort."

"No. Just before we started down, I saw a big body of water that way. It must be about fifteen miles away, at least. But you know how deceiving distances are here."

Directly below them, about two hundred feet away, was the living log jam. The humans resumed their rolling but at an angle across the ever-steepening slope. McKay's helmet, Kickaha's bow and quiver, and Anana's beamer and ax, impeded their movements but they managed. They fell the last ten feet, landing on their feet or on all fours.

The trees paid them no attention. Apparently, the instinct to save their fellows was dominating the need to kill and eat. However, the plants were so closely spaced that there was no room for the five people to get through the ranks.

They looked up the hill. This side was vertical now and beginning to bulge at the top. Hot air radiated from the hill.

"The roots of the grass will keep that overhang from falling right away," Kickaha said. "But for how long? When it does come down, we'll be wiped out."

The plants moved toward the tangle, side by side, the tips of their branches touching. Those nearest the humans moved a little to their right to avoid bumping into them. But the outreaching tentacles made the humans nervous.

After five minutes, the apex of the hill was beginning to look like a mushroom top. It wouldn't be long before a huge chunk tore loose and fell upon them.

Anana said, "Like it or not, Kickaha, we have to use the beamer."

"You're thinking the same thing I am? Maybe we won't have to cut through every one between us and open ground. Maybe those things burn?"

Urthona said, "Are you crazy? We could get caught in the fire!"

"You got a better suggestion?"

"Yes. I think we should adjust the beamer to cutting and try to slice our way out."

"I don't think there's enough charge left to do that," Anana said. "We'd find ourselves in the middle of this mess. The plants might attack us then. We'd be helpless."

"Burn a couple," Kickaha said. "But not too near us."

Anana rotated the dial in the inset at the bottom of the grip. She aimed the weapon at the back of a tree five yards to her right. For a few seconds, there was no result. Then the bark began smoking. Ten seconds later, it burst into flames. The plant did not seem immediately aware of what was happening. It continued waddling toward the tangle. But those just behind stopped. They must have smelled the smoke, and now their survival instinct—or program—was taking over.

Anana set three others on fire. Abruptly, the nearest ranks behind the flaming plants toppled. Those behind them kept on moving, rammed into them, and knocked a number down.

The ranks behind these were stopped, their tentacles waving. Then, as if they were a military unit obeying a soundless trumpet call to retreat, they turned. And they began going as fast as they could in the opposite direction.

The blazing plants had stopped walking, but their frantically thrashing tentacles showed that they were aware of what was happening. The flames covered their trunks, curled and browned the leaves, shot off from the leaf-covered stems projecting from the tops of the trunks. Their dozen eyes burned, melted, ran like sap down the trunk, hissed away in the smoke.

One fell and lay like a Yule log in a fireplace. A second later, the other two crashed. Their legs moved up and down, the broad round heels striking the ground.

The stink of burning wood and flesh sickened the humans.

But those ahead of the fiery plants had not known what was happening. The wind was carrying both the smoke and the pheromones of panic away from them. They continued to the jam until the press of bodies stopped them. Those in the front ranks were trying to pull up the fallen, but the lack of room prevented them.

"Burn them all!" Red Orc shouted, and he was seconded by his brother, Urthona.

"What good would that do?" Kickaha said, looking disgustedly at them. "Besides, they do feel pain, even if they don't make a sound. Isn't that right, Urthona?"

"No more than a grasshopper would," the Lord said.

"Have you ever been a grasshopper?" Anana said.

Kickaha started trotting, and the others followed him. The passage opened was about twenty feet broad, widening as the retreaters moved slowly away. Suddenly, McKay shouted, "It's falling!"

They didn't need to ask what it was. They sprinted as fast as they could. Kickaha, in the lead, was quickly left behind. His legs still hurt, and the pain in his chest increased. Anana took his hand and pulled him along.

A crash sounded behind them. Just in front of them, a gigantic ball of greasy earth mixed with rusty grass blades had slammed into the ground. It was a piece broken off and thrown upward by the impact. It struck so closely that they could not stop. Both plunged into it and for a moment, felt the oily earth and the scratch of the blades. But the mass was soft enough to absorb the energy of their impact, to give way somewhat. It was not like running into a brick wall.

They got up and went around the fragment, which was about the size of a one-car garage. Kickaha spared a glance behind him. The main mass had struck only a few yards behind them. Sticking out of its front were a few branches, tentacles, and kicking feet.

They were safe now. He stopped, and Anana also halted.

The others were forty feet ahead of them, staring at the great pile of dirt that ringed the base of the hill. Even as they watched, more of the mushrooming top broke off and buried the previous fallen mass.

Perhaps a hundred of the trees had survived. They were still waddling away in their slow flight.

Kickaha said, "We'll snare us some of the trees in their rear ranks. Knock off some more apples. We're going to need them to sustain us until we can get to that body of water."

Though they were all shaken, they went after the trees at once. Anana threw her ax and McKay his helmet. Presently they had more fruit than they could carry. Each ate a dozen, filling their bellies with food and moisture.

Then they headed toward the water. They hoped they were going in the right direction. It was so easy to lose their bearings in a world of no sun and constantly changing landscape. A mountain used as a mark could become a valley within one day.

Anana, walking by Kickaha's side, spoke softly.

"Drop back."

He slowed down, with no reluctance at all, until the others were forty feet ahead. "What is it?"

She held up the beamer so that he could see the bottom of the grip. The dial in the inset was flashing a red light. She turned the dial, and the light ceased.

"There's just enough charge left for one cutting beam lasting three seconds at a range of sixty feet. Of course, if I just use mild burning or stun power, the charge will last longer."

"I don't think they'd try anything against us if they did know about it. They need us to survive even more than we need them. But when—if— we ever find Urthona's home, then we'd better watch our backs. What bothers me is that we may need the beamer for other things."

He paused and stared past Anana's head.

"Like them."

She turned her head.

Silhouetted on top of a ridge about two miles away was a long line of moving objects. Even at this distance and in this light, she could see that they were a mixture of large animals and human beings.

"Natives," he said.

5

THE THREE MEN HAD STOPPED AND WERE LOOKING SUSPI-
ciously at them. When the two came up to them, Red Orc greeted them.

"What the hell are you two plotting?"

Kickaha laughed. "It's sure nice traveling with you paranoiacs. We were
discussing that," and he pointed toward the ridge.

McKay groaned and said, "What next?"

Anana said, "Are all the natives hostile to strangers?"

"I don't know," Urthona said. "I do know that they all have very strong
tribal feelings. I used to cruise around in my flier and observe them, and
I never saw two tribes meet without conflict of some kind. But they have
no territorial aggressions. How could they?"

Anana smiled at Urthona. "Well, Uncle, I wonder how they'd feel if you
were introduced to them as the Lord of this world. The one who made this
terrible place and abducted their ancestors from Earth."

Urthona paled, but he said, "They're used to this world. They don't
know any better."

"Is their lifespan a thousand years, as on Jadawin's world?"

"No. It's about a hundred years, but they don't suffer from disease."

"They must see us," Kickaha said. "Anyway, we'll just keep on going in
the same direction."

They resumed their march, occasionally looking at the ridge. After two
hours, the caravan disappeared over the other side. The ridge had not
changed shape during that time. It was one of the areas in which topolog-
ical mutation went at a slower rate.

"Night" came again. The bright red of the sky became streaked
with darker bands, all horizontal, some broader than others. As the
minutes passed, the bands enlarged and became even darker. When
they had all merged, the sky was a uniform dull red, angry-looking, menacing.

They were on a flat plain, extending as far as they could see. The mountains had disappeared, though whether because they had collapsed or because they were hidden in the darkness, they could not determine. They were not alone. Nearby, but out of reach, were thousands of animals: many types of antelopes, gazelles, a herd of the tuskless elephants in the distance, a small group of the giant moosoids.

Urthona said that there must also be big cats and wild dogs in the neighborhood. But the cats would be leaving, since they had no chance of catching prey on this treeless plain. There were smaller felines, a sort of cheetah, that could run down anything but the ostrich-like birds. None of these were in sight.

Kickaha had tried to walk very slowly up to the antelopes. He'd hoped they would not be alarmed enough to move out of arrow range. They didn't cooperate.

Then, abruptly, a wild chittering swept down from some direction, and there was a stampede. Thousands of hooves evoked thunder from the plain. There was no dust; the greasy earth just did not dry enough for that, except when an area was undergoing a very swift change and the heat drove the moisture out of the surface.

Kickaha stood still while thousands of running or bounding beasts raced by him or even over him. Then, as the ranks thinned, he shot an arrow and skewered a gazelle. Anana, who'd been standing two hundred yards away, ran toward him, her beamer in hand. A moment later, he saw why she was alarmed. The chittering noise got louder, and out of the darkness came a pack of long-legged baboons. These were truly quadrupedal, their front and back limbs of the same length, their "hands" in nowise differentiated from their "feet."

They were big brutes, the largest weighing perhaps a hundred pounds. They sped by him, their mouths open, the wicked-looking canines dripping saliva. Then they were gone, a hundred or so, the babies clinging to the long hair on their mothers" backs.

Kickaha sighed with relief as he watched the last merge into the darkness. According to Urthona, they would have no hesitation in attacking humans under certain conditions. Fortunately, when they were chasing the antelopes, they were single-minded. But if they had no success, they might return to try their luck with the group.

Kickaha used his knife to cut up the gazelle. Orc said, "I'm getting sick of eating raw meat! I'm very hungry, but just thinking about that bloody mess makes my stomach boil with acid!"

Kickaha, grinning, offered him a dripping cut.

"You could become a vegetarian. Nuts to the nuts, fruits to the fruits, and a big raspberry to you."

McKay, grimacing, said, "I don't like it either. I keep feeling like the stuff's alive. It tries to crawl back up my throat."

"Try one of these kidneys," Kickaha said. "They're really delicious. Tender, too. Or you might prefer a testicle."

"You really are disgusting," Anana said. "You should see yourself, the blood dripping down your chin."

But she took the proffered testicle and cut off a piece. She chewed on it without expression.

Kickaha smiled. "Not bad, eh? Starvation makes it taste good."

They were silent for a while. Kickaha finished eating first. Belching, he rose with his knife in his hand. Anana gave him her ax, and he began the work of cutting off the horns of the antelope. These were slim straight weapons two feet high. After he had cut them off from the skull, he stuck them in his belt.

"When we find some branches, we'll make spear shafts and fix these at their tips."

Something gobbled in the darkness, causing all to get to their feet and look around. Presently the gobbling became louder. A giant figure loomed out of the dark-red light. It was what Kickaha called a "moa," and it did look like the extinct New Zealand bird. It was twelve feet high and had rudimentary wings, long thick legs with two clawed toes, and a great head with a beak like a scimitar.

Kickaha threw the antelope's head and two of its legs as far as he could. The lesser gravity enabled him to hurl them much farther than he could have on Earth. The huge bird had been loping along toward them. When the severed pieces flew through the air, it veered away from them. However, it stopped about forty feet away, looked at them with one eye, then trotted up to the offerings. After making sure that the humans were not moving toward it, it scooped up the legs between its beaks, and it ran off.

Kickaha picked up a foreleg and suggested that the others bring along a part, too. "We might need a midnight snack. I wouldn't recommend eating the meat after that. In this heat, meat is going to spoil fast."

"Man, I wish we had some water," McKay said. "I'm still thirsty, but I'd like to wash off this blood."

"You can do that when we get to the lake," Kickaha said. "Fortunately, the flies are bedding down for the night. But if morning comes before we get to the water, we're going to be covered with clouds of insects."

They pushed on. They thought they'd covered about ten miles from the hill. Another two hours should bring them to the lake, if they'd estimated its distance correctly. But three hours later, by Anana's watch, they still saw no sign of water.

"It must be farther than we thought," Kickaha said. "Or we've not been going in a straight line."

The plain had begun sinking in along their direction of travel. After the first hour, they were in a shallow depression four feet deep, almost a mile wide, and extending ahead and behind as far as they could see. By the end of the second hour, the edges of the depression were just above their heads. When they stopped to rest, they were at the bottom of a trough twelve feet high but now only half a mile wide.

Its walls were steep, though not so much they were unclimbable. Not yet, anyway.

What Kickaha found ominous was that all the animal life, and most of the vegetable life, had gotten out of the depression.

"I think we'd better get our tails up onto the plain," he said. "I have a funny feeling about staying here."

Urthona said, "That means walking just that much farther. I'm so tired I can hardly take another step."

"Stay here then," the redhead said. He stood up. "Come on, Anana."

At that moment, he felt wetness cover his feet. The others, exclaiming, scrambled up and stared around. Water, looking black in the light, was flowing over the bottom. In the short time after they'd become aware of it, it had risen to their ankles.

"Oh-oh!" Kickaha said. "There's an opening to the lake now! Run like hell, everybody!"

The nearest bank was an eighth of a mile, six hundred and sixty feet away. Kickaha left the antelope leg behind him. The quiver and bow slung over his shoulder, the strap of the instrument case over the other, he ran for the bank. The others passed him, but Anana, once more, grabbed his hand to help him. By the time they had gotten halfway to safety, the stream was up to their knees. This slowed them down, but they slogged through. And then Kickaha, glancing to his left, saw a wall of water racing toward them, its blackish front twice as high as he.

Urthona was the first to reach the top of the bank. He got down on his knees and grabbed one of McKay's hands and pulled him on up. Red Orc grabbed at the black's ankle but missed. He slid back down the slope, then scrambled back up. McKay started to reach down to help, but Urthona spoke to him, and he withdrew his hand.

Nevertheless, Orc climbed over the edge by himself. The water was now up to the waists of Kickaha and Anana. They got to the bank, where she let go of his hand. He slipped and fell back but was up at once. By now, he could feel the ground trembling under his feet, sonic forerunners of the vast oncoming mass of water.

He grabbed Anana's legs, boosted her on up, and then began climbing after her. She grabbed his left wrist and pulled. His other hand clutched the grass on the lip of the bank, and he came on up. The other three were standing near her, watching them keenly. He cursed them because they'd not tried to help.

Orc shrugged. Urthona grinned. Suddenly, Urthona ran at Orc and pushed him. Orc screamed and fell sideways. McKay deftly pulled the beamer from Anana's belt. At the same time, he pushed with the flat of his hand against her back. Shrieking, she, too, went into the stream.

Urthona whirled and said, "The Horn of Shambarimen! Give it to me!"

Kickaha was stunned at the sudden sequence of events. He had expected treachery, but not so soon.

"To hell with you!" he said. He had no time to look for Anana, though he could hear her nearby. She was yelling and, though he couldn't see her, must be climbing up the bank. There wasn't a sound from Red Orc.

He lifted the shoulder strap of the instrument case holding the Horn and slipped it down his arm. Urthona grinned again, but he stopped when Kickaha held the case over the water.

"Get Anana up here! Quickly! Or I drop this!"

"Shoot him, McKay!" Urthona yelled.

"Hell, man, you didn't tell me how to operate this thing!" McKay said.

"You utter imbecile!"

Urthona leaped to grab the weapon from the black man. Kickaha swung the instrument case with his left hand behind him and dropped it. Hopefully, Anana would catch it. He dived toward McKay, who, though he didn't know how to fire the beamer, was quick enough to use it as a club. Its barrel struck Kickaha on top of his head, and his face smacked into the ground.

Half-stunned, he lay for a few seconds, trying to get his legs and arms moving. Even in his condition, he felt the earth shaking under him. A roaring surged around him, though he did not know if that was the flood or the result of the blow.

It didn't matter. Something hit his jaw as he began to get up. The next he knew, he was in the water.

The coldness brought him somewhat out of his daze. But he was lifted up, then pushed down, totally immersed, fighting for breath, trying to swim. Something smashed into him—the bottom of the channel, he realized dimly—and then he was raised again. Tumbling over and over, not knowing which way was up or down, and incapable of doing anything about it if he had known, he was carried along. Once more he was brought hard against the bottom. This time he was rolled along. When he thought that he could no longer hold his breath—his head roared, his lungs ached for air, his mouth desperately wanted to open—he was shot upward.

For a moment, his head cleared the surface and he sucked in air. Then he was plunged downward and something struck his head.

6

KICKAHA AWOKE ON HIS BACK. THE SKY WAS BEGINNING TO TAKE
on horizontal bands of alternating dark-red and fiery-red. It was "dawn."
    He was lying in water that rose halfway up his body. He rolled over and
got to all fours. His head hurt abominably, and his ribs felt as if he'd gone
twelve rounds in a boxing match. He stood up, weaving somewhat, and
looked around. He was on shore, of course. The roaring wave had carried
him up and over the end of the channel and then retreated, leaving him
here with other bodies. These were a dozen or so animals that had not gotten out of the channel in time.
    Nearby was a boulder, a round-shaped granite rock the size of a house.
It reminded him of the one in the clearing in Anana's world. In this world
there were no rock strata such as on Earth. But here were any number of
small stones and occasionally boulders, courtesy of the Lord of the lavalite
planet, Urthona.
    He remembered Anana's speculation that some of these could conceal
"gates." With the proper verbal or tactile code, these might be opened to
give entrance into Urthona's castle somewhere on this world. Or to other
pocket universes. Urthona, of course, would neither verify nor deny this
speculation.
    If he had the Horn of Shambarimen, he could sound the sequence of
seven notes to determine if the rock did contain a gate. He didn't have it.
It was either lost in the flood or Anana had gotten up the bank with it. If
the latter had happened, Urthona now had the Horn.
    A mile beyond the boulder was a mountain. It was conical, the side
nearest him lower than the other, revealing a hollow. It would not be a volcano, since these did not exist here. At the moment, it did not seem to be
changing shape.
    There were tall hills in the distance, all lining the channel. Most of the
plain was gone, which meant that the mutations had taken place at an accelerating speed.

His bow and quiver were gone, torn from him while he was being scraped against the channel bottom. He still had his belt and hunting knife, however.

His shirt was missing. The undershirt was only a rag. His trousers had holes and rips, and his shoes had departed.

Woozily, he went to the edge of the water and searched for other bodies. He found none. That was good, since it gave him hope, however slight, that Anana had survived. It wasn't likely, but if he could survive, she might.

Though he felt better, he was in no mood to whistle while he worked. He cut a leg off an antelope and skinned it. Hordes of large black greenheaded flies settled on the carcass and him and began working. The bite of one fly was endurable, but a hundred at once made him feel as if he were being sandpapered all over. However, as long as he kept moving, he wasn't covered by them. Every time he moved an arm or turned his head or shifted his position, he was relieved of their attack. But they zoomed back at once and began crawling, buzzing, and biting.

Finally, he was able to walk off with the antelope leg over one shoulder. Half of the flies stayed behind to nibble on the carcass. The others decided after a while that the leg he carried was more edible and also not as active. Still, he had to bat at his face to keep them from crawling over his eyes or up his nose.

Kickaha vented some of his irritation by cursing the Lord of this world. When he'd made this world and decreed its ecosystems, did he have to include flies?

It was a question that had occurred more than once to the people of Earth.

Despite feeling that he'd had enough water to last him a lifetime, he soon got thirsty. He knelt down on the channel-bank and scooped up the liquid. It was fresh. According to Urthona, even the oceans here were drinkable. He ate some meat, wishing that he could get hold of fruit or vegetables to balance his diet.

The next day, some mobile plants came along. These were about six feet high. Their trunks bore spiral red and white and blue stripes, and some orange fruit dangled from their branches. Unlike the plants he'd encountered the day before, these had legs with knees. They lacked tentacles, but they might have another method of defense.

Fortunately, he was cautious about approaching them. Each plant had a large hole on each side, situated halfway down the length. He neared one that was separated from the others, and as he did so, it turned to present one of the holes. The thing had no eyes, but it must have had keen hearing. Or, for all he knew, it had a sonic transceiver, perhaps on the order of a bat's.

Whatever its biological mechanisms, it turned as he circled it. He took a few more steps toward it, then stopped. Something dark appeared in the hole, something pulsed, then a black-red mass of flesh extruded. In the center was a hole, from which, in a few seconds, protruded a short pipe of cartilage or bony material.

It looked too much like a gun to him. He threw himself down on the ground, though it hurt his ribs and head when he did so. There was a popping sound, and something shot over his head. He rolled to one side, got up, and ran after the missile. It was a dart made of bone, feathered at one end, and sharp enough to pierce flesh at the other. Something green and sticky coated the point.

The plants were carnivorous, unless the compressed-air propelled dart was used only for self-defense. This didn't seem likely.

Staying out of range, Kickaha moved around the plants. The one who'd shot at him was taking in air with loud gulping sounds. The others turned as he circled.

They had neither eyes nor tentacles. But they could "see" him, and they must have some way of getting the meat of their prey into their bodies for digestion. He'd wait and find out.

It didn't take long. The plants moved up to the now-rotting carcasses of the antelopes and gazelles. The first to get there straddled the bodies and then sat down on them. He watched for a while before he understood just how they ate. A pair of flexible lips protruded from the bottom of the trunks and tore at the meat. Evidently, the lips were lined with tiny but sharp teeth.

Urthona had not mentioned this type of flesh-eating tree. Maybe he hadn't done so because he was hoping that Kickaha and Anana would venture within range of the poison-tipped darts.

Kickaha decided to move on. He had recovered enough to walk at a fairly fast pace. But first he needed some more weapons.

It wasn't difficult to collect them. He would walk to just within range of a plant, run toward it a few steps, and then duck down. The maneuvers caused him some pain, but they were worth it. After collecting a dozen darts, he cut off a piece of his trousers with his knife, and wrapped the missiles in it. He stuck the package in his rear pocket, and waving a jaunty thanks to the plants, started along the channel.

By now, the area was beginning to fill up with animals. They'd scented the water, come running, and were drinking their fill. He went around a herd of thirty elephants that were sucking up the water into their trunks, then squirting it into their mouths. Some of the babies were swimming around and playing with each other. The leader, a big mother, eyed him warily but made no short threatening charges.

These tuskless pachyderms were as tall as African elephants but longer-legged and less massively bodied.

A half an hour later, he came across a herd attacking a "grove" of the missile-shooting plants. These spat the tiny darts into the thick hides of the elephants, which ignored them. Apparently the poison did not affect them. The adults rammed into the plants, knocked them over, and then began stripping the short branches with their trunks. After that, the plants were lifted by the trunks and stuck crosswise into the great mouths. The munching began, the giant molars crushing the barky bodies until they were severed. The elephants then picked up one of the sections and masticated this. Everything, the vegetable and the protein parts, went down the great throats.

The young weaned beasts seized the fallen parts and ate these.

Some of the plants waddled away unpursued by the elephants. These became victims to a family of the giant moosoids, which also seemed impervious to the darts' poison. Their attackers, which looked like blue-haired, antlerless Canadian moose, tore the fallen plants apart with their teeth.

Kickaha, who was able to get closer to them than to the pachyderms, noted that the moosoids were careful about one thing. When they came to an organ that he supposed contained the darts, they pushed it aside. Everything else, including the fleshy-looking legs, went into their gullets.

Kickaha waited until he could grab one of the sacs. He cut it open and found a dozen darts inside it, each inside a tubule. He put these into the cloth, and went on his way.

Several times, families of lion-sized rusty-colored saber-tooth cats crossed his path. He discreetly waited until they had gone by. They saw him but were not, for the moment at least, interested in him. They also ignored the hoofed beasts. Evidently, their most immediate concern was water.

A pack of wild dogs trotted near him, their red tongues hanging out, their emerald eyes glowing. They were about two and a half feet tall, built like cheetahs, spotted like leopards.

Once he encountered a family of kangaroo-like beasts as tall as he. Their heads, however, looked like those of giant rabbits and their teeth were rodentine. The females bore fleshy hair-covered pouches on their abdomens; the heads of the young "rabaroos" stuck out of the pouches.

He was interested in the animal life, of course. But he also scanned the waterway. Once he thought he saw a human body floating in the middle of the channel, and his heart seemed to turn over. A closer look showed that it was some kind of hairless water animal. It suddenly disappeared, its bilobed tail resembling a pair of human legs held close together. A moment later, it emerged, a wriggling fish between long-whiskered jaws. The prey had four short thick legs, the head of a fish, and the vertical tail fins of a fish. It uttered a gargling sound.

Urthona had said that all fish were amphibians, except for some that inhabited the stable sea lands.

All life here, except for the grass, was mobile. It had to be to survive. An hour later, one of the causes for the locomotive character of life on this world rose above the horizon. The reddish temporary moon moved slowly but when fully in view, filled half of the sky. It was not directly overhead, being far enough away for Kickaha to see it edge-on. Its shape was that of two convex lenses placed back to back. A very extended oval. It rotated on its longitudinal axis so slowly that it had not traversed more than two degrees in a horizontal circle within two hours.

Finally, Kickaha quit watching it.

Urthona had said that it was one of the very small split-offs. These occurred after every twelve major split-offs. Though it looked huge, it was actually very small, not more than a hundred kilometers long. It seemed so big because it was so close to the surface.

Kickaha's knowledge of physics and celestial objects was limited to what he'd learned in high school, plus some reading of his own. He knew, however, that no object of that mass could go slowly in an orbit so near the planet without falling at once. Not in Earth's universe.

But his ideas of what was possible had been greatly extended when he had been gated into Jadawin's world many years ago. And now that he was in Urthona's world, he was getting an even broader education. Different arrangements of space-matter, even of matter-energy conversion, were not only possible, they'd been realized by the Lords.

Someday, Terrestrials, if they survived long enough, would discover this. Then their scientists would make pocket universes in bubbles in space-matter outside of yet paradoxically within Earth's universe. But that would come after the shock of discovering that their extra-solar system astronomy was completely wrong.

How long would it be before the secondary returned to the primary? Urthona couldn't say; he'd forgotten. But he had said that the fact that they'd seen it every other day meant that they must be near the planet's north pole. Or perhaps the south pole. In any event, the split-off was making a spiral orbit that would carry it southward or northward, as the case might be.

That vast thing cruising through the skies made Kickaha uneasy. It would soon fall to the main mass. Perhaps its orbit would end in one more passage around the planet. When it came down, it would do so swiftly. Urthona has said that he did remember that, once it came within twelve thousand feet of the surface, it descended at about a foot every two seconds. A counterrepulsive force slowed its fall so that its impact would not turn it and the area beneath and around it into a fiery mass. Indeed, the final moment before collision could be termed an "easing" rather than a crash.

But there would be a release of energy. Hot air would roar out from the fallen body, air hot enough to fry any living thing fifty miles away. And there would be major earthquakes.

There would be animals and birds and fish and plants on the moon, life forms trapped on it when the split-off occurred. Those on the underside would be ground into bits and the bits burned. Those on the upper surface would have a fifty-fifty chance of surviving, if they weren't near the edges.

Urthona had said, however, that the split-off masses never fell in the neighborhood of the oceans. These were in a relatively stable area; the changes in the land surrounding them were slower.

Kickaha hoped that he was near one of the five oceans.

Of all the manifestations of life, the aerial was the most noticeable. He had passed at least a million birds and winged mammals, and the sky was often blackened by flocks that must have numbered hundreds of thousands. These included many birds that had surely been brought in from Earth. There were some, also, that looked just like those he'd known in Jadawin's world. And many were so strange, often grotesque, that he supposed their ancestors had been made in Urthona's biolabs.

Wherever they came from, they were a noisy bunch—as on Earth. Their cawings, croakings, screams, pipings, warblings, whistlings, chatterings filled the air. Some were fish-eaters, either diving into the water from a height or surface swimmers that plunged after fish or froglike creatures. Others settled down on the elephants and moosoids and pecked at parasites. Others picked food from the teeth of enormous crocodiloids. Many settled down on the branches of various plants and ate the fruit or seeds. The trees did not object to this. But sometimes the weight of the birds was so heavy that a plant would fall over, and the birds, squawking and screaming, would soar up from the fallen plant like smoke from a burning log.

The tentacled plants would hasten to lift their helpless fellows upright again. The untentacled were left to their fate. More often than not, this meant being devoured by the pachyderms and moosoids.

Three hours passed, and the menacing mass above him became tiny. It was the only thing on this world that threw a shadow, and even that was pale compared to the shades of Earth. Physically pale, that is. The emotional shadow it cast, the anxiety and near-panic, was seldom matched by anything in Kickaha's world. A smoking volcano, a violent earthquake, a roaring hurricane were the only comparable events.

However, he had carefully observed the reactions of the birds and animals while it was overhead. They didn't seem to be disturbed by it. This meant to him they somehow "knew" that it posed no threat. Not, at least, this time.

Had Urthona given them the instinctive mechanism to enable them to predict the area in which the split-off would fall? If he had, then that meant that there was a pattern to the splitting-off and the merging of the bodies. However, what about those creatures not made in his biolabs: those that had been brought in from other universes? They hadn't been here long enough for evolution to develop any such instinctive knowledge.

Maybe the importees observed the natives and took their cue from these.

He would ask Urthona about that when he found him. If he found him. Shortly before he killed him.

Kickaha cut off some slices of the antelope leg, and brushing away the flies, ate the meat. It was getting strong, so he threw the rest of the limb away after his belly was satisfied. A number of scarlet crows settled down on it at once. These had gotten no more than a few pieces when two large purple green-winged eagles with yellow legs drove them off.

Watching them made him wonder where birds laid their eggs. In this world, no nest would be safe. A cranny in a mountainside could be closed up or on a plain in a few days.

He had plenty of time to observe, to get the answers to his questions about the zoology of this world. If he lived long enough.

"Day" passed while he walked steadily along the edge of the channel. Near "dusk" it had begun widening. He drove off some birds from some fruit fallen from a plant and ate the half-devoured "papayas." In the middle of the "night," some smaller varieties of the rabaroos hopped by him, two long-legged baboons after them. He threw his knife into the neck of a rabaroo male as it went by. The creature fell over, causing the baboons to return for this easier prey. Kickaha pulled the knife out and threatened the primates. They barked and showed their wicked-looking canines. One tried to get behind him while the other made short charges at him.

Kickaha didn't want to tangle with them if he could help it. He cut off the legs of the rabaroo and walked away, leaving the rest to the baboons. They were satisfied with the arrangement.

Finding a safe place to sleep was almost impossible. Not only was the night alive with prowling predators, but the spreading water was a menace. Twice he awoke inches deep in it and had to retreat several hundred feet to keep from drowning. Finally, he walked to the base of the nearest mountain, which had been only a hill when he had first sighted it. There were several large boulders on its slope. He lay down just above one. When the slope got too steep, the boulder would roll. The movement would awaken him—he hoped. Also, most of the action seemed to be taking place in the valley. The big cats, dogs, and baboons were out, trying to sneak up on or run down the hoofed and hopping beasts.

Kickaha awoke frequently as roars, barks, growls, and screams came up from the valley. None of them seemed to be near, though. Nor was he sure that he hadn't dreamed some of the noises.

Shortly before "dawn," he sat up, gasping, his heart thudding. There was a rumbling noise. Earthquake? No, the ground was not trembling. Then he saw that the boulder had rolled away. It wasn't the only one. About half a dozen were hurtling down the slope, which was even steeper now, shooting off swellings, thumping as they hit the surface again, gathering speed, headed toward the valley floor.

That floor, however, was now all water. The only beasts there were a few big cats, up to their bellies in water, staying only to eat as much of their kills as possible before they were forced to take off. There were millions of birds, though, among them an estimated two hundred thousand long-legged flamingos, green instead of pink like their Terrestrial counterparts. They were eating voraciously in the boiling water. Boiling not with heat, but with life. Fish by the millions.

It was time to get up even if he had not had enough rest. The slope was tilting, so that he would soon be sent rolling down it.

He scrambled down and went into the water up to his knees and then got down and drank from it. It was still fresh, though muddied by all the activity. One of the flamingos came scooting through the water, following a trail of something fleeing under the surface. It stopped when Kickaha rose, and it screamed angrily. He ignored it and plunged his knife down. Its point went into the thing the flamingo had been chasing. He brought up a skewered thing which looked like a mud puppy. It did not taste like mud puppy, however. It had a flavor of trout.

Apparently, the water level was not going to rise higher. Not for a while, anyway. After filling his belly and washing his body, he slogged through knee-deep water along the base of the mountain. In an hour, he'd gotten by that and was walking on a plain. About "noon," the plain was tilting to one side, about ten degrees to the horizontal, and the water was running down it. Three hours later, it was beginning to tilt the other way. He ate the rest of the mud puppy and threw the bones, with much meat attached, on the ground. Scarlet crows settled down on it to dispute about the tidbits.

The split-off had not appeared again. He hoped that when it did fall, it would be far, far away from him. It would form an enormous pile, a suddenly born mountain range of super-Himalayan proportions, on the surface. Then, according to Urthona, within several months, it would have merged with the larger mass, itself changing shape during the process.

Some months later, another split-off would occur somewhere else. But this would be a major one. Its volume would be about one-sixteenth of that of the planet.

God help those caught on it at liftoff. God help those on it when it returned to the mother planet.

One-sixteenth of this world's mass! A wedge-shaped mass the thin end of which would rip out of the planet's center. Roughly, over 67,700,000,000 cubic kilometers.

He shuddered. Imagine the cataclysms, the earthquakes, the staggeringly colossal hole. Imagine the healing process as the walls of the hole slid down to fill it and the rest of the planet moved to compensate. It was unimaginable.

It was a wonder that any life at all remained. Yet there was plenty.

Just before "dusk," he came through a pass between two monolithic mountains that had not changed shape for a day. The channel lay in its center, the surface of the water a few inches below the tops of the banks. There was room on both sides of the channel for ten men abreast. He walked along the channel, looking now and then at the towering wall of the mountain on the right.

Its base curved slowly, the channel also curving with it. He didn't want to settle down for the night, since there was little room to avoid any of the big predators. Or, for that matter, to keep from being trampled if a herd of the hoofed beasts was stampeded.

He pushed on, slowing now and then to get as near the mountain as possible, when big cats or wild dogs came along. Fortunately, they paid him no attention. It could be that they had run into human beings before and so dreaded them. Which said much for the dangerousness of Homo sapiens here. Probably, though, they found him to be a strange thing and so were wary.

In any event, they might not be able to resist the temptation to attack him if they found him sleeping on the ground. He pushed on. By dawn, he was staggering with weariness. His legs hurt. His belly told him it needed more food.

Finally, the mountain ceased. The channel ran almost straight for as far as he could see. He had a great plain to cross before reaching a row of conical mountains in the far distance. There were many plants here, few of them now moving, and herds of animals and the ubiquitous birds. At the moment, all seemed peaceful. If there were predators, they were quiet.

He wondered how long the channel was from its beginning to its end. He'd assumed that the flood had carried him for perhaps ten miles. By now, it was apparent that he could have been borne for fifty miles. Or more.

The earth had suddenly split on a straight line as if the edge of an ax of a colossus bigger than a mountain had smashed into the ground. Water had poured from the sea into the trench, and he'd been carried on its front to the end of the channel and deposited there. He was very lucky not to have been ground into bits on the bottom or drowned.

No, he hadn't experienced great luck. He'd experienced a miracle.

He left the mountain pass and started across the plain. But he stopped after a hundred yards. He turned toward the hoofbeats that had suddenly alerted him.

Around the corner of the mountain to his right, concealed until then by a bulge of the mountain wall, came a score of moosoids. Men were mounted on them, men who carried long spears.

Aware that he now saw them, they whooped and urged their beasts into a gallop.

For him to run was useless. They also serve who only stand and wait. However, this wasn't a tennis match.

7

THE MOOSOIDS WERE OF THE SMALLER VARIETY, A TRIFLE larger than a thoroughbred horse. Like their wild cousins, they were of different colors; roan, black, blue, chestnut, and piebald. They were fitted with reins, and their riders were on leather saddles with stirrups.

The men were naked from the waist up, wearing leather trousers that kept their legs from chafing. Some of them had feathers affixed to their long hair, but they were not Amerindians. Their skin was too light, and they were heavily bearded. As they got close enough, he saw that their faces bore tribal scars.

Some of the spears were poles the ends of which had been sharpened and fire-hardened. Others were tipped with flint or chert or antelope horns or lion teeth. There were no bows, but some carried stone axes, and heavy war boomerangs in the belts at their waists. There were also round leather-covered shields, but these hung from leather strings tied to the saddles. Evidently they thought they didn't need them against Kickaha. They were right.

The first to arrive halted their beasts. The others spread out and around him.

Their chief, a gray-haired stocky man, urged his animal closer to Kickaha. The moosoid obeyed, but its wide rolling eyes showed it didn't like the idea.

By then, the main body of the tribe was beginning to come from around the bend of the mountain. They consisted of armed outriders and a caravan of women, children, dogs, and moosoids drawing travois on which were piled heaps of skins, gourds, wood poles, and other materials.

The chief spoke to Kickaha in an unknown language. Of course. Not expecting them to understand him, Kickaha used test phrases in twenty different languages: Lord, English, French, German, Tishquetmoac, Hrowakas, the degraded High German of Dracheland, several Half-Horse

Lakota dialects, a Mycenaean dialect, and some phrases of Latin, Greek, Italian, and Spanish he knew.

The chief didn't understand any of them. That was to be expected, though Kickaha had hoped that if their ancestors came from Earth, they might speak a tongue that he at least could identify.

One good thing had happened. They hadn't killed him at once.

But they could intend to torture him first. Knowing what the tribes on the Amerind level of Jadawin's world did to their captives, he wasn't very optimistic.

The chief waved his feathered spear and said something to two men. These got down off their beasts and approached him warily. Kickaha smiled and held out his hands, palms up.

The two didn't smile back. Their spears ready for thrusting, they moved toward him slowly.

If Kickaha had been in his usual excellent physical condition, he would have tried to make a run for the nearest moosoid with an empty saddle. Even then, he would have had only one chance in twenty of fighting his way through the ring. The odds had been heavier against him in past situations, but then he had felt capable of anything. Not now. He was too stiff and too tired.

Both men were shorter than he, one being about five feet six inches tall and the other about an inch higher. The bigger man held his spear in one hand while the other reached out. Kickaha thought that he wanted him to hand his knife to him.

Shrugging, Kickaha slowly obeyed. There was a second when he thought of throwing the knife into the man's throat. He could grab the spear, snatch the knife out, run for . . . no, forget it.

The man took the knife and backed away. It was evident from his expression, and those of the others, that he had never seen metal before.

The chief said something. The man ran to him and gave him the knife. The gray-headed graybeard turned it over, gingerly felt its edge with his palm, and then tried it on a leather string holding his warshield.

All exclaimed when the string fell apart so easily.

The chief asked Kickaha something. Probably he wanted to know where his captive had gotten it.

Kickaha wasn't backward about lying if it would save his life. He pointed at the mountains toward which he had been traveling.

The chief looked as if he were straining his mind. Then he spoke again, and the two dismounted men tied Kickaha's hands in front of him with a leather cord. The chief spoke again, and the scouts moved on ahead. The chief and the two aides got down off their beasts and waited. In about fifteen minutes, the front of the caravan caught up with them.

The chief seemed to be explaining the situation to his people, making frequent gestures with his spear toward the direction indicated by his captive. There was a babel of excited talk then. Finally, the chief told them to shut up. During this, Kickaha had been counting the tribe. Including the scouts, there were about ninety. Thirty men, forty women, and twenty children.

The latter ranged from several babes in arms to preadolescents. The women, like the men, were black- or brown-haired. The general eye color was a light brown. Some had hazel; a few, blue eyes. Some of the women weren't bad-looking. They wore only short kilts of tanned leather. The children were naked and, like their elders, dirty. All stank as if they'd been bathless for a month or so.

Some of the beasts of burden, however, carried big water skins of water. A woman milked a cow during the brief stop.

The travois, in addition to the piles of skins and weapons, carried a form of pemmican. There were no tents, which meant that when it rained, the tribe just endured it.

While several men pointed spears at him, he was stripped by others. The chief was given the ragged Levi's and worn boots. From his expression and the tones of his voice, he had never seen anything like them before. When he tried to put on the Levi's, he found that his wide buttocks and bulging paunch would not accommodate them. He solved this problem by slitting them with the knife around the waist. The boots were too large for his feet, but he wore them anyway.

Finding the package of poison darts in the rear pocket of the Levi's, he passed them out to men whose spears lacked flint or chert tips. These tied the darts on the ends with rawhide cords and then had a good time play-jabbing at each other, laughing as they leaped away.

The only possessions left to Kickaha were his holey and dirty jockey shorts.

A big female moosoid was pulled out from the herd, fitted with reins and a saddle, and Kickaha was urged to mount it. He did so, holding the reins in his hands. The chief then said something, and a man tied the ends of a long thong under the beast's belly to Kickaha's ankles. The caravan started up then, an old woman—the only old person he saw—blowing a strange tune on a flute made from a long bone. Probably it was the leg bone of a moa.

The ride lasted about an hour. Then the tribe camped—if you call such a simple quick procedure camping—by the channel. While Kickaha sat on the animal, ignored by everybody except a single guard, the people took their turn bathing.

Kickaha wondered if they meant to keep him on the moosoid until they moved on. After half an hour, during which time he was savagely bitten by a horde of blue flies, his guard decided to untie the leg thongs. Kickaha got down stiffly and waited. The guard leaned on his spear, waiting until he was relieved to take a bath.

Kickaha gestured that he would like a drink of water. The guard, a slim youth, nodded. Kickaha went to the edge of the channel and got down on his knees to scoop up water with his hands. The next moment, he was in the water, propelled by a kick on his buttocks.

He came up to find everybody laughing at this splendid joke.

Kickaha swam forward until his feet touched the bottom. He turned around and cast one longing glance at the other side. It lay about three hundred feet away. He could get over to the opposite shore even with his hands tied before him. His pursuers could swim or ride across on swimming beasts. But he could beat them. If only there had been a wood nearby or a mountain, he would have tried for escape. However, there was a plain about two miles broad there. His captors would ride him down before he got to it.

Reluctantly, he hauled himself onto the bank. He stood up, looking expressionlessly at the youth. That one laughed and said something to the others, and they broke into uproarious laughter. Whatever it was he said, it wasn't complimentary to the prisoner.

Kickaha decided he might as well start his language lessons now. He pointed at the spear and asked its name. At first the youth didn't understand him. When he caught on, he said, *"Gabol."*

Gabol, as it turned out, was not a generic term. It meant a spear with a fire-hardened tip. A spear with a stone tip was a *baros;* with an antelope-horn tip, a *yava;* with a lion-tooth tip, a *grados.*

He learned later that there was no word for humankind. The tribe called itself by a word that meant, simply, The People. Other human beings were The Enemy. Children, whatever their sex, were summed under one word that meant "unformed." Adult males were distinguished by three terms: one for a warrior who had slain an enemy tribesman, one for a youth who had not yet been blooded, and a third for a sterile man. It made no difference if the sterile man had killed his enemy. He was still a *tairu.* If, however, he managed to steal a child from another tribe, then he was a full *wiru,* a blooded warrior.

Women were in three classes. If she had borne a child, she was in the top class. If she was sterile but had killed two enemies, male or female, she was in the second rank. If sterile and unblooded, she was a *shonka,* a name that originally was that of some kind of low animal.

Two days and nights passed while the tribe traveled leisurely along the channel. This was, except for the great conical mountains far ahead of them, the only permanent feature of the landscape. Sometimes it broadened and shallowed, sometimes narrowed and deepened. But it continued to run straight as an Indian chief's back for as far as the eye could see in either direction.

Hunting parties went out while the rest of the tribe either camped or moved at the rate of a mile an hour. Sometimes the younger women went with the men. Unlike the primitives who lived on the World of Tiers, the women of this tribe were not engaged from dawn to dusk in making artifacts, growing food, preparing meals, and raising children. They tended herd and shared the child-raising, and sometimes they fashioned wooden poles into spears or carved boomerangs. Otherwise, they had little to do. The stronger of the young women went hunting and, sometimes, on the raiding parties.

The hunters returned with antelope, gazelle, ostrich, and moa meat. Once a party killed a young elephant that had been separated from its herd. Then the tribe traveled two miles across the plain to the carcass. There they stripped it to the bone, gorging on the raw meat until their bellies looked like balloons.

The cutting of the meat was done with flint or chert knives. Kickaha would find out that these rare stones came from nodules that occasionally appeared when the earth opened up to deliver them. Except for the boulders, these were the only solid mineral known.

The diet included fruit and nuts from various trees. These were usually knocked off by the boomerangs as the hunters rode out of range of tentacle or dart.

Kickaha, though an enthusiastic and quick-learning linguist, took more than a week to master the rudiments of the tribe's speech. Though the tribe had a technology that an Ice Age caveman would have ranked as low, they spoke a complex language. The vocabulary was not great, but the shades of meaning, mostly indicated by subtle internal vowel changes, baffled his ear at first. It also had a feature he'd never encountered before. The final consonant of a word could alter the initial consonant of the succeeding word in a phrase. There was a rule to learn about this, but as in all living languages, the rule had many exceptions.

Besides, the possible combinations were many.

Kickaha thought he remembered reading something about a similar consonant change in the Celtic languages. How similar, he didn't know.

Sometimes he wondered if the Thana, as the tribe called itself, could be descended from ancient Celts. If they were, however, no modern Celt would have understood them. In the course of many thousand years, the speech must have changed considerably. A male moosoid, used for riding, for instance, was called a *hikwu*. Could that possibly be related to the ancient Latin *equus*? If he remembered his reading, done so many years ago, *equus* was related to a similar word in Celtic and also to the Greek *hippos*.

He didn't know. It didn't really matter, except as an item of curiosity. Anyway, why would the original tribe brought in here have named a moose after a horse? That could be because the *hikwu* functioned more like a horse than any animal the tribe had encountered.

During the day, Kickaha either rode, his hands bound, on a *merk*, a female riding-moosoid, or he lazed around camp. When he was in the saddle, he kept an eye out for signs of Anana. So far, he didn't know the language well enough to ask anybody if they had seen pale strangers like himself or a black man.

The tenth day, they came through a mountain pass that seemed to be a permanent feature. And there, beyond a long slope, beyond a broad plain, was the ocean.

The mountains on this side and the flat land were covered with permanently rooted trees. Kickaha almost cried when he saw them. They were over a hundred feet tall, of a score of genuses, plants like pines, oaks, cottonwoods, many fruit- and nut-bearing.

The first question occurring to him was: if this land was unchanging, why didn't the Thana put down their roots here? Why did they roam the ever-mutating country outside the ocean-ringing peaks?

On the way down, clouds formed, and before they were halfway down the slope, thunder bellowed. The Thana halted, and the chief, Wergenget, conferred with the council. Then he gave the order to turn about and pass beyond the mountains.

Kickaha spoke to Lukyo, a young woman whose personality, not to mention her figure, had attracted him.

"Why are we going back?"

Lukyo looked pale and her eyes rolled like a frightened horse's. "We're too early. The Lord's wrath hasn't cooled off yet."

At that moment, the first of the lightning struck. A tree two hundred feet away split down the middle, one side falling, one remaining upright.

The chief shouted orders to hurry up, but his urging wasn't needed. The retreat almost became a stampede. The moosoids bolted, riders frantically trying to pull them up, the travois bumping up and down, dislodging their burdens. Kickaha and Lukyo were left standing alone. Not quite. A six-year-old child was crying under a tree. Apparently she had wandered off for a minute, and her parents, who were mounted, were being carried off against their will.

Kickaha managed to pick up the little girl despite the handicap of his bound wrists. He walked as fast as he could with the burden while Lukyo ran ahead of him. More thunder, more strokes of lightning. A bolt crashed behind him, dazzling him. The child threw her arms around his neck and buried her face against his shoulder.

Kickaha swore. This was the worst lightning storm he had ever been in.

Yet, despite the danger of the bolts, he would have fled into it. It was his first good chance to escape. But he couldn't abandon the child.

The rain came then, striking with great force. He increased his pace, his head low while water poured over him as if he were taking a shower. The frequent bolts showed that Lukyo, propelled by fear, was drawing ahead of him. Even unburdened and in good physical condition, he might have had trouble keeping up with her. She ran like an Olympic champion.

Then she slipped and fell and slid facedown on the wet grass for a few feet uphill. She was up again. But not for long. A crash deafened him; whiteness blinded him. Darkness for a few seconds. A score or more of blasts, all fortunately not as near as the last bolt. He saw Lukyo down again. She was not moving.

When he got near her, he could smell the burnt flesh. He put the child down, though she fought against leaving him. Lukyo's body was burned black.

He picked up the little girl and began running as fast as he could. Then, out of the flickering checkerboard of day-turned-night, he saw a ghostly figure. He stopped. What the hell? All of a sudden he was in a nightmare. No wonder the whole tribe had fled in panic, forgetting even the child.

But the figure came closer, and now he saw that it was two beings. Wergenget on his *hikwu*. The chief had managed to get control of the beast, and he had come back for them. It must not have been easy for him to conquer his fear. It certainly was difficult for him to keep the moosoid from running away. The poor animal must have thought his master was mad to venture into that bellowing death-filled valley after having escaped from it.

Now Kickaha understood why Wergenget was the chief.

The graybeard stopped his beast, which trembled violently, its upper lip drawn back, its eyes rotating. Kickaha shouted at him and pointed at the corpse. Wergenget nodded that he understood. He lifted up the girl and placed her on the saddle before him. Kickaha fully expected him to take off then. Why should he risk his life and the child's for a stranger?

But Wergenget controlled the *hikwu* until Kickaha could get up behind the chief. Then he turned it and let it go, and the beast was not at all reluctant. Though burdened with the three, it made speed. Presently, they were in the pass. Here there was no rain; the thunder and the lightning boomed and exploded, but at a safe distance away.

8

Wergenget handed the child to its weeping, wailing mother. The father kissed his daughter, too, but his expression was hangdog. He was ashamed because he had allowed his fear to overcome him.

"We stay here until the Lord is through rampaging," the chief said.

Kickaha slid off the animal. Wergenget followed him. For a moment, Kickaha thought about snatching the knife from the chief's belt. With it, he could flee into a storm where no man dared venture. And he could lose himself in the forest. If he escaped being struck by lightning, he would be so far away the tribe would never find him.

But there was more to his decision not to run for it just now.

The truth was that he didn't want to be alone.

Much of his life, he'd been a loner. Yet he was neither asocial nor antisocial. He'd had no trouble mixing with his playmates, the neighboring farmers' children, when he was a child, nor with his peers at the country schoolhouse and community high school.

Because of his intense curiosity, athletic abilities, and linguistic ability, he'd been both popular and a leader. But he was a voracious reader and quite often, when he had a choice between recreation with others or reading, he decided on the latter. His time was limited because a farmer's son was kept very busy. Also, he studied hard to get good grades in school. Even at a young age, he'd decided he didn't want to be a farmer. He had dreams of traveling to exotic places, of becoming a zoologist or curator of a natural history museum and going to those fabulous places, deepest Africa or South America or Malaya. But that required a Ph.D., and to get that, he'd have to have high grades through high school and college. Besides, he liked to learn.

So he read everything he could get his hands on.

His schoolmates had kidded him about "always having his nose stuck in a book." Not nastily and not too jeeringly, since they respected his quick temper and quicker fists. But they did not comprehend his lust for learning.

An outsider, observing him from the age of seventeen through twenty-two, would not have known that he was often with his peers but not of them. They would have seen a star athlete and superior student who palled around with the roughest, raced around the country roads on a motorcycle, tumbled many girls in the hay, literally, got disgustingly drunk, and once was jailed for running a police roadblock. His parents had been mortified, his mother weeping, his father raging. That he had escaped from jail just to show how easy it was and then voluntarily returned to it had upset them even more.

His male peers thought this was admirable and amusing, his female peers found it fascinating though scary, and his teachers thought it alarming. The judge, who found him reading Gibbon's *Decline and Fall of the Roman Empire* in his cell, decided that he was just a high-spirited youth with much potentiality who'd fallen among evil companions. The charges were dropped, but Paul was put on unofficial probation by the judge. The young man gave his word that he would behave as a decent respectable citizen should—during the probation period, anyway—and he had kept his word.

Paul seldom left the farm during the probation period. He didn't want to be tempted into evil by those companions whose evil had mostly come from their willingness to follow him into it. Besides, his parents had been hurt enough. He worked, studied, and sometimes hunted in the woods. He didn't mind being alone for long periods. He threw himself into solitariness with the same zest he threw himself into companionship.

And then Mr. and Mrs. Finnegan, perhaps in an effort to straighten him out even more, perhaps in an unconscious desire to hurt him as he'd hurt them, revealed something that shocked him.

He was an adopted child.

Paul was stunned. Like most children, he had gone through a phase when he believed that he was adopted. But he had not kept to the fantasy, which children conceive during periods when they think their parents don't love them. But it was true, and he didn't want to believe it.

According to his stepparents, his real mother was an Englishwoman with the quaint name of Philea Jane Fogg-Fog. Under other circumstances, he would have thought this hilarious. Not now.

Philea Jane's parents were of the English landed gentry, though his great-grandfather had married a Parsi woman. The Parsis, he knew, were Persians who had fled to India and settled there when the Moslems invaded their homeland. So . . . he was actually one-eighth Indian. But it wasn't American Indian, among whom his stepmother counted ancestors.

It was Asiatic Indian, though only in naturalization. The Parsis usually did not marry their Hindu neighbors.

His mother's mother, Roxana Fogg, was the one who'd picked up the hyphenated name of Fogg-Fog. She'd married a distant relative, an American named Fog. A branch of the Foggs had emigrated to the colony of Virginia in the 1600s. In the early 1800s, some of their descendants had moved to the then-Mexican territory of Texas. By then, the extra "g" had been dropped from the family name. Paul's maternal grandfather, Hardin Blaze Fog, was born on a ranch in the sovereign state, the Republic of Texas.

Roxana Fogg had married an Englishman at the age of twenty. He died when she was thirty-eight, leaving two children. Two years later, she went with her son to Texas to look over some of the extensive ranch property he would inherit when he came of age. She also met some of the relatives there, including the famous Confederate war hero and Western gunfighter, Dustine "Dusty" Edward Marsden Fog. She was introduced to Hardin Blaze Fog, several years younger than herself. They fell in love, and he accompanied her back to England. She got the family's approval, despite his barbarian origins, since she announced she was going to marry him anyway and he was a wealthy shipping magnate. Blaze settled down in London to run the British office. When Roxana was forty-three years old, she surprised everybody, including herself, by conceiving. The baby was named Philea Jane.

Philea Jane Fogg-Fog was born in 1880. In 1900, she married an English physician, Doctor Reginald Syn. He died in 1910 under mysterious circumstances, leaving no children. Philea did not remarry until 1916. She had met in London a handsome well-to-do man from Indiana, Park Joseph Finnegan. The Foggs didn't like him because, one, he was of Irish descent, two, he was not an Episcopalian, and three, he had been seen with various ladies of the evening in gambling halls before he'd asked Philea to marry him. She married him anyway and went to Terre Haute, which her relatives thought was still subject to raids by the redskins.

Park Joseph Finnegan made Philea happy for the first six months, despite her difficulty in adjusting to a small Hoosier town. At least, she lived in a big house, and she suffered for no lack of material things.

Then life became hell. Finnegan resumed his spending of his fortune on women, booze, and poker games. Within a short time he'd lost his fortune, and when he found out his thirty-eight-year-old wife was pregnant, he deserted her. He announced he was going West to make another fortune, but she never heard from him again.

Too proud and too ashamed to return to England, Philea had gone to work as a housekeeper for a relative of her husband's. It was a terrible comedown for her, but she labored without complaint and kept a British stiff upper lip.

Paul was just six months old when the gasoline-burning apparatus used to heat an iron exploded in his mother's face. The house burned down, and the infant would have perished with his mother if a young man had not dashed in through the flames and rescued him.

The relative whose house had burned died of a heart attack shortly after. Paul was scheduled to go to an orphanage. But Ralph Finnegan, a cousin of Park's, a Kentucky farmer, and his wife decided to adopt Paul. His foster mother gave him her maiden family name, Janus, as his middle name.

The revelation had shaken Paul terribly. It was after this that he began to suffer from a sense of loneliness. Or perhaps a sense of having being abandoned. Once he'd learned all the details he wanted to know about his true parents, he never spoke of them again. When he mentioned his parents to others, he spoke only of the man and woman who'd reared him.

Two years after Kickaha learned about his true parents, Mr. Finnegan fell ill with cancer and died in six months. That was grief enough, but three months after the burial, his mother had also fallen victim to the same disease. She took a longer time dying, and now Paul had no time to do anything except farm, attend school, and help take care of her. Finally, after much pain, she had died, the day before he was to graduate from high school.

Mingled with his grief was guilt. In some mysterious fashion, he thought the shame they'd felt when he'd been arrested had caused the cancer. Considered rationally, the idea did not seem plausible. But guilt often had irrational origins. In fact, there were even times when he wondered if he hadn't somehow been responsible for his real father's having deserted his real mother and for her death.

His plans to go to college and major in zoology or in anthropology—he couldn't make up his mind—had been deferred. The farm had been mortgaged to pay for the heavy medical expenses of his parents, and Paul had to work the farm and take a part-time job in Terre Haute as a car mechanic. Nevertheless, despite the long hours of work, the lack of money, he had some time to express his innate exuberance. He would drop in occasionally at Fisher's Tavern, where some of the old gang still hung out. They'd go roaring off into the night on their motorcycles, their girls riding behind them, and finally end up in Indian Meadow, where there'd be a continuation of the beer blast and some fighting and lovemaking.

One of the girls wanted him to marry her, but he shied away from that. He wasn't in love with her, and he couldn't see himself spending the rest of his life with a woman with no intellectual interests whatever. Then she got pregnant, though fortunately not by him, and she departed to Chicago for a new life. Shortly thereafter, the gang began to drift apart.

He became alone and lonely again. But he liked to ride a horse wildly through the meadows or his chopper over the country roads. It was a good way to blow off steam.

Meantime, he had visits from an uncle who was a knife-thrower, juggler, and circus acrobat. Paul learned much from him and became proficient at knife-throwing. When he felt gloomy, he would go out into the backyard and practice throwing knives at a target. He knew he was working off his depression, guilt, and resentment at the lot cast for him by the fates with this harmless form of mayhem.

Five years went by swiftly. Suddenly, he was twenty-three. The farm still wasn't paid off. He couldn't see himself as a farmer for the rest of his life, so he sold the farm at a very small profit. But now it was evident that his hopes of entering college and becoming an anthropologist—he'd decided by then his choice of career—would once more have to be set aside. The United States would be getting into the war in a year or two.

Loving horses so much, he enlisted in the cavalry. To his surprise and chagrin, he soon found himself driving a tank instead. Then there was a three-months period in Officers' Candidate Training School. Though he wasn't a college graduate, he'd taken an examination that qualified him to enter it. Pearl Harbor tilted the nation into the conflict, and eventually he was with the Eighth Army and in combat.

One day, during a brief respite in the advance of Patton's forces, Paul had looked through the ruins of a small museum in a German town he'd helped clean out. He found a curious object, a crescent of some silvery metal. It was so hard that a hammer couldn't dent it or an acetylene torch melt it. He added it to his souvenirs.

Discharged from the Army, he returned to Terre Haute, where he didn't plan to stay long. A few days later, he was called into the office of his lawyer. To his surprise, Mr. Tubb handed him a check for ten thousand dollars.

"It's from your father," the lawyer said.

"My father? He didn't have a pot to pee in. You know that," Paul said.

"Not the man who adopted you," Mr. Tubb had said. "It's from your real father."

"Where is he?" Paul had said. "I'll kill him."

"You wouldn't want to go where he is," fat old Tubb said. "He's six feet under. Buried in a church cemetery in Oregon. He got religion years ago and became a fire-eating brimstone-drinking hallelujah-shouting revivalist. But the old bastard must've had some conscience left. He willed all his estate to you."

For a minute, Paul thought about tearing up the check. Then he told himself that old Park Finnegan owed him. Much more than this, true. But it was enough to enable him to get his Ph.D.

"I'll take it," he said. "Will the bank cash it if there's spit on it?"

"According to the law, the bank must accept it even if you crapped on it. Have a snort of bourbon, son."

Paul had entered the University of Indiana and rented a small but comfortable apartment off campus. He told a friend of his, a newspaper reporter, about the mysterious crescent he'd found in Germany. The story was in the Bloomington paper and picked up by a syndicate that printed it nationally. The university physicists, however, didn't seem interested in it.

Three days after the story appeared, a man calling himself Mr. Vannax appeared at Paul's apartment. He spoke English fluently but with a slight foreign accent. He asked to see the crescent; Paul obliged. Vannax became very excited, and he offered ten thousand dollars for the crescent. Paul became suspicious. He pumped the sum up to one hundred thousand dollars. Though Vannax was angry, he said he'd come back in twenty-four hours. Paul knew he had something, but he didn't know what.

"Make it three hundred thousand dollars, and it's yours," Paul said. "Since that's such a big sum, I'll give you an additional twenty-four hours to round up the money. But first, you have to tell me what this is all about."

Vannax became so troublesome that Paul forced him to leave. About two in the morning, he caught Vannax in his apartment. His crescent was lying on the floor, and so was another.

Vannax had placed the two so that their ends met, forming a circle. He was about to step into the circle.

Paul forced him away by firing a pistol over his head. Vannax backed away, babbling, offering Paul half a million dollars for his crescent.

Following him across the room, Paul stepped into the circle. As he did so, Vannax cried out in panic for him to stay away from the crescents. Too late. The apartment and Vannax disappeared, and Paul found himself in another world.

He was standing in a circle formed by crescents just like those he'd left. But he was in a tremendous palace, as splendid as anything out of the *Arabian Nights*. This was, literally, on top of the new world to which Paul had been transported. It was the castle of the Lord who'd made the universe of the World of Tiers.

Paul figured out that the crescents formed some sort of "gate," a temporary opening through what he called the "fourth dimension" for lack of a better term. Vannax, he was to discover, was a Lord who'd been stranded in Earth's universe. He'd had one crescent but needed another to make a gate so he could get into a pocket universe.

Paul soon found himself not alone. Creatures called gworls came through a gate. They'd been sent by a Lord of another world to steal the

Horn of Shambarimen. This was a device made ten millennia ago, when the pocket universes were just beginning to be created. Using it as a sort of sonic skeleton key, a person could unlock any gate. Paul didn't know this, of course, but while hiding, he saw a gworl open a gate to one of the tiers on this planet with the Horn. Paul pushed the gworl into a pool and dived through the gate with the Horn in his hand.

In the years that passed, as he traveled from level to level, the gworl trailing him, he became well acquainted with many sectors of this planet. On the Dracheland level, he took the disguise of Baron Horst von Horstmann. But it was on the Amerind level that he was Kickaha, the name he preferred to be known by. Paul Janus Finnegan was someone in his distant past. Memories of Earth grew dim. He made no effort to go back to his home universe. This was a world he loved, though its dangers were many.

Then an Earthman, Robert Wolff, retired in Phoenix, Arizona, was inspecting the basement of a house for sale when the wall opened. He looked into another world and saw Kickaha surrounded by some gworl who'd finally caught up with him. Kickaha couldn't escape through the gate, but he did throw the Horn through so that the gworl couldn't have it. Wolff might have thought he was crazy or hallucinating, but the Horn was physical evidence that he wasn't.

Wolff was unhappy; he didn't like his Earthly situation. So he blew the Horn, pressing on the buttons to make notes, and he went through the gate. He found himself on the lowest level of the planet, which looked at first like Eden. As time passed, he became rejuvenated, eventually attaining the body he had had when he was twenty-five.

He also fell in love with a woman called Chryseis. Pursued by the gworl, they fled to the next level, meeting Kickaha on the way. Finally, after many adventures, Wolff reached the palace on top of the world, and he discovered that he was Jadawin, the Lord who'd made this little universe.

Later, he and Chryseis were precipitated into a series of adventures in which he met a number of the Lords. He also had to pass through a series of pocket worlds, all of which were traps designed to catch and kill other Lords.

Meanwhile, Kickaha was engaged in a battle with the Bellers, creatures of artificial origin who could transfer their minds to the bodies of human beings. He also met and fell in love with Anana, a female Lord.

While chasing the last survivor of the Bellers, Kickaha and Anana were gated through to Earth. Kickaha liked Earth even less than he remembered liking it. It was getting overcrowded and polluted. Most of the changes in the twenty years since he'd left it were, in his opinion, for the worse.

Red Orc, the secret Lord of the Two Earths, found out that he and Anana were in his domain. Urthona, another Lord, stranded on Earth for some time, also became Kickaha's deadly enemy. Kickaha found out that Wolff, or Jadawin, and Chryseis were prisoners of Red Orc. But they'd escaped through a gate to the lavalite world. Now Jadawin and Chryseis were roaming somewhere on its ever-changing surface, if they were still alive. And he, Kickaha, had lost the Horn of Shambarimen and Anana. He'd never get out of this unpleasant nerve-stretching world unless he somehow found a gate. Finding it wasn't going to do him any good unless he had some open-sesame to activate the gate, though. And he couldn't leave then unless he found Anana, alive or dead.

For that matter, he couldn't leave until he found Wolff and Chryseis. Kickaha was a very bad enemy but a very good friend.

He had also always been extremely independent, self-assured, and adaptable. He'd lived for over twenty years without any roots, though he had been a warrior in the tribe of Hrowakas and thought of them as his people. But they were all gone now, slaughtered by the Bellers. He was in love with the beautiful Anana, who, though a Lord, had become more humane because of his influence.

For some time now, he'd been wanting to quit this wandering always-changing-identities life. He wanted to establish himself and Anana someplace, among a people who'd respect and maybe even love him. There he and Anana would settle down, perhaps adopt some children. Make a home and a family.

Then he'd lost her, and the only means he had to get out of this terrible place was also lost.

It was no wonder that Kickaha, the man sufficient unto himself, the ever-adaptable, the one who could find comfort even in hell, was now lonely.

This was why he suddenly decided to adopt the miserable wretches of the Thana as his people. If they'd have him.

There was also the desire not to be killed. But it was the wish to be part of a community that most strongly drove him.

9

IN HIS STILL LIMITED THANA, HE SPOKE TO WERGENGET OF THIS. The chief didn't look surprised. He smiled, and Kickaha saw in this a pleasure.

"You could have escaped us; you still could," Wergenget said. "I saw the intent in your face briefly, though it closed almost immediately, like a fist.

"I'll tell you, Kickaha, why you have lived so long among us. Usually, we kill an enemy at once. Or, if he or she seems to be a brave person, we honor him or her with torture. But sometimes, if the person is not of a tribe familiar to us, that is, not an old enemy, we adopt him or her. Death strikes often, and we don't have enough children to replace the enemies. Our tribe has been getting smaller for some time now. Therefore, I will decree that you be adopted. You have shown courage, and all of us are grateful that you saved one of our precious children."

Kickaha began to feel a little less lonely.

Several hours later, the storm ceased. The tribe ventured again into the valley and retrieved the body of Lukyo. She was carried into camp with much wailing by the women. The rest of the day was spent in mourning while her body, washed clean, her hair combed, lay on top of a pile of skins. At "dusk" she was carried on a litter borne on the shoulders of four men to a place a mile from the camp. Here her corpse was placed on the ground, and the shaman, Oshullain, danced around her, chanting, waving a three-tined stick in ritualistic gestures. Then, singing a sad song, the whole tribe, except for some mounted guards, walked back to the camp.

Kickaha looked back once. Vultures were gliding toward her, and a band of long-legged baboons was racing to beat them to the feast. About a quarter of a mile away, a pride of the maneless lions was trotting toward the body. Doubtless, they'd try to drive the baboons away, and there would be a hell of a ruckus. When the simians were in great numbers, they would harass the big cats until they forced them to abandon the meat.

On getting back to camp, the shaman recited a short poem he'd composed. It was in honor of Lukyo, and it was designed to keep her memory fresh among the tribe. It would be on everybody's lips for a while, then they'd cease singing it. And, after a while, she would be forgotten except in the memories of her child and parents. The child would forget, too, with the passage of time, and the parents would have other more pressing things to think about.

Only those who'd done some mighty deed still had songs sung about them. The others were forgotten.

The tribe stayed outside the lake country for another day. Wergenget explained that the storm season was almost always over by now. But it had been extended by the Lord, for some reason, and the tribe had made a fatal miscalculation.

"Or, perhaps," the chief said, "we have somehow offended the Lord, and he kept the lightning from going back to the heavens for a day."

Kickaha didn't comment on this. He was usually discreet about getting into arguments about religion. There was also no sense in offending the chief when it might make him change his mind about adopting him.

Wergenget called in the whole tribe and made a speech. Kickaha understood about half of the words, but the tones and the gestures were easily interpreted. Though the Lord had taken away Lukyo with one hand, he had given them Kickaha with the other. The tribe had offended the Lord. Or perhaps it was only Lukyo who had done this. In any event, the Lord still did not hate them altogether. By slaying Lukyo, the Lord had vented his wrath. To show the tribe that it was still in his favor, he'd sent Kickaha, a warrior, to the tribe. So it was up to the tribe to take him in.

The only one who objected to this was the youth, Toini, who had kicked Kickaha when he was bending over the channel. He suggested that perhaps the Lord wanted the tribe to sacrifice Kickaha to him. This, plus Lukyo's death, would satisfy the Lord.

Kickaha didn't know why Toini had it in for him. The only explanation was reactive chemistry. Some people just took an instant and unreasonable dislike to certain people in the first minute of acquaintanceship.

Toini's speech didn't exactly cause an uproar, but it did result in considerable loud argument. The chief was silent during the squabble, but apparently Toini had given him some doubts.

Kickaha, seeing that Toini might swing public opinion to his way of thinking, asked the chief if he could speak. Wergenget shouted for silence.

Kickaha, knowing that height gave a speaker a psychological advantage, mounted a *hikwu*.

"I wasn't going to say anything about a certain matter until after I was adopted by the tribe," he said. "But now I see that I must speak about it."

He paused and looked around as if he were about to reveal something that perhaps he shouldn't.

"But since there are some doubters of the Lord here, I believe that I should tell you about this now, instead of later."

They were hanging on his words now. His grave manner and the serious tones made them think that he knew something they should know about.

"Shortly before you came upon me," Kickaha said, "I met a man. He approached me, not walking, but gliding over the earth. He was in the air above the ground at twice my height."

Many gasped, and the eyes of all but Toini widened. His became narrow.

"The man was very tall, the tallest I've ever seen in my life. His skin was very white, and his hair was very red. And there was a glow about him as if he were wrapped in lightning. I waited for him, of course, since he was not the sort of person you would run away from or attack.

"When he was close to me, he stopped, and then he sank to the ground. I am a brave man, people of the Thana, but he frightened me. Also, he awed me. So I sank to my knees and waited for him to speak or to act. I knew that he was no ordinary man, since what man can float through the air?

"He walked up to me, and he said, 'Do not be afraid, Kickaha. I will not harm you. You are favored in my eyes, Kickaha. Rise, Kickaha.'

"I did as he ordered, but I was still scared. Who could this be, this stranger who soared like a bird and who knew my name, though I had never seen him before?"

Some in the crowd moaned, and others murmured prayers. They knew who this stranger was. Or at least they thought they did.

"Then the stranger said, 'I am the Lord of this world, Kickaha.'

"And I said, 'I thought so, Lord.'

"And he said, 'Kickaha, the tribe of the Thana will soon be taking you prisoner. If they are kind to you, then they will gain favor in my eyes, since I have in mind something great for you to do. You will be my servant, Kickaha, a tool to effect a deed which I wish to be done.'

" 'But if they try to kill or torture you, Kickaha, then I will know they are unworthy. And I will blast them all from the face of this earth. As a matter of fact, I will kill one of them as testimony that I am keeping an eye on them to demonstrate my power. If they are not convinced by this, then I will slay one more, the man who will try to keep you from being adopted by the tribe.' "

Toini had been grinning crookedly up to this moment. It was evident that he was going to denounce the captive as a prevaricator the moment he ceased speaking. But now he turned pale and began to shiver and his teeth started chattering. The others moved away from him.

The shaman was the only one who was looking doubtful. Perhaps, like

Toini, he thought that Kickaha was lying to save his neck. If so, he was waiting for more developments before he gave his opinion.

"So I said, 'I am grateful, Lord, that you are honoring me by using me
as your servant and tool. May I ask what task you have in mind for me?'

"And he said, 'I will reveal that to you in the proper time, Kickaha. In
the meantime, let us see how the Thana treat you. If they act as I wish, then
they will go on to great glory and will prosper and thrive as no other tribe
has ever done. But if they mistreat you, then I will destroy them, men,
women, children, and beasts. Not even their bones will be left for the scavengers to gnaw.'

"And then he turned and rose into the air and moved swiftly around the
side of the mountain. A few minutes later, you showed up. You know what
happened after that."

The effect of his lie was such that Kickaha almost began to believe in
it. The tribe surged around him, fighting to touch him as if to draw to
them the power he must have absorbed just by being close to the Lord.
And they begged him to consider them as his friends. When the shaman,
Oshullain, pushed through the mob and seized Kickaha's foot and held on
as if he were absorbing the power, Kickaha knew he'd won.

Then the chief said loudly, "Kickaha! Did the Lord say anything about
you leading us?"

Wergenget was concerned about his own position.

"No, the Lord did not. I believe that he just wanted me to take a place
in the tribe as a warrior. If he had wanted me to be chief, he would have
said so."

Wergenget looked relieved. He said, "And what about this wretch,
Toini, who said that perhaps you should be sacrificed?"

"I think he knows he was very wrong," Kickaha said. "Isn't that right,
Toini?"

Toini, on his knees, sobbing, said, "Forgive me, Kickaha! I didn't know
what I was doing."

"I forgive you," Kickaha said. "And now, Chief, what should we do?"

Wergenget said that since it was now obvious that the Lord was no
longer angry, it was safe to go into the sea-country. Kickaha hoped that the
thunderstorm season was indeed over. If another storm occurred, then
the tribe would know he'd been lying. Which meant it'd probably tear him
apart.

For the moment, he was safe. But if anything went wrong, if it became evident that the tribe wasn't favored by the Lord, then he'd have to
think up another lie fast. And if he wasn't believed, curtains for Kickaha.

Also, what if they should run into Urthona, the real Lord of this universe?

Well, he'd deal with that situation when it happened.

Anyway, if he saw any sign of Anana, any evidence that she was in the sea-land, he'd desert the Thana. It seemed to him that if she'd survived, she would have gone to this area. She'd know that if he'd lived, he would go there too.

Also, Urthona and McKay would go to where the land was relatively stable and where there'd be plenty of water. And where they were, the Horn would be.

He wondered if Orc had been caught in the flashflood that had carried him away. Or had he only been swept a little distance, enough to take him out of reach of Urthona and McKay?

Such thoughts occupied him until the caravan reached the sea. There they drank the water and let the moosoids satisfy their thirst. Some of the women and children gathered nuts and berries from the trees and bushes. The men waded around in the waves and jabbed their spears at the elusive fish. A few were successful.

Kickaha got a small portion of the raw fish, which he examined for worms before eating.

Then the Thana formed a caravan again and began the march over the white fine sand of the beach. They had come in on the right side of the channel, so they turned right. To cross the channel where it emerged from the sea, they would have had to swim a quarter mile of deep water. They passed many trees and animals felled by the lightning. The carcasses were covered with scaly amphibians, teeth flashing or dripping blood, tails flailing to sweep their competitors away, grunting and croaking, snapping. The birds were busy, too, and at many places, the uproar was almost deafening.

When the tribe came across a lightning-blasted female elephant and calf, it drove away the multitude of sea, land, and air life and carved up the bodies for itself. Kickaha took some large cuts but put off eating them. When "night" came, he piled branches and twigs to make a fire and he fashioned a bow-drill to start a fire. The others gathered around to watch. He worked away until the friction of the drill generated smoke, then added twigs and presently had a small fire going.

Kickaha borrowed a flint knife and cut off some smaller portions. After cooking a piece of leg and letting it cool off, he began eating as if he'd never stop. The chief and shaman accepted his invitation to dine. Though they were suspicious of cooked meat, their fears were overcome by the savory odors.

"Did the Lord teach you how to make that great heat?" Oshullian said.

"No. Where I come from, all people know how to make this . . . fire. We call it fire. In fact, your ancestors knew how to make fire. But you have forgotten how to do it.

"I think that your ancestors, when first brought here, must have wandered for many generations before finding a sea-land. By then, the scarcity of wood had made your people forget all about fire. Still, I can't understand why you didn't reinvent fire-making when you did find the sea-land, which has plenty of trees."

He didn't say that the most primitive of humans had had fire. Wergenget might have thought he was insulting him. Which he was.

He thought about Urthona. What a sadist he was. Why, if he had to make a world and then place humans on it, had he set up such a barebones world? The potentiality of Homo sapiens could not be realized if it had almost nothing to work with. Also, the necessity to keep on the move, the never-ending changing of the earth, the limiting of human activity to constant travel while at the same time seeking for food and water, had reduced them almost to the level of beasts.

Despite which, they were human. They had a culture, one that was probably more complex than he thought, the riches of which he would learn when he became proficient in the language and knew both the customs of the tribe and its individual members.

He said, "Fires are also good for keeping the big beasts away at night. I'll show you how to keep the fires fed."

The chief was silent for a while. Besides his food, he was digesting a new concept. It seemed to be causing him some mental unease. After a while, he said, "Since you are the favored of the Lord, and this tribe is to be yours, you wouldn't bring in any evil to us? Would you?"

Kickaha assured him that he wouldn't—unless the Lord told him to do so.

The chief rose from his squatting position and bellowed orders. In a short while, there were a dozen large fires around the perimeter of the camp. Sleep, however, didn't come easily to it. Some big cats and dogs, their eyes shining in the reflected light, prowled around the edges of the camp. And the Thana weren't sure that the fires wouldn't attack them after they went to sleep. However, Kickaha set an example by closing his eyes, and his simulated snores soon told everybody that he, at least, wasn't worried. After a while, the children slept, and then their elders decided that it was safe.

In the morning, Kickaha showed the women how to cook the meat. Half of the tribe took to the new way of preparing food with enthusiasm. The other half decided to stick to eating the meat raw. But Kickaha was certain that before long, the entire tribe, except for some dietary diehards, would have adapted.

He wasn't too sure, though, that he should have introduced cooking. When the storm season started again, the tribe would have to go outside the great valley again. Out there, because of the scarcity of the firewood, it would have to eat its meat raw again. They might become discontented, then resentful and frustrated, because they could do nothing to ease their discontent.

Prometheuses weren't always beneficial.

That was their problem. He didn't plan on being around when they left the valley.

In the "morning," the caravan went on the march again. Wergenget got them to moving faster than the day before. He was nervous because other tribes would be moving in, and he didn't want his to run into one on the beach. Near the end of the day, they reached their goal. This was a high hill about half a mile inland from the shore. Though it changed shape somewhat, like the rest of the land in the valley, it did so very slowly. And it always remained a hill, though its form might alter.

On its top was a jumble of logs. This had been the walls of a stockade the last time the tribe had seen it. The mutations of the hill had lifted the circular wall a number of times and had broken the vines that held it. The tribe set to work digging new holes with sticks and flint-tipped shovels, then reset the logs. Vines were cut and dragged in and bound to hold the logs together. By the end of the third day, the wooden fortress was restored. Within the walls were a number of lean-tos in which the families could take shelter from the rains, and sleep.

During the rest of the season, the tribe would stay in here at night. During the day, various parties would sally out to fish and hunt and gather nuts and berries. Look-outs would watch for dangerous beasts or the even more dangerous humans.

But, before they started to rest and get fat, it was necessary to initiate Kickaha into the tribe.

This was a great honor, but it was also rough on the initiate. After a long dance and recitation of numerous chants and songs, during which drums beat and bone flutes shrilled, the chief used a flint knife to cut the identification symbols of the tribe on Kickaha's chest. He was supposed to endure this without flinching or outcry.

Then he had to run a gauntlet of men who struck at him with long sticks. Afterward, he had to wrestle the strongest man in the tribe, Mekdillong. He'd recovered entirely from his injuries by then, and he knew a hundred tricks Mekdillong was ignorant of. But he didn't want to humiliate him, so he allowed it to appear that Mekdillong was giving him a hard time. Finally, tired of the charade, he threw Mekdillong through the air with a cross-buttock. Poor Mek, the wind knocked out of him, writhed on the ground, sucking for air.

The worst part was having to prove his potency. Impotent men were driven from the tribe to wander until they died. In Kickaha's case, since he was not of the tribe born, he would have been killed. That is, he would have been if it wasn't so evident that the Lord had sent him. But, as the chief said, if the Lord had sent him, then he wouldn't fail.

Kickaha didn't try to argue with this logic. But he thought that the custom was wrong. No man could be blamed for being nervous if he knew he'd be exiled or slain if he failed. The very nervousness would cause impotency.

At least, the Thana did not demand, as did some tribes, that he prove himself publicly. He was allowed to go into a lean-to surrounded by thick branches set upright into the ground. He chose the best-looking woman in the tribe for the test, and she came out several hours later looking tired but happy and announced that he'd more than passed the test.

Kickaha had some pangs of conscience about the incident, though he had enjoyed it very much. He didn't think that Anana would get angry about this trifling infidelity, especially since the circumstances were such that he couldn't avoid it.

However, it would be best not to mention this to her.

That is, if he ever found her.

That was the end of the trials. The chief and the shaman each chanted an initiation song, and then the whole tribe feasted until their bellies swelled and they could scarcely move.

Before going to sleep, Wergenget told Kickaha that he'd have to pick a wife from the eligible females. There were five nubiles, all of whom had stated that they would be happy to have him as a mate. Theoretically, a woman could reject any suitor, but in practice, it didn't work that way. Social pressure insisted that a woman marry as soon as she was of childbearing age. If any woman was lucky enough to have more than one suitor, then she had a choice. Otherwise, she had to take whoever asked her.

The same pressure was on a man. Even if he didn't care for any of the women available, he had to pick one. It was absolutely necessary that the tribe maintain its population.

Two of the five candidates for matrimony were pretty and well-figured. One of these was bold and brassy and looked as if she were brimming over with the juices of passion. So, if he had to take unto himself a wife, he'd choose her. It was possible she'd turn him down, but according to the chief, all five were panting for him.

Given his pick, he'd have wived the woman he'd proved his manhood on. But she was only borrowed for the occasion, as was the custom, and her husband would try to kill Kickaha if he followed up with a repeat performance.

As it was, the woman, Shima, could make trouble. She'd told Kickaha she'd like to get together with him again. There wasn't going to be much opportunity for that, since she couldn't disappear into the woods by herself without half the tribe knowing it.

Ah well, he'd deal with the various situations as they came along.

Kickaha looked around. Except for the sentinel on top of a platform on top of a high pole in the middle of the fort, and another stationed near the apex of the giant tree, the tribe was snoring. He could open the gate and get away and be long gone before the guards could rouse the others. In their present stuffed condition, they could never catch him.

At the same time he wanted to get out and look for Anana, he felt a counter-desire to stay with these people, miserable and wretched as they were. His moment of weakness, of longing for a home of some sort, still had him in its grip. Some moment! It could go on for years.

Logically, it was just as likely that if he stayed here, she'd be coming along. If he set out on a search, he could go in the wrong direction and have to travel the circuit of this body of water. It could be as big as Lake Michigan or the Mediterranean for all he knew. And Anana could be going in the same direction as he but always behind him. If she were alive . . .

One of these days, he'd have to leave. Meanwhile, he'd do some scouting around. He might run across some clues in this neighborhood.

He yawned and headed for the lean-to assigned him by the chief. Just as he got to it, he heard giggles. Turning, he saw Shila and Gween, his two top choices for wife. Their normally flat bellies were bulging, but they hadn't eaten so much they couldn't see straight. And they'd been pretending to be asleep.

Shila, smiling, said, "Gween and I know you're going to marry one of us."

He smiled and said, "How'd you know?"

"We're the most desirable. So, we thought maybe . . ." she giggled . . . "we'd give you a chance to see whom you like most. There'll never be another chance to find out."

"You must be joking," he said. "I've had a long hard day. The rites, the hours with Shima, the feast . . ."

"Oh, we think you have it in you. You must be a great *wiru*. Anyway, it can't hurt to try, can it?"

"I don't see how it could," Kickaha said, and he took the hand of each. "My place is rather exposed. Where shall we go?"

He didn't know how long he'd been sleeping when he was wakened by a loud hubbub. He rose on one elbow and looked around. Both girls were still sleeping. He crawled out and removed the brush in front of the lean-to and stood up. Everybody was running around shouting or sitting up and rubbing their eyes and asking what was going on. The man on top of the platform was yelling something and pointing out toward the sea. The sentinel in the tree was shouting.

Wergenget, his eyes still heavy with sleep, stumbled up to Kickaha. "What's Opwel saying?"

Kickaha said the sentinel's voice was being drowned out. Wergenget began yelling for everybody to shut up, and in a minute he'd subdued them. Opwel, able to make himself understood, relayed the message of the man in the tree.

"Two men and a woman ran by on the beach. And then, a minute later, warriors of the tribe of Thans came along after them. They seemed to be chasing the two men and the woman."

Kickaha hollered. "Did the woman have long hair as black as the wing of a crow?"

"Yes!"

"And was the hair of one man yellow and the other red?"

"Onil says one man had yellow hair. The other was black-skinned and his hair was the curliest he'd ever seen. Onil said the man was black all over."

Kickaha groaned, and said, "Anana! And Urthona and McKay!"

He ran for the gate, shouting, "Anana!"

Wergenget yelled an order, and two men seized Kickaha. The chief huffed and puffed up to him and, panting, said, "Are you crazy! You can't go out there alone! The Thans will kill you!"

"Let me loose!" Kickaha said. "That's my woman out there! I'm going to help her!"

"Don't be stupid," Wergenget said. "You wouldn't have a chance."

"Are you just going to sit here and let her be run down?" Kickaha yelled.

Wergenget turned and shouted at Opwel. He yelled at Olin, who replied. Opwel relayed the message.

"Onil says he counted twenty."

The chief rubbed his hands and smiled. "Good. We outnumber them." He began giving orders then. The men grabbed their weapons, saddled the moosoids, and mounted. Kickaha got on his own, and the moment the gate was open, he urged it out through the opening. After him came Wergenget and the rest of the warriors.

10

AFTER BEING KNOCKED INTO THE CHANNEL, ANANA HAD BEGUN scrambling back up. The water by then was to her breasts, but she clawed back up the side, grabbing the grass, pulling it out, grabbing more handfuls.

Above her were yells, and then something struck her head. It didn't hurt her much, didn't even cause her to lose her grip. She looked down to see what had hit her. The case containing the Horn of Shambarimen.

She looked toward the black wall of water rushing toward her. It would hit within ten seconds. Perhaps less. But she couldn't let the Horn be lost. Without it, their chances of ever getting out of this wretched world would be slight indeed.

She let herself slide back into the water and then swam after it. It floated before her, carried by the current of the stream rising ahead of the flash flood. A few strokes got her to it. Her hand closed around the handle, and she stroked with one hand to the bank. The level had risen above her head now, but she did not have to stand up. She seized a tuftful of grass, shifted the handle from hand to teeth, and then began climbing again.

By then, the ground was shaking with the weight of the immense body of water racing toward her. There was no time to look at it, however. Again she pulled herself up the wet slippery bank, holding her head high so the case wouldn't interfere with her arms.

But she did catch out of the corner of her eye a falling body. By then, the roar of the advancing water was too loud for her to hear the splash the body made. Who had fallen? Kickaha? That was the only one she cared about.

The next moment, the rumble and the roar were upon her. She was just about to shove the case over the edge of the bank and draw herself up after it when the mass struck. Despite her furious last-second attempt to reach safety, the surface waters caught her legs. And she was carried, crying out desperately, into the flood.

But she managed to hold on to the Horn. And though she was hurled swiftly along, she was not in the forefront of the water. She went under several times but succeeded in getting back to the surface. Perhaps the buoyancy of the case enabled her to keep to the surface.

In any event, something, maybe a current hurled upward by an obstruction on the bottom, sent her sprawling onto the edge of the bank. For a minute, she thought she'd slip back, but she writhed ahead and presently her legs were out of reach of the current.

She released the case and rolled over and got shakily to her feet.

About a half a mile behind her were three figures. Urthona. Orc. McKay.

Kickaha was missing. So, it would have been he who had fallen over into the stream. It also would have been he who'd dropped the Horn into it. She guessed that he must have threatened to throw it in if the others didn't allow her to get out of the channel again.

Then they'd rushed him, and he'd released it and gone into the stream after it. Either of his own volition, which didn't seem likely, or he had been pushed into it.

She could see no sign of him.

He was under the surface somewhere, either drowned or fighting.

She found it difficult to believe that he was dead. He'd come through so much, fought so hard, been so wily. He was of the stuff of survival.

Still, all men and women must die sometime.

No, she wouldn't allow herself to give up hope for him. But even if he were still struggling, he would by now have been swept out of sight.

The only thing to do was to follow the channel to its end and hope that she'd run across him somewhere along it.

Red Orc was by now running away. He was going at full speed in the opposite direction. McKay had run after him but had stopped. Evidently he either couldn't catch him or Urthona had called him back. Whatever had happened, the two were now trotting toward her. She had the Horn, and they wanted it.

She started trotting too. After a while, she was panting, but she kept on and her second wind came. If she stayed by the channel, she couldn't lose them. They'd keep going, though they had no chance with her head start of catching her. Not until utter fatigue forced her to sleep. If they somehow could keep on going, they'd find her.

She believed that she had as much endurance as they. They'd have to lie down and rest, too, perhaps before she did. But if they pushed themselves, rose earlier from sleep, then they might come across her while she slept.

As long as she followed the channel, she couldn't lose them, ever. But across the plains, in the mountains, she might. Then she could cut back to the channel.

There was a chance, also, that she could get lost, especially when the landmarks kept changing. She'd have to risk that.

She turned and started across the plain. Now they would angle across, reducing the lead she had. Too bad. Though she felt the urge to break into a run, she resisted it. As long as she could keep ahead, out of range of the beamer, she'd be all right.

It was difficult to estimate distances in this air, which was so clear because of the almost total lack of dust and because of this light. She thought the nearest of the mountains was about five miles away. Even with the speed with which the landscape changed around here, it would still be a respectably sized mountain by the time she got there.

Between her and her goal were groves of the ambulatory trees. None were so large that she couldn't go around them. There were also herds of grazing antelopes and gazelles. A herd of elephants was about a half a mile away, trotting toward the nearest grove. To her right, in the other direction, some of the giant moosoids were nearing another group of plants. She caught a glimpse of two lions a quarter of a mile away. They were using a grove as cover while sneaking up on some antelopes.

Far in the distance was the tiny figure of a moa. It didn't seem to be chasing anything, but her line of flight would lead her near to it. She changed it, heading for the other end of the base of the mountain.

She looked to her left. The two men were running now. Evidently they hoped to put on a burst of speed and make her run until she dropped.

She stepped up her pace but she did not sprint. She could maintain this pace for quite a while. Seldom in her many thousands of years of life had she gotten out of shape. She had developed a wind and endurance that would have surprised an Olympic marathoner. Whatever her physical potential was, she had realized it to the full. Now she'd find out what its limits were.

One mile. Two miles. She was sweating, but while she wasn't exactly breathing easy, she knew she had a lot of reserve wind. Her legs weren't leaden yet. She felt that she could reach the mountain and still have plenty of strength left. Her uncle was a strong man, but he was heavier, and he'd probably indulged himself on Earth. Any fat he'd had had been melted by their ordeal here, where food hadn't been plentiful. But she doubted that he'd kept himself in tip-top condition on Earth.

The black man was powerfully built, but he wasn't the long-distance-runner type. In fact, sparing a look back, she could see that he'd dropped behind Urthona. Not that her uncle had gained any on her.

The case and its contents, however, did weigh about four pounds. Needing every advantage she could get, she decided to get rid of some of it. She slowed down while she undid the clasps, removed the Horn, and dropped the case. Now, carrying the instrument in one hand, she increased her speed. In ten minutes, Urthona had lost fifty yards. McKay was even farther behind his boss now.

Another mile. Now she was wishing she could abandon the throwing ax and the knife. But that was out. She'd need both weapons when it came to a showdown. Not to mention that even if she got away from them, she had to consider the predators. A knife and an ax weren't much against a lion, but they could wound, perhaps discourage it.

Another half a mile. She looked back. Urthona was half a mile away. McKay was behind Urthona by a quarter of a mile. Both had slowed considerably. They were trotting steadily, but they didn't have a chance of catching her. However, as long as they kept her in sight, they wouldn't stop.

The lions had disappeared around the other side of the trees. These were moving slowly along, headed for the channel. The wind was blowing toward them, carrying molecules of water to their sensors. When they got to the channel, they would draw up along it in a row and extend their tentacles into the water to suck it up.

The antelopes and gazelles stopped eating as she approached, watched her for a moment, their heads up, black eyes bright, then bounded away as one. But they only moved to what they considered a safe distance and resumed grazing.

Anana was in the center of antelopes, with tall straight horns that abruptly curved at the tips, when they stampeded. She stopped and then crouched as big black-and-brown-checkered bodies leaped over her or thundered by. She was sure that she hadn't caused the panic. The antelopes had regarded her as not dangerous but something it was better not to let get too close.

Then she heard a roar, and she saw a flash of brownish-yellow after a half-grown antelope.

One lion had shot out of the trees after the young beast. The other was racing along parallel with its mate. It was somewhat smaller and faster. As the male cut off to one side, the female bent its path slightly inward. The prey had turned to its left to get away from the big male, then saw the other cat angling toward it. It turned away from the new peril and so lost some ground.

The male roared and frightened the antelope into changing its direction of flight again. The female cut in toward it; the poor beast turned toward the male. Anana expected that the chase would not last long. Either the cats would get their kill in the next few seconds or their endurance would peter out and the antelope would race away. If the quarry had enough sense just to run in a straight line, it would elude its pursuers. But it didn't. It kept zigzagging, losing ground each time, and then the female was on it. There was a flurry of kicking legs, and the creature was dead, its neck broken.

The male, roaring, trotted up, his sides heaving, saliva dripping from his fangs, his eyes a bright green. The female growled at him but backed off until he had disemboweled the carcass.

Then she settled down on the other side of the body, and they began tearing off chunks of meat. The herd had stopped running by then. Indifferent to the fate of the young beast, knowing that there was no more danger for the present, they resumed their feeding.

Anana was only forty feet away from the lions, but she kept on going. The cats wouldn't be interested in her unless she got too close, and she had no intention of doing that.

The trees were a species she'd not seen before. About twelve feet high, they had bark that was covered with spiraling white and red streaks like a barber pole. The branches were short and thick and sprouting broad heart-shaped green leaves. Each plant had only four "eyes," round, unblinking, multifaceted, green as emeralds. They also had tentacles. But they must not be dangerous. The lions had walked through them unharmed.

Or was there some sort of special arrangement between the cats and the trees? Had Urthona implanted in them an instinct mechanism that made them ignore the big cats but not people? It would be like her uncle to do this. He'd be amused at seeing the nomads decide that it was safe to venture among the trees because they'd seen other animals do so. And then, stepping inside the moving forest, suddenly find themselves attacked.

For a moment, she thought about taking a chance. If she plunged into that mobile forest, she could play hide-and-seek with her hunters. But that would be too risky, and she would really gain nothing by it.

She looked behind her. The two men had gained a little on her. She stepped up the pace of her trotting. When she'd passed the last of the trees, she turned to her left and went past their backs. Maybe Urthona and McKay would try to go through the trees.

No, they wouldn't. It was doubtful that her uncle would remember just what their nature was. He might think that she had taken refuge in them. So, the two would have to separate to make sure. McKay would go along one side and Urthona on the other. They'd look down the rows to make sure she wasn't there, and then would meet at the rear.

By then, keeping the trees between her and the others, moving in a straight line toward the mountain from the plants, she'd be out of their sight for a while. And they would lose more ground.

She turned and headed toward her goal.

But she slowed. A half a mile away, coming toward her, was a pack of baboons. There were twenty, the males acting as outriders, the females in the middle, some with babies clinging to their backs. Was she their prey? Or had they been attracted by the roaring of the lion and were racing to the kill?

She shifted the Horn to her left hand and pulled the ax from her belt. Her path and theirs would intersect if she kept on going. She stopped and waited. They continued on in the same direction, silently, their broad, short-digited paws striking the ground in unison as if they were trained soldiers on the march. Their long legs moved them swiftly, though they could not match the hoofed plains beasts for speed. They would pick out their prey, a young calf or an injured adult. They would spread out and form a circle. The leader would rush at the quarry, and the frenzied bounding and barking of the others would stampede the herd. The pack would dart in and out of the running, leaping antelopes, under their very hooves, often forced to jump sideways to avoid being trampled. But their general direction was toward their intended kill, and the circle would draw tighter. Suddenly, the running calf or limping adult would find itself surrounded. Several of the heavy powerful male simians would leap upon it and bring it to the ground. The others, excepting the mothers carrying infants, would close in.

Then, within twenty feet of her, the leader barked and the pack slowed down. Had their chief decided that she would be less trouble than running off two hungry lions?

No. They were still moving, heading toward the corner of the square formed by the marching plants.

She waited until the last of the pack was gone by, then resumed trotting.

There was a sudden commotion behind her. She slowed again and turned to one side so she could see what was going on. She didn't like what she saw. Urthona and McKay had burst out of the woods. They'd not circled the plants, as she'd expected, but had instead gone in a straight line through them. So, Urthona had remembered that these were no danger to human beings. Hoping to catch her by surprise, they'd probably run at top speed.

They'd succeeded. However, they were themselves surprised. They'd come out of the trees and run headlong into the baboons. The chief simian was hurling himself toward Urthona, and three big males were loping toward McKay.

Her uncle had no choice but to use his beamer. Its ray sliced the leader from top to bottom. The two halves, smoking, skidded to a halt several feet from him. If he'd been just a little slower reacting, he'd have found the baboon's teeth in his throat.

Too bad, thought Anana.

11

NOW HER UNCLE WAS BEING FORCED TO DISCHARGE EVEN MORE of the precious energy. McKay would be downed within a few seconds. The black was crouched, ready to fight, but he was also screaming at Urthona to shoot. Her uncle hesitated a second or two—he hated to use the beamer because he was saving its charges for his niece—but he did not want to be left alone to continue the chase. Three males tumbled over and over until they came to rest—or their halves did—just at McKay's feet. Under his dark pigment, McKay was gray.

The other baboons halted and began jumping up and down and screaming. They were only angry and frustrated. They wouldn't attack anymore.

She turned and began running again. A few minutes later, she looked back. Her pursuers were moving toward her slowly. They didn't dare run with their backs to the simians. These were following them at a respectable distance, waiting for a chance to rush them. Urthona was shouting and waving the beamer at them, hoping to scare them off. Every few seconds, he would stop and turn to face them. The baboons would withdraw, snarling, barking, but they wouldn't stop trailing them.

Anana grinned. She would get a big lead on the two men.

When she reached the foot of the mountain, which rose abruptly from the plain, she stopped to rest. By then, the baboons had given up. Another one of the pack lay dead, and this loss had made up their minds for them. Now some were gathered around the latest casualty and tearing him apart. The others were racing to see who could get to the remaining carcasses first. A half a mile away, a giant scimitar-beaked "moa" was speeding toward the commotion. It would attempt to scare the simians from a body. Above were vultures, hoping to get a share of the meat.

The slope here was a little more than a forty-five-degree angle to the horizontal. Here and there were swellings, like great gas bubbles pushing out the surface of the peak. She'd have to go around these. She began climbing, leaning forward slightly. There were no trees or bushes for her to hide among. She'd have to keep going until she got to the top. From there, she might be able to spot some kind of cover. It was doubtful that she would. But if she went down the other side swiftly enough, she might be able to get around the base of another mountain. And then her chasers wouldn't know where she was.

The peak was perhaps a thousand and a half feet above the plain. By the time she got there, she was breathing very heavily. Her legs felt as if they were thickly coated with cement. She was shaking with fatigue; her lungs seemed to burn. The two men would be in the same, if not worse, condition.

When she'd started ascending, the top of the peak had been as sharply pointed as the tip of an ice-cream cone. Now it had slumped and become a plateau about sixty feet in diameter. The ground felt hot, indicating an increase in the rate of shape-mutation.

Urthona and McKay were almost a quarter of the way up the slope. They were sitting down, facing away from her. Just above them, the surface was swelling so rapidly that they would soon be hidden from her sight. If the protuberance spread out, they'd have to go around it. Which meant they'd be slowed down even more.

Her view of the plain was considerably broader now. She looked along the channel, hoping to see a tiny figure that would be Kickaha. There was none.

Even from her height, she could not see the end of the channel. About twenty miles beyond the point at which she'd left it, young mountains had grown to cut off her view. There was no telling how far the channel extended.

Where was Red Orc? In all the excitement, she had forgotten about him.

Wherever he was, he wasn't visible to her.

She scanned the area beyond her perch. There were mountains beyond mountains. But between them were, as of now, passes, and here and there were ridges connecting them. On one of the ridges was a band of green, contrasting with the rusty grass. It moved slowly but not so much that she didn't know the green was an army of migrating trees. It looked as if it were five miles away.

Scattered along the slopes and in the valleys were dark splotches. These would be composed of antelopes and other large herbivores. Though basically plains creatures, they adapted readily to the mountains. They could climb like goats when the occasion demanded.

Having attained the top, should she wait a while and see what her pursuers would do? Climbing after her was very exhausting. They might think she'd try to double back on them, come down one side of the mountain, around the corner where they couldn't see her. That wasn't a bad idea.

If the two should split up, each going around the mountain to meet in the middle, then she'd just go straight back down as soon as they got out of sight.

However, if they didn't take action soon, she'd have to do so. The plateau was growing outward and downward. Sinking, rather. If she stayed here, she might find herself on the plain again.

No, that process would take at least a day. Perhaps two. And her uncle and his thug would be doing something in the meantime.

She began to get hungry and thirsty. When she'd started for the mountain, she'd hoped to find water on its other side. From what she could see, she was going to stay thirsty unless she went back to the channel. Or unless those wisps of clouds became thick black rainclouds.

She waited and watched. The edge of the plateau on which she sat slowly extended outward. Finally, she knew she had to get off it. In an hour or so, it would begin crumbling along its rim. The apex of the cone was becoming a pancake. She'd have a hard time getting off it without being precipitated down the slope with a piece of it.

There was an advantage. The two men below would have to dodge falling masses. There might be so many they'd be forced to retreat to the plain. If she were lucky, they might even be struck by a hurtling bounding clump.

She went to the other side—the diameter of the circle was now a hundred feet. After dropping the Horn and the ax, she let herself down cautiously. Her feet dangled for a moment, and she let loose. That was the only way to get down, even though she had to fall thirty feet. She struck the slope, which was still at a forty-five-degree angle, and slid down for a long way. The grass burned her hands as she grabbed handholds; the friction against the seat of her pants didn't make the cloth smoke. But she was sure that if she hadn't succeeded in stopping when she did, the fabric would have been hot enough to burst into flames. At least, she felt that it would.

After retrieving the Horn and ax, she walked down the slope, leaning back now. Occasionally her shoes would slip on the grass, and she'd sit down hard and slide for a few feet before she was able to brake to a stop. Once a mass of the dark greasy earth, grass blades sticking from it, thumped by her. If it had hit her, it would have crushed her.

Near the bottom, she had to hurry up her descent. More great masses were rolling down the slope. One missed her only because it struck a swelling and leaped into the air over her head.

Reaching the base, she ran across the valley until she was sure she was beyond the place where the masses would roll. By then, "night" had come.

She was so thirsty she thought she'd die if she didn't get water in the next half hour. She was also very tired.

There was nothing else to do but to turn back. She had to have water. Fortunately, in this light, she couldn't be seen by anybody a thousand feet from her. Maybe five hundred. So she could sneak back to the channel without being detected. It was true that the two men might have figured out she'd try it and be waiting on the other side of the mountain. But she'd force herself to take an indirect route to the channel.

She headed along the valley, skirting the foot of the mountain beyond that which she'd climbed. There were house-sized masses here also, these having fallen off the second mountain, too. Passing one, she scared something out that had been hiding under an overhang. She shrieked. Then, in swift reaction, she snatched out her ax and threw it at the long low scuttler.

The ax struck it, rolling it over and over. It got to its short bowed legs and, hissing, ran off. The blow had hurt it, though; it didn't move as quickly as before. She ran to her ax, picked it up, set herself, and hurled it again. This time, the weapon broke the thing's back.

She snatched out her knife, ran to the creature—a lizardlike reptile two feet long—and she cut its throat. While it bled to death, she held it up by its tail and drank the precious fluid pouring from it. It ran over her chin and throat and breasts, but she got most of it.

She skinned it and cut off portions and ate the still-quivering meat. She felt much stronger afterward. Though still thirsty, she felt she could endure it. And she was in better shape than the two men—unless they had also managed to kill something.

As she headed toward the plain, she was enshrouded in deeper darkness. Rain clouds had come swiftly with a cooling wind. Before she had gone ten paces onto the flatland, she was deluged. The only illumination was lightning, which struck again and again around her. For a moment, she thought about retreating. But she was always one to take a chance if the situation demanded it. She walked steadily onward, blind between the bolts, deaf because of the thunder. Now and then she looked behind her. She could see only animals running madly, attempting to get away from the deadly strokes but with no place to hide.

By the time she'd reached the channel, she was knee-deep in water. This increased the danger of being electrocuted, since a bolt did not now have to hit her directly. There was no turning back.

The side of the channel nearer her had lowered a few inches. The stream, flooding with the torrential downpour, was gushing water onto the plain. Four-legged fish and some creatures with tentacles—not large— were sliding down the slope. She speared two of the smaller amphibians with her knife and skinned and ate one. After cutting the other's head off and gutting it, she carried it by its tail. It could provide breakfast or lunch or both.

By then, the storm was over and within twenty minutes, the clouds had rushed off. Ankle-deep in water, she stood on the ridge and pondered. Should she walk toward the other end of the channel and look for Kickaha? Or should she go toward the sea?

For all she knew, the channel extended a hundred miles or more. While she was searching for her man, the channel might close up. Or it might broaden out into a lake. Kickaha could be dead, injured, or alive and healthy. If hurt, he might need help. If he was dead, she might find his bones and thus satisfy herself about his fate.

On the other hand, if she went to the mountain pass to the sea, she could wait there, and if he was able, he'd be along after a while.

Also, her uncle and the black man would surely go to the sea. In which case, she might be able to ambush them and get the beamer.

While standing in water and indecision, she had her mind made up for her. Out of the duskiness two figures emerged. They were too distant to be identified, but they were human. They had to be her pursuers.

Also, they were on the wrong side if she wanted to look for Kickaha. Her only path of flight, unless she ran for the mountains again, was toward the sea.

She set out trotting, the water splashing up to her knees. Occasionally, she looked back. The vague figures were drawing no closer, but they weren't losing ground either.

Time, unmeasured except by an increasing weariness, passed. She came to the channel, which had by now risen to its former height. She dived in, swam to the other side, and climbed up the bank. Standing there, she could hear Urthona and McKay swimming toward her. It would seem that she'd never been able to get far enough ahead of them to lose herself in the darkness.

She turned and went on toward the mountains. Now she was wolf-trotting, trotting for a hundred paces, then walking a hundred. The counting of paces helped the time to go by and took her mind from her fatigue. The men behind her must be doing the same thing, unable to summon a burst of speed to catch up with her.

The plain, now drained of water, moved squishily under her. She took a passage between the two mountains and emerged onto another plain. After a mile of this, she found another waterway barring her path. Perhaps, at this time, many fissures opened from the sea to the area beyond the ringing mountains to form many channels. Anyone high enough aboveground might see the territory as a sort of millipus, the sea and its circling mountains as the body, the waterways as tentacles.

This channel was only about three hundred yards across, but she was too tired to swim. Floating on her back, she propelled herself backward with an occasional hand stroke or up-and-down movement of legs.

When she reached the opposite side, she found that the water next to the bank came only to her waist. While standing there and regaining her wind, she stared into the darkness. She could neither see nor hear her pursuers. Had she finally lost them? If she had, she'd wait a while, then return to the first channel.

An estimated five minutes later, she heard two men gasping. She slid down until the water was just below her nose. Now she could distinguish them, two darker darknesses in the night. Their voices came clearly across the water to her.

Her uncle, between wheezes, said, "Do you think we got away from them?"

"Them?" she thought.

"Not so loud," McKay said, and she could no longer hear them.

They stood on the bank for a few minutes, apparently conferring. Then a man, not one of them, shouted. Thudding noises came from somewhere, and suddenly giant figures loomed behind the two. Her uncle and McKay didn't move for a moment. In the meantime, the first of the "day" bands paled in the sky. McKay, speaking loudly, said, "Let's swim for it!"

"No!" Urthona said. "I'm tired of running. I'll use the beamer!"

The sky became quickly brighter. The two men and the figures behind them were silhouetted more clearly, but she thought that she still couldn't be seen. She crouched, half of her head sticking out of the water, one hand hanging onto the grass bank, the other holding the Horn. She could see that the newcomers were not giants, but men riding moosoids. They held long spears.

Urthona's voice, his words indistinguishable, came to her. He was shouting some sort of defiance. The riders split, some disappearing below the edge of the bank. Evidently these were going around to cut off the flight of the two. The others halted along the channel in Indian file.

Urthona aimed the beamer, and the two beasts nearest him fell to the ground, their legs cut off. One of the riders fell into the channel. The other rolled out of sight.

There were yells. The beasts and their mounts behind the stricken two disappeared down the ridge. Suddenly, two came into sight on the other side. Their spears were leveled at Urthona, and they were screaming in a tongue unknown to Anana.

One of the riders, somewhat in the lead of the others, fell off, his head bouncing into the channel, his body on the edge, blood jetting from the neck. The other's beast fell, precipitating his mount over his head. McKay slammed the edge of a hand against his neck and picked up the man's spear.

Urthona gave a yell of despair, threw the beamer down, and retrieved the spear of the beheaded warrior.

The beamer's battery was exhausted. It was two against eight now, the outcome in no doubt.

Four riders came up onto the bank. McKay and Urthona thrust their spears into the beasts and then were knocked backward into the channel by the wounded beasts. The savages dismounted and went into the water after their victims. The remaining four rode up and shouted encouragement.

Anana had to admire the fight her uncle and his aide put up. But they were eventually slugged into unconsciousness and hauled up onto the bank. When they recovered, their hands were tied behind them and they were urged ahead of the riders with heavy blows on their backs and shoulders from spear butts.

A moment later, the first of a long caravan emerged from the darkness. Presently, the whole cavalcade was in sight. Some of the men dismounted to tie the dead beasts and dead men to moosoids. These were dragged behind the beasts while their owners walked. Evidently the carcasses were to be food. And for all she knew, so were the corpses. Urthona had said that some of the nomadic tribes were cannibals.

As her uncle and McKay were being driven past the point just opposite her, she felt something slimy grab her ankle. She repressed a cry. But when sharp teeth ripped her ankle, she had to take action. She lowered her head below the surface, bent over, withdrew her knife, and drove it several times into a soft body. The tentacle withdrew and the teeth quit biting. But the thing was back in a moment, attacking her other leg.

Though she didn't want to, she had to drop the Horn and the amphibian to free her other hand. She felt along the tentacle, found where it joined the body, and sawed away with the knife. Suddenly, the thing was gone, but both her legs felt as if they had been torn open. Also, she had to breathe. She came up out of the water as slowly as possible, stopping when her nose was just above the surface. A body broke the water a few feet from her, dark blood welling out.

She went under again, groped around, found the Horn, and came back up. The savages had noticed the wounded creature by then. And they saw her head emerge, of course. They began yelling and pointing. Presently, several cast their spears at her. These fell short of their mark. But they weren't going to let her escape. Four men slid down the bank and began swimming toward her.

She threw the Horn upon the bank and began clawing her way up it.

Her pursuers couldn't chase her on their beasts on this side. The big creatures could never get up the bank. She could get a head start on the men. But when she rolled over on the top of the bank, she saw that her wounds were deeper than she had thought. Blood was welling out over her feet. It was impossible to run any distance with those wounds.

Still . . . she put her ax in one hand and her knife in the other. The first man to come up fell back with a split skull. The second slid back with two fingers chopped off. The others decided that it was best to retreat. They went back into the water and split into two groups, each swimming a hundred yards in opposite directions. They would come up at the same time, and she could attack only one. That one would dive back into the water while the other came at her on the ground.

By then, ten others were swimming across. Some of them were several hundred yards downstream; others, the same distance upstream. She had no chance to get beyond these. Flight to the mountains a mile away on this side of the channel was her only chance. But she'd be caught because of her steady loss of blood.

She shrugged, slipped off her ragged shirt, tore it into strips, and bound them around the wounds. She hoped the tentacled things hadn't injected poison into her.

The Horn and the ax couldn't be hidden. The knife went into a pocket on the inside of the right leg of her Levi's. She'd sewn the pocket there shortly after she'd entered the gateway into Earth. That was a little more than a month ago, but it seemed like a year.

Then she sat, her arms folded, waiting.

12

HER CAPTORS WERE A SHORT, SLIM, DARK PEOPLE WHO LOOKED as if they were of Mediterranean stock. Their language, however, did not seem to her to be related to any she knew. Perhaps their ancestors had spoken one of the many tongues that had died out after the Indo-Europeans and Semites had invaded the Middle Sea area.

They numbered a hundred: thirty-two men, thirty-eight women, and twenty children. The moosoids were one hundred and twenty.

Their chief clothing was a rawhide kilt, though some of the men's were of feathers. All the warriors wore thin bones stuck through their septums, and many bore dried human hands suspended from a cord around their necks. Dried human heads adorned the saddles.

Anana was brought back to the other side of the channel and flung half-drowned upon the ground. The women attacked her at once. A few struck or kicked her, but most were trying to get her jeans and boots. Within a minute, she was left lying on the ground, bleeding, bruised, stunned, and naked.

The man whose two fingers she'd severed staggered up, holding his hand, pain twisting his face. He harangued the chief for a long while. The chief evidently told him to forget it, and the man went off.

Urthona and McKay were sitting slumped on the ground, looking even more thrubbed than she.

The chief had appropriated her ax and the Horn. The woman who'd beat off the others in order to keep the jeans had managed to get them on. So far, she hadn't paid any attention to the knife inside the leg. Anana hoped that she would not investigate the heavy lump, but there didn't seem much chance of that, human curiosity being what it was.

There was a long conference, with many speeches from both men and women. Finally, the chief spoke a few words. The dead men were carried off in travois to a point a mile away. The entire tribe, except for the few guards for the prisoners, followed the dead. After a half an hour of much wailing and weeping, punctuated by the shaman's leaping-abouts, chanting, and rattling of a gourd containing pebbles or seeds, the tribe returned to the channel.

If these people were cannibals, they didn't eat their own dead.

A woman, probably a wife of one of the deceased, rushed at Anana. Her fingers were out and hooked, ready to tear into the captive's face. Anana lay on her back and kicked the woman in the stomach. The whole tribe laughed, apparently enjoying the screams and writhings of the woman. When the widow had recovered, she scrambled up to resume her attack. The chief said something to a warrior, and he dragged the woman away.

By then, "dawn" had come. Some men ate pieces of one of the moosoids killed by Urthona, drank, and then rode off across the plain. The rest cut off portions for themselves and chewed at the meat with strong teeth. The flesh was supplemented by nuts and berries carried in raw-leather bags. None of the captives were offered any food. Anana didn't mind, since she'd eaten but a few hours ago, and the beating hadn't improved her appetite. Also, she was somewhat cheered. If these people did intend to eat her, it seemed likely that they would want to fatten her up. That would take time, and time was her ally.

Another thought palled that consideration. Perhaps they were saving her for lunch, in which case they wouldn't want to waste food on her.

The chief, his mouth and beard bloody, approached. His long hair was in a Psyche knot through which two long red feathers were stuck. A circle of human fingers on a leather plate hung from a neck-cord over his beard. One eye socket was empty except for a few flies. He stopped, belched, then yelled at the tribe to gather around.

Anana, watching him remove his kilt, became sick. A minute later, while the tribe yelled encouragement, and made remarks that were obviously obscene, though she didn't understand a word, he did what she had thought he was going to do. Knowing how useless it was to struggle, she lay back quietly. But she visualized six different ways of killing him and hoped she'd have a chance to carry out one of them.

After the chief, grinning, got up and donned his kilt, the shaman came up to her. He apparently had in mind emulating the chief. The latter, however, pushed him away. She was going to be the chief's property. Anana was glad for at least one favor. The shaman was even dirtier and more repulsive than the chief.

She managed to get up and walked over to Urthona. He looked disgusted. She said, "Well, Uncle, you can be glad you're not a woman."

"I always have been," he said. "You could run now before they could catch you and you could drown yourself in the channel. That is the only way to cleanse yourself." He spat. "Imagine that! A *leblabbiy* defiling a Lord! It's a wonder to me you didn't die of shame."

He paused, then smiled crookedly. "But then, you've been mating with a *leblabbiy* voluntarily, haven't you? You have no more pride than an ape."

Anana kicked him in the jaw with her bare foot. Two minutes passed before he recovered consciousness.

Anana felt a little better. Though she would have preferred to kick the chief (though not in his jaw), she had discharged some of her rage.

"If it weren't for you and Orc," she said, "I wouldn't be in this mess." She turned and walked away, ignoring his curses.

Shortly thereafter, the tribe resumed its march. The meat was thrown on top of piles on travois, and a more or less orderly caravan was formed. The chief rode at the head of the procession. Since attack from their left was impossible, all the outriders were put on the right.

About three hours before dusk, the men who'd been sent across the plains returned at a gallop. Anana didn't know what they reported, but she guessed that they'd gone up one of the mountains to look for enemies. Obviously, they hadn't seen any.

Why had the tribe been on the move during the night? Anana supposed that it was because many tribes would be going to the sea-country. This people wanted to be first, but they knew that others would have the same idea. So they were on a forced march, day and night, to get through the pass before they ran into enemies.

At "noon," when the sky illumination was brightest, the caravan stopped. Everybody, including the prisoners, ate. Then they lay down with skins over their faces to shut out the light, and they slept. About six stayed awake to be lookouts. These had slept for several hours on travois, though when they woke up, they looked as if they hadn't gotten a wink of sleep.

By then, the captives' hands were tied in front so they could feed themselves. When nap-time came, thongs were tied around their ankles to hobble them.

Anana had also been given a kilt to wear.

She lay down near her uncle and McKay. The latter said, "These savages must've never seen a black man before. They stare at me, and they rub my hair. Maybe they think it'll bring them luck. If I get a chance, I'll show them what kind of luck they're going to get!"

Urthona spoke out of lips puffed up by a blow from a spearshaft. "They might never have seen blacks before, but there are black tribes here. I brought in specimens of all the Earth races."

McKay said, slowly, "I wonder what they'd do to you if they knew you were responsible for their being here."

Urthona turned pale. Anana laughed, and said, "I might tell them—when I learn how to speak their tongue."

"You wouldn't do that, would you?" Urthona said. He looked at her, then said, "Yes, you would. Well, just remember, I'm the only one who can get us into my palace."

"If we ever find it," Anana said. "And if these savages don't eat us first."

She closed her eyes and went to sleep. It seemed like a minute later that she was roused by a kick in the ribs. It was the gray-haired woman in her panties, the chief's woman, who'd taken a special dislike to Anana. Or was it so special? All the women seemed to loathe her. Perhaps, though, that was the way they treated all female captives.

Obviously, the women weren't going to teach her the language. She picked on an adolescent, a short muscular lad who was keeping an eye on her. Since he seemed to be fascinated by her, she would get him to initiate her into the tribal speech. It didn't take long to learn his name, which was Nurgo.

Nurgo was eager to teach her. He rode on a moosoid while she walked, but he told her the names of things and people she pointed out. By the end of the "day," when they stopped for another two-hour snooze, she knew fifty words, and she could construct simple questions and had memorized their answers.

Neither Urthona nor McKay were interested in linguistics. They walked side by side, talking in low tones, obviously discussing methods of escape.

When they resumed their march in the deepening twilight, the chief asked her to demonstrate the use of the Horn. She blew the sequence of notes that would open any "gate"—if there had been one around. After some initial failures, he mastered the trumpet and for a half hour amused himself by blowing it. Then the shaman said something to him. Anana didn't know what it was. She guessed the shaman was pointing out that the sounds might attract the attention of enemies. Sheepishly, he stuck the Horn into a saddlebag.

Amazingly, the woman with her jeans had so far not been curious about the heavy lump in the leg of the cloth. Since she had never seen this type of apparel before, she must think that all jeans were weighted in this fashion.

Near the end of the "night," the caravan stopped again. Guards were posted, and everybody went to sleep. The moosoid, however, stayed awake and chomped on tree branches. These were carried on the travois or on their backs. The supply was almost gone, which meant that men would have to forage for it. That is, find a grove or forest of walking plants, kill some, and strip off the branches.

At "noon" the following day, the two mountains forming the pass to the sea seemed to be very close. But she knew that distance was deceiving here. It might take two more days before the pass was reached. Apparently the tribe knew how far away it was. The beasts wouldn't make it to the sea before they became weak with hunger.

Twenty of the men and some four adolescents rode out onto the plain. As fortune had it, the necessary food was advancing toward them. It was a square of trees that she estimated numbered about a thousand. The riders waited until it was a quarter of a mile from the channel. Then, holding lariats made of fiber, they rode out. Nearing the trees, they formed an Indian file. Like redskins circling a wagon train, they rode whooping around and around it.

The plants were about ten feet high and coniferous, shaped like Christmas trees, with extraordinarily broad trunks that bulged out at the bottom. About two thirds of the way up, eyes ringed the boles, and four very long and thin greenish tentacles extended from their centers. When the tribesmen got close, the whole unit stopped, and those on the perimeter turned on four barky legs to face outward.

Anana had noticed that a herd of wild moosoids had ignored them. There must be a reason for this. And as the men rode by, about twenty feet from the outguards, she saw why. Streams of heavy projectiles shot from holes in the trunks. Though a long way from the scene, she could hear the hissing of released air.

From much experience with these plants, the humans knew what the exact range of the darts were. They stayed just outside it, the riders upwind closer than those on the downwind side.

She deduced that they knew what the ammunition count for a tree was. They were shouting short words—undoubtedly numbers—as they rode by. Then the chief, who'd been sitting to one side and listening, yelled an order. This was passed on around the circle so that those out of hearing of his voice could be informed. The riders nearest him turned their beasts and headed toward the perimeter. Meanwhile, as if the plants were a well-trained army, those who'd discharged their missiles stepped backward into spaces afforded by the moving aside of the second rank.

It was evident that those behind them would take their places. But the riders stormed in, swung, and cast their lariats. Some of them missed. The majority caught and tightened around a branch or a tentacle. The mounts wheeled, the ropes stretched, the nooses closed, and the unlucky plants were jerked off their feet. The riders urged their beasts on until the trees had been dragged out of range of the missiles. The other end of the lariats were fastened to pegs stuck into the rear of the saddles. All but one held. This snapped, and the plant was left only ten feet from the square. No matter. It couldn't get up again.

The mounts halted, the riders jumped down and approached the fallen plants. Taking care to keep out of the way of the waving tentacles, they loosened the lariats and returned to their saddles.

Once more, the procedure was repeated. After that, the riders ignored the upright trees. They took their flint or chert tools and chopped off the tentacles. Their animals, now safe from the darts—which she presumed were poisoned—attacked the helpless plants. They grabbed the tentacles between their teeth and jerked them loose. After this, while the moosoids were stripping a branch, their owners chopped away branches with flint or chert tools.

The entire tribe, men, women, children, swarmed around the victims and piled the severed branches upon travois or tied bundles of them to the backs of the beasts.

Later, when she'd learned some vocabulary, Anana asked the youth, Nurgo, if the missiles were poisoned. He nodded and grinned and said, *"Yu, messt gwonaw dendert assessampt."*

She wasn't sure whether the last word meant *deadly* or *poison*. But there was no doubt that it would be better not to be struck by the darts. After the plants had been stripped, the men carefully picked up the missiles. They were about four inches long, slim-bodied, with a feathery construction of vegetable origin at one end and a needle-point at the other. The point was smeared with a blue-greenish substance.

These were put into a rawhide bag or fixed at the ends of spearshafts. After the work was done, the caravan resumed marching. Anana, looking back, saw half of the surviving plants ranged alongside the channel. From the bottom of each, a thick greenish tube was extended into the water, which was being sucked up into these. The other half stood guard.

"You must have had a lot of fun designing those," Anana said to Urthona.

"It was more amusing designing them than watching them in action," her uncle said. "In fact, designing this world entertained me more than living on it. I got bored in less than four years and left it. But I have been back now and then during the past ten thousand years to renew my acquaintance with it."

"When was the last time?"

"Oh, about five hundred years ago, I think."

"Then you must have made another world for your headquarters. One more diversified, more beautiful, I'd imagine."

Urthona smiled. "Of course. Then I also am Lord of three more, worlds that I took over after I'd killed their owners. You remember your cousin Bromion, that bitch Ethinthus, and Antamon? They're dead now, and I, I rule their worlds!"

"Do you indeed now?" Anana said. "I wouldn't say you were sitting on any thrones now. Unless you call captivity, the immediate danger of death and torture, thrones."

Urthona snarled, and said, "I'll do you as I did them, my *leblabbiy-*loving niece! And I'll come back here and wipe out these miserable scum! In fact, I may just wipe out this whole world! Cancel it!"

13

ANANA SHOOK HER HEAD. "UNCLE, I WAS ONCE LIKE YOU. THAT is, utterly unworthy of life. But there was something in me that gave me misgivings. Let us call it a residue of compassion, of empathy. Deep under the coldness and cruelty and arrogance was a spark. And that spark fanned into a great fire, fanned by a *leblabbiy* called Kickaha. He's not a Lord, but he is a *man*. That's more than you ever were or will be. And these brutish miserable creatures who've captured you, and don't know they hold the Lord of their crazy world captive . . . they're more human than you could conceive. That is, they're retarded Lords . . ."

Urthona stared and said, "What in The Spinner's name are you talking about?"

Anana felt like hitting him. But she said, "You wouldn't ever understand. Maybe I shouldn't say *ever*. After all, I came to understand. But that was because I was forced to be among the *leblabbiy* for a long time."

"And this *leblabbiy*, Kickaha, this descendant of an artificial product, corrupted your mind. It's too bad the Council is no longer in effect. You'd be condemned and killed within ten minutes."

Anana ran her gaze up and down him several times, her expression contemptuous. "Don't forget, Uncle, that you, too, may be the descendant of an artificial product. Of creatures created in a laboratory. Don't forget what Shambarimen speculated with much evidence to back his statement. That we, too, the Lords, the *Lords*, may have been made in the laboratories of beings who are as high above us as we are above the *leblabbiy*. Or should I say as high above them as we are *supposed* to be.

"After all, we made the *leblabbiy* in our image. Which means that they are neither above nor below us. They are us. But they don't know that, and they have to live in worlds that we created. Made, rather. We are not creators, any more than writers of fiction or painters are creators. They make worlds, but they are never able to make more than what they know. They can write or paint worlds based on elements of the known, put together in a different order in a way to make them seem to be creators. "We, the so-called Lords, did no more than poets, writers, and painters and sculptors. We were not, and are not, gods. Though we've come to think of ourselves as such."

"Spare me your lectures," Urthona said. "I don't care for your attempts to justify your degeneracy."

Anana shrugged and said, "You're hopeless. But in a way, you're right. The thing to talk about is how we can escape."

"Yeah," McKay said. "Just how we going to do that?"

"However we do it," she said, "we can't go without the knife and the ax and the Horn. We'd be helpless in this savage world without them. The chief has the ax and the Horn, so we have to get them away from him."

She didn't think she should say anything about the knife in the jeans. They'd noticed it was gone, but she had told them she'd lost it during her flight from them.

A man untied their hobbles, and they resumed the march with the others. Anana went back to her language lessons with Nurgo.

When the tribe got to the pass, it stopped again. She didn't need to ask why. The country beyond the two mountains was black with clouds in which lived a hell of lightning bolts. It would be committing suicide to venture into it. But when a whole "day" and "night" passed, and the storm still raged, she did question the youth.

"The Lord sends down thunder and lightning into this country. He topples trees and slays beasts and any human who is foolish enough to dare him.

"That is why we go into the sea-country only when his wrath has cooled off. Otherwise, we would live there all the time. The land changes shape very slowly and insignificantly. The water is full of fish, and the trees, which do not walk, are full of birds that are good to eat. The trees also bear nuts, and there are bushes, which also do not walk, that are heavy with berries. And the game is plentiful and easier caught than on the open plains.

"If we could live there all the time, we would get fat and our children would thrive and our tribe would become more numerous and powerful. But the Lord, in his great wisdom, has decreed that we can only live there for a little while. Then the clouds gather, and his lightning strikes, and the land is no place for anyone who knows what's good for him."

Anana did not, of course, understand everything he said. But she could supply the meaning from what phrases she had mastered.

She went to Urthona and asked him why he had made such an arrangement in the sea-country.

"Primarily, for my entertainment. I liked to send my palace into that land and watch the fury of the lightning, see the devastation. I was safe and snug in my palace, but I got a joy out of seeing the lightning blaze and crack around me. Then I truly felt like a god.

"Secondarily, if it weren't for their fear of being killed, the humans would crowd in. It'd be fun to watch them fight each other for the territory. In fact, it was fun during the stormless seasons. But if there were nothing to keep them from settling down there, they'd never go back into the shifting areas.

"There are, if I remember correctly, twelve of those areas. The seas and the surrounding land cover about five million square miles. So in an area of two hundred million square miles, there are sixty million square miles of relatively stable topography. These are never separated from the main mass, and the split-offs never occur near the seas.

"The lightning season was designed to drive beast and human out of the sea-country except at certain times. Otherwise, they'd get overcrowded."

He stopped to point at the plain. Anana turned and saw that it was now covered with herds of animals: elephants, moosoids, antelopes, and many small creatures. The mountains were dark with birds that had settled on them. And the skies were black with millions of flying creatures.

"They migrate from near and far," Urthona said. "They come to enjoy the sea and the wooded lands while they can. Then, when the storms start, they leave."

Anana wandered away. As long as she didn't get very far from the camp, she was free to roam around. She approached the chief, who was sitting on the ground and striking the ground with an ax. She squatted down before him.

"When will the storms cease?" she said.

His eyes widened. "You have learned our language very quickly. Good. Now I can ask you some questions."

"I asked one first," she said.

He frowned. "The Lord should have ceased being angry and gone back to his palace before now. Usually, the lightning would have stopped two light-periods ago. For some reason, the Lord is very angry and he is still raging. I hope he gets tired of it and goes home soon. The beasts and the birds are piling up. It's a dangerous situation. If a stampede should start, we could be trampled to death. We would have to jump into the water to save ourselves, and that would be bad because our *grewigg* would be lost along with our supplies."

Grewigg was the plural of *gregg,* the word for a moosoid.

Anana said, "I wondered why you weren't hunting when so many animals were close by."

The chief, Trenn, shuddered. "We're not stupid. Now, what tribe is yours? And is it near here?"

Anana wondered if he would accept the truth. After all, his tribe, the Wendow, might have a tradition of having come from another world.

"We are not natives of this . . . place." She waved a hand to indicate the universe, and the flies, alarmed, rose and whirled around buzzing. They quickly settled back, however, lighting on her body, her face, and her arms. She brushed them away from her face. The chief endured the insects crawling all over him and into his empty eye socket. Possibly he wasn't even aware of them.

"We came through a . . ." She paused. She didn't know the word for *gate*. Maybe there wasn't any. "We came through a pass between two . . . I don't know how to say it. We came from beyond the sky. From another place where the sky is . . . the color of that bird there."

She pointed to a small blue bird that had landed by the channel.

The chief's eye got even larger. "Ah, you came from the place where our ancestors lived. The place from which the Lord drove our forefathers countless light-periods ago because they had sinned. Tell me, why did the Lord drive you here, too? What did you do to anger him?"

While she was trying to think how to answer this, the chief bellowed for the shaman, Shakann, to join them. The little gray-bearded man, holding the gourd at the end of a stick to which feathers were tied, came running. Trenn spoke too rapidly for Anana to understand any but a few words. Shakann squatted down by the chief.

Anana considered telling them that they'd entered this world accidentally. But she didn't know their word for accident. In fact, she doubted there was such. From what she'd learned from Nurgo, these people believed that nothing happened accidentally. Events were caused by the Lord or by witchcraft.

She got an inspiration. At least, she hoped it was. Lying might get her into even worse trouble. Ignorant of the tribe's theology, she might offend some article of belief, break some taboo, say something contrary to dogma.

"The Lord was angry with us. He sent us here so that we might lead some deserving tribe, yours, for instance, out of this place. Back to the place where your ancestors lived before they were cast out."

There was a long silence. The chief looked as if he were entertaining joyful thoughts. The shaman was frowning.

Finally, the chief said, "And just how are we to do this? If the Lord wants us to return to *sembart* . . ."

"What is *sembart*?"

The chief tried to define it. Anana got the idea that *sembart* could be translated as paradise or the Garden of Eden. In any event, a place much preferable to this world.

Well, Earth was no paradise, but given her choice, she wouldn't hesitate a second in making it.

"If the Lord wants us to return to *sembart,* then why didn't he come here and take us to there?"

"Because," Anana said, "he wanted me to test you. If you were worthy, then I would lead you from this world."

Trenn spoke so rapidly to Shakann that she could comprehend only half of his speech. The gist, however, was that the tribe had made a bad mistake in not treating the captives as honored guests. Everybody had better jump to straighten out matters.

Shakann, however, cautioned him not to act so swiftly. First, he would ask some questions.

"If you are indeed the Lord's representative, why didn't you come to us in his *shelbett?*"

A *shelbett,* it turned out, was a thing that flew. In the old days, according to legend, the Lord had traveled through the air in this.

Anana, thinking fast, said, "I only obey the Lord. I dare not ask him why he does or doesn't do this or that. No doubt, he had his reasons for not giving us a *shelbett.* One might be that if you had seen us in one, you would have known we were from him. And so you would have treated us well. But the Lord wants to know who is good and who isn't."

"But it is not bad to take captives and then kill them or adopt them into the tribe. So how could we know that we were doing a bad thing? All tribes would have treated you the same."

Anana said, "It's not how you treated us at first. How you treated us when you found out that we came from the Lord will determine whether you are found good or bad in his eyes."

Shakann said, "But any tribe that believed your story would honor you and take care of you as if you were a baby. How would you know whether a tribe was doing this because it is good or because it is pretending to be good from fear of you?"

Anana sighed. The shaman was an ignorant savage. But he was intelligent.

"The Lord has given me some powers. One of them is the ability to look into the . . ."

She paused. What was the word for heart?

"To look inside people and see if they are good or bad. To tell when people are lying."

"Very well," Shakann said. "If you can indeed tell when a person lies, tell me this. I intend to take this sharp hard thing the chief took from you and split your head open. I will do it very shortly. Am I lying or am I telling the truth?"

The chief protested, but Shakann said, "Wait! This is a matter for me, your priest, to decide. You rule the tribe in some things, but the business of the Lord is my concern."

Anana tried to appear cool, but she could feel the sweat pouring from her.

Judging from the chief's expression, she doubted that he would let the shaman have the ax. Also, the shaman must be unsure of himself. He might be a hypocrite, a charlatan, though she did not think so. Preliterate medicine men, witches, sorcerers, whatever their title was, really believed in their religion. Hypocrisy came with civilization. His only doubt was whether or not she did indeed represent the Lord of this wretched cosmos. If she were lying and he allowed her to get away with it, then the Lord might punish him.

He was in as desperate a situation as she. At least, he thought he was.

The issue was: was he lying or did he really intend to test her by trying to kill her? He knew that if she were what she said she was, he might be blasted with a bolt from the sky.

She said, "You don't know yourself whether you're lying or telling the truth. You haven't made up your mind yet what you'll do."

The shaman smiled. She relaxed somewhat.

"That is right. But that doesn't mean that you can see what I'm thinking. A very shrewd person could guess that I felt that way. I'll ask you some more questions.

"For instance, one of the things that makes me think you might be from the Lord is that thing which cut the men and the *grewigg* in half. With it, he could have killed the whole tribe. Why, then, did he throw it away after killing only a few?"

"Because the Lord told him to do so. He was to use the deadly gift of the Lord only to show you that he did not come from this world. But the Lord did not want him to slay an entire tribe. How then could we lead you out of this place to *sembart?*"

"That is well spoken. You may indeed be what you say. Or you might just be a very clever woman. Tell me, how will you lead us to *sembart?*"

Anana said, "I didn't say I will. I said I might. What happens depends upon you and the rest of your tribe. First, you have to cut our bonds and then treat us as vicars of the Lord. However, I will say this. I will guide you to the dwelling palace of the Lord. When we get to it, we'll enter it and then go through a pass to *sembart.*"

The shaman raised thick woolly eyebrows. "You know where the Lord's dwelling is?"

She nodded. "It's far away. During the journey, you will be tested."

The chief said, "We saw the dwelling of the Lord once countless light-periods ago. We were frightened when we saw it moving along a plain. It was huge and had many . . . um . . . things like great sticks . . . rising from it. It shone with many lights from many stones. We watched it for a while, then fled, afraid the Lord would be offended and deal harshly with us."

Shakann said, "What is the purpose of the thing that makes music?"

"That will get us into the dwelling of the Lord. By the way, we call his dwelling a palace."

"*Bahdahss?*"

"That's good enough. But the . . . Horn . . . belongs to me. You have no right to it. The Lord won't like your taking it."

"Here!" the chief said, thrusting it at her.

"You wronged me when you raped me. I do not know whether the Lord will forgive you for that or not."

The chief spread his hands out in astonishment. "But I did no wrong! It is the custom for the chief to mount all female captives. All chiefs do it."

Anana had counted on avenging herself someday. She hadn't known if she'd be satisfied with castrating him or also blinding him. However, if it was the custom . . . he really hadn't thought he was doing anything evil. And if she'd been more objective about it, she would have known that, too.

After all, aside from making her nauseated, he hadn't hurt her. She'd suffered no psychic damage, and there wasn't any venereal disease. Nor could he make her pregnant.

"Very well," she said. "I won't hold that against you."

The chief's expression said, "Why should you?" but he made no comment.

The shaman said, "What about the two men? Are they your husbands? I ask that because some tribes, when they have a shortage of women, allow the women to have more than one husband."

"No! They are under my command."

She might as well get the upper hand on the two while she had the chance. Urthona would rave, but he wouldn't try to usurp her leadership. He wouldn't want to discredit her, since her story had saved his life.

She held out her hands, and the chief used a flint knife to sever the thongs. She rose and ordered the chief's mother to be brought to her. Thikka approached haughtily, then turned pale under the dirt when her son explained the situation to her.

"I won't hurt you," Anana said. "I just want my jeans and boots back."

Thikka didn't know what *jeans* or *boots* meant, so Anana used sign language. When they were off, Anana ordered her to take the jeans to the channel and wash them. Then she said, "No. I'll do it. You probably wouldn't know how."

She was afraid the woman might find the knife.

The chief called the entire tribe in and explained who their captives, ex-captives, really were. There were a lot of oh's and ah's, or the Wendow equivalents, and then the women who'd beaten her fell on their knees and begged forgiveness. Anana magnanimously blessed them.

Urthona's and McKay's bonds were cut. Anana told them how she had gained their freedom. However, as it turned out, they were not as free as they wished. Though the chief gave each a moosoid, he delegated men to be their bodyguards. Anana suspected that the shaman was responsible for this.

"We can try to escape any time there's an opportunity," she told her uncle. "But we'll be safer if we're with them while we're looking for your palace. Once we find it, if we find it, we can outwit them. However, I hope the search doesn't take too long. They might wonder why the emissaries of the Lord are having such a hard time locating it."

She smiled. "Oh, yes. You're my subordinates, so please act as if you are. I don't think the shaman is fully convinced about my story."

Urthona looked outraged. McKay said, "It looks like a good deal to me, Miss Anana. No more beatings, we can ride instead of walking, eat plenty, and three women already said they'd like to have babies by me. One thing about them, they ain't got no color prejudice. That's about all I can say for them, though."

14

ANOTHER DAY AND NIGHT PASSED. THE THUNDER AND LIGHT-
ning showed no signs of diminishing. Anana, watching the inferno from the
pass, could not imagine how anything, plants or animals, escaped the fury.
The chief told her that only about one sixteenth of the trees were laid low
and new trees grew very quickly. Many small beasts, hiding now, in bur-
rows and caves, would emerge when the storms were over.

By then, the plains were thick with life and the mountains were zebra-
striped with lines of just-arriving migrators. The predators, the baboons,
wild dogs, moas, and big cats, were killing as they pleased. But the plain
was getting so crowded that there was no room to stampede away from the
hunters. Sometimes the frightened antelopes and elephants ran toward the
killers and trampled them.

The valley was a babel of animal and bird cries, screams, trumpetings,
buglings, croakings, bellowings, mooings, roarings.

At this place, the waterway banks were about ten feet above the surface. The ground sloped upward from this point toward the sea-land pass,
where the banks reached their maximum height above the surface of
the water, almost a hundred feet. The chief gave orders to abandon the
moosoids and swim across the channel if a stampede headed their way. The
children and women jumped into the water and swam to the opposite
bank and struggled up its slope. The men stayed behind to control the
nervous *grewigg*. These were bellowing, rolling their eyes, drawing their
lips back to show their big teeth, and dancing around. The riders were busy
trying to quiet them, but it was evident that if the storm didn't stop very
soon, the plains animals would bolt and with them, the moosoids. As it was,
the riders were not far behind the beasts in nervousness. Though they
knew that the lightning wouldn't reach out between the mountains and
strike them, the "fact" that the Lord was working overtime in his rage
made them uneasy.

Anana had crossed the channel with the women and children. She hadn't liked leaving her *gregg* behind. But it was better to be here if a stampede did occur. The only animals on this side were those able to get up the steep banks: baboons, goats, small antelopes, foxes. There were a million birds on this side, however, and more were flying in. The squawking and screaming made it difficult to hear anyone more than five feet away even if you shouted.

Urthona and McKay were on their beasts, since it was expected that all men would handle them. Urthona looked worried. Not because of the imminent danger but because she had the Horn. He fully expected her to run away then. There was no one who could stop her on this side of the channel. It would be impossible for anyone on the other side to run parallel along the channel with the hope of eventually cutting her off. He, or they, could never get through the herds jammed all the way from the channel to the base of the mountains.

Something was going to break at any minute. Anything could start an avalanche on a hundred thousand hooves. She decided that she'd better do something about the tribe. It wasn't that she was concerned about the men. They could be trampled into bloody rags for all she cared. Nor, only two years ago, would she have been concerned about the women and children. But now she would feel—in some irrational obscure way—that she was responsible for them. And she surely did not want to be burdened with them.

She swam back across the channel, the Horn stuck in her belt, and climbed onto the bank. Talking loudly in the chief's ear, she told him what had to be done. She did not request it, she demanded it as if she were indeed the representative of the Lord. If Trenn resented her taking over, he was discreet enough not to show it. He bellowed orders, and the men got down from the *grewigg*. While some restrained the beasts, the others slid down the bank and swam to the other side. Anana went with them and told the women what they should do.

She helped them by digging away at the edge of the bank with her knife. The chief apparently was too dignified to do manual labor even in an emergency. He loaned his ax to his wife, telling her to set to with it.

The others used their flint and chert tools or the ends of their sticks. It wasn't easy, since the grass was tough and the roots were intertwined deep under the surface. But the blades and the greasy earth finally did give way. Within half an hour, a trench, forty-five degrees to the horizontal, had been cut into the bank.

Then the men and Anana swam back, and the moosoids were forced over the bank and into the water. The men swam with them, urging them to make for the trench. The *grewigg* were intelligent enough to understand what the trench was for. They entered it, one by one, and clambered, sometimes slipping, up the trench. The women at the top grabbed the reins and helped pull each beast on up, while the men shoved from behind.

Fortunately, there was very little current in the channel. The *grewigg* were not carried away past the trench.

Before all, including the moosoids, had quit panting, the stampede started. There was no way to know how it started. Of a sudden, the thunder of countless hooves reached them, mixed with the same noises they had heard but louder now. It wasn't a monolithic movement in one direction. About half of the beasts headed toward the pass. The other part raced toward the mountains outside those that ringed the sea-land. These had resumed their cone shape of two days ago.

First through the pass was a herd of at least a hundred elephants. Trumpeting, shoulder to shoulder, those behind jamming their trunks against the rears of those ahead, they sped by. Several on the edge of the channel were forced into the water, and these began swimming toward the pass.

Behind the pachyderms came a mass of antelopes with brownish-red bodies, black legs, red necks and heads, and long black horns. The largest were about the size of a racing horse. Their numbers greatly exceeded those of the elephants; they must have been at least a thousand. The front ranks got through and then a beast slipped, those behind fell over or on him, and within a minute, at least a hundred were piled up. Many were knocked over into the channel.

Anana expected the rear ranks to turn and charge off along the base of the right-hand mountain. But they kept coming, falling, and others piled up on them. The pass on that side of the channel was blocked, but the frantic beasts leaped upon the fallen and attempted to get over their struggling, kicking, horn-tossing, bleating fellows. Then they too tripped and went down, and those behind them climbed over them and fell. And they too were covered.

The water was thick with crazed antelopes that swam until bodies fell on them and then others on them and others on them.

Anana yelled at the chief. He couldn't hear her because of the terrifying bedlam, so loud it smothered the bellow of thunder and explosion of lightning beyond the pass. She ran to him and put her mouth to his ear.

"The channel's going to be filled in a minute with bodies! Then the beasts'll leap over the bodies and be here! And we'll be caught!"

Trenn nodded and turned and began bellowing and waving his arms. His people couldn't hear him, but they understood his gestures. All the moosoids were mounted, and the travois were hastily attached to the harness, and the skins and goods piled on them. This wasn't easy to do, since the *grewigg* were almost uncontrollable. They reared up, and they kicked out at the people trying to hold them, and some bit any hands or faces that came close.

By then, the spill into the channel was taking place as far as they could see. There were thousands of animals, not only antelopes now, but elephants, baboons, dogs, and big cats, pressed despite their struggles into the water. Anana caught a glimpse of a big bull elephant tumbling headfirst off the bank, a lion on its back, its claws digging into the skin.

Now added to the roaring and screaming was the flapping of millions of wings as the birds rose into the air. Among these were the biggest winged birds she'd seen so far, a condor-like creature with an estimated wingspan of twelve feet.

Many of the birds were heading for the mountains. But at least half were scavengers, and these settled down on the top of the piles in the water or in the pass. They began tearing away at the bodies, dead or alive, or attempting to defend their rights or displace others.

Anana had never seen such a scene and hoped she never would again. It was possible that she wouldn't. The sudden lifting of the birds had snapped the moosoids' nerves. They started off, some running toward the birds, some toward the mountains, some toward the pass. Men and women hung on to the reins until they were lifted up, then lowered, their bare feet scraping on the ground until they had to let go. Those mounted pulled back on the reins with all their might, but to no avail. Skins and goods bounced off the travois, which then bounced up and down behind the frenzied beasts.

Anana watched Urthona, yelling, his face red, hauling back on the reins, being carried off toward the pass. McKay had let loose of his moosoid as soon as it bolted. He stood there, watching her. Evidently he was waiting to see what she would do. She decided to run for the mountains. She looked back once and saw the black man following her. Either he had orders from her uncle not to let her out of his sight or he trusted her to do the best thing to avoid danger and was following her example.

Possibly he was going to try to get the Horn from her. He couldn't do that without killing her. He was bigger and stronger than she, but she had her knife. He knew how skilled she was with a knife, not to mention her mastership of the martial arts.

Besides, if he attempted murder in sight of the tribe, he'd be discrediting her story that they were sent by the Lord. He surely wouldn't be that stupid.

The nearest mountain on this side of the channel was only a mile away. It was one of the rare shapes, a monolith, four-sided, about two thousand feet high. The ground around it had sunk to three hundred feet, forming a ditch about six hundred and fifty feet broad. She stopped at the edge and turned. McKay joined her five minutes later. It took him several minutes to catch his normal breathing.

"It sure is a mess, ain't it?"

She agreed with him but didn't say so. She seldom commented on the obvious.

"Why're you sticking with me?"

"Because you got the Horn, and that's the only way to get us out of this miserable place. Also, if anybody's going to survive, you are. I stick with you, I live too."

"Does that mean you're no longer loyal to Urthona?"

He smiled. "He ain't paid me recently. And what's more, he ain't never going to pay me. He's promised a lot to me, but I know that once he's safe, he's going to get rid of me."

She was silent for a while. McKay was a hired killer. He couldn't be trusted, but he could be used.

"I'll do my best to get you back to Earth," she said. "I can't promise it. You might have to settle for some other world. Perhaps Kickaha's."

"Any world's better than this one."

"You wouldn't say that if you'd seen some of them. I give you my word that I'll try my best. However, for the time being, you'll pretend to be in my uncle's employ."

"And tell you what he plans, including any monkey business."

"Of course."

He was probably sincere. It was possible, though, that Urthona had put him up to this.

By then, some of the tribe had also gotten to the base of the mountain. The others were mostly riders who hadn't so far managed to control their beasts. A few were injured or dead.

The stampede was over. Those animals still on their hooves or paws had scattered. There was more room for them on the plain now. The birds covered the piles of carcasses like flies on a dog turd.

She began walking down to the channel. The tribe followed her, some talking about the unexpected bonus of meat. They would have enough to stuff themselves silly for two days before the bodies got too rank. Or perhaps three days. She didn't know just how fastidious they were. From what she'd seen, not very.

Halfway to the channel, McKay stopped and said, "Here comes the chief."

She looked toward the pass. Coming down the slope from it was Trenn. Though his *gregg* had bolted and taken him into the valley itself, it was now under control. She was surprised to see that the heavy black clouds over the sea-country were fading away. And the lightning had stopped.

A minute later, several other *grewigg* and riders came over the top of the rise. By the time she got to the channel, they were close enough for her to recognize them. One was her uncle. Until then, the moosoids had been trotting. Now Urthona urged his into a gallop. He pulled the sweating panting saliva-flecked beast up when he got close, and he dismounted swiftly. The animal groaned, crumpled, turned over on its side and died.

Urthona had a strange expression. His green eyes were wide, and he looked pale.

"Anana! Anana!" he cried. "I saw it! I saw it!"

"Saw what?" she said.

He was trembling.

"My palace! It was on the sea! Heading out away from the shore!"

15

OBVIOUSLY, IF HE'D BEEN ABLE TO CATCH UP TO IT, HE WOULDN'T be here.

"How fast does it travel?" she said.

"When the drive is on automatic, one kilometer an hour."

"I don't suppose that after all this time, you'd have the slightest idea what path it will take?"

He spread out his hands and shrugged his shoulders.

The situation seemed hopeless. There was no time to build a sailing boat, even if tools were available, and to try to catch up with it. But it was possible that the palace would circle around the sea and come back to this area.

"Eventually," Urthona said, "the palace will leave this country. It'll go through one of the passes. Not this one, though. It isn't wide enough."

Anana did not accept this statement as necessarily true. For all she knew, the palace contained devices that could affect the shape-changing. But if Urthona had any reason to think that the palace could come through this pass, he surely would not have told her about seeing it.

There was nothing to be done about the palace at this time. She put it out of her mind for the time being, but her uncle was a worrier. He couldn't stop talking about it, and he probably would dream about it. Just to devil him, she said, "Maybe Orc got to it when it was close to shore. He might be in the palace now. Or, more probably, he's gated through to some other world."

Urthona's fair skin became even whiter. "No! He couldn't! It would be impossible! In the first place, he wouldn't dare venture into the sea-land during the storm. In the second place, he couldn't get to it. He'd have to swim . . . I think. And in the third place, he doesn't know the entrance-code."

Anana laughed.

Urthona scowled. "You just said that to upset me."

"I did, yes. But now that I think about it, Orc could have done it if he was desperate enough to risk the lightning."

McKay, who had been listening nearby, said, "Why would he take the risk unless he knew the palace was there? And how could he know it was there unless he'd already gone into the sea-land? Which he wouldn't do unless he knew . . ."

Anana said swiftly, "But he could have seen it from the pass, and that might have been enough for him."

She didn't really believe this, but she wasn't too sure. When she walked away from her uncle, she wondered if Orc just might have done it. Her effort to bug Urthona had backfired. Now *she* was worried.

A few minutes later, the storm ceased. The thunder quit rolling; the clouds cleared as if sucked into a giant vacuum cleaner. The shaman and the chief talked together for a while, then approached Anana.

Trenn said, "Agent of the Lord, we have a question. Is the Lord no longer angry? Is it safe for us to go into the sea-land?"

She didn't dare to show any hesitation. Her role called for her to be intimate with the Lord's plans.

If she guessed wrong, she'd lose her credibility.

"The wrath of the Lord is finished," she said. "It'll be safe now."

If the clouds appeared again and lightning struck, she would have to run away as quickly as possible.

The departure did not take place immediately, however. The animals that had bolted had to be caught, the scattered goods collected, and the ceremonies for the dead gone through. About two hours later, the tribe headed for the pass. Anana was delighted to be in a country where there were trees that did not walk, and where thick woods and an open sea offered two ready avenues of flight.

The Wendow went down the long slope leading to sand beaches. The chief turned left, and the others followed. According to Nurgo, their destination lay about half a day's travel away. Their stronghold was about fifteen minutes' walk inland from the beach.

"What about the other tribes that come through the pass?" she said.

"Oh, they'll be coming through during the next few light-periods. They'll go even farther up the beach, toward their camps. We were lucky that there weren't other tribes waiting at the pass, since the storms lasted longer than usual."

"Do you attack them as they pass by your stronghold?"

"Not unless we outnumber them greatly."

Further questioning cleared up some of her ignorance about their pattern of war. Usually, the tribes avoided any full-scale battles if it was possible. Belligerence was confined to raids by individuals or parties of three to five people. These were conducted during the dark-period and were mainly by young unblooded males, and sometimes by a young woman ac-companied by a male. The youth had to kill a man and bring back his head as proof of his or her manhood or womanhood. The greatest credit, how-ever, was not for a head, but for a child. To steal a child and bring it back for adoption into the tribe was the highest feat possible.

Nurgo himself was an adopted child. He'd been snatched not long after he'd started walking. He didn't remember a thing about it, though he did sometimes have nightmares in which he was torn away from a woman without a face.

The caravan came to a place that looked just like the rest of the terrain to Anana. But the tribe recognized it with a cry of joy. Trenn led them into the wooded hills, and after a while, they came to a hill higher than the oth-ers. Logs lay on its top and down its slope, the ruins of what had been a stockade.

The next few days were spent in fishing, gathering nuts and berries, eating, sleeping, and rebuilding the fort. Anana put some weight back on and began to feel rested. But once she had all her energy back, she became restless.

Urthona was equally fidgety. She observed him talking softly to McKay frequently. She had no doubts about the subject of their conversation, and McKay, reporting to her, gave her the details.

"Your uncle wants to take off at the first chance. But no way is he going to leave without the Horn."

"Is he planning on taking it from me now or when he finds his palace?" she said.

"He says that we, us two, him and me, that is, would have a better chance of surviving if you was to go with us. But he says you're so tricky you might get the upper hand on us when we sight the palace. So he can't make up his mind yet. But he's going to have to do it soon. Every minute passes, the palace is getting farther away."

There was a silence. McKay looked as if he was chewing something but didn't know if he should swallow it or spit it out. After a minute, his ex-pression changed.

"I got something to tell you."

He paused, then said, "Urthona told you and Kickaha that this Wolff, or Jadawin, and his woman—Chryseis?—had been gated to this world. Well, that's a lie. They somehow escaped. They're still on Earth!"

Anana did not reply at once. McKay didn't have to tell her this news. Why had he done so? Was it because he wanted to reassure her that he had indeed switched loyalties? Or had Urthona ordered McKay to tell her that so she would think he was betraying Urthona?

In either case, was the story true?

She sighed. All Lords, including herself, were so paranoiac that they would never be able to distinguish between reality and fantasy. Their distrust of motivation made it impossible.

She shrugged. For the moment, she'd act as if she believed his story. She looked around the big tree they'd been sitting behind, and she said, "Oh-oh! Here comes my uncle, looking for us. If he sees you with me, he'll get suspicious. You'd better take off."

McKay crawled off into the bushes. When Urthona found her, she said, "Hello, Uncle. Aren't you supposed to be helping the fish spears?"

"I told them I didn't care to go fishing today. And, of course, since I'm one of the Lord's agents, I wasn't challenged. I could tell they didn't like it, though.

"I was looking for you and McKay. Where is he?"

She lifted her shoulders.

"Well, it doesn't matter."

He squatted down by her.

"I think we've wasted enough time. We should get away the moment we have a chance."

"We?" she said, raising her eyebrows. "Why should I want to go with you?"

He looked exasperated. "You surely don't want to spend the rest of your life here?"

"I don't intend to. But I mean to make sure first that Kickaha is either alive or dead."

"That *leblabbiy* really means that much to you?"

"Yes. Don't look so disgusted. If you should ever feel that much for another human being, which I doubt, then you'll know why I'm making sure about him. Meanwhile . . ."

He looked incredulous. "You can't stay here."

"Not forever. But if he's alive, he'll be along soon. I'll give him a certain time to come. After that, I'll look for his bones."

Urthona bit his lower lip.

He said, "Then you won't come with us now?"

She didn't reply. He knew the answer.

There was a silence for a few minutes. Then he stood up.

"At least, you won't tell the chief what we're planning to do?"

"I'd get no special pleasure out of that," she said. "The only thing is . . . how do I explain your French leave? How do I account for a representative of the Lord, sent on a special mission to check out the Wendow tribe, my subordinate, sneaking off?"

Her uncle chewed his lips some more. He'd been doing that for ten thousand years; she remembered when she was a child seeing him gnaw on them.

Finally, he smiled. "You could tell them McKay and I are off on a secret mission, the purpose of which you can't divulge now because it's for the Lord. Actually, it would be fine if you'd say that. We wouldn't have to sneak off. We could just walk out, and they wouldn't dare prevent us."

"I could do that," she said. "But why should I? If by some chance you did find the palace right away, you'd just bring it back here and destroy me. Or use one of your fliers. In any event, I'm sure you have all sorts of weapons in your palace."

He knew it was useless to protest that he wouldn't do that. He said, "What's the difference? I'm going, one way or the other. You can't tell the chief I am because then you'd have to explain why I am. You can't do a thing about it."

"You can do what you want to," she said. "But you can't take this with you."

She held up the Horn.

His eyes narrowed and his lips tightened. By that, she knew that he had no intention of leaving without the Horn. There were two reasons why, one of which was certain. The other might exist.

No Lord would pass up the chance to get his hands on the skeleton key to the gates of all the universes.

The Horn might also be the ticket to passage from a place on this planet to his palace. Just possibly, there were gates locked into the boulders. Not all boulders, of course. Just some. She'd tried the Horn on the four big rocks she'd encountered so far, and none had contained any. But there could be gates in others.

If there were, then he wasn't going to risk her finding one and getting into the palace before he did.

Undoubtedly, or at least probably, he would tell McKay just when he planned to catch her sleeping, kill her, and take the Horn. Would McKay warn her? She couldn't take the chance that he would.

"All right," she said. "I'll go with you. I have just as much chance finding Kickaha elsewhere. And I am tired of sitting here."

He wasn't as pleased as he should have been. He smelled a trap. Of course, even if she'd been sincere, he would have suspected she was up to something. Just as she wondered if he was telling her the truth or only part of it.

Urthona's handsome face now assumed a smile. In this millennia-long and deadly game the Lords played, artifices that wouldn't work and that both sides knew wouldn't work, were still used. The combats had been partly ritualized.

"We'll do it tonight, then," Anana said.

Urthona agreed. He went off to look for McKay and found him within two minutes, since McKay was watching them and saw her signal. They talked for fifteen minutes, after which the two men went down to the beach to help in the fishing. She went out to pick berries and nuts. When she returned on her first trip with two leather bags full, she stood around for a while instead of going out again. She managed to get her hands on three leather-skin water bags and put these in her lean-to. There was little she could do now until late in the night.

The tribe feasted and danced that evening. The shaman chanted for continued prosperity. The bard sang songs of heroes of the olden days. Eventually, the belly-swollen people crawled into their lean-tos and fell asleep. The only ones probably awake were the sentinels, one in a treetop near the shore, one on a platform in the middle of the stockade, and two men stationed along the path to the stockade.

Urthona, Anana, and McKay had eaten sparingly. They worked inside their lean-tos, stuffing smoked fish and antelope and fruits and berries and nuts into provision bags. The water bags would be filled when they got to the lake shore.

When she could hear only snores and the distant cries of birds and the coughing of a lion, she crawled out of the frail structure. She couldn't see the guard on top of the platform. She hoped he had fallen asleep, too. Certainly, he had stuffed himself enough to make him nod off, whatever his good intentions.

Urthona and McKay crawled out of their respective lean-tos. Anana signaled to them. She stood up and walked through the dark reddish light of "midnight" until she was far enough away from the sentinel-platform to see its occupant. He was lying down, flat on his back. Whether he was asleep or not, she couldn't determine, but she suspected he was. He was supposed to stay on his feet and scan the surrounding woods until relieved.

The two men went to the corral that held the moosoids. They got their three beasts out without making too much noise and began to saddle them. Anana carried over the water bags and a full provision bag. These were tied on to a little leather platform behind the saddle.

Anana whispered, "I have to get my ax."

Urthona grimaced, but he nodded. He and his niece had had a short argument about that earlier. Urthona thought that it was best to forget about the ax, but she had insisted that it was vital to have it. While the two men led the animals to the gate, she walked to the chief's lean-to, which was larger than the others. She pushed aside the boughs that surrounded it and crawled into the interior. It was as dark as the inside of a coal mine. The loud snores of Trenn and his wife and son, a half-grown boy, tried to make up for the absence of light with a plenitude of sound. On her hands and knees, she groped around, touching first the woman. Then her hand felt his leg. She withdrew it from the flesh and felt along the grass by it. Her fingers came into contact with cold iron.

A moment later, she was out of the structure, the throwing ax in one hand. For just a second, she'd been tempted to kill Trenn in revenge for his violation of her. But she had resisted. He might make some noise if she did, and anyway, she had already forgiven if not forgotten. Yet . . . something murderous had seized her briefly, made her long to wipe out the injury by wiping the injurer out. Then reason had driven the irrational away.

The gate was a single piece composed of upright poles to which horizontal and transverse bars had been tied with leather cords. Instead of hinges, it was connected to the wall by more leather cords. Several thick strips of leather served as a lock. These were untied, and the heavy gate was lifted up and then turned inward by all three of them.

So far, no one had raised an outcry. The sentinel might wake at any moment. On the other hand, he might sleep all night. He was supposed to be relieved after a two-hour watch. There was no such thing as an "hour" in the tribe's vocabulary, but these people had a rough sense of the passage of time. When the sentinel thought that he'd stood watch long enough, he would descend from the platform and wake up the man delegated to succeed him.

The beasts were passed through, the gate lifted and carried back, and the cords retied. The three mounted and rode off slowly in the half-light, heading down the hill. The moosoids grunted now and then, unhappy at being mounted at this ungodly hour. When the three were about a hundred yards from where they knew the first sentinel was placed, they halted. Anana got off and slipped through the brush until she saw the pale figure sitting with its back against the bole of a tree. Snores buzz-sawed from it.

It was an easy matter to walk up to the man and bring down the flat of her ax on top of his head. He fell over, his snores continuing. She ran back and told the two it was safe to continue. Urthona wanted to slit the man's throat, but Anana said it wasn't necessary. The guard would be unconscious for a long while.

The second sentinel was walking back and forth to keep himself awake. He strode down the hill for fifty paces or so, wheeled, and climbed back up the twenty-degree slope. He was muttering a song, something about the heroic deeds of Sheerkun.

In this comparative stillness, it would be difficult to make a detour around him without his hearing them. He had to be gotten out of the way.

Anana waited until he had turned at the end of his round, ran out behind him, and knocked him out with the flat of her ax. She went back and told the others the way was clear for a while.

When they could see the paleness of the white-sand shore and the darkness of the sea beyond, they stopped. The last of the sentinels was in a giant tree near the beach. Anana said, "There's no use trying to get to him. But he can yell as loudly as he wishes. There's nobody to relay his message to the village."

They rode out boldly onto the sand. The expected outcry did not come. Either the sentinel was dozing or he did not recognize them and believed some of his tribesmen were there for a legitimate reason. Or perhaps he did recognize them but dared not question the agents of the Lord.

When they were out of his sight, the three stopped. After filling the water bags, they resumed their flight, if a leisurely pace could be called a flight. They plodded on steadily, silent, each occupied with his or her own thoughts.

There didn't seem to be any danger from Trenn's tribe. By the time one of the stunned men woke up and gave the alarm, the escapees would have too much of a head start to be caught. The only immediate peril, Anana thought, was from Urthona and McKay. Her uncle could try to kill her now to get the Horn in his own hands. But until they found the palace, she was a strong asset. To survive, Urthona needed her.

"Dawn" came with the first paling of the bands in the sky. As the light increased, they continued. They stopped only to excrete or to drink from the sea and to allow their beasts to quench their thirst. At dusk, they went into the woods. Finding a hollow surrounded by trees, they slept in it most of the night through. They were wakened several times by the howling of dogs and roars of big cats. However, no predators came near. At "dawn," they resumed their journey. At "noon," they came to the place that would lead them up to the pass.

Here Anana reined in her moosoid. She made sure that she wasn't close to them before she spoke. Her left hand was close to the hilt of her sheathed knife—she was ambidextrous—and if she had to, she could drop the reins and snatch out her ax. The men carried flint-tipped spears and had available some heavy war boomerangs.

"I'm going up to the pass and look over the valley from there," she said. "For Kickaha, of course."

Urthona opened his mouth as if to protest. Then he smiled and said, "I doubt it. See." He pointed up the slope.

She didn't look at once. He might be trying to get her to turn her head and thus give him a chance to attack.

McKay's expression, however, indicated that her uncle was pointing at something worth looking at. Or had he arranged beforehand that McKay would pretend to do such if an occasion arose for it?

She turned the beast quickly and moved several yards away. Then she looked up.

From the top of the slope down to the beach was a wide avenue, carpeted by the rust-colored grass. It wasn't a man-made path; nature, or rather, Urthona, had designed it. It gave her an unobstructed view of the tiny figures just emerging from the pass. Men on moosoids. Behind them, women and children and more beasts.

Another tribe was entering the sea-land.

16

"Let's split!" McKay said.

Anana said, "You can if you want to. I'm going to see if Kickaha is with them. Maybe he was captured by them."

Urthona bit his lip. He looked at the black man, then at his niece. Apparently he decided that now was no time to try to kill her. He said, "Very well. What do you intend to do? Ride up to them and ask if you can check them out?"

Anana said, "Don't be sarcastic, Uncle. We'll hide in the woods and watch them."

She urged her *gregg* into the trees. The others followed her, but she made sure that they did not get too close to her back. When she got to a hill that gave her a good view through the trees, she halted. Urthona directed his beast toward her, but she said, "Keep your distance, Uncle!"

He smiled and stopped his moosoid below her. All three sat on their *grewigg* for a while, then, tiring of waiting, got off.

"It'll be an hour before they get here," Urthona said. "And what if those savages turn right? We'll be between the Wendow and this tribe. Caught."

"If Kickaha isn't among them," she said. "I intend to go up the pass after they go by and look for him. I don't care what you want to do. You can go on."

McKay grinned. Urthona grunted. All three understood that as long as she had the Horn, they would stay together.

The *grewigg* seized bushes and low tree limbs with their teeth, tore them off, and ground the leaves to pulp. Their innards rumbled as the food passed toward their big bellies. The flies gathered above beasts and humans and settled over them. The big green insects were not as numerous here as on the plains, but there were enough to irritate the three. Since they had not as yet attained the indifference of the natives, their hands and heads and shoulders were in continuous motion, batting, jerking, shrugging.

Then they were free of the devils for a while. A dozen little birds, blue with white breasts, equipped with wide flat almost-duckish beaks, swooped down. They swirled around the people and the beasts, catching the insects, gulping them down, narrowly averting aerial collisions in their circles. They came very close to the three, several times brushing them with their wings. In two minutes, those flies not eaten had winged off for less dangerous parts.

"I'm glad I invented those birds," Urthona said. "But if I'd known I was going to be in this situation, I'd never have made the flies."

"Lord of the flies," Anana said. "Beezlebub is thy name."

Urthona said, "What?" Then he smiled. "Ah, yes, now I remember."

Anana would have liked to climb a tree so she could get a better view. But she didn't want her uncle to take her *gregg* and leave her stranded. Even if he didn't do that, she'd be at a disadvantage when she got down out of the tree.

After an almost unendurable wait for her, since it was possible, though not very probable, that Kickaha could be coming along, the vanguard came into sight. Soon dark men wearing feathered headdresses rode by. They carried the same weapons and wore the same type of clothes as the Wendow. Around their necks, suspended by cords, were the bones of human fingers. A big man held aloft a pole on which was a lion's skull. Since he was the only one to have such a standard, and he rode in the lead, he must be the chief.

The faces were different from the Wendows', however, and the skins were even darker. Their features were broad, their noses somewhat bigger and even more aquiline, and the eyes had a slight Mongolian cast. They looked like, and probably were, Amerindians. The chief could have been Sitting Bull if he'd been wearing somewhat different garments and astride a horse.

The foreguard passed out of sight. The outriders and the women and children, most of whom were walking, went by. The women wore their shiny raven's-wing hair piled on top of their heads, and their sole garments were leather skirts of ankle length. Many wore necklaces of clamshells. A few carried papooses on backpacks.

Anana suddenly gave a soft cry. A man on a *gregg* had come into sight. He was tall and much paler than the others and had bright red hair.

Urthona said, "It's not Kickaha! It's Red Orc!"

Anana felt almost sick with disappointment.

Her uncle turned and smiled at her. Anana decided at that moment that she was going to kill him at the first opportunity. Anyone who got that much enjoyment out of the sufferings of others didn't deserve to live.

Her reaction was wholly emotional of course, she told herself a minute later. She needed him to survive as much as he needed her. But the instant he was of no more use to her . . .

Urthona said, "Well, well. My brother, your uncle, is in a fine pickle, my dear. He looks absolutely downcast. What do you suppose his captors have in mind for him? Torture? It would be almost worthwhile to hang around and watch it."

"He ain't tied up," McKay said. "Maybe he's been adopted, like us."

Urthona shrugged. "Perhaps. In either case, he'll be suffering. He can spend the rest of his life here with those miserable wretches for all I care. The pain won't be so intense, but it'll be much longer-lasting."

McKay said, "What're we going to do now we know Kickaha's not with them?"

"We haven't seen all of them," Anana said. "Maybe . . ."

"It isn't likely that the tribe would have caught both of them," Urthona said impatiently. "I think we should go now. By cutting at an angle across the woods, we can be on the beach far ahead of them."

"I'm waiting," she said.

Urthona snorted and then spat. "Your sick lust for that *leblabbiy* makes me sick."

She didn't bother to reply. But presently, as the rearguard passed by, she sighed.

"Now are you ready to go?" Urthona said, grinning.

She nodded, but she said, "It's possible that Orc has seen Kickaha."

"What? You surely aren't thinking of . . . ? Are you crazy?"

"I'm going to trail them and when the chance comes, I'll help Orc escape."

"Just because he might know something about your *leblabbiy* lover?"

"Yes."

Urthona's red face was twisted with rage. She knew that it was not just from frustration. Distorting it were also incomprehension, disgust, and fear. He could not understand how she could be so much in love, in love at all, with a mere creature, the descendant of beings made in laboratories. That his niece, a Lord, could be enraptured by the creature Kickaha filled him with loathing for her. The fear was not caused by her action in refusing to go with them or the danger she represented if attacked. It was—she believed it was, anyway—a fear that possibly he might someday be so perverted that he, too, would fall in love with a *leblabbiy*. He feared himself.

Or perhaps she was being too analytical—*ab absurdum*—in her analysis.

Whatever had seized him, it had pushed him past rationality. Snarling, face as red as skin could get without bleeding, eyes tigerish, growling, he sprang at her. Both hands, white with compression, gripped the flint-headed spear.

When he charged, he was ten paces from her. Before he had gone five, he fell back, the spear dropping from his hands, his head and back thudding into the grass. The edge of her ax was sunk into his breastbone.

Almost before the blur of the whirling ax had solidified on Urthona's chest, she had her knife out.

McKay had been caught flat-footed. Whether he would have acted to help her uncle or her would never be determined.

He looked shocked. Not at what had happened to her uncle, of course, but at the speed with which it had occurred.

Whatever his original loyalty was, it was now clear that he had to aid, and to depend upon, her. He could not find the palace without her or, arriving there, know how to get into it. Or, if he could somehow gain entrance to it, know what to do after he was in it.

From his expression, though, he wasn't thinking of this just now. He was wondering if she meant to kill him, too.

"We're in this together, now," she said. "All the way."

He relaxed, but it was a minute before the blue-gray beneath his pigment faded away.

She stepped forward and wrenched the ax from Urthona's chest. It hadn't gone in deeply, and blood ran out from the wound. His mouth was open, his eyes fixed; his skin was grayish. However, he still breathed.

"The end of a long and unpleasant relationship," she said, wiping the ax on the grass. "Yet . . ."

McKay muttered, "What?"

"When I was a little girl, I loved him. He wasn't then what he became later. For that matter, neither was I. Excessive longevity . . . solipsism . . . boredom . . . lust for such power as you Earthlings have never known . . ."

Her voice trailed off as if it were receding into an unimaginably distant past.

McKay made no movement to get closer to her. He said, "What're you going to do?" and he pointed at the still form.

Anana looked down. The flies were swarming over Urthona, chiefly on the wound. It wouldn't be long before the predators, attracted by the odor of blood, would be coming in. He'd be torn apart, perhaps while still living.

She couldn't help thinking of those evenings on their native planet, when he had tossed her in the air and kissed her or when he had brought gifts or when he had made his first world and come to visit before going to it. The Lord of several universes had come to this . . . lying on his back, his blood eaten by insects, the flesh soon to be ripped by fangs and claws.

"Ain't you going to put him out of his misery?" McKay said.

"He isn't dead yet, which means that he still has hope," she said. "No, I'm not going to cut his throat. I'll leave his weapons and his *gregg* here. He might make it, though I doubt it. Perhaps I'll regret not making sure of him, but I can't . . ."

"I didn't like him," McKay said, "but he's going to suffer. It don't seem right."

"How many men have you killed in cold blood for money?" she said. "How many have you tortured, again just for money?"

McKay shook his head. "That don't matter. There was a reason then. There ain't no sense to this."

"It's usually emotional sense, not intellectual, that guides us humans," she said. "Come on."

She brushed by McKay, giving him a chance to attack her if he wanted to. She didn't think he would, and he stepped back as if for some reason, he dreaded her touch.

They mounted and headed at an angle for the beach. Anana didn't look back.

When they broke out of the woods, the only creatures on the beach were birds, dead fish—the only true fish in this world were in the sea-lands—amphibians, and some foxes. The *grewigg* were breathing hard. The long journey without enough sleep and food had tired them.

Anana let the beasts water in the sea. She said, "We'll go back into the forest. We're near enough to the path to see which way they take. Either direction, we'll follow them at a safe distance."

Presently the tribe came out onto the beach on the night side of the channel. With shouts of joy, they ran into the waves, plunged beneath their surface, splashed around playfully. After a while, they began to spear fish, and when enough of these had been collected, they held a big feast.

When night came, they retreated into the woods on the side of the path near where the two watchers were. Anana and McKay retreated some distance. When it became apparent that the savages were going to bed down, they went even farther back into the woods. Anana decided that the tribe would stay put until "dawn" at least. It wasn't likely that it would make this spot a more or less permanent camp. Its members would be afraid of other tribes coming into the area.

Even though she didn't think McKay would harm her, she still went off into the bush to find a sleeping place where he couldn't see her. If he wanted to, he would find her. But he would have to climb a tree to get her. Her bed was some boughs she'd chopped and laid across two branches.

The "night," as all nights here, was not unbroken sleep. Cries of birds and beasts startled her, and twice her dreams woke her.

The first was of her uncle, naked, bleeding from the longitudinal gash in his chest, standing above her on the tree-nest and about to lay his hands on her. She came out of it moaning with terror.

The second was of Kickaha. She'd been wandering around the bleak and shifting landscape of this world when she came across his death-pale body lying in a shallow pool. She started crying, but when she touched him, Kickaha sat up suddenly, grinning, and he cried, "April fool!" He rose and she ran to him and they put their arms around each other, and then they were riding swiftly on a horse that bounced rather than ran, like a giant kangaroo. Anana woke up with her hips emulating the up-and-down movement and her whole being joyous.

She wept a little afterward because the dream wasn't true.

McKay was still sleeping where he had lain down. The hobbled moosoids were tearing off branches about fifty meters away. She bent down and touched his shoulder, and he came up out of sleep like a trout leaping for a dragonfly.

"Don't ever do that again!" he said, scowling.

"Very well. We've got to eat breakfast and then check up on that tribe. Did you hear anything that might indicate they are up and about?"

"Nothing," he said sullenly.

But when they got to the edge of the woods, they saw no sign of the newcomers except for excrement and animal and fish bones. When they rode out onto the white sands, they caught sight, to their right, of the last of the caravan, tiny figures.

After waiting until the Amerinds were out of sight, they followed. Sometime later, they came to another channel running out of the sea. This had to be the waterway they had first encountered, the opening of which had swept Kickaha away. It ran straight outward from the great body of water between the increasingly higher banks of the slope leading up to the pass between the two mountains.

They urged their beasts into the channel and rode them as they swam across. On reaching the other side, they had to slide down off, get onto the beach, and pull on the reins to help the moosoids onto the sand. The Amerinds were still not in view.

She looked up the slope. "I'm going up to the pass and take a look. Maybe he's out on the plain."

"If he was trailing them," McKay said, "he would've been here by now. And gone by now, maybe."

"I know, but I'm going up there anyway."

She urged the moosoid up the slope. Twice, she looked back. The first time, McKay was sitting on his motionless *gregg*. The next time, he was coming along slowly.

On reaching the top of the pass, she halted her beast. The plain had changed considerably. Though the channel was still surrounded by flatland for a distance of about a hundred feet on each side, the ground beyond had sunk. The channel now ran through a ridge on both sides of which were very deep and broad hollows. These were about a mile wide. Mountains of all sizes and shapes had risen along its borders, thrusting up from the edges as if carved there. Even as she watched, one of the tops of the mushroom-shaped heights began breaking off at its edges. The huge pieces slid or rotated down the steep slope, some reaching the bottom, where they fell into the depressions.

There were few animals along the channel, but these began trotting or running away when the first of the great chunks broke off the mushroom peak.

On the other side of the mountains was a downward slope cut by the channel banks. On the side on which she sat was a pile of bones, great and small, that extended down into the plain and far out.

Nowhere was any human being in sight.

Softly, she said, "Kickaha?"

It was hard to believe that he could be dead.

She turned and waved to McKay to halt. He did so, and she started her beast toward him. And then she felt the earth shaking around her. Her *gregg* stopped despite her commands to keep going, and it remained locked in position, though quivering. She got down off it and tried to pull it by the reins, but it dug in, leaning its body back. She mounted again and waited.

The slope was changing swiftly, sinking at the rate of about a foot a minute. The channel was closing up, the sides moving toward each other, and apparently the bottom was moving up, since the water was slopping over its lips.

Heat arose from the ground.

McKay was in the same predicament. His moosoid stubbornly refused to obey despite its rider's beatings with the shaft of his spear.

She turned on the saddle to look behind her. The ridge was becoming a mountain range, a tiny range now but it was evident that if this process didn't stop, it would change into a long and giant barrow. The animals along it were running down its slopes, their destination the ever-increasing depressions along its sides.

However, the two mountains that formed the pass remained solid, immovable.

Anana sighed. There was nothing she could do except sit and wait this out, unless she wanted to dismount. The *gregg*, from long experience, must know the right thing to do.

It was like being on a slow-moving elevator, one in which the temperature rose as the elevator fell. Actually, she felt as if the mountains on her side were rising instead of the ground descending.

The entire change lasted about an hour. At the end, the channel had disappeared, the ridge had stopped swelling and had sunk, the hollows had been filled, and the plain had been restored to the bases of the mountains just outside the sea-land. The animals that had been desperately scrambling around to adjust to the terrain-change were now grazing upon the grass. The predators were now stalking the meat on the hoof. Business as usual.

Anana tick-ticked with her tongue to the *gregg*, and it trotted toward the sea. McKay waited for her to come to him. He didn't ask her if she'd seen Kickaha. He knew that if she had, she would have said so. He merely shook his head and said, "Crazy country, ain't it?"

"It lost us more than an hour, all things considered," she said. "I don't see any reason to push the *grewigg*, though. They're not fully recovered yet. We'll just take it easy. We should find those Indians sometime after dark. They'll be camped for the night."

"Yeah, someplace in the woods," he said. "We might just ride on by them and in the morning, they'll be on our tails."

About three hours after the bright bands of the sky had darkened, Anana's *gregg* stopped, softly rumbling in its throat. She urged it forward with soft words until she saw, through the half-light, a vague figure. She and McKay retreated for a hundred yards and held a short conference. McKay didn't object when she decided that she would take out the guards while he stayed behind.

"I hope the guard don't make any noise when you dispose of him," he said. "What'll I do if he raises a ruckus?"

"Wait and see if anyone else hears him. If they do, then ride like hell to me, bringing my *gregg*, and we'll take off the way we came. Unless, that is, most of the Indians are in the woods. Maybe there's only a guard or two on the beach itself. But I don't plan on making a mistake."

"You're the boss," McKay said. "Good luck."

She went into the woods, moving swiftly when there was no obstruction, slowly when she had to make her way among thick bushes. At last she was opposite the guard, close enough to see that he was a short stocky man. In the dim light, she couldn't make out his features, but she could hear him muttering to himself. He carried a stone-tipped spear in one hand and a war-boomerang was stuck in a belt around his waist. He paced back and forth, generally taking about twenty steps each way.

Anana looked down the beach for other guards. She couldn't see any, but she was certain there would be others stationed along the edge of the woods. For all she knew, there might be one just out of eyesight.

She waited until he had gone past her in the direction of McKay. She rose from behind the bush and walked up behind him. The soft sand made little sound. The flat of her ax came down against the back of his head. He fell forward with a grunt. After waiting for a minute to make sure no one had heard the sound of the ax against the bone, she turned the man over. She had to bend close to him to distinguish his facial features. And she swore quietly.

He was Obran, a warrior of the Wendow.

He wasn't going to regain consciousness for quite a while. She hurried back to McKay, who was sitting on his mount, holding the reins of her beast.

He said, "Man, you scared me! I didn't think you'd be coming back so quick. I thought it was one of them Indians at first."

"Bad news. Those're Trenn's people. They must have come after us after all."

"How in hell did they get by us without us seeing them? Or them Indians?"

"I don't know. Maybe they went by the Indians last night without being detected and then decided to trail them in hopes of getting a trophy or two. No, if they did that, they wouldn't be sleeping here. They'd be stalking the Indian camp now.

"I don't know. It could be that they held a big powwow after we escaped and it took all day for them to get the nerve up to go after us. Somehow, they passed us while we were up in the pass without them seeing us or us seeing them. The point is, they're here, and we have to get by them. You bring the *grewigg* up to the guard and make sure he doesn't wake up. I'll go ahead and take care of the other guards."

That job lasted fifteen or so minutes. She returned and mounted her beast, and they rode slowly on the white sand, reddish in the light, past another fallen man. When they thought they were out of hearing of the Wendow sleeping in the woods, they galloped for a while. After ten minutes of this, they eased their animals into a trot.

Once more they had to detect the guard before he saw them; Anana slipped off the *gregg* and knocked out three Amerinds stationed at wide intervals near the edge of the woods.

When she came back, McKay shook his head and muttered, "Lady, you're really something."

When they had first been thrown together, he had been rather contemptuous of her. This was a reflection of his attitude toward women in general. Anana had thought it strange, since he came from a race that had endured prejudice and repression for a long time, and still was in 1970. His own experience should have made him wary of prejudice toward other groups, especially women, which included black females. But he thought of all women, regardless of color, as inferior beings, useful only for exploitation.

Anana had shaken this attitude considerably, though he had rationalized that after all, she was not an Earth female.

She didn't reply. The *grewigg* were ridden to where the last unconscious sentinel lay, and they were tied to two large bushes where they could feed. She and McKay went into the woods on their bellies and presently came on the first of the sleepers, a woman with a child. Luckily, these people had no dogs to warn them. Anana suspected that the Amerinds probably did own dogs but, judging from their leanness, the tribe had been forced to eat them during the journey to the sea-land.

They snaked through a dozen snorers, moving slowly, stopping to look at each man closely. Once a woman sat up suddenly, and the two, only a few feet behind her, froze. After some smackings of lips, the woman lay back down and resumed sleeping. A few minutes later, they found Red Orc. He was lying on his side within a circle of five dead-to-the-world men. His hands were tied behind him, and a cord bound his ankles together.

Anana clamped her hand over her uncle's mouth at the same time that McKay pressed his heavy body on him. Red Orc struggled and almost succeeded in rolling over, until Anana whispered in his native language, "Quiet!"

He became still, though he trembled, and Anana said, "We're here to get you away."

She removed her hand. The black stood up. She cut the rawhide cords, and Orc rose, looked around, walked over to a sleeper and took the spear lying by his side. The three walked out of camp, though slowly, until they came to an unsaddled *gregg*. Cautiously, they got a saddle and reins and put the reins on. Orc carried the saddle while Anana led the beast away. When they got to the two *grewigg* tied to the bushes, Anana told Orc some of what had happened.

The light was a little brighter here on the beach. When she stood close to him, she could see that her uncle's face and body were deeply bruised.

"They beat me after they caught me," he said. "The women did, too. That went on for the first day, but after that, they only kicked me now and then when I didn't move quickly enough to suit them. I'd like to go back and cut the throats of a few."

"You can do that if you like," she said. "After you've answered a question. Did you see Kickaha or hear anything about him?"

"No, I didn't see him and if those savages said anything about him, I wouldn't have known it. I wasn't with them long enough to understand more than a dozen words."

"That's because you didn't try," she said. She was disappointed, though she really hadn't expected anything.

Red Orc walked over to the still-unconscious sentinel, got down on his knees, put his hands around the man's neck, and did not remove them until he had strangled the life out of him.

Breathing hard, he rose. "There. That'll show them!"

Anana did not express her disgust. She waited until Orc had saddled up his animal and mounted. Then she moved her animal out ahead, and after ten minutes of a slow walk, she urged her *gregg* into a gallop. After five minutes of this, she slowed it to a trot, the others following suit.

Orc rode up beside her.

"Was that why you rescued your beloved uncle? Just so you could ask me about your *leblabbiy* lover?"

"That's the only reason, of course," she said.

"Well, I suppose I owe you for that, not to mention not killing me when you got what you wanted from me. Also, my thanks, though you weren't doing it for my benefit, for taking care of Urthona. But you should have made sure he was dead. He's a tough one."

Anana took her ax from her belt and laid its flat across the side of his face. He dropped from the *gregg* and landed heavily on the sand. McKay said, "What the . . . ?"

"I can't trust him," she said. "I just wanted to get him out of earshot of the Indians."

Orc groaned and struggled to get up. He could only sit up, leaning at an angle on one arm. The other went up to the side of his face.

"Bring his *gregg* along with you," she told McKay, and she commanded hers to start galloping. After about five minutes of this, she made it trot again. The black came up presently, holding the reins of Orc's beast.

"How come you didn't snuff him out, too?"

"There was a time when I would have. I suppose that Kickaha has made me more humane, that is, what a human should be."

"I'd hate to see you when you felt mean," he said, and thereafter for a long time, they were silent.

Anana had given up searching for Kickaha. It was useless to run around, as he would have said, "like a chicken with its head cut off." She'd go around the sea, hoping that the palace might be in sight. If she could get in, then she'd take the flying machine, what the Wendow had called the *shelbett,* and look for Kickaha from the air. Her chances of coming across the mobile palace seemed, however, to be little.

No matter. What else was there to do here but to search for it?

For a while, they guided their *grewigg* through the shallow water. Then they headed across the beach into the woods, where she cut off a branch and smoothed out their traces with its leaves. For the rest of the night, they holed up on top of a hill deep in the forest.

In the morning, the *grewigg* got nasty. They were tired and hungry.

After she and McKay had come close to being bitten and kicked, Anana decided to let them have their way. A good part of the day, the animals ate, and their two owners took turns observing from the top of a tall tree. Anana had expected the Indians to come galloping along in hot pursuit. But the daytime period had half passed before she saw them in the distance. It was a war party, about twenty warriors.

She called McKay and told him to have the *grewigg* ready for travel, whether the animals liked the idea or not.

Now she realized that she should have taken the animals through the water at once after leaving the camp. That way, the Indians wouldn't have known which direction to take in pursuit, and they might have given up. The precaution was too late, like so many things in life.

The warriors went on by. Not far, though. About two hundred yards past the point where the refugees had entered the wood, the party stopped. There was what looked like a hot argument between two men, one being the man holding the lion's skull on the end of the pole. Whoever wanted the party to go back won. They turned their *grewigg* around and headed back at a trot toward the camp.

No, not their camp. Now she could see the first of a caravan. It was coming at the pace of the slowest walker, and the hunters met them. The whole tribe halted while a powwow was held. Then the march resumed.

She told McKay what was happening. He swore and said, "That means we got to stay here and give them plenty of time to go by."

"We're in no hurry," she said. "But we don't have to wait for them. We'll cut down through the woods and come out way ahead of them."

That was the theory. In practice, her plan turned out otherwise. They emerged from the woods just in time to see, and be seen by, two riders. They must have been sent on ahead as scouts, or perhaps they were just young fellows racing for fun. Whatever the reason for their presence, they turned back, their big beasts galloping.

Anana couldn't see the rest of the tribe. She supposed that they were not too far away, hidden by a bend of the shore. Anyway, she and McKay should have a twenty minutes' head start, at the least.

There was nothing else to do but to force the tired animals into a gallop. They rode at full speed for a while, went into a trot for a while, then broke into a gallop again. This lasted, with a few rest periods, until nightfall. Into the woods they went, and they took turns sleeping and standing watch. In the morning, the animals were again reluctant to continue. Nevertheless, after some savage tussles and beatings, the two got the *grewigg* going. It was evident, however, that they weren't up to more than one day's steady travel, if that.

By noon, the first of the hunters came into view. They drew steadily though slowly nearer as the day passed.

"The poor beasts have about one more good gallop left in them," Anana said. "And that won't be far."

"Maybe we ought to take to the woods on foot," McKay said.

She had already considered that. But if these Indians were as good trackers as their Terrestrial counterparts were supposed to be, they'd catch up with their quarry eventually.

"Are you a strong swimmer?" she said.

McKay's eyes opened. He jerked a thumb toward the water. "You mean . . . out there?"

"Yes, I doubt very much that the Indians can."

"Yeah, but you don't *know*. I can swim, and I can float, but not all day. Besides, there may be sharks, or worse things, out there."

"We'll ride until the beasts drop and then we'll take to the sea. At least, I will. Once we're out of their sight, we can get back to shore some distance down, maybe a few miles."

"Not me," McKay said. "No way. I'm heading for the woods."

"Just as you like."

She reached into a bag and withdrew the Horn. She'd have to strap that over her shoulder beforehand, but it didn't weigh much and shouldn't be much of a drag.

After an hour, the pursuers were so close that it was necessary to force the *grewigg* to full speed. This wasn't equal to the pace of the less tired animals behind them. It quickly became evident that in a few minutes, the Indians would be alongside them.

"No use going on any more!" she shouted. "Get off before they fall down and you break your neck!"

She pulled on the reins. When the sobbing foam-flecked animals began trotting, she rolled off the saddle. The soft sand eased the impact; she was up on her feet immediately. McKay followed a few seconds later. He rose and shouted, "Now what?"

The war party was about a hundred yards away and closing the gap swiftly. They whooped as they saw their victims were on foot. Some cut into the woods, evidently assuming that the two would run for it. Anana splashed into the shallow water and when it was up to her waist, shucked her ragged jeans and boots. McKay was close behind her.

"I though you were going for the trees?"

"Naw. I'd be too lonely!"

They began swimming with long slow strokes. Anana, looking back, saw that their pursuers were still on the shore. They were yelling with frustration and fury, and some were throwing their spears and hurling boomerangs after them. These fell short.

"You was right about one thing," McKay said as they dog-paddled. "They can't swim. Or maybe they're afraid to. Them sharks . . ."

She started swimming again, heading out toward the horizon. But another look behind her made her stop.

It was too distant to be sure. But if the redheaded man on the *gregg* charging the Indians by himself wasn't Kickaha, then she was insane. It couldn't be Red Orc; he wouldn't do anything so crazy.

Then she saw other riders emerging from the woods, a big party. Were they chasing Kickaha so they could aid him when they caught up with him, or did they want his blood?

Perhaps Kickaha was not charging the Indians single-handedly, as she'd first thought. He was just running away from those behind him, and now it was a case of the crocodile in the water and the tiger on the bank.

Whatever the situation, she was going to help him if she could. She began swimming toward the shore.

17

WHEN KICKAHA RODE OUT OF THE WOODS, HE HAD EXPECTED the people chasing Anana to be far ahead of him. He was surprised when he saw them only a hundred yards away. Most of them were dismounted and standing on the shore or in the water, yelling and gesticulating at something out in the sea.

Neither Anana nor McKay were in sight.

The discreet thing to do was to turn the *hikwu* as quickly as possible and take off in the opposite direction. However, the only reason for the strangers—whom he instantly identified as Amerinds—halting and making such a fuss here was that their quarry had taken to the sea. He couldn't see them, but they couldn't be too far out. And his tribe, the Thana, couldn't be very far behind him.

So, repressing a war cry, he rode up and launched a boomerang at the gray-headed, red-eyed man sitting on his *hikwu*. Before the heavy wooden weapon struck the man on the side of the head and knocked him off his seat, Kickaha had transferred the spear from his left hand to his right. By then, the few mounted warriors were aware of his presence. They wheeled their beasts, but one, another gray-haired man, didn't complete the turn in time to avoid Kickaha. His spear drove into the man's throat; the man fell backward; Kickaha jerked it out of the flesh, reversed it, and using the shaft as a club, slammed it alongside the head of a warrior running to his *merk*.

Having run past all the men, he halted his beast, turned it, and charged again. This time, he didn't go through the main body but skirted them, charging between them and the woods. A man threw a boomerang; Kickaha ducked; it whirred by, one tip just missing his shoulder. Crouched down, holding the shaft of the spear between his arm and body, Kickaha drove its tip into the back of a man who'd just gotten on to his animal but was having trouble controlling it. The man pitched forward and over the shoulder of his *hikwu*. Kickaha yanked the spear out as the man disappeared from his beast.

By then, the first of the Thana had shown up, and the mêlée started.

It should have been short work. The Amerinds were outnumbered and demoralized, caught, if not with their pants down, on foot, which was the same thing to them. But just as the last five were fighting furiously, though hopelessly, more whoops and yells were added to the din.

Kickaha looked up and swore. Here came a big body of more Amerinds, enough to outnumber the Thana. Within about eighty seconds, they'd be charging into his group.

He rose on his stirrups and looked out across the waves. At first, he couldn't see anything except a few amphibians. Then he saw a head and arms splashing the water. A few seconds later, he located a second swimmer.

He looked down the beach. A number of riderless *hikwu* had bolted when he'd burst among them, and three were standing at the edge of the forest, tearing off branches. Their first loyalty was to themselves, that is, their bellies.

Speaking of loyalties, what was his? Did he owe the Thana anything? No, not really. It was true that they'd initiated him, made him a sort of blood brother. But his only choice then was to submit or die, which wasn't a real choice. So, he didn't owe his tribe anything.

Still standing up in the stirrups, he waved his spear at the two heads in the waves. A white arm came up and gestured at him. Anana's, no doubt of that. He used the spear to indicate that she should angle to a spot farther down the beach. Immediately, she and McKay obeyed.

Good. They would come out of the water some distance from the fight and would be able to grab two of the browsing moosoids. But it would take them some time to do so, and before then, the Amerinds might have won. So, it was up to him to attempt to give Anana the needed time.

Yelling, he urged his *hikwu* into a gallop. His spear drove deep into the neck of a redskin who had just knocked a Thana off his saddle with a big club. Once more, Kickaha jerked the spear loose. He swore. The flint point had come off the wood. Never mind. He rammed its blunt end into the back of the head of another Indian, stunning him enough so that his antagonist could shove his spear into the man's belly.

Then something struck Kickaha on the head, and he fell half-conscious onto the sand. For a moment, he lay there while hooves churned the sand, stomped, missing him narrowly several times, and a body thumped onto the ground beside him. It was a Thana, Toini, the youth who'd given him a hard time. Though blood streamed from his head and his shoulder, Toini wasn't out of the battle. He staggered up, only to be knocked down as a *hikwu* backed into him.

Kickaha got up. For the first time, he became aware that he was bleeding. Whatever had struck him on top of the head had opened the scalp. There was no time to take care of that now. He leaped for a mounted Indian who was beating at a Thana with a heavy boomerang, grabbed the man's arm, and yanked him off his saddle. Yelling, the warrior came down on Kickaha, and both fell to the sand.

Kickaha fastened his teeth on the redskin's nose and bit savagely. One groping hand felt around, closed on testicles, and squeezed.

Screaming, the man rolled off. Kickaha released his teeth, spun around on his back, raised his neck to see his enemy, and kicked his head hard with the heels of his feet. The man went limp and silent.

A hoof drove down hard, scraping the side of his upper arm. He rolled over to keep from being trampled. Blood and moosoid manure fell on him, and sand was kicked into his eyes. He got to his hands and knees. Half-blind, he crawled through the fray, was knocked over once by something or other, probably the side of a flailing *hikwu*-leg, got up, and crawled some more, stopped once when a spear drove into the sand just in front of his face, and then, finally, was in the water.

Here he opened his eyes all the way and ducked his head under the surface. It came up in time for him to see two mounted battlers coming toward him, a Thana and an Amerind striking at each other with boomerangs. The male beast of one was pushing the female of the other out into the water. If he stayed where he was, he was going to be pounded by the hooves. He dived, his face and chest scraping against the bottom sand. When he came up, he was about twenty feet away. By then, he recognized the Thana who was being driven from the shore. He was the chief, holding in one hand Kickaha's metal knife and in the other, a boomerang. But he was outclassed by the younger man. His arms moved slowly as if they were very tired, and the redskin was grinning in anticipation of his triumph.

Kickaha stood up to his waist in the water and waded toward them. He got to the chief's side just as a blow from the young man's boomerang made the older's arm nerveless. The boomerang dropped; the chief thrust with his left arm, but his knife missed; the enemy's wooden weapon came down on his head twice.

Wergenget dropped the knife into the water. Kickaha dived after it, skimmed the bottom, and his groping hands felt the blade. Then something, Wergenget, of course, fell on him. The shock knocked the air out of Kickaha's lungs; he gasped; water filled his throat; he came up out of the sea coughing and choking. He was down again, propelled by the redskin, who had jumped off his *hikwu*. Kickaha was at a definite disadvantage, trying to get his breath, and at the same time, feeling for the knife he'd dropped.

His antagonist wasn't as big as he was, but he was certainly strong and quick. His left hand closed over Kickaha's throat, and his right hand came up with the boomerang. Kickaha, looking up through watery eyes, could see death. His right leg came up between the man's legs and his knee drove into the warrior's crotch. Since the leg had to come out of the water, its force wasn't as strong as Kickaha had hoped. Nevertheless, it was enough to cause the redskin some pain. For a moment, his hand loosed the throat, and he straightened up, his face contorted.

Kickaha was still on his back in the water, and his choking hadn't stopped. But his left hand touched something hard, the fingers opened out and closed on the blade. They moved up and gripped the hilt. The Indian reached down to grab the throat of what he thought was still a much-disadvantaged enemy. But he stood to one side so Kickaha couldn't use the crotch kick again.

Kickaha drove the end of the knife into the youth's belly just above the pubic region. It slit open the flesh to the navel; the youth dropped the boomerang, the hand reaching for the throat fell away; he looked surprised, clutched his belly, and fell face forward into the water.

Kickaha spent some time seemingly coughing his lungs out. Then he scanned the scene. The two beasts ridden by the chief and the Indian had bolted. Anana and McKay were still about four hundred feet from the shore and swimming strongly. The battle on the beach had tipped in favor of the Amerinds. But here came more of the Thana, including the women and Onil and Opwel, who had come down from their sentry perches. He doubted that the redskins could stand up under the new forces.

After removing Wergenget's belt, along with the sheath, he wrapped it around his waist. He picked up a boomerang and waded until the water was up to his knees. He followed the line of the beach, got past the action, went ashore, and ran along the sand. When he got near some riderless moosoids, he slowed down, approached them cautiously, seized the reins, and tied them to the bushes. Another unmounted *hikwu* trotted along but slowed enough when Kickaha called to him to allow his reins to be grabbed. Kickaha tied him up and waded out into the sea to help the swimmers. They came along several minutes later. They were panting and tired. He had to support both to get them in to shore without collapsing. They threw themselves down on the sand and puffed like a blacksmith's bellows.

He said, "You've got to get up and on the *hikwu.*"

"*Hikwu?*" Anana managed to say.

"The meese. Your steeds await to carry you off from peril." He jerked a thumb at the beasts.

Anana succeeded in smiling. "Kickaha? Won't you ever quit kidding?"

He pulled her up, and she threw her arms around him and wept a little. "Oh, Kickaha, I thought I'd never see you again!"

"I've never been so happy," he said, "but I can become even happier if we get out of here now."

They ran to the animals, untied them, mounted, and galloped off. The clash and cry of battle faded away, and when they rounded another big bend, they lost both sight and sound of it. They settled into a fast trot. Kickaha told her what had happened to him, though he discreetly omitted certain incidents. She then told her tale, slightly censored. Both expected to supply the missing details later, but now did not seem like a good time.

Kickaha said, "At any time, when you were up in a tree, did you see anything that could have been the palace?"

She shook her head.

"Well, I think we ought to climb one of those mountains surrounding the sea and take a look. Some are about five thousand feet high. If we could get to the top of one of those, we could see, hmm, it's been so long, I can't remember. Wait a minute. I think from that height, the horizon is, ah, around ninety-six statute miles.

"Well, it doesn't matter. We can see a hell of a long way, and the palace is really big, according to Urthona. On the other hand, the horizon of this planet may not be as far away as Earth's. Anyway, it's worth a try."

Anana agreed. McKay didn't comment since the two were going to do what they wanted to do. He followed them into the woods.

It took three days to get to the top of the conical peak. The climb was difficult enough, but they had to take time out to hunt and to allow themselves and the beasts to rest. After hobbling the animals, Anana and Kickaha set out on foot, leaving McKay to make sure the *hikwu* didn't stray too far. The last hundred feet of the ascent was the hardest. The mountain ended in a sharp spire that swayed back and forth due to the slightly changing shape of the main mass. The very tip, though it looked needle-sharp from below, actually was a dirt platform about the size of a large dining-room table. They stood on it and swept the sea with their gaze and wished they had a pair of binoculars.

After a while, Kickaha said, "Nothing."

"I'm afraid so," Anana said. She turned around to look over the vista outside the sea-land, and she clutched his arm.

"Look!"

Kickaha's eyes sighted along the line indicated by her arm.

"I don't know," he said. "It looks like a big dark rock, or a hill, to me."

"No, it's moving! Wait a minute."

The object could easily have been hidden by one of two mountains if it had been on the left or right for a half a mile. It was moving just beyond a very broad pass and going up a long gentle slope. Kickaha estimated that it was about twenty miles away and of an enormous size.

"That *has* to be the palace!" he said. "It must have come through a pass from the sea-land!"

The only thing damping his joy was that it was so far away. By the time they got down off the mountain, traveled to the next pass and got through it, the palace would be even farther away. Not only that, they could not depend upon the two mountains to guide them. By the time they got there, the mountains could be gone or they could have split into four or merged into one. It was so easy to lose your bearings here, especially when there was no east or north or south or west.

Still, the range that circled the sea-lands would be behind them and it changed shape very little.

"Let's go!" he said, and began to let himself backwards over the lip of the little plateau.

18

IT WAS ELEVEN DAYS LATER. THE TRIO HOPED THAT WITHIN A few days, they would be in sight of the palace. The twin peaks between which it had gone had become one breast-shaped giant. Deep hollows had formed around it, and these were full of water from a heavy rain of the day before. It was necessary to go about ten miles around the enormous moat.

Before they rounded it, the mountain grew into a cone, the hollows pushed up, spilling the water out. They decided to climb the mountain then to get another sight of Urthona's ex-abode. Though the climb would delay them even more, they thought it worth it. The mobile structure could have headed on a straight line, turned in either direction, or even be making a great curve to come behind them. According to Anana's uncle, when it was on automatic, its travel path was random.

On top of the mountain, they looked in all directions. Plains and ranges spread out, slowly shifting shape. There was plenty of game and here and there, dark masses that were groves and forests of traveling plants. Far off to the right were tiny figures, a line of tribes people on their way to the sea-land.

All three strained their eyes, and finally Kickaha saw a dot moving slowly straight ahead. Was it an army of trees or the palace?

"I don't think you could see it if it was composed of plants," Anana said. "They don't get very high, you know. At this distance, that object would have to be something with considerable height."

"Let's hope so," Kickaha said.

McKay groaned. He was tired of pushing themselves and the animals to the limit.

There was nothing to do but go on. Though they traveled faster than their quarry, they had to stop to hunt, eat, drink, and sleep. It continued on at its mild pace, a kilometer an hour, like an enormous mindless untiring turtle in tepid heat looking for a mate. And it left no tracks, since it floated a half meter above the surface.

For the next three days, it rained heavily. They slogged on through, enduring the cold showers, but many broad depressions formed and filled with water, forcing them to go around them. Much mileage was lost.

The sixth day after they'd sighted the palace again, they lost Anana's beast. While they were sleeping, a lion attacked it, and though they drove the lion off, they had to put the badly mauled *hikwu* out of its misery. This provided for their meat supply for several days before it got too rotten to eat, but Anana had to take turns riding behind the two men. And this slowed them down.

The sixteenth day, they climbed another mountain for another sighting. This time, they could identify it, but it wasn't much closer than the last time seen.

"We could chase it clear around this world," McKay said disgruntledly.

"If we have to, we have to," Kickaha said cheerfully. "You've been bitching a lot lately, Mac. You're beginning to get on my nerves. I know it's a very hard life, and you haven't had a woman for many months, but you'd better grin and bear it. Crack a few jokes, do a cakewalk now and then."

McKay looked sullen. "This ain't no minstrel show."

"True, but Anana and I are doing our best to make light of it. I suggest you change your attitude. You could be worse off. You could be dead. We have a chance, a good one, to get out of here. You might even get back to Earth, though I suppose it'd be best for the people there if you didn't. You've stolen, tortured, killed, and raped. But maybe, if you were in a different environment, you might change. That's why I don't think it'd be a good idea for you to return to Earth."

"How in hell did we get off from my bitching to that subject?" McKay said.

Kickaha grinned. "One thing leads to another. The point I'm getting at is that you're a burden. Anana and I could go faster if we didn't have to carry you on our moosoid."

"Yours?" McKay blazed, sullenness becoming open anger. "She's riding on my *gregg!*"

"Actually, it belongs to an Indian. Did, I should say. Now it's whoever has the strength to take it. Do I make myself clear?"

"You'd desert me?"

"Rationally, we should. But Anana and I won't as long as you help us. So," he suddenly shouted, "quit your moaning and groaning!"

McKay grinned. "Okay, I guess you're right. I ain't no crybaby normally, but this . . ." He waved a hand to indicate the whole world. "Too much. But I promise to stop beefing. I guess I ain't been no joy for you two."

Kickaha said, "Okay, let's go. Now, did I ever tell you about the time I had to hide out in a fully stocked wine cellar in a French town when the Krauts retook it?"

Two months later, the traveling building still had not been caught. They were much closer now. When they occasionally glimpsed it, it was about ten miles away. Even at that distance, it looked enormous, towering an estimated 2600 feet, a little short of half a mile. Its width and length were each about 1200 feet, and its bottom was flat.

Kickaha could see its outline but could not, of course, make out its details. According to Urthona, it would, at close range, look like an ambulatory *Arabian Nights* city, with hundreds of towers, minarets, domes, and arches. From time to time, its surface changed color, and once it was swathed in rainbows.

Now, it was halfway on the other side of an enormous plain that had opened out while they were coming down a mountain. The range that had ringed it was flattening out, and the animals that had been on the mountainsides were now great herds on the plains.

"Ten miles away," Kickaha said. "And it must have about thirty miles more to go before it reaches the end of the plain. I say we should try to catch it now. Push until our *hikwu* drop and then chase it on foot. Keep going, no matter what."

The others agreed, but they weren't enthusiastic. They'd lost weight, and their faces were hollow-cheeked, their eyes ringed with the dark of near-exhaustion. Nevertheless, they had to make the effort. Once the palace reached the mountains, it would glide easily up over them, maintaining the same speed as it had on the plain. But its pursuers would have to slow down.

As soon as they reached the flatland, they urged the poor devils under them into a gallop. They responded as best they could, but they were far from being in top condition. Nevertheless, the ground was being eaten up. The herds parted before them, the antelopes and gazelles stampeding. During the panic the predators took advantage of the confusion and panic. The dogs, baboons, moas, and lions caught fleeing beasts and dragged them to the ground. Roars, barks, screams drifted by the riders as they raced toward their elusive goal.

Now Kickaha saw before them some very strange creatures. They were mobile plants—perhaps—resembling nothing he'd ever come across before. In essence, they looked like enormous logs with legs. The trunks were horizontal, pale gray, with short stubby branches bearing six or seven diamond-shaped black-green leaves. From each end rose structures that looked like candelabra. But as he passed one, he saw that eyes, enormous eyes, much like human eyes, were at the ends of the candelabra. These turned as the two moosoids galloped by.

More of these weird-looking things lay ahead of them. Each had a closed end and an open end.

Kickaha directed his *hikwu* away from them, and McKay followed suit. Kickaha shouted to Anana, who was seated behind him, "I don't like the look of those things!"

"Neither do I!"

One of the logoids, about fifty yards to one side, suddenly began tilting up its open end, which was pointed at them. The other end rested on the ground while the forelegs began telescoping upward.

Kickaha got the uneasy impression that the thing resembled a cannon, the muzzle of which was being elevated for firing.

A moment later, the dark hole in its raised end shot out black smoke. From the smoke something black and blurred described an arc and fell about twenty feet to their right.

It struck the rusty grass, and it exploded.

The moosoid screamed and increased its gallop as if it had summoned energy from somewhere within it.

Kickaha was half-deafened for a moment. But he wasn't so stunned he didn't recognize the odor of the smoke. Black gunpowder!

Anana said, "Kickaha, you're bleeding!"

He didn't feel anything, and now was no time to stop to find out where he'd been hit. He yelled more encouragement to his *hikwu*. But that yell was drowned the next moment when at least a dozen explosions circled him. The smoke blinded him for a moment, then he was out of it. Now he couldn't hear at all. Anana's hands were still around his waist though, so he knew she was still with him.

He looked back over his shoulder. Here came McKay on his beast, flying out of black clouds. And behind him came a projectile, a shell-shaped black object, drifting along lazily, or so it seemed. It fell behind McKay, struck, went up with a roar, a cloud of smoke in the center of which fire flashed. The black man's *hikwu* went over, hooves over hooves. McKay flew off the saddle, struck the ground, and rolled. The big body of his *hikwu* flip-flopped by, narrowly missing him.

But McKay was up and running.

Kickaha pulled his *hikwu* up, stopping it.

Through the drifting smoke, he could see that a dozen of the plants had erected their front open ends and pointed them toward the humans. Out of the cannonlike muzzles of two shot more smoke, noise, and projectiles. These blew up behind McKay at a distance of forty feet. He threw himself on the ground—too late, of course, to escape their effects—but he was up and running as soon as they had gone off.

Behind him were two small craters in the ground.

Miraculously, McKay's moosoid had not broken its neck or any legs. It scrambled up, its lips drawn back to reveal all its big long teeth, its eyes seemingly twice as large. It sped by McKay, whose mouth opened as he shouted curses that Kickaha couldn't hear.

Anana had already grasped what had to be done. She had slipped off the saddle and was making motions to Kickaha, knowing he couldn't hear her. He kicked the sides of the beast and yelled at it, though he supposed it was as deaf as he. It responded and went after McKay's fleeing beast. The chase was a long one, however, and ended when McKay's mount stopped running. Foam spread from its mouth and dappled its front, and its sides swelled and shrank like a bellows. It crumpled, rolled over on its side, and died.

Its rear parts were covered with blood.

Kickaha rode back to where Anana and McKay stood. They were wounded, too, mainly in the back. Blood welled from a score of little objects half-buried in the skin. Now he became aware that blood was coming from just behind and above his right elbow.

He grabbed the thing stuck in his skin and pulled it out. Rubbing the blood from its surface, he looked at it. It was a six-pointed crystalline star.

"Craziest shrapnel I ever saw," he said. No one heard him.

The plants, which he had at once named cannonlabra, had observed that their shelling had failed to get the passersby. They were now heading away, traveling slowly on their hundred or so pairs of thin big-footed legs. Fifteen minutes later, he was to see several lay their explosive eggs near enough to an elephant calf to kill it. Some of the things then climbed over the carcass and began tearing at it with claws that appeared from within the feet. The foremost limbs dropped pieces of meat into an aperture on the side.

Apparently McKay's dead animal was too far away to be observed.

Anana and McKay spent the next ten minutes painfully pulling the "shrapnel" from their skins. Pieces of grass were applied to the wounds to stop the bleeding.

"I'd sure like to stuff Urthona down the muzzle of one of those," Kickaha said. "It'd be a pleasure to see him riding its shell. He must have had a lot of sadistic pleasure out of designing those things."

He didn't know how the creature could convert its food into black gunpowder. It took charcoal, sodium or potassium nitrate, and sulfur to make the explosive. That was one mystery. Another was how the things "grew" shell casings. A third was how they ignited the charge that propelled the shells.

There was no time to investigate. A half hour had been lost in the chase, and McKay had no steed.

"Now, you two, don't argue with me," Kickaha said. He got off the *hikwu*. "Anana, you ride like hell after the palace. You can go faster if I'm not on it, and you're the lightest one, so you'll be the least burden for the *hikwu*. I was thinking for a minute that maybe McKay and I could run alongside you, hanging on to the saddle. But we'd start bleeding again, so that's out. You take off now. If you catch up with the palace, you might be able to get inside and stop it. It's a slim chance, but it's all we got. We'll be moseying along."

Anana said, "That makes sense. Wish me luck."

She said, "*Heekhyu!*"—the Wendow word for "Giddap!"—and the moosoid trotted off. Presently, under Anana's lashings, it was galloping.

McKay and Kickaha started walking. The flies settled on their wounds. Behind them, explosions sounded as the cannonlabra laid down an artillery barrage in the midst of an antelope herd.

An hour passed. They were trotting now, but their leaden legs and heavy breathing had convinced them they couldn't keep up the pace. Still, the palace was bigger. They were gaining on it. The tiny figures of Anana and her beast had merged into the rusty grass of what seemed a never-ending plain.

They stopped to drink bad-tasting water from the bag McKay had taken off his dead *hikwu*. McKay said, "Man, if she don't catch that palace, we'll be stranded here for the rest of our life."

"Maybe it'll reverse its course," Kickaha said. He didn't sound very optimistic.

Just as he was lifting the bag to pour water into his open mouth, he felt the earth shaking. Refusing to be interrupted, he quenched his thirst. But as he put the bag down, he realized that this was no ordinary tremor caused by shape-shifting. It was a genuine earthquake. The ground was lifting up and down, and he felt as if he were standing on a plate in an enormous bowl of jelly being shaken by a giant. The effect was scary and nauseating.

McKay had thrown himself down on the earth. Kickaha decided he might as well do so, too. There was no use wasting energy trying to stand up. He faced toward the palace, however, so he could see what was happening in that direction. This was really rotten luck. While this big tremor was going on, Anana would not be able to ride after the palace.

The shaking up-and-down movement continued. The animals had fled for the mountains, the worst place for them if the quake continued. The birds were taking off, millions salt-and-peppering the sky, then coalescing to form one great cloud. They were all heading toward the direction of the palace.

Presently, he saw a dot coming toward him. In a few minutes, it became a microscopic Anana and *hikwu*. Then the two separated, both rolling on the ground. Only Anana got up. She ran toward him or tried to do so, rather. The waves of grass-covered earth were like swells in the sea. They rose beneath her and propelled her forward down their slope, casting her

on her face. She got up and ran some more, and once she disappeared behind a big roller, just like a small boat in a heavy sea.

"I'm going to get sick," McKay said. He did. Up to then, Kickaha had
been able to manage his own nausea, but the sound of the black man's
heavings and retchings sparked off his own vomit.

Now, above the sounds he was making, he heard a noise that was as
loud as if the world were cracking apart. He was more frightened than he'd
ever been in his life. Nevertheless, he got to his hands and knees and
stared out toward where Anana had been. He couldn't see her, but he
could see just beyond where she'd been.

The earth was curling up like a scroll about to be rolled. Its edges were
somewhat beyond where he'd last seen Anana. But she could have fallen
into the gigantic fissure.

He got to his feet and cried, "Anana! Anana!" He tried to run toward
her, but he was pitched up so violently that he rose a foot into the air.
When he came down, he slid on his face down the slope of a roller.

He struggled up again. For a moment, he was even more confused
and bewildered, his sense of unreality increasing. The mountains in the far
distance seemed to be sliding downward as if the planet had opened to
swallow them.

Then he realized that they were not falling down.

The ground on which he stood was rising.

He was on a mass being torn away to make a temporary satellite for the
main body of the planet.

The palace was out of sight now, but he had seen that it was still on the
main body. The fissure had missed by a mile or so, marooning it with its
pursuers.

19

THE SPLIT-OFF NOW WAS ONE HUNDRED MILES ABOVE THE PRI-
mary and in a stable, if temporary, orbit. It would take about four hundred
days before the lesser mass started to fall into the greater. And that descent
would be a slow one.

The air seemed no less thick than that on the surface of the planet. The
atmosphere had the same pressure at an altitude of 528,000 feet as it had
at ground zero. Urthona had never explained the physical principles of
this phenomenon. This was probably because he didn't know them.
Though he had made the specifications for the pocket universe, he had left
it up to a team of scientists to make his world work. The scientists were
dead millennia ago, and the knowledge long lost. But their manufactures
survived and apparently would until all the universes ran down.

The earthquakes had not ceased once the split-off had torn itself away.
It had started readjusting, shaping from a wedge form into a globe. This
cataclysmic process had taken twelve days, during which its marooned life
had had to move around much and swiftly to keep from being buried.
Much of it had not succeeded. The heat of energy released during the
transformation had been terrible, but it had been alleviated by one rain-
storm after another. For almost a fortnight, Kickaha and his companions
had been living in a Turkish bath. All they wanted to do was to lie down
and pant. But they had been forced to keep moving, sometimes vigorously.

On the other hand, because of the much weaker gravity, only one sixteenth that of the primary, their expenditure of energy took them much
more swiftly and farther than it would have on the planet. And there were
so many carcasses and dead plants around that they didn't have to hunt for
food. Another item of nourishment was the flying seed. When the separation had started, every plant on the moon had released hundreds of seeds
that were borne by the wind on tissue-thin alates, or masses of threads.

These rose, some drifting down toward the parent world, others falling back onto the satellite. They were small, but a score or so made a mouthful and provided a protein-high vegetable. Even the filmy wings and threads could be eaten.

"Nature's, or Urthona's, way of making sure the various species of plants survive the catastrophe," Kickaha said.

But when the mutations of terrain stopped and the carcasses became too stinking to eat, they had to begin hunting. Though the humans could run and jump faster, once they learned the new method of locomotion, the animals were proportionately just as speedy. But Kickaha fashioned a new type of bola, two or three antelope skulls connected by a rawhide cord. He would whirl this around and around and then send it skimming along the ground to entangle the legs of the quarry. McKay and Anana made their own bolas, and all three were quite adept at casting them. They even caught some of the wild moosoids with these.

Those seeds that fell back on the split-off put down roots, and new plants grew quickly. The grass and the soil around them became bleached as the nutritional elements were sucked up. The plantling would grow a set of legs and pull up the main root or break it off and move on to rich soil. The legs would fall off but a new set, longer and stronger, would grow. After three moves, the plants stayed rooted until they had attained their full growth. Their maturation period was exceedingly swift by Terrestrial standards.

Of course, many were eaten by the elephants, moosoids, and other animals that made plants their main diet. But enough survived to provide countless groves of ambulatory trees and bushes.

The three had their usual troubles with baboons, dogs and the feline predators. Added to those was a huge bird they'd never seen before. Its wingspread was fifty feet, though the body was comparatively small. Its head was scarlet; the eyes, cold yellow; the green beak, long, hooked, and sharp. The wings and body were bluish, and the short thick heavily taloned legs were ochre. It swooped down from the sky just after dusk, struck, and carried its prey off. Since the gravity was comparatively weak here, it could lift a human into the air. Twice, one of them almost got Anana. Only by throwing herself on the ground when Kickaha had cried a warning had she escaped being borne away.

"I can't figure out what it does when there is no satellite," Kickaha said. "It could never lift a large body from the surface of the primary. So what does it live on between-times?"

"Maybe it just soars around, living off its fat, until the planet spits up another part of it," Anana said.

They were silent for a while then, imagining these huge aerial creatures gliding through the air fifty miles up, half-asleep most of the time, waiting for the mother planet to propel its meat on a moon-sized dish up to it.

"Yes, but it has to land somewhere on the satellite to eat and to mate," he said. "I wonder where."

"Why do you want to know?"

"I got an idea, but it's so crazy I don't want to talk about it yet. It came to me in a dream last night."

Anana suddenly gripped his arm and pointed upward. He and McKay looked up. There, perhaps a half a mile above them, the palace was floating by.

They stood silently watching it until it had disappeared behind some high mountains.

Kickaha sighed and said, "I guess that when it's on automatic, it circles the satellite. Urthona must have set it to do that so that he could observe the moon. Damn! So near, yet so far!"

The Lord must have gotten pleasure out of watching the shifts in the terrain and the adjustments of people and animals to it. But surely he hadn't lived alone in it. What had he done for companionship and sex? Abducted women from time to time, used them, then abandoned them on the surface? Or kicked them out and watched them fall one hundred miles, perhaps accompanying them during the descent to see their horror, hear their screams?

It didn't matter now. Urthona's victims and Urthona were all dead now. What was important was how they were going to survive the rejoining of primary and secondary.

Anana said that her uncle had told her that about a month prior to this event, the satellite again mutated form. It changed from a globe to a rough rectangle of earth, went around the primary five times, and then lowered until it became part of the mother world again.

Only those animals that happened to be on the upper part had a chance to live through the impact. Those on the undersurface would be ground into bits and their pieces burned. And those living in the area of the primary onto which the satellite fell would also be killed.

Urthona had, however, given some a chance to get out and from under. He'd given them an instinctive mechanism that made them flee at their fastest speed from any area over which the satellite came close. It had a set orbital path prior to landing, and as it swung lower every day, the animals "knew" that they had to leave the area. Unfortunately, only those on the outer limits of the impact had time to escape.

The plants were too slow to get out in time, but their instincts made them release their floating seeds.

All of this interested Kickaha. His chief concern, however, was to determine which side of the moon the three would be on when the change from a globe to a rectangle was made. That is, whether they would be on the upper side, that opposite the planet, or on the underside.

"There isn't any way of finding out," Anana said. "We'll just have to trust to luck."

"I've depended on that in the past," he said. "But I don't want to now. You use luck only when there's nothing else left."

He did much thinking about their situation in the days and nights that slid by. The moon rotated slowly, taking about thirty days to complete a single spin. The colossal body of the planet hanging in the sky revealed the healing of the great wound made by the withdrawal of the split-off. The only thing for which they had gratitude for being on the secondary was that they weren't in the area of greatest shape-change, that near the opening of the hole, which extended to the center of the planet. They saw, when the clouds were missing, the sides fall in, avalanches of an unimaginable but visible magnitude. And the mass shrank before their eyes as adjustments were made all over the planet. Even the sea-lands must be undergoing shakings of terrifying strength, enough to make the minds and souls of the inhabitants reel with the terrain.

"Urthona must have enjoyed the spectacle when he was riding around in his palace," Kickaha said. "Sometimes I wish you hadn't killed him, Anana. He'd be down there now, finding out what a horror he'd subjected his creations to."

One morning Kickaha told his companions about a dream he'd had. It had begun with him enthusiastically telling them about his plan to get them off the moon. They'd thought it was wonderful, and all three had started at once on the project. First, they'd walked to a mountain, the top of which was a sleeping place for the giant birds, which they called rocs. They'd climbed to the top and found that it contained a depression in which the rocs rested during the day.

The three had slid down the slope of the hollow, and each had sneaked up on a sleeping roc. Then each had killed his or her bird by driving the knives and a pointed stick through the bird's eye into its brain. Then they'd hidden under a wing of the dead bird until the others had awakened and flown off. After which they'd cut off the wings and tail feathers and carried them back to their camp.

"Why did we do this?" Anana said.

"So we could use the wings and tails to make gliders. We attached them to fuselages of wood, and—"

"Excuse me," Anana said, smiling. "You've never mentioned having any glider experience."

"That's because I haven't. But I've read about gliders, and I did take a few hours' private instruction in a Piper Cub, just enough to solo. But I had to quit because I ran out of money."

"I haven't been up in a glider for about thirty years," Anana said. "But I've built many, and I've three thousand hours' flight time in them."

"Great! Then you can teach Mac and me how to glide. Anyway, in this dream we attached the wings to the fuselage and to keep the wings from flexing, we tied wood bars to the wing bones, and we used rawhide strips instead of wires—"

Anana interrupted again. "How did you control this makeshift glider?"

"By shifting our weight. That's how John Montgomery and Percy Pilcher and Otto and Gustave Lilienthal did it. They hung under or between the wings, suspended in straps or on a seat, and they did all right. Uh . . . until John and Otto and Percy were killed, that is."

McKay said, "I'm glad this was just a dream."

"Yeah? Dreams are springboards into reality."

McKay groaned, and he said, "I just knew you was in earnest."

Anana, looking as if she was about to break into laughter, said, "Well, we could make gliders out of wood and antelope hide, I suppose. They wouldn't work once we got into the primary's gravity field, though, even if they would work here. So there's no use being serious about this.

"Anyway, even if we could glide down a mountain slope here and catch an updraft, we couldn't go very high. The moon's surface has no variety of terrain to make thermals, no plowed fields, no paved roads, and so on."

"What's the use even talking about this?" McKay said.

"It helps pass the time," she said. "So, Kickaha, how did you plan to get the gliders high enough to get out of the moon's gravity?"

Kickaha said, "Look, if we shoot up from our viewpoint, we're actually shooting downward from the viewpoint of people on the surface of the primary. All we have to do is get into the field of the primary's gravity, and we'll fall."

McKay, looking alarmed, said, "What do you mean—*shoot?*"

He had good reason to be disturbed. The redhead had gotten him into a number of dangerous situations because of his willingness to take chances.

"Here's how it was in the dream. We located a battery of cannonlabra, killed four of them, and carried them to our camp. We cut off their branches and eyestalks to streamline their bodies. Then—"

"Wait a minute," Anana said. "I think I see where you're going. You mean that you converted those cannon-creatures into rockets? And tied the gliders to them and then launched the rockets and after the rockets were high up, cut the gliders loose?"

Kickaha nodded. Anana laughed loudly and long.

McKay said, "It's only a dream, ain't it?"

Kickaha, his face red, said, "Listen, I worked it all out. It could be done. What I did—"

"It would work in a dream," she said. "But in reality, there'd be no way to control the burning of the gunpowder. To get high enough, you'd have to stuff the barrel with powder to the muzzle. But when the fuel exploded, and it would, all of it at once, the sudden acceleration would tear the glider from the rocket, completely wreck the structure and wings of the glider, and also kill you."

"Look, Anana," Kickaha said, his face even redder, "isn't there some way we could figure out to get controlled explosions?"

"Not with the materials we have available. No, forget it. It was a nice dream, but . . . oh, hah, hah, hah!"

"I'm glad your woman's got some sense," McKay said. "How'd you ever manage to live so long?"

"I guess because I haven't followed through with all my wild ideas. I'm only half-crazy, not completely nuts. But we've got to get off here. If we end up on the underside when it changes shape, we're done for. It's the big kiss-off for us."

There was a very long silence. Finally, Anana said, "You're right. We have to do something. We must look for materials to make gliders that could operate in the primary's field. But getting free of the moon's gravity is something else. I don't see how—"

"A hot-air balloon!" Kickaha cried. "It could take us and the gliders up and away and out!"

Kickaha thought that if the proper materials could be found to make a balloon and gliders, the liftoff should take place after the moon changed its shape. It would be spread out then, the attenuation of the body making the local gravity even weaker. The balloon would thus have greater lifting power.

Anana said that he had a good point there. But the dangers from the cataclysmic mutation were too high. They might not survive these. Or, if they did, their balloon might not. And they wouldn't have time after the shape-change to get more materials.

Kickaha finally agreed with her.

Another prolonged discussion was about the gliders. Anana, after some thought, said that they should make parawings instead. She explained that a parawing was a type of parachute, a semi-glider, the flight of which could be controlled somewhat.

"The main trouble is still the materials," she said. "A balloon of partially cured antelope hide might lift us enough, considering the far weaker gravity. But how would the panels be held together? We don't have any adhesive, and stitching them together might not, probably will not, work. The hot air would escape through the overlaps. Still . . ."

McKay, who was standing nearby, shouted. They turned to look in the direction at which he was pointing.

Coming from around a pagoda-shaped mountain, moving slowly toward them, was a gigantic object. Urthona's palace. It floated along across the plain at a majestic pace at an estimated altitude of two hundred feet.

They waited for it, and after two hours, it reached them. They had retreated to one side, far enough for them to get a complete view of it from top to bottom. It seemed to be cut out of a single block of smooth stone, or material that looked like stone. This changed color about every fifteen minutes, glowing brightly, running the spectrum, finishing it with a rainbow sheen of blue, white, green, and rose-red. Then the cycle started over again.

There were towers, minarets, and bartizans on the walls, thousands of them, and these had windows and doors, square, round, diamond-shaped, hexagonal, octagonal. There were also windows on the flat bottom. Kickaha counted two hundred balconies, then gave up.

Anana said, "I know we can't reach it. But I'm going to try the Horn anyway."

The seven notes floated up. As they expected, no shimmering prelude to the opening of a gate appeared on its walls.

Kickaha said, "We should've choked the codeword out of Urthona. Or cooked him over a fire."

"That wouldn't help us in this situation," she said.

"Hey!" McKay shouted. "Hey! Look!"

Staring from a window on the bottom floor was a face. A man's.

20

THE WINDOW WAS ROUND AND TALLER THAN THE MAN. EVEN at that distance and though he was moving, they could see that he was not Urthona or Red Orc. It was impossible to tell without reference points how tall the young man was. His hair was brown and pulled tightly back as if it were tied in a ponytail. His features were handsome. He wore a suit of a cut that Kickaha had never seen before, but that Anana would tell him was of a style in fashion among the Lords a long time ago. The jacket glittered as if its threads were pulsing neon tubes. The shirt was ruffled and open at the neck.

Presently the man had passed them, but he reappeared a minute later at another window. Then they saw him racing by the windows. Finally, out of breath, he stopped and put his face to the corner window. After a while, he was out of sight.

"Did you recognize him?" Kickaha said.

"No, but that doesn't mean anything," Anana said. "There were many Lords, and even if I'd known him for a little while, I might have forgotten him after all those years."

"Not mean enough, heh?" Kickaha said. "Well then, if he isn't one of them, what's he doing in Urthona's palace? How'd he get there? And if he's interested in us, which he was from his actions, why didn't he change the controls to manual and stop the palace?"

She shrugged. "How would I know?"

"I didn't really expect you to. Maybe he doesn't know how to operate the controls. He may be trapped. I mean—he gated into the palace and doesn't know how to get out."

"Or he's found the control room but is afraid to enter because he knows it'll be trapped."

McKay said, "Maybe he'll figure out a way to get in without getting caught."

"By then, he won't be able to find us even if he wants to," she said.

"The palace'll be coming around again," Kickaha said. "Maybe by then . . ."

Anana shook her head. "I doubt the palace stays on the same orbit. It probably spirals around."

On the primary, the palace was only a few feet above the ground. Here, for some reason, it floated about a hundred feet from the surface. Anana speculated that Urthona might've set the automatic controls for this altitude because the palace would accompany the moon when it fell.

"He could go down with it and yet be distant enough so the palace wouldn't be disturbed by the impact."

"If that's so, then the impact must not be too terrible. If it were, the ground could easily buckle to a hundred feet or more. But what about a mountain falling over on it?"

"I don't know. But Urthona had a good reason for doing it. Unfortunately for us, it removes any chance for us to get to the palace while it's on the moon."

They did not see the palace. Evidently, it did follow a spiral path.

The days and sometimes the nights that succeeded the appearance of the building were busy. In addition to hunting, which took much time, they had to knock over and kill trees and skin the antelopes they slew. Branches were cut from the trees and shaped with ax and knife. The skins were scraped and dehaired, though not to Anana's satisfaction. She fashioned needles from wood and sewed the skins together. Then she cut away parts of these to make them the exact shape needed. After this, she sewed the triangular form onto the wooden structure.

The result was a three-cornered kite-shape. The rawhide strips used as substitutes for wires were tied onto the glider.

Anana had hoped to use a triangular trapeze bar for control. But their efforts to make one of three wooden pieces tied at the corners failed. It just wasn't structurally sound enough. It was likely to fall apart when subjected to the stress of operation.

Instead, she settled for the parallel-bar arrangement. The pilot would place his armpits over the bars and grasp the uprights. Control would be effected, she hoped, through shifting of the pilot's weight.

When the bars and uprights were installed, Anana frowned.

"I don't know if it'll stand up under the stress. Well, only one way to find out."

She got into position underneath the glider. Then, instead of running, as she would have had to do on the planet, she crouched down and leaped into the wind. She rose thirty-five feet, inclined the nose upward a little to catch the wind, and glided for a short distance. She stalled the machine just before landing and settled down.

The others had bounded after her. She said, grinning, "The first

antelope-hide glider in history has just made its first successful flight."
She continued making the short glides, stopping when she had gone
two miles. They walked back then, and Kickaha, after receiving instructions
again—for the twentieth time—tried his skill. McKay succeeded him without mishap, and they called it a day.

"Tomorrow we'll practice on the plain again," she said. "The day after,
we'll go up a mountain a little way and try our luck there. I want you two
to get some practice in handling a glider in a fairly long glide. I don't expect you to become proficient. You just need to get the feel of handling it."

On the fifth day of practice, they tried some turns. Anana had warned
them to pick up plenty of speed when they did, since the lower wing in a
bank lost velocity. If it slowed down too much, the glider could stall. They
followed her prescription faithfully and landed safely.

"It'd be nice if we could jump off a cliff and soar," she said. "That'd really give you practice. But there are no thermals. Still, you'd be able to glide
higher. Maybe we should."

The men said that they'd like to give it a go. But they had to wait until
a nearby mountain would form just the right shape needed. That is, a
mountain with a slope on one side up which they could walk, and more or
less right angles vertically on the other side. By the time that happened, she
had built her parawing. This was not to be folded for opening when the
jump was made. The hide was too stiff for that. It was braced with lightweight wood to form a rigid structure.

They climbed the mountain to the top. Anana, without any hesitation,
grabbed the wing, holding it above her head but with its nose pointed
down to keep the wind from catching in it. She leaped off the four-
thousand-foot-high projection, released her hold, dropped, was caught in
the harness, and was off. The two men retreated from the outthrust of
earth just in time. With only a slight sound, the ledge gave way and fell.

They watched her descend, more swiftly than in the glider, pull the
nose cords to dive faster, release them to allow the nose to lift, and then
work the ropes so that she could bank somewhat.

When they saw her land, they turned and went back down the mountain.

The next day, McKay jumped and the following day, Kickaha went off
the mountain. Both landed without accident.

Anana was pleased with their successful jumps. But she said, "The
wing is too heavy to use over the primary. We have to find a lighter wood
and something that'll be much lighter than the antelope hides for a wing
covering."

By then the covering was stinking badly. It was thrown away for the insects and the dogs to eat.

She did, however, make another wing, this time installing steering slots and antistall nose flaps. They took it up another mountain, the cliffside of which was only a thousand feet high. Anana jumped again and seemed to be doing well, when a roc dived out of the sky and fastened its claw in the wing. It lifted then, flapping its wings, which had a breadth of fifty feet, heading for the mountain on which it roosted.

Anana threw her throwing ax upward. Its point caught on the lower side of the bird's neck, then dropped. But the bird must have decided it had hold of a tough customer. It released the parawing, and she glided swiftly down. For a few minutes, the bird followed her. If it had attacked her while she was on the ground, it could have had her in a defenseless situation. But it swooped over her, uttering a harsh cry, and then rose in search of less alien and dangerous prey.

Anana spent an hour looking for the ax, failed to find it, and ran home because a moa had appeared in the distance. The next day, the three went back to search for it. After half a day, McKay found it behind a boulder that had popped out of the earth while they were looking.

The next stage in the project was to make a small test balloon. First, though, they had to build a windbreak. The wind, created by the passage of the moon through the atmosphere at an estimated ten miles an hour, never stopped blowing. Which meant that they would never be able to finish the inflation of the balloon before it blew away.

The work took four weeks. They dug up the ground with the knives, the ax, and pointed sticks. When they had a semicircle of earth sixteen feet high, they added a roof, supported by the trunks of dead plants of a giant species.

Then came the antelope hunting. At the end of two days' exhausting hunting and transportation of skins from widely scattered places, they had a large pile. But the hides were in varying stages of decomposition.

There was no time to rest. They scraped off the fat and partially dehaired the skins. Then they cut them, and Anana and Kickaha sewed the panels together. McKay had cut strips and made a network of them.

Dawn found them red-eyed and weary. But they started the fire on the earthen floor of the little basket. Using a gallows of wood, they hoisted the limp envelope up so that the heat from the fire would go directly into the open neck of the bag. Gradually it inflated. When it seemed on the brink of rising, they grabbed the cords hanging from the network around the bag and pulled it out from under the roof. The wind caught it, sent it scooting across the plain, the basket tilting to one side. Some of the fire was shifted off the earth, and the basket began to burn. But the balloon, the envelope steadily expanding, rose.

Pale-blue smoke curled up from the seams.

Anana shook her head. "I knew it wasn't tight enough."

Nevertheless, the aerostat continued to rise. The basket hanging from the rawhide ropes burned and presently one end swung loose, spilling what remained of the fire. The balloon rose a few more feet, then began to sink, and shortly was falling. By then, it was at least five miles away horizontally and perhaps a mile high. It passed beyond the shoulder of a mountain, no doubt to startle the animals there and to provide food for the dogs and the baboons and perhaps the lions.

"I wish I'd had a camera," Kickaha said. "The only rawhide balloon in the history of mankind."

"Even if we find a material suitable for the envelope covering," Anana said, "it'll be from an animal. And it'll rot too quickly."

"The natives know how to partially cure rawhide," he said. "And they might know where we could get the wood and the covering we need. So, we'll find us some natives and interrogate them."

Four weeks later, they were about to give up looking for human beings. They decided to try for three days more. The second day, from the side of a shrinking mountain, they saw a small tribe moving across a swelling plain. Behind them, perhaps a mile away, was a tiny figure sitting in the middle of the immensity.

Several hours later, they came upon the figure. It was covered by a rawhide blanket. Kickaha walked up to it and removed the blanket. A very old woman had been sitting under it, her withered legs crossed, her arms upon her flabby breasts, one hand holding a flint scraper. Her eyes had been closed, but they opened when she felt the blanket move. They became huge. Her toothless mouth opened in horror. Then, to Kickaha's surprise, she smiled, and she closed her eyes again, and she began a high-pitched whining chant.

Anana walked around her, looking at the curved back, the prominent ribs, the bloated stomach, the scanty white locks, and especially at one foot. This had all the appearance of having been chewed on by a lion long ago. Three toes were missing, it was scarred heavily, and it was bent at an unnatural angle.

"She's too old to do any more work or to travel," Anana said.

"So they just left her to starve or be eaten by the animals," Kickaha said. "But they left her this scraper. What do you suppose that's for? So she could cut her wrists?"

Anana said, "Probably. That's why she smiled when she got over her fright. She figures we'll put her out of her misery at once."

She fingered the rawhide. "But she's wrong. She can tell us how to cure skins and maybe tell us a lot more, too. If she isn't senile."

Leaving McKay to guard the old woman, the others went off to hunt. They returned late that day, each bearing part of a gazelle carcass. They also carried a bag full of berries picked from a tree they'd cut out of a grove, though Kickaha's skin had a long red mark from a lashing tentacle.

They offered water and berries to the crone, and after some hesitation, she accepted. Kickaha pounded a piece of flank to make it more tender for her, and she gummed away on it. Later, he dug a hole in the ground, put water in it, heated some stones, dropped them in the water, and added tiny pieces of meat. The soup wasn't hot, and it wasn't good, but it was warm and thick, and she was able to drink that.

While one stood guard that night, the others slept. In the morning, they made some more soup, adding berries for an experiment, and the old woman drank it all from the proffered gourd. Then the language lessons began. She was an eager teacher once she understood that they weren't just fattening her up so they could eat her.

The next day, Kickaha set out after the people who'd abandoned her. Two days later, he returned with flint spearheads, axes, hand scrapers, and several war boomerangs.

"It was easy. I sneaked in at night while they were snoring away after a feast of rotten elephant meat. I picked what I wanted and took off. Even the guards were sleeping."

Learning the old woman's language proceeded swiftly. In three weeks, Shoobam was telling them jokes. And she was a storehouse of information. A treasure trove, in fact.

Primed with data, the three set to work. While one of the three guarded Shoobam, the others went out to get the materials needed. They killed the plants that she had told them were likely to contain gallotannin, or its equivalent, in certain pathological growths. Another type of tree that they caught and killed had an exceptionally lightweight wood, yet was stress-resistant.

Kickaha made a crutch for Shoobam so she could become mobile, and Anana spent some time every day massaging the old woman's semiparalyzed legs. She was not only able to get around better, she began to put on some weight. Still, though she enjoyed talking to the three and felt more important than she had for a long time, she wasn't happy. She missed the tribal life and especially her grandchildren. But she had the stoic toughness of all the natives, who could make a luxury out of what was to the three the barest necessity.

Several months passed. Kickaha and company worked hard from dawn to long past dusk. Finally, they had three parawings much superior in lightness of weight, strength, and durability to the original made by Anana. These were stiffened with wooden ribs and were not to be folded.

Told by Shoobam about a certain type of tree, the bark of which contained a powerful poison, Kickaha and Anana searched for a grove. After finding one, they pulled a dozen plants over with lariats and killed them. During the process, however, they narrowly escaped being caught and burned with the poison exuded by the tentacles. The old woman instructed them in the techniques of extracting the poison.

Kickaha was very happy when he discovered that the branches of the poison-plant were similar to those of yew. He made bows with strings from goat intestines. The arrows were fitted with the flint heads he'd stolen from Shoobam's tribe, and these were dipped in the poison.

Now they were in the business of elephant hunting.

Though the pachyderms were immune to the venom on the darts propelled by certain plants, they succumbed to that derived from the "yew" trees. At the end of another month, they had more than the supply of elephant stomach lining needed. The membranes weighed, per square yard, two thirds less than the gazelle hides. Anana stripped the hides from the parawings and replaced them with the membranes.

"I think the wings'll be light enough now to work in the planet's field," she said. "In fact, I'm sure. I wasn't too certain about the hides."

Another plant yielded, after much hard work and some initial failures, a gluelike substance. This could seal the edges of the strips that would compose the balloon envelope. They sealed some strips of membrane together and tested them over a fire. Even after twenty hours, the glue did not deteriorate. But with thirty hours of steady temperature, it began to decompose.

"That's fine," Anana said. "We won't be in the balloon more than an hour, I hope. Anyway, we can't carry enough wood to burn for more than an hour's flight."

"It looks like we might make it after all," Kickaha said. "But what about her?"

He gestured at Shoobam.

"She's saved our necks or at least given us a fighting chance. But what're we going to do with her when we lift off? We can't just leave her. But we can't take her with us, either."

Anana said, "Don't worry about that. I've talked with her about it. She knows we'll be leaving someday. But she's grateful that she's lived this long, not to mention that we've given her more food than she's had for a long time."

"Yes? What happens when we go?"

"I've promised to slit her wrists."

Kickaha winced. "You're a better man than I am, Gunga Din. I don't think I could do it."

"You have a better idea?"

"No. If it has to be, so be it. I suppose I would do it, but I'm glad I don't have to."

21

ANANA DECIDED THAT IT WOULD BE BETTER TO MAKE THREE smaller balloons instead of one large one.

"Here's how it is. To get equal strength, the material of a large balloon has to be much stronger and heavier per square inch than that of a smaller balloon. By making three smaller ones instead of one large one, we gain in strength of material and lose in weight. So, each of us will ascend in his aerostat."

She added, "Also, since the smaller ones won't present as much area to the wind, they'll be easier to handle."

Kickaha had lost too many arguments with her to object.

McKay resented being "bossed" by a woman, but he had to admit that she was the authority.

They worked frantically to make the final preparations. Even Shoobam helped, and the knowledge of what would happen on the day of liftoff did not shadow her cheeriness. At least, if she felt sorrow or dread, she did not show it.

Finally, the time came. The three bags lay on the ground, stretched out behind the wall of the windbreak. A net of thin but tough cured membrane strips enclosed each bag. These, the suspension ropes, were attached directly to the basket. Anana would have liked to have tied them to a suspension hoop below which the basket would be hung by foot ropes. This arrangement afforded better stability.

However, it was almost impossible to carve three rings from wood. Besides, if the ring was made strong enough to stand up under the weight of the basket, its passenger, and the fuel, it would have to be rather heavy.

The ends of the suspension ropes were tied to the corners and along the sides of a rectangular car or basket made of pieces of bark glued together. In the center of the car was a thick layer of earth, on top of which were piled sticks. Wood shavings were packed at the bottom of the pile so

the fire could be started easily. A layer of tinder would be ignited by sparks
from a flint and a knife or the ax.

The wall of earth serving as a windbreak had been tumbled over four
times because of the shape-changing of terrain. The fifth one was almost
twice as high and four times as long as the one built for the test balloon. It
was roofed over by branches laid on cross-legs supported by uprights.

Three gallows, primitive cranes, stood near the open end of the enclo-
sure. A cable made of twisted cords ran from the upper sides of the horizontal arm to the top of the balloon. One end was tied around the top of
the balloon.

The three people pulled the envelopes up, one by one, until all three
hung limply below the gallows arm. The ends of the hoist ropes were secured to nearby uprights. McKay, who had wanted to be first to lift off,
probably because it made him nervous to wait, lit the fire. Smoke began to
ascend into a circular skin hanging down from the neck of the balloon.

When the bag had started to swell from the expanding hot air, Anana
lit the fire in her car. Kickaha waited a few minutes and then started a
flame in his basket.

The bands of the "dawn" sky began to glow. Snorts and barks and one
roar came from the animals on the plains, awakening to another day of
feeding and being fed upon. The wind was at an estimated minimum eight-
miles-an-hour velocity and without gusts.

McKay's envelope began to inflate. As soon as it was evident that it
would stand up by itself, McKay leaped up past the balloon, reached out
with his ax, and severed the cable attached to the top. He fell back, landing at the same time the cable did. After rising, he waited another minute,
then pulled the balloon from beneath the gallows by the basket.

When Anana's balloon had lifted enough to support itself, she cut the
cable, and Kickaha soon did the same to his.

Shoobam, who had been sitting to one side, pulled herself up on the
crutch and hobbled over to Anana. She spoke in a low tone, Anana embraced her, then slashed at the wrists held out to her. Kickaha wanted to
look away, but he thought that if someone else did the dirty work, he could
at least observe it.

The old woman sat down by Anana's basket and began wailing a death
chant. She didn't seem to notice when he waved farewell.

Tears were running down Anana's cheeks, but she was busy feeding the
fire.

McKay shouted, "So long! See you later! I hope!"

He pulled the balloon out until it was past the overhang. Then he
climbed quickly aboard the car, threw on some more sticks, and waited.
The balloon leaned a little as the edge of the wind coming over the roof

struck its top. It began rising, was caught by the full force of the moving air, and rose at an angle.

Anana's craft ascended a few minutes later. Kickaha's followed at the same interval of time.

He looked up at the bulge of the envelope. The parawing was still attached to the net and was undamaged. It had been tied to the upper side when the bag had been laid out on the ground. An observer at a distance might have thought it looked like a giant moth plastered against a giant lightbulb.

He was thrilled with his flight in an aerostat. There had been no sensation of moving; he could just as well have been on a flying carpet. Except that there was no wind against his face. The balloon moved at the same speed as the air.

Above and beyond him, the other two balloons floated. Anana waved once, and he waved back. Then he tended the fire.

Once he looked back at the windbreak. Shoobam was a dim tiny figure who whisked out of sight as the roof intervened.

The area of vision expanded; the horizon rushed outward. Vistas of mountains and plains, and here and there, large bodies of water where rain had collected in temporary depressions, spread out for him.

Above them hung the vast body of the primary. The great wound made by the split-off had healed. The mother planet was waiting to receive the baby, waiting for another cataclysm.

Flocks of birds and small winged mammals passed him. They were headed for the planet, which meant that the moon's shape-change wasn't far off. The three had left just in time.

Briefly, his craft went through a layer of winged and threaded seeds, soaring, whirling.

The flames ate up the wood, and the supply began to look rather short to Kickaha. The only consolation was that as the fuel burned, it relieved the balloon of more weight. Hence, the aerostat was lighter and ascended even more swiftly.

At an estimated fifteen miles' altitude, Kickaha guessed that he had enough to go another five miles.

McKay's balloon was drifting away from the others. Anana's was about a half mile from Kickaha's, but it seemed to have stopped moving away from it.

At twenty miles—estimated, of course—Kickaha threw the last stick of wood onto the fire. When it had burned, he scraped the hot ashes over the side, leeward, and then pushed the earth after it. After which he closed the funnel of rawhide that had acted as a deflector. This would help keep the hot air from cooling off so fast.

His work done for the moment, he leaned against the side of the basket. The balloon would quickly begin to fall. If it did, he would have to use the parawing to glide back to the moon. The only chance of survival then would be his good luck in being on the upper side after the shape-change.

Suddenly, he was surrounded by warm air. Grinning, he waved at Anana, though he didn't expect her to see him. The rapid change in the air temperature must mean that the balloon had reached what Urthona called the gravity interface. Here the energy of the counter-repulsive force dissipated or "leaked" somewhat. And the rising current of air would keep the aerostats aloft for a while. He hoped that they would be buoyed long enough.

As the heat became stronger, he untied the funnel and cut it away with his knife. The situation was uncertain. Actually, the balloon was falling, but the hot air was pushing it upward faster than it descended. A certain amount was entering the neck opening as the hotter air within the bag slowly cooled. But the bag was beginning to collapse. It would probably not completely deflate. Nevertheless, it would fall.

Since the balloon was not moving at the speed of the wind now, Kickaha felt it. When the descent became rapid enough, he would hear the wind whistling through the suspension ropes. He didn't want to hear that.

The floor of the car began to tilt slowly. He glanced at Anana's balloon. Yes, her car was swinging slowly upward, and the gas bag was also beginning to revolve.

They had reached the zone of turnover. He'd have to act swiftly, no hesitations, no fumbles.

Some birds, looking confused but determined, flapped by.

He scrambled up the ropes and onto the net, and as he did so, the air became even hotter. It seemed to him that it had risen from an estimated 100 degrees Fahrenheit to 130 degrees within sixty seconds. Sweat ran into his eyes as he reached the parawing and began cutting the cords that bound it to the net. The envelope was hot, but not enough to singe his hands and feet. He brushed the sweat away and severed the cords binding the harness and began working his way into it. It wasn't easy to do this, since he had to keep one foot and hand at all times on the net ropes. Several times his foot slipped, but he managed to get it back between the rope and skin of the envelope.

He looked around. While he'd been working, the turnover had been completed. The great curve of the planet was directly below him; the smaller curve of the moon, above.

McKay's balloon was lost in the red sky. Anana wasn't in sight, which meant that she too was on the side of the balloon and trying to get into the harness.

Suddenly, the air was cooler. And he was even more aware of the wind.

The balloon, its bag shrinking with heart-stopping speed, was headed for the ground.

The harness tied, the straps between his legs, he cut the cord that held the nose of the wing to the net. There was one more to sever. This held the back end, that pointing downward, to the net. Anana had cautioned him many times to be sure to cut the connection at the top before he cut that at the bottom. Otherwise, the uprushing air would catch the wing on its undersurface. And the wing would rise, though still attached at its nose to the balloon. He'd be swung out at the end of the shrouds and be left dangling. The wing would flatten its upper surface against the bag, pushed by the increasingly powerful wind.

He might find it impossible to get back to the ropes and climb up to the wing and make the final cut.

"Of course," Anana had said, "you do have a long time. It'll be eighty miles to the ground, and you might work wonders during that lengthy trip. But I wouldn't bet on it."

Kickaha climbed down the ropes to the rear end of the wing, grabbed the knot that connected the end to the net, and cut with the knife in his other hand. Immediately, with a quickness that took his breath away, he was yanked upward. The envelope shot by him, and he was swinging at the end of the shrouds. The straps cut into his thighs.

He pulled on the control cords to depress the nose of the wing. And he was descending in a fast glide. Or, to put it another way, he was falling relatively slowly.

Where was Anana? For a minute or so, she seemed to be lost in the reddish sky. Then he located a minute object, but he couldn't be sure whether it was she or a lone bird. It was below him to his left. He banked, and he glided toward her or it. An immeasurable time passed. Then the dot became larger and after a while, it shaped itself into the top of a parawing.

Using the control shrouds to slip air out of the wing, he fell faster and presently was at the same level as Anana. When she saw him, she banked. After some jockeying around, they were within twenty feet of each other.

He yelled, "You okay?"

She shouted. "Yes!"

"Did you see McKay?"

She shook her head.

Two hours later, he spotted a large bird-shaped object at an estimated two thousand feet below him. Either it was McKay or a roc. But a long squinting at it convinced him that it must be a bird. In any event, it was descending rapidly, and if it continued its angle, it would reach the ground far away from them.

If it was McKay, he would just have to take care of himself. Neither he, Kickaha, nor Anana owed him anything.

A few seconds later, he forgot about McKay. The first of a mass migration from the moon passed him. These were large geese-type birds that must have numbered in the millions. After a while, they became mixed with other birds, large and small. The air around him was dark with bodies, and the beat of wings, honks, caws, trills, and whistles was clamorous.

Their wings shot through a craggle of cranes that split, one body flapping to the right, one to the left. Kickaha supposed that they'd been frightened by the machines, but a moment later, he wasn't sure. Perhaps it was the appearance of an armada of rocs that had scared them.

These airplane-sized avians now accompanied them as if they were a flying escort. The nearest to Anana veered over and glared at her with one cold yellow eye. When it got too close, she screamed at it and gestured with her knife. Whether or not she had frightened it, it pulled away. Kickaha sighed with relief. If one of those giants attacked, its victim would be helpless.

However, the huge birds must have had other things on their minds. They maintained the same altitude while the parawings continued descending. After a while, the birds were only specks far above and ahead.

Anana had told him that this would not be the longest trip he'd ever taken, but it would be the most painful. And it would seem to be the longest. She'd detailed what would happen to them and what they must do. He'd listened, and he'd not liked what he heard. But his imagination had fallen short of the reality by a mile.

When used as a glider, the parawing had a sinking speed of an estimated four feet a second. Which meant that, if they glided, it would take them twenty hours to reach the ground. By then, or before that, gangrene would have set into their legs.

But if the wing was used as a parachute, it would sink at twenty feet per second. The descent would be cut to a mere six hours, roughly estimated.

Thus, after locating each other, the two had pulled out some panels, and from then on, they were traveling à la parachute. Kickaha worked his legs and arms to increase the circulation, and sometimes he would spill a little air out of the side of the wing to fall even faster. This procedure could only be done at short intervals, however. To go down too fast might jerk the shrouds loose when the wing slowed down again.

By the time they were at an estimated ten thousand feet from the earth, he felt as if his arms and legs had gone off, flying back to the moon. He hung like a dummy except when he turned his head to see Anana. She would have been above him because, being lighter, she would not have fallen so fast. That is, she would not have if she had not arranged for her rip-panels to be somewhat larger than his. She, too, hung like a piece of dead meat.

One of the things that had worried him was that they might encounter a strong updraft that would delay their landing even more. But they had continued to fall at an even pace.

Below them were mountains and some small plains. But by the time they'd reached four thousand feet, they were approaching a large body of water. It was one of the many great hollows temporarily filled with rainwater. At the moment, the bottom of the depression was tilting. The water was draining out of one end through a pass between two mountains. The animals on land near the lower end were running to avoid being overtaken by the rising water. What seemed like a million amphibians were scrambling ashore or waddling as fast as they could go toward higher ground.

Kickaha wondered why the amphibians were in such a hurry to leave the lake. Then he saw several hundred or so immense animals, crocodilian in shape, thrashing through the water. They were scooping up the fleeting prey.

He yelled at Anana and pointed at the monsters. She shouted back that they should slip out some air from the wings. They didn't want to land anywhere near those beasts.

With a great effort, he pulled on the shrouds. He fell ten seconds later into the water near the shore, with Anana two seconds behind him. He had cut the shrouds just in time to slip out of the harness. The water closed over him, he sank, then his feet touched bottom, and he tried to push upward with them.

They failed to obey him.

His head broke the surface as he propelled himself with his fatigue-soaked arms. Anana was already swimming toward the shore, which was about thirty feet away. Her legs were not moving.

They dragged themselves onto the grass like merpeople, their legs trailing. After that was a long period of intense pain as the circulation slowly returned. When they were able, they rose and tottered toward the high ground. Long four-legged and finned creatures, their bodies covered with slime, passed them. Some snapped at them but did not try to bite. The heavier gravity, after their many months of lightness on the moon, pressed upon them. But they had to keep going. The hippopotamus-sized crocodiles were on land now.

They didn't think they could make it over the shoulder of a mountain. But they did, and then they lay down. After they'd quit panting, they closed their eyes and slept. It was too much of an effort to be concerned about crocodiles, lions, dogs, or anything that might be interested in eating them. For all they cared, the moon could fall on them.

22

KICKAHA AND ANANA RAN AT A PACE THAT THEY COULD MAIN-
tain for miles and yet not be worn out. They were as naked as the day they
came into the world except for the belts holding their knives and the Horn
and the device strapped to her wrist. They were sweating and breathing
heavily, but they knew that this time they could catch the palace—if nothing interfered.

Another person was also in pursuit of the colossus. He was riding a
moosoid. Though he was a half a mile away, his tallness and red-bronze hair
identified him. He had to be Red Orc.

Kickaha used some of his valuable breath. "I don't know how he got
here, and I don't know what he expects to do when he catches up with the
palace. He doesn't know the code words."

"No," Anana gasped. "But maybe that man we saw will open a door for
him."

So far, Orc had not looked back. This was fortunate, because ten minutes later, a window—french door, rather—swung open for him. He
grabbed its sill and was helped within by two arms. The moosoid immediately stopped galloping and headed for a grove of moving plants. The door
shut.

Kickaha hoped that the unknown tenant would be as helpful to them.
But if Orc saw them, he'd be sure to interfere with any efforts to help.

Slowly they neared the towering building. Their bare feet pounded on
the grass. Their breaths hissed in and out. Sweat stung their eyes. Their
legs were gradually losing their response to their wills. They felt as if they
were full of poisons that were killing the muscles. Which, in fact, they
were.

To make the situation worse, the palace was heading for a mountain a
mile or two away. If it began skimming up its slope, it would proceed at an
undiminished speed. But the two chasing it would have to climb.

Finally, the bottom right-hand corner was within reach. They slowed down, sobbing. They could keep up a kilometer an hour, a walking pace, as long as they were on a flatland. But when the structure started up the mountain, they would have to draw on reserves they didn't have.

There was a tall window at the very corner, its glass or plastic curving to include both sides. However, it was set flush to the building itself. No handholds to draw themselves up.

They forced themselves to break from a walk to a trot. The windows they passed showed a lighted corridor. The walls were of various glowing colors. Many paintings hung on them, and at intervals, statues painted flesh colors stood by the doors leading to other rooms within. Then they came to several windows that were part of a large room. Furniture was arranged within it, and a huge fireplace in which a fire burned was at the extreme end.

A robot, about four feet high, dome-shaped, wheeled, was removing dust from a large table. A multi-elbowed metal arm extended a fat disc that moved over the surface of the table. Another arm moved what seemed to be a vacuum-cleaner attachment over the rug behind it.

Kickaha increased his pace. Anana kept up with him. He wanted to get to the front before the palace began the ascent. The front would be only a foot from the slope, but since the building would maintain a horizontal attitude, the rest would be too far from the ground for them to reach it.

Just as the forepart reached the bottom of the mountain, the two attained their objective. But now they had to climb.

None of the windows they had passed had revealed any living being within.

They ran around the corner, which was just like the rear one. And here they saw their first hope for getting a hold. Halfway along the front was a large balcony. No doubt Urthona had installed it so that he could step out into the fresh air and enjoy the view. But it would not be a means of access. Not unless the stranger within the palace had carelessly left it unlocked. That wasn't likely, but at least they could stop running. Almost, they didn't make it. The upward movement of the building, combined with their running in front of it, resulted in an angled travel up the slope. But they kept up with it, though once Kickaha stumbled. He grabbed the edge of the bottom, clung, was dragged, then released his hold, rolled furiously, got ahead, and was seized by the wrist by Anana and yanked forward and upward. She fell backward, but somehow they got up and resumed their race without allowing the palace to pass over them.

Then they had grabbed the edge of the balcony and swung themselves up and over it. For a long time they lay on the cool metallic floor and gasped as if each breath of air was the last in the world. When they were breathing normally, they sat up and looked around. Two french doors gave entrance to an enormous room, though not for them. Kickaha pushed in on the knobless doors without success. There didn't seem to be any handles on the inside. Doubtless, they opened to a push-button or a code word.

Hoping that there were no sensors to give alarm, Kickaha banged hard with the butt of his knife on the transparent material. The stuff did not crack or shatter. He hadn't expected it to.

"Well, at least we're riding," he said. He looked up at the balcony above theirs. It was at least twenty feet higher, thus out of reach.

"We're stuck. How ironic. We finally make it, and all we can do is starve to death just outside the door."

They were exhausted and suffering from intense thirst. But they could not just leave the long-desired place. Yet, what else could they do?

He looked up again, this time at dark clouds forming.

"It should be raining soon. We can drink, anyway. What do you say we rest here tonight? Morning may bring an idea."

Anana agreed that that was the best thing to do. Two hours later, the downpour began, continuing uninterruptedly for several hours. Their thirst was quenched, but they felt like near-drowned puppies by the time it was over. They were cold, shivering, wet. By nightfall, they'd dried off, however, and they slept wrapped in each other's arms.

By noon the next day, their bellies were growling like starving lions in a cage outside which was a pile of steaks. Kickaha said, "We'll have to go hunting, Anana, before we get too weak. We can always run this down again, though I hate to think of it. If we could make a rope with a grapnel, we might be able to get up to that balcony above us. Perhaps the door there isn't locked. Why should it be?"

"It will be locked because Urthona wouldn't take any chances," she said. "Anyway, by the time we could make a rope, the palace would be far ahead of us. We might even lose track of it."

"You're right," he said. He turned to the door and beat on it with his fists. Inside was a huge room with a large fountain in its center. A marble triton blew water from the horn at its lips.

He stiffened and said, "Oh-oh! Don't move, Anana. Here comes someone!"

Anana froze. She was standing to one side, out of view of anyone in the room.

"It's Red Orc! He's seen me! It's too late for me to duck! Get over the side of the balcony! There're ornamentations you can hang on to! I don't know what he's going to do to me, but if he comes out here, you might be able to catch him unaware. I'll have to be the sacrificial goat!"

Out of the corner of his eye he watched her slide over the railing and disappear. He stayed where he was, looking steadily at her uncle. Orc was dressed in a splendid outfit of some sparkling material, the calf-length pants very tight, the boots scarlet and with upturned toes, the jacket double-breasted and with flaring sleeves, the shirt ruffled and encrusted with jewels on the broad wing-tipped collar.

He was smiling, and he held a wicked-looking beamer in one hand.

He stopped for a moment just inside the doors. He moved to each side to get a full view of the balcony. His hand moved to the wall, apparently pressing a button. The doors slid straight upward into the wall.

He held the weapon steady, aiming at Kickaha's chest.

"Where's Anana?"

"She's dead," Kickaha said.

Orc smiled and pulled the trigger. Kickaha was knocked back across the balcony, driven hard into the railing. He lay half-sitting, more than half-stunned. Vaguely, he was aware of Orc stepping out onto the balcony and looking over the railing. The red-haired man leaned over it and said, "Come on up, Anana. I'm on to your game. But throw your knife away."

A moment later, she came slowly over the railing. Orc backed up into the doorway, the beamer directed at her. She looked at Kickaha and said, "Is he dead?"

"No, the beamer's set for a low-grade stun. I saw you two last night after the alarm went off. Your *leblabbiy* stud was foolish enough to hammer on the door. The sensors are very sensitive."

Anana said, "So you just watched us. You wanted to know what we'd try?"

Orc smiled again. "Yes, I knew you could do nothing. But I enjoyed watching you try to figure out something."

He looked at the Horn strapped around her shoulder.

"I've finally got it. I can get out of here now."

He pressed the trigger, and Anana fell back against the railing. Kickaha's senses were by then almost fully recovered, though he felt weak. But if Orc got within reach of his hands . . .

The Lord wasn't going to do that. He stepped back, said something, and two robots came through the doorway. At first glance, they looked like living human beings. But the dead eyes and the movements, not as graceful as beings of animal origin, showed that metal or plastic lay beneath the seeming skin. One removed Kickaha's knife and threw it over the balcony railing. The other unstrapped the multi-use device from Anana's wrist. Both got hold of the ankles of the two and dragged them inside. To one side stood a large hemisphere of thick criss-crossed wires on a platform with six wheels. The robot picked up Anana and shoved her through a small doorway in the cage. The second did the same to Kickaha. The door was shut, and the two were captives inside what looked like a huge mouse-trap.

Orc bent down and reached under the cage. When he straightened up, he said, "I've just turned on the voltage. Don't touch the wires. You won't be killed, but you'll be knocked out."

He told the humanoid robots and the cage to follow him. Carrying the Horn, which he had removed from Anana's shoulder, he strode through the room toward a high-ceilinged wide corridor.

Kickaha crawled to Anana. "Are you okay?"

"I'll be in a minute," she said. "I don't have much strength just now. And I got a headache."

"Me, too," he said. "Well, at least we're inside."

"Never say die, eh? Sometimes your optimism . . . well, never mind. What do you suppose happened to the man who let Orc in?"

"If he's still alive, he's regretting his kind deed. He can't be a Lord. If he was, he'd not have let himself be taken."

Kickaha called out to Orc, asking him who the stranger was. Orc didn't reply. He stopped at the end of the corridor, which branched off into two others. He said something in a low voice to the wall, a code word, and a section of wall moved back a little and then slid inside a hollow. Revealed was a room about twenty feet by twenty feet, an elevator.

Orc pressed a button on a panel. The elevator shot swiftly upward. When it stopped, the lighted symbol showed that it was on the fortieth floor. Orc pressed two more buttons and took hold of a small lever. The elevator moved out into a very wide corridor and glided down it. Orc turned the lever, the elevator swiveled around a corner and went down another corridor for about two hundred feet. It stopped, its open front against a door.

Orc removed a little black book from a pocket, opened it, consulted a page, said something that sounded like gibberish, and the door opened. He replaced the book and stood to one side as the cage rolled into a large room. It stopped in the exact center.

Orc spoke some more gibberish. Mechanisms mounted on the walls at a height of ten feet from the floor extended metal arms. At the end of each was a beamer. There were two on each wall, and all pointed at the cage. Above the weapons were small round screens. Undoubtedly, video eyes.

Orc said, "I've heard you boast that there isn't a prison or a trap that can hold you, Kickaha. I don't think you'll ever make that boast again."

"Do you mind telling us what you intend to do with us?" Anana said in a bored voice.

"You're going to starve," he said. "You won't die of thirst since you'll be given enough water to keep you going. At the end of a certain time— which I won't tell you—whether you're still alive or not, the beamers will blow you apart.

"Even if, inconceivably, you could get out of the cage and dodge the beamers, you can't get out of here. There's only one exit, the door you came through. You can't open that unless you know the code word."

Anana opened her mouth, her expression making it obvious that she was going to appeal. It closed; her expression faded. No matter how desperate the situation, she was not going to humiliate herself if it would be for nothing. But she'd had a moment of weakness.

Kickaha said, "At least you could satisfy our curiosity. Who was the man who let you in? What happened to him?"

Orc grimaced. "He got away from me. I got hold of a beamer and was going to make him my prisoner. But he dived through a trapdoor I hadn't known existed. I suppose by now he's gated to another world. At least, the sensors don't indicate his presence."

Kickaha grinned and said, "Thank you. But who was he?"

"He claimed to be an Earthman. He spoke English, but it was a quaint sort. It sounded to me like eighteenth-century English. He never told me his name. He began to ramble on and on, told me he'd been trapped here for some time when he gated from Vala's world to get away from her. It had taken him some time to find out how to activate a gate to another universe without being killed. He was just about to do so when he saw me galloping up. He decided to let me in because I didn't look like a native of this world. I think he was half-crazy."

"He must have been completely insane to trust you, a Lord," Anana said. "Did he say anything about having seen Kickaha, McKay, and myself? He passed over us when we were on the moon."

Orc's eyebrows rose. "You were on the moon? And you survived its fall? No, he said nothing about you. That doesn't mean he wasn't interested or wouldn't have gotten around eventually to telling me about you."

He paused, smiled, and said, "Oh, I almost forgot! If you get hungry enough, one of you can eat the other."

Kickaha and Anana could not hide their shock. Orc broke into laughter then. When he stopped bellowing, he removed a knife from the sheath at his belt. It was about six inches long and looked as if it were made of gold. He shoved it through the wires, where it lay at Anana's feet.

"You'll need a cutting utensil, of course, to carve steaks and chops and so forth. That'll do the job, but don't think for one moment you can use it to short out the wires. It's nonconductive."

Kickaha said fiercely, "If it wasn't for Anana, I'd think all you Lords were totally unreformable, fit only to be killed on sight. But there's one thing I'm sure about. You haven't a spark of decency in you. You're absolutely inhuman."

"If you mean I in no way have the nature of a *leblabbiy*, you're right."

Anana picked up the knife and fingered the side, which felt grainy, though its surface was steel-smooth.

"We don't have to starve to death," she said. "We can always kill ourselves first."

Orc shrugged. "That's up to you."

He said something to the humanoid robots, and they followed him through the doorway into the elevator. He turned and waved farewell as the door slid out from the wall recesses.

"Maybe that Englishman is still here," Kickaha said. "He might get us free. Meanwhile, give me the knife."

Anana had anticipated him, however. She was sawing away at a wire where it disappeared into the floor. After working away for ten minutes, she put the blade down.

"Not a scratch. The wire metal is much harder than the knife's."

"Naturally. But we had to try. Well, there's no use putting it off until we're too weak even to slice flesh. Which one of us shall it be?"

Shocked, she turned to look at him. He was grinning.

"Oh, you! Must you joke even about this?"

She saw a section of the cage floor beyond him move upward. He turned at her exclamation. A cube was protruding several inches. The top was rising on one side, though no hinges or bolts were in evidence. Within it was a pool of water.

They drank quickly, since they didn't know how long the cube would remain. Two minutes later, the top closed and the box sank back flush with the floor.

It reappeared, filled with water, about every three hours. No cup was provided, so they had to get down on their hands and knees and suck it up with their mouths, like animals. Every four hours, the box came up empty. Evidently, they were to excrete in it then. When the box appeared the next time, it was evident that it had not been completely cleaned out.

"Orc must enjoy this little feature," Kickaha said.

There was no way to measure the passage of time since the light did not dim. Anana's sense of time told her, however, that they must have been caged for at least fifty-eight hours. Their bellies caved in, growled, and thundered. Their ribs grew gaunter before their eyes. Their cheeks hollowed; their legs and arms slimmed. And they felt steadily weaker. Anana's full breasts sagged.

"We can't live off our fat because we don't have any," he said. "We were honed down pretty slim from all the ordeals we've gone through."

There were long moments of silence, though both spoke whenever they could think of something worthwhile to say. Silence was too much like the quiet of the dead, which they soon would be.

They had tried to wedge the knife between the crack in the side of the water box. They did not know what good this would do, but they might think of something. However, the knife would not penetrate into the crack.

Anana now estimated that they'd been in the cage about seventy hours. Neither had said anything about Orc's suggestion that one of them feast on the other. They had an unspoken agreement that they would not consent to this horror. They also wondered if Orc was watching and listening through video.

Food crammed their dreams if not their bellies. Kickaha was drowsing fitfully, dreaming of eating roast pork, mashed potatoes and gravy, and rhubarb pie, when a clicking sound awoke him. He lay on his back for a while, wondering why he would dream of such a sound. He was about to fall back into the orgy of eating again when a thought made him sit up as if someone had passed a hot pastrami by his nose.

Had Orc inserted a new element in the torture? It didn't seem possible, but . . .

He got onto his hands and knees and crawled to the little door. He pushed on it, and it swung outward.

The clicking had been the release of its lock.

23

WHILE THEY CLAMBERED DOWN OUT OF THE CAGE, THE BEAM-
ers on the wall tracked them. Kickaha started across toward the door. All
four weapons spat at once, vivid scarlet rays passing before and behind
him. Ordinarily, the rays were invisible, but Orc had colored them so his
captors could see how close they were. Beauty, and terror, were in the eye
of the beholder.

Anana moaned. "Oh, no! He just let us loose to tantalize us!"

Kickaha unfroze.

"Yeah. But those beamers should be hitting us."

He took another step forward. Again the rays almost touched him.

"To hell with it! They're set now so they'll just miss us! Another one of
his refinements!"

He walked steadily to the door while she followed. Two of the beamers swung to her, but their rays shot by millimeters away from her. Nevertheless, it was unnerving to see the scarlet rods shoot just before his eyes.
As the two got closer to the door, the rays angled past their cheeks on one
side and just behind the head.

They should have drilled through the walls and floor, but these were
made of some material invulnerable even to their power.

When he was a few feet from the door, the beamers swung to spray the
door just ahead of him. Their contact with the door made a slight hissing,
like a poisonous snake about to strike.

The two stood while scarlet flashed and splashed over the door.

"We're not to touch," Kickaha said. "Or is this just a move in the game
he's playing to torment us?"

He turned and walked back toward the nearest beamer. It tracked just
ahead of him, forcing him to move slowly. But the ray was always the same
distance away.

When he stopped directly before the beamer, it was pointed at his
chest. He moved around it until it could no longer follow him. Of course,

he was in the line of sight of the other three. But they had stopped firing now.

The weapon was easily unsecured by pulling a thick pin out of a hinge on its rear. He lifted it and tore it loose from the wires connected to its underside. Anana, seeing this, did the same to hers. The other two beamers started shooting again, their rays again just missing them. But these too were soon made harmless.

"So far, we're just doing what Orc wants us to do," he said. "He's programmed this whole setup. Why?"

They went to the door and pushed on it. It swung open, revealing a corridor empty of life or robots. They walked to the branch and went around the corner. At the end of this hall was the open door of the elevator shaft. The cage was within it, as if Orc had sent it there to await them.

They hesitated to enter it. What if Orc had set a trap for them, and the cage stopped halfway between floors or just fell to the bottom of the shaft?

"In that case," Kickaha said, "he would figure that we'd take a stairway. So he'd trap those."

They got into the cage and punched a button for the first floor. Arriving safely, they wandered through some halls and rooms until they came to an enormous luxuriously furnished chamber. The two robots stood by a great table of polished onyx. Anana, in the language of the Lords, ordered a meal. This was brought in five minutes. They ate so much they vomited but after resting, they ate again, though lightly. Two hours later, they had another meal. She directed a robot to show them to an apartment. They bathed in hot water and then went to sleep on a bed that floated three feet above the floor while cool air and soft music flowed over them.

When they woke, the door to the room opened before they could get out of bed. A robot pushed in a table on which were trays filled with hot delicious food and glasses of orange or muskmelon juice. They ate, went to the bathroom, showered, and emerged. The robot was waiting with clothes that fit them exactly.

Kickaha did not know how the measurements had been taken, but he wasn't curious about it. He had more important things to consider.

"This red-carpet treatment worries me. Orc is setting us up just to knock us down again."

The robot knocked on the door. Anana told him to come in. He stopped before Kickaha and handed him a note. Opening it, Kickaha said, "It's in English. I don't know whose handwriting it is, but it has to be Orc's."

He read aloud, "Look out a window."

Dreading what they would see, but too curious to put it off, they hastened through several rooms and down a long corridor. The window at its end held a scene that was mostly empty air. But moving slowly across it was a tiny globe. It was the lavalite world.

"That's the kicker!" he said. "Orc's taken the palace into space! And he's marooned us up here, of course, with no way of getting to the ground!"

"And he's also deactivated all the gates, of course," Anana said.

A robot that had followed them, made a sound exactly like a polite butler wishing to attract his master's attention. They turned, and the robot held out to Kickaha another note. He spoke in English, "Master told me to tell you, sir, that he hopes you enjoy this."

Kickaha read, "The palace is in a decaying orbit."

Kickaha spoke to the robot. "Do you have any other messages for us?"

"No, sir."

"Can you lead us to the central control chamber?"

"Yes, sir."

"Then lead on, MacDuff."

It said, "What does MacDuff mean, sir?"

"Cancel the word. What name are you called by? I mean, what is your designation?"

"One, sir."

"So you're one, too."

"No, sir. Not One-Two. One."

"For Ilmarwolkin's sake," Anana said, "quit your clowning."

They followed One into a large room where there was an open wheeled vehicle large enough for four. The robot got into the driver's seat. They stepped into the back seat, and the car moved away smoothly and silently. After driving through several corridors, the robot steered it into a large elevator. He got out and pressed some buttons, and the cage rose thirty floors. The robot got behind the wheel and drove the vehicle down a corridor almost for a quarter of a mile. The car stopped in front of a door.

"The entrance to the central control chamber, sir."

The robot got out and stood by the door. They followed him. The door had been welded, or sealed, to the wall.

"Is this the only entrance?"

"Yes, sir."

It was evident that Orc had made sure that they could not get in. Doubtless, any devices, including beamers, that could remove the door had been jettisoned from the palace. Or was Orc just making it more difficult for them? Perhaps he had deliberately left some tools around, but when they got into the control room, they would find that the controls had been destroyed.

They found a window and looked out into red space. Kickaha said, "It should take some time before this falls onto the planet. Meanwhile, we can eat, drink, make love, sleep. Get our strength back. And look like mad for some way of getting out of this mess. If Orc thinks we're going to suffer while we're falling, he doesn't know us."

"Yes, but the walls and door must be made of the same stuff, *impervium*, as the room that held the cage," she said. "Beamers won't affect it. I don't know how he managed to weld the door to the walls, but he did. So getting into the controls seems to be out."

First, they had to make a search of the entire building and that would take days, even when traveling in the little car. They found the hangar that had once housed five fliers. Orc had not even bothered to close its door. He must have set them to fly out on automatic.

They also located the great power plant. This contained the gravitic machines that now maintained an artificial field within the palace. Otherwise, they would have been floating around in free fall.

"It's a wonder he didn't turn that off," Anana said. "It would have been one more way to torment us."

"Nobody's perfect," Kickaha said.

Their search uncovered no tools that could blast into the control chamber. They hadn't thought it would.

Kickaha conferred with Anana, who knew more about parachutes than he did. Then he gave a number of robots very detailed instruction on how to manufacture two chutes out of silken hangings.

"All we have to do is to jump off and then float down," he said. "But I don't relish the idea of spending the rest of my life on that miserable world. It's better than being dead, but not by much."

There were probably a thousand, maybe two thousand, gates in the walls and on the floors and possibly on the ceilings. Without the code words to activate them, they could neither locate nor use them.

They wondered where the wall panel was that the Englishman had used to get away from Red Orc. To search for it would take more time than they had. Then Kickaha thought of asking the robots, One and Two, if they had witnessed his escape. To his delight, both had. They led the humans to it. Kickaha pushed in on the panel and saw a metal chute leading downward some distance, then curving.

"Here goes nothing," he said to Anana. He jumped into it sitting up and slid down and around and was shot into a narrow dimly lit hall. He yelled back up the chute to her and told her he was going on. But he was quickly stopped by a dead end.

After tapping and probing around, he went back to the chute and, bracing himself against the sides, climbed back up.

"Either there's another panel I couldn't locate or there's a gate in the end of the hall," he told her.

They sent the robots to the supply room to get a drill and hammers. Though the drills wouldn't work on the material enclosing the control room, they might work on the plastic composing the walls of the hidden hall. After the robots returned, Kickaha and Anana went down the chute with them and bored holes into the walls. After making a circle of many perforations, he knocked the circle through with a sledgehammer.

Light streamed out through it. He cautiously looked within. He gasped.

"Well, I'll be swoggled! Red Orc!"

24

IN THE MIDDLE OF A LARGE BARE ROOM WAS A TRANSPARENT cube about twelve feet long. A chair, a narrow bed, and a small red box on the floor by a wall shared the cube with its human occupant, Orc. Kickaha noted that a large pipe ran from the base of the wall of the room to the cube, penetrated the transparent material, and ended in the red box. Presumably, this furnished water and perhaps a semiliquid type of food. A smaller pipe within the large one must provide air.

Red Orc was sitting on the chair before the table, his profile to the watchers through the hole. Evidently, the cube was soundproof, since he had not heard the drilling or pounding. The Horn and a beamer lay on the table before him. From this, Kickaha surmised that the cube was invulnerable to the beamer's rays.

Red Orc, once the secret Lord of the Two Earths, looked as dejected as a man could be. No wonder. He had stepped through a gate in the control room, expecting to enter another universe, possessing the Horn, the Lords' greatest treasure, and leaving behind him two of his worst enemies to die. But Urthona had prepared his trap well, and Red Orc had been gated to this prison instead of to freedom.

As far as he knew, no one was aware that he was locked in this room. He was doubtless contemplating how long it would be before the palace fell to Urthona's world and he perished in the smash, caught in his own trap.

Kickaha and Anana cut a larger hole in the wall for entrance. During this procedure, Orc saw them. He rose up from his chair and stared from a pale gray face. He could expect no mercy. The only change in his situation was that he would die sooner.

His niece and her lover were not so sure that anything had been changed. If he couldn't cut his way out of the cube, they couldn't cut their way in. Especially when they didn't have a beamer. But the pipe that was Orc's life supply was of copper. After the robots got some more tools, Kick-

aha slicked off the copper at the junction with the *impervium* that projected outside the cube.

This left an opening through which Orc could still get air and also
could communicate. Kickaha and Anana did not place themselves directly
before the hole, though. Orc might shoot them through it.

Kickaha said, "The rules of the game have been changed, Orc. You
need us, and we need you. If you cooperate, I promise to let you go wherever you want to, alive and unharmed. If you don't, you'll die. We might
die, too, but what good will that do you?"

"I can't trust you to keep your word," Orc said sullenly.

"If that's the way you want it, so be it. But Anana and I aren't going to
be killed. We're having parachutes made. That means we'll be marooned
here, but at least we'll be alive."

"Parachutes?" Orc said. It was evident from his expression that he had
not thought of their making them.

"Yeah. There's an old American saying that there's more than one way
to skin a cat. And I'm a cat-skinner par excellence. I—Anana and I—are
going to figure a way out of this mess. But we need information from you.
Now, do you want to give it to us and maybe live? Or do you want to sulk
like a spoiled child and die?"

Orc gritted his teeth, then said, "Very well. What do you want?"

"A complete description of what happened when you gated from the
control chamber to this trap. And anything that might be relevant."

Orc told how he had checked out the immense room and its hundreds
of controls. His task had been considerably speeded up by questioning robots One and Two. Then he had found out how to open several gates. He
had done so cautiously and before activating them himself, he had ordered
the robots to do so. Thus, if they were trapped, they would be the victims.

One gate apparently had access to the gates enclosed in various boulders scattered over the planet below. Urthona must have had some means
of identifying these. He would have been hoping that while roaming the
planet with the others, he would recognize one. Then, with a simple code
word or two, he would have transported himself to the palace. But Urthona
hadn't had any luck.

Orc identified three gates to other worlds. One was to Jadawin's, one
to Earth I, and one to dead Urizen's. There were other gates, but Orc
hadn't wanted to activate them. He didn't want to push his luck. So far, he
hadn't set off any traps. Besides, the gate to Earth I was the one he wanted.

Having made sure that his escape routes were open, Orc had then had
the robots, One and Two, seal the control room.

"So you had our torments all fixed up ahead of time?" Anana said.

"Why not?" Orc said. "Wouldn't you have done the same to me?"

"At one time, I would have. Actually, you did us a favor by letting us loose so we could savor the terrors of the fall. But you didn't mean to, I'm sure."

"He did himself a favor, too," Kickaha said.

Orc had then activated the gate to Earth I. He had stepped through the hole between the universes, fully expecting to emerge in a cave. He could see through its entrance a valley and a wooded mountain range beyond. He thought that it was possibly the same cave through which Kickaha and Anana had gone in southern California.

But Urthona had set up a simulacrum to lull the unwary. To strengthen its impression, Urthona had also programmed the robots in case a crafty Lord wanted to use the gate. At least, Red Orc supposed he had done so. Orc had ordered the robot called Six to walk through first. Six had done so, had traveled through the cave, stepped outside, looked around, then had returned through the gate.

Satisfied, Orc had ordered the robots, One and Two, to seal up the control room door with *impervium* flux. Then he had stepped through.

"Apparently," Orc said, "that wily *shagg*, the ugly weasel, had counted on the robot being used as a sacrifice. So he had arranged it that the robot would not be affected."

"Urthona always was a sneaky one," Anana said. "But he had depended on his technological defenses too long. Thrown on his own resources, he was not the man he should have been."

She paused, then added, "Just like you, Uncle."

"I haven't done so badly," he said, his face red.

Kickaha and Anana burst out laughing.

"No," she said. "Of course not. Just look where you are."

Orc had been whisked away when he was only a few feet from leaving the cave, or what he thought was a cave. The next second, he was standing in the cube.

Kickaha drew Anana to a corner of the room to confer quietly. "Somehow, that mysterious Englishman discovered a gateway to another universe in the wall at the end of the corridor," he said. "Maybe he had found Urthona's code book. Anyway, where one can go through, others can. And the Horn can get us through. But we can't get to the Horn.

"Now, what's to prevent us from getting Orc to blow the notes for us? Then we can make a recording of it and use it to open the gate."

Anana shook her head. "It doesn't work that way. It's been tried before, it's so obvious. But there's something in the machinery in the Horn that adds an element missing in recordings."

"I was afraid of that," he said. "But I had to ask. Look, Anana. Urthona must have planted gates all over this place. We've probably passed dozens without knowing it, because they are inside the walls. Logically, many if not most of them will be quick emergency routes from one place in this building to another. So Urthona could outsmart anyone who was close on his heels.

"But there have to be a few that would gate him to another world. Only to be used in cases of direst emergency. One of them is the gate at the end of the corridor next door. I think . . ."

"Not necessarily," Anana said. "For all we know, it leads to the control room or some other place in the palace."

"No. In that case, the sensors would have shown Orc that the Englishman was in the palace."

"No. Urthona might have set up places without sensors where he could hide if an enemy had possession of the control room."

"I'm the A-Number One trickster, but sometimes I think you sneaky Lords put me to shame. Okay. Just a minute. Let me ask Orc a question."

He went to the cube. The Lord, looking very suspicious, said, "What are you two up to now?"

"Nothing that won't help you," Kickaha said, grinning. "We just don't want you to get a chance to get the drop on us. Tell me. Did the sensor displays in the control room indicate that there were hidden auxiliary sensor systems?"

"Why would you want to know?"

"Damn it!" Kickaha said. "You're wasting our time. Remember, I have to spring you if only to get the Horn."

Hesitantly, Orc said, "Yes, there are hidden auxiliary systems. It took me some time to find them. Actually, I wasn't looking for them. I discovered them while I was looking for something else. I checked them out and noted that they were in rooms not covered by the main system. But since nobody was using them, I assumed that no one was in them. It was inconceivable that anyone in a room where they were wouldn't be trying to find out where I was."

"I hope your memory's good. Where are they?"

"My memory is superb," Orc said stiffly. "I am not one of you subbeings."

Kickaha grimaced. The Lords had the most sensitive and gangrenous egos he'd ever encountered. A good thing for him, though. He'd never have survived his conflicts with them if they hadn't always used part of their minds to feed their own egos. They were never really capable of one-hundred-percent concentration.

Well, he, Kickaha, had a big ego, too. But a healthy one.

The Lord remembered only a few of the locations of the auxiliary sensor systems. He couldn't be blamed for that since there were so many. But he was able to give Kickaha directions to three of them. He also gave him some instructions on how to operate them.

Just to make sure he hadn't been neglecting another source of information, Kickaha asked robots One and Two about the sensors. They were aware of only that in the control room. Urthona had not trusted them with anymore data than he thought necessary for his comfort and protection.

Kickaha thought that if he had been master of this palace, he would have installed a safety measure in the robots. When asked certain questions, they would have refused to answer them. Or pretended that they didn't know.

Which, now that he thought about it, might be just what was happening. But they'd given him data that Urthona might not want his enemies to have. So possibly, they were not lying.

He took One with him, leaving Anana to keep an eye on her uncle. It wasn't likely that he'd be going anyplace or doing anything worth noticing. But you never knew.

The hidden system console was in a room behind a wall in a much larger room on the tenth floor. Lacking the code word to gate through, he and One tore part of the wall down. He turned on the console and with One's aid, checked out the entire building. It was done swiftly, the glowing diagrams of the rooms flashing by too rapidly on the screen for Kickaha to see anything but a blur. But a computer in One's body sorted them out.

When the operation was complete, One said, "There are one hundred and ten chambers that the sensors do not monitor."

Kickaha groaned and said, "You mean we'd have to get into all of them to make sure no living being is in one of them?"

"That is one method."

"What's the other?"

"This system can monitor the control chamber. It's controlled by that switch there." One pointed. "That also enables the operator to hook into the control-room sensories. These can be used to look into the one hundred and ten chambers. The man named Orc did not know that. The switch is not on the panel in the control room, however. It is under the panel and labeled as an energy-generator control. Only the master knew about it."

"Then how did you come to know about it?"

"I learned about it while I was scanning the displays here."

"Then why didn't you tell me?"

"You didn't ask me."

Kickaha repressed another groan. The robots were so smart, yet so dumb.

"Connect this system with the control room's."

"Yes, master."

One strode ponderously to the control board and turned a switch marked, in Lord letters: HEAT. Heat for what? Obviously, it was so designated to make any unauthorized operator ignore it. Immediately, lights began pulsing here and there, a switch turned by itself, and one of the large video screens above the panel came to life.

Kickaha looked into the room from a unit apparently high on the wall and pointing downward. It was directed toward the central chair in a row of five or six before the wide panel. In this sat a man with his back to Kickaha.

For a second, he thought that it must be the Englishman who had helped Orc. But this man was bigger than the one described by Orc, and his hair was not brown but yellow.

He was looking at a video screen just above him. It showed Kickaha and the robot behind him, looking at the man.

The operator rose with a howl of fury, spun out of his chair, and shook his fist at the unit receiving his image.

He was Urthona.

25

THE LORD WAS CLAD ONLY IN A RAGGED SKIN BOUND AROUND his waist. A longitudinal depression, the scar from the ax wound, ran down the center of his chest. His hair fell over his shoulders to his nipples. His skin was smeared with the oily dirt of his world, and a bump on his forehead indicated a hard contact with some harder object. Moreover, his nose had been broken.

Kickaha was shocked for a few seconds, then he went into action. He ran toward the switch to turn if off. Urthona's voice screamed through the video: "One! Kill him! Kill him!"

"Kill who, Master?" One said calmly.

"You blithering metal idiot! That man! Kickaha!"

Kickaha turned the switch and whirled. The robot was advancing on him, its arms out, fingers half-clenched.

Kickaha drew his knife. Shockingly, Urthona's voice came out of the robot's unmoving lips. "I see you, you *leblabbiy*! I'm going to kill you!"

For a second, Kickaha didn't know what was happening. Then illumination came. Urthona had switched on a transceiver inside the robot's body and was speaking through it. Probably he was also watching his victim-to-be through One's eyes.

That had one advantage for Kickaha. As long as Urthona was watching the conflict from the control room, he wasn't gating here.

Kickaha leaped toward the robot, stopped, jumped back, slashed with his knife with no purpose but to test the speed of One's reaction. The robot made no attempt to parry with his arm or to grab the knife, however. He continued walking toward Kickaha.

Kickaha leaped past One, and his blade flickered in and out. Score one. The point had broken the shield painted to look like a human eyeball. But had it destroyed the video sensor behind it?

No time to find out. He came in again, this time on the left side. The robot was still turning when the knife shattered the other eyeball.

By now Kickaha knew that One wasn't quick enough for him. It undoubtedly was far stronger, but here swiftness was the key to victory. He ran around behind One and stopped. The robot continued on its path. It had to be blinded, which meant that Urthona would know this and would at once take some other action.

He looked around quickly. There were stretches of bare wall that could conceal a gate. But wouldn't Urthona place the gate where he could step out hidden from the sight of anyone in the room? Such as, for instance, the space behind the control console. It wasn't against the wall.

He ran to it and stepped behind it. Seconds, a minute, passed. Was Urthona delaying because he wanted to get a weapon first? If so, he would have to go to a hidden cache, since Orc had jettisoned every weapon he could locate.

Or was he staying in the control room, where he was safe? From there, he could order all the robots in the palace, and there were several score or more, to converge on this room.

Or had he gated to a room nearby and now was creeping up on his enemy? If so, he would make sure he had a beamer in his hand.

There was a thump as the robot blindly blundered into the wall. At least, Kickaha supposed that was the noise. He didn't want to stick his head out to see.

His only warning was a shimmering, a circle of wavy light taller than a tall man, on the wall to his right. Abruptly, it became a round hole in the wall. Urthona stepped through it, but Kickaha was upon him, hurling him back, desperate to get both of them in the control room before the gate closed.

They fell out onto the floor, Kickaha on top of the Lord, fingers locked on the wrist of the hand that held a beamer. The other laid the edge of the knife against the jugular vein. Urthona's eyes were glazed, the back of his head having thumped against the floor.

Kickaha twisted the wrist; the beamer clattered on the tile floor. He rolled away, grabbed the weapon, and was up on his feet.

Snarling, shaking, Urthona started to get up. He sank down as Kickaha ordered him to stay put.

The robot, Number Six, started toward them. Kickaha quickly ordered Urthona to command Six to take no action. The Lord did so, and the robot retreated to a wall.

Grinning, Kickaha said, "I never thought the day'd come when I'd be glad to see you. But I am. You're the cat's paw that pulled the chestnuts out of the fire for me. Me and Anana."

Urthona looked as if he just couldn't believe that this was happening to him. No wonder. After all he'd endured, and the good luck he'd had to find a boulder with a gate in it. For all he knew, his enemies were stranded on his world or more probably dead. He was king of the palace again. It must have been a shock when he found the door to the control room welded shut. Somebody had gotten in after all. Possibly a Lord of another world who'd managed to gate in, though that wasn't likely. He must have figured that somehow Orc or Anana and Kickaha had gotten in. But they couldn't get into the control room, where the center of power was. The first thing he had probably done though, was to cancel the decaying orbit of his palace. After setting it in a safe path, he would have started checking the sensory system. The regular one first. No doubt one of the flashing red lights on the central console indicated that someone was in a trap. He'd checked that and discovered that Orc was in the cube.

But he must also have seen Anana. Had he ordered the robot Two to kill her?

He asked Urthona. The Lord shook his head as if he was trying to throw his troubles out.

"No," he said slowly. "I saw her there, but she wasn't doing anything to endanger me for the moment. I started then to check out the auxiliary sensories just to make sure no one else was aboard. I hadn't gotten to the room in which you were yet. You connected with the control room . . . and . . . damn you! If only I'd gotten here a few minutes earlier."

"It's all in the timing," Kickaha said, smiling. "Now let us get on with it. You're probably thinking I'm going to kill you or perhaps stick you in that wheeled cage and let you starve to death. It's not a bad idea, but I prefer contemplating the theory to putting it into practice.

"I promised Orc I'd let him go if he cooperated. He hasn't done a thing to help, but I can't hold that against him. He hasn't had a chance.

"Now, if you cooperate, too, Urthona, I'll let you live and I won't torture you. I need to get Orc, your beloved brother, out of that trap so I can get my hands on the Horn. But first, let's check that your story is true. God help you if it isn't."

He stood behind the Lord just far enough away so that if he tried to turn and snatch at the beamer, he'd be out of reach. The weapon was set on low stun. Urthona worked the controls, and the concealed TV of the auxiliary system looked into the room with the cube. Orc was still in his prison; Anana and Two were standing by the hole in the wall.

Kickaha called her name. She looked up with a soft cry. He told her not to be frightened, and he outlined what had happened.

"So things are looking good again," he said. "Orc, your brother is going to gate you into the control room. First, though, put the beamer down on the table. Don't try anything. We'll be watching you. Keep hold of the Horn. That's it. Now go to the corner where you appeared in the cube when you were gated through. Okay. Stand still. Don't move or you'll lose a foot or something."

Urthona reached for a button. Kickaha said, "Hold it. I'm not through. Anana, you know where I went. Go up there and stand by the wall behind the control console there. Then step through the gate when it appears. Oh, you'll meet a blind robot, poor old One. I'll order it to stand still so it won't bother you."

Urthona walked stiffly to a console at one end of the enormous room. His hands were tightly clenched; his jaw was clamped; he was quivering.

"You should be jumping with joy," Kickaha said. "You're going to live. You'll get another chance at the three of us someday."

"You don't expect me to believe that?"

"Why not? Did I ever do anything you anticipated?"

He directed the Lord to show him the unmarked controls that would bring Orc back. Urthona stepped aside to allow Kickaha to operate. The redhead, however, said, "You do it."

It was possible that the controls, moved in the manner shown, would send a high voltage through him.

Urthona shrugged. He flipped a toggle switch, pressed a button, and stepped away from the console. To the left, the bare wall shimmered for a few seconds. A hemisphere of swirling colors bulged out from it, and then it collapsed. Red Orc stood with his back almost touching the wall.

Kickaha said, "Put the Horn down and push it with your foot toward me."

The Lord obeyed. Kickaha, keeping an eye on both of them, bent down and picked up the Horn.

"Ha! Mine again!"

Five minutes later, Anana stepped out of the same gate through which Kickaha and Urthona had fallen.

Her uncles looked as if this was the end of the last act. They fully expected to be slain on the spot. At one time, Kickaha would have been angered because neither had the least notion that he deserved to be executed. There was no use getting upset, however. He had learned long ago not to be disturbed by the self-righteous and the psychopath, if there was any difference between the two.

"Before we part," he said. "I'd like to clear up a few things, if possible. Urthona, do you know anything about an Englishman, supposedly born in the eighteenth century? Red Orc found him living in this place when he entered."

Urthona looked surprised. "Someone else got in here?"

"That tells me how much you know. Well, maybe I'll run across him some other time. Urthona, your niece has explained something about the energy converter that powers this floating fairy castle. She told me that any converter can be set to overload, but an automatic regulator will cut it back to override that. Unless you remove the regulator. I want you to fix the overload to reach its peak in fifteen minutes. You'll cut the regulator out of the line."

Urthona paled. "Why? You . . . you mean to blow me up?"

"No. You'll be long gone from here when it blows. I intend to destroy your palace. You'll never be able to use it again."

Urthona didn't ask what would happen if he refused. Under the keen eye of Anana, he set the controls. A large red light began flashing on a console. A display flashed, in Lord letters, OVERLOAD. A whistle shrilled.

Even Anana looked uneasy. Kickaha smiled, though he was as nervous as anybody.

"Okay. Now open the gates to Earth I and to Jadawin's world."

He had carefully noted the control that could put the overload regulator back into the line if Urthona tried any tricks.

"I know you can't help being treacherous and sneaky, Urthona," Kickaha said. "But repress your natural viciousness. Refrain from pulling a fast one. My beamer's set on cutting. I'll slice you at the first false move."

Urthona did not reply.

On the towering blank wall, two circular shimmerings appeared. They cleared away. One showed an opening to a cave, the same one through which Kickaha and Anana had entered southern California. The other revealed the slope of a wooded valley, a broad green river at the foot. And, far away, smoke rising from the chimneys of a tiny village, and a stone castle on a rocky bluff above it. The sky was a bright green.

Kickaha looked pleased.

"That looks like Dracheland. The third level, Abharhploonta. Either of you ever been there?"

"I've made some forays into Jadawin's world," Urthona said. "I planned someday to . . . to . . ."

"Take over from Jadawin? Forget it. Now, Urthona, activate a gate that'll take you to the surface of your planet."

Urthona gasped and said, "But you said . . . ! Surely . . . ? You're not going to abandon me here?"

"Why not? You made this world. You can live in it the rest of your life. Which will probably be short and undoubtedly miserable. As the Terrestrials say, let the punishment fit the crime."

"That isn't right!" Urthona said. "You are letting Orc go back to Earth. It isn't what I'd call a first-rate world, but compared to this, it's a paradise."

"Look who's talking about *right*. You're not going to beg, are you? You, a lord among the Lords?"

Urthona straightened his shoulders. "No. But if you think you've seen the last of me—"

"I know. I've got another think coming. I wouldn't be surprised. I'll bet you have a gate to some other world concealed in a boulder. But you aren't letting on. Think you'll catch me by surprise someday, heh? After you find the boulder—if you do. Good luck. I may be bored and need some stiff competition. Get going."

Urthona walked up to the wall. Anana spoke sharply. "Kickaha! Stop him!"

He yelled at the Lord. "Hold it, or I'll shoot!"

Urthona stopped but did not turn.

"What is it, Anana?"

She glanced at a huge chronometer on the wall.

"Don't you know there's still danger? How do you know what he's up to? What might happen when he gives the code word? It'll be better to wait until the last minute. Then Orc can go through, and you can shut the gate behind him. After that, we'll go through ours. And then Urthona can gate. But he can do it with no one else around."

"Yeah, you're right," Kickaha said. "I was so eager to get back, I rushed things."

He shouted, "Urthona! Turn around and walk back here!"

Kickaha didn't hear Urthona say anything. His voice must have been very soft. But the words were loud enough for whatever sensor was in the wall to detect them.

A loud hissing sounded from the floor and the ceilings and the walls. From thousands of tiny perforations in the inner wall, clouds of greenish gas shot through the room.

Kickaha breathed in just enough of the metallic odor to make him want to choke. He held his breath then, but his eyes watered so that he could not see Urthona making his break. Red Orc was suddenly out of sight, too. Anana, a dim figure in the green mists, stood looking at him. One hand was pinching her nose and the other was over her mouth. She was signaling to him not to breathe.

She would have been too late, however. If he had not acted immediately to shut off his breath, he would, he was sure, be dead by now. Unconscious, anyway.

The gas was not going to harm his skin. He was sure of that. Otherwise, Urthona would have been caught in the deadly trap.

Anana turned and disappeared in the green. She was heading toward the gate to the World of Tiers. He began running too, his eyes burning and streaming water. He caught a glimpse of Red Orc plunging through the gate to Earth I.

And then he saw, dimly, Urthona's back as he sped through the gate to the world that Kickaha loved so much.

Kickaha felt as if he would have to cough. Nevertheless, he fought against the reflex, knowing that if he drew in one full breath, he would be done for.

Then he was through the entrance. He didn't know how high the gate was above the mountain slope, but he had no time for caution. He fell at once, landed on his buttocks, and slid painfully on a jumble of loose rocks. It went at a forty-five-degree angle to the horizontal for about two hundred feet, then suddenly dropped off. He rolled over and clawed at the rocks. They cut and tore into his chest and his hands, but he dug in no matter how it hurt.

By then, he was coughing. No matter. He was out of the green clouds that now poured out of the hole in the mountain face.

He stopped. Slowly, afraid that if he made a too vigorous movement, he'd start the loose stones to sliding, he began crawling upward. A few rocks were dislodged. Then he saw Anana. She had gotten to the side of the gate and was clinging with one hand to a rocky ledge. The other held the Horn. Her eyes were huge, and her face was pale.

She shouted, "Get up here and away! As fast as you can! The converter is going to blow soon!"

He knew that. He yelled at her to get out of the area. He'd be up there in a minute. She looked as if she were thinking of coming down to help him, then she began working her way along the steep slope. He crawled at an angle toward the ledge she had grabbed. Several times he started sliding back, but he managed to stop his descent.

Finally, he got off the apron of stones. He rose to a crouch and, grabbing handfuls of grass, pulled himself up to the ledge. Holding on to this with one hand, he worked his way as swiftly as he dared away from the hole.

Just as he got to a point above a slight projection of the mountain, a stony half-pout, the mountain shook and bellowed. He was hurled outward to land flat on his face on the mini-ledge.

The loose rocks slid down and over the edge, leaving the stone beneath it as bare as if a giant broom had swept it.

Silence except for the screams of some distant birds and a faint rumble as the stones slid to a halt far below.

Anana said, "It's over, Kickaha."

He turned slowly to see her looking around a spur of rock.

"The gate would have closed the moment its activator was destroyed. We got only a small part of the blast, thank God. Otherwise, the whole mountain would've been blown up."

He got up and looked alongside the slope. Something stuck out from the pile below. An arm?

"Did Urthona get away?"

She shook her head. "No, he went over the edge. He didn't have much of a drop, about twenty feet, before he hit the second slope. But the rocks caught him."

"We'll go down and make sure he's dead," he said. "That trick of his dissolves any promises we made to him."

All that was needed was to pile more rocks on Urthona to keep the birds and the beasts from him.

26

IT WAS A MONTH LATER. THEY WERE STILL ON THE MOUNTAIN, though on the other side and near its base. The valley was uninhabited by humans, though occasionally hunters ventured into it from the river village they'd seen on coming from the gate. Kickaha and Anana avoided these.

They'd built a lean-to at first. After they made bows and arrows from ash, tipped with worked flint, they'd shot deer, which were plentiful, and tanned the hides. Out of these they made a tepee, well hidden in a grove of trees. A brook, two hundred yards down the slope, gave them clear cold water. It also provided fine fishing.

They dressed in buckskin hides, and slept on bearskin blankets at night. They rested well but exercised often, hiking, berry- and nut-picking, hunting, and making love. They even became a little fat. After being half starved for so long, it was difficult not to stuff themselves. Part of their diet was bread and butter, which they'd stolen one night from the village, two large bagfuls.

Kickaha, eavesdropping on the villagers, had validated his assumption that they were in Dracheland. And from a reference overheard, he had learned that the village was in the barony of Ulrich von Neifen.

"His lord, theoretically anyway, is the duke, or Herzog, Willehalm von Hartmot. I know, generally, where we are. If we go down that river, we'll come to the Pfawe river. We'll travel about three hundred miles, and we'll be in the barony of Siegfried von Listbat. He's a good friend. He should be. I gave him my castle, and he married my divorced wife. It wasn't that Isote and I didn't get along well, you understand. She just wouldn't put up with my absences."

"Which were how long?"

"Oh, they varied from a few months to a few years."

Anana laughed. "From now on, when you go on trips, I'll be along."

"Sure. You can keep up with me, but Isote couldn't, and she wouldn't have even if she could."

They agreed that they would visit von Listbat for a month or so. Kickaha had wanted to descend to the next level, which he called Amerindia, and find a tribe that would adopt him. Of all the levels, he loved this the most. There were great forest-covered mountains and vast plains, brooks and rivers of purest water, giant buffalo, mammoth, antelope, bear, sabertooths, wild horses, beaver, game birds by the billions. The human population was savage but small, and though the second level covered more territory than North and Central America combined, there were few places where the name of Kickaha the Trickster was not known.

But they must get to the palace fortress on top of this world, which was shaped like the Tower of Babel. There they would gate through, though reluctantly, to Earth again. Reluctantly, because neither cared too much for Earth I. It was overpopulated, polluted, and might at any time perish in atomic warfare.

"Maybe Wolff and Chryseis will be there by the time we arrive. It's possible they're already there. Wouldn't that be great?"

They were on the mountain, above the river valley, when he said this. Halfway down the slope were the birches from which they would build a canoe. Smoke rose from the chimneys of the tiny village on the bend of the river. The air was pure, and the earth beneath them did not rise and fall. A great black eagle soared nearby, and two hawks slid along the wind, headed for the river and its plenitude of fish. A grizzly bear grunted in a berry patch nearby.

"Anana, this is a beautiful world. Jadawin may be its Lord, but this is really my world, Kickaha's world."

MORE

THAN FIRE

To Lynn and Julia Carl,
Gary Wolfe, and Dede Weil

1

"THIS'LL BE IT!" KICKAHA SAID. "I KNOW IT, KNOW IT! I CAN feel the forces shaping themselves into a big funnel pouring us onto the goal! It's just ahead! We've finally made it!"

He wiped the sweat from his forehead. Though breathing heavily, he increased his pace.

Anana was a few steps behind and below him on the steep mountain trail. She spoke to herself in a low voice. He never paid any attention to her discouraging—that is, realistic—words, anyway.

"I'll believe it when I see it."

Kickaha the Trickster and Anana the Bright had been tramping up and down the planet of the Tripeds for fifteen years. Their quest was not for the Holy Grail but for something even better: a way to get out of this backwater universe. It had to exist. But where was it?

Kickaha usually looked on the cheerful side of events. If they had none, he lit the darkness with his optimism. Once he had said to Anana, "If your jail's an entire planet, being a yardbird isn't so bad."

Anana had replied, "A prison is a prison."

Kickaha had been carrying the key to unlock the gate leading to other worlds and to the mainstream of life. That key was Shambarimen's Horn, the ancient musical instrument he carried in a deerskin pouch hanging from his belt. During their wanderings on this planet, he had blown the Horn thousands of times. Each time, he had hoped that an invisible "weak" place in the fabric of the "walls" separating two universes would open in response to the seven notes from the Horn and make itself visible. There were thousands of such flaws in the walls.

But so far, he had not been in an area where these existed. He knew that every time he blew the Horn, a flaw, a way out of their vast prison, might be a hundred yards away, just out of the activating range of the Horn. As he had said, knowing that made him feel as if he owned a ticket in the Irish Sweepstakes. The chances of his winning that would be very, very low.

If he could find a gate, an exit deliberately made by a Lord and often evident as such, he would have won the lottery. The natives of this planet had heard rumors of gates, or what could be gates. Countless rumors. Kickaha and Anana had followed these, sometimes for hundreds of miles, to their sources. So far, they had found only disappointment and more rumors to set them off on another long trail. But today, Kickaha was sure that their efforts would pay off.

The trail was leading them upward through a forest. Many of the giant trees smelled to Kickaha like sauerkraut juice mixed with pear juice. The odor meant that the leaves at the tips of the branches would soon be mutating into a butterflylike, but vegetable, creature. The brightly colored organisms would tear themselves away from the rotting twigs. They would flutter off, unable to eat, unable to do anything but soar far away before they died. Then, if they were not eaten by birds on the way, if they landed on a hospitable spot, the very tiny seeds within their bodies would sprout into saplings a month later.

The many marvels on this planet made it easier to endure their forced stay on it, Kickaha thought. But the longer they were here, the more time it gave their archenemy, Red Orc, to track them down. And Kickaha also thought often of his friends, Wolff and Chryseis, who had been imprisoned by Red Orc. Had they been killed by Red Orc, or had they managed to escape?

Kickaha, who on Earth had been named Paul Janus Finnegan, was tall, broad-shouldered, and muscular. The exceptional thickness of his powerfully muscled legs made him look shorter. He was deeply sun-browned; his shoulder-length and slightly curly hair was red-bronze; his face was craggy, long-lipped, and usually merry. His large wide-set eyes were as green as spring leaves.

Though he looked as if he were twenty-five years old, he had been born on Earth seventy-four years ago.

Buckskin moccasins and a belt were his only clothing. His belt held a steel knife and a tomahawk. On his back was a small pack and a quiver full of arrows. One hand held a long bow.

Behind him came Anana the Bright, tall, black-haired, blue-eyed, and also sun-browned. She came from a people who thought of themselves as deities, and she did look like a goddess. But she was no Venus. A classical scholar seeing her slim and exceptionally long legs and greyhound body would think of the hunting goddess, Artemis. However, goddesses did not perspire, and Anana's sweat ran from her.

She, too, wore only moccasins and a belt. Her weapons were the same as Kickaha's except for the long spear in one hand, and she bore a knapsack on her back.

Kickaha was thinking about the natives who had directed them up this path. They had seemed certain that the Door to the Sleeper's Tomb was on top of the mountain. He hoped that the door was a gate. The natives he had questioned had never been to the mountaintop because they did not have the goods to give the Guardian of the Door for answers to their questions. But they knew somebody who knew somebody who knew somebody who had visited the Guardian.

This was probably another disappointing journey. But they could not afford to ignore any rumor or tale about anything that could be a Lord's gate. Anyway, what else did they have to do?

A little more than a decade and a half ago, he and Anana had escaped from the Lavalite World into the World of Tiers. Then, he had been very confident that they would soon be able to do what must be done.

Their adventures on the Lavalite World, that planet of insecurity, instability, and constantly shifting shape, had been harrowing. Kickaha and Anana had rested for several weeks after escaping from it to the World of Tiers. Then, having renewed themselves with rest and fun, they had sought out and found a gate that teleported them to Wolff's palace, now uninhabited. This was on top of the monolith on top of the World of Tiers.

They had armed themselves in the palace with some of the weapons of the Lords, weapons superior to anything on Earth. Then they had activated a gate that had previously passed them to a cave in a Southern California mountain. This was the cave through which Kickaha had first come back to Earth after many years of absence.

But when he and Anana had stepped through the gate, they had found themselves on a planet in this artificial universe, the Whaziss world. The gate had been a one-way trap, and Kickaha did not know who had set it up.

Kickaha had boasted more than once that no prison or trap could hold him long. Now, if those words could be given substance, he would have to eat them. They would taste like buzzard dung sprinkled with wood ashes.

Yesterday, he and Anna had stopped two-thirds of the way up the mountain and camped for the night. They had continued their climb at dawn and thus should, by now, be close to the top.

Five minutes later, he heard the voices of children drifting down the path. Within two minutes, they stepped over the edge of the small plateau.

The village in the middle of the plateau was much like others in this area. A circular wall of upright and pointed logs enclosed approximately forty log houses with conical roofs. In the center of the village was a temple, a two-story log building with a round tower on top and many carved-wood idols in and around it.

If the natives' stories were true, the temple could contain a gate. According to these, the building contained a vertical structure of "divine" metal. Its thin beams formed a six-sided opening into the world of the gods. Or, as some stories said, a door to the world of the demons.

The natives also said that the hexagon had been on the top of the hill before the natives were created by the gods. The gods—or the demons—had used the opening long before the natives came into being and would use it long after the natives had become extinct.

The first one to tell Kickaha this story was Tsash. He was a priest of a deity that had once been very minor but was now up-and-coming, and perhaps destined to be number one on this island the size of Earth's Greenland.

Tsash had said, "The Door to the Otherworld is open. Anyone may step through it. But he will only find himself on the other side of the six-angled door and still in our world unless he can utter the magical word. And there is no assurance that he who does know the word will like what he finds on the other side."

"And just where is this door?" Kickaha had said.

Tsash had waved his hand westward. The gesture took in a lot of territory, since he was standing in a temple on a cliff on the shore of the Eastern Sea.

"Out there. It is said that the Door is in a temple—dedicated to what god, I do not know—which is on a hilltop. But then, all temples are on the tops of high hills or mountains."

"How many temples are there in this land?" Kickaha had said.

"Only the gods could count them, they are so numerous!"

He had lifted both four-fingered hands above his head, and he had cried, "Do not use the Door even if you find the magical word to open it! You may awake the Sleeper! Do not do that! You will die the Undying Death!"

"Which is what?" Kickaha had said.

"I do not know, and I do not wish to know!" Tsash had shouted.

Kickaha had asked more questions, but Tsash seemed to have submerged himself in prayer. His huge eyes were closed, and the mouth under the green hair growing all over his face was murmuring something rhythmic and repetitive.

Kickaha and Anana had left the temple and set out westward. Fifteen years later, after going up and down and around but always working toward the Western Sea, they were on another mountaintop with a temple on it.

Kickaha was excited. He believed that the long-sought gate was inside the building. Despite the many failures and consequent disappointments, he allowed himself to believe that their quest was at an end. Perhaps "allowed" was not the correct word. He had no control over his enthusiasms. They came and went as they pleased; he was the conduit.

If Anana was delighted or expectant, she did not show it. Many thousands of years of life had rubbed away much of her zest. Being in love with Kickaha and sharing his adventures had restored some of this—far more, in fact, than she had expected. Time was a chisel that had reshaped the original substance of her spirit. Yet it had taken that relentless dimension a long, long time to do it.

"This has to be it!" Kickaha said. "I feel it in the bones of my bones!"

She patted his right cheek. "Every time we get to a temple, our chances to succeed increase. Provided, of course, that there is any gate on this planet."

The children playing outside the wall ran screaming toward them. Kickaha figured that they must have been forewarned. Otherwise, they would have run screaming away from them. The children surrounded the two and milled around, touching them, chattering away, marveling at the two-legged beings. A moment later, a band of armed males chased the youngsters away. Immediately afterward, the priest appeared in the village gate and waved a long wooden shaft at them. The outer end of this sported a scarlet propellor spun by the wind. Halfway down the shaft was a yellow disc bearing on its surface several sacred symbols.

Behind the priest came two minor priests, each whirling above his head a bull-roarer.

All the natives were naked. They were, however, adorned with bracelets and with ear-, nose-, and lip-rings. Their heads and faces were covered with a short greenish fur except for the chin region.

And they were three-legged.

Ololothon, the Lord who had long ago made their ancestors in his biology factory, had been very cruel. He had made the tripeds as an experiment. Then, having determined that they were functional though slow and awkward, Ololothon had let them loose to breed and to spread over this planet. They had no generic name for themselves, but Kickaha called them the Whazisses. They looked so much like the illustrations of a creature called a Whaziss in a fantasy, Johnny Gruelle's *Johnny Mouse and the Wishing Stick*, which Kickaha had read when very young.

Kickaha called out in the dialect of the locals, "Greetings, Krazb, Guardian of the Door and holiest priest of the deity Afresst! I am Kickaha, and my mate is Anana!"

Word of mouth had carried the news of the funny-looking bipeds and their quest to Krazb many months ago. Despite this, protocol forced him to pretend ignorance and to ask many questions. It also required that the council of elders and shamans invite the two strangers into the council house for the drinking of a local brew, for much talking, for a slow working up to the reason why the strangers were here (as if the Whazisses did not know), and for dancing and singing by various groups.

After three hours of this, the priest asked Kickaha and Anana what brought them here.

Kickaha told him. But that caused much more explaining. Even then, Krazb did not understand. Like all the natives, he knew nothing of the Lords or artificial pocket universes. Apparently, the long-ago-dead Lord had never revealed himself to the natives. They had been forced to make up their own religion.

Though Kickaha did not succeed in making everything clear in Krazb's mind, he did make him understand that Kickaha was looking for a Door.

Kickaha said, "Is there one in your temple or is there not? Anana and I have entered more than five hundred temples since we started our search fifteen years ago. We are desperate and about to give up the search unless your temple does indeed contain a Door."

Krazb gracefully got to his feet from his sitting position on the ground, no easy movement for a triped.

He said, "Two-legged strangers! Your long quest is over! The Door you seek is indeed in the temple, and it's unfortunate that you did not come here straightaway fifteen years ago! You would have saved yourself much time and worry!"

Kickaha opened his mouth to protest the injustice of the remark. Anana put a hand on his arm. "Easy!" she said in Thoan. "We have to butter him up. No matter what he says, smile and agree."

The Whaziss's lips tightened and the place where his eyebrows should be under the green fur was drawn down.

"Truly, there is a Door here," he said. "Otherwise, why should I be called the Guardian?"

Kickaha did not tell him that he had met twenty priests, each of whom titled himself "Guardian of the Door." Yet, all of their Doors had been fakes.

"We had no doubt that your words were true," Kickaha said. "May we be allowed, O Guardian, to see the Door?"

"Indeed you may," the priest said. "But you surely are tired, sweaty, dirty, and hungry after your journey up the mountain, though you should no longer be thirsty. The gods would be angry with us if we did not treat you as hospitably as our poor means permit us. You will be bathed and fed, and if you are tired, you will sleep until you are no longer fatigued."

"Your hospitality has already overwhelmed us with its largesse," Kickaha said.

"Nevertheless," Krazb said, "it has not been enough. We would be ashamed if you left us and went to other villages and complained about our meanness of spirit and of material generosity."

Night came. The festivities continued under the light of torches. The humans fought their desire to vent their frustration and boredom. At last, long past midnight, Krazb, slurring his words, announced that it was time for all to go to bed. The drums and the horns ceased their "music," and the merrymakers who had not passed out staggered off to their huts. A minor official, Wigshab, led the humans to a hut, told them that they were to spend the night there on a pile of blankets, and wobbled off.

Having made sure that Wigshab was out of sight, Kickaha stepped outside the hut to check out the situation. Highly looped Krazb must have forgotten to post guards. Except for the drunken sleepers on the ground, not a Whaziss was to be seen.

Kickaha breathed in deeply. The breeze was cool enough to be pleasant. Most of the torches had been taken away, but four bright brands on the temple wall made enough light in this moonless night to guide them.

Anana stepped out from the hut. Like Kickaha, she had drunk very lightly.

"Did you hear Krazb when he said something about the price for admission to the Door?" she said. "That sounds ominous."

2

"It was too noisy. What did he say about the price?"

"That we'd talk about it in the morning. That there were two prices. One was for just looking at the Door. Another, the much higher price, for using the Door."

The price, Kickaha knew, would not be in money. The Whaziss economy was based only on the trading of goods or services. The only item of any value Kickaha could offer was the Horn of Shambarimen. Krazb wouldn't know what it could do. He would desire it just because there was nothing like it anywhere on his world.

Thus, he and Anana were not going to get through the Door unless they gave up the Horn. If they did not surrender it, they would have to fight the Whazisses, whom Krazb would use when no one was watching.

He told Anana his thoughts while they stood in the doorway of the hut.

"I think we should sneak into the temple right now and find out if there is a gate. If there is, we go through it. Provided we can."

"That's what I expected," she said. "Let's go."

While they were putting on their belts, backpacks, and quivers, Kickaha was thinking; What a woman! No hesitancies, no shilly-shallying for her. She quickly figures out what the situation is—probably had it figured out before I did—and then acts as the situation demands.

On the other hand, he did get irritated sometimes because she knew what his thoughts were before he voiced them. And lately, she obviously was having the same reactions to him that he was having to her.

For far too long, they had rarely been out of each other's sight, and they had been without the company of other human beings. The Whazisses were unsatisfactory substitutes for "people." They had a very stunted sense of humor and of art, and their technology had not progressed for thousands of years. Though they could lie, they were unable to conceive of the big whoppers that humans told just for the fun of it. Nowhere had Kickaha heard a Whaziss express an unconventional thought, and their cultures differed very little from each other.

Anana, holding her spear in one hand and a torch in the other, led the way. Tomahawk in hand, Kickaha walked a few steps back from her side until they reached the temple. The log building was dark. The guards who should have been here were drunk and snoring in the village square. While Anana followed him and cast the light of the torch around for him, he went around the temple to check for other entrances. But it had only one, the big wooden two-sectioned door in its front.

That had a thick wooden beam across the sections. He pulled it back from one of its slots and then swung a section back. Torchlights burning in wall sockets showed a smaller building in the center of the temple floor. It was a duplicate of the temple.

No Whaziss was here, unless he was inside the House of the Door, as the priest had called it.

Kickaha shot back the bar on the small door and swung a section open. Anana got close behind him. He stayed outside the building but leaned far in to look around it. The two torches there lit up a structure flanked by two wooden idols.

Anana said, "At last!"

"I told you that this was it."

"Many times."

Both had seen gates like the one before them. It was an upright six-angled structure composed of arm-thick silver-colored metal beams. It was wide enough to admit two persons abreast.

They walked into the building and stopped a few inches from the hexagonal gate. Kickaha thrust the head of his tomahawk into the space enclosed by the beams. It did not, as he had half expected, disappear. And when he went to the other side and stuck the tomahawk in it, it was clearly visible.

"Unactivated," he said. "Okay. We don't need the code word. We'll try the Horn."

He put the tomahawk shaft inside his belt and opened the bag hanging from his belt. He withdrew the Horn of Shambarimen from it. It was of a silvery metal, almost two and a half feet long, and did not quite weigh a fourth of a pound. Its tube was shaped like an African buffalo's horn. The mouthpiece was of some soft golden substance. The other end, flaring out broadly, contained a web or grill of silvery threads a half-inch inside it. The underside of the Horn bore seven small buttons in a row.

When the light struck the Horn at the right angle, it revealed a hieroglyph inscribed on the top and halfway along its length.

This was the highly treasured artifact made by the supreme craftsman and scientist of the ancient Thoan, which meant "Lords." It was unique. No one knew how to reproduce it because its inner mechanism was impenetrable to X rays, sonic waves, and all the other devices of matter penetration.

Kickaha lifted the Horn and put its mouthpiece to his lips. He blew upon it while his fingers pressed the buttons in the sequence he knew by heart. He saw in his mind seven notes fly out as if they were golden geese with silver wings.

The musical phrase would reveal and activate a hidden gate or "flaw" if one was within sound range of the Horn. The notes would also activate a visible gate. It was the universal key.

He lowered the Horn. Nothing seemed to have happened, but just-activated gates did not often give signs of their changed state. Anana thrust the blade of her spear into the gate. The blade disappeared.

"It's on!" she cried, and she pulled the blade back until it was free of the gate.

Kickaha trembled with excitement. "Fifteen years!" he howled. Anana looked at him and put a finger to her lips.

"They're all passed out," he said. "What you should be worried about is what's on the other side of the gate."

He could stick his head through the gate and see what waited for them in another universe. Or perhaps somewhere in this universe, since this gate could lead to another on this planet. But he knew that doing that might trigger a trap. A blade might sweep down (or up) and cut his head off. Or fire might burn his face off. Sometimes, anything stuck through a gate to probe the other side conducted a fatal electrical charge or a spurt of flaming liquid or guided a shearing laser beam or any of a hundred fatal things.

The best way to probe was to get someone you didn't care for, a slave, for instance, if one was handy. That was the way of the Lords. Kickaha and Anana would not do that unless they had captured an enemy who had tried to kill them.

Her spear had come back from that other world without damage. But a trap could be set for action only if it detected flesh or high-order brainwaves.

Anana said, "You want me to go first?"

"No. Here goes nothing—I hope not."

"I'll go first," Anana said, but he jumped through the empty space in the hexagonal frame before she could finish.

He landed on both feet, knees bent, gripping his tomahawk and trying to see in front of him and on both sides at the same time. Then he stepped forward to allow Anana to come through without colliding with him.

The place was twilit without any visible source of light. It was an enormous cavern with dim stalagmites sticking up from the ground and stalactites hanging down from above. These stone icicles were formed from carbonate of calcium dissolving from the water seeping down from above. They looked like the teeth in the jaws of a trap.

However, except for the lighting, the cavern seemed to be like any other subterranean hollow.

Anana jumped through then, her spear in one hand, a blazing torch in the other. She crouched, looking swiftly around.

He said, "So far, so good."

"But not very far."

Though they spoke softly, their words were picked up, inflated, and, like Frisbees, spun back toward them.

Ahead was the cavern, huge as far as they could see. It also extended into darkness on both left and right. He turned to look behind him. The six-sided gate was there, and beyond it was more vast cave. Air moved slowly over him. It cooled off his sweating body and made him shiver. He wished that he had had more time to prepare for this venture. They should have brought along clothes, food, and extra torches.

The Lord who had set this gate up had probably done it thousands of years ago. It might have been used only once or twice and then been neglected until now. The Lord knew where other gates were and where they led. But Kickaha and Anana had no way of knowing what to do next to get out of this world. There was one thing he could do that might work.

He lifted the Horn to his lips and blew the silver notes while his fingers pressed on the seven buttons. When he was finished, he lowered the Horn and thrust the tomahawk head through the gate. The head disappeared.

"The gate's activated on this side!" he cried.

Anana kissed him on his cheek. "Maybe we're getting lucky!"

He withdrew the tomahawk, and he said, "Of course . . ."

"Of course?"

"It might admit us back to the world we just left. That'd be the kind of joke a Lord would love."

"Let's have a laugh, too," she said. She leaped through the hexagon and was gone.

Kickaha gave her a few seconds to move out of his way and also to come back through if she had reason to do so. Then he jumped.

He was pleased to find that he was not back in the Whaziss temple. The stone-block platform on which he stood had no visible gate, but it was, of course, there. It was in the center of a round, barn-sized, and stone-walled room with a conical ceiling of some red-painted metal. The floor was smooth stone, and it had no opening for a staircase. There was no furniture. The exits were open arches at each of the four cardinal points of the compass; a strong wind shot through the arch on his left. Through the openings he could see parts of a long, rolling plain and of a forest and of the castlelike building of which this room was a part. The room seemed to be five hundred feet above the ground.

Anana had left the room and was pressed against a waist-high rampart while she looked at the scene. Without turning to look at him, she said, "Kickaha! I don't think we're where we want to be!"

He joined her. The wind lifted up his shoulder-length bronze-red hair and streamed it out to his right. Her long, glossy, and black hair flowed horizontally like octopus ink jets released in a strong sea current. Though the blue but slightly greencast sun was just past the zenith and its rays fell on their bare skin, it was not hot enough to withstand the chill wind. They shivered as they walked around the tower room. Kickaha did not think the shivering was caused only by the wind.

It was not the absence of people. He had seen many deserted castles and cities. Actually, this castle was so tall and broad that it could be classified as a large town.

"You feel uneasy?" he said. "As if there's something unusually strange about this place?"

"Definitely!"

"Do you feel as if somebody's watching you?"

"No," Anana said. "I feel . . . you'll think I'm being irrational . . . that something is sleeping here and that it'll be best not to wake it."

"You may be irrational, but that doesn't mean you're crazy. You've lived so long and seen so much that you notice subtleties I can't . . ."

He stopped. They had walked far enough that he could see part of the view from the other side. Past the roofs of many structures, up against a hill of rock, was a round, bright blue structure. He resumed walking around the tower until he could see all of it. Then he stopped and gazed a while before speaking.

"That globe must be four or five miles from here. But it still looks huge!"

"There are statues around it, but I can't see the details," Anana said.

They decided that they would walk through the castle-city to the enormous globe. But the room had no staircase. They seemed to be imprisoned in the top room of the tallest tower in the castle. How had the former citizens gotten to this room? They busied themselves intently going over every inch of the inside and outside of the tower room. They could find no concealed door, no suspicious hollow spaces, nor anything to indicate a secret exit or entrance.

"You know what that means?" Kickaha said.

Anana nodded and said, "Test it."

He went to the side of the invisible hexagon opposite that from which they had stepped out. He lifted the Horn and blew the seven notes. Nothing visible happened, but when he thrust his tomahawk through the space where the hexagon must be, the weapon disappeared up to his hand. As they had suspected, each side was a gate.

"It's probably part of a gate maze," she said.

He leaped through the hexagon, landed on both feet, and stepped forward. Two seconds later, Anana followed. They were in a large, doorless, and windowless room made of a greenish, semitransparent and hard substance. The room could have been carved out of a single huge jewel. The only light came from outside it. It showed unmoving objects too dim to be seen clearly. Against the wall opposite him was the outline of a hexagon in thin black lines. Unless a trick was being played upon them, the lines enclosed a gate.

The air was heavy, thick, stale, and unmoving. Near his feet were two skeletons, one human and one semihuman. In the midst of the bones were two belt buckles, golden rings set with jewels, and one beamer. Kickaha leaned over and picked up the pistollike beamer. That made him breathe deeper than he should have. The lack of oxygen was making his heart beat overfast, and his throat was beginning to tighten.

"I think," Anana said, "that we don't have much time to spend trying to get through the gate. Our predecessors didn't have the code, and so they died quickly."

Theoretically, the two previous occupants of the room should have used up all the oxygen in it. But there was enough here to keep the two from beginning to strangle at once. Obviously, the owner of the gate had brought in some oxygen to replace what the dead intruders had used. Just enough to torture the next occupants with the knowledge of their sure fate.

"We've got maybe a minute!" Kickaha said.

He pressed the button on the beamer that indicated the amount of energy left in the fuel supply. A tiny digital display by the button showed that enough fuel was left for ten half-second full-power bursts. After shoving the barrel of the beamer between his waist and his belt, he put the mouthpiece of the Horn to his lips. It was not necessary to blow hard. The output of the seven notes was at the same noise level, regardless of the input.

As the last silvery note bounced around in the small room, Anana thrust the head of her spear into the area of wall on which the lines were painted. It disappeared. Then she withdrew it. It showed no signs of damage or fire. That did not mean much, as both knew. Nevertheless, by now Kickaha's lungs were sending signals to him, and his throat seemed to be falling in on itself. Anana's face showed that she, too, was feeling panic.

Despite his increasing need for fresh air, he turned around and blew the seven-note sequence again, directing it at the blank wall opposite the inscribed one. It was possible that there was a gate there also, one its maker had hidden there. The gate with the hexagon might be a deadly trap for the uncautious.

He could not see any change in the wall, but Anana drove her spear hard against it at different places to determine if an invisible gate was there. The metal head clanged and bounced off the glassy substance, which boomed as if it were a drum. They would have to take the one way open.

Anana, her spear held out, leaped through the gate. He followed her several seconds later. As usual, he winced a little when it seemed that he would slam into the wall. Though his conscious mind knew that he would not do so, he could not convince his unconscious mind. As he passed through the seeming solid, he glimpsed the hexagonal structure a foot beyond the gate. Then he was through a second gate and had landed by Anana. She looked astonished. This was the first time she had encountered a second gate immediately beyond the first.

Fresh air filled his lungs. He said, "Ah! My God, that's good!"

If they had not had the Horn, they would be dead by now.

"Less than a second in one world and on to the next," Anana said.

They did not have much time to look around. Now, they were in an enormous room. The ceiling was at least a hundred feet high, and it and the walls were covered with paintings of creatures he had never seen before. The bright light came from everywhere.

And then the room was replaced by a sandy plain that stretched unbroken to a horizon much more distant than that on Earth, an orange sun, and a purple sky. The air was heavy, and Kickaha suddenly felt as if gravity had increased.

Before he could say anything, he and Anana were on the top of a peak, a flat area so small that they had to cling to each other to keep from falling off. For as far as they could see, mountains extended all around them. The wind blew strong and cold. Kickaha estimated it must be producing a chill factor of zero or lower. The sun was sinking below the peaks, and the sky was greenish-blue.

There was nothing to indicate that a gate was nearby. It was probably buried in the rock on which they were standing.

A few seconds later, they were on a beach that seemed to be tropical. It could have been on Earth. The palm trees waved behind them in the sea breeze. The yellow sun was near its zenith. The black sand under their bare feet was hot. They would have had to run for the trees if they had not built up such thick calluses on the bottom of their feet.

"I think we're caught in a resonant gate circuit," Kickaha said.

But hours passed, and they were not moved on. Tired of waiting for something to happen, they walked along the beach until they came to the place where they had started.

"We're on an island—actually, an islet," Kickaha said. "About half a mile in circumference. Now what?"

The horizon was unbroken. There could be a land mass or another island just beyond the horizon, or the sea could go for thousands of miles before its waves dashed against a beach. Kickaha studied the trees, which had seemed at first glance to be palm trees. But they bore clusters of fruit that looked like giant grapes. If they were not poisonous, they could sustain life for some time. Maybe. The trees could be cut down and trimmed to make a raft with the beamer. However, there were no vines to bind the logs together.

The Lord who had arranged for his victims to stop here had meant for them to starve to death eventually.

Kickaha walked along the beach again while he blew the Horn. Then he walked in decreasing circles until the range of the notes had covered every bit of ground. There were no flaws or unactivated gates here. That the Horn could not reactivate the gate that had admitted them here meant one thing. It was a one-way gate. The Lord who had set this up had put a "lock" on it, a deactivating device. It was seldom used because it required much energy to maintain it. Also, not many Lords had this ancient device.

"Eventually, the lock will dissolve," Anana said, "and the circuit will be open again. But I think we'll have died before then. Unless we can get away from here to a large landmass."

"And then we won't know where we are unless we've been to this universe before."

He used the beamer to cut a cluster of the baseball-sized fruits from a branch. The impact of the fall split some open. Though he was forty feet from the cluster, its odor reached him immediately. It wasn't pleasant.

"Phew! But the stink doesn't mean they're not edible."

Nevertheless, neither offered to bite into the fruit. When they became hungry enough, they would try it. Meanwhile, they subsisted on the rations in their backpacks.

On the evening of the third day, they lay down on the beach to sleep. This area was where they had entered the universe, and they stayed within it as much as possible. If the gate was reactivated, they would be within its sphere of influence.

"The Lord has not only made us prisoner on this islet," Kickaha said. "He has also confined us to a cell of sorts. I'm really getting tired of being in a prison."

"Go to sleep," Anana said.

The night sky was replaced by bright sunlight. They scrambled up from their sand beds as Kickaha said, "This is it!" He and Anana grabbed their backpacks and weapons. Three seconds later, they were standing on a narrow platform and looking down into an abyss.

Then they were in a cave, bright sunlight coming from its opening. He lifted the Horn to his lips. Before he could below it, they were on a tiny rock elevated a few feet above a sea. He gasped, cutting off his blowing of the Horn, and Anana cried out. A gigantic wave was charging toward them. Within seconds, it would carry them off the rock.

Just before the base of the wave reached the rock, they were in one of the small rooms so numerous in this circuit. Again, Kickaha tried to blow the Horn and activate a gate that would shuttle them off from this circuit. But he did not have time. Nor did he have during the next twelve stations they whizzed through.

Like it or not—and they did not—they were caught in the dizzying circle. Then, when they were again in the room at the top of the tower set in the deserted city, he had just enough time to complete the seven notes. And they were transmitted to the most amazing and unexpected place they had ever encountered.

"I think we've broken the circuit!" Kickaha said. "Have you ever heard of a place like this?"

Anana shook her head. She seemed to be awed. After living so many thousands of years, she was not easily impressed.

3

THE SCALY MAN WAS THE CENTERPIECE OF THE ENORMOUS room.

Whether he was a corpse or in suspended animation, he had perhaps been born one or two hundred thousand years ago. The two intruders in this colorful and vibrant tomb had no way of testing its antiquity. They just felt that the tomb had been built when their own exceedingly remote ancestors had not been born yet. It seemed to sweat eons.

"Have you ever heard of this person?" Kickaha whispered. Then, realizing that he had no need to whisper, he spoke loudly.

"I get this feeling that we're the first to be here since that . . . creature was laid to rest here."

"I'm not so sure that he is permanently resting. And no, I've never heard of this place. Or of him. Not of his name, anyway, whatever his name is. But . . ."

Anana paused, then said, "My people had stories about a sapient but nonhuman species who preceded us Thoan. They were said to have created us. Whether the tales were originally part of the prehistoric Thoan cultures or were early fiction, we don't know. But most Thoan insist that we originated naturally, that we were not made by anybody. My ancestors did make the *leblabbiys,* your kind. These, with a multitude of lifeforms, were made in my ancestors' biofactories to populate their artificial pocket universes. But that we Thoan could be artificial beings, never!

"However, the stories did describe the Thokina as somewhat like that creature there. But the Thokina were a different species from us. We were supposed to have invaded their universe and killed all but one. I don't know. There were conflicting legends about them."

In the middle of the room was a short, massive pillar on top of which was a large, transparent, and brightly lit cube. The being, its seemingly dead eyes open, was suspended inside the cube.

"One of the early tales was that the one Thokina who survived the war hid somewhere. He placed himself in an impenetrable tomb. Then he went into a sleep from which he will not be awakened until the worlds are in danger of destruction."

"Why should he care if the worlds are destroyed?"

"I'm just telling you the story as it was handed down for countless generations," she said. "But how do you explain him? Or this place? Part of the legend was that he was keeping an eye on the world. Look at all those images on the wall. They show many universes. Some of them look contemporary."

"How could he keep an eye on the worlds? He's unconscious or, for all we know, dead."

Anana spread her hands out. "How would I know?"

Kickaha did not reply. He was looking around the dome-shaped chamber, which was larger than a zeppelin hangar. In the sourceless light filling the room, the intensely blue ceiling dazzled him. Despite this, he could, by squinting his eyes, see that thousands of shifting forms were spaced along the curve of the ceiling. Most of them seemed to be letters of a strange alphabet or mathematical formulae. Sometimes, he glimpsed art forms that seemed to have been originated by an insane brain. But that was because of his own cultural mindset.

Horizontal bands of swiftly varying colors and hues sped around the wall. Set among the bands were seemingly three-dimensional scenes, thousands of them. These flashed on and were replaced by others. Kickaha had walked around the wall and looked at the scenes that were at eye level. Some were of landscapes and peoples of various worlds he had visited. One was a bird's-eye view of Manhattan. But at its lower end was a twin-towered skyscraper higher than the Empire State Building.

The images came and went so swiftly. His eyes ached after watching them for a few minutes. He closed them for a moment. When he opened them, he turned to look at the main attraction. The base of the tomb was round, and vertical bands of colors and hues raced up and down it. The creature inside the cube was naked and obviously male. Its testicles were enclosed in a globular sac of blue cartilage with air holes on its surface. Its penis was a thick cylinder with no glans or foreskin and bore thin, tightly coiled tentacles on each side.

Anana, first seeing these, had grunted and then said, "I wonder . . . ?"

"What?" Kickaha had said.

"Its mate must have had an extra dimension of sex, of sexual pleasure, I mean. True, those tentacles could have just been used for purely reproductive purposes. But they may have titillated the female in some way I can't imagine."

"You'll never know," he had said.

"Maybe I won't. However, the unexpected happens as often as the expected. It certainly does when I'm in your neighborhood."

The creature was about seven feet long. Its body was very similar in structure to a man's, and the four-toed feet and five-fingered hands were humanoid enough. Its massive muscles were gorilloid. The skin was reptilian; the scales were green, red, black, blue, orange, purple, lemon-yellow, and pink.

The spine, ridged like a dinosaur's, curved at its top so that the very thick neck bent forward.

Seven greenish plates that could be of bone or cartilage covered the face. The eyes were dark green and arranged for stereoscopic vision, though much more widely apart than on a man's face.

A bony plate just below the jaw made it seem that the creature was chinless. Its lipless, slightly opened mouth was a lizard's. From it hung a tongue looking like a pink worm.

The nose and the rest of the face above it formed a shallow curve. Halfway up the head, short, flat-lying, and reddish fronds began and proceeded down around the back of the head to its columnar neck. If there were bony plates under the mat, they did not show.

The tiny ears were manlike but set very far back on the head.

"You don't suppose," Anana said, "that that thing could actually be the last of the Thokina?"

She answered herself. "Of course not! It's just coincidence!"

They stood silently for a while and stared around. Then Kickaha said, "There's no way we can find answers to our questions here. Not unless we stay a long while, and we don't have the food, water, and instruments needed to do that. Yet, we should spend some time here."

"We have to get out of here," she said, "and we don't know we can do that. I suggest we find out how to do that now!"

"There's no danger. Not any we know about, anyway. I think we should stay here a while and see what we can find out. It might come in useful someday."

They had enough food and water to last four days if they were conserved. There was no place to get rid of their body wastes, but a corner in this immense chamber could serve. It seemed to Kickaha that doing that desecrated the place, but that was an irrational feeling.

"What if something happens here that makes it imperative we leave at once?" she said.

Kickaha thought for a moment, then said, "Okay. You're right."

He walked to the place near the wall where they had stepped through the gate, and he blew the Horn of Shambarimen. As it often did, the music evoked in him images of marvelous beasts, wondrous plants, and exotic people. It seldom failed to send shivers along the nerves of those who heard it and to summon up from the depths of their minds things and beings never imagined before.

The last note seemed to hover like a mayfly determined to have several more seconds of its short life. A shimmering area about five feet wide and ten feet high opened before Kickaha. The flashing wall of the chamber behind it disappeared. He was looking at a stone floor and stone walls. He had seen them before and not long ago. From the room they formed, he and Anana had gated through to this gigantic tomb. It was an escape avenue, but he preferred to take another gate, if it was available. This one would lock them into the circuit again.

The room faded away after five seconds. The walls of the chamber and the on-off bursts of light were views of parts of other universes.

"Find another gate if you can," Anana said.

"Of course," he said, and he began walking slowly along the wall and blowing the Horn over and over again. Not until he had gotten halfway around the chamber did a gate open. He saw a large boulder twenty feet ahead of him. Around and beyond it was a flat desert and blue sky.

He did not know in what universe this landscape was located. For all he knew, it could be somewhere on the planet on which he now stood. Gates could also transport you only a few feet or halfway around the planet.

The rest of the walk along the wall found no more gates. He then began a circuit twenty feet out from the wall. But Anana, a few feet from him, called.

"Come here! I just saw something very interesting!"

He strode to her side. She was looking up at a spot where images seemingly shot out of the wall and then shot back into it.

"It showed Red Orc!" she said. "Red Orc!"

"Recognize the background?"

"It could have been on any one of a thousand worlds. A body of water, could have been a large lake or a sea, was behind him. It looked as if he were standing on the edge of a cliff."

"Keep watching it," he said. "I'm going to work my way around the wall again in a smaller circle. But I'll be looking for other views of Orc. Or anything familiar. Oh, I did find another gate. But it led to a desert. We won't take it except as a last resort."

She nodded, her gaze still locked onto the images.

Before he turned to go, he saw a flash of what had to be downtown Los Angeles. There was the Bradbury Building. The next twenty views were of unfamiliar places.

Then he saw briefly a landscape of the Lavalite planet, the world from which he and Anana had escaped. A mountain was slowly rising from the surface, and the river at its base was spreading as its channel flattened out.

What was the use to anyone of all these monitor views when no one was here to see them?

He felt creepy.

There were too many questions and no answers. The practical thing to do was to quit thinking about them. But being pragmatic did not stop him.

After completing the circuit, he stopped. The Horn had opened no more gates. And he had not seen any more scapes of things familiar. Nor could he see the higher views on the curving wall.

He started when Anana yelled, "I saw Red Orc again!"

Before he could get to her, the view was gone.

"He was about to walk through a gate!" she said. "He was on the same cliff by the sea, but he'd walked over to a gate. An upright hexagon!"

"Maybe he's not doing that right now. The view could be a record of the past."

"Maybe, maybe not."

Kickaha went back to his work with the Horn. When he was done, he had opened no new gates. Anana had not seen their most dangerous enemy again.

He started toward the tomb to examine it when Anana cried out a Thoan oath, "Elyttria!"

He wheeled just in time to see the last two seconds of the view. It showed part of the interior of the great chamber and the nearer half of the tomb and occupant. Very close were himself and Anana staring slightly upward.

"Us!" he bellowed.

After a few seconds of silence, she said, "That should not surprise us. If so many worlds and places are being monitored, it's only natural that this place should be. For one thing, the monitors should know when this room has been invaded. And we are intruders."

"Nothing has been done about us."

"So far, no."

"Keep an eye on the views," he said. He walked to the tomb and felt around the base but could not detect any protuberances or recesses. The controls, if there were any, were not on the base.

The cube resisted his efforts to raise it from the base.

After that, he toured the wall again. Inside of an hour, he had examined the wall for as far as he could see up. He even pressed his hand against the displays to find out if this disclosed any means of control. He also hoped that the pressure would swing open a part of the wall and offer access to somewhere else. As he expected, it did not happen. It was not logical that it would, but he had to try. If there was any central control area, it was not visible. And it was not available.

Meanwhile, the hidden monitors in this chamber would be recording his actions.

That thought led to another. Just how did these monitors record so many places in so many worlds? They certainly would not do it by the machines Earth people or the Lords used. The "cameras" on these worlds would be of an indetectible nature. Permanent magnetic fields of some sort? And these transmitted the pictures through gates of some sort to this place?

If they were stored as recordings, they would have to be in an immense area. Inside this planet?

He just did not know.

There had to be some purpose to all this.

"Kickaha!" Anana called.

He ran to her. "What?"

"That man who was wearing the clothes of Western Earth people of the late eighteenth or early nineteenth century," she said, looking excited. "The man we saw inside that floating palace on the Lavalite planet. I just saw him!"

"Know where he was?"

She shook her head but said, "He wasn't in the house. He was walking through a forest. The trees could have been on Earth or the World of Tiers or any of hundreds of worlds. I didn't see any animals or birds."

"Curiouser and curiouser," he said in English.

He looked around again, then said, "I don't think we can do anything more here. We can't just wait around hoping to see flashes of Red Orc or the stranger or, I wish to God we would, Wolff and Chryseis."

"But we might be able to retrace our gate routes back to here someday."

"We'll do it. Meanwhile, let's go. I don't like to reenter the tower room, but we have no choice."

They walked to the wall area enclosing the gate through which they had entered the chamber. He raised the Horn to his lips and blew into the mouthpiece. The air shimmered, and they could see the room in the tower they had left a short time ago. Anana stepped through with Kickaha on her heels. But he turned around for a last view of the chamber.

He saw that the cube was being filled with many beams of many colors and hues. They flashed and died and were replaced within a blink of an eye by other beams. An orange light surrounded the corpse, which was sinking slowly toward the floor of the cube.

"Wait!" he cried out.

But the view faded swiftly. Not, however, before he saw the lid of the cube beginning to raise up.

He did not explain to Anana why he was blowing the Horn again. This time, the gate to the gigantic room did not open. Instead, they were in another place.

He was in despair. It seemed impossible that they could ever retrace their route to the tomb.

Nevertheless, he automatically blew the Horn again and again as they were shot through a circuit. And then they were on a plain on which two-feet-high grass flourished. Far beyond that was a thick forest, and beyond that, a wall of rock towering so high that he could not see its top. It ran unbroken to his right and his left. The sky was bright green, and the sun was yellow and as bright as Earth's.

They had time to run out of the area of influence of the gate before it shuttled them onward. They leaped like two jackrabbits startled by a coyote, and they ran. They had known instantly where they were.

They were in the universe of the planet called Alofmethbin. In English, the World of Tiers. This was his most beloved planet of all the universes. The vast wall of rock many miles in front of them was one of the five truly colossal monoliths forming the vertical parts of the Tower-of-Babylon-shaped planet. And they were standing on top of one of them, though they did not as yet know which.

After they had stopped running, Anana said, "Didn't it seem to you that the gate lasted suspiciously long? We had plenty of time to get away from it, and we never did in any of the others."

"I thought of that," he said, "but we can't be sure of it. However, it did seem like we were on a nonstop train that slowed down long enough for us to jump off."

She nodded. Her face was grim.

"I think someone set it up so we'd get off here."

"Red Orc!"

4

"THAT SEEMS MOST PROBABLE," ANANA SAID. "HOWEVER, HE might've set up the circuit and the trap for one of his numerous enemies. And done so long before you and I appeared on the scene. Or it might've been his emergency escape route."

"Nothing is certain until it happens. To quote your Thoan philosopher, Manathu Vorcyon, 'Order is composed of disorder, and disorder has its own order.' Whatever that means. In any case, I'm mighty suspicious."

"Whenever were you not?"

"When I was still living on Earth, though even there I was what you might call wary. The things that happened after I came here have made me trust very few people. And they've made me consider what might happen in every situation before it could happen. You look at all the angles or you don't live long. It's not paranoia. Paranoia is a state of mind in which you suspect or are certain about things that really don't exist. The dangers I've been suspicious of have existed or could exist."

"Almost every Lord is paranoiac. It's a deeply embedded part of our culture, such as it is. Most of them don't trust anybody, including themselves."

Kickaha laughed, and he said, "Well, let's go on into Paranoia Land."

They began walking across the plain. They were as constantly watchful as birds, glancing up often at the sky, at the grass just ahead of them, and at the vista beyond their feet. The grass could conceal snakes or large crouching predators. Something dangerous could suddenly appear in the sky. But for the first hour, they saw only insects in the grass and herds of large four-tusked elephantlike and four-horned antelopelike beasts in the distance.

Then a black speck emerged from the green sky. It was behind them, but Anana saw it during one of her frequent glances behind her. After a few minutes, it came low enough for them to see a bird with a ravenlike silhouette. It got no lower then but continued in the same direction as they.

When they saw it circle now and then before resuming the same path, they suspected that it was following them.

"It could be one of those giant language-using ravens that Vannax made in his laboratory for spying and message-carrying when he was Lord of this world," Kickaha said.

He added, "Looks more and more like Red Orc is watching us."

"Or somebody is."

"My money's on Orc."

He and Anana stopped to rest a while in the knee-high, blue-stalked, and crimson-tipped grass.

"I suppose it could be a machine disguised as a bird," he said. "But if it's a machine, it's being controlled by a Lord. That doesn't seem likely."

"When did we ever come across anything but the unlikely?"

"Seems like it. But it's not always so by any means."

He was on his back, his hands behind his head, looking at the dark enigma in the sky. Anana was half lying down, leaning on one hand, her head tilted back to watch the bird or whatever it was.

"That figure eight the bird's now making in the sky," Kickaha said, "looks from here like it's on its side. That reminds me of the symbol for infinity, the flattened figure eight on its side. One of the few things I remember from my freshman mathematics class in college. Which I never finished. College, I mean."

"The Thoan symbol is a straight line with arrowheads at each end pointing outward," she said. "If the line has a corkscrew shape, it's the symbol for time."

"I know."

Visions of Earth slipped past in his mind like ghosts in coats of many colors. In 1946, he had been twenty-eight years old, a World War II veteran going to college on the G. I. Bill. Then he had been hurled into another universe, though not unwillingly. This was the Lord-created artificial universe that contained only the tiered planet, Alofmethbin.

This was, he had found, only one among thousands of universes made by the ancient Thoan, the humans who denied that they were human. Here was where he, Paul Janus Finnegan, the adventure-loving Hoosier, had become Kickaha the Trickster.

And, since coming to the World of Tiers, he had seldom not been fleeing his enemies or attacking them, always on the move except for some rare periods of R&R. During these relatively infrequent times, he had usually gotten married to the daughters of a tribal chief on his favorite level, the second, which he called the Ameridian level.

Or he had become involved with the wife or daughter of a baron on the third level, which he called the Dracheland level.

He had left a trail of women who grieved for him for a while before inevitably falling in love with another man. He had also left a trail of corpses. The debris, you might say, of Finnegan's wake.

Not until 1970 did he return to Earth, and that was briefly. He had been born in A.D. 1918, which made him fifty-two or fifty-three Terrestrial years old now. But he was, thank whatever gods there be, only twenty-five in physiological age. If he'd stayed on Earth, what would he be there? Maybe he would have gotten a Ph.D. in anthropology and specialized in American Indian languages. But he would have had to be a teacher, too. Could he have endured the grind of study, the need to publish, the academic backbiting and throat-slitting, the innumerable weary conferences, the troubles with administrators who regarded teachers as a separate and definitely inferior species?

He might've gone to Alaska, where there was, in 1946, a sort of frontier, and he might have been a bush pilot. But that life would eventually have become tedious.

Perhaps by now he would own a motorcycle sales-and-repair shop in Terre Haute or Indianapolis. No, he couldn't have stood the day-to-day routine, the worrying about paying bills, and the drabness.

Whatever he would have been on Earth, he would not have had the adventurous and exotic life, albeit hectic, he had experienced in the Thoan worlds.

The beautiful woman by his side—no, not a woman, a goddess, poetically speaking—was many thousands of years old. But the chemical "elixirs" of the Lords kept her at the physiological age of twenty-five.

She said, "We're assuming that the raven is on an evil mission, bad for us. Perhaps it's been sent to keep an eye on us, but by Wolff. He and Chryseis might have escaped from Red Orc's prison and gotten to this world and now be in the palace. And they may have ordered the Eye to watch over us."

"I know."

She said, "It seems to me that we've been saying a lot of 'I knows.'"

"Maybe it's time we took a long vacation from each other."

"It wouldn't do any good," she said. Then, looking slyly sidewise at him, "I know."

She burst into laughter, fell on him, and kissed him passionately.

Kickaha kissed her back as enthusiastically. But he was thinking that they might have been isolated from other human beings too long. They needed lots of company, not all the time, but often enough so that they did not rub against each other, as it were.

Her comments about "knowing" probably indicated a sadness born out of expectation based on hindsight. Because she had lived for many millennia, she had had far more experience than he. She had lived with hundreds of male Lords and had had a few children. Her longest time with a man had been about fifty years.

"That's about the limit for a faithful couple, if you don't age at all," she had said. "The Lords don't have the patience of you *leblabbiy*, a word I don't mean in a derogatory sense. But we are different in some respects."

"But many couples have lived together for thousands of years," he had said.

"Not continuously."

He was not tired or bored with her. Nor did she seem to be so with him. But being able to look backward on so many experiences, she was unable to keep from looking forward. She knew that a time would come when they must part. For a while, a long while, anyway.

He was not going to worry about that. When the time came to deal with it, he would. Just how, he did not know.

He rose, drank water from his deerskin canteen, and said, "If Wolff had sent that Eye, he would have told it to tell us that it was watching for us. And he would have told the Eye to give us directions to get to wherever he is. So it definitely was not sent by Wolff."

He paused, then said, "Do you want to go now?" He knew better than to order her to leave with him. She resented any hint of bossiness by others. After all, though more empathetic and compassionate than most of her kind, she was a Lord.

"It's time."

They put their knapsacks and quivers on their backs and started walking again. He thought: On top of the many thousands-of-feet-high monolith ahead of us is, probably, the level called Atlantis. And on top of that is the monolith, much more narrow and less lofty than the others, on top of which is the palace Wolff built.

Three hours passed while they strode toward the forest. By now, they could see that another hour would bring them to its edge. Kickaha stepped up his pace. She did not ask why he was in such a hurry now. She knew that he did not like being on the plain for very long. It made him feel too exposed and vulnerable.

After about ten minutes, Kickaha broke the silence between them.

"I suspect that no one had come through that gate in the tomb until we did. There were no signs of previous entry. And, surely, the thing in the tomb or whoever put him there had set up many safeguards. Why, then, were we able to use the gate?"

"What do you think?"

He said, "There was some reason we and only we were allowed in. Emphasis on the 'allowed.' But why were we?"

"You don't know that we were the first there. You don't know that we were 'allowed' in."

"True. But if someone else did get in, he or she didn't trigger the raising of the cube and, I bet, the resurrection of the scaly man."

"You don't know that for sure."

"Yes, but I think that only someone with the Horn of Shambarimen could have penetrated that tomb."

She smiled and said, "Perhaps. But the scaly man must've put himself in that tomb eons before the Horn was made. He couldn't have known that the Horn would be made or that its frequencies would open the way to the tomb."

"How do you know that he didn't know it would be made? In his time, a device similar to the Horn could have been available."

She laughed and said, "No one can predict the future. Besides, what significance did our entering there have?"

"It started a chain of events that's only begun. As for predicting, maybe it's not a matter of predeterminism or predicting. Maybe it's a matter of probabilities. Don't forget that that chamber contains devices surveying many universes. I think that when certain events are observed, the scaly man is raised from the tomb. After that, I don't know."

"You don't know. That's it."

"Okay, you're probably right!" he said. "But if I'm right, I expect you to apologize and kiss my foot, among other things, and be humble and obedient thereafter to the end of eternity, amen."

"Your face is red! You're angry!"

"You're too skeptical, too blasé, too jaded. And too almighty sure of yourself."

"We'll see. But if you're wrong, you can do to me what I was supposed to do to you."

They did not speak for some time afterward. While crossing the last few miles to the edge of the forest, detouring once to avoid a herd of giant bison, they looked back twice. The raven was still following them but was much lower.

"Definitely an Eye of the Lord," Kickaha said.

She said, "I know," laughed, and then said, "I've got to quit saying that."

They entered the shade of the thousand-foot-high sequoialike trees. The forest floor was thick with dead leaves. That was strange, since there was no change of season on this planet. But when he saw a few leaves flutter down from the trees, he realized that it shed old leaves and replaced them with new ones. A few other plants on Alofmethbin did that.

The undergrowth was sparse, though here and there, thorny bushes forced the two to go around them. Many small, blue-eyed creatures that looked like furry and wingless owls watched them from the safety of the brambles.

Monkeys, birds, and flying and gliding mammals screamed, hooted, and chittered in the branches. But in the immediate area of the humans, silence fell, only to be broken after they had passed.

Once a weasel the size of a Rocky Mountain lion looked around the side of a tree trunk at them but did not charge them. The two humans knew that a predator was there before the weasel revealed itself. The clamor in the area ahead of them had ceased.

Kickaha and Anana had already strung their bows. There was no predicting what dangerous man or beast dwelt in this twilit but noisy place. They had also loosened the straps of their knife scabbards.

They had gone a mile when they came to a clearing about sixty feet wide. This had been made by two sequoias that had fallen together. That had been a long time ago, judging by the rottenness of the wood. Kickaha looked up in time to see the raven just before it settled down on a branch halfway down a tree next to the open ground. The big leaves of a parasitic plant hid it then.

"Okay," Kickaha muttered. "No doubt of it now. It's ahead of us but may not know it is. It may be waiting for us to come by here since we were walking in a more or less straight line. I don't know how it's kept its eye on us so far."

Since the raven was the size of a bald eagle, it could not flit from branch to branch.

"Maybe it knows where we're going," Kickaha said.

"How could that be? We don't know ourselves where we're going except in a general direction. And the woods are thick here. It couldn't have followed us. Oh, I see! It followed the silences falling around us."

They withdrew a few feet into the shade. Then he whispered, "Let's watch from here."

Presently, just as he had expected, he saw the big, black bird spiral down and land on a branch projecting from one of the fallen and decaying behemoths. Then it glided to the ground, its wings half-outspread, and walked toward them. Kickaha thought that it had come to the ground to find out where they were. It would hide and listen for the two humans.

But it could, at the moment, neither see them nor, in the still air, smell them. Kickaha and Anana were lucky that they had spotted it before it saw them.

Kickaha placed a finger to his lips, then whispered very softly in Anana's ear.

"It can see like a hawk and hear almost as well as a dog. Let's move on. We won't be quiet. It can follow us until we're ready to catch it."

"If it's sent by a Lord, that might mean that a Lord is in Wolff's palace."

"If there is, we'll be lucky to elude the traps there."

"Lots of ifs."

Kickaha pointed a finger at the huge, black bird and then touched his lips. Deliberately, he stepped on a dry branch. The loud crack made the raven whirl around and waddle swiftly to a hiding place behind a low-growing bush on the side of the clearing across from the two. No doubt, after they had passed it, it would return to the clearing and use it as a runway so it could take to the air again. But if it saw that the humans were walking slowly, it might just follow them on foot. Ravens, however, did not like to walk far.

Thinking that it had located them without being detected, it would be as smug as a raven could be. In this universe, as on most, smugness often caused a tumble into the dust.

"We must take it alive," Kickaha said.

"I know."

"For God's sake!" he said in English. Then, seeing her smile slightly, he knew that she was just having fun with him.

They crossed the clearing slowly, looking left and right and, now and then, behind them. If they did not behave cautiously, the raven would know that they were pretending carelessness to deceive an observer.

Nor did they swing wide of the bush. Silently, they passed within a few feet of it. Kickaha looked at the bush but could not see the bird. Now, if he were so inclined, would be the time for him to break suddenly into a run. Anana would do so a half-second behind him, but she would head for the side of the bush opposite the one he would be racing for. The raven would flee, but it would not have time to take to its wings or to hide again.

Anana said nothing. She was waiting to see what Kickaha would do. He walked on by the bush and into the forest. He did not have to tell her that they were going to pretend they were not aware of the bird. Let the raven follow them. Eventually, they would find out why it was stalking them.

And then he almost halted. He grunted.

Anana noticed the break in stride and heard his suppressed exclamation. Instead of looking around and thus notifying whatever had startled him that she was aware of its presence, she looked straight ahead. She said quietly, "What is it?"

"I wish I knew," he said. "I saw . . . off to the right . . . just a flash . . . a something like a man but not human. Not quite, anyway. Maybe my mind's playing tricks. But he, if it was male, looked like he was human. He was very big and very hairy for a human being. Only . . ."

She waited several seconds, then said, "Well?"

"His face, I don't know. It was not quite human. There was something, uh, bearlike about it. I've been all over this planet and have never seen or heard of anything like it. On the other hand, this planet has more land area than Earth. So, I just never knew anybody who knew about it."

She looked to the left, then to the right.

"I see nothing."

He half-stepped out from behind a tree, then stepped back. "Angle casually over toward the tree."

She went in the direction he had indicated by bending his head. She must have noticed that the arboreal animals in the branches five hundred feet above her had fallen silent. But, like him, she must have thought that it was their approach that had caused this.

They went approximately a hundred feet before he spoke.

"The one just ahead."

It was one of the gigantic sequoialike plants. Its bark was as shiny as if thousands of pieces of mica were embedded in it.

"I hope there's only one of him," he said.

He lifted his bow with an arrow and started to go around on the left side of the enormous trunk. She headed toward the right side. Anybody still on the back side of the tree would be caught between them.

When they came around the trunk, they saw only each other. Though the thing Kickaha had glimpsed did not look as if it had claws, he looked upward along the bole. No creature clung to it, and not even a squirrel could have gotten to the branches this fast. Anana had stepped back so she could see more of the other side of the trunk. The tree was so huge, however, that a section of it was invisible to both of them. After telling Anana to stay where she was but to keep looking upward, he ran around the tree. At the same time, he kept his gaze on the upper reaches of the bole. But he saw no living creature.

When he returned to Anana, he said, "It was too heavy to climb up the trunk even if it'd had claws a foot long. I had to make sure, though."

She pointed at the thick piles of dead leaves on the ground. He was already looking at them. They were scattered in so many directions that he could not tell if the creature had been coming to or going from the tree.

He sniffed. There was a faint musky odor in the still air.

"I smell it, too," she said. "Maybe we should capture the raven. It might know what the thing is. In fact, it could be working for it."

She paused, then said, "Or it could be working for the raven."

"Why don't we wait a while before we grab the bird?"

They pushed on at a faster pace. Now and then, they looked behind them but saw neither the bird nor the bear-thing. After a few minutes, they smelled a whiff of wood smoke. Silently, they walked toward the odor, guided by its increasing strength. They waded through a narrow creek to the other side. When they heard voices, they slowed their pace and made sure they did not step on dry sticks. The voices became louder. They were women's, and it seemed to Kickaha that he heard only two speakers. He made a few signs to Anana, who crept away to circle around the place. She would be his unseen backup if he got into trouble. Or vice versa.

He got down on the ground and wriggled forward very slowly to keep from rustling the dead leaves. He stopped when he was behind a thick bush between two massive tree trunks. He peered through the lower part of the bush and saw a small clearing. In its center was a small fire with a small iron pot suspended by its handle from a horizontal wooden stick set between two forked wooden uprights. Kickaha smelled boiling meat.

A blonde who was beautiful despite her disarrayed hair and dirtied face stood near the fire. She was speaking Thoan. Crouching down on the other side of the fire was a red-haired woman. She was as good-looking as the blonde and equally disheveled and dirty.

Both wore ankle-length robes reminding Kickaha of illustrations of the type of dress worn by ancient Greek females. The material was thin, clinging, and far from opaque. At one time, the robes had been white, but brambles and thorns clung to them, and dirt and blood smeared them.

On the far side of the clearing were two knapsacks and a pile of Thoan blankets, paper-thin but very heat-keeping. Three light axes, three heavy knives, and three beamers, which looked like pistols with bulbs on the muzzles, were on top of the blankets.

A butchered fawn was lying on the far side of the clearing. No flies buzzed around it; the planet Alofmethbin lacked flies. But crawling and scavenging insects were beginning to swarm on the carcass.

Kickaha shook his head. The women were not very cautious, hence not very bright, if they had not kept the weapons close at hand. Or, perhaps this was a trap.

He turned and looked behind him and up into the tree branches, but neither saw nor heard anything to alarm him. Of course, the raven could be hidden among the leaves overhead. After he had turned around toward the women, he lay for a while watching and listening.

Though the two looked to be no more than twenty-five, they had to be thousands of years old. They spoke in the same archaic Thoan that Anana fell into sometimes when she was excited. Except for a few words and phrases, Kickaha understood it.

The blonde said, "We can't survive long in this horrible place. We must find a gate."

"You've said that a thousand times, Eleth," the auburn-haired woman said. "I'm getting sick of hearing it."

"And I'm sick of hearing nothing practical from you, Ona," the blonde snarled. "Why don't you figure a way out for us, suggest just how we can find a gate?"

Ona said, "And I'm about to vomit from your childish bickering and screaming."

"So, throw up," Eleth said. "At least you'd be doing something instead of sitting on your ass and whining. And vomiting certainly wouldn't make this place stink more than it does, even if your puke stinks more than anybody else's."

Ona got up and looked into the pot. "It seems to be done, but I still don't know how to cook."

"Who does?" Eleth said. "That's slave work. Why should we know anything about it?"

"For Shambarimen's sake!" Ona said, and she shook her head so violently that her long auburn hair swirled like a cloak around her shoulders. "Can't we do anything but talk about things that don't matter? A fine pair of sisters we are. Lords one day, and the next, we're no better than slaves."

"Well, at least we don't have to worry about putting on weight," Eleth said, and she grinned.

The redhead looked hard at her.

"I'm trying to be as lighthearted as possible," Eleth said. "We have to keep our spirits up or they'll be so heavy they'll sink down to our toes and ooze out onto the ground. And we'll die or become *leblabbiys*. We'll get eaten by some beast or, worse, be captured and raped by *leblabbiys* and spend the next hundred years or more as wives of some stupid, ignorant, dirty, smelly, snot-wiping-on-their-hands, wife-beating savages. They'll be our Lords."

"You really know how to make me feel good," Ona said. "I'd kill myself before I'd submit to a *leblabbiy*."

"It wouldn't be hopeless. We could escape and find a gate and then find Red Orc and get revenge by killing him. After some suitable tortures, of course. I'm thinking about eating Red Orc's balls just as he ate his father's. Well-cooked, though, and with a suitable garnish, not eaten raw as Red Orc did."

"Speaking of cannibalism," Ona said, "we may have to resort to that before we find a way out of this mess. Now, who should be the eaters and who the eaten?"

"Stop that!"

But both burst out laughing.

Kickaha knew the Lords well enough to doubt that Ona was jesting. If they did starve, one of them would kill and eat her companion.

He listened several minutes to their bickering but did not learn much. The only thing he knew for sure was that their predicament was caused by Red Orc and that they had escaped from him with the few possessions in the clearing.

The two women fell silent while they were looking into the pot. By now, they were getting ready to dip out deer stew with rough spoons made of bark.

Suddenly, Anana stepped out from the bushes into the clearing. She held her bow and an arrow at the ready.

"Hail, iron-hearted daughters of Urizen and Ahania!" she called. "Your cousin Anana greets you in peace! What brings you here?"

THE TWO WOMEN SHRIEKED AND JUMPED AS IF THEY HAD stepped on biting ants. The redhead, however, flashed out of her paralysis and darted toward the beamers near the edge of the clearing. After a few steps, she halted, then walked slowly back to Eleth. She had realized that she could not get to the weapons before Anana's arrow drove through her.

"Ona the Baker!" Anana called to the redhead. "You were always the quickest witted, the coolest, and the most dangerous in physical combat. But how could you be so stupid as to leave your arms out of reach?"

Ona scowled and said, "I am very tired."

Anana addressed the blonde. "Eleth the Grinder, also known as Eleth the Worrier! You were the planner, the thinker, and so in many ways the most dangerous!"

The blonde was not so pale now. She smiled, and she bowed. "Not as dangerous as you, Anana the Bright, Anana the Hunter!"

Anana said, "Ona, you and your sisters, Eleth the Grinder, and Uveth the Kneader, now dead, were known as the kind-hearted daughters of Ahania. Now you are called iron-hearted! But you have always been the kindliest and sweetest of the three!"

"That was long ago, Anana," Ona said.

"Your father, Urizen the Cold, changed you three from kittens to ravening tigers," Anana said. "Your hatred for him is well known."

She paused, then said, "Do you know that he is dead?"

Eleth said stonily, "We had heard that he was. But we were not sure that it was true."

Ona said, "Nor are we sure now. That you say our father is dead does not make it true. But if your news is true, we're glad."

"Except that we would be sad that we were not the ones who killed him," Eleth said.

During this talking, Kickaha had been moving stealthily around the clearing to make sure that no one else was watching the scene. Though he looked for the raven and the bearish creature, he did not see them. Nor was there any sign of anyone lying in ambush.

When the two women saw him step into the clearing, they started only slightly. Evidently, they had suspected that Anana was not alone. Eleth said, "Who is this, Anana?"

"Surely you have heard of Kickaha? Kickaha the Trickster, the killer of so many Lords, the man who slew the last of the Black Bellers? You have also heard of ancient Shambarimen's prophecy that a *leblabbiy* will destroy the Lords. Some say that Kickaha is the man of whom Shambarimen prophesied."

Eleth bit her lower lip. "Yes, we have heard of the *leblabbiy* who has been so lucky so far. We have also heard that he is your lover."

"He is a *leblabbiy*," Anana said cheerily, "and he is such a lover as you should wish you had."

"Thanks," Kickaha said, and he grinned broadly.

"You killed our father?" Eleth said to Kickaha. Her tone indicated that she did not believe Anana.

"No," Kickaha said. "I wish I had. But it was Jadawin, the Lord also known as Wolff, who killed him."

"You saw Jadawin kill him?"

"No. But Jadawin told me that he did, and Jadawin does not lie. Not, at least, to me."

Anana herded the sisters to the end of the clearing most distant from the pile of weapons. Then she ordered them to sit down. She did not frisk them. Their filmy robes made it evident that they were not carrying concealed weapons.

"We're starving," Eleth said. "We were just about to eat the soup. Such as it is."

Kickaha looked inside the pot. "Nothing but meat. Very unhealthy. Why didn't you put some vegetables in?"

"We don't know what plants are good to eat and what're poisonous," Eleth said.

"But all Thoan, male or female, are given survival courses," he said. "You should know that . . ."

Ona said, "We don't know this planet."

"You can get up now and eat," Anana said. "By suppertime, we'll have much better food for you. If, that is, we stay with you. That depends upon how open and truthful you are with us. Now, I heard enough while you were talking to believe that Red Orc is responsible for your being here. Tell me—"

"Red Orc!" Eleth said viciously, and she spat on the ground. "There's a man who needs killing!"

"After suitable torture," Ona said. "He killed Uveth years ago and came close recently to killing us. It's because of him that we're stranded in this wretched wilderness."

Anana let them rave and rant for a while about what they would do to Orc when they captured him. Then she said, "Tell us just how you came to be here."

They stood by the pot, and Eleth was the first to speak. Ona ate while her sister talked, then Ona talked while Eleth ate. After fleeing Red Orc, not for the first time, they had managed to "take over" Nitharm, the universe in which they had taken refuge. "Take over" was a euphemism for slaying the Lord of Nitharm and his family. Since there were no male Thoan in that world, they had taken *leblabbiys* for lovers. This practice was acceptable by Thoan standards because their lovers were their slaves, not their equals, and were often replaced by others.

They had been happy there, they said. The only thing lacking to make their happiness complete was that they had not yet been able to find and kill their father. Then Red Orc had somehow evaded the traps they had set at the two gates into their world. He had taken them by surprise despite their security systems.

At this point in the story, Eleth had interrupted Ona.

"I told them many times that we should just close all gates and stay there forever. That would have kept any Lord from invading our world."

"Yes, you fearful, trembling, sniveling little bitch!" Ona had said. "And just how then would we be able to go to other worlds and make sure that our father was dead!"

"Don't call me names, assface!" Eleth fired back.

The rest of the story was longer than Kickaha wished to hear. But he and Anana let them ramble on since they might reveal something about themselves that could later be used against them.

Red Orc would have killed them if they had not happened to be very close to a gate to another world. They had been able to grab some weapons before they fled. After passing through a circuit of gates, they had come out on this level of the World of Tiers. Since then, they had been trying to survive while searching for another gate. This, they hoped, would not take them to another world but to the palace on top of the topmost monolith of the World of Tiers. There, they knew, was the structure that had been Jadawin's, then Vannax's, and, once again, Jadawin's stronghold. They had heard that no Lord now lived there. Thus, they planned to become the new Lords.

Their story could be true, but if so, it certainly showed them as inept. Kickaha did not believe that they really were, though he knew that Red Orc was ingenious enough to defeat even the most competent.

Anana said, "Then you'll be willing to join us in the fight against Red Orc?"

They agreed enthusiastically.

"What good will they be to us?" Kickaha said loudly. "We don't need them! In fact, they'll be a big liability!"

"You are wrong," Ona said. "You need information, and we know many things about Red Orc that you don't."

Anana, who was aware of what Kickaha was doing, spoke. "That's right, Kickaha. They must know about gates and his activities and strongholds we don't know. Isn't that right, daughters of Urizen?"

They spoke as one. "That is correct."

"Very well," he said. "We're a band, and I'm the leader. What I order must be obeyed immediately and without question. If, that is, the situation calls for action at once. If it's not pressing, I'm open to suggestions."

Eleth, the blonde, looked hard at Anana. "He's a *leblabbiy.*"

Anana shrugged and said, "He and I spun a flat stone marked on one side up into the air, and he called out the right side that fell uppermost on the ground. We had agreed beforehand that the one who did this would be the leader. In times of emergency, he is not to be questioned or disobeyed.

"As for his being a *leblabbiy,* what of it? He's a better man than any Thoan I've ever met. You two should try to get over your absurd opinion of *leblabbiys* as inherently inferior to the Lords. It's nonsense! Dangerous nonsense because it makes Lords underestimate them. By the time the Lord gets killed, he finds out how wrong he was. About Kickaha, anyway."

Eleth and Ona said nothing, but their expressions showed disbelief.

"You'll learn the hard way," Anana said.

The sisters protested when Anana took their beamers.

"How can we protect ourselves?"

"You'll be given them when we think you're one-hundred-percent trustworthy," he said. "Meantime, you can carry your axes, spears, and bows. We'll camp here tonight. Come morning, we start that way."

He pointed west.

"Why that way?" Eleth said. "Are you sure that's the right direction? What if—"

"I have my reasons," Kickaha said, interrupting her. "You'll know why when we get there."

They would be heading toward a gate on this level that would transmit them to the palace. It would take them days to get there, and perhaps days to find the gate after they got there. The area in which it was placed was immense, and he was not sure of its exact location. By the time the party reached it, he and Anana would know if the two women could be trusted. Or the sisters would be dead. Possibly he and Anana would have been slain by them, though he much doubted that.

That night, around a small fire, they all lay down to sleep. The sisters had eaten well, or at least much better than they had been eating. Kickaha had foraged in the woods and brought back various edible plants. He had also shot a large monkey, which had been roasted on a spit.

The sisters had washed their robes in the nearby creek and scrubbed off their body dirt, though they complained about the coldness of the water. The robes quickly dried on sticks thrust into the ground near the fire. When time for bedding-down came, Kickaha took the first watch. The sisters slept near the fire in their thin but warm blankets. Anana, wrapped in her blanket, her head pillowed on her knapsack, lay close to the edge of the clearing. Kickaha stationed himself for a while on the opposite side of the clearing. After a while, he stepped into the forest and prowled around the clearing. He carried two beamers in his belt and another in his hand.

He looked out for big predators, of which one could be that huge, hairy creature he had glimpsed. He also kept an eye on the sisters. If they were going to attack their captors, they might try tonight. However, none of them stirred during his and Anana's watches.

In the morning, when Urizen's daughters wanted to leave the campsite together to empty their bowels in the forest, he insisted that they go one at a time. It was impossible to watch all of them at the same time unless they all went together. But he wanted them alone out among the trees. If a confederate was hanging out around there, he, she, or it might make contact with one of the two. Kickaha watched each of them, but he was hidden behind bushes.

No one approached Eleth while she was in the forest. While Ona was squatting, a raven waddled out from behind a big tree. No, not *a* raven, Kickaha thought. It's *the* raven, the one who's been following us. He watched as the big bird silently came from behind Ona and stood in front of her. She did not look surprised.

They spoke to each other briefly and in low tones. Kickaha was too far away to make out the words. He did not need to do so. A conspiracy was flourishing. But who besides the sisters and the raven was involved?

After the bird had gone back into the woods and Ona started back to camp, Kickaha followed the raven. The bird led him for less than a mile before it came to a clearing large enough for it to wing away. Kickaha plunged into the woods then to gather more plants and to catch several large insects that he knew were delicious eating. He got a perverse pleasure out of insisting that the sisters eat them.

"They contain several vital ingredients lacking in the other plants," he said. "Believe me, I know."

"You're not trying to poison us, are you?" Eleth said.

"Stupid, he doesn't have to do that if he wants to kill us," her sister said.

"I wouldn't say that," Kickaha said, grinning.

"You demon!" Eleth said. "Just knowing that you might do it makes me want to throw up."

"It'll be good for you if you do," Kickaha replied cheerfully. "Your stomach needs emptying after all that heavy meat-eating you've been doing."

Ona giggled and said, "Don't vomit in the pot. I'm really hungry."

Kickaha did not trust Ona at all, but he liked her spirit.

On the way westward that day, Kickaha asked Eleth where the sisters had been heading after they had come through the gate.

"Nowhere in particular," she said. "Of course, we got away from the area of the gate as swiftly as possible because Red Orc might be following us. Then we traveled in the direction of the monolith. If we didn't find a gate on this level, we were going to climb the monolith, though we were not happy about having to do that. It looks formidable."

"It is and then some," he said. "It has the jawbreaking name of Doozvillnavava. It soars sixty thousand feet high or more. But it's climbable. I've done it several times. Its face, which looks so smooth from a long distance, is full of caves and has innumerable ledges. Trees and other plants grow on its face, which also has stretches of rotten rock that crumble underfoot. Predators live in its caves and holes and on its ledges. There thrive the many-footed snakes, the rock-gripping wolves, the boulder apes, the giant axe-beak birds, and the poison-dripping downdroppers.

"There are others I won't mention. Even if you could climb to the plateau on top, you would then have to travel about five hundred miles through a vast forest teeming with many perils, and after that, a plain with no less dangerous creatures and humans. And then you'd come to the final monolith, atop which is Jadawin-Wolff's palace. The climb is hard, and the chances that you'd evade the traps set there are very low."

"We didn't know the details," Eleth said, "but we supposed that climbing the mountain would not be enjoyable. That's why we were looking for a gate, though we knew we probably wouldn't recognize one if we saw it. Most of them must be disguised as boulders and so forth. But some might be undisguised. You never know."

During their journey so far, Kickaha had not taken the Horn of Shambarimen from its deerskin bag. If the sisters knew that he had it, they would not hesitate to murder him and Anana to get it. However, the time would soon come when he would have to use it.

Once a day, while the others rested, he or Anana climbed to the top of a high tree and scanned the country around them. Most of this consisted of the waving tops of trees. But far away and toward the monolith, was a three-peaked mountain. This was his destination. At its foot was a huge boulder shaped like a heart, its point deep in the ground. This contained a gate to a gate that transmitted its occupant to the palace of the Lord of Alofmethbin. Though Kickaha had forgotten the code word activating it, he had the Horn, the universal key.

If the raven was following them, it was keeping well hidden. And there had been no sign of the bearish creature. His brief encounter with it might have been accidental, though that did not seem probable.

Next day, during the noonday halt, he went out into the woods for a pit call but stayed there to watch. Presently, Eleth left the campsite, seemingly for the same reason he had left it. Instead of selecting a tree behind which to squat, she went deeper into the forest. He followed her at a distance. When he saw her stop in a small clearing, he hid behind a bush.

Eleth stood for a while haloed in a sunbeam shooting through a straight space among the branches overhead. She looked transfigured, as if she were indeed the goddess she thought she was. After a while, the raven waddled out from behind a bush. Kickaha began crawling slowly so that he could get within hearing distance. After a few minutes of very cautious progress in a semicircle, he stopped behind the enormous flying-buttress root of a giant tree.

". . . repeats that you are not to kill them, no matter what the temptation, until he has found the gate," the raven said.

"Which will be when?" Eleth said.

"He did not tell me, but he said that it will probably not be long."

"What does he mean by 'not long'?" she said. She looked exasperated. "A day? Two days? A week? This is a hard life. My sister and I long for a high roof, warmth, clean clothes, a shower, good things to eat, much time to sleep, and plenty of virile *leblabbiy* men."

"I don't know what he means by 'not long,'" the raven said. "You'll just have to do what he says. Otherwise . . ."

"Yes, I know. We will, of course, continue to obey his orders. You may tell him that—if you're in communication with him."

The raven did not reply. She said, "What about the oromoth?"

Kickaha did not know what an oromoth was. He would have to ask Anana about it.

"It is trailing you for your protection. It won't interfere unless it sees that you're in grave danger from those two."

"If that happens," Eleth said, "it may be too slow. Or it might be off taking a piss somewhere at that time."

The raven sounded as if it were trying to imitate human laughter. When it stopped that, it said, "That's the chance you have to take. That's better than what will surely happen if you fail. I wouldn't even think about betraying him by telling Kickaha and Anana what's going on and throwing in your lot with theirs."

"I wouldn't dream of it!" Eleth said.

The raven laughed again and said, "Of course not! Unless you thought you'd have a better chance to come out on top! Just remember what he will do to you if you turn traitor!"

Eleth said, stonily, "Is there anything else you have to tell me? If not, get out of my sight, you stinking mess of black feathers!"

"Nothing else. But don't think I'll forget your insult! I'll get my revenge!"

"You stupid snakebrain! We won't even be in this world! Now, get the hell away from me!"

"You Thoan don't smell so nice yourselves," the raven said.

It turned and disappeared into the forest. Eleth looked as if she were about to follow it. But she turned and walked into the woods. As soon as Kickaha was sure that she could not see him, he rose, and he ran bent over along the edge of the clearing. Then he went more slowly and in a straight line. Presently, he saw the raven. It had entered a large clearing and was heading for a fallen tree lying half within the other trees and half into the clearing. The raven hopped up onto the trunk, clawed its way to the upper part, and began ascending that. Obviously, it planned on leaping off the end, which was about thirty feet above the ground, and flapping in a circle around the big clearing until it could get high enough to fly above the treetops.

Kickaha took the beamer from its holster. The weapon was already set on half power. Just as the raven leaped from the end of the fallen tree, Kickaha aimed at the bird and pressed the trigger. A faintly scarlet, narrow beam shot part of the raven's right wing off. It squawked, and it fell.

Kickaha ran around the tree. The bird was flopping on the ground and crying out. He grabbed it from from behind by its neck and choked it. When its struggles had become feeble, he released it. It lay on the ground gasping for air, its legs upraised, its huge black eyes staring at him. If ravens could turn pale, it would have been as white as a snowbird.

He waved the beamer at the raven.

"What is your name, croaker?" he said harshly.

The bird struggled up onto its two feet.

"How do you like Stamun?"

"A good enough name. But what is yours?" Kickaha said. He stepped closer and shoved the end of the beamer close to the raven's head. "Now is not the time for wisecracking. I don't have much patience."

While he spoke, he kept glancing around. You never knew what might be creeping up on you.

"Wayskam," the raven said.

"Who sent that message to Eleth?"

"Awrk!"

Kickaha translated that as an expression of surprise mingled with dismay.

"You heard us?"

"Yes, dummy. Of course I did."

"If I tell you, will you let me live? And not torture me?"

"I'll let you go," Kickaha said, "and I won't touch you."

"You could not touch me and still could torture me," it said.

"I won't give you any pain," Kickaha said. "Unlike the Lords, I take no pleasure in doing that. But that doesn't mean I won't make you talk if I have to. So, talk!"

The raven was doomed to be killed or to die of starvation. It could never fly with half of its right wing sheared off. But the bird was still in shock and had not thought of that.

Or could it, like Lords, regenerate amputated limbs?

It did not matter. It would not survive long enough in the forest to grow back the severed part.

"I'll talk if you'll take me back to your camp and nurse me until I can fly again. And then release me. Not that my life will be worth much if Red Orc finds out I betrayed him."

The raven was thinking more clearly than Kickaha had expected it would. Also, its remark that it could, if given time, fly again showed that Eye-of-the-Lord ravens could grow new parts.

"I promise I'll take good care of you," he said, "if you tell me the truth."

"And will you protect me from the iron-hearted daughters of Urizen? Those bitches will try to kill me."

"I'll do my best," Kickaha said.

"That's all I can ask for. You have a reputation for being a trickster, but it is said that your word is as solid as Kethkith's Skull."

Kickaha did not know that reference, but its meaning was obvious.

"Talk! But keep to the point!"

Wayskam opened its beak. A squawk grated from it. Out of the corner of his eye, Kickaha saw something dim and moving. He jumped to one side and at the same time, started to whirl. His beamer shot its scarlet ray, but it did not hit his attacker. Something—it looked like a paw moving so fast it was almost a blur—struck his right shoulder. He was slammed down onto the ground; pain shot through his shoulder. For a second, he was not fully conscious.

However, his unconscious mind had taken over, and he automatically rolled away. The thing growled like the birth of thunder. Kickaha kept on rolling for several yards, then started to get up on a knee. The thing moved very swiftly toward him. Kickaha raised the beamer. A paw knocked it loose from his grip and numbed his hand. Then the creature was on him.

Its sharp teeth closed on his shoulder, but it did not sink them deeply into his flesh. Its breath was hot, though it did not have the stink of a meat-eater. It quickly released the bite as a paw hooked itself under his crotch and lifted him up and away.

Kickaha was vaguely aware that he was soaring through the air and that his groin was hurting worse than his shoulder. When he struck the ground, he blacked out.

Through the slowly evaporating mists, Anana's face passed from a dark blurry object into lovely features and bright black hair. Her face was twisted with concern, and she was crying, "Kickaha! Kickaha!"

He said, "Here I am. Down but not out, I think."

He tried to get up. His knees could not keep their lock. He sank back onto his buttocks and gazed around. The creature was lying faceup and unmoving on the ground. The raven was not in sight.

"You got here barely in time," he said. "What were you doing? Following me?"

She looked relieved but did not smile.

"You were gone too long just to be urinating. And I smelled trouble. That's nonsense, I suppose, but I have developed a feeling for the not-quite-right. Anyway, I did go after you, and I got here just in time to see that thing throw you away as if you were a piece of trash paper. So, I beamed it."

Kickaha did not reproach her for killing a source of possibly very important information. She must have had to do it.

"The bird?"

"I never saw a bird. You mean the raven?"

He nodded slightly. "The one I told you about. As we suspected, the sisters are working for Red Orc. Willingly or unwillingly, I don't know which."

"Then Red Orc must know we're here!"

6

"**Not necessarily the exact spot**," **he said. "We can't as-**sume he's keeping close tabs on us."

He told her how he had spied on Eleth and the raven, and how noise-lessly and swiftly the bearlike thing had attacked him.

"I'm glad you got here in the proverbial nick of time. But I think I would've gotten away from it and managed to kill it with the beamer."

"Your lack of confidence is pathetic," she said, smiling. "You stay here and get your strength back. I'll go after the raven. If I catch it, we'll get the rest of its story out of it."

"Don't look for it more than twenty minutes. If you haven't caught it by then, you'll never find it."

Before leaving, however, she ran to a small creek nearby and returned with her deerskin canteen full of fresh water. She poured water over his wounds, held the container to his lips so that he could drink deeply, then stood up.

"There! That'll hold you for a while."

She touched her lips with her thumb and forefinger together, forming an oval, and snapped the fingers of her other hand, a Thoan gesture sym-bolizing a kiss. Then she disappeared among the trees. He lay staring up into the bright green sky. After a while, he slowly and painfully got to his feet. Everything seemed to whirl around him, though he did not fall. His shoulder hurt more than his crotch did. His lower back was stiff and would be worse soon. He was bleeding from the shoulder, though not heavily, and from less deep claw marks on his belly and testicles.

When he got to the corpse, he studied it—her—in detail. The first thing he noted, though, was that Anana had shot the beam through the forehead just above the eyes. Though she had had to take swift aim, she had coolly decided to pierce its brain and had done so.

The creature was at least seven feet long and formed like a hybrid of woman and bear. The face lacked the ursine snout, but its jaws bulged out as if they would have liked to have become a bear's. That forehead indicated that she was highly intelligent. The structure of her mouth and the teeth, however, showed that she might have had much trouble pronouncing human words. Whether or not she could speak well, she must have understood Thoan speech.

It was then that Kickaha remembered some stories told by the Bear People, an Amerindian tribe on the second level. These were narratives he had thought were tribal myths until now. They spoke of creatures descended from a union between the original Great Bear and the daughter of the original human couple. Indeed, the Bear People claimed that they, like the Man-Bear, were descended from this couple. But this creature's first ancestors must have been made in some Lord's laboratory. Probably, the Thoan was Jadawin, he who became Wolff on Earth I.

By now, the scavenging beetles and ants, attracted by the odor of decaying flesh, were scuttling across the clearing. Kickaha walked woozily into the forest and sat down near the edge of the clearing, his back against a giant above-ground root. He watched from there. Presently, Anana walked into the clearing for a few feet and looked around. Her stance showed that she was ready to dive back into the woods if she saw or heard anything suspicious.

He hooted softly, imitating the call of a small tree-dwelling lemuroid. She hooted back. He got up stiffly and approached her.

"The raven was already dead when I found it," she said. "One of those giant weasels was eating it."

They talked for a few minutes. Having decided on their course of action, they started back to the camp. Kickaha's plan to shock the sisters into confessing their part in Red Orc's plan had been discarded. He had wanted to cut the head off the Man-Bear and to throw it down at the women's feet. But he agreed with her that it was best to keep them in the dark. For a while, anyway.

By the time they reached the camp, they had concocted a story to explain his wounds. Though a big cat had attacked him, he said, he had gotten away from it. Anana had supported him while he limped into camp. That needed no acting by him, nor did his lying on the ground and groaning with pain.

"We'll have to stay here until I've recovered enough to resume walking," he said.

Whether or not Eleth and Ona accepted his story, he had no way of determining. That they were Thoan made them suspicious of even the most simple and straightforward statement.

Two days later, he was ready to go. Like all humans in the Thoan universes, except for the two Earths, he had remarkable powers of physical recovery. Except for faint scars, which would disappear entirely, his gashes were healed over. However, he had to take in far more food and water than he would have normally eaten. A faster healing required more fuel.

During this time, Anana trailed the sisters into the woods whenever they went there for privacy.

"It's obvious they're trying to get into contact with the raven, and they're upset because it isn't showing up."

"Let them seethe in their sweat," he said.

"Their bickering and quarreling is getting on my nerves."

"On mine, too. They're ten-thousand-year-old infants. They hate each other, yet they feel as if they have to stay together. Maybe it's because each is afraid that the other will be happy if she isn't around to make her life miserable."

She said, "Most Thoan couples are like that. Are Earth mates the same way?"

"Too many."

He paused, then said, "I suppose you know both asked me to roll in the leaves with them."

She laughed, and she said, "They've asked me, too."

On the early morning of the third day, they broke camp and set out toward the target mountain. Two days afterward, they left the great forest. About two days' journey across a vast plain was before them. They crossed it without harm, though they were attacked twice by the sabertooths, which dined chiefly on mammoths, and once by six of the moalike birds called axebeaks. And then they came to the foothills of the mountain named Rigsoorth.

"Here we make camp for the night," Kickaha said. He pointed to an area halfway up the steep three-peaked mass. "By late noon tomorrow, if we push hard, we'll be there."

Only he and Anana knew that he was not indicating the place where the gate was located. He seldom revealed to strangers what he truly intended to do. Misdirection, sleight of hand, and deviousness were traits stamped with the label: KICKAHA.

Eleth said, "The gate is in a large heart-shaped boulder?"

"That's what I said," Kickaha replied.

Just before they got under their blankets that night in the entrance of a small cave, Anana said, "If they think they're that close to the gate, they might try to murder us tonight."

"I doubt it. I think Red Orc has other plans for us. On the other hand, maybe they might try it. I'll take the first watch." He kissed her lips. "Sleep well."

After fifteen minutes, he slipped out from the blankets and crossed by the seemingly sleeping sisters. He crawled up the rocky slope to a boulder and climbed onto its top. After wrapping himself in a blanket, he sat and watched the small fire in the cave opening and the three women around it. Now and then, he looked in all directions. And he listened intently. Once, a huge dark body snuffled around fifty feet below the cave, kicked a few rocks, and sent them sliding noisily down the slope. Then it disappeared. Once, a long-winged bird—or was it a flying mammal?—swooped down and seized a small animal that squeaked once, and then predator and prey were gulped by the darkness.

Night thoughts covered Kickaha as if a black parachute were collapsing over him.

Foremost and most often recurring of the images that questioned him was Red Orc's.

Kickaha was certain that the Lord was nudging him and Anana toward a trap. Even if he had not overheard the raven and Eleth, he would have been sure. So far, he had gone along with with the Lord's plot, whatever it was. That Red Orc had not tried to have them killed proved to Kickaha that the Lord wanted him and Anana alive. He was planning something special for them. Such as intense physical torture or a long imprisonment involving mental pain, or both.

Kickaha thought back to when he and Anana had been in Los Angeles and Orc and his men had been trying to catch them. Now that he considered the events, it seemed to him that Orc's men had been rather inept. And Orc's organizing had not been of the best.

Was that because Orc was playing with him?

It seemed likely. One of the rules of the games Lords played with each other was that the opponent was always given a slight chance to escape a trap. If, that is, the enemy was quick and ingenious enough. And also had a certain amount of luck.

The opening was always so slight that many Lords had been killed trying to get through their foes' trapped gates into those foes' private universes. Thus far, Kickaha and Anana had been fortunate. Their enemies, not they, had died or been forced to flee their strongholds.

But it seemed to Kickaha that Red Orc had not tried hard enough, up to now, to capture or kill them.

However, Red Orc might have gotten tired of the game and determined to get rid forever of his archenemies.

Kickaha did not intend to allow that to happen.

But Red Orc did, and he was not one to be ignored. Of all the Lords, he was the most dangerous and the most successful. No other Thoan had invaded so many universes or killed so many of their owners. No one else was so dreaded. Yet, it was said, according to what Anana and others had told Kickaha, that he had been a somewhat compassionate and loving youth. That is, by Thoan standards.

But the unjust and harsh treatment by his father, Los, had metamorphosed Orc into a brutal and vindictive man. That was some people's theory. But Kickaha believed that the change was caused by the genetic viciousness of the Lords. Whatever the reason, Orc had rebelled against his father. After a long struggle with him, during which several planets in several universes had been ruined, he killed Los. He had then taken his mother, Enitharmon—and his aunt, Vala—as his mates. This was not against Thoan morality, nor was it uncommon.

Much later, Enitharmon had been killed by a raiding Lord. Red Orc had tracked the killer down, captured her, and tortured her so hideously that the Lords, though proficient and merciless torturers, were shocked.

"It was shortly after this, only a thousand or so years afterward, but at least fifteen thousand Terrestrial years ago," Anana had said, "that Red Orc became the secret Lord of both Earths. But you know that."

"Yes, I know," Kickaha had said. "And Red Orc made the universes of the two Earths about then."

"That's what I told you," she had said. "When I told you that, I thought Red Orc had made them and that it was he who populated both planets with artificial human beings. But I believe now that I was mistaken. You see, there is also a story that the two Earths were made by a Lord named Orc. Not our Red Orc. He was one of the very first to make pocket universes. He was born many millennia before Red Orc. But he was killed by another Lord. The two Earths had no Lord for a long time. Then, one called Thrassa took over. But Red Orc, who was born long after the original Orc, killed Thrassa and became the Lord of the two Earths."

Kickaha, his mind leaping ahead to form a conclusion, had said, "The original Orc became confused with Red Orc."

She had nodded. "That's it. Or something like it. During all those thousands of years and with the Lords' failure to keep records and the infrequent communication among the Lords of the many universes, Red Orc became identified with the original Orc. Red Orc, he's my uncle, you know, my mother's brother, and Los and Enitharmon are my grandparents. Jadawin, who is also Wolff, is my half-brother . . ."

"Don't confuse me," Kickaha had said. "Stick to the story."

"Sorry. Red Orc now sincerely believes that he did make the last of the universes to be made, the universes of Earth One and Earth Two. He is not sane, though he functions extremely well. Very few Lords are, in fact, entirely sane. Living so long seems to unbalance the mind of all but the most stable."

"Such as yourself," he had said, grinning.

"Yes. Let me tell you how I arrived at this conclusion."

"That too long a life makes it hard for the brain to continue accepting reality and thus slips into unreality?"

She had smiled and had said, "I wasn't referring to that, though what you say is close to the truth. One night, some time ago when we were on the planet of the Tripeds, while you were sleeping soundly but I could not sleep at all, I got to thinking about Orc and Red Orc. And I saw what the true story has to be."

"Why didn't you tell me about it in the morning?"

"Because that was the night we were attacked by the Shlook tribe. Remember? We fought our way out but had to run for two days before we shook off the last of those three-legged cannibals. That made me forget about it until now. In fact, I was lucky to be able to recall it. After thousands of years, my brain, like all of the long-lived Thoan, stores only certain significant memories. It seems there's only room enough—"

"A struldbrugian's lot is not a 'appy one," Kickaha had said in English.

"What?"

"Never mind. The true story, as you call it."

"You have these two stories about who made the two Earths. The one about the original Orc doing it is not now widespread. Most people now accept the story that Red Orc did it, and his claim that he did so has reinforced that belief. But he could not have done it."

She had paused so long that Kickaha had said, "Well?"

"There's the tale I've heard from several unhostile Lords; not many of those, I'll admit. It's supposed to have come from Red Orc's boasting to his various mistresses, though he has a reputation for being close-mouthed about his personal life.

"It concerns the time when he was stranded by his father on Anthema, the Unwanted World. Los thought his son would die there, though he did have a very slight chance to survive and a lesser chance to find the gate out of that world. But if he did find it, it would only lead him to Zazel's World, also called the Caverned World. And there was no way out of that. Or so thought Los.

"Red Orc did find the gate, and he went into Zazel's World. This, according to Red Orc's story, was a single vast computer but with countless caves and tunnels inhabited by plants and animals. Zazel had died long ago, but an artificial being was still the caretaker of it. This thing eventually let Red Orc talk it into sending him out through a gate Los knew nothing about. But Red Orc intended to reenter that world if he could—after he'd killed his father. That took several thousands of years, an epic in itself.

"The reason my uncle wanted to get back into the Caverned World was that its memory contained the data for making a Creation-Destruction engine."

"Ah!"

"You know what I'm talking about?"

"Sure," Kickaha had said. "The ancient Lords used such engines to make their artificial universes. But as time went by and then during the millennia-long and very destructive war of the Lords against the Black Bellers, the engines were destroyed or lost. And the data for making them were lost, too. Am I right?"

"Right! But Red Orc found out that the data were still in the Caverned World's circuits. He was in no position to get it then, but he was determined to come back someday and do so. Unfortunately for him, fortunately for us, he could not get back in. The creature that ruled the world must have sealed up the gate. Red Orc's been trying to find a way to penetrate that world, though he hasn't tried continuously. Other things, such as warring against the Lords, have kept him busy. But I think that he's almost given up the effort. He's been frustrated too often."

"From what I know of him, I doubt that," Kickaha had said.

One of the recent things occupying Red Orc would have been trying to find Kickaha and Anana. The Thoan's pride would be deeply wounded because the two had eluded him so successfully and for such a long time. He would be in one of his well-known rages. God help the people around him; God help the men he had sent to track down and catch Kickaha and Anana. However, these people were no innocents. Anything bad that happened to them, they deserved.

He might know by now that his greatest two enemies were on—had been on—the Whaziss planet. But he did not know exactly where they were. Or did he?

Though Orc might never have completely lost the trail on Earth of Kickaha and Anana, he must have lost it when they escaped to the Lavalite planet. He must have been trying to find them during the fifteen years they were on the Whaziss planet.

Just what else had the Thoan been up to during that decade and a half? How many Lords had he killed, and how many of the pocket universes were now his?

Who was the mysterious Englishman costumed in early nineteenth-century clothes who had been in that aerial mansion on the Lavalite planet?

Where were Wolff and Chryseis now?

Then the ancient sleeper with the insectile face swam into Kickaha's mental sea. He was an enigmaed enigma. Why had he awakened just as the intruders from a much later time had left that curious chamber? Just how and why had they blundered into that room, which must surely be heavily guarded by whatever guarded it?

Kickaha did not believe that they had "blundered" into it or that the awakening was a coincidence. Coincidences might happen, but even these, he believed, if dug into deeply enough, would reveal the connections.

Anana came to take over her watch. They talked in whispers for about ten minutes. When they were clear on what to do the next day, Kickaha went to the cave to sleep, though not deeply. Thus the night passed, with each taking turns on the boulder. He was on it when a brief gray light announced that the sun was just around the curve of the planet.

The sisters had not once gotten up, though they had shifted around a lot trying to find a comfortable position on the hard rock.

After they had spattered some water on their faces and eaten their simple breakfast, they scattered to various boulders and rocky projections behind which to evacuate. After returning to the camp, they loaded up their gear and set out, Kickaha leading. Before they had put a half-mile behind them, Eleth called a halt.

"This is not the way you told us we'd be going!"

Kickaha said, "I pointed out the spot we'd travel to. But we don't take a direct route. This way will be much easier."

After two hours, the sisters complained that they were taking a hell of a long way roundabout.

Kickaha stopped in front of an eighty-foot-high monolith of reddish granite. Its base was within a few feet of the edge of the cliff on which the group stood. Ten feet up from the base, a half-sphere of glossy black rock extruded from the granite. It looked like a cannonball that had been shot at close range into the monolith.

"Is that the gate?" Eleth said, pointing at the stone pillar.

"No," Kickaha said.

"Then where is it? Are we anywhere near it?"

"It's not the gate, but the gate site is in it."

He opened the deerskin bag attached to his belt and pulled out the silvery trumpet.

Eleth, eyes wide, sucked in air noisily. "The Horn of Shambarimen!"

Ona was too awed at first to make any sound. Then she and Eleth broke into high-pitched chatter. Kickaha let them go on for about a minute before calling for silence.

He raised the Horn to his lips and blew. As soon as the last note had faded away, an arch-shaped area seven feet high and five feet wide formed at the base of the rock. It shimmered as if made of heat waves. Kickaha thought that he could almost see through the ripplings to the other side and that something huge and dark was there. But that was, of course, an illusion.

"We have ten seconds before it closes!" he said loudly. He waved the Horn. "Everybody into it! Now!"

Anana and he pulled out their beamers and shoved the sisters toward the gate. Eleth was shouting, "No! No! How do we know it's not a trap you've set for us!"

She tried to run away. Anana tripped her with an extended leg and then kicked her in the buttocks as she struggled to get up on her feet.

Looking terrified, Ona stumbled toward the entrance, then darted to one side and tried to get past Anana. Anana knocked Ona down with the side of her hand against her neck.

Eleth also ran, holding up the hem of her robe; then she stumbled and fell flat on the ground. She refused to get up, though Kickaha shouted that he would cut her in half.

The shimmering on the face of the rock was gone.

He and Anana stepped back so that they could cover the sisters with their beamers.

"It's plain as the nose on a camel that you two don't want to go through that gate," Kickaha said. "Yet, a moment ago, you seemed quite willing to go with us. Why're you so reluctant all of a sudden?"

Eleth got onto her feet and tried to rub the dirt from the front of her white robe. She said, "We really don't trust you."

"A very weak excuse!" Anana said loudly. "What is the real reason you tried to get away? You know something's waiting for us there? Were you hoping to lead us into a trap?"

"We panicked!"

"Yes," Ona said, faking a snuffling, "we got scared."

"Of what?" Anana asked.

Kickaha bellowed, "You were afraid that Red Orc would catch you along with us, betray you, and kill you, too? Is that right?"

Whatever surprise Eleth felt, she did not reveal it. But Ona winced as if he had struck her with a fly swatter.

"Red Orc?" she screeched. "What does he have to do with that?" She half turned and waved at where the gate had been.

Kickaha walked up to her until his nose almost touched hers. He spoke even more loudly. "I overheard your raven, Wayskam, talking to Eleth! So I know all! All!"

He thought, I don't by any means know all. But I'll scare them into confessing everything. If I can't, I'll let Anana loose on them. Her heart isn't as soft as mine. I hope I can stand the screaming.

The sisters said nothing. That he knew the name of the raven showed them that he was on to them.

"Your protector, the bear-woman," he said, "is dead. Anana killed it."

Eleth smiled slightly and said, "Ah! It wasn't a big cat that clawed you! It was . . ."

"I didn't catch her name," Kickaha said. "Yes, she did tear me up a little. Anana shot her before I could do it."

Eleth still kept silence, but Ona said, "We couldn't help ourselves! We . . ."

Eleth screamed, "Shut up! They don't know anything! They're just trying to get you to talk!"

"Tell you what, Ona," Anana said. "You tell us everything—I mean everything, nothing left out—and I'll spare your life. As for Eleth . . ." She stabbed the beamer at Ona.

"Spill it all!"

Eleth spoke with a diamond-hard voice. No quaverings in her. "If we talk, we'll die. If we don't talk, we'll die. It's better not to talk. Ona, I absolutely forbid you to say another word about it!"

"You think Red Orc'll save us now?" her sister said, sneering. "He'll pop up just in time to save us? How could he? Besides, what does he care about us? I think—"

"That's enough!" Anana said. "You've both said enough to damn yourselves. Not that we needed a word from you to know that. Eleth, you talk first. If you hold anything back, and Ona then reveals that you have been holding back, you die! Immediately!"

Eleth looked around as if she expected Red Orc to come riding down from the mountains to rescue her. No savior was in sight, and Eleth was realist enough to know that none was coming. She began talking.

It was much as Kickaha had expected it to be. The sisters had not, as they had claimed, escaped from Orc when he invaded their palace. They had been caught before they could get to a gate. Instead of killing them, Red Orc had forced them to be tools to catch Kickaha and Anana.

At this point, Anana snorted and said, "Forced? You, the iron-hearted daughters of Urizen, had to be forced to become our enemy?"

"We never claimed to be friends of yours," Eleth said. "But we would never have gone out after you."

"You're too lazy," Anana said.

"He did not tell us why he thought you were there," Eleth said. "We were not in a position to ask him questions about his methods and results."

The Lord had not been able to determine just where the two were on Whazzis. But he did find the only gate existing, the one that Kickaha and Anana eventually came to. The hexagon in the Tripeds' temple had long been there. Orc had rechanneled it, making it a resonant circuit, and then gone elsewhere.

"He did say that it would lead to a certain area on the World of Tiers. When the alarm was set off—where, I do not know—Red Orc would know that the circuit had been entered. Of course, he could not be sure that some other Lord had not activated it. But he said that he was approximately ninety-percent sure that you two would do it."

"How could he be sure that we could survive all the traps?" Kickaha said.

"He apparently had great faith that you two would. He did pay you both a compliment. He said that if anybody could get through the circuit, you could."

"I had Shambarimen's Horn."

"He never mentioned that."

"He wouldn't. If you'd known that, you would've been tempted to betray him and risk everything for this great treasure."

"You're right," Eleth said.

The Lord, or perhaps a servant of his, had gotten them somehow to the middle of the forest where Kickaha and Anana had found them. The sisters had been unconscious during the entire journey from their world to this.

"I can assure you that there is no gate in that forest," Kickaha said. "I know. I've seen the diagram of the gates, in Wolff's palace. You must have been sent through another gate somewhere on this world and then transported by air to the forest."

"There couldn't be gates of which you have no knowledge? Red Orc could not have opened a new gate?"

Kickaha shrugged.

The women had awakened among the trees. For fifty-five days, they had had to struggle to survive there. Orc had given them only a few necessities, the stuff they might have taken with them during a very hasty departure.

"We had almost given up on your getting here," Eleth said. "It wasn't certain that you would survive the circuit or that you would find us. But Red Orc, may he suffer the tortures of Inthiman, did not care if we starved to death or were killed by predators! We had decided we'd stay there five days more. If you hadn't shown up by then, we'd set out for Jadawin's palace."

"A noble ambition," Anana said. "But you had little chance to make it up the two monoliths."

Eleth did not have much to add to her story. She only said that she and her sister did not know why Red Orc wanted them to lead the two to this gate. Ona said that that was true.

Kickaha and Anana withdrew from the women to talk softly.

"They probably don't know why," he said. "Red Orc wouldn't tell them. What I'd like to know is how he knew about this gate."

"I'm not sure that he did or does know," she said. "He may be following us now to see where we go. When he sees us open the gate, he'll pounce."

She looked up the mountain slope and then down it and across the great plain.

"Or, if not he, then someone in his service," Kickaha said.

"He or whoever may be a hundred miles away. Across the plain or up there in an aircraft. One missile would wipe us out."

"He wouldn't blow us apart," Kickaha said. "He wants us alive. We're in a Hamletish situation. There're so many ifs and buts to consider, we're being paralyzed. Let's do something now, and ride out the consequences."

He blew the Horn again. Anana herded the sisters, who protested strongly but vainly, through the shimmering curtain in the rock. She stepped in on their heels. He dropped the Horn into the bag and leaped through the shimmering. On its other side was a hemispherical chamber. The floor was as covered with the opaque brightness as the walls. He could, however, feel bare and level rock under his feet.

Ona screamed and darted by Kickaha. He thrust out an arm to catch her. She ducked it and leaped back through the curtain. The upper part of her body had disappeared when the shimmering snapped off. Only part of her robe, her buttocks, her long legs, and some blood remained. Eleth shrieked and then began sobbing loudly.

Without warning, they were in another place, some sort of pit cut out of rock. Crouching, he spun around, his beamer ready, taking in all that was his new environment. There did not seem to be anything that demanded immediate defense or attack. A man whom Kickaha recognized stood at one end of the pit, but his open hands were held high above his head in a sign of peace.

Kickaha's gaze passed from him to examine the prison they were in. It was a hole twelve feet square and approximately ten feet deep. Straight above was a bright blue sky. The sun was out of sight, and the shadows of the vast cliff on one side were moving swiftly toward the opening of the hole.

They were in a pit at the bottom, or up on one side, of an immense abyss. Both sides went up at a thirty-degree angle from the horizontal, though they had many ledges and holes. Here and there on the walls, some puny trees grew, extending at forty-five-degree angles from the steep slopes. Great patches of some green mosslike stuff covered parts of the walls.

The heat was a vicious magical wand that tapped him and brought forth from his skin a spring of water. He estimated that the temperature was approximately 101°F.

He did not waste time. He took the Horn from its bag and blew it. The seven notes died, but no gate appeared on the walls of the pit. Red Orc had trapped them, no doubt of that.

He put the Horn back in the bag and turned to face the man at the end of the pit. He was tall and handsome and looked twenty-five years old, though he must have lived at least a century and a half ago, possibly more.

His long hair was brown and pulled tightly back into a ponytail. His suit of clothes was of a style in fashion among the Lords a long time ago. But he must have had them made in some Thoan universe. The threads of the jacket pulsed with green, red, white, blue, and yellow as if they were colored tubes. His once-white shirt was ruffed and open at the neck. His trousers were a bottle-green velvety material ending at the calves in a tight band. A scarlet triangular patch covered his groin.

On the middle finger of his left hand was a heavy ring of silver. It wound around the finger three times. Though Kickaha had glimpsed the ring when he had entered the pit, he now saw it in detail. He was startled. It was in the form of the scaly man. That insectile head on the ring looked exactly like the head of the being in the chamber of the dead.

"We meet again," the man said in English, smiling. His pronunciation, though, was not like any English Kickaha had ever heard.

"I am Eric Clifton. At your service. Like you, I am the prisoner of Red Orc. At least, I assume that that loathsome Lord brought you here against your will."

7

ELETH WAS NOW WAILING LOUDLY. KICKAHA SHOUTED, "STOP that caterwauling! You hated your sister, yet you're carrying on something awful, as if she was very dear to you!"

Eleth stared with red eyes at him while she choked back her grief. Sniffling, she said, "But I did love Ona! Just because we disagreed now and then . . ."

"Disagreed? Now and then?" He laughed. "You and your sister were bound in a ring of loathing and spite! The only reason you didn't kill each other was because you'd lose somebody you could hate!"

"That's not true," Ona said. She sobbed once, then said, "You wouldn't understand."

"No, I wouldn't."

He turned back to Eric Clifton.

"I'm Kickaha. You may have heard of me. This is Anana the Bright. She was born at the beginning of the war with the Black Bellers, so that gives you an idea of how long she's lived. This wailer is Eleth, one of the hard-hearted daughters of Urizen, once known as the gentle-hearted daughters of Ahania, Urizen's wife. You may have heard of them."

He paused, then said, "Anana and I saw you briefly when you were in the floating palace of Urthona, Lord of the Shapeshifting World. Anana and I had a hard time with Urthona and Red Orc when we were passing through Urthona's World. But we killed him. Red Orc was also a prisoner on the palace, but he escaped."

"I wondered what happened to you," Clifton said.

"Details later. You can explain to us just how you got into the Thoan universes from Earth and how you happen to be here. And how in hell did you get that ring?"

While he was talking, he was looking at the sides of the pit. An oily substance filmed them.

"It's a long story," Eric Clifton said. "Shouldn't we be thinking just now about how to get out of here before Red Orc shows up?"

"I'm doing that," Kickaha said. "But that won't interfere with my hearing your story. Keep to the highlights, though."

Clifton said that he was born somewhere around 1780 of very poor parents in London, England. His father had managed to work his way up from a day laborer to owner of a bakery shop. When that failed, he and his wife and six children had been put in debtor's prison. There his father and three children had died of malnutrition and fever. His mother had gone insane and was sent to Bedlam. Not long after he and his siblings had been released, his fourteen-year-old brother was caught and hanged for having stolen a pair of shoes. His younger sister became a whore at the age of twelve and died at eighteen of syphilis and gonorrhea.

At this point, Clifton sucked in a deep breath, and tears filmed his eyes.

"That was a very long time ago, but as you see, I am still affected by the memory of . . . never mind . . . anyway . . ."

He had been very fortunate in being adopted, though not legally, by a childless couple. That had saved him from being deported to Australia.

"Though that could have been my great chance to be a free man and, perhaps, a rich man," Clifton said.

The man who raised him was Richard Dally. "A bookseller and publisher. He and his wife taught me to read and write. I became acquainted with Mr. William Blake, the poet, engraver, and painter, when my stepfather charged me with delivering a book to him. Mr. Blake—"

"Does this have anything to do with the main story?" Kickaha said.

"Very much so. I cannot leave it out. Do you know Blake's poetry?"

"I read some of his poems when I was in high school."

Blake had been born, if he remembered correctly, in 1757 and had died in 1827. He was an eccentric who was Christian, but his ideas about religion differed much from the views of his time. Or from any other views then and in Kickaha's time. That much he had learned from his English teacher.

Clifton said, "Did you know that Blake wrote poetic works in which he made up his own mythology?"

"No."

"He mixed them with Christian elements."

"So?"

"His didactic and symbolical works were apocalyptic poems in which the characters were gods and goddesses he invented, or said he invented. He conceived his own mythology, and the deities in them had names such as Los, Enitharmon, Red Orc, Vala, and Ahania."

"What? You must be . . . no, you're not kidding!" Kickaha said.

He turned to Anana. "Did you know this?"

Her eyes widened. "Yes, I did, but don't get angry with me. The subject just didn't come up, though I've met Blake."

"You met Blake?"

Kickaha was so flabbergasted that he spluttered. Yet he knew that she must be telling the truth. This Blake matter had meant little to her, and she would have recalled it if he had mentioned the poet's name.

He said, "All right. It's okay. I was just surprised." He turned to Clifton. "Tell me how this happened."

"Mr. Blake was a mystic visionary and exceedingly eccentric. His eyes were the wildest, the brightest, and the piercingest I've ever seen. His face was like an elf's, one of the dangerous elves. Mr. Dally said that Blake claimed that when he was a child, he saw angels in a tree and the prophet Ezekiel in a field. It was also said that he had seen the face of God at his bedroom window. If you saw him and heard him talk, you'd believe that these stories were true.

"A few times, Mr. Blake visited Mr. Dally to buy a book on credit. He was very poor, you know. Twice, I overheard him and Mr. Dally in conversation, though Mr. Blake did most of the talking. Mr. Dally was fascinated by Mr. Blake, though Mr. Dally felt uneasy when Mr. Blake was indulging in his wild talk. I did too. He seemed possessed by something strange, something not quite of this world. You'd have to talk to him to know exactly what I mean.

"Anyway, one afternoon, Mr. Blake, his eyes looking more wild than I'd ever seen them, more spiritual or more visioning, I should say, told Mr. Dally that he had seen the ghost of a flea. I don't know what he meant by a flea since the ghost, as he described it, had very little of the flea in it. It looked just like the figure on this ring, except that its hand did not hold a cup for drinking blood."

Clifton held up the hand with the ring on its finger.

"The flea was just one of what he called his 'visitations.' That is, the figures of beings and things from the supernatural. Though sometimes he spoke of them as visitors from other worlds."

Anana said, "Sometimes he called them emanations from the unknown worlds."

"From whom did you hear this?" Kickaha said.

"I heard it directly from Blake. As you know, after Red Orc made the universe of Earth and the universe of Earth's twin, he forbade any Lords to visit them. But some did go there, and I was one of them. I've told you that I've been on Earth One several times, though I didn't mention all the times and places I've been there. When I was living in London, a fascinating though disgusting place, I was disguised as a wealthy French noblewoman. Since I collected some of the best of the primitive art of Earth-men, I went to see Blake. I purchased some engravings and tempera sketches from him but asked him not to tell anyone I'd done so. There didn't seem to be the slightest chance that Red Orc would hear about it, but I wasn't taking any risks."

"And you didn't tell me about this?" Kickaha said.

"You know how it happened that I didn't. Let's hear no more of that."

"All right," he said. "But how could Blake have known anything of the Thoan worlds?"

Clifton opened his mouth to say something, but she spoke first.

"We Thoan who know about Blake have wondered that, too. Our theory is that Blake was a mystic who somehow tuned in, you might say, to a knowledge of the people inhabiting the other universes. He had a sensitivity, perhaps neural, perhaps from a seventh sense we know nothing about. No other Earth person has ever had it. At least, we haven't heard of his like, though there is a theory that some Earth mystics and perhaps some insane Earth people . . ."

"No theories unless they're absolutely relevant," Kickaha said.

Anana said, "We just don't know. But somehow Blake received some—what should I call them? visions? intimations?—of the artificial pocket universes. Perhaps of the original Thoan universe, or of that universe that some say preceded the Thoan's. In any event, it couldn't have been coincidence that he knew the exact names of many Lords and some of the situations and events in which they played their parts.

"But his, ah, psychic receptions of them were distorted and fragmentary. And he used them as part of his personal mythology and mingled Christian mythology with them. The mixture was Blakean, highly imaginative and shaped by his own beliefs. Blake was a freak, though of a high order."

Kickaha said, "Very well. Anyway, what he saw as the flea's ghost was the scaly man we saw in that curious tomb. No Thoan knew about the scaly man, yet Blake saw him."

"Obviously."

"Remarkable!"

"All universes and everything in them are remarkable," Anana said.

"Some more than others," Kickaha replied.

He pointed at the ring. "What about that, Clifton? How'd you get it?"

"And how did you get into the Thoan worlds?" she said.

Clifton shook his head. "That is the strangest thing that's ever happened to an Earthman."

"I doubt it's any stranger than how I happened to get to the World of Tiers," Kickaha said.

"I have some ability at drawing," Clifton said. "Mr. Blake's description of the flea's ghost so intrigued me that I drew a sketch of it. I showed it to a friend, George Pew. Like me, he had been a child of the streets, a cutpurse who also was a catchfart for a jeweler named Robert Scarborough."

Kickaha said, "Catchfart?"

"A footboy," Anana said. "A footboy was a servant who closely followed his master when he was out on the street."

Clifton said, "Pew showed the sketch to his employer, Mr. Scarborough, though he did not mention its source. Mr. Scarborough was so taken up with the sketch that he told a customer, a wealthy Scots nobleman, Lord Riven, about it. Lord Riven was very intrigued and ordered that a ring based on the sketch be made for him. It was done, but it was never delivered because it was stolen."

Clifton paused to hold up the ring to look at it. Then he said, "My friend Pew was one of the gang that stole it. He gave it to me to hide because his employer suspected him. I didn't really want to have anything to do with it, though to be truthful, I did consider plans to obtain permanent possession of it. I was at that time not as honest as the rich people would wish me to be, and you might not be if you had been me."

"We're not judges," Kickaha said.

"Pew had told me that only he knew he'd given me the ring for safekeeping. But Pew was killed while fleeing the constables. Thus, I considered the ring to be my property. But I did not plan to sell it until much time had passed. The constabulary had a good description of it; it was dangerous to try to sell it.

"And then, one fine summer day, that event happened that resulted in my being propelled willy-nilly into these other worlds and resulted in my being confined in this pit. Though just what Red Orc plans for me, for us, I don't know."

Thunder, amplified by the deep chasm, rumbled in the distance. With the suddenness of a Panzer attack, dark clouds were speeding from the west. In a few seconds, they had covered the bright sky, and a wind whistled over the top of the pit. The air that reached down into the pit blew away the sweltering heat and chilled Kickaha's naked body.

He said, "We'll hear the rest of your story later, Clifton. We've got to get out of this hole."

Anana did not have to ask him why they had to vacate the pit. She knew what a big downpour in this chasm would do.

Kickaha had considered using the beamers to make a forty-five-degree channel from the bottom of the hole to the surface. They might be able to escape from the pit that way. But there was no time to use the beamers.

Kickaha gave his orders. The two men stood side by side, their faces close to the north side of the pit. Anana, who was very strong and agile, climbed up onto them and stood with one foot on Kickaha's right shoulder and one foot on Clifton's left shoulder. By now, Eleth had recovered enough to join them in their effort. The lightest in the group and very athletic, she had no difficulty climbing up until she was on Anana's shoulders. The thin rope taken from Kickaha's backpack was coiled around Eleth's waist. A few seconds later, she called down.

"The edge is just too slippery for me to get a hold."

"What do you see?" he said. "Anything that might hold a grappling hook?"

"Nothing at all!" Eleth sounded desperate. A bellow of thunder and the cannon blast of nearby lightning tore her next words to shreds. She shrieked and fell backward off Anana. But she twisted around and landed, knees bent, on her feet.

After Anana had come down, she said, "What were you going to say?"

Eleth's reply was again shattered by thunder and lightning. A few raindrops fell on them. Then she shouted, "I saw a torrent of water pouring down the mountainsides! We're all going to drown!"

"Maybe," Kickaha said, grinning. "But we might be able to swim out of this pit."

He sounded more hopeful than he felt.

"Red Orc wouldn't put us here just so we could drown!" Eleth shrilled.

"Why not?" Anana said.

"Besides," Kickaha said, "he may have overlooked the possibility of flash floods. He may have picked this place out but not been around when it rained."

By then, a darkness not as black as midnight but blacker than the last gasp of dusk filled the pit. The wind was stronger and colder, though it was not in its full rage. Suddenly, a heavy rain fell upon them. Whips of lightning exploded near them. A few minutes later, water spilled over the edges of the pit. The water rose to Kickaha's ankles.

Eleth cried, "Elyttria of the Silver Arrows, save us!"

A wave of cold water crashed into the pit and knocked all of them down. Before they could struggle to their feet, a second and larger one fell on them. And then a third wave, the edge of the flood, cataracted into the pit.

Kickaha was rammed against the wall. He almost became unconscious but struggled to swim upward, though he did not know where upward was. When his hand struck stone, he knew that he had been swimming downward. Or had he gone horizontally and felt the side of the pit?

Somebody bumped into him. He grabbed for him or her but missed. Then he was sliding and bumping against stone for an indeterminable time. Just as he thought that he had to suck air into his lungs or die, his head rose above water. He gulped air before he was again drawn down. But he had seen a mass to his right, a mass darker than the darkness around him.

It must be a mountainside, he thought. Which means that I've been carried out of the pit.

He swam again in the blackness. If he had not been turned upside down, he was going for the surface. His chances for surviving were few, since he could, at any moment, slam into a mountainside. He kept struggling, and his head was suddenly out of the water, though a wave at once slapped his mouth and filled it. Choking and spitting, he got rid of the water.

It was no use to call out. The lightning and thunder were still cursing the earth. No one could hear him, and what if they did?

Now he was also in danger of being electrocuted. Lightning was plunging into the flood. But he could see in their flashes that he was being sped past solid rock that soared almost straight up into a darkness not even the lightning could scatter.

A roaring louder than the thunder's was now ahead of him. A waterfall? And he was swept over the edge and fell he knew not how far. When he struck the bottom of the raging river and was scraped along it, he was again half out of his wits. By the time he had recovered them, he was on top of a maelstrom. It whirled him around and around, and then, once again, he slammed into something hard.

When he awoke, he was lying on rock, his upper body out of the stream. It tugged feebly at him. Lightning still blazed through the darkness, though it was not near him.

He lay choking and coughing for a while. After he had gotten back his wind, he crawled painfully up the sloping rock. His face, feet, knees, ribs, hands, elbows, buttocks, and genitals felt as if they had been skinned with a knife. He hurt too much to crawl far. He rolled over; the scene was briefly lit by the lightning. He was on a triangular shelf of stone that dipped its apex into the storming river. Across it was a straight-up God-knows-where-its-top-is wall.

He turned, grunting with pain, sat up, and looked upward. Another flash showed him the wall that towered there. It was only about fifty feet from him. When the rain first came down its side, it must have been a torrent. But now it was a shallow brook.

Kickaha's luck, he thought. One of these days, though. . . .

He got up and staggered through a thin waterfall and under a wide shelf of stone. He sat down. After a while, the thunder and lightning retreated far down the canyon. Somehow, despite the cold and wetness, he fell asleep. When he woke, he saw daylight. Hours passed, and then the sun had come over the edge of the seemingly sky-high mouth of the chasm. It seemed to him that he was even deeper in it than when he had been in the pit.

He said, "Anana!"

His equipment and most of his weapons had been torn from him. He still had his belt and the beamer in its holster. Somehow, the bag containing the Horn of Shambarimem had not been torn from the loop on his belt . . . he grinned then, because he would have given up even the knife and the beamer in exchange for the Horn.

By the time that the sun was directly overhead, he rose stiffly. The storm had cooled the air, but tomorrow the heat would be stifling. He had to get to the top of the chasm. He went back and forth as far as he could along the base of the cliff. When he found cracks and fissures and plants to hold on to—even at this depth, little treelike plants projected at angles from the wall—he began to climb. His hands ached, and some skin had been ground off four of his fingers. Gritting his teeth and groaning, he got to an estimated eighty feet above the river. By then, the water had ceased falling down the wall. And he saw, fifty feet above him, the side of a large nest sticking out from a small ledge.

Maybe the nest contained eggs that he could eat.

When, shaking with fatigue and hunger, he got to the nest, he found that it was made of sticks and twigs and a gluey substance that had dried out. Inside the nest were four mauve eggs, each twice as large as a hen's. He looked around to make sure that the mother was not in sight. After piercing the eggs with the point of his knife, he sucked some yolk from each. Then he broke them open to disclose embryonic chicks. He ate these raw except for the heads and the legs.

Having rested a while, he rose to climb again. It was then that he heard a scream. He whirled. Mama Bird was home, and she was so angry she had dropped the rabbit-sized animal she had been bringing home. It fell, and he did not see it strike the river because he was busy defending himself. The sky-blue bird, somewhat larger than a bald eagle, slammed into him. He gutted it with a slash of his knife, though not before its beak had slashed open an arm and its talons had sunk deep into his chest.

He had thought he could not hurt more than he had. He was wrong.

After defeathering the bird, he butchered it and ate part of it. Then he spent the rest of the day and all of the night on the ledge. At least the night air was warm.

Twelve days later, he got to the top of the chasm. He had eaten on the way, though not much. Despite the regenerative powers of his body, it still had many abrasions and bruises. But these had been acquired recently.

He pulled himself over the edge after he had looked to make sure that nothing dangerous was there. Then he lay on his side, panting. After several minutes, he rose.

It was as if the vessel had appeared out of the air, and perhaps it had. It was a silvery and shiny craft, a cylinder with a cone at each end. Under the transparent canopy at the end nearest Kickaha was a cockpit that ran half of the length of the cylinder. From two sides of the craft, four struts extended to the ground to stabilize the vessel while it was on the ground.

The airboat landed, and the forepart of the canopy rose. The man sitting in the front seat climbed out and strode toward Kickaha, who by then had risen shakily to his feet.

The pilot was tall and muscular; his face was handsome; his flowing hair was shoulder-length and red-bronze. He was clad in a black-and-white-striped robe that came down to his calves. A belt set with many jewels held a holster. It was empty because the beamer it had held was in the man's hand.

The man smiled broadly, exposing very white teeth.

He spoke in Thoan. "Kickaha! You are truly a remarkable man to have survived! I respect you greatly, so much that I could almost just salute you and let you go on your way! However . . ."

"You're full of howevers, Red Orc," Kickaha said. "Not to mention other things."

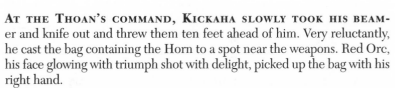

8

AT THE THOAN'S COMMAND, KICKAHA SLOWLY TOOK HIS BEAM-
er and knife out and threw them ten feet ahead of him. Very reluctantly,
he cast the bag containing the Horn to a spot near the weapons. Red Orc,
his face glowing with triumph shot with delight, picked up the bag with his
right hand.

He gestured with his weapon. "Turn your back to me, reach for the sky,
and get down on your knees. Stay in that position until I tell you otherwise."

Kickaha obeyed, but he was considering what his chances were if he
leaped up, ran to the chasm's edge, and jumped. He might go out far
enough to avoid the projecting parts of the side of the chasm and fall into
the river. But would he survive the plunge into the water? Would the
Thoan be able to shoot him before he got to the chasm's edge?

The answer to the first was no; to the second, yes. Anyway, he was
crazy even to think of such a plan. But it might be better to die thus than
to get what Red Orc could have in mind for him.

He never heard the man's footsteps. He did hear a slight hissing and
feel something against his back. When he awoke, he was in the back seat
of the vessel. A long sticky cord bound him around and around and secured
him to the seat of the chair and its back. His wrists were tied together, and
his feet were also bound. His head ached; his mouth was very dry. When
he looked through the canopy, he saw that the boat was at least a thousand
feet in the air and was heading northward.

Red Orc, seated before the control panel, was looking at the TV screen
to one side and above him. He could see Kickaha in it. He rose, having set
the vessel on automatic, and walked back in the narrow aisle between two
rows of seats.

The Thoan stood about four feet from his captive. "You've always gotten away before this," he said. "But you've come to the end of the road."

Kickaha spoke huskily. "I'm still living."

"And you may live for quite a while. But you'll be wishing that you were dead. Perhaps. I really haven't decided what I'm going to do with you."

Kickaha glanced through the canopy and saw the chasm he had climbed or, perhaps, another chasm. At this point, it was at least forty miles wide and went down so far that he could not see the dark bottom. He did not think that erosion had caused this. There must have been one hell of a cataclysm at one time on this planet.

Apparently, Red Orc guessed what he was thinking. He said, "This is the planet Wanzord, created by Appyrmazul. My father, Los, and I fought each other here. Los had a weapon of terrifying destructive powers. I don't know where he got it. Probably he found it buried in some ancient vault. He used it on me and my forces, and I was forced to gate out, leaving my men behind me. That chasm was caused by Los's weapon."

"What happened to it?" Kickaha said. His voice rasped.

"My father won that campaign. Eventually, during an attack on his army, I got hold of the ravener, as it was called. But I had to destroy that ancient weapon. Luck went against me, I was forced to retreat, and I didn't want my father to have it. So, I blew it up.

"However, as you may have heard, the final victory was mine. I captured my father. After I'd tortured him almost enough to satisfy me, I killed him. A long time before that, I had cut off his testicles and eaten them, after I stopped him when he was trying to kill my mother. I should have slain him then. When his testicles regrew, he launched an all-out war against me.

"But in the end, I won, and I burned his body and mixed the ashes in a glass of wine and drank him down. That was not quite the end of him. The next day, I flushed him down the toilet."

Red Orc laughed maniacally. And maniac he is, Kickaha thought. But he's quite rational and logical in most matters. Very cunning, too.

"That's interesting and informative," Kickaha said. "But what about Anana, Clifton, and Eleth?"

Red Orc smiled as if he was pleased by what he was going to tell his prisoner.

"While you were struggling to get out of the chasm, I was looking for the others. Eleth's body was left on a large rock when the flood subsided. The face was torn off, and one side of her head was caved in and the scalp ripped from it. But enough of her blond hair was left to identify her. Thus ended the last of the iron-hearted daughters of Urizen. No one will mourn them.

"Clifton is probably buried under tons of silt and gravel. End of his story. He was in the pit because he was caught in one of my resonant-circuit traps and directed to the same terminal, the pit, to which you and your party were channeled. That pit and the circuit in which Clifton was caught were made by Ololothon long ago. But I took over ownership. In fact, he arranged it as a sort of catch-as-catch-can for any Lord who came along. But it got the Englishman for me. I had almost forgotten about him after I last saw him in Urthona's floating palace on the Lavalite World. Urthona got away from there with you two. What happened to him?"

"Urthona was killed just after we escaped from the palace and gated through to the World of Tiers. He got caught in his own trap, you might say. Cheated me out of killing him."

Red Orc raised his brows and said, softly, "Ah! One more of the very old Lords is dead. I am unhappy about that, but only because I wanted to be the one who killed him. Since he was my father's ally, I had him down in my books."

Kickaha said, "What about Anana?"

A ghost of a smile hovered over the Thoan's lips. He knew that Kickaha knew that he was delaying his account of her to torment him.

"Anana? Yes, Anana?"

Kickaha leaned forward, preparing himself for very bad news. But Red Orc said, "I had expected Ona to be caught in the pit, too, but I assume that something happened to her while she was with you. Or did she escape from you to wander around on Alofmethbin?"

"She died trying to escape. What about Anana?"

"You must be wondering just how you were trapped. Only I could have done it. The many obstacles and the little time to get the necessary things would have been too much for anyone else. Fortunately, the circuit in which you two were caught, originally set up by Ololothon, had a three-day delay holding you in one gate before you were sent forward again. That gave me the time I needed to bring in the necessary equipment in an air-boat through a gate from my base. You have heard of Ololothon?"

"For Christ's sake!" Kickaha said in English. Then, speaking in Thoan, "You are going to drag out the suspense, aren't you? Although you've lived so long, you're juvenile as hell!"

"I am not above taking pleasure in small things," Red Orc said. "If you are almost immortal, you find that there are long intervals between pleasures, and these are short-lived. So, even the smallest pleasures are welcome, especially when they are unexpected."

He paused, meeting Kickaha's glare with his unwavering gaze.

Then he said, "Ololothon?"

"We were on his world, the planet of the Tripeds," Kickaha said. "You know that."

"I know it now," the Thoan said. "Before you told me, I had only suspected that you were there. But I could not be sure. What I was sure about was that if you took the only exit gate on Ololothon's world, you would be caught in the resonant circuit he set up. Long, long ago, after I invaded his palace and slew him, I studied the charts of his gates and recorded them to file in my bases. I might need to use them someday. And I was right: I did. Very few Lords, perhaps none, have such foresight."

Brag, brag, brag, Kickaha thought. However, he was interested in knowing just how the Thoan's plot had been carried out.

"Eleth and Ona were very clever. They managed to escape from my prison on my base while I was elsewhere. I suspected that they had bribed the guards, but I did not have time to torture the truth out of anyone. I killed all of them. However, the corruption might have spread throughout my palace. So, I completely depopulated it. I did not slay their children, of course. I made sure that they were adopted by a native tribe."

Just like that, Kickaha thought. Torture and murder, and then he compliments himself for his mercy.

"It took me some time to track the sisters down to this planet and then locate them. I found them wandering half-starved and totally miserable in the forest where you came across them. Instead of immediately punishing them as I had promised, I decided to use them against you and Anana. They were in such terror, wondering if they would be released without harm, as I had promised they would be if they cooperated. Or would I break my word? I also arranged for a raven, an Eye of the Lord, and an oromoth to work with them, to keep a watch on you and Anana when you showed up and also to make sure the sisters did not betray me. The Eye and the oromoth would get a suitable reward, but I promised them they would die if they tried treachery. I—"

"Anana and I know about that," Kickaha said. "We killed both of them."

Red Orc's face crimsoned. Glaring, he shouted, "Do not speak unless I give you permission!"

When he had regained his composure, he said, "I was faced with a problem. You had the Horn, or at least I assumed you still had it. The Horn changed normal conditions for those in a circuit. With it, you might escape even if caught in one. And then the alarms I had set up in the circuit sounded through the series of gates and registered in my base. I knew then that you and Anana had entered the gate from the planet of the Tripeds.

"The gate-circuit chart I inherited from Ololothon after I killed him so many years ago showed that one of the brief stops would be on Alofmethbin. But it would be for only a few seconds. I gambled that you would recognize Alofmethbin and would run out of the area of influence of the gate before it could send you on. Or that you would be sounding the Horn at that time and that would nullify the action of the gate. And I was right, of course. I would have preferred that you be much closer to the sisters when you exited, but I had to work with what was available. Nor did I know, of course, whether or not there was a flaw near the gate.

"For this reason, I could not erect a cage there to imprison you and Anana when you entered. You would only have to blow your Horn and you would escape through the flaw, if there was one. The probability that there would be was about fifty-fifty."

Kickaha opened his mouth to ask a question, thought better of it, and closed his lips.

"I knew you would head in a straight line for the nearest gate, the one in the boulder. My usual good fortune held because I knew about the gate. Ololothon was on this planet several times when Wolff was its Lord, found four gates, and charted them. He connected the gate in the boulder to the pit."

Kickaha cleared his throat, then said, "Permission to speak?"

Red Orc waved his hand.

"What happened to Anana?"

"I have a story to tell!" the Thoan said harshly. "It will enlighten you so that you will know whom you are up against! Now, be silent! Ololothon must have dug that pit shortly after the chasm was made by my father's engine of destruction during my campaign against him on Wanzord. I found the pit a long time ago when I went briefly to the planet Wanzord. I like to prowl around universes and gather data that I may use later. You never know when it will be useful. Then, when you two disappeared from the circuit for a few hours, a delay that came too soon for you to be on the islet . . ."

He paused, then said, "You used the Horn to escape the circuit before you got to the islet, of course. But you got caught in it again?"

Kickaha nodded. Though he did not see how the Thoan could use knowledge of the scaly man's existence to his own advantage, it was best to keep him ignorant. Never give anything away; you might regret it.

"Few things make me anxious," the Thoan said, "but I am not above admitting that your disappearance gave me a bad time. But I went ahead with my plan. However, there might be a flaw in the walls of the pit. It was not likely there was, but I could not take the chance. One blast from the Horn and you might escape through that. So, I placed a generator near the pit—you could not see it from the bottom of the pit—and set it to form a one-way gate completely around the pit and just below the surface of the rock wall. As long as that one-way gate shield was there, even the Horn could not open a flaw."

Red Orc paused.

"Permission?" Kickaha croaked. His throat and mouth were very dry, but he'd be damned if he'd ask the Thoan for a glass of water.

"Go ahead."

"Why didn't you just wait for night, while we were on the plains or in the forest, then swoop in in your aircraft and capture us?"

"Because I take no chances unless I am forced to do so. You might have had enough time to use the Horn and escape through a flaw. Once you were in the pit, you could not escape. Your Horn could not get you out of it."

"But you overlooked the flash floods," Kickaha said.

The Thoan's face became red again. He shouted, "I had not been on the planet long enough to know that there were floods caused by rainstorms! That planet is very dry! I never saw a cloud while I was there!"

Kickaha said nothing. He did not want to goad the Thoan into doing something painful, such as burning his eye out with a beamer ray. Or God knew what else.

"So!" Red Orc said. "I got a bonus! That Englishman, Clifton, apparently escaped from the floating palace of Urthona in the Lavalite World. But he fell at last into one of my traps in another world, and I shuttled him into the pit! All my most elusive enemies—except for Wolff and Chryseis—were collected like fish in a net!"

"Wolff? Chryseis?" Kickaha murmured.

"Wolff and Chryseis!" Red Orc howled. His voice was so loud in the narrow area of the boat that Kickaha was startled again.

The Thoan yelled, "They escaped! They escaped! I should have dealt with them as soon as I caught them!"

"You don't know where they are?" Kickaha said softly.

"Somewhere on Earth!" the Thoan said, waving one hand violently. "Or perhaps they managed to gate through to another world! It does not matter! I will catch them again! When I do . . . !"

He stopped, took a deep breath, and then smiled. "You can quit being so happy about them! I did find Anana!"

Kickaha knew that Red Orc wanted him to ask about her. But he gritted his teeth and clamped his lips. The Thoan was going to tell him anyway.

"Anana's body, what was left of it, was sticking out from under a small boulder! I left her for the scavengers!"

Kickaha shut his eyes while a tremor passed over him, and his chest seemed to have been pierced by a spear. But the Lord could be lying.

When he felt recovered enough to speak in a steady voice, he said, "Did you bring back her head to show me?"

"No!"

"Did you photograph her body? Not that I'd believe a photo."

"Why should I do either?"

"You're lying!"

"You will never know, will you?"

Kickaha did not reply. After waiting for a few moments for his captive to say something, the Thoan returned to the pilot's seat.

Kickaha looked out through the canopy again. Though he saw no more vast chasms, he did see a world the surface of which had been swept clear of soil and vegetation. Yet new growth had managed to get a roothold here and there. Some species of birds, as he well knew, had survived, and he supposed that some animals had escaped the apocalyptic raging. Perhaps somewhere were small bands of humans. They must not be eating well, though.

He became more angry than usual at the arrogance and scorn for life of the Lords. They would destroy an entire world and think little of doing it.

It was a miracle that Anana was not like her own kind.

In ten minutes, the vessel began to slow, then hovered in the air for a few seconds before sinking swiftly. It landed by a corrugated monolith of stone that bent halfway up in a thirty-degree angle from the horizontal. At its base was an enormous reddish boulder roughly shaped like a bear's head. The Thoan squeezed several drops of a blue liquid from a container onto a small part of the sticky rope. A moment later, the rope became smooth and was easily loosened by Kickaha's efforts. But the bonds tying his hands before him were still sticky.

He was shepherded out of the vessel. After the Thoan had commanded the craft to close the canopy, he guided Kickaha toward the boulder. Then he spoke a code word, and part of the side of the boulder shimmered with bands of red and violet. Looking steadily at it hurt Kickaha's eyes.

"Go ahead," Red Orc said.

Kickaha entered the gate into a small chamber in the rock. The next second, he was in a large windowless room made of greenish marble and furnished with carpets, drapes, chairs, divans, and statuary. A few seconds later, part of the seemingly solid wall opened and Red Orc stepped inside the room.

He motioned with the beamer. "Sit in that chair there."

After his captive had obeyed, Red Orc sat down in a chair facing Kickaha's. He smiled, leaned back, and stretched out his legs.

"Here we are in one of my hideaways on Earth Two."

"And?"

"Are you hungry? You may eat and drink while I'm discussing a certain matter with you."

Kickaha knew he would be foolish to refuse just because his enemy offered it. He needed the energy to get free, if he was going to do that, and he had no doubt that he would. "When," not "if," was the way it was going to be.

He said, "Yes."

Orc must have given some sort of signal, or he had assumed that his captive would not refuse a meal. A door-sized section of the wall opened. A woman pushed in a cart on which were goblets, covered dishes, and cutlery. She was a black-haired, brown-eyed, and dark-skinned beauty. She wore only some sort of silvery and shimmering hip band from the front of which hung a foot-long fan-shaped band of the same material. A peacock feather was inserted into her hair. She stopped the cart by a table, bowed to Red Orc, transferred the food and drink to the table, and pushed the cart out of the room, her narrow hips swaying. The section swung shut.

"You may not only have the best food and drink this planet offers, but her, too," the Thoan said. "And others equally as beautiful and skilled in the bodily arts. If, that is, you accept my proposal."

Kickaha arched his eyebrows. Proposal? Then Red Orc must need his help in some project. Since he was not the man to draw back from danger, he had something near-suicidal in mind.

Afterward? If there was an afterward?

Kickaha held up his bound wrists and pointed a finger at the table. Red Orc told him to raise his arms high and to hold them as far apart as he could. Kickaha did so. There was approximately an inch between his wrists.

"Hold steady," the Thoan said, and he drew his beamer so swiftly his arm seemed to be a blur. A yellow ray lanced out; the bond was cut in half; the beamer was holstered. It was done within two eyeblinks.

Very impressive, Kickaha thought. But he was not going to tell Red Orc that. And what kind of beamer projected a yellow ray?

"I'll be back when you've finished eating," the Thoan said. "If you wish to wash first or need a toilet, utter the word 'kentfass,' and a bathroom will extrude from the wall. To make it go back into the wall, say the same word."

A curious arrangement, Kickaha thought. But Red Orc had a curious mind.

The Thoan left the room. Though Kickaha did not have much appetite, he found that the food, which consisted of various vegetables, fruits, and different kinds of fish, was delicious. The wine was too heavy for his palate, but it did have an inviting don't-know-what taste and went down easily. Afterward, he used the bathroom, which was decorated with murals of undersea life. It slid into the wall, and the wall section swung shut. Some of these sections must conceal gates.

A few minutes later, the Thoan entered. Now he wore a longer robe and sandals. With him were three dark men wearing conical helmets topped by peacock feathers, short kilts, and buskins. All were armed with spears, swords, and knives. They took positions behind Red Orc, who had drawn up a chair shaped like a spider and sat down in it facing his captive. He was unarmed.

"You must be very puzzled," he said. "You're asking yourself why I, a Lord, require the assistance of a *leblabbiy*?"

"Because you've got something to do that's too big for you to handle by yourself," Kickaha said.

Red Orc smiled. He said, "I suppose you're wondering what your reward will be if you succeed in carrying out my desires. You also doubt that I'd keep my word to reward you."

"You have an astounding ability to read my mind."

"Sarcasm has no place here. I have never broken my word."

"Did you ever give your word?"

"Several times. And I honored it, though my natural inclination is to break it. But there have been situations . . ."

He was silent for a few seconds. Then he said, "Have you heard about Zazel of the Caverned World?"

"Yes," Kickaha said. "Anana . . ."

He choked. Even speaking her name summoned up grief like a thick glutinous wave and burned his heart.

After clearing his throat, he said, "Anana told me something about him. He created a universe that was a ball of stone in which were many tunnels and caves. Which, in my opinion, only a nut would do. According to her, Zazel was a melancholy and gloomy man, and he eventually killed himself."

"Many Lords have committed suicide," Red Orc said. "They are the weaklings. The strong kill each other."

"Not fast enough for me. What does he have to do with us?"

"When I was a youth, I mightily offended my father. Instead of killing me, he gated me through to a world unfamiliar to me and very dangerous. It was called Anthema, the Unwanted World. I wandered around on it, and then I met another Lord, Ijim of the Dark Woods. He had gated through to Anthema while being pursued by a Lord whose world he had tried to invade. For forty-four years he had tried to find a gate through which he could travel to another universe."

The Thoan paused. He looked as if he were recalling his hard times on that planet.

He spoke again. "His long solitude had made him paranoiac. But we teamed up, though of course each of us was planning to kill the other if we escaped that very undesirable world. We did finally find a gate, but it had been placed by Los inside a structure built by some fierce predators. Nevertheless, we got inside, found the gate, and jumped through it. It was a shearing gate. That is, Los had set it up so that we had to calculate the few seconds when it was safe to enter. Otherwise, we would be cut in half.

"Ijim was halved like an apple, and I lost some skin and a slice of flesh on the end of my heels and on my buttocks. After wandering through tunnels, I came to a very large cavern. There I met Dingsteth, a creature made by Zazel to be his overseer, or manager. After Zazel committed suicide, Dingsteth was the only sentient being in that vast ball of stone perforated with tunnels and large caverns.

"Dingsteth was very naive. It did not kill me at once as it should have done. It wasn't loneliness, a desire for companionship, that stopped it. It did not know what loneliness was. At least, I think it does not suffer from that emotion. There were certain signs . . ."

Red Orc again became silent. He looked past Kickaha as if he were viewing a screen displaying images of the Caverned World. Then he spoke.

"I found out from Dingsteth that the whole stone world was a computer, semi-protein and semi-silicon. It held enormous amounts of data put there by Zazel. Much of that data has been lost to the rest of us Lords."

The Thoan paused, licked his lips, and said, "So far, only I have entered Zazel's World. Only I know of the priceless data-treasures contained in it. Only I know about the gate that gives access to it. Only I know about certain data that would give me complete power over the Lords and their universes."

"Which is?" Kickaha said.

Red Orc laughed loudly. Then he said, "You are not only a trickster, you are a jester. It's not necessary that you know what I am specifically looking for, and you know that. I know that, if you should somehow get into Zazel's World, you will make a desperate effort to find out what I so greatly desire. I won't tell you because I won't take the slightest chance that knowledge of it should ever get to other Lords. And I certainly would not trust you with that knowledge."

"How can I tell anybody else about something I'm ignorant of?" Kickaha said.

"You can't. But some Lords might be able to guess what it is."

This reasoning did not seem entirely logical to Kickaha. But he could not expect the Thoan to be completely rational. Hatred and a passion for power had driven Red Orc insane. Or vice versa.

Nor did he expect Red Orc to keep any promise or give any lasting reward. The Thoan knew that Kickaha would not give up revenge for Anana's death. Even if Anana had somehow survived, she had come near death because of Red Orc. That was unforgivable.

He said, "What do you need me for?"

"We know that I am using you as a pawn whom I will sacrifice if the oc-

casion demands it. However, I swear by Shambarimen, Elyttria, and Manathu Vorcyon that if you succeed, you will be set free, and—"

"Anana, too, if she didn't die?"

Irritation at the interruption flitted across Red Orc's face. But he spoke
evenly.

"Anana, too."

Kickaha asked the Thoan what he wanted him to do.

"Get into Zazel's World. When you've done that, you can communicate
with me, and I'll come swiftly."

Kickaha bit a corner of his lip. "Why can't you do it yourself?"

Red Orc smiled and said, "You know why. It'll be a dangerous project,
and your chances of surviving are small. But if you die, I'll know what
killed you and avoid it. I can do that because I have the Horn. Besides, I'd
like to determine if you are the greatest of Tricksters, which some Lords
claim you are. My experience with you has impressed me even though
you are a *leblabbiy.*"

"You enjoy deadly games?"

"Yes. So do you."

"You did catch me," Kickaha said. "Several times."

"And up until now, you slipped away from me. When we were chasing
you through the city of Los Angeles, I was playing with you. My hired
criminals were not very bright, and luck favored you. And then I was
caught in the Lavalite World and came too close to being trapped there forever. I suspect you were responsible."

Kickaha did not confirm that. Let him guess.

"In any event," Red Orc said, "I will no longer be playing cat-and-
mouse with you."

"I will try to do what you want me to do, and I won't attempt to escape,"
Kickaha said. Probably Red Orc did not believe him any more than Kickaha believed Red Orc. But Red Orc described in detail how he had gotten
into and out of the Caverned World.

Los, Red Orc's father, had gated his son from the family world to a cave
on Anthema. Red Orc still did not know exactly where the Antheman gate
was. But Los could have had more than one on that planet.

He and Ijim had found the gate from Anthema to Zazel's World because his father had provided his son with a map. But that had been cryp-
tic and very difficult to figure out, and he might never have been able to
read it.

"I was able to leave the Caverned World because Dingsteth showed me
the gate out," Red Orc said. "However, it allowed exit but not entrance.
The same was true for the gate by which I got from Anthema to Zazel's
World. You will have to find a gate that is at present unknown. Or, if you

can find it, use the gate Ijim and I used. I've been trying so long to find it again, and I've been so obsessed with it that I'm going around in a circle. I need someone to search for it whose view is fresh. Someone who's also ingenious, or at least has the reputation for being so. Thus, I'm asking you to volunteer for the venture."

"Give me the Horn," Kickaha said. "That can open any gate, and it reveals weak places in walls among the universes."

"You can't stop joking, can you?"

Kickaha said, "No. Very well. I must know more about these gates and the worlds in which they're located. And other items, too."

After an hour, Red Orc left the room, though the evil that Kickaha imagined as emanating from him still hung in the air. What the Thoan required was clear. His secret motives were not. For one thing, Red Orc had been in Zazel's World when he was eighteen years old. That was at least twenty thousand Terrestrial years ago. What had he been doing in the meantime? Why hadn't he stormed the fort, so to speak, and invaded the Caverned World to get the data he wanted? Or had he tried again and again and always failed? If the Thoan had tried many times to do that, then he was indeed desperate. It would be almost impossible to succeed where the Thoan had failed, yet he was turning over the job to a despised *leblabbiy.*

Almost impossible. But Kickaha was convinced that as long as something was one-thousandth of one-thousandth of one-half percent possible, he could do it. Though he sometimes laughed at his own egotism, he believed that he was capable of everything but the impossible, and he was not so sure that he could not defeat those odds, too.

During the next three days, Kickaha did not see his captor. He exercised as vigorously as possible in this large room, which was not large enough, ate well, and mostly chafed and fumed and sometimes cursed. The beautiful servant made it evident through signs that she would bed him if he so desired. He refused her. Not until he was certain that Anana was dead could he even consider another woman.

He indulged in fantasy scenes about how Anana could have lived through the flash flood. And Red Orc, searching in his aircraft up and down the chasm, might have missed her because she was in a cave or under a ledge, or because he just did not see her even if she was in the open.

After a while, he quit imagining these scenarios. He would just have to wait and see.

The afternoon of the third day, Red Orc entered the chamber. His beamer was in his holster, and a sheath hanging from his belt carried a long dagger. In his right hand was a large bag. Behind him came five armed bodyguards, one of them a bowman. He did not greet his captive but said,

"Come with me." The men grouped around him. Kickaha was conducted from the room and through a series of exotically decorated halls, all empty of natives. Then he was taken into a vast room blazing with the light of a thousand torches. The ceiling was six or seven stories high. Its gold-plated walls bore many figures of animals and human beings, all outlined in jewels. It had no furniture. At the far end was a gigantic bronze statue of a man with an enormous upright phallus, four arms, and a demon's face. Twenty feet before it was an altar with a block of stone at its base. The block was stained with old blood. A stone platform half its height surrounded it, and stone steps led up to it.

"Am I to be sacrificed?" Kickaha said, grinning.

The Thoan's smile seemed to be carved from granite.

"Not as part of a religious rite."

He spoke in the mellifluous native tongue, and the guards marched out through the main door. One of them shut the door and slammed a huge bolt shut. The bang sounded to Kickaha like a note of doom. But he had met many dooms and defeated them.

Red Orc said, "Go to the block, walk up the steps, and stand by the block."

When Kickaha turned around to face the Thoan, his back almost touching the stone, which still was higher than his head, he saw Red Orc swinging the bag backward. Then the bag soared up and landed with a thump near Kickaha's feet.

"Empty the bag," the Thoan said loudly. His words echoed.

Kickaha removed a beamer, a bundle of batteries, a long knife, a canteen full of water, and a smaller bag. He dumped its contents: a bundle of clothes, a belt holding a holster and a sheath, a pair of shoes, a smaller knife, and a box of compressed rations.

"There is no battery in the beamer," Red Orc said. "After you reach your next destination, you can put the battery in it."

"And after you're out of knife range," Kickaha said. "You're taking no chances."

"I'm not as reckless as you, *leblabbiy*. You have your instructions and as much useful information as I am able to give you. Rebag those items, them climb up on the top of the stone."

When Kickaha was standing up on the top of the block, he looked at the Thoan. He was smiling as if he was deeply enjoying the procedure. He called, "I would really prefer to keep you prisoner, work my pleasure on you, and eventually drink your ashes down as I did my father's. But I am pragmatic. I give you sixty days to complete your mission, and—"

"Sixty days?" Kickaha bellowed. "Sixty days to do what you couldn't do in ten thousand years!"

"That's the way it's going to be! By the way, Trickster! Here's an additional incentive for you to return to me! Your traitor bitch, Anana, is in the room next to the one you occupied!"

He paused, then shouted, "Or am I lying?"

Kickaha felt as if a giant icicle had slammed through him. Before he could unfreeze, he heard Red Orc scream out a code word.

The hard stone beneath his feet became air, and he dropped straight down.

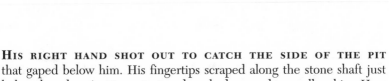

9

His right hand shot out to catch the side of the pit that gaped below him. His fingertips scraped along the stone shaft just below the edge. A gate, not a trapdoor, had opened to swallow him. How typical of Red Orc not to warn him that he was going to fall!

Holding the bag in his left hand close to his side, he struggled to maintain his vertical attitude. The light that had come through the gate was cut off. Total darkness was around him as he pierced the air. The shaft down which he hurtled must have narrowed by now. Its circular wall seemed to be an inch away from his body. Then he became aware that it was twisting. The soapy texture of the stone kept the skin of his back from burning— so far.

By then, he had begun counting seconds. Twenty of them passed. He had dropped perhaps five seconds before starting to time his descent. Four more passed before the shaft began curving gently and then became horizontal. The darkness was tinged with a dusklike light. It quickly became brighter.

Oh-oh, he thought. Here it comes!

He cannonballed from the hole. Above him was a wall of stone lit by a strong light. He began twisting around so that he could land on his feet. As he did so, he saw that he was in a chamber of stone about twenty feet wide and thirty feet high. What he had thought was a wall was a ceiling. Below him was a pool of water, and he was about to strike it. Though he tried to go in feet first, he crashed on his side with enough force to plunge him to the bottom. He struggled upright despite his half-daze and shoved upward toward the light. With the bag still in his hand, he swam to the side of the pool. It was only several inches above the water, and thus it was easy to drag himself onto the rock floor.

"Damn!" he said loudly.

His voice came back hollowly. After sitting up to catch his breath and to look around, he stood up. The light was sourceless—nothing new to him. It showed three tunnel openings in the walls. Kickaha undid the string on the bag and removed most of its contents. Though he was wet, he donned the snug jockey shorts and long-sleeved shirt. After drying his feet with the short kilt, he put that on and then the socks and the shoes. These were much like tennis shoes. It did not take him long to fasten the belt around his waist, sheath the beamer and knife, and attach the bag to the belt.

"It's been fun, so far."

Not much fun was his uncertainty about Anana's fate. The demon son of a bitch Thoan had given him a brief joy when he had said that Anana was still living. Then he had blown out the joy as if it were a candle when he said that he might be lying. That, of course, was said to bedevil Kickaha throughout his mission.

Red Orc was left-handed. Was that a clue that the left tunnel was the right one to take? Or were they all the right ones? It would be like Red Orc to do that.

He entered the tunnel on his left. It was filled with the same source-less and shadowless light as the room, though the illumination was no stronger than twilight. He walked slowly, wary of any signs of traps, although it seemed to him that Red Orc would have deactivated these. He would not want to stop the mission just after it had begun. Not even Red Orc was that crazy.

After an estimated fifteen minutes, the tunnel turned to the left and then, after ten minutes, to the right. Soon it straightened out. Presently, he came to a brightly lit chamber. He laughed.

Just as he had anticipated, three tunnels opened into it and only one tunnel led from it. Red Orc had set it up so that the person who had to choose one of three in the room of the pool would torment himself with anxiety. That Red Orc had not given him instructions on choosing the correct tunnels meant that the Thoan was not going to make it too easy for him.

The stone wall seemed to be unbroken, but some part of it could hold a disguised TV receiver. The Thoan might be watching him now. If he were, he would be grinning.

Kickaha gave the invisible watcher the finger.

He walked more swiftly than before down the single tunnel. It, too, was filled with a dusky light. After about a mile, the light began to get brighter. Within forty or so steps, he was in a straight tunnel. Bright daylight was at its end. When he stepped out of its mouth, he was on a ledge on the side of a mountain. It towered straight up, its surface smooth, and below the ledge it was just as straight and smooth. If he cared to jump into the river at the foot of the mountain, he would fall an estimated thousand feet. A wind blew cold up the face of the mountain.

Where was the gate?

Some seconds later, he felt warm air on his back. He turned to see a shimmering area ten feet within the tunnel. Beyond it were the vague shapes of chairs and tables.

"Play your little game, Red Orc," Kickaha murmured.

He started to walk toward the shimmering but stopped after a few steps. Another shimmering wall had appeared in front of the first and blanked it out.

This was the first time he had ever experienced that.

"Now what?"

Through this gate, he could dimly see what looked like the trunk of a tree at one side beyond the wavering curtain. He could make out nothing other than that. He shrugged and, beamer in hand, leaped through the gate. He landed in a crouch and looked around him. When he saw nothing threatening, he straightened up.

Trees twice the size of sequoias were around him. A red-and-green-striped plant, something like Spanish moss, hung from the branches of many trees. Now and then, a tendril twitched. The ground was covered with a soft, thick, pale-yellow moss. Large bushes bearing reddish berries grew here and there. The forest rang with many types of melodious bird-calls. Around him was a soft dappled light and a cool air, which made him quite comfortable.

He waited for a while for someone to appear. When they did not, he walked on into the forest, not knowing or caring if he was going deeper into it or approaching its edge. Since he lacked directions from Red Orc, he would do what seemed best to him or go wherever his whim led him.

He was thinking about the puzzling appearance of the second gate in the tunnel when a man stepped out from behind a giant tree. Kickaha stopped, but not one to be caught easily from behind, glanced to his rear, too. No one was there. The man was as tall as he, had long straight black hair done in a Psyche knot, wore no clothes, and was barefoot. The crimson feather of a large bird stuck out of his hair, and his cheeks were painted with slanting parallel bars: green, white, and black. A long blue band that fell halfway to his knees was tied around his penis. He was unarmed and was holding up his hand, palm outward, in a peace gesture.

Kickaha advanced toward the man, who smiled. The high cheekbones, the snub nose, and the epicanthic folds were definitely Mongolian. But the eyes were hazel.

The stranger called out in a Thoan that differed from the standard speech but was understandable. "Greetings, Kickaha!"

"Greetings, friend!" Kickaha said. But he was on guard again. How in hell could this man have known his name?

"I am Lingwallan," the man said. "You won't need that weapon, but you may keep it if you prefer to. Please follow me." He turned and started to walk in the same direction Kickaha had been going.

Kickaha, after catching up with him, said, "What is this world? Just where on it are we? Where are we going? Who sent you?"

"If you'll be patient, you'll soon have the answers to your questions."

Kickaha saw no reason to balk. If the man was leading him into an ambush, he had an unconventional way of doing it. But it was effective. His "guest" was too curious to reject the invitation. Besides, he had a hunch that he was in no danger. Not that his hunches had always been right.

During the several-miles-long hike, Kickaha broke the silence once. "Do you know of Red Orc?"

Lingwallan said, "No."

They passed a band of some deerlike animals feeding on the mossy stuff. They raised their heads to look once, then resumed grazing. After a while, the two men passed near a young man and young woman, both nude. These sat with their backs against the trunk of a tree. Between the woman's navel and pubes was a triangle painted in green. The man sported a long orange ribbon tied around his penis. He was playing a primitive kind of flute; she was blowing on a curved wooden instrument that had a much deeper tone. Whatever tune the two were playing, it was a merry one. It also must have been erotic, if the male's erection was an indicator.

Kickaha put the beamer into the holster. Presently they heard the loud and shrill voices and the laughter of children playing. A moment later, they stepped into a very broad clearing in the center of which was a tree three times as large as a sequoia and swarming with birds and scarlet-faced monkeys. Round houses with cone-shaped roofs made from the branches and leaves of a palmlike plant formed nine concentric circles around the tree. Kickaha looked for the gardens usually found on Earth among preliterate tribes but saw none.

There were also none of the swarming and stinging insects that infested such Terrestrial hamlets.

When he and Lingwallan had stepped out of the forest into the light cast by a sun that had passed beyond the treetops, a silence fell over the place. It lasted only several seconds. Then the children and the adults surged forward, surrounding the two. Many reached out to touch Kickaha. He endured it because they obviously were not hostile.

His guide conducted him through an aisle formed by the wider separation of houses. When they got to the inner circle, the crowd stopped, though its chatter did not. Before then, Kickaha had seen the windows cut into the trunk of the Brobdingnagian tree and the large arched entrances at its base. Except for the arch directly in front of him, all the apertures were crowded with brown faces.

In the arch stood a giantess wearing only a necklace that flashed on and off and a green hipband. A huge red flower was in the hair on one side of her head. She held a long wooden staff on which carved snakes seemed to crawl upward.

Though almost seven feet tall, her body would make any man's knees turn to jelly. Her face would bring him to his knees. Kickaha felt a warmth in his loins. She seemed to radiate almost visible rays. No man, no matter how insensitive and excited, would dare to try to board her without her permission. Truly, she not only looked like a goddess, she was surrounded by a goddess's invisible aura.

Her leaf-green eyes were bright in the golden-skinned face. Their color is just like mine, Kickaha thought, though my handsomeness is not in the same league as her beauty.

Lingwallan ran ahead of Kickaha and sank to one knee at her feet. She said something, and he rose and ran back to Kickaha.

"Manathu Vorcyon bids you to come to her. She says that she does not expect you to bow to her."

"Manathu Vorcyon!" Kickaha murmured. "I should have known."

Almost all of the Lords he had encountered he considered to be deeply evil. They were really only human beings, as he well knew, despite their insistence that they were a superior breed to Homo sapiens in kind and in degree. They cruelly exploited their human subjects, the *leblabbiys*.

But Manathu Vorcyon, according to the tales he had heard, was an exception. When she had created this universe and peopled it with artificial human beings, she had devoted herself to being a kind and understanding ruler. The *leblabbiys* of her world were said to be the happiest of people anywhere in the thousands of universes. Kickaha had not believed this because all except two of the Lords he had met were intolerably arrogant and egotistic and as bloody-minded as Genghis Khan, Shaka, or Hitler.

Wolff and Anana were two Thoan who had become really "human." But both had been, at one time, as ruthless and murderous as their kin.

He walked up to Manathu Vorcyon. And then, despite his determination never to bow to any man or woman, he dropped to one knee. He could not help himself; he was overwhelmed with the feeling that she did shed the radiance of a goddess. Never mind that his brain knew that she was no more divinely born than he. His knee bent as if he had been conditioned to do so since childhood.

Now that he was closer to her, he saw that her necklace was made of living fireflylike insects tied together.

He started. Lingwallan's voice had sounded loudly behind him.

"Manathu Vorcyon! The Great Mother! Our Lady! The Grandmother of All! I present to you Kickaha!"

"Rise, Kickaha, the many-angled man, the man of countless wiles, the man who is never at a loss!" Manathu Vorcyon said. Her voice was so melodious and powerful that it rippled his skin with cold. "Enter this house as my guest."

There were many things to note when he entered the great room just behind the entrance. The tree, though still flourishing, had been cut into to make rooms and winding staircases. Following just behind Lingwallan, he climbed one of the staircases. The lighting was only from the sun, in the daytime anyway, but what devices transmitted it, Kickaha did not know. The furniture in the rooms he saw as he passed the doorless entrances was carved from the tree and was not removable. There were thick carpets and paintings and statuary and fountains in every room.

But he was too eager to know why he had been whisked here by Manathu Vorcyon to take time to inspect the artifacts. After being shown into his own room, he showered by standing in a waterfall that ran alongside the outer wall and disappeared down many small holes in the floor. When he stepped out, he was toweled dry by a young woman who could win any Miss America contest on Earth. After drying him off, she handed him a pair of sandals. Thus dressed, making him think that sandals were probably formal wear here, he went down a polished staircase. Lingwallan met him and conducted him into the feasting room. It was large but unfurnished except for a very thick carpet. The ruler of this world sat cross-legged on it with her guest and two large but very good-looking men and two large and beautiful women. Manathu Vorcyon introduced them and then said, "They are my bedmates."

All at one time? Kickaha thought.

She added, "They are also my lovers. There is, as you know or should know, a widely separated difference in meaning between bedmate and lover."

The food was brought by servants, including Lingwallan, who seemed to be a sort of head butler. The dishes held a variety of fruit and vegetables, some unfamiliar to Kickaha, and roasted pig, venison, and wild bird. The buttered bread was thickly coated with a jam that made his eyes roll and his body quiver with ecstasy.

The goblets were formed from some sort of seashell and held four different kinds of liquors. One contained water; one, a light and delicious wine; one, a watered-down whiskey; one, a liquor that he had never before tasted.

He ate and drank just enough to satisfy his belly, though he went easy on the meat so that he could have another slice of bread with jam. Manathu Vorcyon nodded approvingly at his restraint. The truth was that he would have liked to get a big buzz on, not stuff himself. But this was not the time or place for that.

What would be appropriate, he thought, would be to stop the small talk and get answers to his questions. The Great Mother seemed to be in no hurry, which could be expected from a woman who had lived more than thirty thousand years.

After dinner, they went outside to watch a ceremony in honor of the guest. The dances were colorful and noisy, and the songs were full of references to myths and legends about which Kickaha knew nothing. Lingwallan, standing by his side, tried to explain what these were but gave up because he could not be heard above the din. Kickaha did not care about any of them. He wanted to get the inside information about his predicament from the one who should know, Our Lady, Manathu Vorcyon.

Tired and bored though somewhat agitated, he went to bed in his room. After an hour of sighing, yawning, and turning to both sides on the thickly padded blankets on the floor, he managed to get to sleep. But he was awakened by a vivid dream in which he saw Anana's face, looking very distressed, appear out of gray and menacing clouds.

The next morning, after he had showered and done all those things that are necessary but time-consuming, he went down the staircase and out of the tree to breakfast, served near the entrance. The giantess did not show up until after Lingwallan had conducted Kickaha through the hamlet and shown him all the sights and spoken of their history and meaning. Kickaha was disgusted. No matter what the universe, a guest had to go through a visiting fireman's tour.

However, he did learn what kind of Lord the giantess was. She was a benevolent despot. That is, she had determined what kind of environment the *leblabbiys* would live in and also what kind of society they would have. Jungles and forests and many rivers and lakes occupied most of the landmass. There were no deserts, though there were many low mountain ranges.

Through the dense vegetation wandered small families or somewhat larger tribes. Hunting, fishing, and food-gathering occupied a few hours a day. Agriculture was limited to small gardens. Their leisure time was spent in conversation (the *leblabbiys* were very gabby), raising the young, council meetings, arts, athletic contests, and copulation. The latter was sometimes a public game, which was why male winners wore penis-ribbons and female winners had painted deltas on their stomachs. Those sporting blue, green, and orange awards had won first, second, and third places in the very popular competition.

Women and men had equal rights. Instead of warring against other groups, the men and women engaged in intense and sometimes very rough athletic games with neighboring tribes.

If Kickaha was to believe Lingwallan, Manathu Vorcyon's subjects were as happy as human beings could be.

Kickaha, who had lived among many preliterate tribes, knew that the closeness and security of tribal life demanded a rigid conformity. A rebel threatened cultural unity and was usually treated harshly. If he did not submit after harsh censure and then the silent treatment, he was exiled or killed. The rebel usually preferred being slain. Being ousted from the tribe was unendurable to the members.

He asked Lingwallan about this.

"Our Lady has decreed that innovators in the arts and technology are not to be discouraged. But explosive powder and firearms will not be tolerated, nor will engines needing fuels be made. She says that things of iron, except as art objects, breed poisons in the land, air, and water. She has told us of what is happening to your native planet, Earth One."

He paused, shuddered, then said, "We do not want that, and if we did, She would not permit it."

"But there's no chance for overpopulation here," Kickaha said. "All Thoan maintain a limit on the number of births in every universe except those of Earth One and Two. For instance, Jadawin, once Lord of the World of Tiers, reduced the rate of births among his subjects by making sure of an ample supply of an antifertility chemical in the waters."

"I know nothing of him or the other Lords," Lingwallan said. "But Our Lady wisely made our bodies so that we are fertile only after long intervals."

"You don't have murders or theft or hatred of neighbors or sex crimes?"

Lingwallan shrugged and said, "Oh, yes. The Great Mother says that that is unavoidable since we are human beings. But the tribal councils settle arguments, from which there is no appeal except to Manathu Vorcyon. It's very difficult to escape detection if you murder someone. It is rare, anyway. As for sex crime, that too is rare. The punishment for sex with a child under the age of twelve is death. After that age, the couple who mate must do so only by a mutual agreement."

He thought for a moment, then said, "Treating a child brutally, physically, mentally, or emotionally, is punished with death or exile. But I have never heard of such a thing in any tribes I know. Children are our most precious possessions, if, that is, a child can be owned."

Kickaha did not ask him if he resented being dictated to by the Great Mother. He would have wondered about Kickaha's sanity if the question had been uttered.

"Everybody's happy, in ecstasy?" Kickaha said. "It's all advantage and no disadvantage?"

Lingwallan shrugged, then said, "Where in this world or any others are there not disadvantages?"

Kickaha knew that he would be bored if he stayed long here.

Manathu Vorcyon greeted him at the main entrance to the tree and said, "We will talk now about Red Orc, you, and me. About many things." She led him up the central staircase to the sixth story and through a doorless entrance into a large room. Against one wall was a twelve-foot-high mirror. On the only table was a silver pitcher and three silver goblets, all with figures of humans and beasts in alto-relief. One of these caught his eye. It was an image of the scaly man.

Manathu Vorcyon told him to sit down on one of the two chairs in the room.

"This place is taboo, except for me and my guests, of course. We won't be interrupted."

After she sat down, she filled two goblets with a greenish liquor. She said, "Among other questions, you want to ask me just why and how you were transported from Red Orc's place to here."

Kickaha nodded and then sipped the liquor. It tasted . . . only one way for him to describe it—like layers of sunlight, moonlight, and starlight liquefied. His heart beat faster; his head seemed to expand slightly; his body became pleasantly warm.

"Don't drink it swiftly," she said.

Kickaha was used to nudity, but those huge, round, and unsagging breasts across the table from him aroused a strange feeling. It was partly sexual and partly . . . what? It evoked an image of himself as an enwombed fetus and the sloshing of the amniotic sea rocking him back and forth while he slept and dreamed dreams without words. No, without any knowledge of words. He just thought. And he thought not only without language. He thought without images. He was without words, and his brain was equally empty of images. He was floating and rocking in pure emotion. He was safe and well-fed and quite cozy and never wanted to leave this place. Here was heaven, and outside it was hell.

Quickly, the feeling slipped away. The amniotic ocean receded with a low roar as if there were a hole in the sac and it was pouring out in a waterfall. Panic shot through him, and then he was again the man he had been a second ago.

He shook his head slightly and swore silently that he would drink no more of the green liquor. Not in this room and not when she was present, anyway.

Manathu Vorcyon smiled as if she knew of his moment of transport. She said, "I have been aware for a very long time of Red Orc and his plans. For a much shorter time, I have also been aware of you. And I know somewhat what has been happening in many of the worlds."

Not looking behind her, she stabbed a backward-pointing thumb at the silvery mirror on the wall. "Through that, I hear and see people and events in other worlds. It's hooked up to gates made by others and to gates that I've made in the weak places in the walls among the universes. The transmission is not always good, and I often have trouble maintaining the frequency lock on the gates. But I can keep watch on certain key places.

You could say that I have my finger on the pulsebeat of many worlds. My people believe it's a magic mirror."

Kickaha wanted to ask her if the device was an ancient one she had inherited or if she had made it herself. Anana had told him stories about her. One was that she was the only scientist, with the possible exception of Red Orc, among the Lords. But, true or not, she did have the device, and that was all that mattered now.

"I have heard about you, and now and then seen you," she said. "But until recently, when you were detected by the glindglassa"—she indicated the seeming mirror again—"I had set no traps to gate you through to me. I had no strong reason then to do so. As soon as I had a reason, I set up more traps—no easy thing to do by remote control—hoping to catch you someday. I also connected alarms to the gates to sound when you and you alone were in one."

"How did the detectors know me?" Kickaha said.

"The skin of every person has unique patterns in its electric field. The glindglassa detects these and also registers the individual's mass. It employs a visual detector, which I don't use very often because it's so difficult to keep a lock on it. But I had put your physical description, which I got from other sources, into the computer. It stores a display of every person caught in its field. When you were finally detected, it emitted an audio and visual notice along with your image and frequency field.

"From then on, the traps were set to detect you when you were in the range of the glindglassa and to shunt you here. The probability that you would be caught was very low because there are thousands, maybe hundreds of thousands, of gates, and I could lock into only a thousand."

"Why don't you also trap Red Orc?"

"I doubt that he knows that I would like to do that. But he probably knows that such a device as the glindglassa exists. I believe that he carries a frequency-emitter canceler."

Kickaha said, "Wouldn't the absence of a frequency field at the same time that a mass is detected identify Red Orc? And what about the visual detector?"

She smiled. "You're not just a tricky but simple killer of Lords. For one thing, the visual-detection field often drifts away from the transmission-reception lock. For another, Red Orc has never entered any of my traps—not to my knowledge, anyway. He may have a visual-detector damper and a false-mass emitter. You're not the only wily one."

"Why did you gate me through into the forest instead of directly to your tree?"

"You needed time to adjust and to be peacefully greeted by Lingwallan. Who knows what might have happened if you had appeared among strangers? You're very quick. You might have used your beamer before you understood the situation."

"Not me."

"You don't lack self-confidence. That's beneficial for a person, up to a point."

Kickaha did not believe her explanation. The probable truth was that she was very cautious. She just did not want anyone she had gated through to be close to her when they came through. The gatee might carry a very powerful bomb or some other very destructive weapon. The trees around him when he came through doubtless held hidden detectors. They would notify her if he carried any such weapons.

She said, "This is not the time for minor questions. But I will answer one you must have. Why did I not shunt to here all persons in my traps? One of them might have been Red Orc. I did try that method for a long time, five hundred years to be exact. I quit doing that when I learned that he was somehow able to avoid being caught.

"Now. Hold your tongue until I tell you that you may loose it."

10

MANATHU VORCYON HAD LONG AGO KNOWN ABOUT RED ORC, his wars against his father, Los, and against other Lords after he had slain his father.

"I also have heard about you, Kickaha. Many Lords fear you. They identify you with the *leblabbiy,* who, an ancient prophecy says, will destroy all Lords. Prophecies are nonsense, of course, unless they're self-fulfilling. Despite their mighty powers, the Lords are not only decadent, but superstitious."

So far, Red Orc had not tried to invade her universe. She had too many weapons of the ancients for him to attack her even if he brought about the death of all other Lords.

"That is," she said, "I thought so until recently. But he now has the Horn of Shambarimen. That may give him the courage to try to invade my world. And I have heard through my spies that he is again striving to get into Zazel's World, though he had ceased doing that several millennia ago. The Horn may enable him to enter it. It is said that he knows that the last of the ancient creation-destruction machines is buried in there. My spies have told me that Red Orc has often said that he would destroy all universes except one if he could get his hands on the creation-destruction engine."

Ah! Kickaha thought. So that's it! Red Orc would tell me only that he wanted "certain data" in the Caverned World. That data was this creation-destruction engine, whatever that is.

"Your pardon for interrupting, Great Mother," Kickaha said. "Hearing you say that, I just can't keep quiet. That is not accurate information. The machine is not there. However, the data to build it is. I know, because Red Orc himself told me so. I mean, he might just as well have told me that he wanted to find the data, plans, schematics, I don't know. But from what you said, I'm sure the engine itself isn't there."

She raised her thick and glossy-black eyebrows. "That is so? He is the Lord of all liars and may not have told you the truth."

"He thought I was unable to escape him and that I was certain to return to him. Thus he revealed much that he would not otherwise have told. He is indeed a great liar. I don't hold that against him since I've indulged in a few untruths myself. In this case, however, he had no reason to lie."

Manathu Vorcyon was silent for a half-minute. Then she said, "It may be best that you do speak now. First, tell me how you, an Earthman, came to the World of Tiers. I have heard parts of your story. These may or may not be true. Tell me your story from the beginning until now, but do not make an epic of it. I need only a swiftly told outline."

Kickaha did as she commanded. But when he described the scaly man, he heard her gasp.

Her eyes opened very wide, and she cried, "The Thokina!"

"What's the matter?"

"Just go on. I'll tell you later. What happened after you first saw him?"

Kickaha told her how the scaly man, whom they had thought dead, had begun to move just as he and Anana gated out of the tomb.

She got to her feet and began pacing back and forth while vigorously swinging her arms. She looked disturbed.

He thought: Even goddesses can lose their composure.

"The Thokina! The Thokina!" she muttered. "It can't be!"

"Why not?"

She swung around to face him. "Because they are only creatures of folklore and legend born of primitive fears and imagination! When I was a child, my parents and the house slaves told me stories about them. In some of these, the Thokina were a nonhuman species who were the predecessors of the Thoan. In other tales, they made the first Thoan and enslaved them. Then the Thoan revolted and killed all but one. That sole survivor fled to some unknown universe, according to the story, and put himself into a sort of suspended animation. But the tale, which was a very spooky one for a child, told of how he would rise one day when the time was ripe and would join the greatest enemy of the Thoan and help him slay all of them. That greatest enemy would be a *leblabbiy*.

"The tale also described how he would then kill the last Thoan and become the Lord of all the worlds.

"But another story said that he would join the *lablabbiy* and help them overthrow the Lords. The tales made enjoyable hair-raising stories for the children. But that the Thokina could actually be . . . that . . . that . . ."

"I am not lying," he said. "And I was wondering about the image of the scaly man I saw on a goblet during the feast."

"If a Thokina has risen from his sleep and is somewhere out there, what does he intend to do?"

"All you know now is that they did and do exist. You really don't know if he'll be hostile or friendly."

He wondered if some of that fright she'd felt as a child when hearing the tale was still living in her.

She sat down, leaned toward him, and clamped her hand around his wrist. He winced as his wristbones seemed to bend in toward each other. Her grip was as strong as he imagined a gorilla's would be. He certainly did not want to tangle with her, not in a fight, anyway.

"This scaly man is an unknown factor. Therefore, until we know better, he's a danger. Tell me. Did you tell Red Orc about him?"

"I did not. I wouldn't tell him anything that he might use."

She loosed her grip. Kickaha felt like rubbing his wrist, but he was not going to let anyone, not even a goddess, know that her grip was so powerful that she had hurt him.

She said, "Good. We have that advantage. Another is that Red Orc does not know where you are. Now, when you resume your journey to the Caverned World, you—"

One does not twice interrupt a goddess, but he did it anyway.

"Resume my journey?"

"Of course. I took it for granted that you would. You did give your word to him that you would, didn't you?"

"It doesn't matter if I did or not. He knew I'd return to him because he said that Anana might be alive and his prisoner. I doubt very much that she did survive the flash flood. But I can't chance it that she didn't."

"You didn't get to tell the rest of your story."

He ended his narration at the point where he had jumped into the trap she had placed before the Thoan's gate.

She said, "You're an extraordinary man, though you've had more luck than most would have had. It may run out soon. Then again . . ."

They talked of other things. Kickaha sipped on the liquor. Near the end of their conversation, he felt even more hopeful than he usually did, and he was almost always high on optimism.

The goddess stood up and looked down at him. Her expression seemed to show fondness for him. He felt more than fondness for her.

"It's agreed that you will go on looking for Zazel's World. You'll have an advantage doing that because I know a gateway that I doubt anyone else knows. My powers are not small, though this is a mammoth project. I will try to keep you within detection range of the glindglassa, though I am not at all sure that I can do that. You will spend several more days here resting and exercising and discussing with me the details of our plan. You look tired. You will go to bed, and you may rise when you feel like it."

"I sometimes rise when I don't feel like it."

She smiled and said, "Unless I'm wrong, you are implying more than appears on the surface of your words."

"I usually do."

"For a *leblabbiy,* you are very brash."

"There's some doubt that I am a *leblabbiy,* completely *leblabbiy,* that is. I may be half-Thoan, but I'm not eager to find out if I am. What is is, and I am what I am."

"We'll talk about that some other time. You are dismissed."

She's really putting me in my place, he thought. Oh well, it was the liquor talking. Or was it?

Anana's bright face arced across his mind. For a moment, he felt as if he were going to weep.

She patted him on the shoulder and said, "Grief is a price paid for admission to life."

She paused, then said, "Bromides help few people in times of sorrow. But there are some things I know that could ease the grief."

She said nothing more. He went up to his room and prepared for bed. When he got into it, he had some trouble getting to sleep. But only fifteen or so minutes passed before he was gone from the waking world. He awoke with a start and reached for the beamer under his pillow. A noise? A soft voice? Something had awakened him. By then, the beamer, which he kept under his pillow, was in his hand. Then he saw, silhouetted in the doorless entrance against the dusk-light of the hallway, a woman's figure. She was so tall that she had to be Manathu Vorcyon. He smelled a faint odor. This might have brought him up out of sleep; the nose was also sentinel against danger. The odor was musky but not perfume from a bottle. It hinted at fluids flowing and fevers floating hot and steamy from a swamp, a strange image but appropriate. The odor was that of the flesh of a woman in heat, though stronger than any he had ever smelled.

She walked slowly toward him.

"Put the beamer down, Kickaha."

He placed it on the floor and waited, his heart thudding as if it were a stallion's hooves kicking against a stall door. She eased herself down on her knees and then on her side against Kickaha. Her body heat was like a wave from a just-opened furnace door.

"It has been eighty years since I have had a child," she whispered. "Since then, I have met no man whose baby I cared to bear, though I have bedded many splendid lovers. But you, Kickaha, the man of many wiles, the man who is never at a loss, the hero of many adventures, you will give me a child to love and and to raise. And I know that I have stirred in you a mighty passion. Moreover, you are one of the very few men not afraid of me."

Kickaha was not sure of that. But he had overcome fear most of his life, and he would ride over this fear, which was not a big one, anyway.

He thought of Anana, though the withdrawal of blood from his brain for nonmental uses paled the thought. If she were dead, she would be no barrier for him to other women. But he did not know if she had died, and he and Anana had sworn faithfulness to each other. They would honor the vow unless they were separated for a long time or were forced by circumstances to suspend it for a while. What they did in such situations was left to each to justify to himself or herself.

Her mouth met his, and the right breast of Mother Earth, in itself a planet, rested on his belly.

He thought, I am in her power. I depend upon her to help me in the battle with Red Orc. The fate of whole universes is on the scales. If I say no to her, I might weigh the balance in favor of Red Orc. No, that's nonsense, but she might not be so enthusiastic in helping me. Also, a guest does not offend a hostess. It's not good manners.

Mainly, though, I want to do this.

He sighed, and he said, "I am indeed deeply sorry, Great Mother. But Anana and I swore absolute fidelity to each other. Much as I desire you, and I've desired only Anana more than you, I will not do this."

She stiffened, then got up. Looking down at him, she said, "I honor your vow, Kickaha. Even though I can see plainly in this dim light that you are not at all indifferent to me."

"The body does not always override the dictates of the mind."

She laughed, then said, "You know the Thoan proverbs well. I admire you, Kickaha. Fidelity is a rare trait, especially when I am the temptress."

"That is the truth. Please go before I weaken too much."

Three days later, Kickaha and Manathu Vorcyon were standing before the silvery screen of the glindglassa. Kickaha was fully clothed and well armed with various weapons. His backpack contained food, water, and some medical supplies. His head was full of advice from the Great Mother.

She leaned close to the glindglassa and whispered a code word. Its surface instantly shimmered and expanded slightly, then contracted slightly. Kickaha looked into it but could see nothing beyond.

Manathu Vorcyon turned, enfolded him in her arms, pressed him close to her breasts, and kissed his forehead.

"I shall miss you, Kickaha," she murmured. "May you succeed in your mission. I will be attempting to keep you under surveillance as much as possible, but even that will not be much."

"It's been more than fun," he said. "It's been very educational. And you have highly honored me."

She released him. He stepped toward the gate. She lightly touched the back of his neck and ran the tip of her finger down his spine. A shiver ran through him. It felt as if a goddess had blessed him.

She said, "If anyone can stop Red Orc, you'll be the one."

He wondered if she really meant it. It did not matter. He agreed wholeheartedly with her. However, his best might not be enough.

He stepped through the wavering and shimmering curtain.

11

Though Kickaha had been told by the giantess that he would find nothing dangerous during his first transit, he was ready for the unexpected. He was crouching, beamer in hand, when he was suddenly surrounded by darkness. Per Manathu Vorcyon's instructions, he walked forward three steps. Bright sunlight dazzled him. Before him was an open plain—no surprise, since the Great Mother had told him what to expect. He straightened up, looked around, and reholstered the weapon.

The sky seemed to be one vast aurora with shifting and wavering bands of violet, green, blue, yellow, and gray. The plain was covered with tall yellow grasses except for groves of trees here and there. Far away, a large herd of huge black animals was grazing. Behind him was a house-sized and roughly pyramid-shaped boulder of some smooth, greasy, and greenish stone.

He had fifty seconds to get to the other side of the boulder. The Great Mother had arranged this detour to mystify any enemy who might be traveling through the gateways. He ran around the stone and saw a shimmering on its side. But he stopped for several seconds. Here was something not even the Great Mother could have anticipated. Two tiger-sized beasts with long snouts and predators' teeth were standing in front of the gate. They roared but did not charge.

Kickaha, yelling, ran at them, his beamer again in his hand. One beast bounded away; the other held its ground and crouched down to spring at him. His beamer ray drilled through its head. It slumped and was silent. He leaped over the carcass, which stank of burnt flesh, and through the gate. A roar filled his ears. The other beast had turned and was, he supposed, charging him. He envisioned the gate disappearing and the animal bouncing off the suddenly hard side of the boulder. But he was rammed forward by its flying body and slammed into a wall. The force of the impact stunned him.

When, after an undeterminable time, he regained his senses, his groping hand felt a sticky liquid. An odor like a weasel's filled his nostrils. But he also smelled blood. He felt the device on his wrist and pressed a button. Light sprang from it, momentarily dazzling him. It lit up a small chamber cut out of stone like the first one. But he doubted that he was in the same boulder, if it was a boulder. He got to his feet and noted as he stepped over the big predator that only its front part had gotten through the gate.

He walked toward the wall through which he had just entered. There were shimmerings on each of the other walls. The Great Mother had told him that two were false gates containing devices that would spray poison on the intruder. He jumped throught the safe gate while hoping that he had not been delayed too long by the animal. As he emerged on the other side and yelled out the code word, he landed on top of a six-foot-square and six-inch-deep metal box. It was poised a thousand feet in the air above a land of bare stone. The sky was blue, and the wind whistling past him was cold. Below were row on row of Brobdingnagian busts carved out of monoliths. They extended to the horizons. Manathu Vorcyon had told him that this was the world of Arathmeem the strutter. That Lord, long since slain by Red Orc, had made a planet of which a fourth consisted of billions of rock or jewel busts of himself.

He was glad that he had not arrived when an electrical storm was in full rage. Thunder and lightning and a strong wind might have drowned out the code word. In which situation, the metal box would have automatically turned over and dumped him.

On the bottom of the box, near the edge, was a slightly raised metal plate. He got down on his belly, reached over the edge, felt the plate, and pressed it. Then he was, as the Great Mother had said he would be, in darkness and enclosed by a very thick fluid. It pressed on him and flowed up his nostrils and into his ears. He had not been given an oxygen mask because he would not be in this gate-trap very long. But an enemy of Manathu Vorcyon would be unless he knew what Kickaha knew.

He reached out with his right hand and felt up and down the wall until his fingers came to a rounded protuberance. He pushed with the flat of his hand on it, and he was free of the strangest trap he had ever been in. It was inside a massive rock on Wooth's World, a stone that was a living-nonliving thing, analogous to a virus. The slow-moving fluid eventually emerged from fissures in the rock and dripped onto the ground outside the gigantic boulder. From this lava were born—if that word could be used for the bizarre process—small balls flat on the bottom.

The natives on this planet worshiped the "mother," and they would take the "babies" and set them in the center of their villages. These minor gods grew into stones as large as the mother. Moreover, there was a thriving trade in "babies." Those villages that had a monopoly on the supply sold them to those who lacked them. Many wars had been fought to protect or to seize a source of the most precious commodity on this planet.

Dripping with the heavy gray fluid, Kickaha stood motionless until it had oozed away from him and spread in a puddle around him. Then he jumped to the ground beyond the puddle. He began walking toward the east. Manathu Vorcyon, during millennia of the use of spies and eaves-dropping via gates she had tapped into, had a rough idea of where the gate to Zazel's World was located on this planet. It was up to Kickaha to find the exact location, but he knew the direction he should go from her gate.

Getting there was not easy. He was on the Unwanted World, a planet so crowded with dangerous beasts, birds, plants, and other forms of life that it was a wonder they had not killed each other off long ago. After some days of avoiding or shooting these, Kickaha had great respect for the survival abilities of Red Orc. After ten days, four of them spent in hiding from a five-foot-high and city-block-wide creature that oozed across the ground and emitted a deadly gas, Kickaha topped a high ridge. Below him was a plain and a river. Near the river were the remains of the gigantic square nest built by some kind of creatures. Manathu Vorcyon did not know what they were. The structure was built with a concrete-like substance made in the creatures' bellies and spat out to dry.

Los had set up a gate there, the only entrance, as far as anyone knew, to Zazel's World. When Red Orc had finally returned to this place, he had slain all of the creatures living in it. Unable to find the gate, he had destroyed the construction. Believing that the creatures had broken the gate off at its foundation and buried it somewhere, he searched the land for a hundred-square-mile area. He had very sensitive metal detectors that could determine the size and shape of any metal mass a hundred feet down in the ground. The first time he looked for the gate, he did not find it, and he did not succeed during his many other searches.

"The truth," the Great Mother had said, "is that we can't be sure that those creatures removed and hid the gate. Perhaps a Lord did it, though that does not seem likely."

Kickaha had refrained from saying that he had already thought of that. She might, as on previous occasions, be irritated enough to chew him out and thus put him in his place. Sometimes the Great Mother was a Big Mother.

After crossing the plain, spooking a herd of bisonlike animals on the way, he got to the ruins. There were no pieces left from Red Orc's beam-blasting. He must have disintegrated these and burned out a huge hole in the ground. The hole was brim-full of water.

Kickaha took the backpack off and placed it on the ground. After opening it, he took out a device shaped like a big cigar, but twice the size of the largest cigar he had ever seen. Attached halfway along its upper part was a monocular cylinder. He pointed it toward where the building had been. He could see crosshairs and the sky through it. He slowly moved it back and forth, working upward. Then he saw a brightness like a short lightning streak.

He murmured, "I'll be damned! There it is!"

Manathu Vorcyon had told him that the instrument was a gate or crack-in-the-wall detector. Kickaha had not known that such a thing existed until she had handed it to him. It was many thousands of years old, and as far as she knew, the only one.

"Shambarimen is supposed to have made that, too," she had said.

"You must have a hell of a lot of confidence in me," he had said. "What if I lose it or have it taken away from me?"

She had shrugged and had said, "I've been saving it for a truly important time, a serious crisis. This is it."

So, here was the gate or, since the metal hexagram had been removed, the weak spot made by the gate. Red Orc had not known where it was since he did not have the detector.

Kickaha put the detector down. Up there, perhaps fifty feet above the ground, was the crack in the wall between two universes, visible only to his instrument. To reach it, he would have to build a series of platforms and ladders. There was plenty of wood around, and he had the tools he needed.

"Might as well get to work," he muttered.

"Thank you," a voice said loudly behind him.

He whirled, his hand darting at the same time for the holstered beamer.

Red Orc stood forty feet from him. He was smiling, and his beamer was pointing at Kickaha. On the ground behind him was an airboat, its white needle shape gleaming, its canopy open.

"No!" the Thoan said.

Kickaha stopped his hand. At a gesture from Red Orc, he raised both hands above his head. His heart was beating so hard that it seemed to be close to exploding.

"How . . . ?" Kickaha said, then closed his mouth. The Thoan would certainly explain how clever he had been.

"Now you may move your hand slowly. Use two fingers to remove your beamer, and toss it far from you," Red Orc said. "Then throw the finder to me."

Kickaha obeyed, looking at the same time for Thoan backups. The nearest cover for them was a grove of woods a hundred yards away.

"I knew Manathu Vorcyon had gated you away," the Lord said. "I detected her trap long ago, and I deliberately sent you through my gate so that she would bring you to her world. I knew that she would probably give you some device to find the crack—I admit I didn't know why the hexa-gram was no longer there—and that you would use her gates to get here."

Kickaha had many questions. One was how Red Orc knew that Man-athu Vorcyon had been the one to whisk him away to her world. But he would not ask them. What mattered was that he was in as bad a situation as he had ever been.

"I don't intend to kill you just now," Red Orc said. "Rest a while while I use her device."

Keeping his eyes on Kickaha, he bent down and picked up the finder. Then he pointed the beamer at Kickaha. He must have set it only for stun power, but the ray hit Kickaha in the chest and knocked him backward and down. The effect was as if Kickaha had just opened a door and a team of men running with a big rammer had slammed its end into his chest. The world grew dim around him; his breath was knocked loose from him. He could not get up though he strove to do so.

By the time that he could draw in enough air and raise himself on one elbow, he saw Red Orc looking through the device. A second later, he took it from his eye. He turned with a grin of delight and triumph toward Kick-aha.

A bright flash blinded Kickaha, and a roar deafened him.

Pieces of bloody flesh struck his face and chest. Then the smoke sur-rounding Red Orc was blown away by the wind. His left hand and much of his lower arm gone, his head and torso a red ruin, the Lord lay on the ground.

Kickaha fell back onto the grass and stared at the bright and blue sky. He just could not grasp what had happened. The man of many wiles, the man never at a loss, was bewildered. Not until his heart had slowed down to near a normal rate and his chest pain had eased was he able to think straight.

Anger replaced the pain. Manathu Vorcyon had betrayed him. She had used him as a pawn, not caring that he might be mutilated or killed. Her "detector" was a fake designed to lure Red Orc. The light, the supposed crack in the wall, automatically came on a few minutes after he had turned the instrument on. And something, he did not know what, triggered the ex-plosives when the Thoan came within a certain range. That her decoy also could be killed had not stopped her.

The Great Mother was a great bitch.

"She could at least have warned me," he muttered.

Her reasoning for not doing so would have been that he might act dif-ferently if he knew the true intent of the finder. And she would have ex-plained that Red Orc was such a danger to everybody in the universes, to the existence of the universes themselves, that any means to kill him was justified.

Not to me, he thought. Now I have to kill Manathu Vorcyon. I won't go after her, but if I should ever happen to run across her, I'll deal her the dead man's hand.

Then he groaned. A thought had inserted itself in the flow of his images of revenge against the Great Mother. Only Red Orc knew whether or not Anana had drowned in the flash flood, and he was dead.

Groaning again, he rolled over on his side to get ready to stand up. He said, "God!" Shock had come after shock. Standing not ten feet from him was Red Orc. He held a beamer pointed at his enemy and was smiling as the slain man had been smiling. Behind him was another airboat, the exact duplicate of the first one.

Kickaha looked at where Red Orc had been—where he still was. He was a corpse. Yet the living man was here. It was too much to understand. But if his mind could not handle the inrush of events, his body was able to struggle to its feet. Weaving back and forth slightly, he spoke hoarsely.

"You have nine lives!"

"Not quite as many as a cat," Red Orc said.

Kickaha waved at the dead man but did not speak.

"Clones, flesh of my flesh, genes of my genes," the Lord said. "I raised them from babies and educated them. Being, in a sense, I, they have my inborn drive toward power, so I have seen to it that they don't have a chance to usurp me. I wouldn't turn my back to any of them. Since they're as intelligent as I am, though not nearly as well educated or experienced, they were reared to be staked-out goats, decoys with highly expendable lives. Four of them have been sacrificed so far, including that man there, but I did avenge the first three."

He paused, smiled, then said, "Of course, you could be talking to one of them now, not the real Red Orc."

"But how did you get here? How did you know when I got here?"

"Manathu Vorcyon is not the only one who has secrets. Tell me what happened here. I assume that the device was not able to detect a crack and that it was a trick to blow my head off. You must also have thought of the high probability that your head could have gone the way of my clone's. However, I take nothing for granted. There wasn't a gate or a crack, was there?"

"No."

Red Orc smiled. "I know there isn't. I tried the Horn here, and nothing happened. If I'd known that when I sent you out, I would've told you not to waste your time or mine."

He gestured with the beamer and said, "Walk ahead of me to the boat."

Kickaha obeyed. He wondered where the Horn was now. Probably it was in the Lord's boat. Then the same thing that had happened when Red

Orc caught him at the cliff top occurred again. He felt a slight prick in his back, and he awoke in an unfamiliar room, a twenty-foot cube. He was not bound, and he was naked. There was in the cube no furniture, rugs, door, or window. In one corner was a hole in the floor, apparently for excretion, but it looked and smelled clean. Cool air moved slightly over him, piped in through a nozzle on a wall near the ceiling.

His chest still hurt. When he looked down, he could see the five-inch-wide black-and-blue bruise across his breast. But his head was clear, and he no longer felt emotional shock. What he did feel was frustration and rage.

To work off the stiffness in his muscles and his emotions, he exercised as vigorously as the chest pain would allow him. Then he began pacing back and forth while waiting for Red Orc to make his next move. Hours must have gone by before a cough behind him startled him. Red Orc or one of his clones stood there, holding a beamer. Kickaha was beginning to think that the weapon had been grafted to the Lord's hand. And the Lord had popped out of a gate or had opened a section of the wall while his captive's back was turned to him.

"Turn around," the Thoan said.

Kickaha did so, and the upper and lower sections of the wall before him parted. The top section slid into the ceiling; the lower, into the floor. At the Lord's command, Kickaha marched down a very wide and high hallway, doorless and windowless, then went around a corner and down a similar corridor. Two men armed with spears stood by the sides of a door twelve feet high. Their square steel helmets and bulging cuirasses were arabesqued in gold, and their short kilts were crimson and embroidered with small green female sphinxes. Kickaha had never seen such armor or dress before. The guards stepped aside, their spears ready to plunge into Kickaha. The door slid to one side into the wall.

The two, followed by the guards, entered an enormous room furnished with laboratory equipment, most of it strange to Kickaha. They walked down a half-mile-long aisle past many tables and big machines. When a wall barred farther progress, Red Orc told Kickaha to stop. The Thoan spoke a code word swiftly, but not too fast for Kickaha to understand it and to store it in his memory.

A huge square area of the wall became transparent. Kickaha could not help crying out. Anana, unclothed, was in the room beyond the wall. She was bound into a chair, her head held in a brace. Her eyes were closed. Above her head was what at first seemed to be a giant hair dryer.

He whirled around and snarled. "What are you doing to her?"

"I would think you'd be overjoyed because she is alive. If I had left her on that ledge just above the floodwaters, she would have died. She had a broken leg and arm, three broken ribs, and a slight concussion. Now she's in excellent physical shape because of my medical skills. You're a hard man to please, Trickster."

"What are you doing to her?"

The Lord waved his free hand. "What you see, *leblabbiy*, is a process I conceived and built and experimented with during those many times I worked to relieve myself of the inevitable boredom that comes to all immortals. The machine there is not an ancient device I inherited. I invented it."

He paused, but Kickaha said nothing. If Red Orc was waiting for another outburst, he was not going to get it.

The Lord spoke sharply. "Look at her, Kickaha! And say good-bye to the Anana you knew!"

Reluctantly, Kickaha turned to the window.

"That machine is removing her memory. It's doing so slowly, because a quick process injures the brain, and I do not want a mindless mistress."

Kickaha quivered but did not move or speak.

"The machine requires an hour a day for ten days to remove all memory back to when she was approximately eighteen years old. When the process is completed, she will believe—and in a sense, it will be true—that she is on her native planet and her parents and siblings are still living. It will be as if she has journeyed back in time, but without any knowledge of the thousands of years that have passed since she was eighteen."

Kickaha could not speak for a moment, and when he did, he croaked. "She won't remember me."

"Not at all. Nor will she remember me. But I will introduce myself and in time, make her love me. I can make any woman love me."

"What about when she finds out the truth?"

"She won't," Red Orc said, and he laughed. "I'll see to that. Of course, when I get tired of her, if I do . . ."

"Do you plan to do the same thing to me? Or do you have something painful in mind?"

"I could remove your memory up to the time, say, when you were a college student on Earth and went through Vannax's gate to the World of Tiers. Or I could torture you until you scream for death. Any man, no matter how brave, can be made to do that, even I. Or, if you volunteered to kill Manathu Vorcyon and succeeded, you could earn your freedom. First, though, you would have to complete the mission of finding a way into the Caverned World. If you do so, you will get the gift of keeping all your memories. That would indeed cause you great pain because of your memories of Anana."

Kickaha had no trouble choosing one of the options. But he would not tell Red Orc his decision until he was forced to do so. Just now, he could think only of Anana.

If we ever get free and are reunited, Kickaha thought, I'll see that she loves me again. And I'll tell her about our life together in detail.

Red Orc spoke another code word. The window became the wall. All four marched off through three halls and entered a large room ornately furnished in a style that Kickaha assumed was that of the natives. He and the Thoan sat down in comfortable chairs, facing each other across a large table of polished red wood in which were spiral green streaks. The table legs were carved with the figures of mermen and merwomen. Food and drink were brought in by a man and a woman, one of whom stood behind the Lord and the other behind Kickaha.

"You may bathe, eat, and rest after we've finished here," the Lord said. "Now! I assume you've decided that you'll try to carry out the two missions for me and for your own sake. I would certainly do so. While you live—"

"While I live, I hope," Kickaha said.

"I know that. Let us eat."

"I am not at all hungry," Kickaha said. "I would choke on the first bite."

"Sometimes the belly overrides everything. Very well. You may eat later in your own quarters."

The Thoan waited until he had chewed and swallowed several bites and drank some wine before he spoke again.

"Describe your experiences while with the ogress slut."

Kickaha did so, holding nothing back except what the Great Mother had said about the scaly man. Red Orc might know something of what his "guest" had said and done while with Manathu Vorcyon. It did not seem likely, but he did not know what kind of espionage system his "host" might have.

When Kickaha had finished, Red Orc said, "I did not want to drag her into my affairs. Not yet, anyway. But she did it when she snatched you away from me. By the way, she did not gate you through to the forest because she was considerate of you and wanted you to have time to get adjusted to her world before she met you. She did so to protect herself. If I had implanted a small atom bomb in you and set it to explode as soon as you arrived in her world, she would have been beyond its range."

He laughed, then said, "But I don't have that capability. To make atom bombs, I mean. If I wanted to take the time and do the research to find the data for making one and then go through the long tedious process of mining the metals needed and building a reactor . . . you get the idea."

He drummed his fingers for a moment before speaking again.

"Two days should be enough for you to recover. After that, ready or not, you will go out again. And this time I will launch you through a series of gates that I am sure Manathu Vorcyon has not trapped."

Kickaha had not yet eased his grief when he stepped through the gate the Lord had picked for him. At the second gate, he had time to slip a battery into his beamer before being shunted to the next station. Within three minutes, he had passed through five gates. One of these was in a cave high on a mountain. Before he was passed on, he glimpsed a valley at the bottom of which was a river. Near it was a tiny village and above that was a castle. He cried out with the joy of recognition. It was the keep of Baron von Kritz, an enemy of his when he had lived on the Dracheland level of the World of Tiers, the world he loved most. And then he was in the next station.

But this was not the place described by Red Orc. It was a windowless cell with a heavily barred jailhouse door, and it was bare of furniture except for a toilet, a washbowl with a soap dish, towels on a wall rack, and a pile of blankets in one corner.

It did have an occupant, whom Kickaha recognized at once though the man was unclothed.

Eric Clifton!

The Englishman was standing in a corner and looking confused.

Before either could say anything, Kickaha felt his senses leaving him. Clifton was now down on his knees, his face going slack. When Kickaha regained consciousness, he was lying on the floor. Like his cellmate, he was nude. And his beamer, holster, belt, and backpack were gone.

He struggled to his feet. Clifton was beginning to stir. Kickaha looked through the bars and gasped.

The scaly man was standing outside the cell.

12

"**I did not think that anyone save me could have been** spared death from the flood," Eric Clifton said softly behind him. "But it might have been better if you and I had perished in it. Now we are in the merciless hands of a demon from Hell, perhaps the Prince of Darkness himself. Our very souls are in extreme peril."

Kickaha was aware of the words, but he was too intent on studying his captor to take in their full meaning. Close up, the creature looked even more monstrous and dangerous than when in the "coffin." The massive muscles and thick skeleton were a Hercules'. The gold and green scales of his skin gleamed in the naked light above him. Around his neck from just below the jaw and to the shoulders were interlocking bands of bone on the surface of which were the snakish scales. And lines on his face revealed what Kickaha had not seen before. Bony plates underlay the scales there, too. But they seemed to be of thinner bone than on his neck and body.

Now the scaly man opened his mouth to reveal long, sharp teeth like a lion's, though the canines were much shorter.

No fruit or vegetable eater, this thing, thought Kickaha. However, bears had a predator's teeth, and their diet was more vegetarian than carnivorous.

The long and very narrow tip of its tongue slid out like a reptile's. It was a green tendril extending from a red tongue that looked like a man's.

Its large, green eyes were set an inch or so farther back than in a human skull. Though they reminded Kickaha of a crocodile's, they had eyelids that blinked regularly.

Behind him, on the other side of the hall, were two cells similar to his.

"How long have you been here?" he said softly to Clifton.

On hearing Kickaha's voice, the creature's flat ears moved outward and formed cups.

Clifton whispered, "Since two days ago. I came close to drowning in the flood, and I was much battered. But I did manage to grab a tree trunk and float far down the flood. I was swept over the edge of a great cataract but still survived, thanks to God and my guardian angel. However, I was carried to the very deeps of the chasm, so deep that its top was a very thin ribbon of light and I was in the darkness of the bowels of Hell. I like to have died of the heat and the moisture, but I strove to reach the shore of the waters, which had become a mere river again by then. I groped around blindly, and once more, God and my guardian angel bestowed salvation upon me."

The scaly man had moved forward, closed his huge hands on two bars, and was eyeing the captives intently. Kickaha was startled when he saw on the creature's right index finger the ring Clifton had worn in the pit. He turned swiftly and glanced at the Englishman's right hand. The ring was gone. He turned back to face the scaly man. If he had taken the ring from Clifton, he had made it larger so that it could fit his huge finger.

Kickaha said, "Cut the lengthy narrative. How did you get here?"

"God bless us all! I did not think we were short of time in this prison. To be brief, I climbed as high as I could, falling several times but only short distances, until, thoroughly exhausted, I found a ledge large enough for me to sleep on despite my fatigue."

"I told you to get to the point."

"When I awoke, I felt around the ledge and discovered that it projected from a cave. I heard running water inside. I was very thirsty and too high above the river to get a drink. So I went into the cave, very slowly, you may be sure, sliding my feet along the rock floor and making sure that I was not at the edge of an abyss. Presently, I came to a cataract within the cave itself. And then light blazed around me. I was on a high mountain in another world. In short, I had gone through a gate hidden in a cave in the chasm. Placed there by some Lord long ago after the battle on that planet between Los and his son, Red Orc."

"That could have been many thousands of years ago," Kickaha said. "Probably a Lord named Ololothon did it."

"Yes. But I did not stay more than a few seconds on the projection of rock high on the mountain. I was gated to another place, then another, then another. That was the last stage. I arrived in this cell inside the circle you see drawn on the floor in that corner. I advise you not to enter that circle because somebody else might be gated through at any moment. If you were standing within it when that happened, an explosion might occur."

For the first time, Kickaha noticed the orange circular line in the corner. He said, "I doubt that would happen. If this cell is equipped with sensors, and most gates are, the gate would not be activated as long as anyone was already in that circle."

"But you don't know that there are sensors in this cell."

"What happened to your ring?"

"Oh, shortly after my arrival here, I became unconscious. I suppose it was gas released by the demon. That would account for my becoming unconscious immediately after I'd entered the cell. It would also account for both of us becoming senseless when you entered. That thing came into the cell afterward and removed our clothes and possessions. Anyway, when I woke up after arriving here, the ring was gone. He is now wearing it."

Clifton pointed at the creature's finger.

"I saw it," Kickaha said. "Now—"

The scaly man spoke then with a deep resonant voice while the tendril flopped around in his mouth. His words were an incomprehensible gabble. When he stopped speaking, he cocked one ear toward Kickaha as if he expected a reply.

Kickaha replied in Thoan, "I don't understand you."

The scaly man nodded. But to him, a nod must mean a no. He turned away and shambled off down the corridor.

"Now," Kickaha said, "you never finished your account of how you got into the Lords' worlds."

"I—"

Clifton stopped, and his jaw dropped. Kickaha turned and saw that a cell across the hall from his had just been filled. The man in it was crumpling, his knees sagging. Then he lay on his side inside the circle where he had appeared. Kickaha recognized at once the long bronze-reddish hair and the angelically handsome face.

"Red Orc!"

Clifton gasped, and he cried, "The devil has caught the devil!"

An alarm must have been set off somewhere to notify the scaly man. Kickaha heard his heavy footsteps and then saw him coming down the corridor. Just before the creature got to Red Orc's cell, Kickaha became unconscious again.

He woke befuddled, deaf, and against the wall opposite the barred door. His head felt as if it had swelled to twice its normal size. Smoke stung his nostrils and made his eyes smart, but it did not have the odor of gunpowder. He reached out on both sides of him. His right hand touched, then moved up and down, flesh and ribs. By his side was Clifton, still knocked out. He was blackened with smoke and smeared with blood and fragments of bloody flesh. When Kickaha looked down at his own body, he saw that he was also blackened and bloody. Still stunned, he flicked gobbets of flesh from his chest, stomach, and right leg. What had happened?

By then, the smoke had drifted out of the cell and down the corridor. The bars of the door were coated with blood; pieces of skin and muscle clung to the bars and lay on the floor. An eye was on the floor near Kickaha's feet.

Slowly, he came out of his daze. He tried to get to his feet, but he was trembling so much that he could not do it. Also, his back hurt, and his legs were strengthless. He closed his eyes and sat against the wall for a while. When he opened his eyes, he had a clear idea of what had to have happened. Not Red Orc but a clone sent by Red Orc had been caught in the scaly man's trap. But that meant that the Thoan had sent his clone after Kickaha, for what purpose he did not know.

No. Kickaha, his brain now starting to operate on all cylinders, realized what the purpose was. Red Orc had detectors that told him that he, Kickaha, had been taken away from the course set for him by the Thoan. Red Orc must have been surprised—and very alarmed—when Kickaha had once again vanished. But Red Orc had sent a clone along the same path after Kickaha. How quickly he must have acted! He had placed a bomb in the clone's backpack, a bomb set to explode a few seconds after its carrier reached the point at which Kickaha had been snatched away. The clone, of course, had not known that Red Orc had put the bomb in the knapsack.

Though Red Orc could not have known what was occurring after Kickaha had vanished from the detectors, he had guessed that only an enemy would do it. He might have reasoned that Manathu Vorcyon had abducted Kickaha again. Whoever was responsible, he or she possessed a device Red Orc lacked. So that person must be destroyed even if Kickaha was also turned into a shower of fragments.

Despite his pain and violent shaking, Kickaha got up and limped to the door of his cell. The bars of the clone's cell had been bent outward. The vagaries of the explosion had left a leg, severed at the upper part of the thigh, standing against the bars, a hand lying on the floor outside the bars, and what looked like a rib.

He pressed his shaking face against the bars and looked down the corridor. The scaly man was standing about twelve feet from the door of Kickaha's cell, but he was moving his head vigorously up and down and to both sides. It was as if he was trying to move the scattered pieces of his brain back into their previous positions. Though he was clean of blood and gobbets, his bright gold-and-green scales were dulled by smoke.

Kickaha turned to look at Clifton. The man's eyes were open, and his mouth was working. Kickaha still could not hear anything. He started to walk toward the Englishman but never made it. His senses faded.

When he awoke, he was lying on his back on a bed in a big room. Its ceiling and walls were huge screens displaying unfamiliar animals and many scaly men and women moving through exotic and brilliantly colored landscapes. All of his pains and the shaking were gone. As he sat up, he could hear the rustling of the sheets. He pushed away the covers to expose his legs. The smoke, blood, and flesh pieces had been washed off.

Near him, Eric Clifton lay on a similar bed under a glowing crazy quilt just like his own. Kickaha was noting that the room had no windows or doors when a section of the wall sank into the floor. The scaly man entered. For a moment, he turned his head. The profile was an unbroken arc from the back of his neck to just below his lower lip except for the small protrusion of the tip of his nose. The line described by his profile was like the somewhat flattened arc of a mortar shell. The insectile appearance was increased when he came straight on to Kickaha's bed. But when he stopped in front of the bed and spoke, he seemed more human than insect. The tone of his voice and the look in his eyes seemed as if they were expressing concern.

"I don't understand," Kickaha said.

The scaly man lifted his hands and turned their palms upward. But if that gesture meant that he also did not know Kickaha's speech, he certainly was not going to be frustrated.

During the next two months, Kickaha and Clifton spent at least four hours a day teaching Thoan to him. Meanwhile, they lived in luxurious rooms a story above the hospital room and were served food, some of which was tasty and some of which repulsed them. They also exercised vigorously. And the scaly man had returned Clifton's ring, now resized to fit the Englishman's finger.

Their host's name was Khruuz. His people had been called Khringdiz. He, the lone survivor, had never heard of Thokina, the name given his kind in Thoan legend. But Kickaha thought that the Lords had adapted Khringdiz to their own pronunciation.

They were deep underground below the "tomb"—itself very deep—to which Kickaha and Anana had gated. Khruuz did not know why they had been transported to his place of millennia-long rest. But when Kickaha told him that he had used the Horn of Shambarimen, a sonic skeleton key to all gates, Khruuz understood. He said that it was still an accident that they had gone through the gate there. What had happened was that the gate, like many closed-circuit gates, had a "revolving node." Anywhere from ten to a hundred gates were continuously "whirled" in the node. The gatee might be passed through any one of them, his entrance being determined by which one he encountered when a gate became activated by an energized portion of the node. The Horn had been blown just as a "crack" or flaw opening to the tomb had come by in its rotation. The flaw was not a true gate, that is, it had not been made by a Lord, but existed in the fabric. But the Horn had made the difference.

"That means that Red Orc might know how to get into here," Kickaha told Khruuz. "You used a series of gates to trap us and the Thoan's clone. If he has detectors, and I think he does, he may get into here. Or he may send another clone, somebody anyway, with a bomb a thousand times more powerful than the one the clone carried. Of course, he can't know just where the clone went or what happened after he got here."

By then, Khruuz had heard everything that Kickaha knew about Red Orc. He had also been told as much of the history of the Thoan people as Kickaha knew.

Khruuz spoke in his heavily accented and just barely understandable Thoan. His tongue-tendril now and then struck parts of his palate and formed sounds that were not in Thoan and probably only in his language.

"I have closed all the gates for the time being. That keeps anyone from coming in, but it also does not permit me to gather information from the outside."

Khruuz had told Kickaha that parts of the outline of the legends about the Khringdiz were close to the truth. But the details were usually wrong. When the Thoan people had killed off all of the Khringdiz except for him, he had made this underground retreat. After being there for a while, he had stopped the molecular motion of his body and settled down for a very long "sleep." The fuel to drive the machine for maintaining the chamber, to record the events on various parts of various universes, and to "awaken" him was nuclear power. When the fuel was almost gone, the machinery would bring him out of molecular stasis.

"By then," Khruuz had said, "the probabilities that the situation would be considerably changed were high. The Lords might have died out. Their numbers were comparatively few at the time I went into stasis. And their descendants, if these existed after such a long time, might be different in culture and temperament. They could be much more tolerant and empathetic. Or some other sentient species, higher on an ethical level than the Lords, might have replaced the Thoan. In any event, whoever inhabited the universes might be willing to accept me, the last of the Khringdiz. If such was not the situation, I would have to deal with the evil as best I could.

"My fuel would have lasted for some time yet. But I had also set up the security system so that any intrusion into the chamber would awaken me. You entered, and I was brought out of stasis prematurely. But the process takes some time. It did not bring me out of stasis in time for me to speak to you. You got away because of the Horn. That, by the way, must contain machinery the design for which was stolen from my people. The Thoan did not have such technology."

"What?" Kickaha had said. "The Horn was invented by the ancient Lord, Shambarimen!"

"This Shambarimen must have gotten the data from one of us, undoubtedly after he killed the Khringdiz who owned it. But instead of sharing it with his fellow Lords, he kept it secret. He incorporated it in the artifact that you called the Horn. That has to be what happened."

"But there must have been other designs, or even the machinery itself!" Kickaha had said. "If the devices for opening gates or flaws were used by the Khringdiz, surely some would have fallen into Thoan hands!"

"No. They were few and well guarded. They gave us an advantage over the Thoan because we could enter their gates and flaws. But those of us who survived the initial onslaught were too few to use the openers effectively. At last, only I survived. However, those who did have the openers must have destroyed or hidden all the designs and the machines before they were hunted down and killed. You know the rest of the story."

"So, Shambarimen lied about inventing the Horn," Kickaha had said. "There goes another legend into the dust!"

Khruuz had shrugged his massive shoulders in a quite human gesture. He had said, "From what you tell me and from my experience since being awakened, it's evident that the Lords are still here and that very few have changed."

Kickaha had said, "You'd like to get revenge, wipe them out?"

The scaly man had hesitated, then had said, "I can't deny that I would be happy if all my original enemies, the Lords who existed when we were being exterminated, were to be killed and I was the one who did it. But that is impossible. I must somehow make peace with them. If I cannot do that, then I am doomed."

"Don't feel hopeless," Kickaha had said. "I am the enemy of almost all Lords because they tried to kill me first. They must be killed before there will be peace in all the universes. You and I would make wonderful allies. How about it?"

The scaly man had said, "I will do my best to help you. You have my word on that, and in the days when there were other Khringdiz, the word of Khruuz was enough."

Kickaha had asked him if he knew how the Thoan came into being. Khruuz replied that his people would never have made beings so unlike themselves.

"Some questions have no answers," Khruuz had said. "But our universe was not the only one. Somehow, the Thoan broke through the wall between our universes. Instead of treating us as if we were peaceful and nonviolent sentients, which we were, they behaved as if we were dangerous animals. We were treacherously attacked, and in the first blow, the Thoan wiped out more than three-quarters of us. We survivors were forced to become killers. The rest of the story you know."

"And now?" Kickaha had said.

"When I opened a gate and connected it to a circuit, I had no way of knowing if the Thoan were still violent beings. So I decided to collect various specimens. You two were the first to be caught. I did not know that you were not Thoan but from a planet that did not even exist when I took refuge. The third was a Thoan. You know what happened then."

"We can help you, and you can help us," Kickaha had said. "Red Orc must be killed. In fact, all those Lords who would slay us must be killed. But first I have to get into Zazel's World before Red Orc does."

"He really intends to destroy all of the universes and then make his own?"

"He says he does. He's capable of doing it."

Khruuz rolled his eyes and spat, his tongue-tendril straight out from his mouth. At that moment, he looked serpentine. Kickaha told himself to quit comparing Khruuz to insects and reptiles. The Khringdiz was as human as any member of Homo sapiens and much more human than many of them. At least, he seemed to be so. He could be lying and so hiding his true feelings.

Man, I've tangled with too many Lords! he thought. I'm completely paranoiac. On the other hand, being so has saved my life more than once.

Khruuz had promised to study the data re gates, which his bank contained. He had set his machines to scan that section, to abstract significant data, and to print it out. That took only two hours, but he had an enormous amount of data to read in the—to Kickaha—exotic alphabet of the Khringdiz.

"Most of this is what my people knew about gates," the scaly man said. "But I assume that the Thoan made some advances in their use since I went into the long sleep. I was trying to get information on these when I had to close my gates. Unfortunately, Zazel must have made his Caverned World after that. However, we may yet find out something about his gate setup. Not until Red Orc is dealt with, though."

"If we do that, we won't have to worry about getting into Zazel's World," Kickaha said.

"Yes we will. Some other Lord might get the creation-destruction engine data. The data should be in safe hands or destroyed. Though it makes me shudder to think of doing that to scientific data, it is better than chancing that it might be stolen or taken by violence."

Kickaha thought for a moment, then said, "At one time, every Lord must have had the engine. Otherwise, how could they have made their own private universes? What made them all disappear? Why don't at least some of them now have the data for making the engines?"

"You're asking the wrong person," Khruuz said. "I was out of the stream of the living for thousands of years. There may be some Lords who have the engines or the designs for them, but they don't know it. As for your first question, I think that every Lord who successfully invaded another's universe destroyed his enemy's creation-destruction engine. The successful invader would not want others who might invade during the owner's absence to find one. And then another Lord would slay the previous invader. In time, very few engines would be left. But I really don't know."

Several weeks after this conversation, Khruuz summoned Kickaha and Clifton to a room they had never seen before. This was huge and had a domed ceiling. The ceiling and walls were black but strewn with tiny sparkling points and lines connecting them. They formed a very intricate web.

Khruuz waved a hand and said, "You see here the results of my data-collecting. The points are gate nodes, and the lines connecting them show the avenues traveled between and among gates. Those lines are drawn there just for the sake of the viewer. They separate the gates so that the viewer may more easily distinguish among them. Actually, the transit time between one gate and the next is zero."

Kickaha said, "I saw a gate map once when I was with Jadawin in his palace. But it was nowhere nearly as complicated as this. Isn't it something!"

Khruuz's dark eyes regarded Kickaha. "Yes, it is something, as you say. But what is displayed is a map of all nodes known to me. Mostly, they're Khringdiz gates, and the majority were opened into Thoan universes when my people were still battling the enemy. Thus, many of them connect with various Thoan gates, though the connection was done by accident."

Khruuz admitted that he did not know where many of the nodes and routes were. If someone took these from Khruuz's world, that person would have to go in ignorance to where the routes took him. And there were many nodes that intersected with closed-circuit routes.

"Is there a chance that a Khringdiz route might end at a gate leading into the Caverned World?" Kickaha said. "From what I've heard, there's only one gate, or there was one gate, giving entrance to Zazel's World. But what if there's an ancient gate to it made by the Khringdiz?"

"There is a chance. But I don't know what gate, if any, would take you there. It might take you a hundred years to travel every gate and route, and you still would not find the right one. Moreover, your chances of survival during this search would be very small."

"But Red Orc must think that there is one. Otherwise, why would he have sent me out to find it?"

Eric Clifton said, "You should know by now that he seldom tells you the true reason for what he does."

"I guess so. But he didn't have to lie about that."

During their time with Khruuz, Kickaha insisted that Clifton finish his often-interrupted narrative of how he had gotten into the Thoan universes.

"Where was I? Oh, yes! First, a recapitulation of the events leading up to the point at which the flash flood stopped my telling of the tale."

Kickaha sighed and sat back. There was no hurry just now, but he wished Clifton were not so long-winded.

"The madman Blake described to his friend the vision he had had of the flea's ghost, which you and I now know was of the Khringdiz. I was so fascinated by this that I drew a sketch of the scaly man as described by Mr. Blake. I showed it to my closest friend, a boy named Pew. He worked for a jeweler, a Mr. Scarborough. He showed my sketch to his employer, and Mr. Scarborough showed the drawing to a wealthy Scots nobleman, a Lord Riven, who then ordered that a ring be made based on the sketch. But poor stupid Pew stole the ring. Knowing that there would be a hue and cry and that he would be the most suspected, he gave the ring to me to hold for him. That shows you how brainless he was. At that time, I had not repented of my sins and sworn to God that I would no more lead a dishonest life."

Kickaha, his patience gone despite the abundance of time he had, said, "Get on with it."

"Very well. The constables searched for Pew, who had taken refuge with the gang of homeless street boys he had joined before working for Mr. Scarborough. But the constables found him, and he was killed while fleeing from them. A shot in the back of the head, I believe, sent the poor devil's soul downward to Hell.

"That meant, as far as I was concerned, that I owned the ring. But I knew that much time would have to pass before I could chance selling it. And it would be better if I went to a far-off city before I attempted that transaction. But I could not quit my employer, Mr. Dally, the bookseller and printer, immediately. I would be suspected, and the constables might discover my association with George Pew. If I was convicted, I would hang."

Baron Riven was determined to find the ring and the person who had stolen it. One of his agents questioned Clifton about the theft. The agent had unearthed the fact that Clifton was one of Pew's closest friends, perhaps his only friend. Clifton was terrified, but he denied everything except knowing Pew. That was a lie Clifton knew would be eventually exposed. One night, shortly after the interview, he fled, his destination the city of Bristol. He planned to board any ship that would carry him out of England. He had no money, so he would have to find work aboard as a cabin boy. Or any job he could get.

"I snatched a purse and with the money got lodgings in a cheap dockside tavern," he said. "I also applied at a dozen ships for work to pay for my passage. Finally, I got one as a cook's helper aboard a merchantman."

The night before he was to ship out, while he was walking the streets near the waterfront, he felt a hand on his shoulder and then a pinprick in his neck. He tried to run away, but his legs failed him, and he fell unconscious onto the cobblestones. When he awoke, he was in a room with Lord Riven and two men. He was naked and was strapped to a bed. The baron himself injected a fluid into one of Clifton's arteries. Contary to Clifton's expectation, he stayed conscious. When Lord Riven questioned him about the ring, Clifton, despite his mental struggles, told him the truth.

"A truth drug," Kickaha said.

"Yes, I know. My sack, containing my few worldly possessions, had been examined. The baron now wore the ring. I expected to be turned over to the constables and, eventually, hanged. But it turned out that the baron did not want the authorities to know about me or the ring. He ordered his men, very rough and brutal-looking scoundrels, to cut my throat. He tossed them some guineas and started to walk to the door with a splendidly decorated and large leather bag in his hand. But he stopped after a few steps, turned, and said, "I have a more severe punishment in mind for him. You two leave now!"

They did so quickly. Then he took out from his bag two large semicircular flat pieces of some silvery metal.

"Portable gates!" Kickaha said.

"Ah, then you know what I am talking about?"

"They're the means I used to get into the universe of the World of Tiers," Kickaha said.

"Ah! But I did not have the slightest idea then what their purpose or origin was. I thought that they were tools of torture. In a way, they were just that. He placed their ends close together on the floor so that they formed a slightly broken circle. Then he untied me. I was too terrified to resist, and I wet my pants again, though I believe that I had emptied my bladder when I awoke tied to the bed."

Lord Riven untied the Englishman, leaving his hands bound behind his back but his feet free. Then he picked up Clifton by the back of his neck with one hand. He carried him as if he were a small rabbit and stood him inside the two crescents. He told Clifton not to move unless he wanted to be cut in half.

"My teeth were chattering, and I was shaking violently. Though he had warned me not to speak, I asked him what he intended doing to me. He replied only that he was sending me directly to Hell instead of killing me first."

Clifton believed that he was in the power of a devil, perhaps Satan himself. He begged for mercy, though he expected none. But Lord Riven bent down swiftly, shoved the ends of the semicircles together with his fingertips, stood up, and moved back several feet. For several seconds, nothing happened.

"Then the room and the baron disappeared. Actually, I was the one to disappear, as you well know. The next second, I was aware that I was in another world. It did not look like Hell. There were no capering devils or flames issuing from the rocks. But I was indeed in Inferno. It was a dying planet in one of the worlds of the Lords."

He paused, then said, "Remembering that calls up the absolute panic and horror possessing me then. But I managed to get my hands unbound, and I managed to live, though I experienced the torments of the damned."

"What year was it that you gated through?" Kickaha said.

"The year of Our Lord eighteen hundred and seventeen."

"Then you've been about one hundred and seventy-five years in the Thoan worlds."

"Good God! That long! I've been so busy most of the time."

The Englishman sketched his life since then. He had been many places, had passed safely through many gates, had been a slave many times to both Thoan and humans, had been a chief of a small tribe, and had finally settled down into a comparatively happy life.

"But then I got an itch for adventure. I took a gate that led me eventually through many worlds until I fell into the trap, the pit, set up by Red Orc. I did not know whose it was until I saw the man who appeared in Khruuz's cell and was blown to bits."

He paused briefly, "That man looked exactly like Lord Riven."

"I had guessed that," Kickaha said. "The baron was Red Orc, living at that time on Earth One and disguised as a Scotch nobleman."

13

THOUGH KICKAHA KEPT BUSY SO THAT HE WOULD NOT THINK about Anana, he could not keep her out of his mind. With the images of her came anguish and fury. By now, the Thoan should have finished his memory-erasing on Anana, and she would think that she was only eighteen years old.

Red Orc would explain to her that she had had amnesia and was now in his care. Or that she had been given as his ward to him by her father and then had suffered a memory loss. He would make sure that she did not learn how many millennia had passed since that supposed event.

Even now, he might be attempting to seduce her. Or he might be forcing her to his bed. Kickaha tried shutting out the visions of her making love to Red Orc. But it was not as easy as pulling down a window blind.

Two months passed. On the third day of the third week of the third month (a good omen, if you believe in omens), Khruuz told Kickaha and Clifton to come to the gates-display room. The vast chamber was unlit except for the light-points on the ceiling dome and the walls. They were much brighter than during the first visit. A single light illuminated Khruuz and the control panel before which he sat. When they entered, he rose with an expression that the two knew by now was intended for a smile.

He rubbed his hands together just as humans did to express their joy or high satisfaction. "Good news!" he said. "Very promising!"

He stabbed a finger at the ceiling. Bending his neck, Kickaha saw a huge point that had not been there when he was in the chamber. Many lives ran from it to many smaller points. He also saw that one bright point had changed from white to orange. Several lines leading to it were also orange. One of them ended at the big point.

"The orange point leads to Zazel's World—if my calculations are correct."

"Are you sure?" Kickaha said.

Khruuz sat down before the huge indicator-control panel. "I just said that I was not sure. If the computer is correct, I'm sure. But I don't know if it is correct. The only way to know will be to gate someone to it."

"How did you do it?" Kickaha said.

"I set the computer to tracing all the lines you see in this room. Since you were here last, many new points and lines have been added."

"But you said that you had shut down all the gates leading to here because of Red Orc," Clifton said.

"True. I had. But I took the chance that Red Orc would not detect the new gates I opened. These were opened for some microseconds before closing down. In that time, the computer did its tracing. The results of millions of tracings in the microsecond intervals are now displayed."

Kickaha wondered what it was that made the Khringdiz believe that he had found the gate to the Caverned World. Before he could ask, Khruuz said, "Look at the point that is far larger than the others. Now, do you see the orange line leading from it to the smaller orange point? The large point is a cluster of points so close together they look to your eye as if they were one point."

He looked up and smiled again. "The big point represents something I do not believe that the Thoan know about."

"Is that the all-nodes gate you asked me about two months ago?" Kickaha said. "I wondered about that, but you didn't say anything more when I said I'd never heard of it."

"Your answer was enough, even though you are only an expert on gates by experience. But you are not a scientist. Also, if Red Orc knew of the revolving or all-nodes gate, he would have used it."

He said something into the panel, and the screen before him showed a different display. In its center was a big light, the cluster of points that made up the all-nodes gate. Now Kickaha could see a small separation among the points.

Khruuz said one word in his harsh language. The screen zoomed in toward the point until the image almost filled it. By it appeared a word in small Khringdiz letters.

"That indicates the gate in the all-nodes cluster that leads to two places, what you call cracks, in the 'wall' of Zazel's World. Note that the faults are much dimmer than the active gates. One fault is a once-active gate; the other, a weakness that was in the wall when that universe was made. The once-active gate was the gate that was closed, I believe, by the creature that rules the Caverned World. That being—you said his name is Dingsteth—not only closed the gate, he moved the fault. That implies great knowledge and a vast power source. Even my machines are not capable of doing that. But my machines can detect that the fault has been moved. Look closely. I'll turn the power up so that it may be better seen."

He spoke another word. A very faint line appeared. One end was at the dim point, and the other end was at an even dimmer point.

"Traces of the operation," the scaly man said. "There are thousands of light-points on the chart. But this is the only one showing the path of a gate or fault that has been moved. Of course, what Dingsteth did was to shut down the shearing trap in the one-way gate that Red Orc had used to get into his world. Then he made it into a two-way gate just long enough to disintegrate the hexagonal structure. He would not have to leave his own world to do that since the beamer rays he used on the inner side of the metal hexagon would disintegrate it in his world and in the other.

"After doing this, he remade the gate into a one-way entrance. Having done that, he moved the fault to another location, a feat beyond the power of present-day Thoan technology. That's why Red Orc could not find it on the Unwanted World. What you saw through Manathu Vorcyon's device was, as you realized later, a false light."

"That's wonderful!" Kickaha said. "But what about the one-way gate through which Dingsteth let Red Orc out of the Caverned World?"

Khruuz held his opened hands palms up in another human gesture. "It's been closed down, made into a no-way fault. I doubt that Red Orc has detectors sensitive enough to locate the fault. The lack of these also accounts for his failure to detect the entrance gate and the path it made when it was relocated. Even though the gate had been a two-way momentarily, the creature had means to cancel the trace of the two-way gate's existence. But you'll have to reopen the exit gate after you get in there."

"I'll handle it!" Kickaha said. "Let's get going!"

"Not so fast. Here's the machine that will open, or should open, the entrance point Dingsteth closed."

Khruuz said something, and a drawer slid out from the wall below the control panel. From it, he took a black metallic cube, four inches across. An orange button was on its top; the bottom part was curved; a strap dangled from one side of it.

"The key to the gate to the Caverned World," Khruuz said. "Your Horn of Shambarimen is the only other key."

He held up the black box. "I inherited this from a friend, a great scientist, who was killed a few days after he gave it to me. As far as I know, it's the only one in all the universes. Strap this gate-opener onto your wrist. Without it, you might as well stay here."

The preparations for the trip took two days. Eric Clifton argued that he should go with Kickaha. Khruuz said that the chances were high that Kickaha would fail in his mission. If Clifton went with Kickaha, he might die, too. Khruuz needed Clifton's knowledge of the universes of the Lords if he was to be effective in the battle against them.

"Besides," Khruuz confessed to Kickaha when Clifton was not present, "I would get very lonely, even if he is not a Khringdiz."

Thus, though impatient, Kickaha had to wait until Khruuz told him when the correct time for entering the all-nodes gate arrived.

"The node does not really revolve," the Khringdiz said. "But I use 're-volve' as a convenient term. Launching you requires exact timing. You have an interval of twenty seconds to get into the node and to take the gate that should lead you to the fault in Zazel's World. If you are delayed by ten microseconds, you'll enter another gate taking you to somewhere else."

The Khringdiz had built a nine-angled metal structure to mark the place for Kickaha to enter. An hour before the time to go, Kickaha put on an oxygen mask, an oxygen bottle, a pair of dark goggles, weapons, a back-pack filled with supplies, and, strapped to his left wrist, the cube contain-ing the device for opening the fault. Kickaha called it "the can opener."

Eric Clifton was there to see his fellow Earthman off. "God be with you," he said, and he shook Kickaha's hand. "This is a war against the Devil, so we are destined to win."

"God may win against Satan," Kickaha said. "But how about the casu-alties along the way?"

"We will not be among them."

A display in Khringdiz numbers on the wall indicated the time. Kick-aha had learned what these meant. When he had two minutes to go, he checked a Khringdiz watch on his right wrist. It was synchronized with the wall instrument. He stood before the nonagonal structure, and when he had thirty seconds to go, made ready to enter the gate. Though Khruuz had told him that he would meet no one else, Kickaha had unstrapped the beamer in his holster.

Khruuz said, "Get ready to go. I'll give the word twenty seconds from now."

It seemed that he had just quit talking when he shouted in Thoan, "Jump!"

Kickaha leaped. He passed through the nonagon and was momentar-ily bewildered. He seemed to be stretched far out. His legs and feet looked as if they were very elongated. His feet were at least twenty feet from his torso. His hands, at the ends of beanpole arms, were ten feet from his shoulders.

He felt, at the same time, a shock, as if he had fallen into a polar sea. His numbed senses began to fade. Khruuz had not told him that this would happen—but then, Khruuz did not know what would happen. It was up to him, Kickaha thought, to do what was required.

He was enveloped in a dim greenish light. His rapidly chilling feet felt as if they were on a floor, but he could not see it. Nor were there any walls around him. It was like being in an invisible fog.

Then a slightly brighter light glowed behind the dusk. He walked toward it, if "walking" was the right word. More like wading through molasses, he thought. He did not know how many seconds had passed since he had entered this place—if it was a place. But it was no use wasting time in looking at the wristwatch. Either he got there in time or he did not.

The greenish dusk brightened; the light on its other side—if there was any such thing as another side here—increased. That should be the node "revolving" there. The light should be the gate he wanted.

Then the light began to fade. He strove to step up his pace. By all the holies! He had thought that twenty seconds were more than enough time to get to the gate. But now it seemed an impossibly short time. And he was beginning to feel as if his stomach, lungs, and heart were as distorted as his limbs. He felt very sick.

If he vomited in the mask, he would be in a bad way indeed.

Then the light was around him. Very slowly, or so it seemed to him, he reached for the opening device given him by Khruuz. It, too, was distorted. His right hand missed it altogether. He felt close to panic, a cold panic sluggishly moving up from wherever panics came from. He did not have much time to press the button. At least, he thought he did not. But he was sure that if he did not activate the little machine very quickly, he would not be within his allotted time.

He reached across his chest and felt his left shoulder, though that, too, took time to find. How many seconds did he have left? Finally, his fingers touched his shirt. He slid them downward, at the same time seeing an arm bent in a zigzag course, as crooked as the cue stick W. C. Fields had used in a movie, the title of which Kickaha could not remember. Then his middle finger was on the button, which had a concavity on top of it that had not been there when he had leaped through the gate. But he pressed on it.

Now he was in a tunnel illuminated with a first-flush-of-dawn light. He no longer felt sick; his legs and feet had snapped back to their normal size. The cold had given way to warmth. He breathed easily then. Maybe he had been holding his breath while he was in that awful space. His wristwatch told him that he had been in the half-space or no-space for eighteen seconds.

He turned off the oxygen and removed the mask and bottle. Immediately, he noticed that the air was not moving. It was hot and heavy and gave the impression of having died a long time ago. After putting the oxygen equipment down at his feet to mark the point of entrance, he looked around. The tunnel went through smooth crystalline stone and was wide enough for twenty men to march abreast. In the middle of the floor was a shallow and curved ditch filled with running water. Some sort of thick lichen grew on the walls and ceiling in large patches. The dim light was shed by greenish knobs on the ceiling, walls, and floor. Hanging from the ceiling or lying on the floor were the dried-out bodies of six-angled insectile creatures. He had no idea of their function or of what had killed them.

The strangest feature of this tunnel, though, the one giving him the most pause, was the characters moving slowly in a single-file parade along each wall. They were black and four inches high and slightly above his eye level. When they came to a lichen patch, they disappeared but emerged from beneath the patches on the bare spaces. They could be symbols or alphabet or ideogram characters. That some looked vaguely familiar, resembling some Greek, Cyrillic, Arabic, and Chinese writing, did not mean anything. They were coincidences.

The still air continued to oppress him. He decided to scratch a big X on the wall as a starting point. Then he placed the oxygen mask and bottle in his backpack.

Now, which way should he go?

Upstream was as good a direction as any. That was also the way in which the characters were going.

For five hours, he walked steadily through the tunnel in a silence that filled his ears with a humming. The only living thing was the luciferous lichen. But it could be that the knobs were also live plants. Every half-hour, he stopped to scratch an X upon the wall. The air continued to be hot and thick, and he often was tempted to use the bottle. But he might need it for an emergency.

By now, he was convinced that he was in Zazel's World. Though the Thoan legends were sketchy in their descriptions of it, they certainly sounded like the tunnel he was in. Jubilation at having done what Red Orc had found impossible to accomplish spurred him on. He'd show the bastard.

Near the beginning of the sixth hour of his walk, he came to a fork. A tunnel opening was on his left, and one was on his right. Without hesitation, he took the left one. He regarded the left as lucky—to hell with the superstitions concerning sinistrality—and he was betting that the chosen avenue would lead him to the heart of this planetary cavern. He found evidence for this when he came across the first of many animal skeletons. They strewed his path as he stepped past or over them. Some seemed to have died while locked in combat, so intertangled were their bones. Alarmed, he started to jog. Something bad had happened.

A few minutes later, he stepped over bones and through the tunnel exit into a gigantic cave. It was lit by the knobs, which were much more closely placed than those in the tunnels. But their illumination did not enable him to see very far into the cave.

He walked down a slope and onto the flat stone floor. Here, as in the tunnel, lay the bones of many different kinds of animals and birds. The plants once growing here had been eaten down to the soil on the stone floor. However, enough fronds and fragments were left for him to identify them as of vegetable origin. He supposed that the animals had devoured the dead or dying plants. But they had killed each other off before all the plant remnants could be eaten.

On the wall nearest him, the symbols moved in their arcane parade as far as he could see.

According to what he had heard, the entire world was a colossal computer. But Zazel had made fauna and flora to decorate his large caves and to amuse himself. They and the computer had failed to preserve his desire to live, and he had committed suicide.

Where was the operator of this place, the sole sentient, the lonely king, the artificial being whom Zazel had left to watch over this dismal universe?

Kickaha called out several times to alert Dingsteth if he should be within hearing range. His voice echoed, and no one answered him. He shrugged and set out for the other end of the cavern. When he looked back, he could not see the entrance. The shadows had taken it. After another hour, he came to the end of the vast hollow and was confronted by six tunnel openings. He took the one on the extreme left. After thirty-five minutes, he came to another. The same spectacle as in the previous place was before him. The bones and shreds of plants lay together in the silence.

But the train of symbols still moved along the walls and disappeared into the darkness ahead. The computer was still alive. Rather, it was still working.

Nowhere had he seen any controls or displays. To operate the computer, he figured, you had to speak to it. He did not have the slightest knowledge of how to ask it questions, and the strange symbols were unreadable. Probably Zazel had made his own language to operate the machine. That meant that Kickaha's mission was a failure. Worse, he was stuck in this godawful place with only enough food to last him twelve days. If, that is, he ate very lightly.

He thought, if I can find Dingsteth or he finds me, it'll be fine. That is, it'll be okay if he cooperates.

Dingsteth, however, was beyond helping anybody, including himself. Kickaha found what was left of him in a chair carved out of stone. The bones had to be his. They were of a bipedal manlike being, but too different in many respects to be a genuine specimen of Homo sapiens. Among the bones were tiny plastic organs and wires attached to them. The skull, which had fallen into the lap, was definitely not a man's.

I'm very lucky to have found this place so soon after I got here, Kickaha thought. After all, when I came to this world, I was gambling that I'd find Dingsteth. I could have wandered through this maze, which probably goes for thousands of miles throughout this world of stone. But here I am in the place I was looking for. And in a relatively short time, too.

On the other hand, his luck hadn't been so good. The only one who could tell him where the engine data was was no longer talking and never would talk again.

Kickaha could find nothing to reveal how Dingsteth had died. The skull and skeleton bore no obvious marks of violence. Maybe he had become bored with his futile and purposeless life and had taken poison. Or it could be that Zazel had constructed Dingsteth so that he died after a certain span of time. Whatever had killed him, he had left behind a world that was running down.

Kickaha said loudly, "I just don't know!" And then he howled with frustration and rage and seized the skull and hurled it far across the floor. That did not help his predicament any, but it did make him feel a little less angry. His voice and his cry were hurled back at him from the faraway walls. It was as if this world were determined to have the last word.

He was galled by the thought that Dingsteth's death did not mean that the creation-destruction data would never be available to anyone. If Red Orc got here, he might be able to operate the computer. He was a scientist, and he was intelligent enough to figure a way to communicate with the computer. Kickaha certainly could not hang around here until the Thoan arrived, if he ever did.

He smacked his fist, not too hard, against the back of the stone chair. He shouted, "I'm not beaten yet!"

14

THE SYMBOLS ON THE WALL COULD BE GOING IN A CIRCUIT AND ending up where they had started. But they might be heading toward a control room. He decided to go deeper into the cavern-tunnel complex. A little more than a mile was behind him when he stopped. The light-shedding knobs and lichen here were turning brown. At least half of the knobs had fallen from the ceiling to the floor, and the rest looked as if they would not be able to cling to the ceiling much longer. If this rot spread, all the tunnels and caves would be totally dark, and the plants' oxygen production would cease.

Unable to give up any project easily, he walked onward, marking the wall with an X every hundred feet. The rot had now become almost complete. There was plenty of fresh water, though. No, there was not. Ten minutes later, the stream had quit running. Within five minutes, the groove in the middle of the floor was filmed with water. Even that would soon be gone in the increasing heat.

By now, so many knobs were dead that he could see only five feet in front of him. He stopped again. What was the use of pushing on? This world would soon be dead. Though the characters were still moving along the wall, that meant only that the great computer had not completely died. It would probably keep working as long as its energy supply did not run out. That might be for an unguessable number of millennia.

He turned around and began walking toward the huge cave. To make sure that he was following the right path, he had to stay close to the wall marked with X's. After a few minutes, he was forced to take his flashlight from his backpack. He attached this to his head with a band and walked faster. Then the air became so heavy and oxygenless and his breath so short that he brought the bottle out of the backpack and carried it by a strap over his right shoulder. After putting the mask over his face, he turned on the air. Now and then, though, he would turn it off and slide the mask to one side. He was able to get along without the oxygen for a few minutes before he had to replace the mask and breathe "fresh" air.

At least, no one would have to worry that Red Orc would possess the engine. That made him feel better. He could now dedicate himself completely to killing the Thoan and rescuing Anana.

Following the X's, he finally came to the huge cave. They ceased then because he had seen no reason to mark the wall here. He would continue to its other side and find the X marked by the mouth of the tunnel from which he had entered the cave. Instead of going along the wall, he walked through the center toward the middle tunnel. The headbeam fell on the dead pieces of plants and the bones of the animals, some of which were very curious. Then he stopped.

There was the stone chair. But where was the skeleton of Dingsteth?

He went close to the empty chair and turned around and around to flash his light throughout the cavern. It did not reach to the ceiling or the walls. He walked in the direction in which he had hurled the skull. Though he inspected a wide area where it could have fallen, he could not find it.

He removed the oxygen mask.

"Dingsteth! Dingsteth!" he called again and again. The name roared back at him from the distant walls. When the echoes had ceased, he put the mask back on and listened. All he heard was his blood thrumming in his hears. By now, though, the hidden watcher must know that the intruder was aware that he was not the only living creature in the Caverned World.

Kickaha waited for five minutes before shouting out the name twelve times. Echoes and then silence came once more.

He called out, "I know you're here, Dingsteth! Come out, wherever you are!"

Presently, he went to the chair and sat down. He might as well be comfortable, if a stone chair could be that. He waited the ten minutes he had allotted himself. After that, he had to get going. Someday, though, he would come back with much larger supplies and resume the search. Khruuz would probably be with him and would determine if he could do anything to get this world's electrical juices to flowing again.

Two minutes had passed. He was thinking that that was enough time to wait, since he was not absolutely sure that he had enough air. Then he straightened up. His eyes tried to pierce the darkness beyond the beam. He thought that he had heard a very faint chuckle. He stood up and turned around slowly. Before he had completed a three-quarters circle, he was struck hard on the right side of his head. The object hurt him but did not daze him. He jumped forward and reached up and turned off the headlight. Then he ran forward about ten steps more and flopped onto the hard floor.

His beamer in his hand, he listened. He knew what had hit him. As he had dashed away from the chair, he had seen, out of the corner of his eye, the skull of Dingsteth rolling out into the blackness.

He listened as if his life depended upon his ears—which, indeed, it did. After a few seconds, another chuckle, louder this time, came from behind him. He rolled away for a few turns, then crouched. Whoever had thrown the skull probably had means for seeing without photonic light. So did he. After removing the backpack and groping around in it, he brought out a pair of goggles and put them on. He moved a small dial on the flashlight and looked through the goggles in the ghostly light.

No one was visible. The only hiding place would be behind the stone chair. But the attacker would know that Kickaha knew that. Where else could he—or she—hide? The water channels in the cave were deep enough for a stretched-out man to conceal himself. The nearest was thirty feet away.

Hold it a minute! Kickaha thought. He who jumps to conclusions is often concluded. The attacker may be figuring out what I'm thinking. So he really is behind the chair. He pots me while I'm on my way to check out the water channels. But then, he could have done it easily any time. Why did he throw the skull at me and thus give me warning?

Whoever's doing this is a Thoan. Only one of them would play with me as a cat would play with a mouse. However, I'm no mouse, and the Thoan must know that. The higher the danger, the more the fun in the game. That's what he's thinking. So, let's give him a lot of fun and then have the last laugh.

It's highly probable, of course, that more than one is lurking out there. If the game starts to go against the skull-thrower, his buddy shoots me.

He could do nothing about that for the present. He would keep watching for other players, however.

He rose, whirled three times, holding the backpack out like a throwing hammer, and hurled it at the chair. The pack fell by the side of the stone carving. No one poked his head from behind it or looked around its side. Then he switched the night-vision light to photonic, hoping to startle his enemy into betraying himself. A glance showed that no one had fallen for the trick. He switched back to night vision.

He approached two channels cautiously, looking back quite often. These were empty for as far as he could see in the light beam. But his attacker or attackers could be in the darkness. He felt the dial on the side of the beamer barrel near the butt. Without looking down at it, he advanced it to what he guessed would be a two-hundred-yard range. Suddenly, he started spinning, the trigger pulled all the way back. The beam from its end, a black pencil as seen through his goggles, described a circle as it pierced into the darkness. If anyone was hit, he did not yell.

Just as he completed his spin, he ran toward the chair. At the same time, he released his pressure on the trigger. Too much battery energy had already been expended. Anyone behind the chair would hear his pounding footsteps and would know he would have to do something quickly.

A goggled head, followed by very broad shoulders, rose from behind the carving. Even before his chest reached the top of the chair, his beamer was spitting its ray. Firing, Kickaha threw himself down. The stone floor smoked an inch from his left shoulder. But his ray had gone through the Thoan's neck and beyond. No doubt of that.

He rose and made a wide curve while walking toward the chair. Though he could hear his own soft steps, he doubted that the fallen man could. He also doubted that the man could hear cymbals clashing next to his ear.

While approaching the chair, he glanced behind and to both sides of him. If there was another enemy out there, he should have fired by now. However, he could be lying wounded in the dark, though not so hurt that he was out of the action permanently.

After making sure that his beam had gone through the man's neck, Kickaha took off the corpse's goggles. As he had thought it would be, the face was Red Orc's. But the real Red Orc could have sent a clone in his place. Kickaha would never know unless he ran across another one and that one confessed that he was the original Red Orc.

Unlikely event, Kickaha thought. This one, though, did not have the Horn. Would Red Orc let it out of his sight? No, he would not. So, it seemed probable that the dead man was a clone. But he could not have gotten into this world without the Horn. Thus, Red Orc had blown the Horn and then sent this clone through. Or was he along with him and now somewhere in the darkness?

Few things were ever certain.

He picked up the man's beamer and held it so that the headlight showed him its every detail. Its dial was set on stun range within a hundred feet. That meant that he had intended to knock his enemy out, not kill him. Whoever he was, he had been having fun by playing around with his enemy. When the Thoan tired of that, he would have stunned the Earthman and taken him back to Red Orc's headquarters as a prisoner.

Quickly, though frequently looking around, Kickaha took the man's oxygen bottle, beamer, battery pack, headlight, food rations, and canteen. Waste not, and you might not get wasted. As he left the cave burdened with two backpacks and went into the tunnel, he wondered if Red Orc could be in this tunnel and waiting for him, hoping to ambush him.

Kickaha switched to the night-vision light and goggled, walked more swiftly. The long journey was uninterrupted. No other person suddenly appeared ahead of him. Nor did his frequent glances backward show him any follower.

Sweating, his nerves still winched up tight, he got to the last X, the mark showing where he had come through the gate. He stood before the wall and uttered the code word Khruuz had given him. He was not looking forward to going through the cold and twisted and terrifying ordeal of the core-gate again. To his surprise, he was spared that. He stepped through the wall and was immediately in a forest.

He looked around and groaned. The trees were like those he had seen when he had gated to the world of Manathu Vorcyon. Before he could adjust to the unexpected, he was surrounded by big brown men with long straight glossy-black hair, snub noses, and black eyes with epicanthic folds. Their long spears were pointed at him.

"Hey, I'm the Great Mother's friend!" he said. "Don't you know me?"

Though they obviously did know him, they said nothing. They marched him through the forest. An hour later, they entered a clearing in the center of which was the gigantic tree in which Our Lady lived. Forthwith, he was conducted into the arboreal palace and up the winding stairway to the dimly lit sixth floor. They left him standing before a big door.

"You may come in now," Manathu Vorcyon said from behind the door. He pushed the polished ebony door open. Light rushed out upon him. He squinted, then saw a large round table in the center of a luxuriously furnished room. The giantess was on a large well-padded chair facing him. On one side of her was seated Eric Clifton; on the other, Khruuz, the scaly man.

He said, "I've had a lot of surprises, but this one jolts me the most. How in hell did you two get here?"

She waved a hand. "Sit down. Eat. Drink. And tell us of your adventures in the Caverned World. Under other circumstances, I would allow you time to bathe and to rest before dining. But we are very eager to know what you discovered."

Kickaha sat down. The chair felt good, and he was suddenly tired. A sip of yellow wine from a wooden goblet gave him a glow and pushed away his fatigue. While he ate, he talked.

When he was done, he said, "That's it. Red Orc can now get into that world. A lot of good it'll do him. As for his finding the way in, I don't know how he did it."

"Obviously," Khruuz said, "he put some kind of tracer on your passage from my place to Zazel's World. That is not good news. He has means of tracking he did not have before. That is, to my knowledge."

"He can track intergate passage to my world, too," Manathu Vorcyon said. "Especially since he has the Horn."

"But I doubt that he has the device I used on the Unwanted World," Kickaha said. "Okay, I've told you my story. How did you three get together?"

"It was Khruuz's idea," the Great Mother said. "He sent Eric Clifton as his envoy to me to propose that we band together against Red Orc."

"And I set up the gating from Zazel's World so that you would come directly here," Khruuz said.

"Your world is unguarded now?" Kickaha said. "Red Orc'll—"

"Try to get into it," Manathu Vorcyon said. "But he does not know that it's unguarded. Anyway, Khruuz has set up traps."

Though Khruuz's face was nonhuman, it showed a quite human annoyance. He said, "I believe that Kickaha was addressing me and expected me to reply."

The giantess's eyes opened. She said, "If I offended you, I regret doing so, though I did not intend offense."

Kickaha smiled. Already there was friction, however slight, between the two allies. Manathu Vorcyon was used to doing exactly what she wanted to do. That included interrupting people when they were talking. Apparently, Khruuz was not used to being regarded as an inferior. To Manathu Vorcyon, everybody else was inferior. Was she not Our Lady, the Great Mother, the Grandmother of All? Did not everybody in her world and the others regard her with awe? Even Red Orc had not contemplated attacking her until recently. And that was only because she had entered the battle early.

"If I am not speaking out of turn," Kickaha said, carefully keeping sarcasm out of his voice, "I suggest that our best defense is attack against Red Orc. We shouldn't wait until he storms into this world or any other. We should go after him with everything we have."

"Good thinking, although it's superfluous," she said. "We have already decided that is the best policy. We also agree that you should be our spearhead."

"I'm used to being cannon fodder," he said. "It started during World War Two—that was on Earth when I was a youth—and it's never let up since. But I won't be used as a mere pawn. I insist on full membership in this council of war. I've earned it."

"There was never a thought that you would not be an equal in the council," she said smoothly. "However, it has been well known for millennia that a military committee is useful only for advice. An army must have a single leader, a general who makes quick decisions, whose orders are to be obeyed even though the soldier questions that they are the right thing to do.

"You, Clifton, have no military experience. You, Kickaha, are essentially a loner, a man of action, one excellent, perhaps unexcelled, in situations involving very few persons. You are no master strategist or at least have had no experience in planning strategy. You, Khruuz, are an unknown element, though your ability to survive when all your people died is testimony to your wiliness. You also must be an invaluable repository of scientific and technological knowledge. But you really do not know humans or their past and present situations. Nor have you had any experience as a military leader."

She paused, breathed deeply, then said, "The choice of your leader is obvious. I have all that you lack and also those abilities you do have."

The others were silent for a minute. Then Kickaha said, "I don't give a damn about being the general. That's not my style. But I insist I not be treated like a sacrificial piece on a chessboard. When I'm in the field, I make my own decisions, right or wrong, even if it goes against orders. The foot soldier is the only guy who knows what's needed in his immediate area."

He took in a deep breath, then looked straight at Manathu Vorcyon.

"Something is sticking in my craw, choking me. It's a bone I have to pick with you."

"I expected this," she said. "If you had kept silent about it, I would not have respected you."

"Then I'll say out loud for Clifton's and Khruuz's benefit what's bugging me. You sent me to the Unwanted World to locate the gate to Zazel's World. You gave me a gate detector. But you didn't tell me the detector was a fake or that it was a booby trap. You knew that it would explode after a certain time. And—"

"No. It would explode only when Red Orc or his clones came within a certain distance of it. And after a certain time interval. I did not know the pattern of his electrical skin fields or what his body mass was. But using your descriptions of his physical features, I estimated his probable mass. I doubt that that was off more than a pound or two."

"You didn't care if I was killed, too!" Kickaha blurted.

"No. I cared very much. That is why the bomb was set so that it would not go off until the one who took it from you was out of range of you. Out of killing range, anyway."

"But you didn't know if the person who took it away from me was Red Orc or not!"

"Whoever did take it was likely to be your enemy."

"Well," Kickaha said slowly and less vehemently, "I suppose you want an apology from me for suspecting you didn't care if I was killed as long as Red Orc bought the farm."

"What does . . . ?"

"In English, it means dying in combat."

"Ah! But, no, I don't wish for an apology. No reason to give me one. You didn't know all the facts . . ."

"Damned few facts," Kickaha muttered. "In fact, none."

"I had to expose you to a certain amount of danger. You are used to that. As it turned out, you were only stunned."

She looked at the others. "You agree that I am the general in this war?"

Khruuz shrugged. "You have presented your case logically. I cannot argue with you."

"Thanks for even allowing me my say," Clifton said. "Who am I to question you three mighty ones?"

"Kickaha?"

"Agreed."

"Very well. Here is what I have in mind as our next move."

15

KICKAHA WAS ON ONE OF RED ORC'S PROPERTIES, EARTH II.

Just exactly where he was there, he did not know. He had gated through, courtesy of the Great Mother, to an area on Earth II corresponding to the California region on Earth I.

"Red Orc has forbidden any Lord to enter either Earth," Manathu Vorcyon had told him. "But as you know, other Lords, including Jadawin and Anana, made gates to both these worlds and entered them.

"Long ago, I made several gates there for possible future entrances, though I have not used any so far. You will take the gate on Earth Two closest to where you think Red Orc has a palace. It's possible that he has discovered this gate and trapped it."

"How well I know that."

Before stepping through the glindglassa, he had been embraced by her. For a few seconds, his head was buried in the valley between her breasts. Ah, delicious sensation!

After releasing him, she held him at arm's length, which was a considerable distance. "You are the only man who has ever rejected me."

"Anana."

She nodded and said, "I know. But you'll get me in the end."

"It's not your end I'm thinking about."

She laughed. "You're also the only man whom I could forgive. But you have forgiven me for placing you in such danger without telling you. On your way, and may the luck of Shambarimen be with you."

The legendary Hornmaker's luck had run out eventually, but Kickaha said nothing about that. He stepped through the seeming mirror into a warm desert of rocks and few plants. Behind him was the boulder holding the gate. He looked around and saw only some buzzards, weeds, more boulders, and some angular rock formations, strata that had been tilted upward. When and where had he seen them?

The sky was cloudless. The sun was at a height that made him believe that the time was around ten in the morning. The air seemed to be a few degrees above 75° Fahrenheit.

The Great Mother had not been able to tell him how close the gate was to the area corresponding to the Los Angeles region of Earth I. Nor did she know in what direction it was from that place.

As usual, on my own, he thought. But that was a milieu he loved.

He had been facing west when he came out of the boulder. South was on his left hand. He always favored the left, his lucky side. If he found out that he was going in the wrong direction, he would just turn around and head the right way. He walked down the rough and exotic rocks, slipping a few times though not falling, until he got to more or less level ground. During this, he passed close to a diamondback snake, whose warning rattle made him feel comfortable. He was, in a sense, home. However, the last time he had really been on his native planet and in Los Angeles, he had not liked it. Too many people, too much traffic, noise, sleaze, and foul air.

A little later, he came across a huge tarantula. Its tiny vicious eyes reminded him of some of the black-hearted villains he had encountered in many worlds. That, too, warmed him. Meeting them had sharpened his survival skills; he owed them a debt of gratitude. Too bad they were all dead. He could not now thank them.

He wore a wide-brimmed straw hat for shade, a dark maroon shirt open at the neck, a leather belt, baggy black pants, black socks, and sturdy hiker's shoes. A holster holding a beamer was at his side, and a canteen full of water hung from his belt on his right. His backpack was stuffed full with items he considered necessary for this expedition.

Shortly after he began walking on the road, he stopped. Of course! Now he knew where he was. Those stone formations and boulders! How many times he had seen them in Western movies! They were the Vasquez rocks, an area used many times in shooting those films. Thus, his destination was south, though he did not know how far away. He set out confidently in the direction of the 30th parallel.

Ahead of him was what Earth I called the Los Angeles area. The geography was the same as on Earth I, but its architecture and inhabitants were different.

After a while he came to a well-traveled and wheel-rutted path. Five miles or so had spun out from his feet when he heard something behind him. He turned around and saw a cloud of dust a half-mile north. It was boiling up from a body of men on horseback. Their helmets flashed in the sun. Two men at the front of the cavalcade held aloft flapping banners on long poles. And now the reflection from lanceheads struck his eyes as if it were from sunbeam javelins. It twanged nerves that evoked images of the many raids he had made when with the Bear People tribe on the Amerind level of the World of Tiers. And when he had been in jousts on the Dracheland level of that same world. The flashing lights were transformed into the blood-thumping calls of war horns.

However, the last thing he wanted was to be arrested by soldiers. His clothing would make them curious. If they paused to question him, he would not be able to answer them in any tongue they knew. In this world, a suspicious alien equaled the calaboose.

The country on his left was flat, but a wash was forty feet away. The hills on his right were a hundred and fifty feet from him. He ran toward the dry streambed, hoping that the cavalry would not see him. But if he could see them, they could see him. Too bad. Nothing to do about it except run.

He jumped into the wash, turned around at once, and looked over the edge of the bank. His head was partly hidden by a clump of sagebrush. Presently, the standard-bearers rode by. Each of their crimson flags bore the figure of a huge brown bear with relatively longer legs than a grizzly's. The face was also relatively shorter than a grizzly's.

Maybe the giant short-faced bear that died out on Earth I has survived here, he thought.

The officers behind the standard-bearers were clean-shaven and wore round helmets with noseguards and curved neck-protectors, topped by black plumes—something like the armor of ancient Greek warriors. They also wore plum-colored capes and crimson tunics with gold braiding on the fronts. Their legs were bare, and their feet were shod in leather sandals. Scabbards with short swords were on their broad crimson-chased belts. Their body armor, casques something like those of the Spanish conquistadores, was in a basket behind each rider. It was too hot to don these unless a battle was coming up.

Actually, the sun was too strong for wearing helmets. But he supposed that their military regulations required them even when the heat forbade them.

The dogfaces carried spears in their hands and long swords in their scabbards. They were as clean-shaven and as dark-skinned as the officers. But whereas the officers had short hair, the rank-and-file had long, dark, wavy, and unbound hair. They did not look Mediterranean. Their faces were broad and high-cheekboned, the eyelids had slight epicanthic folds, and their noses were, generally, long. A dash, perhaps only a savor, of Amerind ancestors, he thought.

About two score of archers followed these out of the dust cloud.

Behind these came a number of men and women on horseback or driving wagons loaded with bundles of supplies. They wore soiled, yellow, high-crowned, floppy, wide hats. Their varicolored tunics were dust-smudged, and they carried no weapons. They were undoubtedly American Indians and were civilian servants or slaves. Behind this section rode a few companies of lancers and archers.

"They've got horses," Kickaha mumbled. "I need a horse. Ergo, I'll get a horse. But I suppose they hang horse thieves just as they did in the Old West. Well, it won't be the first time I stole a horse. Nor the last, I hope."

After the group had passed, the dust had settled down, and he was sure no soldiers were coming back to get him, he went back to the road. He walked for an hour in the increasing heat. When he saw two men ride down from a pass in the hills on his right, he increased his pace. By the time the two had gotten to the road, he was only forty feet from them. He called out to them, and they reined in their horses.

Two tougher customers he had never seen. Their hats were like the wagon drivers'. Their black and food-dotted beards flowed down to their chests. Their black eyes were hard, and their hawklike faces were sun-seamed and looked as if they had never smiled. They wore dirty blue tunics and full, leg-length boots. Quivers full of arrows hung from their backs; their bows were strung; their scabbards held long swords and long knives.

Kickaha put his pack down, reached in, and brought out a small ingot of gold. Holding it up and pointing with the other hand at the nearest animal, he said, "I'll give you this for a horse."

Of course, they did not understand his words, but they understood his gestures. They spoke softly to each other, then turned their horses and charged him, swords in hand. He had expected this, since they looked to him like outlaws. His beamer ray, set at stun power, knocked them off their steeds. He caught one horse by the reins and was dragged for a few feet before it stopped. The other animal kept on running. After doffing all his clothes except for his pants and donning the stinking boots and tunic of the larger man, he rode away. He also had the man's bow and quiver. He had kept his own pants because they would ease the chafing from riding. He had left the gold ingot on the ground by the unconscious bandits. They didn't deserve it, but what the hell?

The ride was far longer than he wanted, because he did not press his horse, and he had to find water and feed for it. As he neared the city, he encountered an increasingly heavier traffic. Farmers with wagons piled high with produce were going into the city, and wagons holding bales of goods rattled out of it. Once he passed a slave caravan, mostly Indian men and women linked together by iron collars and chains. The unchained children followed their parents. Though he felt sorry for the wretches, he could do nothing for them.

Finally, he came to a pass that led down to the city, which was still some miles away. By then, he had exchanged some gold for local money, round copper or silver coins of various sizes and values. On each was stamped the profile of some big shot, and circling close to the rim were three words in an alphabet unfamiliar to him.

This was a large city by the citizens' standards, he supposed. His estimate was approximately one hundred thousand to one hundred fifty thousand population. It had a few squalid dwellings on the edge of the municipality. Their number increased as he rode closer to the ocean, though it was still miles from where he was. Here and there among these shacks and rundown stores were walled estates with huge houses. The streets seemed to have followed the paths of drunken cows until he was halfway along what would be the Hollywood Hills on his native planet. Then the dirt streets straightened out and became paved with large hewn-stone blocks.

Here and there were some tall, square, white stone buildings with twin domes, large front porches, and columns bulging in the middle and covered with the carved figures of troll-like heads and of dragons, lions, bears, and, surprisingly, elephants. Or were they mammoths? The streets were unpaved in this area. Narrow ditches along their sides were filled with water that stank of sewage. He supposed that there were stone-block or cobblestoned streets nearer to the coast, but he did not have time to see them.

This city had its equivalent of the L.A. smog. The smoke from thousands of kitchen fires hung heavy over the valley.

While he rode, he had been using his gate-detector. The light in it did not come on until he swept the "Hollywood Hills" area. Unlike the hills he had seen while on Earth I in 1970, these slopes were bare except for a score or so of mansions. Emanating from one on the very top of a hill were several bright spots. Gates.

He could not be sure, but he thought that the large white building topped by two domes was where the Griffith Observatory would be on his native planet. If he remembered correctly what he had been told while in Los Angeles, a road led up through a park and ended at the observatory. It seemed probable that on this world, a private road to the same spot would have been laid out to the mansion. There was only one way to find out.

It took several hours of searching to find it, because he could not ask directions of passersby. Finally, he came to a dirt road that led him to a road paved with large flat stones. That led toward the ocean and followed a course at the foot of the hills. But a road that wound to the top of the hill was dirt. He rode unhurriedly up it. The steep slope would be hard on a horse if it galloped or even cantered.

While he was on a narrow lane flanked by tall trees, he figured out what he would do when he got close to the mansion. Though Red Orc lived in it now and then, he was probably unknown to most of the citizens. He had bribed some prominent citizen to front for him and to put the property in his name. Red Orc might not even leave his grounds. The mansion would be well guarded, and any entrance gates in the house would be trapped.

At this moment, the Thoan might not be in the house. He was said to have other houses on several continents of Earth II. He gated from one to the other, depending upon what area he was interested in at the time. His spies reported indirectly to him on the current state of affairs in that part of this world, and he no doubt also read the news periodicals.

Though the creator and hidden observer of both Earths, Red Orc made it a policy to interfere as little as possible with human affairs. The planets were his studies. He had made both in the image of his own planet, that is, the geological and geographical image of his now-ruined native world. But they had been been copies of his world when the human inhabitants were in the Early Stone Age.

He had made artificial humans, then cloned one set, and put one on Earth I and one on Earth II. Each was exactly like the other in genetic makeup, and each had been placed in the same geographical location as the other. They were both in the same primitive state, and each of the corresponding tribes had spoken the same language. Thus, those placed in, say, what would be Algeria on Earth I and the exact same area on Earth II would speak the same language.

Red Orc had observed the tribes on both Earths during the last twenty thousand years. Some Thoan said it was thirty thousand years, but no one except Red Orc knew the correct period of time. Whatever the date, he had watched the prehistory and history of humans on both planets. He had not devoted all of his time to observation there. He apparently just dropped in now and then to bring his information up to date. Or to conduct some of his nefarious business.

Both planets were vast experiments in divergence. Though the various tribes had been, in the beginning, the exact counterparts of their duplicates on the other planet, including not only their physical forms but their languages, customs, and even names, there was a great difference after twenty thousand years.

Kickaha did not have time to compare in detail how these people had diverged from those of Earth. Red Orc might have spies watching for him. The Thoan left as little to chance as possible; he guarded his own rear end. For all Kickaha knew, word of his coming might have reached Red Orc days ago.

So be it.

Halfway up the road, he came to a high stone wall across it and extending up into the hills. A dozen armed men were lounging in front of the gate. He turned around and rode back into town. There he managed to trade some of his small coins for lodging for his horse. The owner of the stables did not seem very curious. There were too many foreigners in this harbor city for him to be surprised to meet one, even out here, miles from the metropolitan area.

Or it could be that he had been told by a Red Orc agent to pretend indifference.

Kickaha walked back to the bottom of the hill and went into the woods a few yards from the road. Here he waited for nightfall, meanwhile napping and then eating his own rations and drinking from his own canteen. Though he was theoretically immune to any disease, he did not want to chance the local food or the water. After a long time, midnight came. By then, the sky was overcast. But he wore the headband and its attached night-vision device. He worked uphill through the trees some distance from the road until he came to the wall. Though it was ten feet high, he got over it easily by throwing a grappling hook and climbing up the rope.

When he was on top and had drawn the rope up, he took from the backpack a sensor-detecting instrument given him by Khruuz. He swept the immediate area with it. It registered nothing. That only meant, however, that any sensors planted out there were not active. There could be plenty of passive detectors camouflaged as rocks or tree bark. It did not matter. He was pressing onward and upward.

He let himself down to the ground and whipped the hook free. After coiling it and hanging it from a strap on his belt, he climbed up almost vertical slopes. Then he came to less steep ground. Again, he swung the sensor-detector in a semicircle. Its light, set within a recess, did not come on.

After he had climbed to the top of another stone wall, he used the detector again. Now, its indicator glowed. He set it to determine what frequency the detectors were on. Having done that, he rotated a dial on the machine's side until it matched the frequency. Then he pressed a recessed button in its side. Immediately, the inset light turned off. The machine had now passively canceled the transmitted waves so that they would not register his body. But the alarms in Red Orc's house might go off if this action was detected.

He was, he thought, in a tiny canoe moving on a river of uncertainty and ambiguity, a craft leaking from holes, with the paddle on the point of breaking. But if it sank, he would swim on upstream.

He wiped the sweat from his forehead and drank deeply from the canteen. This he had emptied and refilled a dozen times during his trip with water from clean streams flowing from the hills. He pushed through the thick bushes among the trees for a few yards, stopping when he saw the lights in the upper-story windows of the great mansion. The ground floor had no windows. Like those large houses in the valley, this building was constructed of white stone blocks.

Kickaha removed his night-vision goggles and looked behind him and down. The valley was in darkness except for a few widely scattered lights, probably clusters of torches. He resumed his walk toward the east side of the house. The ground was level, and the gravel path he was following wound through beds of flowers. Forty feet from the house, the lawn began. Glancing at his detector now and then, Kickaha proceeded to the corner of the house and stuck his head around it. Lit by torches set in brackets on the front wall was a wide porch. Along the front edge of the porch were seven columns covered by carved figures.

Two spearmen stood before the eight-foot-high arched doorway.

He took two minutes to stun them with the beamer, tie their hands behind them and their feet together, and slap tape on their mouths. He did not know when the change of guard would be and did not care. There was no lock on the big iron door. Since it resisted his push, he supposed that it had been barred from the inside. His beamer cut through the door and the big rectangular wooden bolt behind it.

The only noise was the sputter of melting metal and the clang as the bolt and metal bracket on the other side fell onto the floor. He had to push them aside when he entered. He stepped inside a well-lit room big enough to hold a medium-sized sailing ship. The illumination was the sourceless lighting of Thoan technology. Cool air was blowing from a wall vent near him.

No one appeared to defend the house. After searching through the ground floor and finding no one there, he went up a wide staircase to the second story. There he found the room in which Anana had been subjected to the memory-uncoiling. It was as empty of people as the first floor. The third revealed nothing useful except the lights he saw through his gate-detector. So far, he had found gates on every floor, ten in all. Red Orc believed in having many escape routes close at hand.

The "attics," the twin domes, were entered by trapdoors in the ceiling of the third story. Though he did not expect to find anything significant there, he was wrong. Each dome housed an airboat. If Red Orc failed to get to a gate fast enough, he could use one of these to escape. Kickaha got into the cockpit of one and reacquainted himself with the controls and instruments. Having done that and started the motor, he pushed the button that energized the control mechanism of the dome door. It slid to one side, showing a still-cloudy sky.

The airboat lifted and pointed toward the doorway. He was going to fly back to the Vasquez rocks and regate there to Manathu Vorcyon's World. Since he was one-hundred-percent sure that all the gates in the house were trapped, he would take none. He was beginning to feel that Red Orc had guessed that he would break into the house. It was a wonder that the Thoan had not fixed it so that the house would blow up when any unauthorized person entered it.

He pressed down on the acceleration pedal. The craft surged forward, pressing him against the back of the pilot's chair. He should go slowly until he was out of the dome, but he was in a hurry.

That haste was his undoing. Or maybe it wouldn't have made any difference.

In any event, when he saw the shimmering, which was a few inches outside the dome-hangar door, it was too late to stop.

He howled, "Trapped!"

The airboat passed through the shimmering curtain, the gate that Red Orc had set to be triggered when the craft approached it.

16

JUST AS HE BULLETED THROUGH THE VEIL, HE PRESSED TWO
buttons to fire big and powerful "cannon" beamers, one on each side of the
nose of the boat. Whatever was waiting for him on the other side was going
to be blasted. Metal would melt, and flesh would be a cloud of atoms.

No, they would not. The cannons failed to spit out the ravening beams
that destroyed everything in their range.

He should have checked them out before taking off. Red Orc had deactivated them.

Though furious at himself for not testing the beamers, he did what
was needed to keep the airboat from slamming into the opposite wall of the
gigantic hangar he had shot into. His foot lifted from the acceleration
pedal. At the same time, he turned the magnetic retro-fire dial to the full-
power position. His body surged forward slightly, but the pressure was so
intense he felt crushed. The magnetic restraining field kept him from
breaking his chest bones against the steering wheel. Its nosetip almost
touching the wall, the boat had stopped.

He slid back the canopy and looked over the side of the cockpit. About
fifty feet below was the hangar floor. Parked at the rear of the vast room
were two score airboats of different sizes and a zeppelin-shaped and -sized
vessel. On the floor near the front of the building, a dozen men were aiming their beamers at him. What he had thought was a wall was the upper
part of the closed hangar door.

Red Orc walked out of the small doorway near the big one. He stood
well back of the armed men and looked up. Though he seemed small at
this distance, his voice was loud.

"Bring the boat down slowly, and give yourself up! If you don't, I'll
detonate the bomb in your boat!"

Kickaha shrugged and then did as ordered. This was most probably the
stonewall end of his life. He was sure that the Thoan did not need the
Trickster anymore. Besides, his enemy had slipped away from him so

slickly so many times that he would no longer chance his doing it again.

But then, you never knew about Red Orc, a slippery and unpredictable customer himself.

Kickaha turned off the motor. At the command of the soldiers' officer, he threw his backpack and weapons out. Red Orc would now have a gate-detector for his own use. He'd be one-up in the ever-shifting conflict between himself and his foes, Khruuz and Manathu Vorcyon. Kickaha got out of the cockpit and stood, hands held high, while the officer ran a metal detector over him and patted him down. The officer spoke in Thoan, and Kickaha put his hands behind his back. The officer used a hold-band to secure his wrists together.

A woman walked through the doorway and then stopped by Red Orc's side. She was beautiful. Her long straight black hair fell past her shoulders. Her dress was a simple red shift; her feet were sandaled.

Kickaha cried, "Anana!"

She looked blankly at him and questioningly at the Thoan.

"She doesn't know you, Kickaha!" Red Orc said. He put one arm around her. "I haven't told her about you, but I will. She'll find out what a vicious and murderous man you are. Not that she'll be very interested in you."

Many bad things had been happening to Kickaha. This seemed the worst to him.

Red Orc told the officer to take the prisoner away.

"We'll see each other soon," he said. "Our final talk will be, in a sense, our last one."

In a sense? What did that mean?

Anana was looking straight at him. Her face showed pity for him. But that would soon change to repulsion when the lying Thoan told her what a cowardly backstabbing lowlife he was.

"Don't believe a word he says about me!" Kickaha shouted at her. "I love you! You loved me once, and you'll love me again!"

She pressed closer to Red Orc. He put his hand on her breast. Kickaha surged forward but was brought to his knees by a beamer butt slamming the back of his head. Dazed, his head hurting, and with vomit rising, he was marched away. Halfway to the building that would be his prison, he got the dry heaves. But his guards urged him on with kicks.

Even though sick, he observed the land around him and the big building he was headed for. It was in a large clearing surrounded by trees. These were growing so closely together that their branches interlocked, moving up and down and sometimes bending around other branches. They looked as if they were feeling each other up. He did not need to be told that they were watchdog trees. Whether or not they just held an escapee or ate him, they were tough obstacles.

The sky was blue and clear except for some very high and thin clouds. The sun was like Earth's. That meant nothing, because many suns in many worlds looked like the Terrestrial sun. Some were as large as the sun; some very tiny, though they looked large.

The guards were tall blue-eyed men with Dutch-bobbed brown, red, or blond hair. They wore yellow calf-length boots and baggy green knee-length shorts attached to a harnesslike arrangement over their shoulders. Broad leather straps running diagonally across their chests bore metal sunburst badges.

Kickaha had never seen such uniforms before. For all he knew, he could still be on Earth II but in a place distant from the "Los Angeles" area.

The building into which he was conducted was onion-shaped, and its front bore clusters of demonic and snakelike figures locked in combat or copulating.

He was marched between two squads through a vast foyer and then halted before an elevator door. Its door did not open. Instead, the shimmering of a gate appeared, and he and one squad walked through it and into a large elevator cage. It was the only one he had ever seen furnished with a washbowl, its stand a rack with towels, a toilet, a fully rotatable blower, a showerhead, a floor drain, and a chair on which was a roll of blankets. The cage accelerated upward for several stories. When it stopped, he expected the door to slide open. But it lurched sideways and began to move swiftly on the horizontal plane.

Presently, the cage stopped. The squad marched out through a shimmering that had appeared over the doorway. As soon as the last man had left the cage, the gate vanished.

So, the cage was also his prison cell. An hour after entering it, he saw a small section of the wall slide up. A revolving shelf came out of the recess. His meal was on it. Okay. He had been served before in just such a manner. And he had gotten more than once out of what seemed to be an escape-proof chamber.

He did not eat for several hours. Though he had recovered somewhat from the blow on the head, he still felt sick. Most of that, though, was because Anana no longer knew him and might never know him again.

When he had seen her in the huge hangar, her face had looked, in a subtle way, much younger. It was as if without his realizing it before, every hundred years of her millennia-long life had placed another microscopically thin mask of age on her face. Yet, she had always looked young to him. Not until the memory-uncoiling had taken her back to when she was eighteen years old had the real difference become apparent. Though still aged, she was now unaged. What previously could not be seen had been made visible. And a long-dead innocence had been reborn. Only he, who knew her so well, could have perceived the lifting of the years.

A square section of the wall glowed, shimmered, then became a solid picture. He saw Red Orc, nude, sitting on a chair behind a table. Behind the Thoan, by the opposite wall, was a huge bed.

He lifted a cut-quartz goblet filled with red wine. He said, "A final toast to you, Kickaha. You led me a hot chase and a quite amusing one. To be frank, you also worried me now and then. But you made the hunt more interesting than usual. So, here's to you, my elusive but now doomed quarry!"

After sipping the wine and setting the goblet down, he leaned back. He looked quite satisfied.

"You did what I could not do during my intermittent searches: you found a way into Zazel's World. But that was because I was too close to the problem. You were fresh. However, I owe you thanks for what you did for me, and you're one of the very few I've ever felt gratitude toward. In fact, I owe you double thanks."

He reached out a hand to something Kickaha could not see. When he brought it within vision, it held the gate-detector device.

"I also owe you great gratitude for your gift even though you were not so willing to tender me this. Thank you, again."

"You call this gratitude?"

"I haven't killed you, have I?"

He sipped again, then said, "I don't know what happened to my son, that is, the clone I sent after you into the Caverned World. I suspect that you killed him. You will tell me in every detail what did happen."

To refuse to tell the Thoan of his experiences there would be useless, even stupid. Red Orc would get it out of him and cause him unendurable pain while doing it. Reluctantly, Kickaha described how he had traveled to the place and what had occurred there. But he did not mention Clifton or Khruuz.

Red Orc looked neither frustrated nor angry. He said, "I believe some of your story, but I'll wait a while for verification for my son Abalos to return. Whether he does or not, I will get into Zazel's World in time. I have no doubt that I'll be able to reactivate it, though it may take a while."

"Time is what you don't have. After all, Manathu Vorcyon has come out from her isolation. She is now your great enemy."

"I was going to tackle her someday anyway."

Kickaha quoted an ancient Thoan saying. "He who is forced to begin attack before he planned to do so has no plan."

"It was Elyttria of the Silver Arrows who said, 'Old sayings are always old but are not always true.'"

Kickaha sat down in the only chair in his room. He grinned, and he said, "Let's quit trading epigrams. Would you be kind enough to tell me exactly how you intend to proceed against Manathu Vorcyon? After all, I'll never be able to warn her. And then would you tell me what you've got in store for me? I like to be prepared."

"I will do the latter, though not completely," Red Orc said. "I'll not tell you one of the things I plan for you. You can watch me do it."

The Thoan stood up and called out, "Anana!" Then he said, "From now on, you'll be able to see what takes place in this room and hear everything. The transmission from your room will be stopped."

A minute later, Anana, as nude as the Thoan, walked into the room. She went into his arms and kissed him passionately. After which, he led her to the bed.

Kickaha yelled, "No! No!" and struck the screen area with his fist. All he did was to hurt his hand, but he did not mind that. Nevertheless, he used the chair to strike the screen many times. Neither the wall nor the chair was damaged. Then he unrolled the blankets and wrapped them around his head and stuck the ends of his little fingers into his ears. When he did that, the sound volume was raised so high that he could hear everything.

He screamed to drown out the noises until his throat was too hoarse to continue. After a long time, the sounds ceased. He came out from under his covers to look at the screen. It was now silent and blank. He croaked a sound of relief. But his mind was still displaying the images and voicing the noises.

Suddenly, the area glowed, shimmered, and became a picture. This one was a replay. Evidently, Red Orc was going to run it and, probably, future scenes over and over again until Kickaha went berserk or withdrew into himself.

He gritted his teeth, pulled up his chair to face the wall and, mask-faced, stared at the images. He did not know if he could concentrate enough to summon up certain mental techniques he had learned a long time ago. While living with the Hrowakas, the Bear People, on the Amerind level of the tiered planet, he had mastered a psychological procedure taught by a shaman. Many years had passed since then. Despite this, he had not forgotten the methods any more than he had forgotten how to swim. They were embedded in his mind and nerves.

Doing them with the needed concentration was the main problem now. It was not easy. He failed after starting them seven times. Then he grimly focused on the movie and did not quit that until hours later. If Red Orc was watching him—he undoubtedly was—he would be puzzled by his prisoner's attitude.

Seeing the film over and over hurt Kickaha as he had never been hurt before. Tears flowed; his chest seemed to be a cavern filled with boiling lead. But he would not quit. After a while, his pain began to ooze away. Later, he became bored. He had attained enough objectivity to see the film as a pornographic show in which the characters were strangers. He felt as if his only punishment was to be doomed to watch the same movie over and over forever.

Now, he was able to start the internal ritual. This time, he succeeded. The screen area suddenly disappeared. Though it was still there to see and to hear, he no longer saw or heard it. He had shut it out.

He thought, Absakosaw, wise old medicine man! I owe you much. But he could never repay Absakosaw. He and his tribe had been slain by one of Kickaha's enemies. Kickaha had killed their killer, but revenge did not make the Bear People rise from the dead.

Three days passed. The screen area remained blank. On the morning of the fourth day, it came alive. This time, the scene was a different bedroom but with the same actors. It was obvious that Anana was deeply in love with Red Orc. But then, she had always been lusty, and she had no reason she knew of to hate the Lord. Nor did she know, of course, that she was being observed.

Either this transmission was a new one or Red Orc had figured out why Kickaha never paid attention to the film. In any event, it was getting through to Kickaha in more than one way. Again, he sat for hours staring at the wall until he was bored. After this, he used Abakosaw's system. When he rose from the chair, he saw only the wall. However, occasional images from the film would pierce his mind. He might be worn down eventually and be unable to make the blanking-out work.

The fifth day, while he was exercising vigorously, he heard the Thoan's voice. He turned. The screen was active. But it did not display the scenes that had driven him close to insanity. Red Orc's head and shoulders filled the screen. That confused Kickaha for a few seconds until he realized what had happened. Only the films were blocked from his mind, and he would receive anything else coming from the wall.

Red Orc said, "You are elusive in more ways than the physical. I'd ask you to teach me your technique, but I have my own. And I could get you to tell me that without rewarding you with a month or so free of mental torture. I'm sure that you have held certain items of information back from me. You've been pleased, perhaps smug, because you've done this. You're going to go to sleep now. When you wake up, I'll know everything you know. Know, at least, those items you've been keeping from me."

The screen faded into blackness. Everything faded. When Kickaha awoke on the bed, he knew that he had been made unconscious, probably by gas. Then he had been questioned. Red Orc had used some sort of truth drug and gotten out of him everything, including the facts about Khruuz. That must have startled and alarmed him considerably. The appearance of the scaly man was something he could not have anticipated.

After Kickaha had eaten his dinner and placed the tray of dirty dishes on the swing-out shelf, he found out what else Red Orc had done. The screen came on. Again, Red Orc and Anana made passionate and polymorphous-perverse love. Grimly, Kickaha went through the old Hrowaka's methods. But this time, five hours went by without his being able to blank the screen out.

Suddenly, it stopped in the middle of the tenth replay. The Thoan's head appeared.

"By now, you have concluded that I canceled the effects of your technique. I did so, of course, with hypnotic commands. You remember the methods, but you can't make them effective."

Kickaha managed to control himself and not throw the chair at the screen. He tried to smile as if he did not care. Instead, he snarled.

"I have decided not to wait for Absalos to return from Zazel's World," Red Orc said. "Your story that you killed him is probably true. I'll find out when I get there. I will be gating out to there in a few minutes. When I come back, I'll have data to make the creation-destruction engine. After that, you and all my enemies and billions who have never heard of me will die. So will their universes. Even my Earths will perish in a beautiful display of energy. I've run them as experiments, but I can now predict what's going to happen to their people. Earth One humans will kill almost all of themselves with their brainless breeding, poisoning of land, air, and sea, and in the end, the collapse of civilization, followed by starvation. Then the survivors, though plunged into savagery, will start the climb back to civilization, science, and technology, only to repeat the same story.

"This will also eventually happen on Earth Two. Why should I continue the experiments when I know by now what the results will be? I'll use the energies of the disintegrated universes to make a new one. One only. This will be the ideal world, ideal for me, anyway.

"I may take Anana with me to my new world. But I may not. While I am gone on my trip, she'll be kept occupied. My son, Kumas, will have her. She will love him as much as she loves me, because she won't know the difference."

He paused, smiled, and said, "That she won't know the difference shows something about true love, doesn't it? It's a philosophical problem in identity. I would like to discuss it with you, though I believe that the discussion would not last long. You're a trickster, Kickaha, but you do not know Thoan philosophy. Or, I suspect, Earthian philosophy. You are, basically, a simple-minded barbarian."

He turned his head to look at something. Perhaps, Kickaha thought, he was checking the time on a chronometer. What did it matter what Red Orc was doing? It didn't, but he was always curious about anything he could not explain.

The Thoan turned his head back to look at Kickaha.

"Oh, yes! Enjoy the movies!"

He walked out of Kickaha's view. Immediately after, the screen shifted to a room in which Red Orc—or was it his clone?—and Anana were at the peak of ecstasy.

Kickaha tried to become deaf, blind, and unfeeling steel. He failed.

There was more than one way to skin a cat. Or, as the Thoan saying went, more than one direction in which to fart. He had used only one of the three techniques taught him by the shaman, Absakosaw.

He sat down and once more watched the films. He was going to sit here until he got bored. Then he would think of Anana and Red Orc as puppets operated by strings. After a while, they should cease being human—in his mind, anyway—and become mere wooden dolls with articulated limbs.

However, as long as the amplified noises came from the screen, he would have much difficulty ignoring that. The sounds that Anana made kept moving the course of his thoughts back to when he and she had been making love. Just as he was on the edge of giving up and trying some other technique, the screen went blank.

A second later, the Lord's face appeared.

"Kickaha! I am Kumas, Red Orc's son!"

Kickaha shot up from his chair. He said, "Are you? Or are you Red Orc playing another trick on me?"

The man smiled despite the strain on his face.

"I don't blame you. My father breeds suspicion as some breed worms for fishing."

"If you are indeed his son . . . his clone . . . how can you prove that? And what if you are? What do you want of me?"

"Partnership. My father has gone to Zazel's World. He has left me in charge because he trusts me most, though that is not saying much. I have always been obedient to him and never shown any sign of ambition. He thinks I am shy and reclusive, far more interested in reading and in writing poetry and in gaining knowledge. In that, he is partly correct. But I have hated him as much as my brothers do. Unlike them, I have succeeded in hiding my true feelings."

He stopped for a moment while he obviously made an effort to slow down his rapid breathing.

Kickaha said, "You want me to help you kill him?"

Kumas gulped audibly and nodded. "Yes! I know much about you, mostly from my father, though I do have other sources of information. I admit that I do not have enough confidence in myself to carry out my plans."

"Which are what?"

Kickaha's heart was beating hard, and he had to control his own heavy breathing. The situation had suddenly changed from hopelessness to hope. Unless, that is, the Thoan was playing another game with him.

"We'll talk about that now. I'll show you that I am not my father by doing something he would not do. Watch!"

Suddenly, a door-sized area of the wall near the screen shimmered.

"Step through the gate into my room."

Though Kickaha was still suspicious, he could not refuse this invitation. He went through the shimmering to find himself in a large room. It was Spartan in its decorations and furniture. Along all the walls were shelves filled with books, rolls of scripts, and computer readout cubes. The bed was old-fashioned, one of those that hung from the ceiling by chains. By the opposite wall was a desk that ran the length of the room.

Kumas, if he was truly Kumas, was standing in the middle of the room. A beamer was on the edge of the desk near Kickaha. He could get to it before the Thoan could. Kumas spread his hands out and said, "See! I have no weapons except that beamer. To prove that I trust you, I'll not stop you from having it. The battery is in it; it's ready to fire."

Though he moved nearer the weapon, Kickaha said, "That won't be necessary—as of now, anyway. Where's Anana?"

Kumas turned toward the empty space of the wall just above the desk. His back was to Kickaha. He said, "Sheshmu," Thoan for "open." The area became a screen showing Anana and several women swimming in an enormous outdoor pool. Anana seemed to be having fun with them. Their cries and shrieks and chatter came clearly.

Kumas spoke another word, and the volume shrank to a barely heard sound.

"As you see, she is quite happy. She has accepted my father's lies that she was rescued by him from Jadawin when Jadawin—so my father said—invaded her parents' universe. She believes that she is only eighteen years old, and she is deeply in love with my father."

Kickaha's chest was, for a moment, again filled with a searing-hot liquid. He murmured, "Anana!" Then he said, "What'll happen when she finds out he's lied? She'll eventually find discrepancies in his story. How's he going to keep her from reading histories or overhearing somebody saying something that'll not contradict what he says?"

Kumas had been looking curiously at him. He said, "I expected you to be concerned only with how we were going to dispose of my father. But your first concern seems to be about Anana. You must really love her."

"No doubt of that! But will she ever love me again?"

Kumas said sharply. "That remains to be seen. Just now, if you'll pardon me, we have something much more important. If we don't do that, you and Anana won't have any future. Neither will I."

"Agreed. It'll be hard not to go to her, though. Very hard. But you're right. Let her stay happy until the time when she must be told the truth."

They sat down at a table. Kickaha outlined his story to the Thoan. When he told him that Red Orc planned to disintegrate all the universes and to start over with a new one, he saw Kumas turn pale and start to shake.

The Thoan said, "I did not know that, of course. He told that only to you, because he thought that you would never be able to pass it on."

"That can wait," Kickaha said. "How many of your brothers are left, by the way?"

"Four of us, unless you really did kill Absalos."

"I did."

"Three out of the original nine still live. Ashatelon, Wemathol, and myself. Ashatelon and Wemathol insist on accompanying us to the Caverned World. They want to be in on the kill."

"The more, the merrier," Kickaha said.

But he was thinking that he could not trust any of the clones, though Kumas seemed to be different from the others. Red Orc might have done some genetic tampering with the clones. Or perhaps environment counted for more than the Lords thought it did. In any event, he would have to watch them closely, though he doubted they would be a danger to him until Red Orc was out of the way. They were afraid of their father, and they would need a leader who was not the least bit scared of him. Then, like jackals who'd helped the lion during the hunt, they might fall upon Kickaha.

Kumas resumed talking. "At least four of my brothers so far have died when our father sent them on suicidal missions. Kentrith was sent into Khruuz's world not knowing that a bomb was in his backpack. We were not aware of it until our father told me about it. He laughed all the while. You would think that he would be kind to us since his father was so cruel to him. But that did not happen. Los seems to have twisted him so much that he takes an especial pleasure in tormenting his own sons. Sometimes I think he brought us into being just so that he could, in a certain way, torture himself."

"What do you mean?" Kickaha said.

"He hates himself, I am sure of that. By punishing us, he is punishing himself. Does that idea seem too farfetched to you?"

"It could be valid. But I don't know if it is. Right or wrong, it doesn't change a thing. You've swept this room for recording devices he might've planted?"

"Of course. So, that leaves me and Ashatelon and Wemathol. Those two are what my father wanted, men of action. I disappointed him because I was too passive. He didn't understand it. After all, I was his genetic dupli-cate. So why didn't I have his nature? He tried to explain it, but—"

Kickaha cut in. "We can always talk about that later. But if we don't stop your father dead in his tracks, and I do mean dead, we won't have a later time."

"Very well. He is now in the Caverned World, if what he told me is true, and I can never be sure about anything he tells me. He should be there a long time. Reactivating that world won't be easy. Our logical next step should be to attack him while he's there. First, if it's possible, we should seal up all gates there except the one we use for entrance. Don't you agree?"

Kickaha nodded. But while listening to Kumas, he could not keep from thinking about Anana. What if she could not love him again? It was then that an idea pierced him like an arrow made of light. If it worked, it would turn her against Red Orc.

He said, excitedly, "Kumas! Listen! We're going to fix your father. In one way, anyway. He seems to anticipate just about everything, but he won't have foreseen this. At least, I hope not. Here's what we're going to do before we leave."

An hour later, Kumas left the room to be with Anana. Kickaha watched them via a screen. By then, she was out of the pool and in a green semi-transparent dress, her long black hair done up in a Psyche knot. She was reading from a small video set while sitting on a bench in the flower gar-den. She looked up when Kumas stopped before her. He handed her the cube he and Kickaha had prepared. He talked to her for a while, then walked away. Frowning, she held the cube in her hand for a long time.

Kickaha turned the screen off when Kumas walked into the room.

"Do you think she'll look at it?" he said.

Kumas shrugged his shoulders. But he said, "Would you be able to re-sist doing it?"

"That depends upon whether or not he made her promise not to listen to any derogatory comments about him. If he did, she probably won't watch it. But I'm betting the Bluebeard syndrome will overwhelm her. She'll drop the cube into the slot and turn on the screen. I hope so, any-way."

"Bluebeard syndrome?"

Kickaha laughed. He said, "Bluebeard was the villain in an old folktale. He married often and killed his wives and hung them up to dry in a locked room. But he had to go off on a trip, so he told his latest wife she could use the key he'd given her. It would open every room in the castle. But she was definitely not to unlock one room. Under no circumstances was she to do that. Then he took off.

"Naturally, her curiosity overcame her wifely duty to obey him. So, after fighting temptation for some time, she surrendered to it. She unlocked the room where the former wives hung from hooks. She was horrified, of course. She told the authorities, and that was the end of Bluebeard."

"We Thoan have a tale similar to that," Kumas said.

"If Red Orc just commanded her not to pay any attention to anything bad she hears about him from his sons, she'll do it anyway. But if she gave her word . . . I don't know. In her mind, she's eighteen years old. The Anana I knew would hardly have waited until he had left her to find out just what it was he didn't want her to know. But eighteen-year-old Anana must have been a different woman from the older woman."

"We'll find out when we come back," Kumas said. "If we do come back."

17

"HERE WE ARE," KICKAHA SAID CHEERILY. "BACK IN THE LAND of the dead."

He and the three clones, the "sons," were in the tunnel of Zazel's World where he had entered it on his first mission. They had not passed directly from Red Orc's mansion to this place. The first step, a comparatively easy one, had been to find a gate to Manathu Vorcyon's World. The Great Mother had told Kickaha before he had been sent on his first passage to Khruuz's World that she was again setting the trap that had whisked him away to her world. He could return to her through that.

On entering the Great Mother's world, the party was in the forest surrounding the great tree in which she lived. Again, warriors appeared from the trees and led them to the palace-tree. After a series of conferences with her, they were sent on to Khruuz's universe. They landed in a room cut out of rock and with no windows or doors. A few minutes later, the gate passed them on to a prison cell. This was in Khruuz's underground fortress. The scaly man had set up a shunt in the gate-passages. This had allowed him to seal all the immediate entrances to his world. But they would be opened when Eric Clifton's instruments told him that the preliminary gate was occupied. Khruuz had gone to Zazel's World, and Clifton had been left behind to monitor the gates.

The Englishman had released them from their cell after he was sure that Kickaha was not the captive of Red Orc's sons. Kickaha had told him immediately of events to the minute he had left for here. Then Clifton had told his news about Khruuz.

"Or at least he started to go there," Clifton had said. "He intended to use the same route you used when you gated there."

"How long has he been gone?"

"Ten days." Clifton had rolled his eyes and looked mournful. "It seems to me that he should have been back five days ago. However, he might have tried to reactivate the world. I didn't know it was dead until you told me, and he wouldn't find out it was until he got there."

"I don't know what he's up to," Kickaha had said. "He should've waited for us. Maybe he thinks he can do just as well without us. I don't know."

"You're suspicious?" Clifton had said.

"Khruuz has never proved that he's trustworthy. On the other hand, he's given me no reason to suspect him. He seems to be very friendly, and he sure needs us. Did need us, anyway. Maybe something's happened so he doesn't need us anymore. But what could he have up his sleeve?"

"His hatred for the human species?"

"He hates the Lords. He wouldn't be human if he didn't. But then, he's not human. Why should he have anything against us *leblabbiys*? We never did anything to him."

"We do look just like the Lords," Clifton had said. "Hatred is not by any means always rational."

"But he's never shown anything but friendliness toward you and me. He'd have to be a hell of an actor to repress his hatred all this time."

"That may be significant. I wouldn't blame him a bit if he frothed at the mouth when he spoke about them. But he seems to have a self-control cast in bronze. Is that in itself suspicious?"

"It could be," Kickaha had said. "But for the time being, there's nothing we can do about it. We go ahead without him."

An hour later, the war party had gated out to Zazel's World, not knowing what reception it might get at its destination. The tunnel, however, was empty. There was one difference, no small one, from Kickaha's first trip. The symbols were again marching along on the tunnel wall.

He said, "Somebody's had some success resurrecting this stone carcass."

"Let's hope the somebody is not Red Orc," Kumas said.

To avoid their confusing Red Orc with the clones in a situation where individual identity was crucial, the clones had changed the color of their hair to purple. They also wore orange headbands and carried light-blue backpacks.

"That those characters on the wall are moving again means that either Khruuz or Red Orc has started the computer up again," Kickaha said. "Let's find out who did it."

This time, he was not going to walk the wearying and time-consuming tunnels. The four men had gated from Red Orc's palace riding small foldable one-seater airboats weighing thirty pounds. They were more like motorcycles than the conventional airboats. But the oxygen and water tanks and the case of supplies and the "small cannon" beamers fixed to the fuselage nose put a strain on the tiny motor.

Their craft were cruising at thirty miles an hour. Nevertheless, in these close quarters, the boats seemed to be going very swiftly.

Through his goggles, the infrared light made the tunnels even more ghostly than in photonic light.

In less than an hour, he saw the two-tunneled fork ahead. He held up his hand and stopped the boat.

"What in hell!"

The entrance to the left-hand tunnel was blocked with a single stone. The symbols disappeared there. But those on the other wall kept marching into the right-hand tunnel.

He got off the craft to inspect the stone. It was smooth and contained many fluorescent chips. It also merged with the sides of the entrance as if it were stone grown from stone. Or as if a stone-welding instrument had been used.

He took from his backpack a square device with a depth indicator on its back. After pressing the front part against the stone, he said, "There's thirty feet of solid stone there. Beyond that is empty space, the continuation of the tunnel, I suppose. Someone has set it up to make us go where he wants us to go."

Kumas's voice came over the tiny receiver stuck to Kickaha's jaw. "I hope Khruuz did it."

"Me, too. But we can't do anything except follow the route so thoughtfully laid out for us. From now on, you and I, Kumas, will be as close to the ceiling as we can get. Ashatelon and Wemathol, you keep your boats several inches above the floor and about ten feet behind us. That way, we can have maximum firepower and yet not shoot each other. I'll be slightly ahead of Kumas."

Although he did not like having the Thoan at his back, he had to be the leader. Otherwise, they would believe he was a coward. He had told Kumas to stay at his side because he was not at all certain that Kumas would know what to do in a fight unless he had orders.

Five minutes later, they decelerated quickly and then stopped. The entrance to the cave was also blocked. But a new hole had been made in the wall by the mouth of the cave. It led at right angles to the tunnel they were in. The symbols had reappeared on the previously blank part of the wall.

"Onward and inward," Kickaha said. "Keep your eyes peeled and your fingers on the firing button. But make sure you don't shoot unless you have to."

"If our father did this," Kumas said, "we're done for."

"Many a Lord has thought that after setting a trap for me," Kickaha replied. "Yet here I am, as healthy and unscarred as a young colt. There my enemies are, dead as the lion who tackled the elephant."

"A braggart is a gas balloon," Wemathol said. "Prick him and he collapses."

Ashatelon spoke harshly. "This man is not called the Slayer of Lords, the man who won the war against the Bellers, for nothing. So why don't you keep your sneering to yourself?"

"We'll discuss this later with knives," Wemathol said.

"Nothing so heartening as brotherly love," Kickaha said. "You Thoan make me sick. You think you're gods, but you haven't graduated from the nursery. And you wipe your asses just like the lowest of *leblabbiy*, though you don't do as good a job of it. From now on, no more squabbling! That's an order! Keep your minds on our mission! Or I'll send you back to your nurses to wipe your noses!"

They did not speak again for some time. The boats took them along a tunnel for a mile before another stone blocked their passage. But this was not stone-welded. The separation between it and the tunnel wall was obvious. Nevertheless, the men were stopped.

Either the symbols had ceased moving or they were somehow slipping through the blocking stone.

Again, Kickaha used the depth sounder. Looking at the indicator, he said, "It's ten feet deep. Then, emptiness."

"Do we turn back?" Kumas said.

"And wander around here until we run out of food?" Wemathol said.

"Maybe we should use the cannon to melt our way through," Ashatelon said. "That might use up much of the battery energy. But what else can we do?"

"We'll blast our way in," Kickaha said.

They did as he ordered and took turns in beaming the stone. Under the force of the rays, the stone melted swiftly and lava ran out on the floor below. Scraping the semiliquid away from the stone was hot and hard work. Their small shovels made the labor longer, but it had to be done. Sweating, making sure they did not come within range of the narrow beams, they succeeded in throwing the glowing stuff away from the tunnel entrance. When one craft had used up half of the battery, the second boat moved in. But a minute after the second boat had started its melting, the stone began to roll into a recess in the wall.

Kickaha told Ashatelon to turn off his beamer.

"It's a wheel!" Kumas cried.

"Tell us what we don't know, stupid," Wemathol said.

They backed the boats away and then waited. The craft noses were pointed at the opening, and the pilots had their fingers on the FIRE button.

"Be ready to shoot," Kickaha said. "But don't be trigger-happy."

"Why would anybody except Red Orc have closed the entrances?" Wemathol said.

"I don't know. Maybe Khruuz did it, though I don't know why. Just don't assume anything."

The huge wheel had completely moved within the wall recess. Beyond that was a cave.

Kumas had removed his goggles at Kickaha's order. He was to determine if photonic light was present. He said loudly, "The cave is lit up!"

The others now took their goggles off. The brightness from the cavern was much stronger than could be given by luminiferous plants. There were no shadows, so the illumination seemed to have no source. That meant that a Thoan was providing it. Maybe.

Now they could see that the cave was gigantic. Cool air brushed their bodies. To test it, Kickaha took off his oxygen mask and breathed deeply. Though the air was delightfully fresh, he said, "We'll keep our masks on for a while."

He could not see the distant walls and ceiling of the cave, so vast was it. But he could see strange-looking plants, some of them tree-tall, growing from the soil on the floor.

Kumas said, "Red Orc is waiting for us in there."

"Somebody is," Kickaha said.

"You go first," Kumas said.

"Of course!" Kickaha said loudly. "If I waited for one of you to lead, we'd sit here until we starved!"

"No man calls me a coward!" Ashatelon said.

Before Kickaha could stop him, Ashatelon had shot his boat forward and through the opening. But he did not stop at once. Instead, he accelerated until he seemed to be going at the maximum speed of the craft, fifty miles an hour. The boat rose. For a moment, it was out of sight. Then it appeared and, a moment later, hovered a few inches above the floor and ten feet in from the entrance. Its nose was pointed toward them.

"Now you may know who's a coward!" Ashatelon bellowed.

His words echoed from the distant walls.

Kickaha's boat moved into the cave. He looked around. A green lichenous stuff covered most of the wall behind him. Somehow, the plants had been given a new life. Or else they had never been dead in this cave. The walls near them were about two miles apart, and the ceiling was about a hundred feet high. The other end was so far away that it shrank to a point. The symbols paraded on both walls and toward the end of the cave until they were too small to see.

The other two Thoan entered. "No one here," Kumas said. He sounded very relieved.

"Someone rolled that wheel aside," Kickaha said. "We'll go on."

He started to press his foot down on the acceleration pedal. Then he felt wet drops on his bare skin, and a fine mist was around him.

When he woke up, he was inside a square cage made of bars. Above him were bars through which he could see the cave ceiling. He got slowly to his feet, becoming aware that they were unshod while he did so. His clothes had been removed and were nowhere in sight. The cage floor was solid metal. In a corner was a pile of blankets. In another was a metal box, and the third corner held another box, the top of which had a toilet-seat hole. In the center of the metal floor was a painted orange-lined circle with a diameter of three feet.

And there were other cages, widely separated, arranged in a circle. Six, including his. Inside each one was a man. One of them, however, was not a member of Homo sapiens.

"Khruuz!" he said hoarsely. He gripped the bars facing the inner part of the circle. For a moment, he was weak and dizzy. Despite wearing oxygen masks, he and the Thoan had been gassed. The gas must have been of the kind that did its dirty work through the skin.

"Must've been sprayed through holes in the wall behind us," he murmured to himself. "It doesn't matter how it was done. We're here."

Red Orc wasn't the one responsible for their captivity. He was in the cage directly across from Kickaha's. Like the others, he was unclothed. His face pressed against the bars, he was smiling at his archenemy. Did that mean that he was pleased that at least the others were also caged? Or did it mean that he was enjoying a secret? Such as that he had brought them here and was now posing as a prisoner? But why would he do that? Time would reveal the truth.

The three clones of Red Orc were in the other cages. Wemathol called out, "So much for your brags, Kickaha!"

He spat through the bars.

Kickaha ignored him. He was about to speak to Khruuz when a . . . creature? thing? semihuman? walked slowly and dignifiedly into the center of the circle. A second before, it had not been present. Where had it come from? A gate, probably.

Though he had never seen it before this, Kickaha knew that it had to be the thing he had thought was dead.

He cried out, "Dingsteth!"

It faced Kickaha, and it said, "Neth thruth," Thoan for "I am it." Carved jewels, not teeth, flashed in its mouth.

Kickaha had heard about Dingsteth from Anana and Manathu Vorcyon. According to them, Dingsteth was an artificial creature made by Zazel as a sort of companion and manager. Before Zazel had killed himself, he had charged his creation to stand guard on and to preserve his world. Just why he would want to keep the dreary universe going, no one knew.

Now the fabled being was standing before Kickaha. It was bipedal and six feet tall. Its skin was lightly pigmented, a Scandinavian pink. It walked slowly, because it had to. The shiny flesh rings around its shoulders, hips, elbows, knees, and wrists did not allow the free movement humans had. Its head, neck, and trunk were proportionally larger than those of a man. The skull was almost square, and the lips were very thin.

Where a man's genitals would have been was smooth skin.

The thing said, "You know my name. What is yours?"

"Kickaha. But I thought this world had died and you with it."

"You were meant to think that," it said, pronouncing its words in a somewhat archaic manner. "But you and the others were too persistent. So I was forced to take appropriate action."

It paused, then said, "I thought the gate was closed."

"This thing intends to keep all of us here forever!" Red Orc shouted. "Dingsteth! I came here in peace!"

Without turning around, the thing spoke to the Thoan. "You may have, and you may not have. The being who calls himself Khruuz says that you are very cruel and violent and obsessed with the desire to have the data for my master's creation-destruction engine. He says that you will destroy all the universes, including Zazel's, to have the energy to make a new world for yourself only."

"He lies!" Red Orc said.

Dingsteth continued to look at Kickaha.

"The semihuman calling himself Khruuz may be lying, and he may be telling the truth. He says that he can bring me proof of his words if I let him return to his own world. But you, Orc, promised to come back soon after I gated you out of here so long ago. You did not. Therefore, you lied to me.

"How do I know that this Khruuz is also not a liar? How can I be sure that you are not all liars? You, for instance, Kickaha. You and Khruuz and the others may never return if I let you leave this world. Or you may come back intending to force me to reveal data that you should not have. I do not know if you are a liar, but you are certainly capable of senseless violence. I saw you throw away the facsimile of my skull. And I saw you kill a man, though that act was in self-defense. Or appeared to be."

Dingsteth walked away from the circle of cages. Kickaha watched it go to a place twenty yards away. It stopped near a "tree," a scarlet plant the branches of which grew closely together and extended to an equal distance from the trunk. Near this cylindrical tree was a large round stone. The keeper of this world was equidistant from the tree and stone. It turned its back to the prisoners. It must have spoken a code word, because it vanished suddenly.

He called to Khruuz, who was two cages away from his, "How did it catch you?"

"Gas. Your question should have been, 'How do we get out of these cages?' "

"Working on it now," Kickaha said. "But I admit that this is one of the toughest problems I've ever had to solve."

"You mean that we have ever had," Khruuz said.

Red Orc said, "Yes, we! I propose that until we do escape, we put aside our hatreds and cooperate fully."

"I won't put them aside," Kickaha said. "I won't allow them, however, to keep me from working with you."

Kumas said, "We're doomed."

"Weakling!" Ashatelon said. "I am ashamed to be your brother. I have been since we played together as children."

Wemathol called, "You're really cooperating, Ashatelon!"

Khruuz's deep and rough voice stopped the snarling and snapping. "Hearing you Thoan makes me wonder how you ever succeeded in conquering my people. I do not believe that the Thoan who killed all of us except myself could be your ancestors.

"I suggest that we act as a harmonious whole until we have dealt with Dingsteth—nonviolently, I hope."

"Don't ask them to give their word they won't stab you in the back before that's done," Kickaha said. "Their word is as worthless as a burning piece of paper."

"I know that," Khruuz said. "But our common danger should be the cement binding us together."

"Ha!"

Red Orc said, "Does anyone have any ideas?"

"Dingsteth may be listening, probably is right now," Kickaha said. "So how do we share ideas if it's going to know what we plan to do? We have no paper to write on, and we couldn't throw notes from cage to cage even if we did have paper. They're too far apart. Besides, Dingsteth'll be watching us."

"Sign language?" Kumas said. The others laughed.

"Think about it, dummy," Wemathol said. "How many of us know sign language? It'd have to taught by one who knows, if any of us do. And we can't do that unless we shout at each other. Dingsteth would hear us and learn along with the rest of us. Thus—"

"I get the idea," Kumas said. "I was just thinking out loud, you worthless, do-nothing, gasbag lout. What's your ingenious idea?"

Wemathol did not reply.

Very little was said for the rest of the day. Night came when the sourceless light was turned off, and the only illumination was from the plants. Kickaha slept uneasily on his pile of blankets, not because he lacked a bed but because he could not stop thinking about how to get out of the cage and what he would do after that. Finally, sleep did come, laden with dreams of his life with Anana. Some of them were nightmares, fragments of desperate situations they had been in. On the whole, though, they were pleasant.

During one dream, he saw the faces of his parents. They were smiling at him and looked much younger than when they had died. Then they receded and were lost in mists. But his feeling about them was happy. He awoke for a while after that. There had been a time when he wondered if they were his biological mother and father. It had been hinted by some Thoan that he was adopted; his true parents were Thoan, possibly Red Orc himself. He had seriously considered questing for the truth when he had time for it. Now he did not care. The biological parent was not necessarily the real parent. Loving and caring made the real father and mother. The poor but decent couple who had raised him from a baby on an Indiana farm were the ones he had known and loved. Thus, they were the only parents about whom he cared. Forget the quest.

Dawn, a less bright light than yesterday's, sprang into being. No false dawn here for Dingsteth. An hour later, it appeared between the tree and the stone and walked into the circle. It was careful not to come close enough to be reached through the bars.

Without the preliminary of a greeting, it spoke. "I heard your talk about escape plans. I have run the possibilities of your succeeding in that through the world. It gives you more than a 99.999999999-percent chance of never doing that. It is trying now to locate what it is that you could do so that the chance will be one hundred percent."

"It has to have complete data from you to calculate that," Kumas said. "You cannot ever know that."

"Make it easier for us!" Wemathol howled. "Blab everything, you anus's anus, king of the cretins!"

Kumas, looking chagrined, lay down on his blanket pile. He refused to say a word after that.

"Nevertheless, I am attempting to consider all factors," Dingsteth said. "Unfortunately, my creator did not install a creator's imagination in me."

"We'll be glad to help you find what you're looking for!" Wemathol yelled.

Dingsteth turned toward Wemathol. "You would? That is most kind of you."

It had to wait until the laughter of the caged men had ceased before it could make itself heard. Even Khruuz vented his short barking laugh.

"That's some kind of human joke, I suppose. I don't understand such. An hour from now, you will hear a signal. You, Kickaha, will immediately stand in that circle on the floor of your cage. You will be gated to an exercise-and-shower area. After you have returned to the cage, the signal will again sound. You, Wemathol, will go then."

It named off each man in turn, made sure that they understood the arrangement, and returned to the gate by the tree. After it had disappeared, Ashatelon said, "It's taking good care of us, though I can't say much for the food. I wonder why it cares at all about our condition?"

"Its seeming concern for us is built in," Red Orc said. "It's part of its command complex. But Zazel put that in for his own good reasons. We may regret that Dingsteth did not kill us at once."

"We shouldn't give a damn about Zazel's reasons just now," Kickaha said. "Let's take advantage of them as soon as possible."

Easier said than done, as the old Terrestrial saying went. By the time that Kickaha had been transported to the exercise area, he had not heard or said anything that might help them. He found himself in a space cut into the stone. It had no exit or entrance—except for the gate that had brought him there—and was ventilated from narrow slits along the walls. Its ceiling was fifty feet high, it was fifty feet wide, and it was a half-mile long. At either end was an unwalled shower, a fountain, a commode, and a heat-dryer.

He warmed up before running swiftly up and down the room for five miles. After a warming-down exercise, he drank, showered, and dried off standing before the blower, after which he stood in the circle and was gated through to the cage. Another loud hooting came, and Wemathol got into his circle.

On the third morning of this routine, Kickaha asked Dingsteth what it planned to do with them eventually.

"You will stay caged until you kill yourself or die through accident, though I do not see how accidents can occur."

It was some time before the hurricane of protests trailed away. There was a silence for several minutes. Then Wemathol said, "We'll be here forever."

Dingsteth said, "Forever is only a concept. There is no such thing. However, if you had stated that you would be here for a very long time, you would be correct."

"We'll go crazy!" Kumas screamed.

"That is possible. It won't make any difference about your longevity."

Kickaha spoke calmly, though he did not feel like doing so. "Why are you doing this?"

"Zazel's commands are to be obeyed. I myself do not know why he left such orders. I surmise, however, that at the time he gave them to me, he did not foresee that he would one day kill himself. He is dead; his commands are not."

Kumas fainted. Wemathol hurled at Dingsteth every item in his large treasury of insults and obscenities. When he had run through them, he started over. Ashatelon bit on his arms until blood came. The other three said nothing, but Red Orc stared through the bars for a long time. Khruuz wept, a strange sight for the humans, since his insectile face looked as if it hid no more than an insect's emotions. Kickaha leaped up and hung from the bars and grimaced and hooted as if he were an ape. He had to express himself in some way. Just at the moment, he felt as if he had shot backward along the path of evolution. Apes did not think of the future. He would be an ape and not think about it.

He would later realize how twisted his logic was. Just then, it seemed to be quite reasonable. It was only human to go ape.

18

HE HAD COMPLETELY RECOVERED BY THE NEXT MORNING. NOW, looking back at yesterday, he thought that being an ape had been fun. All he had lacked to be a true anthropoid was a fur coat and fleas.

Nevertheless, that brief fall from evolution's ladder was a warning. For too many years, he had been under extreme stress and in near-fatal situations. The breaks between them had been too short. It was true that he seemed almost always to be in top physical and mental condition, ready to take on the universe itself, no holds barred, anything goes. But deep within him, the multitudinous perils, one after the other, had demanded high payment. The latest and worst of the shocks. Anana's permanent memory loss and then an inescapable sentence to life imprisonment, had been the one-two punch knocking him out of the ring.

"Only for a little while," he muttered. "Once I get in shape again, get a long rest, I'll be ready to fight anything, anybody."

Some of his cage-mates were still suffering. When Kumas was addressed by the others, he only grunted. All day long, he stood, his face pressed against the bars, his hands gripping them. He ate very little. Ashatelon cursed and raved and paced back and forth. Wemathol muttered to himself. Only Khruuz and Red Orc seemed to be undisturbed. Like him, their minds were centered on escaping.

Fat chance! He had tried again and again to summon up from his reservoir of ingenuity a possible means to break out. Every idea was whisked off by the hurricane of reality. This prison, compared to Alcatraz, was off the starting blocks and over the finish line before Alcatraz could take a step.

Thirty days passed. Every afternoon, Dingsteth visited them. It spoke for a few minutes to each prisoner except Kumas. He turned his back to it and refused to say a word.

Red Orc tried to talk it into releasing him. Dingsteth always rejected him. "Zazel's orders are clear. If he is not here to tell me otherwise, I am to hold any prisoners until he returns."

"But Zazel is dead. He will never come back."

"True. That makes no difference, however. He did not inform me as to what I should do with prisoners if he died."

"You will not reconsider in light of the changed situation?"

"I am unable to do so."

Kickaha listened closely to the dialogue. The next day, while running in the exercise room, not even thinking of his problems, an idea exploded in his mind. It was as if his unconscious had lit a firecracker. "Might work," he told himself. "Couldn't hurt to try. Depends upon Dingsteth's mental setup."

The following day, when he saw his captor walking stiffly into the circle of cages, he called to it.

"Dingsteth! I have great news! Something marvelous has happened!"

The creature went to Kickaha's cage and stood close, though not close enough to be grabbed. "What is it?"

"Last night while I was dreaming, Zazel's ghost came to me. He said that he had been trying to get through to you from the land of the dead. But he can only do that in dreams. You don't dream."

Kickaha was guessing about that. But it seemed probable that its brain would lack an unconscious mind.

"Since you don't dream, but I am a blue-ribbon dreamer, Zazel, his ghost, that is, used me as his medium to communicate to you!"

Dingsteth's features were incapable of expressing puzzlement. Nevertheless, they managed to hint at it.

"What does 'blue ribbon' mean in the context of your statement?"

"It's a phrase for 'excellent.' "

"Indeed. But what is a ghost?"

"You don't know about ghosts?"

"I have great knowledge, but it is impossible for my brain to hold all knowledge. When I need to know something, I ask the world-brain about it."

"Ask it about ghosts and spirits and psychic phenomena. Now, here's what happened last night. Zazel . . ."

After Kickaha had finished his story, Dingsteth said, "I will go to the world and ask it."

It hurried away. As soon as it had vanished through the gate between the tree and the stone, Red Orc said, "Kickaha! What are you—?"

Kickaha held a finger to his lips while shaking his head slightly. "Shh! Bear with me!"

He paced around the cage. His thoughts were like a swarm of asteroids orbiting a planet. The center of the planet was the idea that had suddenly come to him yesterday. It was a bright comet born in the darkness of his unconscious mind and zooming into his conscious mind, the bright planet—colliding with it, turning it into fire for a moment.

I should have been a poet, he thought. Thank God I have sense enough, though, not to tell others the images, the similes and metaphors, springing up in my brain. They would laugh at me.

Having veered away from the subject of importance to his own self, a failing common to everyone, his mind returned to it. What would he say when Dingsteth came back to tell him he was full of crap?

The ruler of the Caverned World did return within five minutes. When it stood before the cage, it said, "The world informs me that there are in reality no such entities as ghosts or spirits. Thus, you are lying."

"No, I'm not!" Kickaha shouted. "Tell me, when was the data about spiritual things put into the world-brain?"

Dingsteth was silent for a few seconds. Then it said, "It was approximately twelve thousand years ago as time was measured in Zazel's native world. I can get the exact date for you."

"See!" Kickaha said. "The data has long been obsolete! Since then, it's been discovered that what was thought to be a superstition is fact! There are indeed such entities as ghosts and other kinds of spirits! About two thousand years ago, a Thoan named Houdini proved that there are ghosts. He also proved that they can communicate with us, but it's seldom that we can communicate with them. The ghosts appear to be highly sensitive and gifted individuals, such as myself, and make their wishes known. Their method of communication is like a one-way gate. They can speak to us. We can't speak to them!"

He glanced around. By now, all except Kumas were gripping the bars and looking intently at him.

"If you don't believe me, ask them! They'll tell you that what I said is true! Isn't that right, men?"

None of them may have guessed rightly what he was heading for. But they were intelligent enough to play along with him. Kumas might not, but when Dingsteth asked him if Kickaha was telling the truth, the Thoan lay silent on his blankets and stared up through the bars. The others swore that what Kickaha claimed had indeed been public knowledge for a very long time.

"In fact," Red Orc said, "this same Houdini confirmed the existence of ghosts through scientific-psychic experiments. He was able several times to see them, though faintly. But the dead sometimes come through more or less clearly in dreams."

He looked at Kickaha as if to say, "Who the hell is Houdini?"

Kickaha held up a hand and formed an O with the fingers while Dingsteth's back was turned to him. He was delighted that the Thoan had caught on so quickly.

Khruuz spoke loudly. "My people lived before the Thoan! We knew that there were spirits long before the Thoan became aware that we existed!"

Kickaha hoped that the clones did not get so enthusiastic that they made up "facts" that could be exposed as untruths. This game had to be played coolly and close to the chest. When Dingsteth wheeled around to see Khruuz, Kickaha gestured at Ashatelon and Wemathol to say little. Then he stopped. It had occurred to him that Dingsteth's monitor cameras would photograph him.

If the creature did view the films and it had questions about the gestures, it would get some kind of hokey explanation from him.

Wemathol and Ashatelon told the creature that everybody had known for millennia that there was a spiritual world and that ghosts now and then did communicate through dreams. They were, however, more scornful of Dingsteth for its ignorance than Kickaha wished them to be. They could not resist their impulses to insult and demean.

If Dingsteth was affected by them, it did not show it. After turning its back to face Kickaha, it said, "Describe Zazel."

Canny creature! Not so guileless as it seemed.

To put off the answer until he could think of an acceptable one, Kickaha said, "What do you mean? Describe his physical features? His face? His height? The relative proportions of his limbs to his trunk? The color of his hair and eyes? Whether his ears were small or large? How big a nose he had and what its shape was?"

"Yes."

Kickaha breathed in deeply before speaking, hoping to suck in inspiration of mind as well as breath. He spoke loudly so the others could hear him clearly.

"Ah, well, he was shrouded in a mist so I couldn't make out his face clearly. The dead appearing in mists or not clearly to the dreamer is, as I've said before, a common phenomenon. Isn't that right, men?"

"Yes, indeed!"

"No doubt of it! It's been proven!"

"If Houdini were here, he'd tell you himself that it's true!"

"We Khringdiz had the same experiences!"

Kumas rose from his blankets, went across his cage, and screamed, "You're all crazy!" after which he lay down again.

Dingsteth said, "He invalidates your statements."

"Not at all," Red Orc called. "His mind is sliding down into insanity. You will have noticed that he said 'all,' meaning everybody here, you included. You know you're not insane. The rest of us know we're sane.

Therefore, his statement is that of a mentally unhinged man and so does not coincide with reality."

"That seems reasonable," Dingsteth said. "I know that I am quite rational."

He spoke to Kickaha, "What did Zazel say?"

"First, he greeted me. He said, 'Niss Zatzel.' "

Wemathol groaned. He thought that the *leblabbiy* Earthman had really goofed up.

" 'Niss Zatzel.' I didn't know what he meant. Then I realized that he was speaking the Thoan of his time. He was saying 'I am Zazel' in the form of his tongue when he lived. Fortunately, the language has not changed that much. I could understand almost everything he said. When I couldn't, I could figure it out from the context. Also, his words did not come through the mists without some distortion, some muffling, too. Both the appearance of ghosts and their voices come through as if a slightly malfunctioning gate were transmitting them."

"I am pleased to find that out. 'Niss Zatzel.' You are not a Thoan, hence you would not be likely to know the ancient language."

Kickaha decided to quote Zazel's supposed words indirectly from here on. About all he knew of the archaic Thoan was a few words Anana had told him. He was glad that he remembered some of their conversation, which had taken place long ago.

"What did he say after that?" Dingsteth said.

Kickaha spoke slowly, his thoughts only a few words ahead of his tongue.

"He said he had learned much from the other spirits and from the Supreme Spirit who rules their land. He sees now what errors and mistakes he made while in the land of the living."

Don't get carried away, Kickaha told himself. Make it effective but short. The less I say, the more chance I won't say something that'll betray me.

"To be brief, he told me that he could not get in contact with you except through a human who was open to psychic channels. That one was me. It took him some time and energy to do it since I was emotionally upset about being imprisoned. Finally, last night, he did it in a dream of mine. He told me to tell you that we should be released and treated as guests, though Red Orc is to be watched carefully because he's dangerous. But you are not to give anybody the data on the creation engine. You should destroy it and then let each of us go our own way."

After a slight pause, Kickaha said, "He also told me, insisted, in fact, that the Horn of Shambarimen, which you took from Red Orc, should be given to me. It is my property, and as Zazel said, I won't misuse it."

Red Orc's face paled, and it twisted into a silent snarl. But he dared not say anything that would make Dingsteth refuse to release him. On the other hand, Kickaha had to include the Thoan in the people to be freed. If he did not, Red Orc would expose him for the liar he was.

"Zazel ordered that you erase all the data about the engine because it's a great danger to every living thing in every universe. You must do this immediately. And you must make sure the data is not retrievable. By that, he means that none of it is to be left stored in the world-brain. No one'll be able to call it up from the world.

"Then you will let us out of our cages and permit us to gate out of this world. But Zazel ordered that Red Orc's weapons not be given back to him and that his airboat be stripped of its beamers. We will fly our machines to the departure gate. All of us will leave together and gate through to Red Orc's palace on Earth Two."

Red Orc glared. He knew why Kickaha was making these terms.

Kickaha continued: "Zazel did not tell me why he wants us to do that. He must have some reason he didn't care to tell me. But it'll be for the best, I'm sure. The dead know everything."

Dingsteth did not speak for several minutes. Its eyes were as unmoving as those in a statue, though it did blink. It did not shift slightly or twitch minutely as a human would have done in that rigid posture. The caged men, Kumas excepted, did not take their gazes from him.

Kickaha murmured to himself, "Is Dingsteth going to buy it?"

His fabrication would not work on any Thoan or most Earth people. But the creature was not human, and it had had almost no experience with the supreme prevaricator species, Homo sapiens.

At long last, Dingsteth spoke. "If Zazel ordered it, it will be done. If only I could dream, he might speak to me!"

For a moment, Kickaha felt sorry for it. Maybe it was more human than he had thought. Or maybe it just wanted to be.

They would be released within an hour, and they would be gated to the cave wherein their craft were stored. But it took longer to carry out "Zazel's instructions" than Kickaha had anticipated. The unforeseen, as so often happened, took place. Khruuz was the first to be gated through to the place where Dingsteth had put the aircraft. Kumas was to follow Khruuz, after which Red Orc would be transmitted to the storage place. Kickaha had requested this gating order because he wanted Red Orc not to be the first in the storage place. No telling what that wily bastard could do if he were alone or had only his clones to deal with. But Khruuz was powerful enough to overcome him if the need arose.

The Khringdiz disappeared from the circle in his cage. Dingsteth had trouble getting Kumas to obey its orders. Kumas, lying on his blankets, turned his back to Dingsteth. Finally, Dingsteth said, "I have means to make you do as I wish. They involve much pain for you."

For a half-minute, Kumas was silent. Then, his face expressionless, his eyes dull, he rose. He shambled to the center of the circle and stood in it. Dingsteth pointed one end of the small instrument in its hand at the circle and pressed a button. Though the radio signal from it started the process, five seconds would pass before the gate was fully activated.

Kumas must have been counting the seconds. Just before he would have vanished, he moved to one side and stuck his right leg beyond the circle.

Then he was gone. But the leg, spurting blood, remained in the cage. It toppled over immediately.

"Killed himself!" Red Orc shouted. The other humans were silent with shock. Dingsteth may have been, but it did not show it. It said, "Why did he do that?"

"It's as I told you," Kickaha said. "He was crazy, poor bastard."

Dingsteth said, "I do not understand the instability and twisted complexities and frequent malfunctionings of human beings."

"We don't either," Kickaha said.

Dingsteth put off cleaning up the mess until after its "guests" had left its world. Or perhaps it was not going to bother with it. It gated the others to the cave in which their aircraft were stored, but sent them to a different circle in the cave from the one originally intended. When Kickaha stepped out of his circle, he saw the Thoan's body in a circle nearby. After a glance at it, he was busy getting ready. That did not take much time. When they were all mounted on the seats of their boats, Dingsteth opened a door to the cave by speaking a code word. A section of the wall slid into the recess, and they flew out into a tunnel. Dingsteth had given them directions for getting to the gate that Red Orc had used for entrance to this world. Red Orc rode behind his clones, Khruuz and Kickaha behind him.

Twenty minutes later, they were at the gate. Kickaha dismounted from his boat and brought out of his backpack a wrist-binding band. Before Red Orc could react, the clones and Khruuz had seized him. He might have gotten away from Ashatelon and Wemathol, but Khruuz was as strong as a bear. Obeying the orders Kickaha had whispered in the hangar-cave, the Khringdiz held the Thoan's arms behind him, and the clones gripped Red Orc's legs. Dingsteth, watching them via the world-brain, must have wondered what was going on. Kickaha quickly secured Red Orc's wrists together at his back.

Exultantly, Kickaha took the Horn from his pack and blew the seven notes. Immediately, a section of the wall shimmered. Red Orc, who had been silent throughout, was hurried by Khruuz into the gate. A minute later, all were in the palace that held Anana. They were busy for a little while defending themselves against the guards, who had attacked them when they saw that their master was a prisoner. That did not take long. A few beamer shots killed some, and the others scattered.

Soon, however, the guards rallied and took up defensive positions. It looked as if the invaders would have to take the place by room-to-room fighting. But Kickaha called for the captain, who replied from behind a barricade of furniture in a hall. After Kickaha, Wemathol, and Ashatelon talked to the captain, they made an agreement. The captain then conferred with his lieutenants and some of the rank and file. The parley took over an hour, but the result was that the guards swore loyalty to Kickaha and the clones. They did not love Red Orc and did not care who paid them, especially since Kickaha had doubled their wages and reduced their working hours.

Kickaha was delighted. "I'm sick of bloodshed. Necessary or unnecessary, it goes hard against my grain. Besides, some of us would've been killed if they'd put up a fierce resistance. One of us might've been me."

Wemathol and Ashatelon did not trust the soldiers. To prevent assassination or mutiny, they took some guards aside. These were promised large sums if they would spy on their fellows and report any likely troublemakers or actual plots. Then the clones, not telling Kickaha what they were doing, approached other guards to keep their eyes on Kickaha's spies. He found out about this when some of the clones' spies informed him of this. They expected a reward for the betrayal, and they got it.

Kickaha then hired other soldiers and some servants to watch the clones. For all he knew, though, the clones had taken into their secret service the same people he employed. These would spy on him. Undoubtedly, Wemathol and Ashatelon also had their own agents to spy on each other.

This made him laugh uproariously. If the process kept up, all of the guards and the servants would be double or triple or even quadruple agents.

After making reasonably sure that the guards would give no immediate trouble, Kickaha visited Anana. She was in the garden and in a lounging chair by the swimming pool, which was large enough to be a small lake. The sun of Earth II, near its zenith, blazed down on her. On a small table by her was a tall glass containing ice cubes and a dark liquid. Though the noise from the dozen or so women attendants in the water was a happy one, she did not look contented. Nor did she smile or ask him to sit down when he reintroduced himself.

"By now," he said, "Wemathol has told you the truth. I sent him ahead of me to explain what's really happened to you because I didn't think you would listen to me at all. But I'm ready to tell you all over again what Red Orc did to you and to add any details Wemathol left out."

Her voice was dull, and she did not look directly at him. "I heard him through to the end, though it cost me much not to scream at him that he was a liar. I don't wish to hear your lies. Now, will you go away and never come back?"

He pulled up a chair and sat down.

"No, I won't. Wemathol told the truth, though being Thoan, it may have hurt him to do so."

He longed to take her in his arms and kiss her.

She looked at him. "I want to speak to Orc in person. Let him tell me the truth."

"For Elyttria's sake!" he said, speaking more loudly and impatiently than he had intended. "Why bother with that when he'll only lie!"

"I'll know if he's telling the truth or not."

"That's illogical! Irrational!"

He tried to master his anger, born from frustration and despair.

She said coldly, "I do not tolerate a *leblabbiy* speaking to me like that. Even when he has me in his power."

"I . . ."

He closed his mouth. This was going to be very difficult and would require great self-control and delicacy.

"I apologize," he said. "I know the truth, so it's hard for me to see you so deceived. Very well. You may speak to Red Orc face-to-face."

"You'll be watching us, hearing us?"

"I promise you that no one will be observing you two."

"But you'll be recording us. Then you'll run off the tape, and technically, not be lying to me."

"No. I promise. However . . ."

"What?"

"You won't believe me. But Red Orc might kill you unless you're guarded."

She laughed scornfully. "He? Kill me?"

"Believe me, I know him far better than you do. He could revenge himself on both of us by breaking your neck and depriving me altogether of you."

"I would never have loved you, *leblabbiy*. So how could he deprive you of me?"

"This is taking us in a circle. I'll give you what you want. You'll be in a room with Red Orc, and neither human nor machine will be watching or listening to you two. But there'll be a transparent partition between you and him. I won't take any chances with him. That's my decision, and it's unchangeable."

Khruuz was not human. He could monitor Anana and Red Orc. In a literal sense, no human or machine would observe them. But I can't do that, he thought. I've never lied to her.

For the same reason, I'll also not carry out a plan I had. Putting We-mathol or Ashatelon in their father's place and having one of them pretend to be a repentant and now truthful Red Orc . . . that's out, too. But the temptation is so powerful it hurts me deeply to reject it.

Anana did not seem to be grateful even when he told her that she could take all the time she wanted for the meeting. That turned out to be two hours. When she came out of the room, she was weeping. But as soon as she saw Kickaha, she managed to make her face expressionless. A Thoan did not show "weak" emotions before a *leblabbiy*. Instead of responding to his questions, she walked swiftly to her room.

Red Orc had been held in the room in which he had talked to Anana. Kickaha went to it and sat down on the chair she had occupied. That it was still warm made him feel as if he had touched her.

He looked through the transparent metal screen at the Thoan, who met his gaze unflinchingly.

"You have won this round," Kickaha said. "Big deal. You're not going to get out of this alive. Not unless I decide you will. You do have a chance, but I won't lie to you. I find it almost impossible to kill a man in cold blood or to order others to do what I'm not willing to do. Believe me, your clones want to torture you for a long time before killing you. They can't understand why I won't let them do it."

The Thoan was silent for a moment before replying. He said, "I don't understand either. As for escaping from here, you ought not to be so sure. We are alike in many respects, Kickaha, more than you admit, I believe. But that's nothing to waste time with. You've opened a door for me, if I understand your implications. That opening, however, won't be freedom for me. You will not just kill me, but you will keep me prisoner, or attempt to do so, until I kill myself from frustration and boredom. Correct?"

Kickaha nodded.

"You stupid *leblabbiy!*" the Thoan screamed. His entire skin was suddenly a poisonous red, and his face was knotted with fury. He shook his fist at Kickaha, then he spat. Tiny bubbles quickly gathered at the corners of his mouth, broke, and were replaced by other bubbles. His eyeballs were shot with blood; the arteries on his forehead swelled as if they were cobras puffing up their hoods. And then he began banging his forehead against the screen.

Kickaha had jumped with surprise when Red Orc screamed, and had stepped back. But he now went up to the screen to observe the Thoan closely. Blood was running from his forehead and spreading over his face. Blood had smeared the screen. He truly looked red with a capital R. Though the Thoan had earned his title primarily because he had shed so many people's blood, he was also known throughout the many universes for his rages. They did not happen often, because of his glacial self-control. But when they did erupt, they were fearsome to behold.

This, Kickaha thought, was the granddaddy of all furies.

If it was true that the child was the father of the man, ancient hurts were thrusting themselves up from his soul. Though the very long-lived Lords remembered only the most significant events of their remote past, Red Orc had never forgotten his earliest years, his hatred of his father, his deep love for his mother, and his grief when she had been killed. Nor the numerous frustrations and disappointments since then. His many victories had never canceled these.

Watching the Thoan, who was now tearing at his face with his fingernails and still screaming, Kickaha wondered why the Thoan had not tried some system of mental healing. Or perhaps he had, but it had not been successful.

Now Red Orc was rolling over the floor until he banged against a wall, then rolled back until stopped by the opposite wall. He was, however, no longer screaming. Blood from the scratches and gashes on his face, chest, stomach, and legs marked his passage on the floor.

Suddenly, he stopped rotating. He lay on his back, his mouth gaping like a fish out of water. His legs and arms were extended to form a crude X, and he was staring at the ceiling.

Kickaha waited until the Thoan's massive chest was no longer rising and falling so quickly. Then he said, "Are you over your tantrum?"

Though Red Orc did not reply, he did rise to his feet. His face was composed under the blood covering it. After a minute, during which he stared at Kickaha, he spoke calmly.

"I know what you are going to propose. If I am to stay alive, I will have to tell Anana the truth about what I did to her."

Kickaha nodded.

"I need some time to think about it," the Thoan said.

"Okay," Kickaha said. "You have ten seconds."

For a moment, Kickaha thought that Red Orc was going to rocket off in another rage. He had pressed his lips together, and his eyes began looking crazy again. But then he breathed out deeply and smiled.

"I was thinking about a week to make up my mind. Very well. No, I will not tell Anana the truth."

"I didn't think you would," Kickaha said. "However, I have another offer. If you accept it, you'll escape lifelong imprisonment. But the offer depends upon an answer to my question. Did you store Anana's memory? If you did, can you give it back to her?"

RED ORC SAT STILL, HIS EYES FOCUSED ON A POINT A FEW inches from Kickaha's head. That he did not answer at once showed that he was going to be very careful about what he would say.

Kickaha tried to think as the Thoan was thinking. Red Orc knew whether or not he could give Anana's memory back to her. He was wondering if he should lie. If he was able to restore her memory, he would say that he could not do so. Though a no from him would confine him for life in a seemingly escape-proof cell, Kickaha had found a way to get out of Dingsteth's cages. What the *leblabbiy* could do, he, Red Orc, could do.

If he said yes, only he would operate the machine. Anana would be in his power, and he could kill her with a jolt of electricity or whatever else was available. He would not enjoy his revenge long. A few seconds later, he would die.

Finally, he said, "No. I cannot restore her memory. Even if it could be filed, it would take a vast storage space, a capacity that only Zazel's World would have. And I am not certain of that. Destroying is far easier than creating."

"You should know," Kickaha said. "You have taken Anana's memory from her. What's been done to her can be done to you. How would you like to be stripped of your memory?"

The Thoan shuddered slightly.

"I'll see to it that the memory-uncoiler takes you back to when you were only five," Kickaha said. "You were, if my informants are to be believed, a loving person at that age. That way, I don't have to kill you—I hope I don't—and you'll be given a second chance. You'll not be confined to a cell, but you won't be allowed to go out of this palace. Or wherever you're kept. Not until I'm one-hundred-percent satisfied that you'll stay on the right path, that you're a real pussycat.

"Maybe it'd be better to take you back to the age of three. Or even two. That'd make it easier for us to help you form a different persona, or at least reshape you. Your destructive tendencies could be channeled into creative drives. Despite what you said, it's sometimes easier to create than destroy."

"Thousands of years of knowledge and experience lost," Red Orc murmured.

Kickaha had expected that the Thoan would go into another rage. But the first one seemed to have exhausted him.

"It happened to Anana."

The Thoan breathed deeply, looked at the ceiling, then into Kickaha's eyes.

"But you forget something. Only I know how to operate the memory-uncoiler."

"I haven't forgotten," Kickaha said. "You'll be injected with a hypnotic that'll make you answer all questions."

"That won't do anything to me," the Thoan said. He smiled. "I have taught myself certain mental techniques that will automatically block out the effects of any hypnotics available to you."

"I won't hesitate to cause you such pain you'll be happy to tell me much more than I want to know about operating the uncoiler. I've seldom tortured a man before this, only when it was absolutely necessary to save lives. Do you doubt that?"

"You're a man of your word," Red Orc said sarcastically. "But whose life are you saving if you torture me?"

Kickaha grinned. "Yours. However, I don't have to torture you. I have another card up my sleeve. I won't have to hurt you, physically, that is. Khruuz will be able to figure out how to operate the machine."

It was the Thoan's turn to grin. "I anticipated long ago that someone with the Khringdiz's knowledge might be available. The machine will not turn on until it has identified me as the operator. It must read my voice frequencies and pattern of intonation. It also requires my handprint, my eye-prints, my odorprint, and a small patch of my skin so that it may read my DNA. It also must receive a code phrase from me, though you will be able to get that out of me by torture. That will not be necessary. I'll give you the code phrase, much good it will do you."

"And?" Kickaha said.

"Ah! You have anticipated another barrier to operating the machine. You are right in doing that. Certain numerous components of the machine, after a certain delay, will explode unless I am the operator. That will disintegrate the machine and annihilate everything within three hundred feet of the blast and do extensive damage for another three hundred."

"That's a lot of trouble," Kickaha said. "What you did, you set up the self-destruction system to keep your clones from being able to use it, right?"

"Of course, you idiot!"

"This idiot will find a way to fool the machine," Kickaha said. "You're holding back one item of information about how the machine identifies you. It's something that marks you as different from your duplicates. I can get that out of you if you hurt enough. I don't like the idea, but as I said, I'll use torture. It's a tool that almost always works."

"It would get you what you want. But that information would not aid you one bit. The machine would explode even if you used Ashatelon or Wemathol."

Red Orc paused, then said, "My sons could be the operators if it were not for one insurmountable factor. I may as well tell you what it is since I don't care to be disintegrated, and it is the factor that makes it impossible to use the memory-stripping on me. Not even I can cancel it. If I am the person whose memory is to be stripped, the machine will blow up. It will know that I am the subject, because it can detect my age. The clones are much younger than I. Therefore, the machine will be triggered when it reads the age difference."

"How can that be?" Kickaha said. "Your body cells are replaced every seven years. It won't be any older, within a seven-year limit, than your clones' bodies."

"True. But the machine will scan my memory before it starts the stripping process. That will determine that I am indeed the original person, because my clones have shorter memories. There is nothing that I can do about that. I cannot remove that circuit without causing the machine to explode. That is a command that now that I've installed it, cannot be canceled."

Red Orc stood up. "I'm tired of this. Gate me back to my cell."

Kickaha also rose from his chair. "You're leaving when I'm having so much fun?"

Red Orc was now standing inside the circle on the floor, waiting to be transmitted to his cell. He called out, "Take my advice, Kickaha! Watch Khruuz! Do not trust him!"

As Kickaha left the room, he admitted to himself that he was stymied. The situation was a Mexican standoff. Red Orc was suicidally stubborn. Though he'd been offered a deal far better than he deserved, he'd rather die than lose his memory and, thus, his precious identity.

Kickaha went to the control room, a huge chamber with a very deep carpet on which were various mathematical formulae. The Khringdiz was sitting on a chair before a panel with many displays and controls. He wheeled his seat around and looked up at Kickaha. "It seems that you must either kill him or imprison him until he dies."

"Keeping him locked up is a bad idea. Sometime during the thousands of years he may yet live, he'd find a way to escape. I hate to think of him on the loose again."

"My advice is to end his misery."

"Misery?"

"Yes. Sometimes, so I've been told, he is quite calm, at one with himself because he feels superior to all other humans. Then he is even kind to people. He believes that he is truly a god. But this feeling only lasts a certain time. He tortures himself because he cannot make himself peaceful and serene. He cannot get people to love him, though this feeling largely comes from the unconscious, and he is not aware of it. By love, I don't mean sexual love—that is, lust. During the thousands of years he has lived, he has not found a way to be at peace with himself or with others. He was driven to madness by others because he drove them to hate him.

"Now he is given the opportunity to erase that madness, to start over again. But despite his misery and suffering, he loves his madness. He cannot give it up. He thinks of himself as a very strong person, which he is in many respects. Yet he is also what he despises most, a weakling."

Kickaha laughed loudly, then said, "Thank you, Doctor Freud!"

"Who?"

"Never mind. But, though nonhuman, you certainly seem to know much about the human psyche."

"I'm convinced that there is not a significant basic degree of difference between any two sapient species, or among the members of the same species."

"You may be right. Anyway, I gave Red Orc a most generous offer, considering what he's done. He isn't going to accept it. That's that."

Khruuz rolled his huge eyes upward. Kickaha did not know what that meant. Disgust? Wonder at the craziness of human beings?

The Khringdiz said, "Red Orc was trying to make you suspicious of me when he told you to watch me. I hope that you dismissed his warning for what it is, a lie."

"Oh, sure. I know what he's doing," Kickaha said. "He's always in there pitching."

Damn Red Orc! he thought. He's brought up from the deep of my mind what's been lurking down there. I knew it was there—I'm never entirely without suspicion—but I just had no valid reason at all to suspect Khruuz of evil intentions. I don't have any now. I should rid my mind of Red Orc's warning—though, come to think of it, Manathu Vorcyon did say that I might trust the Khringdiz too much. But she admitted that she didn't have any basis for her remark. Except that you shouldn't trust anybody unless they'd been through the fires with you, and maybe not even then.

Usually, I breathe in suspicion with the air. But Khruuz had such impressive credentials for hating the Lords. I don't doubt that he has. But who else does he hate? All humans? Could he be as crazed as Red Orc but have much better control at concealing his feelings? I certainly can't accuse Khruuz. No basis for doing that.

But it's possible he's up to something I won't like at all. How do I determine what he really thinks and feels? I could lock him up, keep him out of the way. But I need him badly, and I'd be unfair and unjust if I imprisoned him without good reason.

Ah! Idea! Ask him to submit to a lie detector! No. He might be able to fool the machine or any truth drugs through mental techniques. If Red Orc can do that, Khruuz probably can do it. Anyway, his metabolism and neural reactions probably differ from those of humans. The machine or the drugs wouldn't work as they do with us. If I ask him to volunteer, I'll mightily offend him. I just can't do that. Or should I do it anyway?

He looked at the Khringdiz and wondered what was going on in that grasshopper head.

Khruuz said, "Do you plan to execute Red Orc soon?"

"I haven't made up my mind. He should be killed. But I hate doing it— that's my weakness—and I'd have to do it personally, press the button to flood his cell with gas or whatever. I won't delegate it to someone else. That's a coward's way."

"I do not see that it is," Khruuz said. "Do you yourself kill the animal that others serve you on the table?"

"I usually kill my own meat. But you have a point. Not much of one, though. Red Orc is not an animal, despite what many say about him. And despite the fact that he intended to kill me and then eat me as if I were an animal."

"I hope you soon resolve your dilemma," the Khringdiz said. "Meanwhile, I have been thinking that I should return to my world and stay there for a while."

Red Orc's warning was a hand plucking at his mind as if it were made of harp strings. The music—discord, rather—was high notes of suspicion. Damn Red Orc again! But he said calmly, "Why?"

"As you know, I've been trying to get through Red Orc's access codes here to enter various sections of the computer. His data banks may have the information we need to make another memory-uncoiling machine and to operate it. If so, we can strip him of his memory to any age we select, and thus avoid the unpleasantness of executing him. But there's another far more compelling reason. He may be lying when he says that he has not stored that part of Anana's memory that he took from her. It may be in the bank. If it is, we can give her memory back to her."

Kickaha was so excited that all thoughts of doubt about the Khringdiz scattered like a flock of birds under gunfire. After all, what evidence did he have that Khruuz was plotting something sinister? Not a bit. The

Khringdiz had been invaluable in the conflict with Red Orc. Moreover, he was a likable person despite his monstrous features.

"Do you really think so?" he said.

"It is possible. We cannot afford to ignore anything, no matter how difficult it may be to obtain it. It is well worth the time and the effort."

"I could kiss you!" Kickaha cried.

"You may do so if it pleases you."

"I should have said I feel like kissing you," Kickaha said. "I was speaking emotionally, not literally."

"But I need to go to my planet," the Khringdiz said. "I have an enormous amount of data stored there, data inherited from my ancestors and data stolen or taken from the Thoan. There is much there of which I am not aware. It's possible that I might not only find the means there to crack Red Orc's codes, but find data on building memory-uncoiling machines. Who knows?

"Also, our friend, Eric Clifton, must be very lonely. I will transmit him to here so that he will have human companionship."

"Oh, man!" Kickaha said.

"What?" Khruuz said.

"Nothing."

"I've noticed that when you humans say 'nothing' in the context of your conversation, you mean 'something.' "

"Very observant of you," Kickaha said. "But in this case, I was struck by a completely irrelevant thought. Something I'd forgotten to do, that's all."

His suspicions of the Khringdiz had been like a bag of garbage he'd thrown from the beach into the ocean. It had drifted off, almost out of sight, and then a tidal wave had picked the bag up and hurled it back against him, knocking him off his feet.

He said, "That's damned decent of you, considering Clifton's feelings. But I'd rather he stayed with you for a while."

"Why?"

Kickaha was taken aback. Mentally, he stuttered. But a second later, he said, "Clifton can't help you with anything technological, I think. But he can be helpful in other matters. As for companionship, you need that, too. And Clifton likes you. Also, I'm sure there are things you could tell him, enlighten him. He's intelligent and eager to learn."

Weak, weak! he thought. But it's the best I could come up with. I hope what I said doesn't make Khruuz suspect that I suspect him.

"Very well," Khruuz said. "He stays. I like Clifton, and he does provide companionship. But he must want to be with his own kind, and I offered to send him here because of that."

He paused, then said, "I thank you for considering my feelings of loneliness."

"You're welcome," Kickaha said. The Khringdiz certainly did not behave as if he wished to get Clifton out of the way. If Khruuz was up to no good—but why should he be?—he could easily kill Clifton, who would not be on his guard.

"I would like to return immediately so that I may get started quickly on the research," the Khringdiz said. "I'm eager to grapple with the problem."

He punched a button on the control panel and rose from the chair. Suddenly, the room seemed to crackle with emotional static. Khruuz was smiling, but that did not make his face seem less sinister. It looked that way no matter what his expression. The tendril on the end of his tongue was writhing; his stance was subtly changed. Like a lion who's been drowsing but has just smelled a strange lion, Kickaha thought. He's ready to defend his territory. Ready to charge the intruder.

But the Khringdiz spoke calmly. "You are making much from nothing. I sense that you have unaccountably become hostile. I cannot as yet easily read subtle human expressions or understand certain inflections of voice. But it seems to me that you—what should I say?—have become suspicious of me. Am I wrong?"

"You're right," Kickaha said as he withdrew his beamer from its holster and pointed it at Khruuz. "I may be completely wrong to doubt your intentions. If I am, I'll apologize. Later, that is. But the stakes are too high for me to take a chance with you. For now, you'll be locked up until I determine if I'm right or wrong. I'll explain later."

He waved the beamer. "You know where the gates to the special cells are. I'll be right behind you. Don't try anything. If you do, I'll know you're guilty."

"Of what?" Khruuz said.

"Get going."

They walked toward the door. Khruuz, instead of making a beeline toward it, veered a few feet to the left. Kickaha said, loudly, "Stop!"

The Khringdiz took two more steps, halted, and began to turn. Kickaha had his finger on the trigger. He had advanced the power dial on the side of the beamer to a setting for a more powerful stun charge. Khruuz, he calculated, would have more resistance to the normal charge than most human beings.

Khruuz was saying something in his native language while he turned around to face Kickaha. Then he was gone.

For several seconds, Kickaha was too surprised to react. When he recovered, he smacked his forehead. "Code word! That's what he was saying! For God's sake! He'd set it up! Slick! They don't fool me often, but . . . !"

The Khringdiz had formed a gate inside a loop of the symbol for eternity, the figure eight, one of the designs on the carpet. Standing in the area of the gate, he had uttered the code word and was now, most probably, in the underground fortress in his planet.

Clifton was doomed. Khruuz would kill him at once.

Kickaha strode to the control panel and called for an all-stations attention. Then he ordered Wemathol and Ashatelon to report to the nearest screen. A minute later, both their faces were in the panel screens. He told them what had happened. Both looked alarmed. Wemathol, distinguishable from his brother by his green headband, said, "What do you think he's planning to do?"

"I don't know," Kickaha said. "Listen! He may pop back through the gate or another gate at any moment. Can either of you set up a one-way exit gate covering the floor of this room? That'll stop him if he tries to reenter."

Wemathol said, "We both know how to do that."

"Then get up here on the run and do it!"

Ashatelon, wearing a crimson headband and crimson boots, was the first to appear. Several seconds later, his brother entered the room. Ashatelon, breathing hard, said, "The Khringdiz could have set up gates anywhere in the palace."

"I know that, but we can't cover the floors in every room! Can we?"

"Yes, but it would take time. If we did that, then the gates we use now would be closed. You could not transport food to my father, for instance. Not that I would mind if he starved to death."

"Besides," Wemathol said, "Khruuz could have set up gates in the walls. Or even in the ceilings."

"Just cover the floor of this room," Kickaha said. "Get to work, you two."

They seated themselves before control panels. Kickaha called the captain of the guards and told him some of the situation. "Put your men on a twenty-four-hour roving patrol. Work in three shifts. If the Khringdiz shows, shoot him."

He doubted that Khruuz would come back soon. He suspected that the scaly man would be returning to Zazel's World, or trying to do so. Khruuz wanted the data for the creation-destruction engine as fiercely as Red Orc desired it. Or so it seemed reasonable to assume. Just why, Kickaha did not know. But he would not put it past the Khringdiz to use it to destroy all but one universe.

Doing that would make him the most solitary of all sentient beings. Unless he had means for cloning himself and changing some of the duplicates into females. He might even have the data in his files for altering the genes of the clones. That would make a genetically varied people.

No use speculating. Get done at once what needs to be done.

He used a recorder to send a message to Manathu Vorcyon and had it taken by a runner to the gate that channeled to her world. She might come up with an idea for invading Khruuz's World. Kickaha did not like sitting around waiting for the Khringdiz to attack. Attack as soon as possible was his motto. By the time that the messager reported that the recorder had been placed in the gate, the clones had finished setting up the one-way exit gate over the control-room floor.

Wemathol said, "It does not interfere with the operation of the controls, however."

When Kickaha was convinced that there was nothing more to do, for the moment anyway, he went to Anana's suite of rooms. The entrance to this was a door with a huge monitor screen on it. He called to her. The screen became alive. He saw her walking back and forth just beyond the door. A caged tigress, he thought, and even more beautiful. She hates me and would kill me if she could. That was a thought to choke his mind. Whoever would have thought that his beloved would one day tear him to bloody rags of flesh if she had the opportunity?

He asked for permission to enter. She stopped pacing and whirled around, her face twisted with anger.

"Why do you keep up this charade of politeness and of caring for me? You're the master here! You can do anything you wish to do!"

"True," he said. "But I would never harm you. However, I can't trust you—as yet. I'll be gone for a while. I don't have time to explain the situation to you, and it wouldn't change your mind about me, anyway. I'm putting you in a special suite for your own safety and for mine. Someday, maybe you'll understand why I'm doing this. That's all."

He had intended to enter her suite and talk face-to-face with her. But he had changed his mind. He went to another screen section on the wall and called Wemathol and Ashatelon.

"New plan," he said. "Here's what you must do at once. Gate Anana into Cell Suite Three. Pick four trusted women servants to gate food and water and other necessary supplies to her and Red Orc while we're gone. Send all but fifty guards off on a paid vacation. Those left—and they must be the most trusted men you know—will continue the twenty-four-hour patrol. After that's done, close up the palace, bar all gates, lock all lower-story windows. I give you two hours and thirty minutes to do the job. Then report to me. Be ready to go to Zazel's World."

The clones started to protest that there was not enough time to carry out his orders. He said "Do it!" and turned the screen off. Ten minutes later, he had sent another message to Manathu Vorcyon. This brought her up to date on the situation. Then he verified that Anana had been transmitted to the escape-proof suite. At the time he had set for them, Wemathol and Ashatelon appeared on their one-man airboats.

Kickaha said, "Let's go." He lifted the Horn to his lips.

20

THEY HAD EXPECTED A WORLD MADE ALIVE AGAIN BY DING-
steth. But it was as dead as when they had left it. However, it was not quite
as it had been during their previous visit. And it looked as if someone had
blasted through a section of a wall. The new hole led to a very large cave
containing live plants and animals and an area with chairs, tables, dishes,
cutlery, a kitchen, and a bathroom. Dingsteth must have lived here, though
there were no signs of struggle.

"Khruuz has been here," Kickaha said, "and he captured Dingsteth
despite its traps. Nothing subtle or easy, just powered his way through
them, destroying them. So, we go to Khruuz's World."

"Elyttria!" Wemathol said. "How do we get into his world? And would
it be wise to go there?"

"No," Kickaha said. "Not if you want to live forever. We'll have no trouble, though, transmitting ourselves there. The Great Mother is helping
us. She told me some time ago how we could do it. The way is now set up."

They flew back to the final X marking the gate through which they
had entered. Here, Kickaha blew three times on the Horn. Manathu Vorcyon had also arranged that blowing it thrice at this point would alert her
to open the passage to Khruuz's World. Kickaha did not know how she did
this, but the important thing was that she could. She was now willing to use
the knowledge she had kept to herself for so many millennia.

After warning them, though unnecessarily, to be alert, Kickaha led them
into the gate. They came into the many-tunneled place a long way from
Khruuz's headquarters. Using the detector Manathu Vorcyon had gated to
him days ago, Kickaha saw where the cluster of gates was located and rode
off in that direction. Though the Khringdiz must have assumed that he had
closed all the gates, they still glowed faintly in the detector and so could be
found. The Great Mother had indeed provided well for them.

They had expected traps in the form of explosions, deadly gases, or gates switching them into a circuit or to a desolate universe. But they encountered none. Khruuz seemed to have assumed that no one could gate to his complex unless he permitted them entrance. Finally, after searching the scaly man's living quarters, which were empty, they got to the entrance to Khringdiz's control chamber.

Kickaha was the first to go into it. He halted; the others crowded around him. They stared at the smears of dried blood on the floor directly before the main control panel. Then Kickaha saw the body on the floor fifty feet from the stains. Clifton was lying there on his face. His outstretched hand still gripped a beamer. He had not been taken completely by surprise by Khruuz.

Kickaha strode to the body, noting on the way that there were no bloodstains between the smears and Clifton. Kneeling down, he put his finger on Clifton's neck. No pulse. He had not expected one. Clifton was wearing only a kilt, sandals, and a belt with a holster. On the back of the left arm was a cauterized hole, and close to the lower spine was a similar hole. He had been shot twice with a narrow beamer ray.

He turned the Englishman over. The two wounds in the front matched those in the back. Rising, he said, "Khruuz must've been in a hell of a hurry. He didn't even take the time to get rid of the body."

He ordered Wemathol to take the corpse into the hall some distance away and disintegrate it with the big beamers on his airboat. The Thoan put on his gas mask and began dragging the body from the room. Kickaha went back to the smears before the main control panel. He looked at them more closely.

"Clifton did get off some shots before he died. It looks as if Khruuz was wounded. But not bad enough to lay him low."

Again, he got down on one knee, and he examined one edge of the stains. He said, "Ah! Here's the imprint of the front part of a foot! It's not human! And it's not Khruuz's! Has to be Dingsteth's! It was standing close to Khruuz when the beamer fight was going on!"

Ashatelon got close to the half-print. When he arose, he said, "You're right. But was Dingsteth a prisoner, or did it come with Khruuz voluntarily?"

"I doubt very much it came willingly."

Ashatelon said, "Why would Khruuz take Dingsteth with him? If Dingsteth obeyed your orders, it would have erased all data about the creation engine."

He stopped, then said, "Oh, I see! I think I do, anyway. The data in the computer could be erased, Dingsteth having followed your orders. But it could be in Dingsteth's brain!"

Kickaha nodded. "I goofed up. I should have thought of that Dingsteth wouldn't have told me the data was in its mind unless I'd asked it if it was. Khruuz was smarter. He may even have thought of it when we were there. But he kept quiet about it for his own reasons."

The clone said, "He's hellbent for revenge. He's going to do what Red Orc meant to do! Destroy all universes except one!"

Kickaha said, "We don't know that for sure. But you're probably right. We're going back to the palace but not until we see Manathu Vorcyon. Bad as the situation is, she may want to join us. I think Khruuz is already in the palace. He'll expect us to be treading on his heels. We may have hurried him so much he didn't take time to prepare for us. Let's hope so. In any case, we're going to take a detour, see Manathu Vorcyon first."

If the giantess was surprised by their sudden appearance, she did not show it. As soon as she had been informed of the latest events, she said, "I'm going with you. I have not left my world for many thousands of years, but I have not forgotten how to fight. It will take a few hours to get ready. Meanwhile, eat. You need the rest and the food."

What she did during this time, the others did not know. But when she appeared before them, she wore a suit like a firefighter's, a transparent globe over her head, gloves, and an oxygen tank on her back. A harness over her torso held at least a dozen weapons, some of them unfamiliar to Kickaha. Behind her were four servants carrying similar outfits. These were given to the men.

She is indeed the goddess of war, he thought. But Athena never looked so formidable. And it was at once evident that she had assumed command. Though Kickaha did not like that, he knew that it was best for all of them. Her millennia of experience made him look like, pun intended, a babe in arms.

"Follow me," she said, her voice coming through a speaker in her helmet. "We're going to a place where only I have been. You may put on the suits when we get to it."

They went up the winding staircase in the tree to her room. She spoke a code word. The glindglassa, the huge mirror, shimmered. Kickaha, the first in line behind her, stepped through it into a gigantic room with many doors. He did not have time to marvel at its many objets d'art, some of which must have been twenty thousand years old, nor at the stuffed bodies of men and women standing here and there, all arranged in various postures, their faces expressing a range of emotions. These, he supposed, were enemies she had killed during the ancient Time of Troubles. Unique mementos—and dust-free, too.

She led them from the room into a hallway at least four hundred feet long. Near its end, she turned into a fifty-foot-high entrance. Beyond it was a huge hangar housing scores of aircraft. At her orders, the four donned the clothes. The holsters on their harness, however, contained only the familiar: beamers, hand grenades, knives, and tasers. She told them how to snap the globes into the metal rings at the top of the suits and secure them with a tiny snap lock on the rim. Inside the globes were transmitters to bring in outside noises. She also gave them instructions on the operation of the oxygen apparatus. After their helmets were on, they heard her voice only through a transmitter-receiver attached to the globes.

A minute later, they got into a transparent-hulled vessel shaped like a blimp envelope minus the rudder and fins, but with top and bottom turrets. She showed them their posts and how to operate the big rotatable beamers spaced around the ship to be able to fire from every side of the craft. Two of them were instructed briefly on the operation of the retractable turrets. She pointed out the six foldable single-pilot craft secured along the hull.

"They operate just like those you rode into Zazel's World. Be ready to use them."

She got into the pilot's seat and instructed them in the use of the simple controls. After that, the others strapped themselves into the swivel chairs at the beamer stations. Wemathol occupied the bottom turret; Ashatelon, the top turret. Kickaha was the rear gunner. He preferred to be the pilot or, if he could not be that, the top turret operator. But the Great Mother had ordered otherwise. Like the rest of the crew, he took ten minutes familiarizing himself with the turret and beamer controls. Then Manathu Vorcyon lifted the ship from its landing supports and drove it slowly into the wall at the back of the hangar. The gate, unlike so many, did not display a shimmering as the vessel went through it.

For a moment, they were at an altitude estimated by Kickaha to be five thousand feet. The sun was bright, the blue sky was clear, and the land beneath was forest-covered. Whether or not they were still in Manathu Vorcyon's world he did not know. Then they were suddenly surrounded by water and a feeble light from above. A minute later, they were again flying, this time in a moonless night.

The Grandmother of All certainly made it difficult for an enemy to track her through the gates.

Kickaha recognized the constellations. He had seen them every night while in Red Orc's stronghold. They were flying above Earth II. Their attack would be from outside the palace instead of inside it.

Manathu Vorcyon's voice came through his helmet receiver.

"In two minutes, we'll be within the palace! If you can take Khruuz alive, do it! He is the repository of knowledge that we do not possess. And he is the last living person of his species. He may plan to destroy all living creatures in all the universes. He cannot be condemned for his madness, though he cannot be excused.

"We Thoan cannot repay him for what we did to his people. Nevertheless, we cannot allow empathy or guilt to interfere in this. If you have to do it, kill him!"

A minute passed. She cried out, "We're going in!"

The night sky vanished. They were inside the well-lit and enormous dining hall for the guards and servants. Approximately forty corpses of guards, severed by beamer rays, were scattered through the hall. Three of the four maids left in charge of gating food to Red Orc and Anana were dead on the floor near a table. The overturned chairs and the half-eaten food on the dishes showed that they had been interrupted in their meal. The ten remaining guards had either fled the palace or were dead somewhere in it, or perhaps hiding.

By now, Kickaha thought, the alarms Khruuz must have set up will have told him an intruder is in the palace.

The doorway into the dining hall was just large enough for the vessel, despite its top and bottom turrets, to scrape through. Like the dining-room walls, ceiling, and floor, the hallway was blackened from beamer rays. The ship emerged into another huge room. It was also blackened. The fried or severed bodies of five guards sprawled there.

Manathu Vorcyon's voice came to Kickaha. "The fourth maid was probably kept alive so that Khruuz could question her. He would want from her the code words allowing him to gate through whatever he wishes to send to Red Orc's and Anana's quarters."

Kickaha gritted his teeth. The scaly man could send explosives or poisonous gas through the small food gates. Given enough time, Khruuz might be able to figure out how to expand the food gates to a size large enough to gate a person in or out. That is, he might if he wanted them in his presence for some reason.

Sweat poured over him when he envisioned the scenario. He groaned softly. A high imagination was both a blessing and a curse.

". . . might have done that before he resumed his interrogation of Dingsteth," Manathu Vorcyon said. "He may have the engine data by now, or he may still be trying to get it out of Dingsteth. That depends on how long he has been here, and what the situation is."

The ship squeezed through another hall. The scars and the broken-off parts of the walls and ceiling showed that Khruuz had entered the palace in a craft similar in size to theirs. But they were quickly in another wide, long, and high room. This was for receiving many guests, even though Red Orc never gave parties. In its center, sitting unoccupied and unlit, was a ship much like Manathu Vorcyon's. But its hull was rounded fore and aft, and its bottom was flat.

"Khruuz has gone ahead on foot, because the hallways are too narrow for his ship unless he blasted his way through them," the giantess said.

Her vessel settled down. The bottom turret withdrew into the hull while Wemathol scrambled out of it. When the ship was resting on the floor just behind the scaly man's she said, "Get out the fliers."

While the men were unfolding the aircraft outside the hull, she investigated Khruuz's vessel. It did not take her long. When she returned, she said, "Its door seems to be locked. Here is my plan. We go in two parties to make scouting forays. Kickaha, you and Ashatelon will go together down the nearest hall. Wemathol, you and I will go into the far hallway. That leads to the control room if what you told me about the layout, Kickaha, is correct. Report at once if you need help."

She told them the code words for unlocking the two doors of her craft and for turning the power on in the big vessel. Anybody who had to run for it would return to it and use it as the situation required. They would have no trouble operating it. The controls were clearly marked.

As Kickaha rode off with Ashatelon's machine by his side, he said, "You know, Khruuz may have already flown the coop. If he did, he probably left a bomb strong enough to blow this building to bits."

"You're the most encouraging man I've ever met," the Thoan replied. "Why don't you keep all that cheer to yourself?"

Kickaha laughed, though not as enthusiastically as he usually did.

In twenty minutes of cursory search, they had been in every room and corridor on the first floor in the eastern half of the palace. Kickaha reported their findings. Manathu Vorcyon's voice quickly followed his. She and Wemathol were in the second story and outside the door to the control room.

"We've found the fourth maid. She is lying in the hallway. Her body is covered with small burns, her eyes are burned out, and her head is sliced off. Evidently, she had to be tortured before she would tell him what he wanted to know. A very brave woman, though it was foolish of her not to reveal her secrets. She could have spared herself all the pain."

She paused, then said, "All of you come up here. I'll wait for you before I enter the control room."

When Kickaha and his partner got there, they found that Manathu Vorcyon's beamers had cut the door away from the wall. It was lying in the hall. She was now carving out a large circular area in the wall thirty feet from the doorway. It was large enough to admit her and the airboat.

"Kickaha and Ashatelon, make another entrance on the other side of the door at the same distance from it as this one."

While they were doing that with the large beamers of their vehicles, they heard the other section fall crashing into the room. Shortly thereafter, Kickaha rammed his flier into the section he and the clone had cut out. The impact would have knocked him off his seat if he had not been belted to it. The section fell inward and crashed onto the floor.

He looked through it, wary of a beamer ray or a grenade. The huge room contained many control screens and panels, but it also had many machines, their purpose unknown to him. He reported that he could see part of the room. No one was in his view, but he'd be happy to stick his head through the hole to see all of the room. He was relieved, however, when Manathu Vorcyon forbade that. Did he want his head sliced off just to show how brave he was?

She continued, "The part of the room I can see seems to be unoccupied. Nor do my sensors indicate any body heat in there. Nevertheless, he may be shielded by something—if, that is, he is indeed in there. When I give the signal, we'll all go in at the same time. As I said, I prefer that we just wound him, but that will probably be impossible."

She held her hand up. Then she shouted, "Go!"

Kickaha pressed down on the acceleration pedal of his craft. It shot through the hole so swiftly that he was pressed back against the upright support behind him. Just as he entered the room, he raised the airboat so that it lifted in a tight curve to his right. His head almost touched the ceiling, which was forty feet above the floor. He straightened out the machine as his retrofield fired. It slowed down so abruptly that he was pushed forward against the restraining belt.

Ashatelon's vehicle, which had curved to the left, stopped in front of Kickaha's. It was so close to his that the cone noses almost touched. Ashatelon's flight path was supposed to end at a level lower than his partner's, but he had miscalculated. No time for reproaches. Kickaha was too busy looking around below him for Khruuz. He did not see him.

He grunted when he saw Dingsteth stretched out facedown behind a massive machine set out a few feet from the back wall. Its hands were tied together behind its back. A trail of blood in front of the machine led around it to Dingsteth.

Khruuz must have walked out of the room before his pursuers got there or he had gated out of it. The latter, probably. His enemies had interrupted him just as he had shot Dingsteth. Since the Khringdiz did not have time to finish it off, he had fled through a gate or down the hallway.

Kickaha, along with the others, rode down to the console behind which Dingsteth lay, landed, and got off his craft. Manathu Vorcyon ordered Wemathol to stand guard by the doorway. She did not want Khruuz to surprise them by doubling back from a gate. Then she strode around the console. The others crowded behind her. Kickaha was turning Dingsteth over on its back.

He looked up as she stopped by him. "Beamed through a shoulder and a leg," he said. "His pulse is weak."

The giantess said, "Khruuz has not been gone long. Dingsteth's blood is fresh."

Kickaha started to stand up. A strange disorienting feeling passed through him. He seemed to be floating. It was as if he were in a very swiftly descending elevator. When he straightened up, he looked up through the giantess's helmet at her face, twisted with alarm. She opened her mouth. Before she could say anything, a great noise stopped her.

Then the floor came up at him. He struck it very hard, and it buckled and broke open against his fallen body. He was vaguely aware that the console was skittering over the floor, hurling aside Ashatelon, who had been standing at its corner. Something hit him hard in the back, and he lost consciousness. The last things he heard were a deep rumbling, a crashing like an avalanche, and his own feeble voice crying out.

21

Pain awoke him. His head, nose, neck, lower back, and right elbow hurt. His legs were numb from his hips downward. But they were not so deadened that he could not feel the heaviness pressing them down. All he could see through the helmet, which was covered with a very thin layer of white dust, was the tiled floor. A large crack in it was just below him. His nose was flattened against the front of his globed helmet. When he licked his lips, he tasted blood.

The room was silent except for a single muffled groan from somewhere. He called out. Silence answered him.

He tried to roll over, but his legs were pressed down against the floor. While struggling to pull himself free, he saw green boots sticking out from a pile of cement blocks mixed with fragments of various materials. They were lightly covered by the plaster dust covering everything in the room. But parts of the boots were not so veiled that he could not see that they were green. Ashatelon was the only one wearing green footwear.

When he lowered his head and turned it to his right, his vision was blocked by a metal ceiling beam an inch from his helmet. Torn loose from its wall support, the beam had probably struck one side of his curved helmet. The impact had hurled him to one side so that his shoulder had just missed being crushed by the beam.

He strove to drag himself forward to escape whatever it was that felt like a Titan's thumbs pressing down on his legs. Not until he was breathing very hard and was exhausted did he stop. At least, he had managed to move forward several inches. Or was that wishful thinking?

After lying still a few minutes, he began struggling again. He quit that when he suddenly saw the huge, dusty, light-blue boots of Manathu Vorcyon before him. Her voice filled his helmet.

"Lie still, Kickaha. I'll try to lift this beam from your legs."

The boots disappeared. Presently, after much grunting and many expletives, she said, panting, "I cannot do it. I will get my boat, if I can find it in this mess, and use it to haul up the beam. There is a rope in the supply bag on the boat."

While she was gone, Wemathol came to Kickaha. He croaked when he spoke. "She told me to dig the debris from around the beam. Just lie still, Kickaha. You cannot do anything until she gets back."

"As if I didn't know that," Kickaha muttered. He longed for a tall glass of iced water.

He heard scraping sounds and a loud panting for some time. Then Wemathol said, "There is a chance your legs might not be crushed. They were buried in debris before the beam fell on top of the pile."

"I can feel something now," Kickaha said. "The numbness is going away."

The giantess came on an airboat. She had had to tear away a mass of debris before she could uproot it. It was not hers, but it was the only one she could find. She helped the clone dig out the debris on top of and around the massive beam. Then she got the rope through the space beneath it. Within a few minutes, it was lifted up far enough for Wemathol to drag Kickaha out from under it. She landed the boat and got off it to examine Kickaha.

His legs would not yet obey him. He sat leaning against the pile of debris while Manathu Vorcyon felt his legs through the cloth. She reported that they did not seem to be broken, but she would have to examine them after his clothes were off. Then she said, "Ashatelon is dead."

"I'm surprised he is. He seemed to be a survivor."

"Time makes sure that nobody is."

Kickaha looked up at what was left of the ceiling. Only its outer part was left, but the collapsed story above that had plugged up the hole. Parts of it looked as if they would soon fall through. Moreover, the broken wall of this room had spilled out into the hallway. While he was looking at the damage, the building shifted slightly, and the other walls became even more cracked. The far end of the ceiling collapsed with a roar and a cloud of white plaster dust, plunging into the room and forming a great mound that reached up through the gaping hole.

He said, "Maybe we should get out of here."

Before she could reply, Wemathol came into the room after exploring the hallway.

"We're not on Earth Two!"

Kickaha and the giantess spoke as if they were one person. "What? How do you know?"

"I could see the sky through a small opening in a part of the hallway ceiling. A stone pillar must have fallen from the palace roof and pierced through all the floors of the rooms above. There is not much of the sky to see, but it is enough. It is green."

Kickaha said, "That means—"

"It means," the Great Mother said, "that Khruuz wrapped up the entire palace, perhaps some of the surrounding grounds, in a gate and transported it to this universe. That took great power. It would also take some time to be arranged. He must have set it up before he came to this room with Dingsteth. When the palace came through the gate, it was up in the air, by accident or design, and it fell. It could not have been very high above the surface or we would be dead."

"Just what I was going to say," Kickaha said. He looked around. "Where's Dingsteth?"

"It's either buried under a pile or it woke up before we did and walked off. It may have been in a daze. But I would assume that if it did wander away, it will not get far because of its wounds."

"It was half flesh and half electronic circuits," Kickaha said. "Its recovery powers must be greater than ours. Is there a trail of blood leading out of the room?"

"No," she said. "But Dingsteth was next to you when the palace collapsed. It should have been hit by the same beam that came close to smashing you."

"Or it's seeking Khruuz so it can get revenge," Wemathol said.

"With its hands bound behind its back?" the giantess said.

Kickaha cried, "Anana!" He tried to get up, but his legs were still too weak. At least they were showing signs of getting their strength back.

The woman and the clone looked at each other but said nothing. They knew what Kickaha was envisioning: Anana in a suite of rooms inside the building but sealed off from the rest of it. The only access was through a gate. But the wall containing the gate activator could be buried under rubble.

Red Orc would be in a similar situation. Kickaha was not worried about him.

Manathu Vorcyon, however, was more concerned than he about the Thoan. She said, "It is possible that the collapse might not have buried them. It could have opened a way for Anana, and Red Orc, too, to get out of their rooms."

"Not very likely," Wemathol said.

"Anything is possible. But we cannot take a chance. We have to locate Khruuz and also determine if Red Orc did get away."

"Aren't you going to look for Anana?" Kickaha said.

"Later," Manathu Vorcyon said. "Wemathol, you come with me. I am sorry, Kickaha, but we cannot wait for you to recover. Khruuz would not have stayed inside the palace when he gated it to this place. He would have taken another gate to it after it was transported. He would not care to be in the palace when it was transmitted to here, wherever this is. It is certain that he'll be looking for us. I am surprised that he has not come back to this room by now."

"He's somewhere around here, waiting to ambush us," Wemathol said. He looked around nervously.

The Great Mother decided that they should remove their tanks, back-packs, helmets, and suits.

"They slow us down, and I doubt we have to guard against poison gas," she said. When she and the clone had stripped down, they put on their weapons belts. Then they removed Kickaha's suit and helped him strap on his belt. In addition to his weapons, the Horn of Shambarimen was attached to the belt.

Wemathol removed the radio sets, which were attached by suction discs to the interior of the globed helmets. The three stuck these on their wrists.

The air was dusty and getting hot. The palace must have landed in a tropical area, Kickaha thought.

He watched the two ride away on the boat, which had two seats in tandem and was a very thin and lightweight metal structure supporting a small motor, a small storage space, and two rotatable beamers. The Great Mother was at the controls. Wemathol sat behind her. Kickaha was to stay behind the pile but keep on guard. His gate detector was in a small pouch hanging from the belt. A canteen was by him, and his beamer was in his hand, ready to shoot if the scaly man or Red Orc appeared. Though the room did not seem to be accessible behind him, he looked there now and then. The large masses of rubble might conceal an opening into the room approachable from the other side of the wall.

All was silent except for the occasional creaks caused by the shifting parts of the ruins. Anybody in here with good sense should get out of the structure before all of it crashes, he thought. But anybody with good sense wouldn't be in this mess in the first place. And I still hurt very much.

It seemed improbable that Khruuz could be tuned in to their radio frequencies, but it was best not to chance it. They were to use the radios only if a situation absolutely required it.

He felt helpless. Though he usually was content to be alone, he would have been glad to hear a human voice. Also, that the entire building might collapse and bury him at any moment made time seem to stretch out like a glowing-hot wire in a drawing machine. If it got too thin, it snapped. That would be when the debris suspended above him fell through the ceiling.

He was beginning to sweat a lot from the increasing heat. However, the numbness of his legs seemed to be completely gone. Though they still pained him, he stood up. He was shaky but getting stronger. He drank deeply from the canteen Manathu Vorcyon had given him. A few minutes later, he walked out of the room. No use staying here. Not when Khruuz was prowling around out there and armed with God only knew what.

The going was not so tough at first. Though what was left of the hallway was jammed halfway up to the open ceiling, he could scramble up, slipping sometimes, crawl through the space between the top of the mound and the ceiling, where there was ceiling, and slide down the other side of the mounds. A beam of pale light slanted from the opening Wemathol had mentioned. Kickaha looked up through it. No mistake. The sky was green.

Beyond the hallway was a room the size of two Imperial palace ballrooms. But it was shattered. He was confronted with numerous obstacles: hillocks and dales of plaster chunks, pieces of wood, stone slabs and blocks, broken and unbroken marble pillars, marble chunks, and greater-than-life-sized stone statues. Many of the slabs and pillars and statues were sticking up at a slant from the mounds like cannons from the ruins of a fort. Also protruding were jagged broken-off legs and backs of chairs and tables; dented metal and wooden cabinets; broken bottles, the odors of spilled beer and wine making the air pungent; twisted and broken chandeliers; and warped frames of large paintings, the cloth fragments hanging from them. Getting over or around these made him sweat. The perspiration mingled with the white dust, covered his body and hair, and ran down into his eyes, stinging them. He thought that he must look like a pale ghost with scary red eyes.

Now and then, he took the gate-detector out of a belt pouch and turned it on. The instrument lit up a dozen times. But he could not use the Horn now to open the gates. Khruuz might be within hearing range.

The Great Mother had said that she and Wemathol would go to the northeast corner of the palace. From there, they would separate for individual searches. Once the scaly man was taken care of, they would find each other by radio. Kickaha headed toward the northeast section of the palace, but he was forced to take a circuitous path. Despite his strenuous climbing, his legs were gaining, not losing, strength.

When he got to the tremendous heap of debris on the other side of the huge room, he seemed to have deviated from a straight path. Manathu Vorcyon and Wemathol had probably ascended through an opening to the second story and then to the third. But he could not even see entrances to the next room. Towering peaks of debris blocked his view.

He began going up the slope of rubble but slid back now and then. The sliding material made noises. Near the top of the mound was an opening to a tunnel of sorts. It seemed to go through the pile and into the wall, which was somehow still standing. He used a tiny flashlight to illuminate the interior of the tunnel, which had been formed by accident. Two huge marble columns coming in almost parallel angles to each other but slanting somewhat downward had punched through the wall and stopped side by side. The big hole they must have made in the wall had been plugged up by a mass of large fragments. Stone slabs had crashed down to make a roof over the pillars. The pillars were not so close to each other that there was no space for him to move forward, molelike, between them. Some debris half-blocked the passageway, which pointed upward at about ten degrees from the horizontal. But he had room enough to pass the stuff half-blocking the tunnel behind him. Beyond the dark tunnel was light, feeble but brighter than that in this cramped space. If he could get through it to the next room, he would be coming out in a place an enemy lurking there would not expect. He began worming his way through it.

Though he was making as little noise as possible, he was not quiet enough. For a second, he envisioned Khruuz standing to one side at the end of the tunnel, waiting for anyone who came through it. No. If the scaly man was there, he would shoot his beamer rays down its length when he heard noise in the tunnel and would slice his enemy. In any event, he, Kickaha, could not stop going forward. And why would the scaly man be there? He wouldn't know there was a tunnel there.

When he cautiously poked his head from the thirty-foot-long passageway, he saw that he was near the top of a mountain of debris. Most of the ceiling of this gigantic room had fallen through, and perhaps some of the floor of the third story. He took his time looking at the ruins below him. If anyone was hiding down there, he would have to be behind a very large mound near the wall at the other side.

His beamer in one hand, he slid down on his back. He silently cursed the noise he could not help making. When he got to the bottom, scratched and bleeding from small gashes and smarting from plaster dust in the wounds, he waited a while for an attack. None came. He went over smaller piles and then found behind the second mountainous ruin a gaping hole in the wall. It was large enough for a Sherman tank to pass through. In fact, it looked as if a tank had made the hole. He did not know what kept the rest of the much-cracked wall from collapsing.

He stepped through the hole after sticking his head through it to scout the territory. Above him, all the stories had partly fallen through. Down here, the light was almost that of dusk. Up there, it was bright. He could see a much larger piece of the green sky than he had seen in the hallway.

The heavens around the World of Tiers were the same color. Could Khruuz have gated the palace to the planet shaped like the Tower of Babylon? If so, why did he choose it? Or . . . no use speculating.

A pile of timbers and stone stuck out several feet from a twenty-foot-high jumble to his left. He had just seen something stir in the darkness under the ledge. The shapeless mass, covered with white dust, could be a man. He looked closely at it and finally determined that it had its back to him. That might be a ruse. Whoever it was could have seen him, then turned away to make him think he saw a dead or badly injured person. When he heard Kickaha's footsteps, he would twist his body to face him and would shoot. Maybe.

Kickaha got into a sort of ready-made foxhole in the rubble and then fired a beam near the figure's head. That would startle anyone who didn't have absolute control of his nerves. But the man did not move. Kickaha got out of the hole with the least noise possible and walked slowly along a curve toward the ledge. When he got within twenty feet of it, he saw that the figure was neither Khruuz nor Red Orc. It was Dingsteth. But its hands were no longer tied behind its back.

The creature must have ceased bleeding. It certainly had left no trail. Kickaha still did not go directly to it. When he stopped by it, he was half-concealed by the pile. He leaned over and poked the back of its head with the end of his beamer. It groaned.

"Dingsteth!" Kickaha said.

It muttered something. He dragged it out from under the ledge and turned it over. Under the dust on its skin were many black spots. Burns? Unable to hear distinctly what it was saying, Kickaha glanced around, then got to his knees and put an ear close to Dingsteth's mouth. Though his position made him feel vulnerable, he kept it.

"It's me, Kickaha," he said softly.

It said, "Khruuz . . . not believe that . . ."

"What? I can't hear you."

"Kickaha! Khruuz . . . when I said . . . not have data . . . in my brain . . . tortured me . . . did not believe me . . . took me along . . . got away . . . Zazel . . . proud of me."

"I'll get help for you," Kickaha said. "It may take some time . . ."

He stopped. Dingsteth's eyes were open. His mouth, filled with the diamond teeth, was still.

He had to break radio silence. Manathu Vorcyon would want to know about this. He called her at once, and she replied at once. After he told her what had happened, she said, "I am still where I told you we were going. I sent Wemathol to look for you. If he does not find you at the end of ten minutes, he will return to me."

If Wemathol was going to take only ten minutes for the search, he would be in the airboat. After twelve minutes had passed, he used the radio to ask Wemathol to report. But the clone did not reply.

Manathu Vorcyon's voice came immediately. "Something may have happened to Wemathol! I will give him two more minutes to report."

Which is mostly up and down and around and along, he thought. Fifteen minutes later, he stopped to give his aching legs time to recharge.

When he felt stronger, he got to his feet and plodded on. Shortly thereafter, he came to another large area. Parts of the roof had fallen down on it. The sun blazed down through the opening but was past its zenith. It shone near one end of the room where a winding staircase by the wall had somehow escaped being smashed. Its upper part, shorn of its banister, protruded from the peak of a very high mound. He climbed to its top, though not without slipping and sliding and making noise. The staircase, made of some hardwood, seemed to be stable. He went up it slowly, looking above and below him at every step.

But with only twenty steps to go, he had to get down and grab the edge of the rise. From somewhere nearby, something had crashed with a roar as if it were a Niagara of solid parts. The staircase shook so much that he thought it was going to break from the wall. Screeching, it separated from the landing above. It swayed outward, then swayed inward and slammed up against the wall. The stone blocks of the wall moved, and some were partly displaced. He expected the wall to fall apart and carry the staircase with him. If that did not happen, the swaying and banging of the staircase would snap it off and tumble it to the heap thirty feet below.

Though he gripped the edge of the rise, he was moved irresistibly sideward toward the open side of the staircase. A few more such whipping movements would shoot him off the steps even if the structure did not fall. And he could now see for only a few feet around him. Thick dust raised by the newly fallen mass stung his eyes and clogged his nostrils.

Suddenly, it was over except for a shuddering of the stairs. When that ceased, Kickaha began climbing on hands and knees. The structure was leaning away from the wall, though not quite at the angle of the Tower of Pisa. Not yet, anyway. The higher he climbed, the more the structure bent at its apex and the louder it creaked and groaned.

By then, he had to lean to the right to compensate for the leftward slant of the steps. When his hands clung to the rise of the highest step, he slowly and awkwardly stood up, balancing himself precariously, his left leg straighter than his right. Before him was the floor of the second story, exposed like a dollhouse by the ripping away of its wall. It was bending in the middle, groaning under the weight of a gargantuan pile of debris. It could collapse at any moment. He had to leap through the eight feet of space between him and the floor. Do it at once.

Or he could go back down the staircase, though it might snap off before he got far.

He reholstered the beamer. He would need both hands to grip the edge of the exposed floor if he could not soar out and up to it. Under normal circumstances, he could have made such a jump easily and landed on the floor with his feet. After glancing around, he crouched down and propelled himself outward. The staircase gave way then, bending down under the force of his jump. It was too much for it. It snapped and the upper part fell down and struck the heap with a loud crash.

Although the recoil of the staircase made the leap longer than he had planned, he reached the floor. His belly was even with the edge of the floor just before he began to fall. His arms banged against the floor, and his chest struck the edge. He was supporting his body with the upper part of his arms while his legs dangled. He twisted and threw his right leg up over the edge and pulled himself entirely onto the floor.

He was panting, and he wanted to lie on his back for a minute to recover his strength. But the wood underneath was bending, and he could feel alarming vibrations running through it. Maybe the floor, overburdened by the immense pile in the middle of the room, had been close to the point of breaking before his weight was added to it.

He scrambled to his feet, drawing the beamer from its holster as he did so. As he sped toward the nearest door to the north, he heard a great cracking noise. The floor suddenly slanted down. He was almost caught by its shifting, but he leaped through the doorway just in time. For a few seconds, he came close to being borne backward with the avalanche. A pile of debris plugged all but a narrow opening in the upper part of the doorway. He landed on its slope and clawed away at the rubble to keep going as it spilled out onto a floor that was no longer there. Dust billowed out from behind him and blinded him.

He managed to get over the top of the pile in the doorway, though it was like running on a ground that was moving in the opposite direction. When he got to the bottom of the pile on the other side, he was suddenly facedown on the floor of a room. Most of the heap was gone, having avalanched into the emptiness of the room he had just left. Even so, his legs were now dangling over the bottom of the doorway. And the floor of the room that was to be his refuge was moving downward.

He pulled himself away from the edge, got up, and sprinted up the increasingly slanting surface of this floor, which was attached to the wall on the other side but would not be for long. Leaping over small piles of debris sliding toward him, racing around the larger heaps also sliding toward him, he strove to get to the exit to the room beyond this one. He did not make it. He was deafened by another roar, and he fell through to the room below. Somehow, he landed on his feet and rolled down a mound and ended, his breath and his wits knocked out of him, upon the back of a huge divan. He had been fortunate not to have been buried.

Also, the edge of the riven floor had missed by a few inches slamming into him. It undoubtedly would have killed him. As it was, it had only half killed him.

It took him an undeterminable time to regain all of his senses. Then he was aware of how much he hurt and of how many places on him were painful. But he got up. His beamer was still clutched in his hand, and the bag containing the Horn had not been torn from his belt. While the dust was still settling, he walked slowly forward. Though he felt like coughing, he suppressed it. And then he heard a cough from somewhere ahead of him.

He stopped. A vague form was moving slowly in the dust toward him. It seemed to be in the air a few feet from the surface. Wemathol in his air-boat? Instead of calling out, he dropped behind a small mound and pointed his beamer at the object. Never assume anything—even if he had broken that rule now and then.

More debris fell in the next room, the one from which the unknown had come into this room. More dust billowed out, enveloping the object. He squinted toward where it had been, his eyes stinging and wet. If that was not Wemathol, then it must be Manathu Vorcyon. Or, if Khruuz had somehow gotten hold of an airboat, he could be riding it out there.

He waited. A minute passed by. Then he was startled by another crash-ing sound. This was followed by four less-loud collapses. The dust thick-ened. He held his nose and breathed out through his mouth to avoid sneezing. But a sneeze was building up in him that he would not be able to control. And then, someone out in the dust went "Ah! Choo!" This was followed by a series of nose blasts.

Kickaha, despite heroic efforts not to do so, sneezed mightily.

Though it was hard to do while the nasal explosions racked his body, he reached out and felt what seemed to be a large piece of broken crockery. He tossed it as far as he could to his right. If it made a noise that the hid-den person could hear, it wasn't audible to him. His own sneezing drowned it out. There was no reaction from the being. No ray beam cutting through the dust; no voice.

He could not wait until the dust settled. The rider might have heat de-tectors or be wearing night-vision goggles. Or he could be lifting the boat up high so that he could spot anyone in the room after the dust settled down.

He crawled away from behind the mound, trying to do it silently and keeping down close to the floor. The best thing for me to do, Kickaha thought, is to stand up and get out of this room swiftly. But if he did that, he could not avoid making a lot of noise and stumbling into and over de-bris. Moreover, he did not know where the exits were.

When he felt a large pile in front of him, he went behind it. To hell with radio silence. He called. Manathu Vorcyon's voice, much softer than usual, came at once. "What do you want?"

Kickaha whispered, "You still in the same place? I ask because there's someone on an airboat very close to me. I can't see him because of the dust."

"It is not I. And Wemathol would have answered you if he were capable of doing so. Make sure, though, before you shoot, that it is not he."

"Off," he said.

Kickaha groped around until he felt several large chunks of plaster. He cast these into the dust before him. But the unknown did not fire at the source of the noise. Probably his boat was hovering high up and he was making sure of his target before he attacked.

That person had to be Khruuz.

He stood up and began making his way toward the far wall. After a few steps, he jumped to one side. Something wet had fallen on his left shoulder. He felt the spot with his right hand. Though he had to bring his fingers close to his eyes, he saw a dark mass of dust and something liquid.

Was it raining blood?

He looked upward. The particles were beginning to settle down. It would not be long before he would be able to distinguish any dark object near where the ceiling had been. Especially since the light was brighter up there.

He started walking again, then stopped. He had heard a low moan. After listening carefully for a moment, he stepped forward. He jumped aside with a suppressed oath. Something heavy had struck the floor near him. He walked as slowly and as silently as possible toward the source of the thump. It could be a trick, but he doubted it. The impact had sounded like the body of a man striking the earth. Wood or stone would have made a different sound. There had been a hint of a splat in the sound, flesh giving way and bone broken against the unyielding stone floor.

At last, he saw the thing. It was indeed Khruuz. He was lying on his back, his eyes open. Blood had spread out from under his body as if Death had unrolled a scarlet carpet for him. Even that thick skull had caved in. Coming closer to the corpse, though still warily, Kickaha saw that a wide and thick bandage was wrapped around its left thigh. Blood had trickled from it down the side of the leg. Clifton must have shot the scaly man before he was killed by him. Khruuz had only taken time enough to bandage himself before he gated Dingsteth with him for the invasion of the palace. He must have been aflame with desire for revenge. He could not wait to get it; he had lauched his attack despite his injury. But the slow loss of blood had weakened him so much that he had fallen off his airboat.

Score one for Clifton.

He radioed Manathu Vorcyon the news. She said, "It is unfortunate that we did not take him alive; he was such a repository of knowledge and the last of his kind. But I am also much relieved that he is no longer a danger to us. By the way, I can see the landscape around the palace. Khruuz gated not only the building, but the lawns and gardens around it. They're wrecked, but I believe that Khruuz gated himself and Dingsteth to a lawn or garden after the palace had been transmitted here. He would not have wanted to be inside the palace when it landed. Then he entered it to finish the killing."

Kickaha said, "Now we can look for Anana and Red Orc."

"I understand your wish to do that," she said. "But first, we have to find Wemathol."

They talked for a few minutes. She would proceed from the northeast corner of the palace and search. He would be looking for the clone while he headed for her. They would keep in radio contact and describe where they were every five minutes.

Kickaha signed off. The airboat was hovering about fifty feet above him. He had no way to get to it. He shrugged and started walking and climbing. Eventually, he found an archway that was not entirely jammed with debris. Halfway through the next room, he saw a man propped up in the semidarkness against the side of a fallen and broken marble pillar. He turned his flashlight beam on the figure. It was Wemathol, unmoving, his eyes shut. Dust did not conceal the crimson color of his boots and headband. His chest was smeared with blood mixed with dust. His beamer was not in sight, and his only weapon was a dagger in a scabbard.

Kickaha cried out, "Wemathol!"

His voice was bounced back to him from the vast walls. The clone did not stir.

Kickaha lifted the wrist radio to his lips, then decided to determine Wemathol's exact condition before reporting. He came close to him and, bending over, spoke his name.

Wemathol's right foot kicked the beamer from Kickaha's hand.

22

THOUGH LOCKED UP BY SURPRISE FOR ONE OF THE FEW TIMES in his life, Kickaha unfroze in a sliver of a second. He hurled himself at the man, stabbing at the same time with his pen-sized flashlight.

The Thoan had snatched out his long dagger as he straightened up. Kickaha grabbed the wrist just above the hand holding the dagger. At the same time, his flashlight drove toward his attacker's left eye. It would have punched through to the brain if the Thoan had not turned his head slightly. It caught in the corner of his eye, gashed it, and slid on. Kickaha dropped the flashlight and twisted the Lord's left wrist. At the same time, he turned his body sideways to prevent the man from kneeing him in the testicles. Though Kickaha had rotated his antagonist's wrist with such force that it should have been broken, he was unable to do more than half turn it. The man was indeed powerful. But his dagger dropped to the ground.

Kickaha leaned back then and jerked the man forward, at the same time shifting his footing so that his sidewise stance would enable him to swing the man around. But the man did not resist. He allowed Kickaha to whirl him around and cast him away as if he were a throwing hammer. He spun for ten feet, fell, rolled several times on the ground, and bounded to his feet as if he were a leopard.

Kickaha had charged him even while he was rolling. The Lord dashed for the beamer, which was lying between two small piles. Kickaha changed direction to intercept him. The Lord bent down to scoop up the weapon on the run. Kickaha leaped and struck with both feet the buttocks presented to him. The man cried out as he toppled forward. But he did not let loose of the gun even as he slid on his face and chest.

Though Kickaha had fallen on his back with a thump, he stood up quickly. The Lord turned over, blood welling from deep scratches and shallow gashes on his face, chest, and belly. Then he bent his torso up off the ground, swinging the beamer upward. Just before he pulled the trigger, Kickaha's throwing knife sped like a dark barracuda in a half-lit sea. Its point drove about an inch into the man's left biceps, and he dropped the beamer. But he jerked the dagger out and gripped it in his right hand. Then he rose to his feet with astonishing swiftness. Bending over, he reached with his left hand for the beamer.

Roaring, Kickaha leaped, and his feet slammed into the man's chest just as he straightened up. The beamer shot once, its violet ray slicing the twilight. Kickaha's right wrist burned. The weapon skittered across the floor. The breath drove out of the Lord's chest as he went backward. The dagger fell from his hand as he flailed his arms to keep his balance. But he fell on his back.

Kickaha had managed to twist so that instead of slamming onto the ground on his back after his kick, he landed on his feet in a crouch. But he did not take the time to pick up the dagger. Hoping to catch the man while he was still lying down or in a vulnerable position while rising, Kickaha ran toward him. The Lord sprang upright as if he had been lifted by an invisible hand. He was holding something; he hurled it at Kickaha.

For a moment, Kickaha was halfdazed. His brain and body seemed numb. The stone had come flying out of the duskiness, slammed into his forehead, and stopped his charge. A chunk of red, apple-sized marble lay bloodstained on the ground. That it had not killed him or knocked him completely unconscious showed that the Lord was weakened. Or had made a bad pitch.

His own condition was not up to par. And he was at a disadvantage because the Lord had picked up the dagger. But he was also wheezing for breath, and blood was flowing from the wound in his upper arm.

Kickaha wiped his own blood from his forehead and his eyelids. When his wind was back, he would attack again.

Between gasps, he said, "Red Orc! How'd you escape! What did you do to Wemathol before you took his boots, headband, and dagger?"

The Thoan managed to smile. He said, "I did fool you!"

"Not for long."

"Long enough! Before I tell you how I got away from my prison, tell me what happened here."

Red Orc wanted to put off renewing the combat until he regained his breath. That was all right with Kickaha. He needed time, too. Time, he suddenly realized, to call Manathu Vorcyon. She would come a-flying. If, that is, she could find him. When he started to raise his arm, he saw that the radio was no longer on it. Where it had been was a burn wound. Red Orc's one shot had cut through the suction disc holding the radio and taken some skin with it. He was lucky that the ray had not severed his wrist.

Losing the radio was no handicap. He did not need her help, and he would be very disappointed if she, not he, killed Red Orc.

His breathing was not so quick now. He said, "Khruuz gated the entire palace to another universe. The World of Tiers, I believe. The rest you can figure out easily. Now, what's your story?"

While he had been talking, he had looked around hoping to see the beamer. No luck.

"Ah!" Red Orc said. "So that is it! Is the Khringdiz still alive?"

"No. Did Anana escape with you?"

"I do not know. I was able to crawl out from my prison after it collapsed. I lost much skin getting through some very tight openings. And then I saw Wemathol riding his airboat. I jumped down on him from a pile and knocked him off the boat. Unfortunately, that kept on going. During the struggle with Wemathol, his beamer fell through a hole in the floor and I could not find it later. When I broke his neck, I put on his boots and headband and took his dagger. I deceived you long enough to get you into this situation. And now I am here to end the saga of Kickaha."

"I'll see about that. What makes you believe that you can defeat me? You're inferior to me, though you're a Lord and I'm a *leblabbiy*."

"How can you say that?" Red Orc said loudly.

"You had to use me to get into Zazel's World after you had failed during a search of many thousands of years. I was the one who deceived Dingsteth and talked it into releasing us. You didn't have the imagination to think of the ghost-of-Zazel idea. I had you at my mercy when I locked you up here. You'd still be there if Khruuz hadn't gated the palace. So, what makes you think you're a better man than I am?"

"You're a *leblabbiy,* a descendant of the artificial humans we Thoan made in our factories!" Red Orc howled. "You are inherently inferior because we made your ancestors inferior to us! You were made less intelligent than we! You were made less strong and less swift! Do you think that we would be stupid enough to make beings who were our equals?"

"That may have been the case when you first made them," Kickaha said. "But there is such a thing as evolution, you know. If I am indeed one of a lowly lesser breed, why is it I have killed so many Lords and gotten out of so many of their traps? Why do they call me the Trickster, the Slayer of Lords?"

"You have slain your last Lord!" Red Orc bellowed. "From now on, I will be known also as Kickaha's Killer."

"Old English saying: 'The proof is in the pudding.' Get ready to choke on what I'm going to feed you," Kickaha said.

Red Orc was getting into a terrible fury, and that would shape his judgment. Or was he just pretending to be overwhelmed with anger so that his enemy would be too confident?

"I'm pleased you have the dagger," Kickaha said. "It gives you an advantage you really need."

"*Leblabbiy!*" the Thoan screamed.

"Don't just stand there and call me names like some ten-year-old kid," Kickaha said. "Try me! Attack! Let's see what you got!"

Red Orc yelled and ran at Kickaha, who stooped and picked up the marble chunk that had struck him in the forehead. He wound up like a baseball pitcher, which he had been when in high school. He aimed the stone for the Thoan's chest. But Red Orc stabbed at it, and it struck the point of the dagger. This was knocked loose from his grasp. No doubt, it also paralyzed his hand for a moment. In that time, Kickaha, yelling a war cry, was on him. Red Orc tried to dodge him, but Kickaha slammed into him and squeezed his hands around the thick neck and forced him to stagger backward. The Thoan tried to box both Kickaha's ears; Kickaha ducked his head so that he was struck on its upper part. The blows made his head ring, but he pulled the Thoan close to him, banged his head against Red Orc's (it was a question who was more dazed by this), and then fastened his teeth on Red Orc's neck.

The Thoan fell backward, taking Kickaha with him. Red Orc came out the worse from the fall. His breath whoofed out, and he had to fight Kickaha at the same time that he was trying to get his wind back. Kickaha was now in his own rage. He saw red, though it might have been his own blood or the Thoan's. Despite the impact and his loss of breath, Red Orc managed to turn over, taking Kickaha with him, and they rolled until they were stopped by a debris heap. Kickaha had fastened his teeth on the Lord's jugular vein and was biting as deep as he could. He did not expect to cut through the vein. He was no sharp-fanged great ape, but he strove to shut off the flow of blood.

Kickaha's body was pressed against Red Orc's left arm so tightly that, for some seconds, Red Orc could not get it free. But he brought the other arm up and over, a finger hooked. It dug deeply into Kickaha's right eye, and then was yanked back toward Red Orc. Kickaha's eye popped out and hung by the optic nerve. He was not aware of his other pains; his fury overrode them. But this one pierced through the haze of red.

Nevertheless, he kept on biting the vein. Red Orc then began slamming the side of Kickaha's head with the edge of his hand. That hurt and dazed Kickaha so much that he unclamped his teeth and rolled away. He was only vaguely aware that the optic nerve had been torn loose. When he stopped rolling, the lost eye flat, its fluid pressed out of it, stared up at him, a few inches from the other eye.

That sent a surge of energy through him. He got to his feet at the same time that Red Orc rose. He charged immediately. Red Orc turned to meet him. He was borne backward as Kickaha's head slammed into his belly. Kickaha fell, too, but reached out and squeezed the Thoan's testicles. While Red Orc writhed in agony, Kickaha got up and jumped on him with both feet. The Thoan screamed; the bones of his rib cage were fractured.

That should have been the end of the fight. But Red Orc was not the man to be stopped by mere crippling and high pain. His hand shot out and gripped Kickaha's ankle even as he writhed, and he yanked with a strength he should not have possessed. Kickaha fell backward, though he twisted enough to keep from falling completely on his back. His shoulder struck the floor. Red Orc had half turned, his grip still powerful. Kickaha sat up and pried one of the Thoan's fingers loose and bent it back. The bone snapped; the Thoan screamed again and loosed his clutch.

Kickaha got onto his knees and slammed his fist against the Thoan's nose. Its bridge snapped. Blood spurted from his nostrils. Nevertheless, in a wholly automatic reaction, he hit Kickaha's jaw with his fist. It was not the knockout blow it would have been if Red Orc had not been weakened. It did make Kickaha's head ring again. By the time his senses were wholly back, he saw that Red Orc was getting back onto his feet. And now he was swaying as he stood above Kickaha.

"You cannot defeat me," he croaked. "You are a *leblabbiy.* I am Red Orc."

"That's no big deal. I am Kickaha."

Kickaha's voice sounded feeble, but he rolled away while the Thoan staggered after him. Red Orc stopped when he saw the dagger on the ground, and he went to it and picked it up.

"I will cut off your testicles, just as I cut off my father's," he said, "and I will eat them raw, just as I ate my father's."

"Easier said than done," Kickaha said. He stood up. "What you did to so many people, especially what you did to Anana, will drive me on, no matter how you try to stop me."

"Let us get this over with, *leblabbiy.* It is no use for you to keep hoping you will overcome me. You will die."

"Sometime. Not now."

The Thoan waved the dagger. "You will not get by this."

Looking at the man's face, squeezed with agony, and at his bent-over posture, Kickaha thought that he might be able to dance around Red Orc until he collapsed. But the chances were fifty-fifty that he might crumble first.

His hand brushed against the deerskin pouch containing the Horn. In his fury, he had forgotten about it. He pulled it out from the pouch and gripped its end as if it were a club. Ancient Shambarimen had not made the instrument to be used as a bludgeon. But it would serve. He advanced slowly toward the Lord, saying, "It will be told that you had to use a knife to kill an unarmed man."

"You would like me to cast it aside. But no one will have seen this fight. Too bad, in a way. It should be celebrated in epic poetry. Perhaps it will be. But I will be the one who tells others of how it went."

"Always the cowardly liar," Kickaha said. "Use the dagger. I'll kill you anyway. You'll gain even more fame as the only man ever to be killed by the Horn."

Red Orc said nothing. He came at Kickaha with the knife. The Horn swung and struck the Thoan's wrist as he jabbed. But Red Orc did not drop the knife. Instead, he lunged again, and the blade entered Kickaha's chest. But it only made a shallow wound because Kickaha grabbed the man's wrist with one hand and banged Red Orc over the head with the Horn. Red Orc tore his wrist from the grasp, retreated for several seconds, breathing heavily, then attacked again.

This time, he used one arm as a shield against the bludgeoning while he thrust with his right hand. His dagger sliced across Kickaha's lower arm, but Kickaha brought the Horn down and then up and slammed its flaring end into Red Orc's chin. Though the Thoan must have been dazed by the blow, he managed to rake the edge of the blade across Kickaha's shoulder and then gash the hand holding the Horn. Kickaha dropped it; it clanged on the ground.

Red Orc stepped swiftly forward. Kickaha retreated.

"You can run now," the Thoan said hoarsely. "That is the only way you can escape me. For a while, anyway. I will track you down and kill you."

"You have a lot of confidence for a beaten man," Kickaha said.

He stooped to pick up the bloody marble chunk. For a few seconds after he had straightened up, he was dizzy. Too much blood lost; too many blows on the head. But Red Orc was in as bad a condition. Who won might depend upon who passed out first.

He wiped the blood from the marble chunk on his short trousers, and he held it up for Red Orc to see.

"It's been used twice, once by you, once by me. Let's see what the third time does. I doubt you'll be able to bat it again."

Red Orc, wincing, crouched, his knife held out.

"When I was a youth on Earth," Kickaha said, "I could throw a baseball as if it were a meteorite hurtling through space. And I could throw a curve ball, too. A scout once told me I was a natural for the big league. But I had other plans. They didn't work out because I came to the World of Tiers, and from there to other universes of the Lords. Let's see now how an Earthly sport is good for something besides striking out a batter."

He wound up, knowing that he was out of practice and that the irregularly shaped chunk was no lightweight ball. Also, he did not have much strength left. But he could summon it. And he was only ten feet from Red Orc.

The chunk flew spinning from his hand. Just as it did, the Thoan dropped to his knees and leaned to one side. But the stone, far from going into its target, the chest, veered off the path Kickaha had intended for it.

It thudded against Red Orc's head just above his hairline. The Thoan fell over on his side, dropping the dagger. His eyes and mouth were open; he did not move.

Kickaha picked up the dagger while keeping his one eye on the Thoan. Then he slammed his boot into the man's side. The body moved, but only because it had been kicked.

Kickaha knelt down and ripped off the man's shorts. He held up the testicles and prepared to cut them off. He might eat them raw. He did not know if he was up to it. But despite his exhaustion, he was still raging. This Thoan must suffer what he had intended to inflict upon his enemy.

Manathu Vorcyon's voice came to him. "Kickaha! You cannot do that! You are better than he! You are not the savage he is!"

Kickaha looked up at the Great Mother with his good eye. She was sitting on her airboat. But both were blurred. The good eye was not so good.

"The hell I'm not!" he said. His own voice seemed far away. "Watch me!"

He did it with one swipe. And then everything rushed away from him, and the darkness of nothing rushed in to fill the space.

23

KICKAHA'S WOUNDS WERE HEALED, AND A NEW EYE HAD GROWN
in the socket. The latter process had taken forty days, during part of which
time his eye had been a nauseating jellylike mass. But he was as fit and as
whole as ever.

He sat near the edge of the monolith on which was the palace Wolff
had once occupied as Lord of this world. Now and then, Kickaha sipped a
purplish liquor from a cut-quartz goblet. He looked up at the green sky and
yellowish sun and then at the vast panorama below him, unique among the
many universes.

The palace was on top of a massive and soaring stone pillar, the highest point of this Tower of Babylon–shaped planet. It soared from the center of a circular continent, the Atlantis tier. This, in turn, was on top of a
larger monolith, the Dracheland tier. Below this tier was the still larger tier
that Kickaha called the Amerind, his favorite stomping grounds. Below this
was the Okeanos level. A person on its edge would see nothing but space,
empty except for the air filling it. If you jumped over the edge, you fell for
a very long time. Where you ended up, Kickaha did not know.

Theoretically, if you had a very powerful telescope and the humidity
was very low, you could see to the lowest tier, the outer part of it, anyway.
He was content with the view he had.

Anana had survived the collapse of her prison suite, but when she was
carried out of the room five days after Khruuz had gated the palace, she
was severely injured and much dehydrated. Kickaha had stayed with her
until she had recovered. Despite his nursing, she still had hated him.

Red Orc's wounds had healed themselves. Though not imprisoned, he
was closely watched. Red Orc was no longer his name; it was now just
Orc. He had not been given a choice of lifelong incarceration or having his
memory shorn to the age of five. The Great Mother had worked with the
Thoan's computer until she had found the access code that opened up all

the files. She was probably the only one in the many universes who could have done it, and that took her a long time.

After the machine had been built, the Thoan was placed in a chair and subjected to the memory-stripping process. Now he was only five years old in mind. Those raising him, volunteer native house servants, would give him the love and attention every child required. Kickaha was not glad that he had not killed the man who had robbed him of the Anana whom Kickaha had known. But he could not hate the man who was no longer Red Orc. However, it would be a long time, if ever, before he would like him.

One problem with Anana had been solved. The machine had been used to strip her awareness of the events following immediately after Orc had taken away her memory.

The ethics of doing this without her consent had bothered Kickaha. But not very much. She was no longer in love with Orc because she did not remember him. And now she did not hate Kickaha. Never mind that she did not love him either. He had already started his campaign to win her back. How could he not succeed? Modesty aside, what other man in all the universes could compare with him?

The Great Mother had returned to her own world, but she and Kickaha would visit each other now and then.

He looked again at the view. Unsurpassed in beauty, in mystery, in promised adventure!

He would never again leave this world, the land area of which was larger than Earth's. To roam in it forever with Anana by his side would be to live in Heaven. Though it would be unlike Heaven in that it had a streak of Hell and he could be killed . . . ah! that gave it its savor.

"My world!" he shouted. And while those words soared out over the planet, they were followed by a roar like a lion notifying everybody that this was his territory.

"Kickaha's World!"